ROUGH

RIDE

P J KING

DEDICATION

For my mother with love.

ACKNOWLEDGMENTS

Rough Ride is a lengthy book and therefore my grateful thanks go to my long suffering family, who listened patiently to me blathering on incessantly and for putting up with my unsociable writing habits, often throughout the night.

To my sister Christine Sparrowhawk, and friends Sam Lintott, and Jan Muller, who read the book in its embryo stage and encouraged me to continue.

To my veterinary surgeon – Michael Byers, from Shotter & Byers, who gave me masses of advice about the drugs and horse related matters.

To my friend Lynne Scott, a detective in the police force, who told me all about police procedure.

To my friend Wendy Scott, who offered fantastic advice and support on the abridging and editing of the original text.

To Vanessa Swain, who diligently edited and painstakingly trawled through the final proof reading.

To James Willis, of Spiffing Covers, who produced the Book Jacket, and was very patient with me when I kept changing my mind.

To all my dear friends who believed in me and promoted the book for me.

Finally to my Mum, and to whom I dedicate this book, sadly not here to see the publication, but the wisest person I have ever known.

CAST OF CHARACTERS

CHARLES PARKER-SMYTHE	Wealthy city boy
JENNIFER PARKER-SMYTHE	Charles' second wife
CELIA PARKER-SMYTHE	Charles' first wife
RUPERT PARKER-SMYTHE	Celia and Charles' son
JESSICA PARKER SMYTHE	Celia and Charles' daughter
IVY BAINBRIDGE	Jennifer's mother
SUSAN BAINBRIDGE	Jennifer's sister
FREDA FULLER	House keeper at Nantes Place
CAITLIN MONTAGUE	Head Groom at Nantes Place
LUCY PHILLIPS	Groom at Nantes Place
PETE BOWYER	Gardener at Nantes Place
FELIX STEPHENSON	Groom at Nantes Place
DORIS WINDRUSH	The daily help at Nantes Place
FRED WINDRUSH	Doris' husband
CHLOE COOMBE	Owns and runs Mileoak Farm
JOHN COOMBE	Married to Chloe
TOBY, LILY AND RORY COOMBE	John and Chloe's children
BIBI SIMMONS	Head girl at Mileoak
SUSIE BENNETT	Groom at Mileoak
SANDY MACLEAN	A barrister & livery at Mileoak
KATHERINE GORDON	A livery at Mileoak
JEREMY GORDON	Katherine's husband

MARCUS AND SUSANNAH	Jeremy and Katherine's kids
PATRICK HODGES	Farrier
SHARON HODGES	Patrick's wife
ANDREW NAPIER	Veterinary Surgeon
JULIA NAPIER	Andrew's wife
OLIVER TRAVERS	Veterinary Surgeon
SUSE TRAVERS	Oliver's wife
ALICE CAVAGHAN	Veterinary Surgeon
PAULENE GODWIN	Practice Manager at Vet's
GARY RUTHERFORD	Accountant for Vet's
KAREN RUTHERFORD	Gary's wife, a book-keeper
GRACE ALLINGTON	Hunt supporter
COLIN ALLINGTON	Grace's husband, an Estate Agent
TOM SNOWHILL	Uni student, hunt supporter
OLI BUXTON	Uni student, hunt supporter
ALEX CORBETT	Local GP
SUSAN MARSH	Psychiatric Social Worker
MIKE LISTER	Hunt supporter – terrier man
RACHAEL PILLSWORTHY	Senior MFH of the Hunt
GILES PILLSWORTHY	Rachael's husband – MFH
IAN GRANT	MFH of the Hunt
ALICE GRANT	Ian's wife
DUNCAN WORTHINGTON-BARNES	Senior MFH of the Hunt

DEIDRE WORTHINGTON-BARNES	Duncan's wife
FELICITY COLERIDGE	Secretary to the Hunt
MICHAEL GAINSBOROUGH	Hunt Treasurer
TRACY GAINSBOROUGH	His wife
LAVINIA APPLETON-LACEY	Chairman of the Hunt
LADY VERONICA HARTWELL	Owns Fittlebury Hall
MARK TEMPLETON	Estate Manager at Fittlebury Hall
ANGUS FERRERS	City boy
VICTORIA FERRERS	His wife
AMANDA LEWINGTON GRANGER	Chairman of the Hunt Supporters
GEORGE KING	Huntsman
MARY KING (DECEASED)	His wife
JAY POTTER	George's assistant
LAVENDER CLARKE	Amateur Whip for the Hunt
HARRY JAMES	Whipper in for the Hunt
FRANK KNAPP	Terrier Man
DICK LEWINGTON	Terrier Man
LIBBY NEWSOME	A floozy who rides with the hunt
FATIMA GUPTA	Owns and runs the village shop
RAVI GUPTA	Married to Fatima
DICK MACEY	Landlord at the Fox
JANICE MACEY	Dick's wife
ANGIE WELLS	Barmaid at the Fox

LAURA	A student
LINDA	A student
SEAN	Linda's boyfriend
EWAN	A Hunt Saboteur
ANNIE	A Hunt Saboteur
RYAN	A Hunt Saboteur
JONTY	A Psychopath
WEASEL	A Villain
TUBBY	A Villain
NORA	A Villain
FREDDIE	A Villain
HAWKEYE	A Villain
JIM FARRELL	SIO- Major Crimes Team
DI TERRY BATES	Detective Inspector - MCT
DC PETER SOUTHERN	Investigating Officer - MCT
SANDRA MAITLAND	Family Liaison Officer
DI RAYMOND BURNS	Local DI seconded into the MCT
DS NEIL BERRY	DS Seconded into the MCT
DC DIANNE SCOTT	DC Seconded into in the MCT

<u>PROLOGUE</u>

Three days earlier…

Slowly, Laura uncurled her aching body from where he'd forced her over the desk, the slap marks were now red and pronounced across the cheeks of her bottom, her ripped thong riding up past her waist. She glared at him as he rocked back on his chair watching her, knowing her face was puce with anger and humiliation. Jerking up her clothes from the floor, from where she'd so casually dropped them earlier, she scrambled into her jeans and tee shirt, stumbling and wobbling around in her haste to get dressed. He laughed nastily in amusement.

"Not quite what you planned eh baby? But you were a nice little fuck. Here, have an extra drink on me" he chortled and pushed some notes over the desk.

"You total bastard" she stammered "you virtually raped me."

A cruel smile spread over his face, "Yes I suppose I did, what did you expect, you asked for it and you loved it, and what's more I paid for it. You fucking students are all the same; two a penny, now piss off and leave me alone."

Her shocked expression hardened, she glowered at him for a long minute "This wasn't in the deal. Nobody treats me like that! Who do you think you are! You'll pay for this, if it's the last fucking thing I do, I'll make sure you pay!"

He rocked back again in his chair amused, "Don't make me laugh! I've paid and paid you well! Push off sweetie, and don't let me see your common little screwed arse again – you're boring me now." He looked down at his desk and started to shuffle some papers ignoring her. She grabbed her jacket and stormed out slamming the door on its hinges, rattling the photographs of his children and Jennifer on the desk.

Sad scrubber he thought carelessly. Stupid little tart, making dumb idle threats, but when she had gone, he put his head in his hands and groaned with disgust and despair, what had made him do that? What was happening to him, he sickened himself.

He looked at the photographs and in particular the beautiful smiling face of Jennifer. He'd been so happy when they'd got married and she had moved into Nantes with him, and Christ knew, he gave her everything she wanted - even divorced Celia, but she had changed. She was no longer fun to be with, didn't laugh anymore, and was a bloody misery when he came home. She had this mad idea that the staff were against her, that his friends didn't like her - well who cared about them anyway? Surely she should only care about him, but the curvy, refreshing, free thinking spirited girl he'd married was now like a stick insect and just as brittle. Their sex life had gone downhill lately too and it had always been brilliant, but Christ - whores weren't the answer, just a temporary stupid fix . He loved her desperately and still did, but their marriage was heading for trouble. Now she was organising this damned party, seemed to think it was important to him, but it was just another bloody black tie function with a lot of hooray henrys and hedge funders in penguin suits. He groaned inwardly at the thought of it all, a bunch of tossers with their trophy wives making idle small talk and bitchily trying to outdo each other in their designer frocks. In fact the more he thought about it, the less and less he wanted to go home anymore.

CHAPTER 1

Three days later ...

Jennifer pushed a stray strand of blonde hair back behind her ear glancing distractedly at her nail polish and then moodily out of the window. She anxiously tapped her Gucci loafered foot on the polished oak floor - here she was in her ivory bloody castle surrounded by all this damned luxury and she had never felt more fed up or miserable in her life. The sun strobed in through the long Georgian windows of the morning room catching crystal glints on the cream silk wallpaper, and the air was heavy with the sickly scent of lilies cascading from a huge glass vase. Beside her on a small French side table lay the remnants of her morning coffee, a Costa Rica blended especially at Fortnum's coupled with one of Mrs Fuller's homemade rock cakes, dusted with icing sugar and reluctantly untouched. "Homes & Gardens" and "Country Life" were cast carelessly aside. Above the fireplace a large antique, gilt edged mirror echoed the ornate Ormolu clock below, flanked by a pair of ugly but valuable Staffordshire dogs, along with enormous rural-scene oil paintings which hung on the walls. It was a stunningly elegant room - but to her it was as cold as a packet of frozen peas.

Jennifer herself, when she wasn't scowling was a strikingly beautiful woman. She was slim, although she seemed to be on a permanent diet these days, and blonde, okay with a bit of help in that department and her hair was cut into a long shaggy bob. Her large baby-blue eyes were fringed with long lashes, high Slavic cheekbones and full lips made heads turn when she came into a room. For a long time now though those sparkling eyes had become dull and misery radiated from them like dark bruises. She twisted her diamond rings nervously on her finger, she knew she should have been perfectly happy, some people would give their right arm to have what she did - she now had a life of luxury, a beautiful house tended by numerous

3

minions, a London flat in Kensington, a chalet in the French Alps, and a very wealthy husband, but Jennifer could not have felt more wretched. In fact her life was a bloody farce. There were wars going on, people starving, atrocities, and the highlight of her day was total trivia by comparison. Here she was fretting about her scorched lawn and her sad floppy roses - what a load of bloody nonsense, but right now to Jennifer in her irrational maelstrom of misery she was busy whipping herself into a right old frenzy.

Bloody drought and bloody Pete she thought agitatedly, he was a lazy good for nothing and after all the money they paid him to keep the garden up to scratch. Didn't he realise that in only two weeks she was hosting her party – to which the entire County had been invited. She so desperately wanted to dazzle all those old fogies who had snubbed her and to make a reputation as being the most perfect hostess - she just had to. It was what Charles would expect of her, just like her predecessor the flawless Celia had been, and in the height of this glorious summer her guests would want to take their champagne onto the terrace and how could they do that when the garden looked such a mess. It seemed as though all the despair she had felt over the last year was funnelling into this pinpoint in time stretching her to breaking point - her wretchedness erupting into blinding rage.

She spotted the bulk of Pete ambling across the lawn, with his drooping shoulders and sluggish walk, as he slouched towards the summer house and the very sight of him was enough to light the blue touch paper to her ticking bomb. She leapt up from her chair storming across the room and out through the open casement doors and strode out across the parched grass.

"Pete!" she screamed unable to contain herself and launching into irrational abuse, "What the hell have you been doing all week? This garden looks a tip, the roses and the lawn need watering, and the state of the hanging baskets are a damned disgrace. You're a lazy bastard, a total waste of space, I don't know why we employ you!"

Pete turned in his slow aggravating way looking her up and down rudely. He was a huge man, not fat just solid muscle, his arms rather too long for his body, his massive hands dangling at his sides. He had an unruly shock of black hair, dark hooded eyes and bushy brows, with a long and hooked nose. He made a sinister figure as he towered above Jennifer, staring down at her peevish cross face his eyes fixed hers with hatred.

"There's water shortage on" he snapped, glaring at her with a barely disguised contempt "I'm not supposed to use the sprinklers or the hose. I shouldn't even be keeping the pool topped up". How dare she speak to him like this he thought, who the hell did she think she was? He'd been so happy at Nantes, it was the only home he'd ever known and he'd tended the garden slavishly for Celia, the woman he'd adored. She'd always been so kind to him treated him with respect; she was a real lady and no mistake. He'd hated this woman from the day he set eyes on her, she'd outed his mistress and he was buggered if he would lift a finger willingly for her.

"Oh for God's sake - to hell with the water shortage!" Jennifer yelled, exploding in exasperation. "This is my party at risk here, and I'm not letting you spoil it for me with your stupid ethics! Get the hose out and do your bloody job – otherwise you'll be out and that means out of the cottage too, and ..." she spat " get that fag out of your mouth" Tossing her blonde shaggy mane of hair, she turned on her heel storming back into the house.

Pete felt his face go red, his temper rising, clenching his fists into a ball and watched her marching back across the grass, "Stupid fucking woman" he muttered, she was a spiteful cow and bitch enough to sack him, which would mean he had nowhere to live either. Since his mother had died and he was alone in the cottage it had become his haven, especially after the traumas of the hospital. He could leave of course, but where'd he go and she would make sure he had a crap reference, then what'd happen to him? He'd have to bloody do what she wanted, he'd no choice, and more hate welled up inside him. What was she but a jumped up typist who married the boss. All the staff loathed her before she even arrived, why should they like her, not one of them was prepared to give her an easy life. Her party would be a failure because she was such a total cow not because of him and the damned garden and serve her right too.

Jennifer was trembling as she stalked back to the house, sinking down into a chair, all the rage evaporating as fast as a hiss of steam and now she just felt like crying. God knows she had tried everything to win them over - but whatever she did, however she behaved the staff were barely civil to her. Now she had finally lost it, shouting at Pete and everyone knew he was a sandwich short of a picnic. She couldn't understand how Celia had continued to employ and put up with him, but when she had complained to Charles, he'd said that he had to stay and wouldn't even discuss it. With a heavy heart she reached out to the table distractingly shoving the rock cake into her mouth, almost choking as she gobbled it down. Quickly she pulled herself up short exasperated, what was she doing, stuffing her face like that! She must pull herself together and not allow this spiral of misery to defeat her. She shook her shoulders and took a deep breath regaining her composure, dusting the crumbs away from her mouth. Brushing down her Jaeger shirt, she stood up and glanced at herself in the mirror, flicked her hair back and marched off to find Mrs Fuller who no doubt had her feet up somewhere.

Just lately Chloe had begun to look more closely at herself in the mirror. She was still slim and that was despite three children. She had a sexy good body kept trim by so much riding and physical exercise. Her hair had not been allowed a trace of grey, it had been highlighted over many years and now it would be impossible to remember exactly what the real colour was anyway. She was an attractive woman, not beautiful or pretty, but sexily rumpled, with twinkling naughty blue eyes framed with thick dark lashes that were totally disconcerting when she turned them up to full beam. Full fleshy lips and a cheeky smile combined to make most people take a second look at her. Chloe did not pretend to be sexy - she just was. Although now she had fine lines in her face which crinkled when she laughed, which was most of the time, but it was true that just lately she had started to notice them more. As she peered into the mirror, her hand touched her face, she pushed her hair back from her forehead, and posed and grimaced and smiled at the reflection that equally grimaced and smiled back at her.

"Oh well" she sighed out loud, "Chloe you're getting older, you'll just have to face it". She tousled her hair with her hands, pouted her lips and then shrugging her shoulders suddenly thought - Christ! Look at the bloody time!

"Toby, Toby, TOBY" she yelled from the bottom of the stairs, "Get off that bloody computer and into the bathroom NOW!"

Every school morning was like this. Why oh why, couldn't

Toby just get a move on? Her firstborn at nine was the most emotionally complicated of her children; he was fixated by any computer game not to mention his beloved X Box. In fact the main body of his conversation revolved around different levels of difficulty and the variations of this or that game. Chloe had learned to appear to take in all the rambling and intricate details, but had become adept at murmuring '*Really*' or '*Wow*' at what seemed to be the strategic moments, and Toby, bless him, rattled on not appearing to notice. Chloe was always crippled with guilt about this lack of interest on her part, but there was a limit to how much she could enthuse about it for Christ's sake. The guilt though always lay like a crouching tiger at the back of her mind, ready to pounce at any opportunity, goading her about how useless she was as a mother. It was a persistent nagging emotion which she had never been able to quite equate with her lifestyle. True she was a busy working mum, but always she lived with this insistent conflict of hopeless inadequacy as far as the children were concerned. She seemed to be permanently juggling one set of values and responsibilities for another, and sometimes she just couldn't manage to keep all the balls in the air.

"Toby, have you brushed your teeth, we have to leave in ten minutes!" she yelled and with exasperation turned to Lily, who was wise in the extreme for her seven years, already waiting patiently and dressed for school. "Darling, can you help Rory put his shoes on?"

Lily was a dream child, beautiful, charming and helpful. She was slim and quite tall for her age, long ringlets tumbling down her back, a round lovely face with a slightly turned up nose and Chloe's blue eyes. Rory too, was an angelic looking five year old. A delightful child, a crazy, chattering blond clone of Chloe at that age, or so her mother said. All three of her children were so exquisitely different and she adored them with pain that was almost excruciating in its intensity. Chloe could not love without this kind of passion, she was a salad of volatile emotions, the down side of which was, that people seldom lived up to her expectations. She had some good and loyal friends with whom she shared a deep empathy, but over the years she had been badly hurt by people -so called friends - falling far short of her own notions.

"Come on, come on, we'll miss the bus!" she screamed up the stairs, agitated by the last minute frenzied rush to cram everyone and everything into the car. Toby dashed through the kitchen, out of the back door to join the others. She ritually sloshed tea into spill proof beakers, which the kids never bothered to drink and ushered all five dogs into the boot room. She bent down and ran her hand over her own beloved dog and whispered "Good boy Sam, I won't be a minute, go to your bed", tossing them all a bunch of dog chews she smiled – how she loved her dogs. Giving a last anxious glance around the hurricane hit kitchen, as she was bound to have forgotten something, she dashed out of the back door balancing the mugs with practised skill and climbed into the farm car, the axiomatic Landrover Discovery. The kids were all in, but arguing about who had got to the front seat first – bedlam was breaking loose. Nothing new there!

"Enough squabbling" she shouted, "put your seat belts on and drink your tea!" Handing them each a beaker, she rammed the car into gear and they were off down the pot-holed farm drive to the five bar gate that had seen better days. The rule was whoever sat in the front had to open the gate. Lily tumbled out, swinging on the gate as she opened it.

"Don't swing on the gate Lily – I've told you a dozen times, gates are for opening…"

"And stiles are for climbing" finished Lily cheekily. Chloe smiled indulgently, thinking how predictable she was becoming along with her wrinkles.

The nubile buds displayed in an early spring had long since burst into a verdant dazzling green, but the hot weather had arrived quickly this year and was baking everything to a crisp, it was so dry the hedgerows were like tinderboxes. Christ knew what the hay crop would be like she wondered. There again she wondered that every year, it was always too hot or too wet. She sped along the road in the rolling filthy car. The kids were all talking at once against the murmur of Radio Sussex. Chloe half listened to fragments of the children's conversation making mental notes and plans for her day ahead. She slowed down to negotiate some treacherous double bends where she often met the milk tanker on its way to the neighbouring farmer's dairy herd. Sure enough, she saw it coming, edged the car over into the hedge, and waved to the driver.

"You should drive slower" remarked Lily.

"Don't be saucy Lily" replied Chloe, although she knew that Lily was probably right.

"Mum, Mum, can you check me on my eight times tables?" wailed Toby, "I've got a test today"

"Toby, why, why why do you do this to me, there simply isn't enough time"

"Please mum … It's not my fault …"

"Of course it's your fault, you must have known!" But she said "okay then let's get on with it."

They all chanted dutifully, the little ones joining in.- making a game of it – singing them out loud, coming to the favourite line when they all shrieked with laughter "eight fives are farty!"

"Come on now, please try and drink your tea" Chloe urged. The Landrover seats were sticky with spilt drinks, discarded sweet wrappers, cardigans, odd shoes, the kids' drawings and bits of Lego. She pulled up to negotiate the T junction, turning right into Cream Pot Lane and almost immediately pulled over into the entrance of a farm and parked at the top of the drive, where the school bus would pick up the children. She switched off the engine and the kids undid their seat belts and craned their head to watch for the bus the tea forgotten. Lily dragged down the front visor and peered at her reflection in the mirror. Chloe smiled, Lily was such a tom boy in many ways, but ironically was careful about her appearance. In the back Rory started to hit Toby.

"He punched me first Mum!" Rory wailed.

"TOBY!" remonstrated Chloe, "Did you punch him?" Toby feigning innocence looked angelically back.

"Of course not, I wouldn't do that" he fibbed.

The full scale row was defused by Lily shouting "here it comes Mum" and sure enough the roof of the old bus was looming above the top of the hedges progressing gingerly down the winding lane. Within moments it had rumbled around the corner and pulled up with a jerk, the doors opening with a hiss. In haste they all scrambled out of the Landover, Toby and Lily storming up the steps to be swallowed up by the bus. Rory rushing not to be left behind tumbled over but before he could cry, was swept up by Chloe who carried him and set him down on the bottom step with a hug and a kiss. He clambered up, he felt very grown up now he was old enough to go on the bus with the other two.

"Morning Bert. Mrs Asher" called Chloe to the old driver and the elderly lady escort sitting at the front of the bus, "another lovely day".

"Morning M'dear" greeted Mrs Asher, tottering up from her seat.

"Morning Chloe" Bert called back "Sure is- we don't seem to have had any rain for weeks."

"Now come on you lot, no mucking about" remonstrated Mrs Asher, how many times do I have to tell you put your belts on and no moving seats."

This made Chloe laugh, Mrs Asher was a right old softie! "Bye my darlings" she called "be good, see you later" She waved to them as the kids pulled faces out of the back window. She watched them superstitiously until they had rolled off out of sight and clambered back into the Discovery. Phew another busy day ahead, she had the farrier due, and the vet coming to rasp some teeth, and several lessons booked, but all at home luckily. Christ before she knew it they would be getting the hunters up again and meanwhile the eventers had to be kept fit – it was bloody endless.

CHAPTER 2

Mrs Fuller did indeed have her swollen feet up, she was resting in the kitchen chair legs akimbo on the pine table – her lisle stockings wrinkled around her knees, with her slippers dangling off her toes listening to the morning story on Radio 4. She was sipping a cup of tea, and enjoying one of her rock cakes. Her kitchen was cosy and homely, with polished wooden kitchen chairs around a scrubbed pine table, a small posy of wild flowers randomly arranged in an earthenware pot in the middle. There was always a smell of fresh baking and the Aga kept the kettle permanently on the boil. Her copper pans shone to perfection hanging on their racks. The old pine dresser took up most of one wall laden with blue striped plates and mugs. Mrs Fuller was from a bygone age, she had worked for the family for years and her reputation as a cook was renowned in the County. If there had ever been a Mr Fuller no-one knew, she never mentioned him and no-one had dared to ask. As housekeeper she ran the place like a well-oiled machine, with the help of dear old Doris the daily and her hubby. She knew everything that there was to know about this house. Suddenly, she stiffened in her chair hearing the familiar groan of the floorboards at the sound of feet coming along the corridor long before Jennifer arrived. She jumped up spilling the tea, the rock cake crumbling as it landed on the floor, as the kitchen door swung open.

"Mrs Fuller," said Jennifer quietly, carefully enunciating her words and trying to sound bright and friendly, "I wondered if we might have a chat about the party? We've only two weeks to go before the big day and I thought it might be a good idea if we organised a bit of plan, you know cleaning the house all that sort of thing…" she finished feebly.

"Well," Mrs. Fuller mumbled her mouth full of cake "I do my

best you know …"

"Oh, I know you do, and of course it's a lot to ask, and we do have Doris to help" Jennifer said, deciding to try the tactful approach. Christ, it was like walking on a minefield she thought, "but if it's too much for you, please you must say, perhaps we could get some extra help in?"

Mrs Fuller glared at Jennifer "Are you saying that I'm not up to the job?"

Jennifer could have slapped her, she knew she was being deliberately difficult, but instead she just swallowed hard saying, "No, no, of course not, just that if you felt that you needed extra help then you must just tell me that's all I meant." Jennifer bit her lip knowing that once again she had offended the old girl. In truth it wouldn't have mattered what she'd said she would have upset her, but the awful reality was that she would be lost without Mrs Fuller. She depended on her so much, she was a housekeeper of the old school, not only for the cooking, organising Doris, the linen, ordering the food and wine and the other stuff that she knew nothing about. Jennifer's life would not run so smoothly without her. It was old Mrs Fuller who knew about managing the house, the protocol, the who's who. So what if the old bat was a bit of a skiver sometimes when it mattered she produced the goods, and there was no doubt she was an amazing organiser, marvellous cook, although fuck knew how on that ancient stove, and not a modern appliance in sight. Without her Jennifer knew she would be lost, and actually Mrs Fuller would pretty soon be poached by someone else. It was that bloody Pete's fault he had wound her up. She took a breath, and started again.

"Mrs Fuller I wouldn't want to offend you for the world and I'm so sorry if it sounded that way. I haven't had a good start to my morning, the garden is looking dreadful, but that's no excuse of course" she apologised, trying to sound as sincere as she could, although for fuck's sake who worked for who around here. "Naturally we must organise the house cleaning together and the preparations for the party, I simply don't know what I'd do without you."

Mrs Fuller gave her a long frosty look. She knew she held the trump card - old fancy pants badly wanted this party to be a success and couldn't do it without her. Let's face it she didn't have a clue about codes of etiquette or behaviour, no idea how to handle staff, let alone run a house. She was always winding up poor old Pete. She was nothing but a trumped up little tart. When Mr Charles had dumped the first Mrs Parker-Smythe in favour of this madam, Mrs Fuller had been furious; she had loved her dear Celia. Now she was a lady she reminisced, charming, cultured, definitely one of the County set - everyone had respected Celia and loved the little ones; how devastated they were when she was ousted by this cow. Mind you, he had always been a bit of a one for the ladies. Now this madam had managed to get her claws into him and was trying to make herself into something she wasn't, even with all the clothes and jewels and her carefully put on '*plummy*' voice. You can take the girl out of the council house, but you can't take the council house out of the girl. Mrs Fuller continued to stare at Jennifer, if she wasn't such a hardnosed cow you could almost feel sorry for her she thought. She could never forgive her though for what had happened to Celia, and the disgrace this floozy had brought to Nantes, and frankly it was hard to be civil at times; but this had been her home for 25 years and she wasn't going to be pushed out by this upstart. She would organise the party for Nantes and the Family as competently as she always did. Meanwhile as for this bitch. I'll put her in her place she thought bitterly - show her what's what.

"Mrs Parker-Smythe" she said finally, "I've been the housekeeper at Nantes Place for many years and if you don't think I can handle your party then I'll be happy to leave it to you. However, I'm prepared to accept your apology, and will of course do my very best to make sure that your party's a success. As it happens, I've all the preparations in hand, and as you're clearly so concerned, I suggest we go over them now."

Jennifer looked thoroughly wretched but with grateful relief sank down heavily at the kitchen table. Mrs Fuller gave her a long triumphant look, and walked into her small neat sitting room just off the pantry and delighted in making Jennifer wait until she came back with a black ledger. The weathered old book which Mrs Fuller referred to as her '*bible*' contained all the details of every dinner party, every function and occasion that had been held at Nantes for many years. She turned to the page marked with a red ribbon and looking up she stared unblinking into Jennifer's strained face.

"I'll need to know how many acceptances have been received," she began "so that I can let the caterers know numbers by the end of this week. Based upon my menu, Mr Charles has approved the choices for the wine, champagne and other drinks and I've ordered these from Fletchers."

Mrs Fuller kept her tone cold and efficiently formal, occasionally glancing at her notes she continued rapping out the arrangements she'd made, her voice like machine gun fire. "Doris, has a couple of girls coming in from the village on the day before, to make sure the house is spotless. The Marquee is being erected two days before, they'll supply the chairs, tables and lighting." She consulted her bible again, "the caterers bring all linen, china and cutlery. Fletchers will deliver the day before, and provide the glassware too. The florist is coming on the morning of the party and I've ordered large pedestal displays for the house and the marquee, with flower centre pieces on the tables. I've chosen a pastel theme of freesias, roses and stephanotis - very fragrant. As for lavatories, we normally use 'Chic Loos', which provide high class discreetly screened facilities, which I've booked to arrive on the Friday afternoon. I've confirmed the string quartet for the champagne reception and the jazz band for later in the evening. Fred Windrush'll be organising the parking, and I'll open up the lower snug as a cloakroom for any coats, where two women from the village will be on duty. I can assure you madam that all's in order, I do not need any help from you," she paused , placing emphasis on the last wounding sentence and then continued, "but naturally if you'd like to check, I'll give you full details." Freda Fuller's face was flushed with victory, she glared at Jennifer, take that you bitch she thought.

Jennifer was reeling, lambasted with the information and felt like she'd just gone ten rounds with Mike Tyson. Old hag she thought, she delights in belittlingly me and making me feel useless and by Christ she had certainly succeeded. She twisted her rings, her anger shrivelled into humiliation and felt tears of self-pity threatening to come. Taking out her handkerchief and blowing her nose, she mustered as much dignity as she could, murmuring, "Thank you Mrs Fuller, good morning" and with that she stood up and shakily walked out of the kitchen feeling very small indeed.

"Hiya" called Chloe. Patrick looked up, hair falling over his eyes, he was bending over, with a horse's foreleg clasped between his knees, expertly fitting a smoking hot shoe.

"Mornin' darlin'" – he smiled at Chloe and straightened up, patted the horse, put down the pritchel, walking over to give her a hug.

"Yum yum, you smell nice" Chloe laughed, twinkling her eyes at him. Actually it was true he did, of burning hooves and horses, the trademark cologne of farriers. Patrick was an old mate, they had known each other for years, her father had been a horse dealer and his father had shod his horses, and between them they carried on the tradition.

"How are you sweet pea? What's the gossip?" asked Chloe

"What I don't know," Patrick laughed, "I'll make up!" It was her standard question and his standard reply. It was true though, farriers as a profession knew more gossip than was good for them and relished passing on any juicy titbits - good and bad.

"Okay seriously"

"Seriously?" teased Patrick his blue eyes lighting up with mischief.

"Yep, come on – give! I know you, you've got something to tell!"

"Well . make a cuppa and a bacon buttie and I might." tempted Patrick

"It'd better be worth it! You coming up to the house or shall I bring it down?"

"Oh I'd love to come up, but I've gotta bit more to do here yet, and plenty else on today."

"Righto, be back in a mo', I'll need to let the dogs out too"

Patrick watched her go as she turned across the yard admiring her tight bum in short shorts as she sped off towards the house, and then went back to his anvil beating and shaping the shoe with easy expertise then tossed it in a bucket of water to cool.

When Chloe and John had moved to Mileoak Farm years ago, it

had been a total risk. It had been a tired old dairy unit set in 150 acres, the buildings although not that old in themselves were in bad repair thanks to the storms in the 80s and 90s, and had not housed cattle for years.

The farmhouse was run down, uncared for and unloved by the divorced tenant farmer who occupied it, and was in need of complete modernisation. He had lived frugally only using one end of the house, drinking his way into oblivion and financial ruin. The kitchen was large though, and at that time was the only warm place in the house, with an ancient Aga and an under stuffed winged chair beside it. There were deep stone ceramic sinks with dirt encrusted wooden drainers which had been used to clean buckets and boots and were long past their sell by date. Free standing units dotted around the walls - the kind with frosted glass panes to the cupboards, and drop down worktops; and an old table covered in chipped formica was in the middle. It was a kitchen straight out of the 50s. At the far end was a walk in larder, with marble shelves for storing food and big iron hooks in the ceiling to hang the meat. Off the kitchen was another room where the farmer slept, it stunk of dirty washing and booze.

The unused part of the house was much older, damp and musty, the tattered wallpaper hanging in festoons off the walls. It still had the original sockets from when electricity had been installed, with cord cables hanging from old brass fittings in the centre of the ceilings. Black oak beams crisscrossed the walls, gaping inglenooks, with debris in the fireplace, and grimy little paned windows. It was full of nooks and crannies and dated back in parts to the 17th century, stepping down a stair here and up another there, ducking heads under the low beams – it was very quaint but in a terrible state of repair. John and Chloe had fallen in love with the house, and against all the advice from family and friends had gone ahead using every penny of the inheritance from John's grandmother and bought the place. Now with much tender restoration and money it was unrecognisable.

Chloe hummed to herself as she let the dogs out of the boot room, they galloped around her and leapt into the air, barking excitedly, sniffing about her legs, and vying for her attention. She bent down to stroke them, ruffling their ears fondly, "now down, get down all of you!" she laughed. She glanced around the room, looking at the aftermath of the breakfast mess, plates, mugs, and cereal bowls, all still on the big pine table. Piles of comics, half made Lego models, Julip ponies pushed to the centre. Hmm, she decided to ignore it for the time being – she had lots to do today. Moving over to the Aga, she heaved down a heavy iron pan onto the hot ring and rummaging about in the fridge found the bacon and threw some into the pan.

John had left for work early again and said he would not be back until late tonight; hopefully she would have time to clear up the mess before he came home. She really needed to make an effort, as although he was fairly long suffering, he had definitely been on a short fuse over the last few months. It had insidiously worried her, nagged at her like an intermittent tooth ache. He was normally such an even tempered man but he seemed to be working later and later, and was distracted with her and the children. To be fair he had a busy job and she knew it was a tricky time for him at work. She had tried to talk to him about it, and had got short shrift and she'd backed off, but she felt bit uneasy. She was pretty sure they were okay and that it was just pressure of work. They had been married for eons and were happy she thought, but her constant guilt thing – perhaps she should make more effort for him. The shrill whistle of the kettle shook her and turning automatically she sloshed the boiling water on top of the teabags, and flipped over the bacon. Finishing off making the sandwich, she determined not to worry about John – it was probably nothing but her own guilty conscience. She picked up the mugs and balancing the whole lot on a tray as the dogs dashed past her, made her way back down to the yard to give Patrick his breakfast.

"Okay, my part of the deal done, one bacon sarnie – what gives then?" she held the tray elusively just out of Patrick's reach.

"Okay, okay- I'll tell you! You'll love it!" He looked at her with a naughty glint in his eye.

"I bet it's nothing at all, just a ruse." she dared, stepping back and nearly falling arse over tit, as the dogs scrapped over some hoof trimmings. "Bugger! And Sod it!" The tea slopped into the tray, narrowly missing the sandwich.

"Give it to me treacle, I can see you spilling the lot!" Patrick reached for the tray and put in the back of his open van. "Now where shall I begin?"

"How about the beginning and don't leave anything out." Grumbled Chloe.

"Okay, okay. Well now, you know that young Caitlin, Head

Groom up at Nantes?"

"Course I do – lovely girl, going out with one of the mounted policeman – Tony"

"Ah well, that is what we all thought eh? I just happened to pick up her phone when I was working up at Nantes last week"

"Whatdya mean you just happened to pick up her phone, how do you '*happen*' to do that then?" exploded Chloe "you are totally incorrigible - remind me not to leave my phone about!"

"D'you want me to go on or not babe?" teased Patrick

"Course I do" said Chloe intrigued

"Well… Whoever Caitlin is texting it isn't Tony, I can tell you! Tony is single, this guy is married. The texts are pretty graphic too!"

"Who is it then? There must have been a number –or a name?"

"Dunno" said Patrick, "I didn't have my spy kit with me – and the name was just listed as someone called Ace."

"Ace? Pretty funny sort of name eh? You sure, or are you just making this all up."

"Chloe, my little cream puff, how can you doubt me, I wouldn't make something like that up, and I haven't told anyone else either- so keep it to yourself!"

"Patrick …" Chloe began, but was irritatingly interrupted by the clatter of hooves coming into the yard "Bugger, bugger, bugger – just as this was getting interesting."

"Hi you two" called a voice from one of the skittering horses, "Lovely morning."

"Hi Katherine, Sandy, you two okay? Have a good ride?" said Chloe, burying her frustration behind a plastered smile.

"Great ride thanks, the horses are as fit as fleas, should be well up for Borde Hill on Saturday" grinned Sandy, "Mind you, I think he may be a little explosive in the dressage!." She inclined her head to the frisky grey horse "Hope the ground won't be too hard, I rang the organisers and they said it would all be aerated, so should be okay".

"He'll be ace Sandy" laughed Patrick. "Mmmmm … Ace" he repeated slowly.

Sandy leapt down from her rangy horse, Seamus, a talented 17hh eventer, landing neatly on her feet. A tiny, glamorous woman, with bright red lipstick, who was friendly and funny and a seriously good livery to have as far as Chloe was concerned. She always paid her bills on time directly into the farm account, and was obsessional about her horse and her belongings. They all made a huge joke about it which she took in good heart, but didn't alter her fastidiousness. As obsessional in her job as she was with her horse, Sandy was a successful barrister and had a nose for guilty people, she looked carefully at Patrick and Chloe, but said nothing. Not her business she thought briskly, but they were talking about something. Instead, she remarked to Patrick.

"Seamus will need doing again in a couple of weeks Patrick, can you book him in? I think we ought to put in two stud holes in each shoe if this weather doesn't break"

"Course – let me get my diary "Patrick, glad of the chance not to look at Chloe, went to rummage in the front of the van.

"Better book me in too" Katherine added, "Save you coming out a few days later"

Chloe moved off to fetch a broom, shouting for Bibi, "Hey Beebs, come and give the girls a hand can you?"

Bibi popped up from behind a stable door, "Coming" she called. Chloe was dying to get back to her conversation with Patrick. That was the trouble with this place, there was never any privacy. She returned with the broom, just as Bibi appeared to take care of the liveries.

"Good ride ladies?" asked Bibi and shepherded them all off to their stables, chatting aimlessly. Chloe started to sweep up the trimmings edging closer to Patrick

"This conversation needs finishing!" she hissed quietly.

"Too right" he replied "but not in front of this lot!" Chloe would just have to wait.

Pete trudged up the uneven flags of the garden path to his little cottage, his head down, muttering to himself. He stomped into the kitchen, closing the door firmly behind him. Fuck, he was hot, the sweat glistened on the rounded muscles of his upper arms, and seeped through the back of his black singlet. He ran his fingers through his greasy hair, and wiped his huge hand across his forehead. He worked hard, broke his back every day in that bloody garden and he was treated like shit, and it never used to be like that. He moved over to the old stone sink and turned on the tap, filling the chipped enamel bowl and reached over for the soap –carbolic, just like his mum had always made him use. Obsessively, he worked it over and over in his hands, lathering it extensively up his long arms. The strong smell comforted him and made him feel really clean. He took a brush and manically scrubbed his fingernails – there that should do it, not a trace of dirt on him now. He reached for the towel and vigorously rubbed himself dry. He emptied the bowl, rinsed it out, put the soap in the dish and hung the damp towel up on its hook carefully. He went back to the bowl and rinsed it out again – satisfied.

On the kitchen table was a loaf of malted brown bread, still quite fresh despite the heat. He had only bought it from the village shop yesterday. He liked the nutty taste although it was quite expensive, he liked plain and simple food, natural food that had not been mucked about with. He moved over to the old fridge, largely empty, just the minimum requirements were all he needed. He took out the butter and the cheese, took a plate from the cupboard, and knives from the drawer, wiping each utensil carefully on a clean teacloth and sat down to eat. He cut himself a hunk of the bread, scraped on cold butter in uneven chunks and sliced the cheese thickly, ladling pickle on top. He chewed slowly, meticulously, 20 times each mouthful, just as his mother had told him. What would she have said about that woman he ruminated? His mother would have known what to do. His resentment festered like an open sore, his thoughts becoming more irrational and disordered. His grudge had deepened into a chasm so wide, his thoughts illogically running ahead of him – she would get her comeuppance and it would be so sweet when it came – so very sweet. But he was prepared to wait his time, he was good at waiting.

Abruptly he stood up, hanging from a peg in the kitchen along with his winter coat was a black balaclava. He took it down from the hook, moving into the sitting room ducking his huge frame under the low blackened beams. It was a small room, immaculately clean with tiny latticed windows hung with short paper thin curtains. An inglenook fireplace at the end was stacked neatly with logs to one side, the fire basket swept immaculately clean. An old TV stood in the corner, a relic from some second hand shop and opposite it was a tired and threadbare sofa, covered in a once garish, now faded velour. There were no ornaments, no books, nothing personal of any kind – it was like a cheap sad holiday let. Pete did not like clutter, everything had to be neat, and he was extremely careful about the exact order and placing of things. On one wall was a small cheap print of some cows in a field, and on the adjacent wall hanging from a tarnished chromium chain was an old mirror, speckled in the corners with age. Pete walked over to it and stared hard at his reflection, his dark hooded eyes glaring back malevolently. His black hair long and lank, he looked down, fingering the thick fabric of the hood and tugged it over his head, enjoying the coarse roughness of the wool as it clung to his face. His eyes peered back at him from the mirror, as he adjusted the hood to fit – yes, it was perfect. He would not go back to the hospital.

CHAPTER 3

The village of Fittlebury, was in an area known as the Rape of Bramber, cradled in the palm of the South Downs, commanding wonderful and panoramic views of the surrounding hills. At its heart, was a large well-kept village green, a small lane dividing it through the centre, coming from Hawkesbury in the south, which forked in the middle of the green into a wide angle and divided into two. The left hand fork, headed towards the nearby village of Cosham and the bypass to Horsham, about 20 miles away to the north. Along the lane was the local school, the village shop, and beyond the recreation ground and pavilion. The road to the right of the fork, led to the doctor's surgery, the tiny police house and the small local garage cum workshop. After leaving the village, it meandered for some miles and eventually led to the hamlet of Priors Cross where the ruins of an old Abbey stood proud but crumbling, onwards towards the larger village of Cuckfield.

The point of the fork was crowned with an ornate village pump, with a four cornered apex roof, tiled with traditional Horsham Slate and supported by gothic carved oak pillars, standing on a brick plinth. It was a quaint old landmark and meeting place, and had seen many trysts over the years. Behind the pump was a row of traditional Sussex cottages, tile hung, with tiny latticed windows, and low but wide front doors. All along their fronts the cottages were bordered with gaudy flower beds, crammed with hollyhocks, delphiniums and roses. White picket fencing and gates, enclosed the tiny front gardens, and lichen encrusted stepping stones led onto the green and the road.

Across the far side of the green was the church, parts of which dated back to the 13th century but it had largely been rebuilt much later; a flint stone wall hugged the churchyard and was entered through a roofed lynch gate, similar to the pump. Lopsided tomb stones tumbled about the grave yard, shaded by the gloomy yew trees, and here and there, some bunches of flowers, made splashes of colour in the tranquillity of the place. To the right of the Church and set well back was the vicarage, it was a lofty old Georgian house, with its original brickwork and sash windows, and an incongruously grandiose porch with dirty white Corinthian pillars. The vicarage was one of the few that had remained in the provenance of the church and had not yet been sold off, although the vicar now served both the parishes of Fittlebury and Cosham. On the opposite side of the green was the village pub, the Fox and Hounds, commonly abbreviated to The Fox and was a popular local watering hole for all and sundry.

The wonderful weather had brought on a real rush for ice-creams and cold drinks in the village shop. Fatima Gupta had suggested to Ravi that it would be a good idea to stock up, so that they had plenty in. She had an uncanny knack of knowing just what people were wanting. Since she and Ravi had bought the failing shop about eight years ago, they had turned the place around. What with the strict rules of the Parish Council and their own innate sense of business, they had kept its character with the double fronted bow windows displaying, local fresh fruit and vegetables and flowers outside, shading them from the sun with a gaudy striped awning. Inside, Mrs Gupta beamed from her counter top; behind her, bottles of spirits stood in marshalled ranks, alongside the cigarettes and the aspirins. On one side of her was a vast array of sweets and on the other a display cabinet packed with freshly baked pasties, golden sausage rolls and Danish pastries. Before they had moved in, they'd had the shop extended, to include a small hardware department, with a refrigerated and frozen section, and put in a little kitchen area where Mr Gupta did his baking. When old Mrs Goldsmith had retired from running the post office from her home they'd applied to have the franchise in the shop, and had cunningly situated it right at the back, so that customers would have to go temptingly right past the shelves brimming with goodies. They'd even extended their opening hours too, and gone from the traditional times, now opening all day on a Sunday to compete with the 24/7 premise of the likes of Tesco Express. Yes, the Guptas had good heads for business and the shop was thriving. It was in a good situation too, on the road to Cosham and Horsham, and right beside the school.

The shop door stood open, as it was so hot and Mrs Gupta had moved the vegetables further under the awning to avoid the direct sun. She fanned her face with one of the leaflets plonked on the counter advertising the forthcoming flower and produce show. The shop had been busy all day and now at 3.15 pm the mums were arriving to pick up their kids from the school, so she was expecting a rush at any moment, and urged Ravi to give her a hand.

She rubbed one foot against the other, their swollen sides spilling over the top of her sandals; she must sit down more - that was what the doctor had told her. Ravi bumbled through from the back of the shop, wiping his hands on his apron – he was a hardworking man, well they both were – and it was a constant source of disappointment to them that neither of their children had been remotely interested in the shop. Ravi had argued that it was their duty to help their family, as he and their mother had done, it was their tradition. Selinda and Ayeesha, however, had other ideas, and were defiant, pointing out that they had been brought up in the 21st century, that they were not living in Pakistan and that they lived within a free society. They wanted a good education and were determined to go to University. Eventually, Mr and Mrs Gupta had agreed and the twins had gone off to Cardiff without a backward glance, to read Philosophy and History. Okay, so they were at home now, but they had their studies, and they did as much as they could Mrs Gupta thought indulgently. Sometimes she wondered what would become of them all. It seemed a million years ago that she and Ravi, living in London then and working in their respective family shops, had defied their parents, scorning the marriage partners they had chosen for them years before. They too, had been rebellious and run away to be married for '*love*'. Whenever she thought about it, she knew that she would not have done things differently and had no regrets, but somehow the intrinsic sense of '*family*' had gone, especially since her and Ravi's parents had died. They were the end of an era. Her daughters were loved and loving, both good girls but they were not shopkeepers.

She sighed, shifting her feet again. Fatima was a heavy woman, with deep brown eyes, hair once a glossy black, now threaded with grey, pulled back into a loose bun. Gold chains dangled around her plump neck and wrists. She had begun to feel her age, sometimes her heart seemed to be beating in her head and her breath came in short gasps. Ravi was concerned about her, she knew that, so she had taken herself off to Dr Corbett, who had tried to make her go to the local hospital in Horsham for some tests but she had refused. She had another appointment to see him in a couple of weeks, and he had given her some tablets, ordering her to rest, but how was she supposed to do that with the shop to run?

Fatima looked up to see a couple of people coming into the shop. They were strangers to her, she knew most of the people who came in from the village, or made a pit stop at the shop for a pie, but she had never seen these two before.

"Afternoon" she beamed, appraising them. They were an odd couple, a man and a woman, young, dressed alike in black vest tops and jeans. The girl had long fair hair, and heavily kohled eyes, she was slender, with a tiny tattoo on her shoulder and her jeans were too big for her, or was that the fashion now Mrs Gupta considered. The lad, was tall, with a baby growth of a beard, one of those little goatee things, rather wispy and pathetic. He had closely cropped hair almost shaved, so that she could see his scalp shining with sweat. He had large disconcertingly light blue eyes, which seemed not to blink as he looked at her. There was something about them - especially him - she didn't like the look of one bit she was thinking.

"Afternoon" the girl replied "small packet of Golden Virginia, and some green Rizlas."

Mrs Gupta turned to get the tobacco, and was just turning back, when she caught a glimpse of the lad nudging the girl with his elbow.

"There we go, anything else you are wanting today?" she asked.

With an apparent effort, the girl smiled at her. Mrs Gupta instinctively did not trust her. No real reason, somehow she was just not likeable.

"No, we're just passing. Any idea where Nantes Cottage is?" she asked.

"Dear me, Nantes Cottage, now let me be thinking" Mrs Gupta paused, "No I can't, I don't recall a cottage of that name, but it may be near to Nantes Place itself. That's just along the lane outside the village. Are you looking for someone in particular?"

The girl hesitated for a fraction of a moment, a moment too long in Fatima's opinion.

"Just looking up an old friend who said she lived round here" the girl improvised "we're just driving through".

"What would her name be then?" asked Fatima, she was looking at them strangely. They were a peculiar couple.

"Oh doesn't matter," the girl dodged the question, I'll give her a ring on her mobile, that'd be best. How much do I owe you?

"If you are sure my dear, sorry I can't be helping; that'll be £5.75 please" the girl counted out a handful of coins and with that the pair of them turned on their heels and left saying no more. Fatima watched them go from her vantage point behind the counter. They jumped into an old Landrover with blacked out windows and roared off. Definitely odd she thought - she turned to see if Ravi had been listening, but at that moment she heard a noisy burst of chattering voices and children's feet running up the pavement and a crowd of them burst into the shop. She turned to face the rush of eager little faces, promptly forgetting all about the strangers.

Chloe was at the end of the lane, waiting for the school bus to bring the children back home. She was in a world of her own, thinking about all the masses of things she had to do when she got back. She was worried about John, she had phoned him twice today, and had only got his voicemail which was unusual, he must be busy with clients she thought. Thank God for Beebs and Susie - what would she do without them, they were good girls, and were great with the clients. The yard was busy at the moment, the eventers taking up a lot her time with the season in full swing. Oliver Travers, her vet had been out today doing routine stuff, rasping teeth and vaccinations, but it had all taken ages, and she had not stopped to draw breath, and she still hadn't touched the house since breakfast time.

In the distance, she heard a throaty engine roaring along the road, and looked up sharply, registering immediately that it was travelling way too fast around these corners. It always seriously pissed her off when people drove like that, supposing they met a horse or a cyclist on the bend. A Landrover hurtled towards her - bloody hell thought Chloe! She glared at the driver, a young bloke with a shaven head and a girl in the passenger seat whom she couldn't see well. The customised long rear windows were blacked out. Hmmm it was no-one she knew which was strange as this lane was pretty quiet and didn't have much passing traffic. The Landrover sped past racing on down the lane. She tutted aloud to herself - bloody idiots driving like maniacs! At that moment, the school bus rumbled into sight, and pulled up. The doors hissed open and the kids tumbled out screaming in unison "Mummmmeeee" – she laughed and jumped out of her car to meet them, sweeping them up in a hug.

Lucy was tired, thirsty and dirty. She wiped a greasy lock of hair back from the sweat on her forehead and idly scratched at the fly bites on her arms. Her day had started well enough, another scorcher. The work at this time of year should have been a lot easier, after the hard grind of the winter, but as usual Caitlin was on her back. The trouble with Caitlin was that she could never sit back and enjoy the leisurely pace of the summer, whilst the hunters were out to grass and the work load was more than halved. No, Caitlin couldn't allow any of them to relax and chill out – she could hear her voice now *'Lucy, I think we'll be painting the inside of the stables today now'*. Lucy's annoyance had hung in the air all of the long hot day, disgruntled and begrudging, as she slowly and with sullen silence had started to empty out the loose boxes of the old shaving beds. Even more annoying was that Caitlin did not even appear to notice her sulking. She just sang along to Heart Radio and meticulously and laboriously ladled out the paint, a small half smile on her lips. Lucy could have knocked her off the stool with her shavings fork - that would have wiped that smirk off her face. She wondered about Caitlin, she really did. Okay they were poles apart, but they both worked for the Parker-Smythes for little reward and much aggro on the whole. Caitlin had been the head groom before Lucy arrived and Lucy had thought she would find an ally, in the *'them and us'* situation, but Caitlin refused to become drawn into any bitching about the family, although Lucy was itching to know more about the scandal that had rocked the whole household shortly before she came to work at Nantes.

Last season Caitlin had become even more condescending, she had taken up with one of the mounted policemen, who occasionally accompanied the Fittlebury & Cosham Hunt. Lucy didn't hold with the police, you always had to watch your back with those buggers. She stubbed out her roll-up carefully, Caitlin of course, wouldn't allow her to smoke in the yard, and would have her knickers in a right old twist if she saw her – that's if she was wearing any she thought bitchily. She made her way back to the stable block, the tops of her thighs rubbing together as she walked and she could feel the sweat trickling between her breasts, this bloody heat was intolerable. In a way it would be a relief to go into the relative cool of the old brick stables. She strolled over the cobbles, through the gate and under the arch, with the clock house perched aloft. As she unlatched the gate and turned to close it she saw Pete standing under the shade of the trees, fag in his mouth, staring at her in that very still way he had about him. She guessed he had been watching her, his eyes running up the length of her legs to fix his eyes on the squashy pertness of her bum cheeks as they oozed out of her shorts. She did not smile at him but ran her hands provocatively over her breasts and turned away towards Caitlin and the radio and the newly painted stables. Pete was always watching her, and she liked to tease him, enjoying his covert dirty desire.

Caitlin looked up and smiled at Lucy. Why oh why was she so nice, thought Lucy, she was just too sweet to be wholesome, but nonetheless she managed to return the smile.

"Well" Caitlin beamed, in her soft husky Irish lilt, "this is a good job done to be sure."

"Couldn't see the point myself" retorted Lucy sarcastically, her eyes becoming hard and contemptuous, she glared at Caitlin, "you should chill out when the season is over, put your feet up"

"Don't be like that Lucy" replied Caitlin, choosing not to rise to the scorn in Lucy's tone "Don't you think it looks grand now?"

Lucy ignored her, sulkily clanking a broom and shovels into her barrow and stomped off. She had already decided she would give this job up after the summer, look for another – maybe a riding school, or a livery yard. She was fed up with having to raise her cap to these toffs, and bloody hell Caitlin was so fucking irritating and holier than thou. She would keep her ideas to herself for the time being though, would make her announcement just as the season had started and land them right in it. It would be difficult trying to replace her at such short notice – she smirked to herself, enjoying with relish her plans to leave them in the lurch.

Caitlin stepped down from her stool, putting down her paintbrush, admiring her handiwork. She flexed her aching shoulders, and watched Lucy banging about with the barrow and the shovel, she was not going to let her sullen moods affect her. She was pretty sure that Lucy was hatching a plan to leave, she kept finding the Horse & Hound open in the tack room at the situations vacant, the silly girl forgetting to shut the magazine. Frankly she wouldn't miss Lucy; her skiving attitude was hard work. Anyway, she herself was happy and nothing would spoil it for her. Her life had turned around - she was in love. She looked at her watch, only ten minutes to go.

"I'm going down to check the horses in the water meadow, I may be a while, once you have swept the yard Lucy, you can finish if you like" she called.

Lucy nodded her head, and wheeled round abruptly with the barrow , "Okay" she said ungraciously, knowing that Caitlin wouldn't be back for at least a couple of hours, she was going to meet her man and that would mean that she could knock off immediately. With luck Lucy could be down to The Fox for happy hour. "See ya then" she replied more pleasantly. She watched Caitlin's tall, slender figure walk away, and wondered just what she saw in that copper – he must be good in bed or something. At one time she had thought that Caitlin had a bit of thing with the boss. He was a smooth bastard. Good looking too, and he knew it – but she had been wrong, pure white Caitlin would never do anything so immoral. Sexy Mr PS on the other hand, was a randy sod and he was surely never being faithful to that frigid cow Jennifer, so if not Caitlin, who was he shagging? Mmmm thought Lucy I wouldn't mind a crack at him myself – she licked her lips – yum yum! Something rather horny about the thought of having the boss right under his wife's nose.

Pete watched Lucy from the shade of the tree, where he had been loitering, pretending to trim back some shrubs. She knew that he was there, and flaunted herself at him, running her hands over her tits like that – she was nothing but a tart, but he couldn't help but stare at her. He would like to run his hands over her tits too, squeeze her bum. He thought about her a lot, sleeping all alone in that tiny stable flat. He had been in there once, when she asked him to change a light bulb in the lofty ceiling of her bedroom. The state of the flat had shocked him, dirty cups and plates in the sink, ash trays brimming over, her dirty knickers on the floor of the bedroom, clothes all over the place. Dust like grey icing coated everything; the floor had obviously never seen a vacuum cleaner. He grimaced; the filth had sickened him, his fastidiousness hardly allowing him to touch anything. His obsessional cleanliness though had been overcome by his lust, and for his sins, he'd picked up her knickers and fondled them in his hand, bringing them up to his face, deeply inhaling her scent. He remembered how he'd had to pull himself together, and thrown them to one side in disgust. He had been compelled to go into the bathroom to manically wash his hands and face. It had been in much the same mess, the washbasin fouled with old toothpaste, and stray pubic hairs clung around the rim of the lavatory. Damp towels abandoned on the floor where she had thrown them. She was a dirty bitch but he was nonetheless fascinated by her.

It was still hot, even this late in the afternoon, and Pete watched Caitlin disappear over the fields towards the water meadow, she was on her way to meet her fellah, that young policeman with the red hair – right tosser he was too. Moments later he heard Lucy run up the outside steps to the door of her flat, lift the latch and the clunk of the door shutting behind her. Pete wondered what she was doing now, stripping, peeling off her little tee shirt. He stood imagining her naked. Her plump little body wriggling out of her shorts, the animal sweat on her body. Oh Mother, he thought forgive me for being so wicked, but he pushed her out of his mind and continued to watch the windows, hoping to catch a glimpse of Lucy.

Lucy on the other hand, could not be bothered to bathe, pulling her sticky tee shirt over her head, she tossed it aside, dragged a baby wipe around her sweaty armpits, and threw it on the floor. She changed her top, to a tiny cropped black vest with the number 3 emblazoned on the front in silver sequins. She picked up some deodorant and squirted it around her body. Checking her face in the mirror, she lashed on some more mascara, rumpled up her hair, pouting her lips, and decided she was okay. Rummaging around for some money she stuffed it in the back pocket of her shorts, picked up her phone, tobacco and papers and without a backward glance, she slammed out of the flat. She took the steps down two at a time, and more sedately she glanced around to make sure Caitlin had not returned. The coast clear, she dashed across the stable yard, through the gate and onto the gravel drive, her feet scrunching on the shingle. She strode towards the entrance gates, passing the shady rhododendrons, and horse chestnut trees, to meet the footpath to the village at the end of the drive. Leaping over the stile, she jumped into the field and made her way along the path at the side of the hedge. God, the ground was hard, it hadn't rained for ages, and large cracks had opened up in the soil. It was a lovely walk down to the village, taking about ten minutes. She ambled through the field, then into a shady spinney, enjoying the momentary reprieve from the sun. She crossed into another small meadow and in the corner was an old wooden kissing gate, leading directly into the Churchyard. Pete watched her go, as she walked across the field and out of sight into the spinney. He was desperately tempted to follow but reluctantly turned around and went back to the garden to water the bloody lawn, secateurs in his hand, and irrational malice in his heart.

CHAPTER 4

This evening the Fox was buzzing. Outside the garden lay to the left and ran behind the pub, with benches and tables festooned with umbrellas. Tonight it was full of locals enjoying the cooling of the day with a pint, before going home for supper. It was a truly traditional old Sussex Inn, an original longhouse, with later additions over the years, giving the place a higgledy-piggledy look. Horsham slates tiled the uneven roof, and the walls were a warm aged red brick with the later newer parts being timber clad and painted white. It had small square paned lead windows set slightly askew and huge hanging baskets in a riot of colours swung from the walls, matching the flower tubs in the garden.

Dick Macey, a retired copper, owned the pub, along with his wife Janice, and they were all that good landlords should be. Dick middle aged and thick set, a ruddy faced chap, with plenty of bonhomie, served a renowned pint. Janice was rather plump with a carefully made up round face, brown hair cut short and was super-efficient. When Dick had retired they had bought the pub from the Horsham Brewery when it had gone bust and since then had turned the place around in terms of trade. Happy Hour at the Fox was the highlight of Lucy's day and she called hello to several people she knew in the garden, and stepped down under the low door onto the uneven flagstone floor of the cool snug.

The bar was crammed with low blackened beams, an inglenook fireplace with a massive fire grate took up almost one wall, complete with the essential horse brasses hanging from the lintel. On small polished tables dotted around the bar, were pretty vases of dianthus and honeysuckle. Angie was behind the bar tonight, the epitome of a barmaid – ample cleavage spilling out over lacy low cut top. Her hair piled up carelessly into a topknot, most of which was escaping in tendrils across her pretty face.

"Hi Luce, how's you?" she said "half or a pint?" She cocked her head to one side, looking at Lucy.

"Oh better make it a pint – I'm bloody gasping" laughed Lucy. "It's been a long day". She liked Angie, she was a good sort and was the same with everyone, no matter who they were.

"Coming up chick" Angie picked up a long straight glass and tilted it under the pumps.

"I'll get that Ange, and one for me too"

Lucy turned and her face lit up as she saw Patrick, coming up behind her – his smiling craggy face beaming into hers. "Why, thanks Patrick, now what've I done to deserve this?" She purred.

"Ah well, you'll have to let me touch your tits now" he joked, holding out both hands to cup her breasts.

Lucy laughed, that was farriers for you, biggest rogues in the world, but would run a mile if you took them on, or would they? Patrick was great fun, a tall, strapping bloke, with messy blonde hair and naughty blue eyes. He was sexily muscular, and Lucy had often admired his tanned body when he was working and stripped off his top in the hot weather. He was a great farrier, lovely with the horses, and knew his job. Lucy enjoyed it when he came to the yard - Patrick loved to gossip.

"How's Sharon?" she asked "still working hard?"

"Ah, she works too hard, and neglects me" he answered with a rueful smile, "I need consoling!" Although he laughed, something in the way he said it made Lucy think that Patrick half believed his bald statement.

"Aw come on, you love her to bits, and she never neglects you" Lucy retorted. "The grass is always greener eh Patrick?" They laughed together, and Ange gave them a hard stare from behind the bar, she never missed a flirty trick. Lucy glanced around, nobody of much interest in here tonight. She nodded to a couple of the terrier men, Dick Lewington, and his crony Frank Knapp. They both nodded at Lucy, but then turned back to their own conversation.

"Let's go and enjoy the sunshine, and I could do with a smoke too"

They turned, taking their drinks and stepped outside. Christ it was so hot. The garden was pretty crowded, lots of people sitting on the wooden benches making the most of the weather. May was such a glorious time of year, and this year had been exceptionally hot so far. There were no wasps yet either and the smell of the honeysuckle and early roses was heavy in the air as the evenings were drawing out the day to its maximum.

"Roll me one Luce" Patrick pleaded "I've left mine in the van." He cocked his head sideways and gave her a wheedling, hang dog look.

"You've always left yours in the van – you bugger"

"Go on, you know you want to" he cajoled. Those innuendoes! Sighing and handing over her pint for Patrick to hold, Lucy took out her tobacco and papers, and swiftly rolled two perfect cigarettes.

"There you go gorgeous, now you owe me one" she countered, licking the end and popping it slowly in his mouth and taking back her drink.

"Any time princess, just say when!" Lucy knew that Patrick was like this with everyone but one day she might just push him a bit further. He was seriously attractive in a rugged way, and had been married to Sharon for years - they had been childhood sweethearts, although Lucy thought there was probably more to his roving eye than a joke though. A pot on the boil perhaps?

"How's things up at Nantes then? Caitlin let you finish early?" queried Patrick, hoping that with a bit of prompting Lucy would go on to tell him more about 'Ace'.

"Oh she's still loved up with that copper, she disappeared to meet him, so I took my chance to finish a bit earlier."

Hmmm thought Patrick, Lucy obviously had no idea who Ace was then? If she had known she would have delighted in imparting this juicy bit of gossip. Patrick didn't like Lucy that much, she was a bit too tarty for him and he knew that given a chance she would fuck anything. But she was working at Nantes and they were good clients to him so it always paid to be nice.

Lucy looked around the garden clearly not interested in

furthering this discussion about the beloved Caitlin. She spotted Grace and Colin Allington who were sitting at a table behind Patrick. "Hi, Grace, Colin," she called.

"Hey Lucy, Patrick, come on over and join us" shouted back Colin "Tom and Oli will be here in a minute. Budge up a bit Grace" said Colin moving along the bench.

"How's tricks with you two?" asked Patrick as he and Lucy walked over plonking themselves down "your horse okay now after that abscess Grace?"

"Yes, seems much better – I'm down to dry poulticing now" replied Grace.

"You're probably okay now with this dry weather" he reassured "want me to take a look, when I'm passing?"

"Oh Patrick would you? I want to make sure he's up and running before hound exercise starts" She looked relieved, "and I hate it when he's in pain"

"Okay, I'll give you a bell then" smiled Patrick.

Colin and Grace were stalwart hunt supporters, riding regularly to hounds and walked the new hunt puppies each year for the huntsman. Grace was a lovely woman, about 35 now, raw boned and hardy with brown curly hair, muddy brown eyes and an ingenuous appeal. A real country gal, she had been brought up in the village on her parents' farm and had met Colin at the hunt ball about 12 years previously where he had gone with a bunch of his cronies. They made a good couple and had a decent solid marriage, but it was pretty common knowledge that they had been trying to have children for a long while and so far had been unsuccessful. Colin was a jovial chap, always dressed the part of the country gent, with tweeds and brogues. He had his own estate agency business in Horsham and he had fallen in love with Grace on that first night, and had been in love with her ever since. It was a traditional courtship, Grace felt so secure and safe with Colin. When she agreed to marry him they had bought an engagement ring, and thrown a party, the wedding taking place a year later. Colin had bought a barn conversion, with a bit of land to house the horses, the chickens and the dogs, which was perfectly situated quite close by to her parents' place. The barn was an amazing restoration keeping the main part of the tithe barn as an open plan sitting room, with a huge staircase up to a galleried landing, with loft rooms above. It had a huge kitchen with a massive four oven Aga where Grace liked to cook for Colin. For Grace her life would have been perfect if she had been able to conceive but meanwhile she threw herself into her Colin, keeping an eye on her parents, who were now in their seventies, and of course her animals. She was happy outwardly but she always felt that there was just that little something missing in her life. Still, she would never show how much it got her down this longing for children, but it did not stop her looking at the baby section in the local department store.

They all sat in the cooling sunshine, with the drone of bees diving into the flowers, and chattering voices, and every now and then a raucous shout of laughter came from one of the other benches. Lucy kicked off her trainers and put her face up to the sun, wriggling her toes on the grass and hoped her feet didn't smell. Patrick wrinkled up his nose and she whacked him on the back.

"Oi you, no comments now!" she threatened. Colin and Grace snorted with laughter, holding their noses. They all gossiped amiably, mainly about the hunting season, and the drought, and the price of the hay. Inevitably, they came around to the subject of Jennifer Parker-Smythe's forthcoming party.

"Jesus Christ" roared Lucy "What a circus it'll be!"

"Have you two been invited?" Patrick asked Colin and Grace. They both squirmed uncomfortably on the bench and after some cajoling admitted that they had.

"Oh b'Jesus Luce, what would Mrs PS say if she saw Colin and Grace, mixing with the riff raff!" Patrick guffawed with laughter

"It's not quite what it seems" stammered Colin, "we've known Charles for years after all, but we hardly know her and frankly were pretty curious to see what kind of show she'd put on so we decided to accept. Time to give her a bit of a chance with the olds" he added, "anyway, it should provide some good sport."

"Should do" laughed Patrick, "from what I hear it is going to be a pretty swanky affair, black tie, champagne, loads of nobs going"

"Yeah right, a load of dressed up wankers!" scoffed Lucy. "No offence intended Colin."

"None taken Luce, but it will be interesting to see if the new Mrs PS can pull it off, she's not exactly skilled at the job after all, not like Celia"

"I never knew Celia, she'd been booted out before I started, and I can't get a word out of Caitlin about any of it"

"Well, actually Celia was pretty unique. Old money and old school, but really one of the decent ones, you know?" defended Colin.

"Well we all know you were in love with her Col" teased Grace, "your stammer was twenty times worse when you spoke to her. And she could be a bloody snob!"

"What happened then?" Lucy urged, she was dying to know.

"Charles had always been a serial shagger of women, quite a reputation for it, one of the bad boys. Drove fast cars, rode mad horses, and a killer instinct in business. Always had some flashy woman or another on his arm, and then as soon as they got serious he ceremoniously dumped them. I don't think any of us thought he would settle down and then he met Celia" Grace reminisced. "Ultimately, I think there was pressure from their families to marry and they were a very well matched couple."

"Blimey" said Luce, "so he has always been a wild child, didn't just have a midlife crisis then? Why on earth did she marry him?"

"I think she wanted to be married, wanted a home and a family, and as I said the parents put the pressure on. They actually met each other out hunting. A bunch of us had an invite to go out with the Churchminster Union, great hunting, with some decent hedges and timber over in their country, and we made a bit of a day of it. We met at Celia's parents' place, and obviously she came out with us. Fantastic rider, and bloody bold over a hedge, and Charles was initially really smitten with her." Colin continued "Of course – he'd turned on his notorious charm, and as Grace said it was a good match, two old county families, so everyone approved. He just went along with it, so to cut a long story short, they were married a year later."

"I always thought she had been a bit namby-pamby, a bit of a wimp" said Lucy, "Just shows you how wrong you can be"

"No she was a quite a catch in those days" informed Grace,

"Celia, had a lot of verve, but marriage, or should I say Charles, changed her a lot. They were both pretty soon disillusioned and after she had the children she stayed at home a lot more and Charles pretty soon got up to his old tricks. Nothing serious until Jennifer came along though".

The sound of a loud throaty engine, and an old Landrover swung into the pub car park. Its canvas tilt was folded down with two lads in the front seat, grinning like idiots. They hung out over the doors

"Yo – you guys, we're gonna get them in, wanna top up?"

"I'm okay" called Patrick "gotta drive"

"I will – make it a pint" shouted Lucy, secretly miffed that Colin and Grace's revelations had been interrupted.

"Be right over" called the dark haired lad "how about you Colin, Gracie?"

"Driving mate, but Grace will have a G&T" shouted Colin.

The previous conversation had been forgotten much to Lucy's frustration and Patrick totally changed the subject asking Grace how the puppy walking had gone.

Grace's face lit up, "Oh they're just wonderful, I'm sure they'll win a prize at the show. Mind you, they've gone back to Kennels now. They drove me mad at the end, always jumping out and destroying everything, quite an unruly couple this year, but God I miss them!" She looked wistful, besides Colin and her parents, her animals were her life.

"Took us bloody ages to get them on a lead, leaping around like salmon, little buggers, but you have got to take them everywhere with you, part of the remit you know!" Colin laughed, smiling indulgently at Grace.

"I remember when you brought them to the point to point" snorted Patrick "bloody little monsters they were too! Ran riot as I recall."

"Ah well they call it socialisation."

"Ha, is that what they call it. I seem to remember them running off with Lady Veronica's picnic. What a drama that was! Never seen the old girl look so cross. Didn't I hear a rumour too that they stole someone's washing off the line and ate it?"

"Oh purleeeese don't remind me! That was a bit embarrassing, but at least they know their names now, even if they don't have many manners" laughed Grace "Anyway, the Puppy Show should be a good afternoon, especially if the weather holds."

Oli and Tom pitched up to join them, carefully balancing the drinks, one in each hand, and plonked Grace's and Lucy's on the table. They were handsome lads, tall and brawny, with good tans and easy smiles. Just starting their long summer break from Uni, they had been helping out with odd jobs for people. They sank onto the grass, and sprawled lazily down beside the others.

"Phew, I needed that, I'm bloody knackered" sighed Oli beer running down his chin, "We've been working over at the Kennels all day".

"It looks brilliant though, got the rings all sorted" said Tom, "worth all the hard work, will be great."

"Old George had us scrubbing and painting, and dead heading the hanging baskets, so the place looks a real showpiece" remarked Oli.

"They've got Col Harry Short, Master of the Crawley and Horsham, and old Bill Treadgold, that crotchety old huntsman from the Ainton, coming to judge so it will be a tough call."

The Annual Puppy Show at the Fittlebury & Cosham Hunt was a big do. Like a glorious country summer garden party. Marquees were erected and served a luscious tea and the champagne flowed. The young hounds that had been walked by members of the hunting community would be shown in a variety of classes and the silver trophies they won fiercely contended. The Hunt Committee, issued invitations to the puppy walkers, farmers over whose land they hunted, and to a lot of local toffs and also to ancillary staff, such as farriers, grooms and the like who had given good service to the hunt, and it was considered an honour to be invited. Judges were drafted in, usually a huntsman and a master from different packs, who took their jobs very seriously. It was a grand day, especially if the weather held, and everyone looked forward to going. It heralded the new entrant of hounds to the pack, and the anticipation of the hunt season to come.

"Blimey – he is a bit old school, a right old tartar. How do you think Nettle and Nimrod will fare Grace?" asked Patrick, who seriously doubted that they would be well behaved enough not to totally disgrace themselves.

"Well, not sure really, they have lovely intelligent heads but Nimrod is a bit weak in the loin. We'll just have to see – fingers crossed." Grace bit her lip, "They were sweeties really!"

"I wouldn't be too confident, if I were you Gracie, I know you love them, but there is some pretty stiff competition, that couple that the Tophams had were quite special – you know the ones I mean, Nigel and Nelson?" said Colin. "Still at least we will get the usual silver spoons; we've quite a collection now!" Colin laughed and took his wife's hand.

"Bout time you had us all round for a Barbie then" remarked Patrick, "this weather is fantastic and it can't last for long."

"You're on for that, I could do my famous chilli ribs" enthused Colin

"Infamous you mean" laughed Grace grinning at her husband. "Bombay bottom springs to mind!"

Lucy was feeling a bit left out, she had never tasted them "I hope that's an open invitation Colin?"

"Course it is – the more the merrier – bring what you want to drink and we'll provide the grub eh Gracie?"

"Sure" replied Grace. She was feeling a bit mixed about Lucy – she was nice enough, but she didn't quite trust her somehow. Her motives seemed shallow and she wasn't certain she would trust her with Colin given the opportunity for a quickie. Not that Colin would give her another glance.

"Drink up Luce" Patrick was getting a bit agitated and looking at his phone, "time's getting on and I need to get home otherwise Sharon will hang my balls on the line, I can drop you off as I go past Nantes" He swilled down the remainder of his pint and got up.

"Coming?"

Lucy was torn between chatting up Tom and Oli, or going home and flirting in the van with Patrick.

"We can drop Lucy back Patrick, no sweat" Oli chimed in.

"Okay then, if you're sure – that okay with you Lucy?

"Yep, fine with me, providing you guys don't mind? But thanks for the offer."

"Fine with us – see ya Patrick" their eyes glittered, Lucy was always up for a good laugh.

"Night you all, don't forget Grace, give me a ring about your horse, or if I'm going past, I'll pop in."

"Thanks Patrick, you're a star!" she replied "Night then"

Lucy watched Patrick stride away across the garden, dodging in and out of the tables, and jump into his van in the car park. He turned to look at her and winked as he drove away. Mmm, she thought, Patrick could wait and she was sure there would be another night for him. Meanwhile, she really fancied the two lads and could see a bit of fun ahead tonight.

"We're off too you lot, have a good evening – see you later" as Colin and Grace stood up, leaving the three of them together , they strolled off across the grass, hand in hand, saying the occasional hello to people they knew. Lucy watched as they got to their Landcruiser and Colin opened the door for Grace to climb in – one of the old school was our Colin.

"Bye – see you later" they all called. Tom looked at Oli, and then at Lucy – "Do ya fancy another one Lucy?"

"Why not, I fancy making it a bit of night – how about you two?" She gave them a knowing look, "We could get some bottles and come back to mine if you like?"

"Sounds great, let's go now shall we?" responded Oli eagerly "I'll go and get some plonk and crisps."

Oli's tall lanky frame stalked off to the bar and Tom turned to look at Lucy, her sprawling tanned legs astride the bench, her bouncy breasts bulging out of her tee shirt. She was bloody sexy and she knew it. Provocatively, she put her index finger, into her open mouth and sucked it, winking at him.

"Can't wait" she murmured. Tom was suddenly a bit tongue tied, he felt his cock start to stiffen, Christ she was horny. "I am going to do things to you, you cannot imagine sweetie" she whispered.

Tom could not believe what he was hearing and willed Oli to return as fast he could. "Oh my God" he muttered, "what about Oli, don't you fancy him then?"

"Why not both – the night is young" she purred, as Oli came back two carrier bags swinging from each hand. "Let's go!"

Driving towards Nantes, Lucy sat in the middle of the front bench seat of the Landrover, Oli driving and Tom in the passenger seat. Lucy had snuggled back and was arching her body up, as Tom stroked the top of her leg, getting closer and closer to her crotch. She stroked her tits, circling her nipples.

"Wow, it's getting hot in here" she sighed, and took off her tee shirt, so that her plump breasts spilled over the top of her bra to be admired.

"Oh my God" the boys said in unison. Oli, put out a hand to fondle her, and the Landrover swerved from one side of the lane to the other. The open top giving a graphic view to anyone they met, but Lucy didn't care, let them look she thought. By the time the drive into Nantes came into view, Tom was working his way up inside her shorts and was pushing a finger up inside her, whilst Oli by this time had almost managed to release her tits. They protruded out over the top of her bra, and she felt a frisson of excitement. They came to the fork in the drive, and Oli veered to the left, up towards the stables, their approach screened from the main house by the shrubbery. The stable yard was empty, Caitlin who lived in the Old Granary, situated closer to the house and garages, would long since have gone home thought Lucy confidently. When Oli pulled up, outside the gate, and turned off the engine, she decided to savour the tantalising, dangerous open air moments a little more. Oli, turned and released her breasts and started to stroke them, bending down and taking each nipple in turn in his mouth. Tom meanwhile began opening her shorts as far as he could. Lucy lay with her head back against the seat, her eyes closed.

"Wow that feels so good!" She murmured "let's go inside". The lads could hardly wait, Lucy not bothering to dress slid over the seat to Tom's waiting arms, Oli picked up the carrier bags and they stumbled up the stairs to the flat, fiddling with the key and they all fell through the door shrieking with laughter.

Outside from his vantage point in the shrubbery, Pete stood watching, his cock hard and excited in his hand. He could only guess what they would be getting up to in the flat. He imagined Lucy sprawled on the bed on all fours, Tom's cock in her mouth and Oli fucking her from behind. He expertly stroked himself harder and faster, moaning as he did so, until his fantasy exploded onto his trousers. His heart beating fast, his breath coming in gasps, he shut his eyes, and tried to calm himself. Slowly recovering and steadying his breathing, he looked down in distaste, zipped himself up and thought – one day soon I will have the real thing, and when he did he would show her.

CHAPTER 5

That night Jennifer luxuriated in the bath after another lonely day. The fragrant steam of the water wafted over her as she washed herself cautiously. She'd had a Brazilian wax at the beauticians in the afternoon and her skin was feeling tender. God she hated having it done, exposing herself so openly to some chit of a girl, but Charles liked it.

How her life had changed. Brought up in the East End of London, her dad had left them when she was a kid, and all she remembered of him was as a frightening man who was always shouting, and whose breath stank when he came near them. After he had left, her mother had scraped a living cleaning at the local Blockbusters and a small electrical shop in the evenings. During the daytime she worked at a drycleaners, her skin and hair always smelling of the fumes. It was strange that certain smells reminded you of things and that smell always reminded her of her mum. Mum had done her best for them though. Always a dinner on the table, even if it was often only egg and chips, and they'd often had to let themselves into the flat until she came home, although when they were younger Auntie Mary next door would keep an eye on them. She made sure that at Christmas and Birthdays they always had presents and it wasn't until later that Jennifer realised that these were all bought on a catalogue and had taken months to pay off.

Jennifer's sister, Susan, was older and had left school with no qualifications to work in a sweet factory. She had been a right one our Susan Jennifer thought – slipping into the vernacular – she'd loved the fellahs and had quite a reputation. Susan told Jennifer if she wanted a man, she had to be prepared to show him the goods. Pretty soon though Susan had got knocked up, the bloke disappeared and she was given a council flat where she still lived with her two children, each from different partners both of whom had eventually left her. Jennifer vowed she would not end up like our Susan – she just couldn't. So she had worked hard at the local comprehensive and was bright. The teachers there encouraged her – they were accustomed to kids who were no hopers and she left school with eight respectable GCSEs and some qualifications in typing. She found herself a job in a stuffy accounts department of local insurance brokers as a junior office assistant. It was a dreary place and the work tedious and boring, but it was a job. She decided she would go to night school, doggedly studying most evenings. Her friends were fed up with her and had stopped calling round to see if she wanted to go out on the town with them. So, whilst they went out clubbing, she struggled on. Eventually, a couple of years later she managed to pass A' levels in Business Studies, and English. Her mother had been so proud of her, telling everyone what a clever kid she had. Susan had scoffed and belittled her – said she had wasted her time and that she could have had a nice little council flat of her own by now, and probably some man to keep her warm and take care of her too. As it was, Susan declared, she would end up spending the rest of her days in that smelly little office, so what was it all for? Susan's words had hit home and Jennifer realised that she was right, she needed to move jobs if she wanted to move up a career ladder.

Jennifer started to scour the papers in the 'situations vacant', until she saw an advertisement for an assistant to a PA, in investment banking in the City. It had been a long shot, and she still remembered her amazement and then apprehension when she was informed she would be seen for an interview. She had dressed very carefully, splashed out on a black tailored suit from New Look, and teamed it with a crisp white shirt and black court shoes. She bought a set of imitation pearls from the homeware department at Tesco, and wore minimal make up. It was a good look, smart but not expensive, and she practised in the mirror her responses to questions she might be asked. She was interviewed by the PA herself, an austere woman whose hair was severely scraped back in a bun and thick rimmed black glasses, and a member of staff from the HR department. She was enthusiastic and keen, and the questions they asked were relatively straightforward. She portrayed an eager, sensible young woman, who worked hard. Two weeks later, she received a letter to say the job was hers, and asking her to let them know when she could start.

In the beginning, she had been in awe of Charles. Whenever, he strode into her office like a dynamic whirlwind he filled it with his presence, rattling out his curt instructions to Cynthia, the PA in his posh voice. Jennifer had kept her head down working away in the corner. Charles was a tall, attractive man, and had floppy streaky blonde hair- a Hugh Grant type. She admired his easy assured manner, the arrogant way he spoke, his wealth, and his privileged life. He was the man she had dreamed of finding and he had the lifestyle she craved – this was the kind of man she wanted, not some numpty from the East End. But how could she make him notice her, up until now she didn't even think he knew her name. So she decided to play the long game. Gradually she started to change her demure appearance, rather than sitting at her chair when he came in she made sure he spotted her with her marginally shorter skirts giving a hint of her stocking tops when she bent over, and the odd discreet flash of cleavage as she moved about the room. She was careful not to be too forward and made no direct overtures – it was all just tiny innuendoes – a flick of her blonde hair, a suck of her pencil, looking at him from under her lashes, her body language as she sat at her desk, that kind of thing. She did her homework and discovered more about him, what music he liked, what sports he played, about his life and what rocked his boat. She made herself indispensable workwise and he began to look for her in the office, making excuses to come in pretending to be looking for things. She would flatter his ego and God what an ego he had, but she tenaciously kept him at arm's length. Cynthia had seen what was going on and kept her working hard, continually disapproved of her clothes and her work, and on one occasion even tried to get rid of her, but Charles over-ruled her. He became the hunter, the more she charmingly declined his attentions the keener he was and the more he wanted her - enjoying the psychological chase, and to be fair she remained elusive. Weeks of flirting with her passed. He took her out for the odd unnecessary business lunch, and to her surprise she found she actually liked him. They laughed a lot, keeping the talk light-hearted, but both seeming to genuinely enjoy each other's company.

Finally, she agreed to a proper date. He took her to an amazing restaurant, in Holland Park, with a maze of tiny rooms. Once the haunt of the hippy generation 40 years ago, it had now become home to the ultra-cool London set, filled with crazy furniture from church pews to pulpits. It was on that night, that shockingly, despite all her cool exterior, she knew that she had fallen in love with him, the man himself, the person he was under that brash bad boy image. When she had kissed him goodbye, seductively brushing her lips lightly on his, she knew that things for her had changed. It was not about the money or just having a shag, or even being his mistress for a while, she wanted the whole fairy tale. She knew he was married with two small children, but through her rose coloured glasses that didn't matter, she had made her plan, determined to pursue her dream when one day she would become his wife.

Gradually over a period of time of wining and dining she could stand it no longer and had succumbed, and they had fallen hungrily into bed together. Their love making had been marvellous after all the months of sexual tension building up between them. She could still recall that first night and the explosion of sexual dynamite between them, and even now it made her smile. Gradually though he had coaxed her more and more into kinky sexual tricks. Jennifer had never been an easy lay, never slept around and was actually quite naïve in the bedroom stakes, and at first had been quite shocked but gone along with more or less anything he suggested. Coached by her sister she pretended to be a tigress in the bedroom, agreeing and inviting what he wanted but eventually discovered that she really didn't need to pretend at all, she was very definitely her own woman and loved every minute of it. He was hooked and she was in love.

When he first decided he would shave her, she squirmed with embarrassment at his minute and intimate examination of her, making her lie still, while he took his time and savoured the job. As he pushed her head back on the pillow and parted her legs, she closed her eyes and then found that it was in fact very sensual and erotic, and her squirming mortification changed to desire. He had been delighted – relishing in his possession of her. A few days later, he surprised her by bringing a stranger to the flat and told her that he wanted her to have a tiny tattoo of his name on her labia and this man was an expert. She was astonished, angry at first at this fait accompli, but as usual he persuaded her. Charles had watched the little Chinese man wash and clean her before beginning, and then stared fascinated as he performed his work, with Jennifer desperately trying not to wriggle. When it was finished he had smiled at her and declared that she was truly his now. Strangely, she had not felt cheapened and humiliated as she had expected but loved and wanted– especially when he photographed her, smoothing oil onto her clitoris to make it shiny for the picture. He enjoyed owning and possessing her, and she liked it too. But she was more than just a tart in the bedroom, she was good enough to take out as a mistress to show off to his friends. She waved goodbye to the East End and he set her up in a flat in Chelsea, and as she gave up her job, he gave her a car and a credit card, and in return she allowed him to do what he liked with her, whenever he wanted and they became inseparable.

As the months rolled by, Charles became more obsessed with her, and she with him, she began to enjoy more and more their bed time romps, but her eventual dream never died, and she started to put the pressure on, especially after she had satisfied his sexual appetite. When he was satiated, and they lay coiled together she would carefully coax and cajole him, planting suggestions of how life could be if they were together and did not have to resort to this subterfuge. She had been clever, never openly criticising Celia, just sowing little seeds of discontent in his mind. Insidiously she wore him down and finally, whilst he was supposed to be away on a business trip, they enjoyed a wonderful week on holiday together, of sun, sea and shagging and he had agreed. The die was cast and after all the months of calculating and careful manipulation, he told her he would get a divorce. God though thinking back she had definitely paid the price and now she wondered - had it all been worth it? She looked round at the steaming bathroom, with its gold taps, and marble sinks, fleecy white towels, the expensive perfumes and lotions and felt so bloody lonely she could have wept.

The 'Wonderful Celia' had of course insisted Charles should reconsider, she had even agreed she would tolerate Jennifer in the London flat and turn a blind eye to the affair, believing that in time he would tire of his mistress. In response, Jennifer had redoubled her efforts, delighting Charles more and more, taking inordinate care with her appearance and clothes, being the perfect sparkling companion in his London life. To Charles, Celia seemed dull by comparison, and was just the snobby bitchy wife at home in the country, and he was drawn more and more magnetically to his bubbly effervescent mistress. Celia intrinsically had known their marriage was long past its sell by date already and that it was too late to salvage it or her reputation in the County. After her initial attempts to regain his affection she implored him to consider her social status, and later her terrible vitriol against Jennifer oozed out like a festering poison. In all the chaos of emotion Celia had hardly mentioned the children. All of which made Charles even more determined, and finally Celia resigned herself to the situation and had agreed to the divorce. It proved to be a bloodless pathetic business, no courts involved. Charles had guiltily settled a very generous allowance upon Celia and the children and bought them a house about 20 miles away, and paid the school fees. In return he was granted access to his children whenever he liked – generally nowadays though he only saw them for the odd weekend, and a week or two during the holidays as Celia made things as difficult as possible for him – there was always one reason or another why it wouldn't be convenient. So, Celia had moved out of Nantes with the children and her dogs and Jennifer had blissfully moved in during the following week, as the new Mrs Parker-Smythe.

For Jennifer all her dreams had come true, but she had been bitterly disappointed by their small and quiet London wedding, which took place in the Chelsea Registry office almost immediately after the divorce had come through. Charles insisted that he just could not tolerate a big affair and only invited a few of his London acquaintances, and the minimum of Jennifer's family. She had badly wanted the big meringue dress, and the whole white wedding circus. Charles reasoned that it would be insensitive to Celia and the children and remained totally adamant on the subject. She had been really pissed off about it, and frustrated by his stubbornness, but she reluctantly could see his point, and at the end of the day she was going to marry him, and that was what mattered. Charles had his way on the wedding arrangements, but as a consolation promised Jennifer that he would make it up to her, so when they drove down to Nantes Place for the first time, she not only had her new wedding ring on her finger but coupled with it, was an enormous solitaire diamond ring.

She remembered vividly the first journey to Sussex and arriving at Nantes; sweeping down the drive which dipped and curled, lined with horse chestnut trees, and crossing the small arched bridge over the brook laced with willows and mallows. Her heart thumped with anticipation as they drove onwards, where the drive forked sharply, a smaller track to the left where a wrought iron sign pretentiously indicated the stable yard; and then grandly around a thickly dense bank of shrubs, where suddenly Nantes Place came into view. The grandeur of the house had almost made her gasp out loud. Of course she had seen photographs of it all, it had been in his family for generations, but the reality was astonishing. It was her Cinderella moment, as she smiled across at Charles and took his hand, he had squeezed hers back and grinned. Quickly she had regained her composure, looking ahead, excitement bubbling inside her and began to relish the vastness of it all. Like a little boy, he took her hand and he proudly showed her around, the beautiful antique furniture and ornaments, the old masters on the wall, the spreading lawns and beautiful gardens, the pool, tennis court, and gym area. She was simply overawed, desperately hoping she had made noises in all the right places, even admiring the stables, despite her terror of horses and managed to make flattering remarks about his glossy hunters. When she was introduced to the staff later that same day, she remembered how good she had felt, thinking how they would all be friends as she confidently beamed at them, and they had gazed back at her stony faced looking like they'd swallowed a bag of lemons.

In those early days of marriage, Charles had loved being with her, never wanting to leave to work in London, insisting she redecorate the house however she wished, no expense spared. They had stayed at home, initially declining invitations from curious cronies. They had made love in every room, in every position. Secretly, she could not wait for their first public appearance together – it was to be a New Year's Eve Ball, held in a swanky manor house hotel. She had been so excited, going up to London, to choose an evening gown, not TK Max for her any longer, she could buy it from wherever she fancied. But she really needed someone to advise her on what to buy, but who? She only had a few friends and they were too orange and 'Essex' to give her any help with this kind of function, and she had made no new women friends since she lived with Charles in the country. In the end she had gone on her own, and had opted for a chic backless Yves St Lauren number, in a sliver of silver, with a plunging neckline, slashed almost to her waist. She had posed in front of the mirror that night, her breasts held into place with some tit tape and taken off her knickers, so that she was totally naked underneath, her curvy body wrapped enticingly in the luxurious fabric. God she had felt sexy, and Charles had told her she was too, tantalisingly running his hand up her back. She had worn a long platinum necklace, with a single diamond, dangling between her breasts and diamond studs in her ears. Her hair, longer then, a silver blonde mane pinned up sexily with a diamond clasp. High silver strappy sandals and clutch bag and she was ready. She had felt a million dollars.

They'd made quite an entrance, Charles, with his smooth tanned face, body toned from the gym and antics in the bedroom, had looked so handsome in his Armani DJ. His eyes sparkled with a mixture of naughtiness and malice as he smiled, and she remembered he had put his hand around her waist running his thumb along her backbone as they walked across the foyer to the champagne reception where the

other members of their table had already grouped. They had all turned
to gape at her, glasses in their hand, mouths open. Charles had made
the introductions, and the men had ogled her cleavage, clapping
Charles on the back, full of '*good on you, old boy*' remarks. Jennifer
recalled smiling warmly to their partners, who despite being not being
so very much older than her, were dressed in much more sober
outfits, bordering on the frumpy, expensive but '*all the gear no idea
look*'. The other women had completely snubbed her, looking at her
with total contempt. They had actually turned their backs on her and
carried on talking to one another. Charles hadn't seemed to notice,
and she was left isolated and ostracised whilst the men chatted at the
bar. It had been no better through the dinner itself, although seated
with a man on either side of her; at least she had had someone to
make conversation with, even if they had spent the whole time
looking down her front. The other women, closed ranks and ignored
her for the whole of the evening. She had tossed her silver mane of
hair and thought '*fuck 'em*'.

The final humiliation though that night, was when she had
overheard in the powder room, whilst perched on the loo, one old
harridan remark to one of the hardnosed bitches in her cut glass voice
"Just a silly little jumped up tart, he will soon tire of her, no social
graces, don't you know? When I think of our poor Celia, how must
she be feeling, dear girl. He should have kept this one in the bedsit
where she belongs and kept his lady at home."

"Did you see her gown – shameless little slut, morals of an alley
cat – bit plump too eh? Wait till I tell Celia!" came the reply.

Jennifer could have wept, and had waited in the loo trembling
with anger and despair until they'd finally gone. How the bloody hell
could she have thought it would be easy to fit in here, she was not like
these awful people. She had crept out and looked at herself critically
in the mirror– thinking defiantly, sod 'em she would make this work,
she would! It was an uphill struggle, battling against the county set
and she was firmly in the chasm that was no man's land - of not being
accepted by anyone in her new life, nor her old either. She had
immediately decided to lose some weight, and she would make them
change their minds about her.

Well over a year had gone past, although now she was wraith-
like thin, but despite her best efforts her life was still bleakly empty.
She had absolutely no friends and the staff hated her – fiercely loyal

to the memory of the wonderful Celia. *WC*, as she had bitterly nicknamed her. In desperation, Jennifer had even taken a couple of secret riding lessons, fantasising that she could accompany Charles whilst he was out hunting this coming season, determined to become a suitably accomplished companion, but she was so rigid with fear and after a few humiliating falls she had given up on the idea. She had gone privately to elocution and etiquette lessons to make sure that she did not make any social faux pas. To an extent this had given her more confidence, but it also made her awkward and the naturally funny zany person she was started to disappear along with the invitations for dinner. Her dreamt of life became a lonely, miserable existence as Charles had insisted that she was expected to remain at Nantes and run his household, whilst he went back to London to work during the week – if only he knew what it was really like, or perhaps he did? So, she'd hatched the idea of this forthcoming party. It would be her chance to shine, and show all those old crows, that she was an excellent wife for Charles, an accomplished hostess, who ran her household like clockwork, and was both chic and cultured. She had asked Mrs Fuller to draw up a list of invitations, it was laughable really, that she had no bloody friends of her own she could ask. She imagined sparkling at the party, with Charles on her arm, and the admiring looks of the men and women alike, surely as hostess they could not be so openly rude to her? Dreams can sometimes become nightmares, and more and more, as the day approached, she wondered why she had ever thought of the idea.

Still Charles was coming home tonight from London, and she was so looking forward to seeing him. She had an army of toys at the ready, ones that she knew would excite him and would oil her skin so that she glistened, and had set out her sexiest underwear. She had it all planned, he always insisted on a formal dinner in the dining room, she would dismiss Mrs Fuller early – God if she knew what Charles was really like! Then she would tempt him into taking her there on the dining table. She imagined him picking her up, and putting her on the edge of the table whilst he swept aside the candelabra, and silver. Just like that scene in Pretty Woman, where Richard Gere fucks Julia Roberts on the piano, she thought dreamily. Then they would move upstairs for the finale, it would be a wonderful evening. She lay daydreaming in the steam, the bubbles covering her small pointed nipples, when her mobile rang.

"Sweetie, it's me," soothed Charles, "I'm just snowed under at

work, so I'll stay in the flat again tonight - sure you understand"
Jennifer's heart sank, this was the second time this week he had
stayed in town – was he was on the cunt hunt again, was he going to
replace her? She just couldn't bear it.

"Oh Charles" she whinged "I can't believe it, I've had a dreadful
day again with Pete and Mrs Fuller hasn't been much better" The
words were out before she could stop herself, she'd been so
determined not to moan about anything "I was so looking forward to
you coming home tonight – I've some surprises for you" she invited
hoping she sounded sexy.

"Sorry darling no can do" he dismissed "just too busy. It's your
job to sort the staff out you know, so just do it eh? See you at the
weekend – ciao." and with that he disconnected. She looked down at
her mobile astonished and unbelieving, and then in wretchedness and
anger hurled it against the marble washbasin where it fell splintering
into pieces on the floor.

CHAPTER 6

Katherine Gordon was a really nice woman, and some might say a lucky one. Her husband Jeremy was a wealthy banker and a decent enough bloke, but had become a bit of a cold fish as he grew older, and he spent a lot of time up in London making money. He had become more and more obsessed with his work and talked gloomily of the recession, consequently driving himself even harder. Their children, Marcus aged 13 and Susannah aged 12 were growing up fast and were away now during term time at boarding school, and oh crikey, how she missed them. It had not been her idea for them to go; she had tried to reason with Jeremy that surely they could find a good local private school, where they could live at home. It had been the source of many arguments for them. Jeremy saying that he had gone to a boarding school and they would have a great time, notwithstanding the good start it had given him at University and later in the City. Katherine claiming that she had done just as well at her day school. In the end they had compromised, the children would go away to school and if they did not settle in the first term, then they could come home and another school would be found. It took a long time and a lot of negotiation but finally Katherine had reluctantly accepted - especially as the children themselves were keen to go. In the build-up to Marcus' departure to school 18 months previously she had become more and more anxious for him and perhaps even more so for herself, dreading him leaving. To Katherine's dismay, he loved being away, he made a lot of friends, and whilst he looked forward to coming home for the holidays and his exeats during the term time, he was a happy, and well-rounded boy. Of course because she loved him so much, she was pleased that he was content, how awful she would have felt had he been miserable. But she had considered - was that a reflection on her own failings as a mother, as he no longer needed her in the way that he once had - was that the end of it all? She fussed over him when he came home which he allowed and tolerated well, and it made her feel better too.

Susannah, buoyed up with Marcus' tales of school life, excitedly left to join her brother this last autumn term. She too had taken to boarding with relish, especially as her friend Lotty had gone as well.

Katherine went as often as she could to the school events and luckily it wasn't too far away, but nonetheless it was hard for her to see them growing so independent of her. At first she had felt that she was redundant as a mother and pretty much the same as a wife with Jeremy being away so much. She suddenly had a lot of time on her hands, the house seemed ominously quiet, and when they were little, the kids had filled up so much of her time. Katherine was adamant that she would not sit around getting fat and feeling sorry for herself and was determined not to mope about the place, making up her mind she would fill her hours to the maximum. They had a big house but rather than rattle around in it during the daytime she shut herself in her kitchen, lap top on the table, built in TV, with Bose surround system installed, her very own little haven. Mind you, as there was no-one around much to mess the rest of the house up, and she had a cleaner who came in on Friday and Monday mornings to dust the place, she could do pretty much as she pleased.

Her total saving grace though was her horse. Riding had now become her passion, and she whiled away her days at the yard, but to ease her conscience for her own self-indulgence she did a couple of stints every week at the local hospice in Horsham. She had had horses as a child, but when she went away to university she had left her hobby behind. She had been quite young when she married Jeremy, having met him in London where she had worked in a PR company. They had spent a few years in town and when they decided to have children had moved to the country within commuting distance to London for him. When Marcus and Susannah had started at their first prep school she had needed to fill that void when they were away and had taken some riding lessons at Chloe Coombe's yard and from that moment she was hooked. The unique smell of horses remembered from her childhood, the touch of supple leather, and the exhilaration of riding itself lured her back to the stables over and over again. Jeremy relieved that she had found a good niche for herself, unlike a lot of his friends' wives, who through boredom had sought affairs, drinking and all sorts, had offered to buy her a horse. He secretly rang Chloe who said she would keep an eye out for something suitable. After a few months they had found Polly, a sweet 16hh, grey mare, she was ten years old, with a lot of experience and a kind and genuine attitude. Katherine had fallen in love with her immediately and kept her at Chloe's yard on a full livery basis. This had worked well, Chloe taking care of the horse, and helping Katherine build up her riding confidence after all the long years out of the saddle. She began riding just to be a happy hacker really, to fill in her hours before the children came home, but Chloe had been an inspiration to her, encouraging her to become more skilled at the dressage and jumping. Not only did Chloe keep Polly beautifully, it was more than that, she had a wealth of expertise and had no problem in sharing her knowledge. Katherine had taken lessons with Chloe, twice a week and had gone from strength to strength. She could now perform a passable dressage test and bounded round cross country fences and show jumps at riding club level. It was all pretty low key, and fitted in well with the needs of her family. When Marcus had gone away, Katherine threw herself even more into the riding, and took Susannah to the yard for some lessons too, although ironically her beloved daughter could take or leave it, unlike lots of little girls who were pony mad. With the impending departure of Susannah to school, the yard was to become her salvation. Polly sadly, just couldn't keep up with the rate of Katherine's progress. The sweet horse tried her heart out but struggled to jump the bigger fences, and make the time on the cross country which was needed if Katherine wanted to have a crack at some affiliated eventing where the fences were much more complicated and demanding. Chloe had gently coaxed her into thinking about finding Polly a new home, one where she would not be over faced and where she could do another person the same service that she'd done for Katherine. So it was with great sadness that Chloe had found her a lovely and perfect home with a nervous lady. Katherine had been sad to let Polly go, the little mare had been a real friend to her and a wonderful confidence booster but she really did need to move on to something more talented if she were to even consider affiliated eventing. The upside of the sadness was that she knew that Polly had found a good home where she was well loved and kept. So last autumn, coinciding with Susannah's excited departure for school, she too was excited, at the prospect of her new horse, which she had bought in the August

It had taken a while for her to become accustomed to him, a glossy 16.2 sports horse by the well know eventing stallion Talisman. Talisman, who was aptly named as something intended to bring good luck, had endowed his progeny with his own innate talent. So Alfie, whose proper name was Aramis, had been found. Alfie had been produced by an eventing friend of Chloe's, a fairly young horse at 7 years old, but he had competed at some BE100 classes and showed very good form, going clear every time cross country and show jumping. His dressage needed some work, but he had a good attitude

and a real '*yes please*' way about him and would be ideal for
Katherine, who had the tenacity to improve his flat work. Katherine
had taken a while to get used to her new ride – he was so different
from Polly, much bigger for a start, it was like the difference between
driving a Mini and a Ferrari, he had so many buttons to push! With
Chloe's help, she had really started to feel at one with him now, and
had hunted him that first season, albeit apprehensively at first. She
discovered he was like a machine across country, but had perfect
manners, never pulling or badly behaved. Katherine had grown to
love him and spent hours with him in the stable, petting and grooming
him. Alfie loved the attention, he was a real softie, mild mannered
and affectionate. Between Katherine and Chloe they had put a lot of
work into the dressage, which was improving all the time. Now it was
half way through May, and Katherine felt ready to tackle anything,
and was to make her debut at her first '*proper*' horse trial at Borde
Hill this coming weekend. It had been hard work, especially juggling
it all round the school holidays, when she devoted herself once again
to the family, but she was ready! Jeremy had made all the right
noises, fuelled by the guilt factor and was happy to indulge her
passion for her hobby. He had even said he would come on Saturday
to watch her compete and would bring a picnic lunch. The only
downside was that the children were still at school, they didn't break
up for half term until next week, but they had sent her little cards and
notes to wish her good luck, and all in all, everything in her life was
happy.

Sandy Maclean scratched her head, whipping the wig off her
short cropped hair which stuck up at right angles as she pulled it off.
It had been a relatively easy afternoon in court, a straightforward
case, which to her satisfaction she had won for her client, a meek
middle aged woman, with a domineering and philandering husband,
who had tried to take his wife to the cleaners. Sandy had won a
sizeable settlement, care custody and control of the children, and
costs – that must have hurt the bastard's pocket she thought. Quite
right too she considered. She had spent a little time with her client
afterwards and the other wigs had gone home, there was no-one left
in the robing room, flinging off her gown she plonked herself down
on a chair, leaning back, hands behind her head. Phew it was damned
hot she thought - despite the air conditioning. She bent forward and
gathered her papers together, tying them carefully with a ribbon

before shoving them into her briefcase. She was glad that the case had finished on time, as now she could start to think about the event on Saturday. Fun time! She was so looking forward to going – Seamus was on top form, and so good now that Katherine was coming too. She thought fondly about her friend, the two women had become quite close, unusual for Sandy, who didn't make friends easily and who was a real career woman, and Katherine a home bird. She enjoyed Katherine's company, her easy affable ways, and she spent a lot of her spare time with her.

Sandy had been a barrister for about 15 years. She had worked her socks off and after receiving a first from University College then went onto the Inns of Court School of Law in London. She was lucky and obtained a pupillage in a London Chambers and was called to the Bar in 1996. She specialised in Family Law now, operating from a branch of the London Chambers in Lewes. She had a reputation for being ruthless and successful, being a favourite amongst solicitors in the South East, her empathy with vulnerable clients and ability to be a tenacious advocate in difficult circumstances was renowned.

She was a very private person though and kept her personal life well out of Chambers. She compartmentalised her life well, work was work, business was business, private life was private, that was the way she liked things. Although she had a good relationship with the Senior Clerk, Simon Wantage, who put a lot of work her way. Simon was probably the only person who knew much about her horse and her hobby, and she occasionally confided in him when she had been particularly successful at an event. Simon was a good Clerk, and knew how to be discreet – he must harbour many secrets she thought.

Sandy was single now and loved it; she had married disastrously a slightly younger man. He had been devastatingly good looking, romantic and the total opposite of her in that he had no real ambition, and was content to live off her earnings. He was a mediocre artist, exhibiting out of a small gallery in Brighton. He flattered her, and was good in the sack, but looking back she knew had been a bit of a waster. She had kept him financially for a few years whilst her glasses were still rose coloured, but finally she faced him with an ultimatum that he had to get a proper job. In response, sensing the good times with her had gone, he had promptly had an affair with another gallery owner who promised to exhibit his paintings – the final humiliation of which was that the gallery owner had been a man.

The rejection at the time had been not just humiliating, but for the first time Sandy doubted her ability to read a situation. How could she have misjudged him so much, she had never seen any signs of his bisexuality when she was with him, but reflecting on their relationship of course they were there. His effeminate ways at times, his fastidiousness, his desire to be a kept man, she felt nothing now of the love - or was it lust - that she once had, and frankly was glad to be without him. Of course no-one knew the real truth, although she suspected rumours abounded, and the divorce, her speciality after all, was simple and quick. Since then she had been involved with a number of men, but wanted no ties and made that clear from the start of any relationship. Her horse was the only constant in her life. Dear Seamus, what a salvation he was. She pulled out her phone and rang Simon at the chambers. Hopefully she would catch him.

"Hey Simon, good result here" she briefly outlined the settlement, "but I've got stuff to do, so won't be back tonight, and I'm not in tomorrow – the tie ups can wait till Monday if you don't mind?"

"That's fine with me Sandy, I've got masses on here, so that would suit me. By the way, I've had Jonathan Field on the phone from Milners, they have a case for you – it sounds interesting, right up your street, so I have pencilled them in your diary for next week."

"Great – keep the work rolling in Simon and I'll give you a nice drink out of it" she smiled into the phone "Have a good weekend". What a good bloke he was, she always saw him right, and it was worth every penny!

"You too" he returned. She ended the call, thinking work was coming in thick and fast at the moment, but she did not want it to interfere with her competing, she must check her event diary to make sure there were no glaring clashes. Her mind wandered back to this morning when she and Katherine had come back from their ride. Chloe and Patrick had certainly been in the throes of good gossip, what could that be about she wondered? They had gone totally quiet when they'd arrived back with the horses and despite not wanting to get involved, it was curious nonetheless. Ah well she smiled no doubt she would find out sooner or later, and with that she picked up her briefcase and went home to change.

CHAPTER 7

Saturday dawned another hot and sunny day. Bloody hell the ground would be hard thought Chloe, as she stood in Seamus' box, carefully plaiting the short grey mane.

"Stand still, you old bugger" she complained, as Seamus started to turn his head to nuzzle in her pockets for a Polo "not much longer. Anyway, you don't deserve one, you were a real shit machine this morning, it's taken me ages to get you clean." She pulled his ears fondly and gave him a Polo. He ate it greedily, snatching it out of her hand "Oi you!" she exclaimed "you nearly had my fingers!"

Beebs in the next door box was having similar problems with Alfie, normally so placid, he was clearly excited. Both horses had been restless, dashing backwards and forwards to their doors, shitting everywhere as Chloe pulled out the truck. Next time, we'll plait you buggers before I do that she thought.

Katherine was in a state of high tension too. Her first affiliated event, it was a big step for her. Of course she had done the riding club ones, but this was serious stuff, going out to play with the grown-ups. She had been really relieved that Chloe had offered to take them both in the lorry, rather than going in their trailers. It made such a difference to have her with them, and all that space for the paraphernalia. Somewhere to sit and collect your thoughts and even a loo for when you got nervous! Her tack was spotless, and now she made a 'check list' of things she needed to take, so that nothing would be forgotten at the event. She cringed when she remembered one of her early competitions, when she'd left her bridle behind – what a drama that had been! Jeremy was coming along later, just before the start of the dressage phase, he knew that with Chloe and Sandy going along, she would have lots of moral support, and God knows she was going to need it!

Frankly, Chloe could have done without going, Susie had today off, so Beebs was left to do the yard on her own. John was spending 'quality' time with the children, and it would have been nice to have spent a bit of time at home together as a family. She loved eventing,

60

and had been relatively successful in her younger days, but since the children had come along and the yard had become so busy, she tended to concentrate more on producing the riders and their horses than competing herself. Although when she got to Borde Hill, she knew she would get those old pangs of desire to get out there again – but in truth, she had as much pleasure in seeing her clients doing well. She really wanted Katherine to have a good run with Alfie, this was an important day for them, it would be nice to get a ribbon, but to come back safely was more important. Sandy, on the other hand, was an old campaigner with a lot more experience, although Seamus could do with more flatwork, and if anything let them down it would be the dressage phase. It was hard for Sandy to put that much work in, she was so busy with her job, and she would rather spend her precious time jumping, Sandy was one of those riders that really attacked fences, she had been perfect for Seamus, as initially he was a bit windy over the big timber. A few seasons of hunting and Sandy's guts and determination gave Seamus such confidence that now he was fluent and fast across country. They had an excellent partnership and should have a good day.

Plaiting finished, she went over to the truck, flicking the switch to bring the ramp down, mentally checking that hay nets had been put ready to go, and that the water tanks were full. She methodically went over to the side lockers, first aid kits, equine and human; brown paper and soft bandages with ice tight clay for the horses' legs; grooming kit, stud kit – check. She pulled down the steps to the living area and glanced about inside.

"Have you put your jackets in?" she called, "Don't forget the horses' passports and your number bibs." Christ, it was worse than talking to Rory or Lily.

"Yes they're all in our trunks, they just need to be loaded" shouted Katherine, "The tack is in too, and I haven't forgotten my bridles!" she laughed. Sandy came out of the tack room struggling to carry her saddles.

"Hold on" said Chloe, "I'll give you a hand." They manhandled the saddles into the lockers, and looked around. "Do you wanna check your list Katherine? I'll put the travel boots on the horses." It was always manic like this packing the truck for a competition, she would be glad to get underway.

Finally they were rattling along the lanes towards Borde Hill, it was their local event in terms of distance, just the other side of Cuckfield. The only dodgy part was on the small lanes the lorries were compelled to use, via the farm at the back of the estate. Chloe slowed to negotiate the entrance gates, flagged by two enormous stone pillars, only just wide enough to get the truck through. Her lorry was a big old bus, but she had been used to driving HGVs for years and it didn't faze her, but what did was the sight of a sea of horseboxes and Landrovers and trailers sprawled over the fields in the distance. Christ what an entry! She could remember when it had been a small event, now it was bloody vast! Stewards were guiding her into the parking area, and with relief she was shepherded into the smaller enclosure, used as an over flow lorry park on the other side of the concrete road. There were a lot of shady oaks there and she managed to get the truck as close as she could to the massive trees, so that the horses would not be baked in the back of the box. She looked at Katherine, who was looking a little pale. Chloe knew that feeling only too well.

"Let's get on with it then" she said kindly, "best to be busy and getting on with things when you're nervous. Jumping out of the cab, she walked round to the back of the box and got the ramp down. The horses were excited, stamping their feet and gazing excitedly out of their windows. She went up the ramp and patted them, they would be fine until they returned. She put on her bum bag, remembering to take the passports out of the living area, locked it all up and they all set off towards the main ring.

It was packed, pretty girls with short shorts and tee shirts lounging about on the grass by the side of the show jumping ring, sipping cans of Coke. Long legged riders stood in white breeches, long boots and open-neck shirts watching how the course was riding. The ice cream stand had a long queue, and thirsty dogs panted on their leads. I am so glad I left Sam at home Chloe thought, bloody stupid people bringing dogs on a day like this. They made their way through the throngs of people towards the secretary's tent, passing all the trade stands without a second glance. There would be time enough for browsing once the important stuff was over. Sandy and Katherine took their horses' passports up to the secretary who checked their vaccinations were up to date, always a heart stopping moment if you had made a bloomer about that! The secretary smiled and handed over their numbers after relieving them of the start fee.

Christ this was getting to be a seriously expensive sport, the entries had been £65 each and that didn't include the cost of getting here.

"Oh! It's my lucky number" squealed Katherine – she held aloft the paper number – '315.' It was a funny thing about riding, you all had lucky numbers, wore lucky pants, lucky breeches, lucky numnahs. The list was endless, all probably a load of rot, but she didn't know anyone who jeopardised their luck and flouted the fantasy. She was just like it herself. They marched off to the walk the cross country course, the loud speakers booming as they approached.

"Number 164, that's Caroline Stanbridge on her own horse Lucky Tiger, storming over number seven, the Huntsman's Hedge, they are really on a roll, oh but Tiger is having a good look at the Trakhener at number eight, Caroline's given him some encouragement and they're over . Well done!"

The setting here was amazing, as they walked up the hill. Looking back, the lovely park spread out before them; little dots of people by the lakes, and the tents and marquees were just visible through the old oaks peppered around the show jumping arena. It was like looking down at a toy farm.

Katherine glanced at her programme. "The BE100 for me has pink numbers and the Novice for you Sandy are the yellow ones" as she spoke, a stunning bay galloped over the finishing line.

"Number 159, Freddie Chandler on Fisherman finishing strongly, horse looking very fit, they've obviously had a fantastic round" reported the commentator.

"That guy has some seriously nice horses, that's a lovely sort" admired Sandy.

Chloe who was anxious to start walking the course, was deep in thought barely acknowledged her. It always took longer than you thought to schlep round the course, and time was ticking on. Borde Hill had a fair but challenging cross country, and some nice easy inviting fences to start, with a good gallop in between, but by fence five some more serious questions were asked of the horse and rider. They began their trek round, passing the first few jumps with hardly a glance, as they were fairly straight forward. They paused panting at fence five, after a steady climb up the hill.

"Now don't take this one for granted Katherine, your horse will be feeling the pull of the slope, just like we are, and you need to steady up a bit here and show jump this combination" she carefully walked the striding between the two elements of the fence, the second one slightly offset from the first. "Find a line that you will aim for, so that you get the angle right" she advised. They stood and looked at the fence for a little while, considering the line. Sandy's fence was similar but larger.

From then on the course asked lots of questions, not necessarily about the height of the fences, which were governed by strict rules, but it was more the angles, approaches and landings that had to be taken into consideration. Chloe punctuated each fence with advice *'You will need to kick on for this one'*, or *'Make sure you have good balance into this'*, *'going from bright sunshine into shade, the horse needs time to adjust to the change in light, so a bit of encouragement might be needed here'*.

Katherine eyed her anxiously , Chloe reassured her, "You will be fine Katherine, just keep your leg on and focus, don't look at the crowds, or take your eye off the game for a moment and Alfie will fly round".

The water complex was the only tricky part of the course really. There had been several fallers, mainly through bad riding, and people taking it too fast.

"Don't forget the drag on your horse's legs in the water will make it lose power, imagine how it is when you try and run through water" advised Chloe, "You need to make sure you have enough impulsion to get out! For you Sandy, there is a jump in the middle, so balance up and don't mistake speed for power, okay?"

At that moment a whistle blew from one of the jump judges, the signal that a horse was approaching, and they all leapt to one side. Around the corner it came, a lathered up chestnut, coming at break neck speed, flying into the water and promptly tripping up and stumbling, the rider falling head over heels into the lake. The horse galloped on with cries of *'loose horse, loose horse'* from the spectators. The rider desperately clambered upright, waterlogged and soggy and put her hands on her knees to steady herself.

"Fuck, fuck fuck" they heard her say disappointedly.

"That is just what I mean, steady up, balance and focus". It was unfortunate to have had that happen, especially to Katherine, who looked white and gritted her teeth. "Let's watch one more eh?" said Chloe. It was a while before the whistle blew again, the loose horse having been caught and reunited with the saturated rider. It was a good call though to watch another one go through, as Polly Summers, one of Chloe's pupils came into view on Night Express. She was seriously covering the ground, but on approach, steadied right up, took a check on the horse and sailed over the first element, splashed through the lake and jumped out onto the bank on the opposite side. "Perfect. That's the way to do it" Chloe was proud of Polly, she was really coming on now.

They walked back to the truck, mulling over the course. Chloe made them wait by the show jumping arena and watch a few rounds. This phase of the competition at Borde Hill was notoriously tricky, the course being built on a slight incline and the working in area was small and overcrowded. There was no opportunity walk the show jumping course, so had to watch the other riders jumping and memorise their way round and it was always good to see how the fences were riding anyway - where to take a check and where to kick on. They watched a few go round with varying degrees of success.

"Come on, let's go and get you tacked up and on board" Chloe urged. Katherine was so tense she'd snap if you touched her, and Chloe was certain she'd feel better once she was mounted. Sandy on the other hand was absolutely icy calm, almost withdrawn. Chloe didn't know which was worse.

The dressage phase took place quite a distance away from the main arena, so as to give the horses as little distraction as possible whilst they performed their tests. They walked the horses down the lorry ramp, tacked them up, put on white bandages, and the worst job of all, screwing the studs into their shoes. God she hated this job, arching her back after the last stud had been put in. She always thought of Patrick, how on earth did he manage to bend over like this all day! Katherine and Sandy emerged from the living in the lorry in their riding gear, looking very smart in their snowy white breeches and shirts, their stocks tied neatly and secured with gold pins.

"Here, give me your jackets, I'll carry them over and you can put them on just before you go, otherwise you'll boil" laughed Chloe. She folded them carefully, stowing them away in a large tote bag - '*old faithful*' as it was known. It was a '*lucky*' item with all sorts of clever pockets, which housed all the gear they might need at the dressage. Rule books, spare studs, bottles of water, copies of their tests, that kind of thing. Sandy had a bit of trouble mounting the excited Seamus, who was dancing about at the mounting block, but Alfie, almost sensing Katherine's anxiety stood rock still while she clambered on. At that moment a black Range Rover Sport hurtled up and screeched to a stop, - Jeremy arriving in the nick of time.

"You cut it a bit fine" snapped Katherine, her nerves jangling "I thought you were going to miss it".

"I'm sorry darling," said Jeremy sheepishly, "I got a bit carried away on the computer, and then when I arrived I couldn't find the lorry, I've been driving around for ages looking for you."

"Oh well, you're here now, we're just off to the dressage"

"Lock up the car Jeremy and we can all go over together" called Chloe handing him '*old faithful*'.

The horses jogged over the parkland, their eyes on the cross country jumps in the distance and listening to the sound of the loudspeakers. Seamus leapt up in the air squealing and farting with excitement.

"Bloody hell! Pack it in Seamus" scolded Sandy, almost unseated. Chloe suggested that Sandy and Katherine push on ahead and they would catch them up.

"Oh God, I hope she does alright, it means so much to her you know" said a concerned Jeremy, his face crinkled up against the sun despite his sunglasses.

"She'll be fine, Alfie's a good horse and he'll take care of her, you just make sure you have that champers cooled for them when it's all over!" laughed Chloe. By the time they had trudged over to the dressage arenas, Sandy and Katherine were both trotting around in circles, suppling up their horses, concentrating hard. Chloe made the odd remark as one or other passed her '*rounder*' or '*more impulsion*', '*make him bend a bit more*'. Checking her watch, she nudged Jeremy and they made their way over towards the arena stewards.

"Hi Becky" called Chloe to a tall, ruddy faced woman wearing a large letter C on her number bib "how are you?"

"Oh, Chloe! Lovely to see you, have to say it'd be better if you were riding though; you could show some of them how to do it! There are some shocking riders here today." Chloe looked pleased at the back handed compliment.

"Aw – thanks Hun! I'm here with a couple of my liveries - you running on time?"

"Yep, spot on" said Becky

"My rider is no 315." Becky consulted her list and ticked off Katherine's number. "By the way who's judging?"

"Righto – now there are three to go before her, oh and it's Penny Robinson judging."

"Thanks, see you later" said Chloe, armed with the information, she made her way back to Katherine. "Three to go before you, and make sure you have him nice and forward, this particular judge likes them that way." Actually, she is a fucking bitch thought Chloe, one of the failed rider types, but she wasn't going to mention that to Katherine. She passed her a bottle of water. "I'll just take off his bandages and give you a shout when it is your turn. You're doing fine, he looks great" She glanced over to Sandy who was having a bit of a battle with Seamus, no real surprise there though, but Sandy didn't seem worried, in fact she had a huge grin, or was it a grimace, on her face.

It was Katherine's turn. Chloe passed up her jacket, checked the girth, took her whip, as they were not allowed to be used in the dressage section of eventing, and with that she was off, trotting around the edge of the small grass arena, marked out with white boards, the judge's car at the end. Chloe did not know what was worse, watching someone else compete or doing it yourself. She so badly wanted Katherine to do well, and for Alfie to give her a super ride. Jeremy got out the video camera, just as the car horn signalled for them to start, and she was coming down the centre line, even managing to smile at the judge. It was a fair test, Alfie made the occasional loss of balance on the turns, but on the whole it was not bad, performing all of the movements, and when Katherine came out, she was beaming. The first hurdle was over and she had not disgraced herself.

Finally, Sandy's turn came, Chloe gave her some last minute instructions as she took off Seamus' bandages and handed her a drink and her jacket. Seamus's eyes were out on stalks and his ears pricked tight listening to the distant sound of the loudspeakers and Chloe made a mental note that she must to talk to Sandy about more flatwork for the horse as he was becoming bloody unruly, but this was not the time right now. Sandy confidently sprang into the ring with an enthusiastic Seamus, who was like a kettle coming up to the boil. He steamed round the outside of the arena with Sandy just managing to control him and the judge tooted the car horn. They shot down the centre line with gusto, Seamus clearly hugely enjoying himself! Sandy sensitively just managed to wagon him around the arena performing all the required movements by the skin of their teeth, but the horse was on the point of explosion! Sandy came out grinning, she had no delusions about the test, but was pleased that she had managed to contain him, even if it was tense to say the least.

Back at the lorry, they swopped the tack over for jumping saddles and bridles, and strapped on boots. Thank the Lord for the makers of Velcro thought Chloe, long gone were the tedious buckles and straps on the boots, bloody fiddle they had been! She checked the studs had not worked loose and replaced the hind ones with something a bit more substantial. The riders mounted again and they headed off to the show jumping. God, it was bedlam. Chloe dodged in and out of the horses flying in all directions as she moved warily to the centre of the working in area and stood beside the practice jumps, so that she could put them back up if they were knocked down. The jumps had to be ridden with the red flags to the right of the riders as they approached so as to avoid any pile ups, but they were having near misses all over the place as they clammered to get priority over the order of jumping and Chloe advised both her riders to work quietly around the outside of the arena, avoiding people and horses as best they could and jump only when they saw a clear space. Seamus came bounding into a fence, jumping out of his skin over the little jump, punctuated by yet another stream of excited farts.

"Christ you would think I fed that horse on baked beans" exclaimed Chloe to herself. Luckily, Alfie, despite being younger was much calmer, his jumping was effortless and smooth. As the time ticked on, Chloe moved over to the edge of the ring and checked timings with the steward, shouting out to Katherine "Four more to go before you!"

All too soon, it was Katherine's turn, she bounded into the ring, her face set in a grim line, and Alfie, sleek and beautiful, his intelligent eyes taking in the jumps and his ears pricked in readiness circled in a slow balanced canter and waited for the bell to start.

"Good luck" called Chloe and Jeremy in unison.

They were the last of Section C to jump and there had been precious few clear rounds. It was an anxious two minutes for her spectators, but once over the first fence Katherine relaxed and started to really ride and enjoy the course. They were a picture to watch, and managed a clear round, with only one dodgy moment when a pole rattled ominously but settled back in its cup and luckily did not fall. Katherine whooped with delight as did the crowd of spectators!

She threw her arms around Alfie, "you super super super star" she breathed into his ear, and the horse shook his lovely head.

"I think you love him more than you love me" moaned Jeremy.

There was a short break, the course was not to be altered for the Novice course but just raised higher and Sandy would be the first to go in her section, so there was no course walk. Normally she would have taken Alfie straight back to the truck, but Katherine had dismounted and loosened off his girth straps and she and Jeremy stood under the shade of a massive oak tree, she desperately wanted to watch Sandy's round. Seamus was on a roll and looked amazing, hardly able to contain himself. Finally, the course was ready, and Chloe beckoned them over, patting Seamus and having a last minute chat with Sandy. Then they were off, prancing into the ring, the bell went and Seamus swung into action, taking every fence with gusto, and clearing them by miles. It was a fabulous round but at the last fence, a deceptive upright, Sandy relaxed and the hot-headed grey horse took control, flattened and steamed off, rolling the top pole. A roar of disappointment came from the crowd.

"Bugger, bugger, bugger" Sandy was so cross with herself, but it had been a great round nonetheless, and he was a tricky horse to hold.

"Well done" shouted Chloe, "he isn't easy and you rode

brilliantly!"

Animated, and back at the truck, both riders glugged back the cans of Red Bull that Chloe had miraculously produced from '*old faithful*'. The best bit was now to come and they were really looking forward to it Chloe re-checked the studs, and taped up the horses' boots, offering the horses a sip of water, as they tried to gulp greedily out of the bucket, but Chloe only permitted them a draught or two. The girls appeared at the lorry door, having changed into their bright cross country colours and put on their back protectors and air jackets. Jeremy stood around helplessly, he was a bit of a spare part, and Chloe teased that he would have to start learning what to do, if he were to become a true eventing groupie.

The riders made their way to the start of the cross country, Chloe and Jeremy hurrying to catch them up, '*old faithful*', had been replenished with water and Chloe had made sure she had her stop watch with her. They toiled back up the hill to the collecting ring for the cross country phase where the girls were already warming up. There was less of a melee of riders here, and the starter was rattling through the competitors and the girls would soon be off.

"Now Katherine, don't hammer him round, the ground is hard and you're going for a clear, and it's more important that you come back safely than worry about the time at this stage," Chloe added "Sandy, don't go too fast! You know what he's like!" Katherine was now clearly enjoying herself, as she moved into the start box, a confident smile on her face.

"*Five, four, three, two, one and go and good luck!*" counted down the starter and she surged off, Alfie, ears pricked galloping into the first fence. Chloe held her breath, but they were over and safe and she watched as they sped off into the distance.

"*Last to go in this BE 100 pre-novice section is Katherine Gordon, on Aramis. This is Katherine's first affiliated event, and they have a good dressage score of 29 and a clear in the show jumping. This may be Katherine's lucky day, if she can just hold it together on this good young horse*" the commentator announced confidently. Chloe thought bugger, I hope she didn't hear that, she doesn't need the pressure, but Katherine had long gone.

"And Katherine Gordon, with Aramis clear at fence five, and making good progress across the long pull up the hill to fence 6, and they're over" came the excited report over the loud speaker.

Oh God, thought Chloe, please let them get round. She superstitiously stood as she always did, with her legs crossed, and her fingers on both hands crossed too. Katherine stormed back into view as the course wound back towards them. The next fence was a big drop down into a sunken road, and out again, to meet a skinny fence on an angle. Chloe saw Katherine steady the big horse, he sized it all up and with a kick from Katherine, flew down the drop, leapt out bravely, but not at quite the right angle for the skinny. Katherine dragged him towards the narrow fence, trying madly to straighten him with brute strength and the honest horse that Alfie was, he leapt over and was off on his way!

"Phew" moaned Chloe "that was a close one!" They were then out of view and she could only wait to hear over the commentary to find out what happened at the water. The delay was awful.

"Katherine Gordon, clear through the water and on her way home now!" came the report over the loud speaker. Chloe started to relax, she just hoped Katherine didn't, not quite all over yet! Then into view came the steaming horse and rider, Alfie a bit steadier now after the long course, and Katherine, red in the face from exhilaration. Just the last jump to go and despite Alfie's tiredness, he made a huge effort, and they were over, steaming through the finishing line. Chloe ran over to meet them, flushed with excitement. Katherine immediately slid of the foaming horse, and handed the reins to her.

"Oh my God, he was amazing, it was simply the best round, he's a machine!" She flung her arms around him, patting him "Good boy Alfie, what a good boy!" The horse blowing hard, nuzzled her neck. One down, one to go thought Chloe and went back to the collecting ring, leaving Jeremy with the excited Katherine, who had dismounted and was leading the tired Alfie back to the lorry.

"We just have to wait for the fence judges to move, and then it's you. Okay?" Sandy nodded in assent, she was quiet, and Chloe knew that she was concentrating and focusing on the course ahead. Chloe knew better than to try and make small talk, the waiting was always the worst, and it seemed to be taking ages too. She could see the judges' cars in the distance moving to the different fences on the novice course, and a motorbike sped around, methodically checking to make sure that everyone was in place before giving the all clear to start the next section.

The minutes ticked past agonisingly, "You're on Sandy" called Chloe, as the steward beckoned her over. Sandy, face fixed, walked over to the start box and waited for the countdown.

"Just started on the course is Sandy Maclean, the first to go in this Novice Section H. She is riding her own Irish Rock, known as Seamus. Sandy has a full time job and events for fun, so go ahead Sandy and enjoy the ride!" Oh my God thought Chloe, this commentator gets more and more cheesy. She cranked her legs and fingers into the lucky position, trying to crane her neck to get a view of the grey flash in the distance, he was covering the ground like a rocket. So far so good, she just hoped Sandy could keep him under control and that in his exuberance he didn't make silly mistakes and tip up.

The commentator, busy now talking about a new starter, was not giving much information, Chloe waited anxiously, and then she saw them hurtling towards the sunken road fence. Christ they were just going too bloody fast, she could hardly bear to watch. Sandy was standing up in her stirrups, tugging like mad at Seamus, struggling to check him to slow down. It must have taken a super human determination, but with a last momentous effort, he rebalanced and she managed to position him just in time, and they were over in a flurry of dust. In no time at all, the commentator had declared them through the water and clear and Chloe saw a blur of grey coming towards the finish, full of running, Sandy tugging and trying to control him. They shot through the finishing line, Seamus clearly was as fit as a flea, but Sandy looked exhausted. She slid off, and handed him to Chloe, with Seamus dancing around on the end of the rein. Sandy gasping, bent double, her hands on her knees for support, then she looked up grinning.

"Fan-bloody-tastic!!" she sighed. Chloe laughed and she hugged Sandy, "you old bugger Seamus."

Back at the truck, the horses washed off, and their studs removed. They had walked them round to cool down and for their breathing to recover, checked their legs for any injuries and wrapped them with ice clay and bandages, and finally loaded them into the lorry.

"What a day! Fantastic success for Mileoak and it's all thanks to you Chloe".

Chloe looked awkward, "you rode them, not me."

"Yes but without you, we couldn't do it" said Sandy.

"Great team work eh? Chloe grinned. "Come on let's sit down and have something to eat, I'm bloody knackered".

Jeremy had produced the most marvellous picnic from the back of the Range Rover. He had spread out on a picnic blanket moist slivers of smoked salmon, bowls of prawns, beef, brie, avocados and tomatoes along with French bread, together with a huge bowl of strawberries. With a flourish he opened a bottle of Moet.

"Here's to a great day" he toasted. They raised their glasses and clinked them together.

It had been a great day indeed. Chattering and laughing, recounting every fence, Sandy and Katherine were animated. Jeremy listened indulgently, thinking he could get into this eventing lark! Chloe shovelled down some food, before the champagne went to her head, she still had to drive home. Home, she wondered what John had been up to with the children and suddenly she had a real longing to get back to Mileoak. She was really tired, the girls had no idea how far she had walked today. Worse than a marathon, she thought, I could do with a bit of TLC myself.

"Come on let's go and see what the scores are like".

"D' you know I'd forgotten all about the scores" laughed Katherine," better go over I suppose and get the bad news!"

"Top up Chloe?" asked Jeremy brandishing the bottle "plenty more and I've another bottle in the car."

"No thanks, I'd love to, but I've got to drive, and I should be getting back really, I've left Bibi on her own today". They put away the picnic, and wandered down towards the main arena. The competition was still in full flow. Jeremy offered to buy them all ice creams, and they certainly did look good, but Chloe could never

73

bother to queue, she was too keen to see the scores. The big scoreboards were housed in an open sided marquee with masses of competitors milling around them. The results for Katherine's class were up, they scanned the long list of scores. Katherine gave a huge whoop to see that she had come 3rd! In her first event too!

"Well done, you really deserved it" cried Chloe and Sandy together.

"Oh my God, I'm in the Prize giving, what time is it? "Katherine gasped, clutching the others in delight.

" ...15 minutes — better get back to the truck, so you can put your jacket on" Chloe glanced at Sandy, who was scrutinising the results of her own section, only a few cross country results had been posted, but so far Sandy had done pretty well. The dressage phase, despite the tension, had gone well, the judge must have liked Seamus, and she was on a 35, with one down in the show jumping which gave her a further 4 penalties, making a 39 so far, she might just be in the money. Chloe knew though the results would be an age, as Sandy had been the first to go in her section, and there were 45 runners altogether. She thought gloomily of all the hanging around. Okay you could browse amongst the trade stands, spending money on stuff you probably didn't need, laze about watching the rest of the sections, but she was agitating to get home.

They found Jeremy who had just paid for the ice creams, he was ecstatic when he heard Katherine's news, throwing his arms in the air, almost hurling the ice creams into orbit.

"I'm so proud of you darling, it was wonderful to come and watch. I'll definitely come again" he beamed.

"You'd better" glowed Katherine "clearly you bring me luck, but y' know Chloe, I couldn't have done it without your help and support, and yours too Sandy". She turned to look at them, "seriously, you've both been an inspiration to me, all that encouragement, and being here with me today."

"You did it, you rode him and you did fantastically" Chloe said, guiltily forgetting that moments before, all she'd wanted to do was to get home. Back at the truck, ice creams melting in the hot sun, Katherine threw on her jacket ready for the prize giving, with Chloe thinking once again, how could she spoil her moment of glory. Sandy glanced at her, catching her mood, her famous intuition kicking in.

"Why don't you drive the horses home Chloe? She suggested, "I'm sure that Jeremy will bring Katherine and me back to the yard, you've spent ages here with us." Chloe looked at Sandy, then at Katherine and Jeremy, who both smiled warmly at her.

"Are you are sure? It is hot and I don't want to leave them baking on the lorry longer than necessary, but I don't want to miss the prize giving either"

Ten minutes later Chloe was on the road home, listening to the radio and thinking how surprised John would be that she was home so early. The miles rolled by, she hummed along to the radio, pleased with the day out, very successful indeed. She groped in her bag, and pulled out an illicit cigarette, lighting it and inhaling deeply. No-one knew she smoked occasionally - well a girl had to have her secrets. Before she knew it she was coming up the lane to the farm and she trundled into Mileoak and down the drive, past the house and into the yard. Funny, she thought I can't see John's car, perhaps he had taken the children out? The yard looked a shambles, unswept, with bandages and whips discarded around all over the place. Bibi greeted her; she had an embarrassed look on her face which Chloe caught immediately.

"Everything okay Beebs?"

"Fine, fine." Bibi reassured, "you're home earlier than I thought"

Chloe looked at her sideways, "what's up Beebs? What's happened?" She had a sinking feeling, Bibi was not a good liar, the look on her face spoke volumes, and something had happened, she knew it. What?

"Well" stammered Bibi "Horses are all fine, and I don't want to be the cause of any trouble y' know Chloe"

"Just bloody tell me" demanded Chloe. "Whatever it is I'll find out pretty soon, so come on, give, what's up?" Chloe thoughts were running wild, had one of the children had had an accident? One of the dogs perhaps? John's car had gone, where was he, he was supposed to spend the day here with them? Was he okay? She'd had her phone with her all day, so they'd have got hold of her at any time if there were any problems.

"Oh Chloe, don't be angry with me" Bibi wailed, " I know the yard looks a right state, but just after you left, John came down and asked me to mind the children whilst he popped out. He promised to be back before you came home, but you're much earlier than normal, and I just couldn't do everything. They're fine, playing in the orchard, so that I could keep an eye on them, but I had to keep popping backwards and forwards to make sure they were all okay, and then I had to get them their lunch ..."

Chloe was shocked, what was John playing at, it wasn't Bibi's job to look after their children, what had happened to make him disappear like that? No wonder the poor kid hadn't been able to do the yard, not surprising at all, and not at all her fault either. I mustn't get angry she thought.

"It's okay, it's not your fault, but if you don't mind getting the horses off and sorting out the truck for me, I'd be really grateful and I'll go up and sort out the kids. Sorry to ask you, I know you've had a real rubbish day, but I'll give you a bit extra this week to make up"

Bibi looked relieved. "Oh Chloe, I'm so sorry, of course, I'll get the horses off and finish up here too, no need for any extra, it's fine honestly". Chloe looked at her gratefully, she was a good girl, and she hated feeling that she'd taken advantage of her, she'd make sure she had a bit of a bonus.

"Thanks, I really appreciate it Beebs, I'll put the truck away later, and be back down when John comes home." She was seething - what the fuck was he up to abandoning the kids like that?

She stalked back to the house, via the orchard. The kids were having a great time it seemed, despite their absent father. They'd made a camp out of an old tarpaulin, and some wooden pallets, dragging a tartan rug underneath for a floor.

"Hello Mummy" called Lily, "we're having such fun, what do you think of our camp? Bibi helped us and she let us have our lunch out here" The boys turned round, grins on their faces.

"You aren't cross are you mummy? You look a bit cross". Quickly Chloe forced a smile onto her strained face.

"Of course I'm not cross darlings, it looks a fabulous camp, and what a good idea to have lunch out here," she plonked herself down under the tarpaulin with them and looked at the remnants of their lunch, half eaten jam sandwiches and biscuits, the dogs would have a field day with the scraps. "Where's Daddy" she asked trying not to seem too concerned.

Lily, licking the jam off her fingers, looked at her innocently. "Oh yes, he left just after you. He was playing about with his phone and got one of those texty messages. He said he had to go out for a bit and asked Bibi to babysit. She was fantastic fun, this camp was her idea and we had a cool lunch, jam sandwiches, you never let us have them" she prattled on, "we even managed to get Toby away from his computer."

What the hell was going on thought Chloe, it wasn't as though it was asking much for him to be with his kids for one day a week, and that bloody phone, he was always funny about it, even took it to the loo with him these days. She rallied herself, stroking Lily's hair.

"Where are the dogs darling?"

"Daddy shut them in the boot room" said Toby, "I told him you'd be cross about that. Are you cross mummy, you have an angry face." Immediately Chloe readjusted her face once again and smiled through her teeth.

"Sweetie, I seriously am not cross, although I'd like the dogs to have been out here with you and enjoying the fun."

Toby looked worried. "I knew you wouldn't like it, shall we go and get them now?" Together they stood up, holding hands and walked towards the house. She opened the door to the boot room and the dogs tumbled out, indignant at their enforced confinement and desperate to be the one who got most of Chloe's attention.

"There, there , it's okay my lovelies, I'm back now." The dogs dashed into the garden, cocking their legs and quarrelling as they went, they were worse than the kids. "Okay, let's go back and finish off that camp, we can put in some cushions and as a treat how about some coke? As it's such a lovely day, we could have a barbeque out there."

Chloe rounded up the children and chattering they disappeared back to the orchard, closely followed by the cavorting dogs, who immediately gobbled up the left overs of the lunch. Chloe tried to concentrate on their game, but her mind constantly strayed back to the same question. Where the hell had John gone in such a rush?

CHAPTER 8

It was a dingy flat, with the constant droning noise of vehicles in the street below floating up through the open window, competing with Judas Priest belting out on the stereo. The shabby curtains were pulsating with the vibrations of the traffic and music. The room was thick with a sweet musky smell and whorls of smoke snaked and curled through the air. Bottles of water and opened cans of coke were strewn everywhere, and discarded sweet wrappers joined the half eaten sandwiches stuffed back in their cellophane boxes which had been chucked on the floor. There were four occupants in the room, a couple draped across the sofa, and two others sprawled on the filthy carpet sharing a spliff between them.

"I've got an attack of the munchies, anything left of those sweets?" sighed the lad lounging on the sofa. He scratched his eyebrow, he'd had it pierced again yesterday and fuck me he thought, it was bloody sore. He yawned, his puffy red eyes squinting to focus. One of the girls chucked him a half-eaten Mars bar, followed by the remains of a sandwich. "Is this all we got? What I really fancy is toast, with loads of butter and jam, or better still Marmite!" He struggled to his feet, swaying his way to the little kitchenette, ""Who wants some?"

"Just make a load and bring it in Sean, we're all starving, and these sandwiches are shit" moaned Linda, her damp black hair clinging to her head, her face chalk white, with its heavy black make up smudged over her eyes. She heaved herself off the sofa, and moved over to the open window, leaning out over the ledge "I'm so fucking hot" she yelled out of the window. She peered further out, looking down into the street below, catching sight of someone she knew "Hey Laura" she bellowed "come on up – blue door", she leaned out further pointing downwards. "Whoa, I nearly fell out" she laughed.

The girl in the street below glanced up, shading her eyes from the glare of the sun."Yo, Linda" called Laura, "okay, I'll come up, having a party?"

What a stroke of luck thought Laura, just the person I was hoping to see. She had actually been loitering around in the hope of catching sight of Linda, who hadn't been at college for a week or more, and Laura knew that this was roughly where she'd said she lived. Laura made her way through a door way, between two shop fronts and climbed up the stairs in front of her. It was filthy in here, litter everywhere, and she was pretty sure she could smell stale piss. The door to the flat was on the latch and she pushed her way in, the reek of the dope was overpowering and she wrinkled her nose, she hated the stuff. Still, if the plan that she'd been carefully germinating was to come to anything, then she'd need help and these dope heads would be perfect. She smiled at them all.

"Hey Linda, good to see you" she greeted, "You okay, missed you at college". Linda pulled back from the window struggling to stay balanced.

"I'm so finished with all that crap, those lecturers bore the shit out of me, and I don't give a flying fuck about the exams" she spat. "Come and have a smoke, let your hair down. This is Ewan and Annie". The couple on the floor looked up at her, and acknowledged her with nods of their heads.

"Hi" said Laura, "No I won't have a smoke thanks, got a raging sore throat, might have a cold coming". This was a total lie, but she didn't want to alienate them. "You finished with college then Linda?" she asked, thinking that this was a bit of a blow to her. She needed to nurture their friendship a little, become Linda's buddy, and college would have been a good environment to do it. If the truth were known, Laura could not think of anything worse than being friends with this Emo, with her gothic make up and her skanky ways, but she wanted to befriend her for her own motives. She was fairly sure that she would be able to make use of them, and they were stupid enough to go along with it. She brushed her shiny fair hair away from her face and over her shoulder. "Yes it's shit there" she lied, in reality she was a bright girl, studying art and fashion design and hoping to get some good qualifications, so that she could go on to get a job in design, if she was lucky enough, in one of the big stores. Trouble was, her allowance didn't go far, and she'd had to supplement her income in a variety of ways, not all of which would have been approved of by her grandparents, who'd brought her up.

"What you been up to then?" she asked trying to sound as

deadpan and flat as were the voices of the others.

"Oh, this and that, y' know" said Linda, "we went up to Parliament Square and did our stint in the protest tents , lucky it was warm though, they must be freezing their bollocks off when it's cold"

"Hard to think it'll be cold, when the weather's like this eh?" At that moment Sean crashed into the sitting room, with a tray, with what must have been a whole sliced loaf of toast piled precariously high on a plate with pots of jam and marmite.

"Lunch is served" he laughed "Waiter service!" Ewan and Annie levered themselves up and dived in, as did Linda. "Whoa, leave some for me you gannets" cried Sean, plonking himself down on the floor, and grabbing a couple of slices. "You want some? I'm Sean by the way" he turned to Laura.

"Ah, mm, no thanks" she stammered, smiling at him.

Sean peered at her, "Haven't I seen you before somewhere?" he asked curiously.

"No, don't think so, hey but maybe once or twice on the Sabs bus?" a genius response thought Laura which was bound to open up the conversation in the direction she wanted, although she'd have to be careful what she said, she knew fuck all about hunt saboteurs or their cranky ways. Sean looked more interested.

"You a member then?" he asked "Which area?"

"Oh Guildford", said Laura vaguely, quickly adding "then a bit up near Oxford way, where I come from. What about you?"

Linda looked at her, "You never told me you were a Sab Laura, kept that quiet."

Laura considered for a brief moment "Well, you never asked me did you? Yeah, I'm dead against those cruel upper crust bastards shredding up foxes and wildlife. They all still hunt illegally despite the ban, and in a way it's worse now, the police do nothing about it at all. Fucking pigs!" She desperately hoped she sounded convincing.

"Too right" remarked Ewan, speaking for the first time, his eyes with hugely dilated pupils finding it hard to focus on her "Annie and I try an' go every week in the winter, just with a few of the hard core, but there are not so many now, and we're well outnumbered, they take all sorts of liberties" he complained.

"I know" said Laura, "they need teaching a bloody lesson really, but unless you make a drastic plan, nothing'll be done".

"Whatdya mean a drastic plan, what else can we do?" said Linda.

"Well" began Laura, "I dunno, something that will make those bastards sit up and take notice. Publicity, that's what we need, so that Joe Public can really see what they get up to. Since the bill went through, they seem to think it's done and dusted, whereas the likes of us know better." She blustered on "it's come out of the public eye now, never makes the papers, so we're forgotten about. Those toffs need teaching a lesson."

Sean eyed her interested "You're right chick, but what can we do?"

Laura stood up, "I really don't know" but she had set the seed in their heads, and she would be back to do more "Look I gotta split, just wanted to make sure you were okay Linda", she raised her hand to them and with that she left. They waited until they heard her go down the stairs.

"Seems a good girl that, eh Linda, nice of her to be concerned about you, and to find another supporter, eh?" "With that he began to roll another spliff, and changed the music to some early Black Sabbath.

Laura walked back out into the sunshine, filling her lungs with fresher air, despite the filthy car fumes. She tossed her blonde mane over her shoulders and her eyes glittered. She was pleased with her visit to Linda and her dope heads. Rebels without a cause they were, well she would certainly give them a cause she smirked, but not quite in the way in which they intended. It was imperative that she took her time though, they needed to trust her , and she needed to take time to build up their faith in her. She didn't give a toss about stinking foxes, or about how they were hunted, but she did care about destroying one man who had used her, and treated her like a slag. It'd been a piece of piss tracking him down, hot shot fucker that he was, well she'd make him eat his own shit by the time she'd finished with him. Smiling to herself, deep in thought she walked back along the hot pavement towards the tube,.

Jennifer lay on a sun lounger alongside the crystal sparkling water of the pool. She was carefully shaded by a vast safari style parasol. She wasn't going to let the sun turn her into a wrinkly prune - like so many of the women around here who clearly had made no attempts to protect their skin. She studied her carefully manicured hands, her nails painted a deep red as they glinted in the sunshine. Perhaps next time, she thought, I may go for a French polish - more discreet. She had learned that lesson after her original gaffe, and the scornful glares at the fated New Year's Eve party. In London, she could be a lot more daring but the dress she had chosen for her own party was simple and understated but even she had to admit was totally chic. Some months ago, she had enlisted the help of a personal shopper, a disconcertingly ebullient girl, who had persuaded her to alter her image to adapt to her new lifestyle. Jennifer, wasn't sure at first, and didn't feel herself at all in her new clothes, when she looked in the mirror she seemed to see someone else. She was getting used to it though, and despite her initial misgivings, she did like the new dress that Sophie had insisted was perfect for her party. It was of cream silk with a sweetheart neck line, and tapering hand beaded straps, fitted to the waist with an A line skirt floating like a cloud to just below the knee, trailing behind to a longer length. The bodice also had tiny beads intricately threaded into small flowers. There was not a flash of a boob, or leg in sight and sighing, she accepted that it probably was '*just right*'. She picked up her book, read a few lines, and then realised that she hadn't digested a word, and flung it aside.

She looked around from behind her huge sunglasses, she had everything she had always dreamed of, but now she had it, her life felt empty and meaningless. The vivacious person she'd once been chasing her elusive rainbows - had found her pot of gold but discovered it had a price tag which had sucked away the sparkle of life. She knew she couldn't go on like this, it was tearing her up, there seemed to be no fun in anything anymore and moreover, no-one to have fun with or to have a passion for. She needed to find something to do - to while away the long hours of the day. What though? She had no friends and no real interests either. She had always enjoyed shopping, but the fun of a bargain disappeared when you could buy anything you wanted, and anyway her wardrobes were stuffed with clothes but she had no occasion to wear them.

Perhaps, she should give Chloe Coombe a ring and start up the riding lessons again. She had been really nice to Jennifer when she went before, although Jennifer had been so nervous and gawky, and then humiliated, which had probably come out as a frosty coldness, which she hadn't meant at all. To be fair too, Chloe had been sworn to silence about her clandestine instruction, and as far as Jennifer knew, no-one had found out. Jennifer, rather meanly, had not invited Chloe to her party for fear that she would blurt out her secret. It would be difficult to re-instate the training after such a deliberate slight. She pondered what to do. To take up the riding again might just be what she desperately needed if she were not to go insane with loneliness. Abruptly, she picked up her wrap and threw it on around her bikini, and gathering up her book and pathetically silent new phone, she went inside to change.

Chloe was up to her neck in shit , mucking out one of the deep litter boxes, her arms ached with the effort of it all. Beebs and Susie were running barrows back and forth to the muck heap, but she was knackered. Still the job had to be done and today was the perfect opportunity, and between the three of them they were steaming on in more ways than one! Mondays were always quiet, the horses' day off, and few people wanting lessons too. She and the girls used these days to do jobs which might have been a bit neglected during the busy week. Numnahs and bandages were drying on the line, and the huge yard washing machine was still whirring away in the tack room. Nearly done she thought, getting stuck in with the fork again - anyway, it was a good way to deal with the anger that she'd felt since the weekend. She had challenged John about his abrupt disappearance when he had finally come home, to find her in the orchard with the children. He'd looked guilty and surprised to see her back, having been caught out. She was impressed with herself that she'd kept her temper, and unbelievably he'd brushed the incident off, saying he'd been called into work urgently. Chloe didn't believe him and he knew it, and to be fair he had tried to make up all of that Sunday, but Chloe had remained distant, and they'd hardly spoken this morning.

"Hey Chloe, you've a visitor" Beebs called appearing with an empty barrow. Chloe shaken out of her deep thoughts looked up surprised, to see a silver Mercedes convertible, with Jennifer Parker-Smythe stepping cautiously across the yard on strappy sandals.

"Blimey, what does she want? Beebs, no taking the piss now" she warned. Chloe put down her fork and went to meet Jennifer, aware that she stank of horse shit, and in her faded old shorts and tee shirt, she must look a right sight. "Hi Jennifer" she greeted "what brings you here?" They must have looked like chalk and cheese, Jennifer in her pale green linen capri trousers, and white camisole top.

"Ah Chloe, I'm so glad that you're here, I wanted to talk to you… And to apologise" she faltered.

Chloe curbed her look of surprise, "Apologise?" she asked "what for? Look do you fancy a glass of lemonade. I could really do with one?" Chloe shouted to Beebs and Susie, "take a break girls, I just have to pop up to the house" she didn't want the girls earwigging this conversation. Beebs and Susie looked knowingly at each other with a *'fine by us'* looks on their tanned faces.

Jennifer followed Chloe up to the house, the dogs lifting an eyelid from dozing in the shade of the back porch. Chloe automatically put a hand down to fondle them, and then kicked off her stinky mucker boots.

"Come on in Jennifer" she invited, "excuse the mess". The kitchen was indeed in its usual chaos, but Jennifer glad of being welcomed so openly, was determined not to make any humorous remarks, which may be misconstrued. Chloe washed her hands and went over to the fridge and pulled out a glass jug "it's homemade, really refreshing, the kids love it." She clunked some ice into two tall glasses and motioned for Jennifer to follow her outside to a small, walled and very secluded terrace area just off the kitchen. "This is one of my favourite places" sighed Chloe "it's so private, and John and I often have our tea out here in the morning or a beer at night." Although not lately she thought sadly. They sat down at the small wrought iron table and chairs, "Now Jennifer, what is it you wanted to talk about?" she asked.

Jennifer, who had been preparing to lie and say Chloe's

invitation to the party had been overlooked, decided that if this was going to work then she needed to be honest right from the start, after all Chloe had proved to be discreet before.

"Look Chloe" she began "I don't know quite how or where to start."

Chloe felt sorry for her, she was like a fish of water down here and nobody had made any effort with Jennifer, including her.

She waited for Jennifer to continue "I haven't found it easy to settle here in the country, I've always lived in London, and not the posh part either. I've really tried to fit in, and perhaps I haven't always gone about it in the right way, but I truly have tried my best. But I'm miserable and I'm lonely. I purposely didn't send you an invitation to our party, because I was afraid that you might mention I'd come to you before when I tried to learn to ride. I realise that this was really wrong of me, and I'd like you very much to come, if you'd consider it now?"

Chloe looked at Jennifer for a long moment, not sure how to respond at first. "You can't think very much of me, if you believe that I'd have said anything, you specifically told me not to" she said testily.

"Please Chloe" whispered Jennifer, wringing her hands together "I do think a lot of you and your endless patience with me in my dismal attempts to ride." She went on "It was a long while ago after all. It was very hard for me to come down here and take over at Nantes from Celia, with all the tradition and stuff that was involved and quite honestly I was out of my depth and still am frankly."

Chloe stared at her, thinking it must have taken a lot for her to come here today, and admit what she just had, it would have been much easier to have lied about the invitation. It was a desperate woman indeed to have said what she just did.

"Actually, Chloe, I want to be completely honest with you, Charles has kind of just dumped me down here, I don't have any friends, and I really badly wanted to fit in, but I just didn't, and don't know how to. I'd love to come back and have another go at riding with you, and equally love you to come to the party"

Chloe was astonished, she must be in a right state, to have come here and disclosed all this personal stuff. "It's okay Jennifer" she responded kindly, "it would never have been easy for you to take Celia's place, so the best piece of advice I can give you, is not to try – just be yourself, and let people like you for who you are"

Jennifer said sadly, "They only see me as a gold digger, who was after Charles for his money, but they don't know the real person or know anything about me at all. Please come to the party Chloe, and teach me again. I really am sorry."

It was hard for Chloe to refuse, given the pleading in her voice, and whilst she was under no illusion that they would become best buddies, Chloe was a real old softie and knew she would be prepared to help her with her riding - if she were serious that was.

"Look Jennifer, okay I'll try and come to the party, but no promises – okay? As for the riding, it's not a problem at all, when d' you want to start again?"

Jennifer looked at her gratefully. "You don't know what this means to me Chloe, thank you. I've an idea though, and I don't know what you think? How about I come down to the stables and help you with other stuff, that way I'd learn to be around the horses - without being so terrified of them all the time. I know I could try with the horses at home, but I don't think that Caitlin, and certainly not Lucy, would be willing to help me".

She had a point there thought Chloe, with that little madam Lucy taking the piss all the time, it would be all round the Fox by teatime. Caitlin she knew would be more sympathetic, but even so, she could see there could be an issue. Actually it may well be a good idea, just get her used to being around the horses a bit more and she could meet some of the other liveries and clients, it might well help she conceded.

"I think that's a good idea Jennifer, when do you want to come? How about tomorrow?"

Caitlin, lay back on the springy grass, her hands behind her head, her pert nipples erect with desire. God she loved him, she thought as she looked down at his mop of hair, he was kissing and licking her tummy.

"Mmmm, that is so lovely" she whispered. Gradually, his head sunk lower towards her pants, and she felt his thumbs hook underneath them, edging them down further, as he worked his mouth more and more downwards. She thought she would explode with craving for him, "don't stop, don't stop" she sighed.

Slowly, he teasingly eased her knickers right down, until she slid her legs out. Naked now, he looked down at her and bent forwards to kiss her gently on the lips. Sitting back and watching her all the time, he deliberately sucked the tip of his finger, opened her legs and softly began to stroke her, watching the rapt expression on her face. She moaned and closed her eyes, and he smiled. God she was gorgeous. He positioned his head between her legs and began to lick and explore her with his tongue, gently at first and then more intensely, as he felt her body stiffening with excitement as she came. "Oh my God, that was amazing" she gasped. Quickly, he undid his trousers, and opening her with his fingers, thrust himself up inside her, she was wet and warm and ready for him. He moved rhythmically, pushing himself in deeper and deeper, her long legs grasping him around his back, caressing his hair with her hands "I love you" she whispered.

"And I you" he said, kissing her all the more, and for the time being it was enough.

Patrick was singing along to Radio 2 in his van, they played all the good songs, ones that you knew. He could play a few of them on his guitar too, he had been taking lessons for a while and they had been going really well lately. The van rattled along, the horseshoes in the back clanking together as he swung round the corners. Jack his dog had his head lolling out of the open window sucking in the air as he drove along. Patrick was quite near to Grace's and he remembered he'd promised to look in when he was passing and see her horse. Patrick had finished early at this last job, just a few trims, and he could pop in there and have a quick look if she was around. He glanced at his watch, yes he had time before he was due at Mileoak.

He pulled over into a small National Trust car park at the edge of

High Ridge Woods, and thought, I'd better ring first, just to make sure she's at home. She often went up to her parents at this time of the day, and he didn't want to make a wasted journey. Bugger - he thought no signal here. Not surprising really he laughed to himself, these woods are pretty dense. Nosily he glanced about, there was one car in the car park, which looked familiar and probably belonged to a dog walker, but it was a pretty isolated spot and there were never many people about. Then he saw it, another car - a Toyota 4 wheel drive, hidden right around the corner of the car park, quite out of sight from the road. It looked like Oliver Traver's - the vet's vehicle. He squinted to look, to see if he could see any sign writing on the side, but it was just too far away. That was odd? Patrick had done quite a lot of work with him on several cases of obscure lameness. Good bloke, a Kiwi, married and lived just outside the village. Why would his car be parked here, so hidden? Curious, he edged his van into gear and moved towards the Toyota, yes it was Oliver's car, he could clearly see the vet's logo on the passenger door now. Very strange indeed! As he was pondering the question, he heard the sound of someone crashing through the woods towards the vehicle, and Oliver himself came into view. A tall, good looking guy, with a tousled head of blonde hair and a good tan, wearing shorts and polo shirt, he was fiddling with his flies. Our Oliver was very popular with the ladies Patrick thought enviously, although he kept them all at arm's length, his wife Suse was a right bitch and known to keep him on a short lead.

"Hi Oliver" hollered Patrick through the open van window "everything alright?"

"Yep, I'm fine thanks buddy, just stopped for a piss," shouted back Oliver, "been desperate for a leak!"

Patrick looked at him and laughed "I know the feeling mate! Well so long as you're okay. See you later, can't stop." He turned the van around, and moved off slowly, fiddling with his phone, bloody signal! He would just go up to Grace's anyway and take a chance.

Chloe was busy in the kitchen, it had been a long day, and she was still surprised about Jennifer Parker Smythe's visit. It was a pain really, she was not sure that she wanted Jennifer hanging around the yard much, she would have to be shown how to do things and that in itself took time, it was often as quick to do it yourself. Still, she had promised her and she was a sucker for a sob story, so she would just have to get on with it now, and see how it panned out. She had told Jennifer to be here at 9.30 tomorrow morning. When she'd mentioned it to Beebs and Susie they'd moaned like stink, saying she would be a stuck up pain in the arse and would try and order them around, not want to get her hands dirty and be a bloody hindrance. Chloe secretly agreed with them but said would they please, for her - Chloe, just give it a try? She also said that they weren't to gossip about it either, which she knew would be hard to do, as it was such a juicy titbit of information, but she wanted them to keep schtum, at least for the time being. They had rolled their eyes and complained but agreed that they would do it just for Chloe and her alone. Relieved Chloe wondered how long it would be before people got to hear about Jennifer's plan, that's if she lasted more than a day. Oh well, not her problem, as long as she wasn't the perpetrator of the gossip.

She flipped the fish fingers over in the pan, God she loved them – real nursery food. Checking the oven chips were crisping nicely, she shoved the peas into boiling water. Lily was drawing at the kitchen table.

"Mummy, what's an erection?"

Chloe gasped "Lily, why do you ask?

"Well Emma said today, that she had overheard her daddy talking about a man who couldn't get an erection" Lily said seriously, concentrating on her picture. Oh no! Chloe hated answering these sorts of questions! Emma was Lily's best friend, and the daughter of Alex Corbett, their local GP.

"Well darling" started Chloe, "it means, when a man's willy gets hard, you know how Rory's and Toby's do sometimes" desperately hoping that Lily wouldn't ask any more.

"Oh" said Lily, "is that all, I thought he couldn't put up a shed or something". Chloe relieved that her daughter was happy to leave it at that, used diversionary tactics.

"Lily be a little love and lay the table please".

"Mummy, I'm in the middle of my drawing, why can't the boys do it, they never do anything!"

"Stop moaning Lily, you are here and they aren't, so please be a good girl and help mummy. Okay?"

Tutting like a grown up, Lily stomped over to the drawer and flung the knives and forks on the table. Chloe slapped the fish fingers onto plates, cutting Rory's up for him, and nicking a bit for herself. Gorgeous! Lily bellowed out the back door to the boys who were mucking about in the garden and they dashed like mad things back into the kitchen and flopped onto their chairs.

"Oh great fish fingers! Yucky peas!"

"Eat your peas, or no ice cream" Chloe bargained.

"Bloody hell" said Lily.

CHAPTER 9

Charles dawdled over his breakfast, half-heartedly reading the FT. It was early yet and he was getting a later train to town this morning. Mrs Fuller had done his favourite kippers, with fresh white bread and butter. What a treasure she was that woman. He thought about last night. He'd been late home, and nearly didn't bother to come back at all, but he'd been conscious that he had been neglecting Jennifer lately, and made an effort. He thought he would get a bollocking from her again when he got in, but to his surprise she had seemed quite animated, although he couldn't think why. He liked her like this - it was what had attracted him to her in the first place, her sense of fun and sparkle which had been sadly lacking of late. In fact they'd had seriously good sex last night too, which was why he was leaving later this morning. She sat across the table from him - quite unusual too, as more often than not, she didn't get up until after he had left. Her negligee fell slightly open, giving the odd glimpse of a bare shoulder, rumpling her hair with her hand, as she glanced at the paper.

"What have you got on today darling?" he asked. She looked up surprised, had he found out somehow about going to Mileoak?

"Nothing much, last minute stuff towards the party" she answered evasively "It's only a week on Saturday. I just hope the weather holds out."

He looked at her, "Well not much we can do it if doesn't is there? It'll be fine whatever." Was this the moment he thought to broach the subject of the children coming to stay?

"By the way, sweetie I have to sort out with Celia, when the children are coming over to stay – what do you think?"

Jennifer put down the paper "Oh I don't mind when they come, but if it could be after the party, that would be better for me really."

Charles was astonished; normally negotiating these visits were as sensitive as the G8 summit and could be downright awkward, the children did not give Jennifer an easy time when they came so he was genuinely surprised that she was so affable about an impending visit.

"Of course darling, absolutely goes without saying. How about the weekend after?"

"Fine with me" she agreed, turning back to her paper. Charles was really pleased, that had been easy - much more so than he'd expected, he'd envisaged a minor tantrum. Now he could ring Celia up later and tell her, and that would shut her up. Good, good, he thought, perhaps after that weekend he would surprise Jennifer with a weekend away somewhere.

Jennifer pretended to read the paper. She was excited at the thought of going to Mileoak this morning. Chloe had been really nice to her yesterday, and her advice of *'just be yourself'* had stuck with her. She had high hopes that things may be turning a corner. She was determined to make her life work.

Oliver Travers kissed his wife goodbye, he'd got an early call to a colic at the hunt kennels and dashed out of the door, leaving her in bed. She turned over when he had gone, wide awake, thinking, why the fuck can't he just leave quietly and not disturb me. She and Oliver had come over from New Zealand about 5 years ago when he'd accepted a post with Andrew Napier, who ran a small equine practice in West Sussex. Oliver was good at his job and pretty soon Andrew had offered him a partnership, which he'd accepted without hesitation or consultation. This had really pissed off Suse, she hated England and missed her family back home. When they had come over, it was supposed to have been for a short period, and the idea was to go back after a few years, now she was bloody stuck here in this godforsaken place. She loved Oliver, he was handsome, clever and full of energy, and had thrived here, whilst she Suse, had vegetated, got fatter, and had a dreary job in Horsham working in an insurance company. She could have lived with it all but she never saw him, he was always on call, or busy visiting clients and she always felt that he put them before her. If it was between one of his clients being saved from a fire and her, she knew he would always choose the client, and she was sick of it all. He often talked about his work, but half the time she couldn't be bothered to listen. She struggled up and looked at the clock - it was 7.00am, she could have another hour in bed before she needed to get up and that was just what she would do. *Fuck you Oliver!* She could hardly bear to look at him these days, and was glad that he'd gone. Her mum had telephoned yesterday and told her all the family news and she missed them all so badly. She dreamed of packing her things and just upping sticks and going, it would serve him right - the prick! She pulled the duvet back over her head and shut out the thoughts.

Oliver sped off, colic was always dangerous and you never knew what the outcome would be. So he needed to get there as fast as he could. More and more he realised that Suse and he were growing apart, she had become a right grumpy old bag, constantly nagging at him, and had absolutely no empathy with the needs of his work. He pulled into the kennels, and glanced at his watch, he had made it in 15 minutes. He swung the car into the stable yard, driving past the kennels themselves and the flesh house. George the huntsman was waiting for him.

"Nero is right poorly, found him about an hour ago, very distressed, sweating and groaning. Usual signs, looking at his gut, getting up and down, stamping his feet, you know." reported George.

"Let's have a look at him then" said Oliver. They moved into a large old fashioned loose box, with a massive straw bed, banked up high on either side. A big roan horse rolled its eyes at Oliver, sweat glistening on its flanks and neck. "There, there old fella, let's see what we can do for you". Oliver took out his stethoscope and listened carefully to the heart, then moved it towards his stomach. "His heart rate is up but there are some gut sounds George, I think you are right about colic – hopefully not a serious one" said Oliver.

"Course I'm right" snapped George "I've been round horses all my life, I know a colic when I see one." Oliver ignored him, old Nero was more important now than any one-up -man ship.

"Has he passed any droppings? Has he been eating and drinking normally?" He asked moving to the front of the horse, and opening its mouth and looking at colour of the gums.

"Eating his bed a bit, drinking okay, but no droppings this past hour."

"That's okay. Just hold him still George while I do a rectal exam". He pushed and prodded the horse about, finally saying "I think we're lucky, you called me well in time, I'll just give him something for the pain, and a shot of Buscopan and see what that produces, with any luck this is just a spasmodic and nothing worse." They waited, Oliver, checking the horse's heart rate, and gut sounds periodically. Since the intravenous Finadyne, he'd been less distressed, and then with an enormous fart, Nero produced a pile of droppings. "Crisis over I'm hoping" laughed Oliver.

"Good old boy, Nero, good lad" George pulled the horse's ears fondly.

"Okay George, make sure he doesn't have any hay, and put him in a box with shavings, not straw, as I think he may have just gorged himself. Keep an eye on him, checking him every half hour or so, and I'll pop back later this afternoon to see him again – but call me in the meantime if you're at all worried – Okay?"

"Thanks very much indeed veterinary, you were here so quick, makes all the difference" said George gratefully.

"Glad I could mate" said Oliver, and George touched his cap in salute.

Oliver pulled out of the kennels, and checked his watch – no point in going back home, Suse would have gone to work. He was secretly relieved, he couldn't face another contretemps with her. He sighed, he knew that it was just a question of time really. God knows, though, he had tried, and to be fair so had she, but they both had to be realistic. Their marriage was well into injury time, had been for ages, and whereas before he put up with it, now things had changed. He sighed again, what would be, would be and he was in too deep now to go back. He decided he would go straight to the office and see what's what. He knew that he and Andrew both had a heavy day ahead, but if it was feasible they always tried to meet at the office before they started off for their calls. He drove towards the village and pulled into the small car park, and parked next to Andrew's identical Toyota. He locked the car carefully, it was chock-a-block with stuff, scanners, scopes and other necessaries, but the biggest haul for any thieves would be the drugs – particularly the Ketamine, which had a huge illicit resale value. Satisfied that it was secure, he loped into the office with his big easy stride, pushing open the door to the small reception area, to be greeted by Paulene their secretary, cum receptionist, cum goffer!

"G' day boss!" she smiled "How's your corks!"

"Hey g' day to you too, my corks are swinging! Lovely day again eh?"

He didn't stop to chat, as he had a lot on and wanted to be on the road as soon as he could. As an equine practice, they didn't have the big waiting room needed in small animal practices, and beyond the reception, was a large admin office which he and Andrew shared, a small kitchen and laboratory area, and the drugs store. He opened the door, to find Andrew sitting behind his desk, phone to his ear. Oliver moved over to the coffee machine, gesturing to Andrew if he wanted one. His desk was piled high with paperwork, and he groaned inwardly, it was all very well being so busy with the practical stuff which he loved, but the behind the scenes work was piling up.

Andrew finished his call and looked up at him "Morning mate – you're late today?"

"Yep, got called out to an early colic at the hunt kennels, responding though, but I'll pop back later, just to make sure" murmured Oliver rifling through the piles of invoices, and insurance reports on his desk.

Andrew glanced over at his partner appreciatively; he had made the right choice when he'd asked Oliver to come into partnership with him. He was a damned good vet, brilliant diagnostician and not afraid of hard work, just a pity about his bitch of a wife.

"What you got on today then?" asked Oliver, slurping his coffee, he knew that Andrew was as busy as he was, and all in all they made a great team, sharing the work load equally, both as dedicated as each other.

"Oh stacks lined up, routines, teeth, vaccinations, a vetting, lameness work out – usual stuff. I'll be out for most of the day I think. How about you?"

"Yep, same for me too, but we do need to make time for our

practice meeting mate."

Oliver and Andrew tried to meet up once a week, workload permitting, to discuss practice policy and future plans. It may be that they would need to take on an assistant if the practice continued to grow as it had, and maybe another person in the office too, they really needed to talk about it all.

"How about this evening, if we finish in time? I'm on call, so if we have the meeting about 7.30, that should give us time to get the routine stuff out of the way" said Andrew.

Oliver's heart sank a little - another late meeting, Suse would be seriously fed up, last night he had been on call and had to go out a couple of times and early this morning too. She'd go apeshit, although to be honest he wasn't sure that he really cared anymore. She did nothing but carp at him the whole time, she had really let herself go too, when she wasn't working, she just slouched about in old jogging pants, rooted to an armchair in front of the TV with a glass of wine in her hand. He used to love being with her, going out with her to social stuff, but she could barely be civil to him, let alone to his friends and clients. Truth was he couldn't see the marriage lasting much longer, it was just a matter of time. Once again, he shoved the thoughts to the back of his mind before replying "Cool with me."

Jennifer glanced at the clock, it was 9am, Charles had finally gone to work, and she had 15 minutes to get ready to be over at Mileoak on time. She was excited and nervous - this was a big thing for her. Chloe had said if she wanted to learn about horses, she would help her but she had to be prepared to shovel shit, clean tack and sweep the yard, no-one was exempt from any task at Mileoak. It wasn't all the fancy glamorous stuff that you read about. Jennifer had no idea what would be expected of her, her only concern was her genuine fear of horses.

She looked in her wardrobe – what to wear though? She thought about what Chloe had been wearing yesterday, denim shorts and a tee shirt – mmm nothing fitted the bill here, all too upmarket. Ruthlessly, she dragged out a pair of Armani jeans, they were nice but they would have to serve a new purpose. Delving around in her nail kit she found a small pair of scissors, and painstakingly hacked the legs off the jeans, the ends were ragged, but she didn't care. She stuffed them into a small leather holdall, together with a simple black tee shirt; she would grab her hunter wellies on the way out. Pulling on a light summer dress and some sandals, she was careful to make it look as though she were just going out for an hour or two and with a deep breath forced herself not to run down the stairs.

Chloe looked at her watch, it had just gone 9.30am, Jennifer probably wouldn't turn up at all she mused. She herself had arrived in the yard at about 8.15, having dropped the kids off at the bus. Beebs and Susie, started at 7.30am and fed and hayed first thing, turning out as many as they could, depending on what each horse's schedule was for that day. They all usually had a quick break together when Chloe came down to discuss the daily chores, before getting stuck into the work. Over coffee, she had spoken to them both quietly and seriously.

"Look I can only say this again, I know this is going to be a pain with Jennifer coming, and it probably won't last long before she gives up, but it may not. I want you both to be mature about this and genuinely help her - no taking the piss, or being rude, but help her understand the work. You don't have to tug your caps to her at all, she is just another worker, but equally don't take any shit either. Treat her like you would want to be treated yourself when you were just starting out, and above all, no-one is supposed to know. So I mean it, no gossip – okay?"

Both Beebs and Susie liked and respected Chloe, she was a fair boss, and was never afraid to get her hands dirty herself. She was a good rider and had masses of experience, from which they had both benefitted immensely. She treated them with respect, but she was without doubt the governor in the yard, so when she made a decision, they stuck to it. Both girls nodded their heads solemnly in agreement.

Jennifer swung into the drive at Mileoak, hooked back the gate and drove through. Better shut it she thought, start as she meant to go on, there were no posh electric gates here! She parked the Mercedes alongside the horse walker and slid out, carrying her bag.

"Morning Chloe" she called, I just have to change if that's okay" as she took in Chloe's astonished look at her dress "I didn't want anyone to know what I was up to" she laughed. Five minutes later, she looked more the part, even if Chloe had never seen anyone mucking out in cut off Armani's before.

She introduced Jennifer to the girls and said that they would be showing her what to do for the next hour or so, but when it came to dealing with the horses themselves, she, Chloe would be there to supervise. Chloe nodded to the girls, just a miniscule warning in her eye, and disappeared into the house, dogs leaping about after her. I just hope it goes okay, she thought to herself. Beebs and Susie could be merciless at times and she hoped she had impressed upon them enough the need for diplomacy. It would be a good management skill for them both to learn though, if nothing else!

Back at Nantes with the breakfast over, Freda Fuller was sitting in her favourite chair at the table in the kitchen. Doris had come in this morning and they'd sat gossiping over a cup of coffee, when they heard the front door slam. Mrs Fuller stood up and went along the back corridor into the vast hallway, looking out of the long windows, just in time to see Jennifer speeding down the drive in her flashy motor. Now where was she off to and in such a hurry thought Freda, she usually was only just up and dressed by this time of the morning. She didn't care, it gave her some breathing space at least, and she and Doris had a lot to do this morning without that madam interfering. She bumbled back to the kitchen, and sat down heavily in her chair, her feet were killing her already.

Doris looked up "What's up?"

"Dunno, the missus has gone off in a tearing hurry, no idea where to. She usually tells me if she's going out. Funny eh?" gossiped Freda. Doris looked at her with a '*great news*' look on her face, she didn't like Jennifer any more than anyone else did.

"Good riddance, we'll have time for another cuppa before we start then eh?" she grinned.

Jennifer had never worked so physically hard before, even a good work out in the gym was nothing compared to this! She could feel the little rivulets of sweat running down her tummy. She was helping the girls with the last of the deep litter muck outs, taking over from where Chloe had left off the previous day. Beebs and Susie were running the barrows and she had been asked to get stuck in with a fork, the acrid, over-powering stench of urine filled her nostrils and tainted her breath.

"Well done Jennifer, you're going great" said Beebs admiringly. She had to admit it, the woman was trying hard and it couldn't have been a filthier job. "We'll soon be done here at this rate, and then we can have a cuppa, before we start the riding"

Jennifer's heart quickened. The riding! She was okay about doing this kind of thing, she'd never been a lazy person, and wasn't afraid of getting her hands dirty, that was until she'd come to Nantes, but her intrinsic fear of horses immediately made her panic.

Beebs saw the look on her face, and thought this woman is really terrified, poor cow. "Look, don't worry about it, Chloe will take great care of you, and she is the best trainer in a country mile, you just never gave it a chance before. Susie and I'll be there to help, so try not to worry."

Jennifer gulped, "Oh you are kind Bibi, I know it's irrational, but where I came from I'd never had an opportunity to be near horses, or any other large animal come to that, and it's the pure size and strength that frightens me."

Bibi nodded "I can understand that, we all will, and we'll take things really slowly to start. Chloe knows her job so please try not to get yourself in a state, the horses pick up on your tension y' know. Perhaps instead of a cuppa, you could have a large G&T !"

Jennifer smiled back bleakly. "Good idea" she laughed, "a bit of the old Dutch courage. I'll bring a bottle up with me tomorrow!"

There was a footstep behind them and Chloe popped her head around the door, looking admiringly at the work.

"Did you do all this Jennifer?" she asked

Beebs answered before Jennifer could speak "yes, she did, and a great job too. We've almost finished this one, making good time boss!" Chloe looked at Beebs and was pleased and surprised, good old Bibi she seemed to have found a good rapport with Jennifer.

"I'll get the kettle on then, whilst you do this last load" she said "Okay with you Jennifer?"

"Cool with me thanks Chloe" Jennifer smiled back. It was the first time in ages that she had felt so content, here with these decent people, up to her neck in shit, who'd have believed it!

They all settled down into the tack room on the old sofa and chairs in the corner, chocolate biscuits in hand. Jennifer looked down at hers, she was starving and after all that physical work, surely she could afford to eat just one.

"Go on" coaxed Bibi, "they're great, Chloe only buys us the nicest biscuits"

"You deserve them ladies" laughed Chloe. "Now let's decide who's riding what. Susie, can you and Beebs go down to long meadow and bring in Rufus and Ben for me? I'll ride Ben and I'm planning to go for a gentle hack with Jennifer. Sandy and Katherine can't come up today, so then, if you don't mind, you could do Alfie and Seamus?" The girls beamed at her, they loved riding those two, and rarely got the chance. Coffee finished, they set off to collect the horses. Chloe turned to Jennifer, "now have you got anything suitable to ride in?"

Jennifer looked dismayed, she had forgotten all about that "Oh God, how stupid of me, I'm so sorry, I totally forgot about that, after my first disastrous attempts, I dumped the lot! I never dreamt that I might ride again."

"Never mind" said Chloe "you're a quite a bit smaller than me, but I'm sure we can kit you out. While the girls are bringing in the nags, come up to the house with me and we'll find you an old pair of breeches and boots."

Beebs and Susie ambled across the fields to fetch in the horses, headcollars and ropes swinging from their shoulders. It was such a perfect day, the sun brilliant in the flawless sky. The grass was meagre, parched with the fierce heat and was going a crispy brown. The hay fields looked sparse with the drought, and the leaves on the

101

trees were shrivelling. They so badly needed some rain.

"Whatdya think about this Jennifer then?" asked Susie "She seems alright, she got right stuck into that shitty mucking out."

"She's better than I thought she'd be, got quite a good sense of humour" replied Bibi "but she was genuinely terrified when I mentioned riding. Chloe should sort her out though, and she's doing it with a bit of a different attitude this time. Not so up her own arse."

"We'll see" said Susie darkly.

Jennifer and Chloe had disappeared up to the house, kicking off their boots at the door; they padded up to Chloe's bedroom. It all looked so normal thought Jennifer, eying the unmade bed and the clothes frothing out of the top of the linen basket. Chloe rummaged around in the bottom of the wardrobe, pulling out a pair of breeches that had clearly seen better days.

"Here, she tossed them to Jennifer, see if they fit." She added "they were always too small for me." Jennifer slid out of her shorts and tugged on the musty breeches, struggling with the zip. It had been a long time since she had worn second hand clothes, even though she had grown up with them.

"They're fine, thanks Chloe, I really appreciate it" she said gratefully.

"Don't give it another thought, they are a bit ancient but they'll certainly do for the time being anyway. You had better leave them in the tack room when you've finished, along with your shorts and tee shirt, if you want to keep this under cover." she advised. Jennifer hadn't thought about that - imagine Mrs Fuller and Doris when they did the laundry finding these! She and Chloe giggled together at the idea.

"Yes you're right Chloe, as long as you don't mind, but I'll try and pop into Horsham and get some of my own, and if it's okay leave it all here with you?"

"Fine by me, I can wash them for you with our stuff, one more load won't make much difference".

By the time Jennifer and Chloe returned to the yard with Jennifer's feet slopping about in Chloe's size 6s, Bibi and Susie had returned with the horses.

"That little sod Rufus would not be caught! We had to drag out Ben, then tempt him with Polos, greedy bugger soon came then" reported Bibi. Rufus was a pretty little horse, with a cheeky eye, but he was a kind old boy and really looked after his rider. Chloe had had him for years, and he was semi-retired now, just being used for the odd hack. Jennifer eyed him apprehensively.

"Right now Jennifer, this is Rufus. Rufus, this is Jennifer" smiled Chloe. "Come and say hello to him." Jennifer edged nervously up to the ginger face and went to pat him, "not directly in front, otherwise they get a bit spooked, approach from the side and pat him." Jennifer moved to the side, and stroked the golden coat tentatively. "Now, be really positive with him and he'll know you are the boss" said Chloe "he needs to know you're his herd leader, because in a minute, after you've brushed him, you're going to tack him up."

Blimey thought Jennifer, on her previous visits, the horses had all been tacked up ready and waiting, and there had been no way she would've wanted to touch them. She gritted her teeth, she would do this! Chloe showed her how to brush the horse, and pick out his feet; gradually Jennifer started to relax a little. The old horse, enjoying the fuss, nuzzled in her pockets for a treat.

"OOOOhhh" squeaked Jennifer, leaping back "what's he doing?" Rufus startled at the response, pulled back in surprise, the girls looked on incredulous – fucking hell this was going to be a long job. Patiently Chloe calmed her down and showed her how to give him a titbit, patting him all the time. Bibi brought out his tack and Chloe painstakingly showed Jennifer the various parts of the bridle and saddle and how to put it all on.

"There" said Chloe "not too difficult eh? Now the last thing we do is put on his boots, which protect his legs from any damage. Then we can be off. Susie, be a love and tack up Ben for me, and find me a leading rein, while I sort out a crash hat for Jennifer" she called.

"All done boss, he's ready"

"Ah thanks so much babe, you're a star" responded Chloe "come on Jennifer let's find you a hat."

Finally they were ready to go. Jennifer wobbled onto the saddle, awkwardly holding the reins and stiff with apprehension. Beebs held Rufus, whilst Chloe swung easily onto her horse, she handed her the leading rein and they moved off. Jennifer's face was tight with fear and Chloe talked reassuringly to her all the whole time.

"Bloody good luck with that" said Susie, "she's got the patience of a fucking saint has Chloe!"

"Yep, it's going to be a long job, that's if she ever comes back!!" Beebs chortled.

CHAPTER 10

Pete watched Jennifer zooming up the drive, the roof down on her car and her silver bobbed hair spiralling in a dizzy vortex. He was pruning the dead heads off the flowers, and tidying up the front beds. The car swept around the drive to the garages at the back and he heard her slam the door as she got out and the quick scrunch of the gravel as she ran into the house. She's in a hurry he pondered, good that means less time for her to have a go at him. Since last week, when she had been so rude he'd been ruminating about her, and how he could extract revenge. Deep down, somewhere in his conscious he knew that this was a bad sign. The doctors had warned him about these irrational thoughts and that he should learn to recognise them, and seek help if he couldn't control them. He didn't care, he hated her.

Jennifer sped directly up the stairs, taking them two at a time, not wanting to risk meeting anyone on her way up to her room before she had time to shower. She was absolutely filthy, and stank of horses. She hadn't felt so happy in a long time she mused. Okay she was tired but it was a good tired feeling. Chloe had been so patient with her, and Beebs and Susie had made her feel so welcome. After she had come back from the ride, they had all sat cleaning the tack, chatting and had really included her. The day had flown past, watching them ride some horses and lunge others. She marvelled at their easy skill, wondering if she could ever ride like them. She had helped the girls wash the horses off, and even took the quiet ones out to the fields. She hadn't had so much fun in ages. She couldn't believe the time, when Chloe announced that she had to go and pick up the children from the bus.

"Can I come tomorrow" she had asked tentatively. She couldn't bear it, if Chloe said no, but Chloe merely remarked that horses were for '*life and not just for Christmas*', and they would expect her again tomorrow, earlier if she could make it.

"Before you go Jennifer" Chloe had said "take this, you might find it useful bedtime reading." Chloe offered her a tattered book, *The Manual of Horsemanship*. "I know this looks old, but it's a really good book to get you started, tells you all sorts of stuff. Enjoy!"

"Thank you so much Chloe!" To Jennifer it was like having the crown jewels.

Laura lay with her arms wrapped around Jonty. They had kicked off the sheets, and lay naked on the top of the bed in the heat of the day. Jonty was thin and lanky, but had strong tattooed arms and long legs, his carefully shaved head showing a miniscule bristle. She had lived with him in his flat in Bethnal Green for about a year now, and she held him in a mixture of adoration and awe. Jonty had respect around here and she liked that, because as his woman she was respected too. She had met him in Brick Lane Market, where he had a stall, selling CDs and other odds and sods from leather bags to belts. Browsing amongst the cardboard boxes full of gear, she had looked up to see him watching her and smiled at him. They started an easy banter and he'd asked her to meet him later for a drink at the Vibe Bar. The place had been packed and she saw him in the corner, holding court with his cronies and he had beckoned her over. It had all started there she remembered, but she had not known the half of what he did until much later. Fundamentally Jonty was a villain, and came from a villain's upbringing. He could be funny and lovely, but he was also ruthless and dangerous, and it was this juxtaposing of personality traits which kept her glued to him. She never knew which mood he would be in or what might prompt it, she just dealt with him on a day to day basis. He accepted her student life and encouraged her to supplement her income when and howsoever she could, and she liked that about him, she could maintain her independence, whilst she basked in his protection. He had other women she knew that, but she also knew not to question it, he always came home to her. It was a strange mixture of earning a living in whatever way they could, and an inherent desire to have stability.

She glanced up at him as he slept. He had been late home last night, coming home in the early hours, but he'd been on a high, exhilarated and bouncing. She knew the signs, he must have been out on a job. He opened one eye and yawned.

"Al 'right princess?" he murmured

"Yep, I'm fine, you go back to sleep, I know you're knackered."

"Too right, long night eh?" he yawned, disentangled himself from her and rolled over.

Laura eased herself off the bed, stooping down to put on her pants, and throwing on an old shirt. She could do some work now, and gently closing the bedroom door, she moved into the living room. Sitting down at the table, she pulled out her notebook, and unscrewed a bottle of water taking a long gulp. She had an assignment which she must finish, and now was the perfect time to be getting on with it, Jonty would not be up for hours yet. She opened her text books and cranked up the lap top. Although she tried to focus, the words just swam around and would not sink in, she must have read and reread the same paragraph a thousand times. It was hopeless she just couldn't concentrate, all she could think of was a bitter sweet revenge and how she would pay that bastard back – respect that was what he needed. Perhaps when Jonty did finally wake up he might enjoy another drive into the country.

Oliver sat with his feet up on his desk, drinking coffee and reading through some blood results that had just come in, marking them carefully with a red pen for action. He had zipped through his day earlier than he had thought, and now was onto the boring stuff. Technically he was still on call till 7pm, and it was only just 5.30. He leafed through his diary, filling out the daily reports, so that Paulene could update the invoices and case records in the morning. She always complained that she couldn't read his handwriting when she came to do them, and by that time he'd usually left on his rounds. She was a beaut was Paulene, and blimey her workload had doubled since he'd got here. He was busy, but so were they all, they badly needed to draft in another pair of hands. He looked up as the office door opened, and Paulene shoved her head around the door.

"I'm off Oli, I've switched the phones through, and put some letters in your out tray for signing, can you be a love and post them when you go?" she asked, "Oh and by the way, I need you to sign the drugs requisition, so that I can get the order in tomorrow"

"Paulene, you're a little corker" smiled Oliver, "where'd we be without you?"

She laughed "Up a bloody gum tree! I'll put the door on the catch as I go out. See you in the morning, have a good night."

Oliver watched her go; he stood up and signed the requisition, glancing at the order, and put it on her desk. He picked up the telephone and started to make calls, updating clients on results, impending visits and insurance claims. To him this was an important part of the job, clients needed to be kept in the loop and that personal element was vital. He never hurried the calls making sure that he answered all of their questions carefully and with no hint to them that there was anyone else more important than they were at that moment. He sighed putting down the phone, it was now 6.30 and he should ring Suse to tell her he would be late. She answered on the first ring.

"Hi, it's only me" he began tentatively, but before he could continue she abruptly interrupted him.

"Don't tell me you're going to be bloody late again Oliver? I'm so sick of this I can't tell you. It's fine for you with your precious job, but to me it feels like I'm living on my own here!" she exploded.

"Suse, don't be like that, you know I can't help it, it's not as though I'm doing it on purpose! I'm really stacked up with work, and you knew what my job was like when you married me."

"Biggest mistake I made" she responded nastily "for two pins, I'd pack my bags and jump on a plane home." This was not the first time she'd made similar remarks, and Oliver had begun to wish she actually would go, rather than harping on to him about it every second.

"Okay Suse, I'm not going to row with you. I've a practice meeting and will be home as soon as I can get away" he said resignedly.

"Don't bother" she snapped and with that she slammed down the phone.

He couldn't blame her in lots of ways. The job did take up a lot of his time - of course it did, because it wasn't like a normal job that's why. Something had to give, and he couldn't see how it could be him or the job. Why Suse couldn't take a leaf out of Julia's book? Andrew's wife never seemed to give him gyp or moan all the time. He heard the sounds of the front door open, it must be Andrew, thank God, they could start the meeting on time, and hopefully he wouldn't be too late.

"You look a bit stressed Ol" remarked Andrew, as he bustled across the office to his desk "anything up?"

"Oh just the usual – Suse fed up with me, complaining that she never sees me" said Oliver, running his hand through his hair. "You never seem to have this trouble – what's your secret?"

"No secret" he smiled ruefully, "Julia is her own woman, plays her tennis, does her bridge club, personal trainer all that garb. I don't think she knows I'm there half the time, only as long as I pay the bills!" He shifted some paperwork on his desk to one side. "Look, I'm on call tonight, I can do this lot later, why don't we start now, and then you can get off? Let me just grab a coffee though."

They sat down amiably enough but they both knew that they'd some serious talking to do.

"Okay" said Andrew "let's look at the staff ratio"

"What staff?" laughed Oliver, they had Paulene, who did all the day to day running of the office, which had been fine when it was just Andrew. Karen Rutherford came in on Fridays, to do the bookkeeping, and her husband Gary was their accountant, so that worked well. At the moment Paulene also ran the hoover around the place, as it was so difficult to get trustworthy casual labour, with all the drugs around even though they were always locked up.

"Right, I think we're both agreed that the practice has grown beyond our expectations, and that we're both stretched to the absolute limit with work. So I think we need to take on an assistant, maybe someone who hasn't long qualified and can do all the routine stuff, and needs to gain some experience."

"Yes, I totally agree with that" said Oliver, "but there is the knock on effect from taking on someone new – another vehicle, stocked with equipment, accommodation - which would cost a lot of money, and we would definitely need more office help then too. Can we financially afford to do it?"

Andrew looked at him, "Oli, there is something else that I want to discuss with you."

"Christ that sounds ominous"

"I've been thinking for a long time about branching out more. We've outgrown these premises really, especially if we take on another vet and an office assistant. I've always wanted to have a more diagnostic base, where clients can bring horses for x-rays, hydrotherapy sessions, small surgery, you know the sort of thing. Up till now it has been a pipe dream, but I heard last week on the QT, that Lady Veronica is thinking of selling up the Old Mill – do you know it?"

Oliver was stunned, this would be a huge step, and all sorts of questions ran through his mind at once. "Is that the old place on the edge of the Fittlebury Hall estate running alongside the river?

"Yes, it is, been empty for about five years now. Old Ted Craddock used to live in it, stayed on there after he had retired as gamekeeper. He moved out to live with his daughter, and it's never been lived in since. It isn't huge, there's the old mill itself and attached to it is the little cottage where he lived. There are some good out buildings though, and we could probably get it with a little bit of land. The access isn't great, but we could put in a better one. The Mill could be the office, and we could convert the outbuildings. Having the cottage is a bonus, as we could use it for assistants. Whatdya think?"

"You seem to have it all sussed out" exclaimed Oliver. "Who told you it was up for sale?

"Well it's not officially, Mark Templeton the estate manager, tipped me off, when I was up there last week" said Andrew "I know Lady Veronica pretty well, I could approach her if you agree."

"Whoa, whoa mate! Can we afford it? We'd have to have a helluva loan"

Andrew looked him straight in the eye, "Yep, I think we could, if we got it at the right price, and we don't have to do it all up straight away. If we bought it, we could take our time on the work, whilst building up the extra business" he reasoned. "Look, shall I run it past Gary, to see if he thinks it's financially viable, then we could go see the bank manager. I must know that you would be on board though mate, I couldn't do it on my own?"

"Well, strike me down, you really are serious" laughed Oliver, "You've got it all worked out mate. Well I'm game on deffo!"

Chloe was spent; she leant against the Aga, with a large glass of chilled wine in her hand. What a day! John had called to say he was on his way home, and she had put the chops in and the jacket potatoes were already cooked and in the bottom oven, they could have it with salad. She was pleased, it was the first time he had been home this early for ages and she really needed to have a proper talk to him. She had even tidied up the kitchen! She would just have time to spend five minutes in the office, doing a bit of paperwork before he came in. She had turned the small room where the farmer had slept just off the kitchen, into the farm office and it was truly her space now, with precious photographs of the family, and of her competing her favourite horses plastered all over the walls. A large old oak desk was under the window, looking out onto their little terrace, and directly behind it, on the opposite wall a long work station, housing the computer with shelves above, crammed with box files. On the long side of the wall, as you came in from the kitchen, was a huge oak dresser. She sank down in her chair at the desk, looking out onto the terrace, the sun still a warm glow in the sky. She had time to think clearly now. What had happened to her and John?

She decided that she really needed to get to the bottom of what was troubling him. He was behaving really strangely, secret phone calls and texts to his mobile, coming home late, disappearing like he did last week. The atmosphere between them was tense, and it was so unlike him to be secretive; they had always had a real friendship, the sort where you could tell each other anything. She was lost in thought, as Lily popped her head around the door

"Wake up mummy!" she called "our programme on the TV has

finished now!"

Chloe smiled down at Lily, "hey cheeky, I wasn't asleep!" adding "what are the boys doing?"

"Three guesses where Toby is? Rory has fallen asleep in the chair" Lily giggled.

"Okay sweetie, let's go scoop him up and put him to bed. How about you? You tired?"

"You do say the silliest things mummy" laughed Lily "me tired, I don't think so!"

Pity thought Chloe, it would have nice to have put them all to bed a bit earlier tonight. She walked through to the playroom, where Rory was fast asleep, his thumb in his mouth. Chloe's heart tightened, she loved them all so much. She gently lifted him up, and he put his little arms around her and nuzzled into her neck. Carefully climbing the stairs, with Lily at her heels, she managed to peel off his clothes, and put him into bed without waking him. Ah, the blissful, untroubled sleep of the young.

"Now it's your turn missus" she said to Lily. Lily turned around and ran away, squealing along the hallway into Toby's room, where he was deeply engrossed in a computer game.

"Get lost Lily" he growled "you're a pain in the ….oh sorry mum, I didn't see you there" he looked at her sheepishly, then back at the screen to some lurid game he was playing.

"If you've done your homework love, you should get into your PJs," she glanced at her watch "then you can have half an hour more on your computer, and then its bed – okay? Lily you little minx, get in your nightie right now! She chased Lily along the end of the corridor to her bedroom, where Lily threw herself on her bed laughing, Chloe collapsed on top of her, tickling her until she was gasping!

"Mummmeeee stop! I will, I will" Lily squeaked, tears of laughter in her eyes.

"Good girl, and don't forget to brush your teeth. You can keep the light on if you like. I'll be back up to see you all in a bit, after I've seen to Daddy's dinner. Listen I can hear his car." Chloe sped off down the old staircase, as the back door opened, and John came in, he looked tired, negotiating his way through the dogs and the boots into the kitchen, throwing his briefcase on the floor.

"I'm home" he called. "What's to eat, I'm starving." He looked at Chloe, took in her dishevelled hair, deepening tan, looking very sexy in her short shorts, and tee shirt, "not working today then I see?" as he glanced at her flip flops.

Chloe was incensed, how bloody dare he? She hadn't stopped all fucking day, and to come out with an opening remark like that, she could kill him. "No, spent all day by the pool with my masseuse" She said sarcastically. "What the fuck do you think I have been doing?"

"No need to swear Chloe" he said evenly, "I was only joking"

"Well don't make stupid jokes like that eh? Do you want your dinner, it's all ready, or shall I serve it on your head?" she snapped. "Perhaps you could go and kiss your children goodnight, that's if you remember what they look like." The atmosphere was electric with an impending row, John gave her a long, hard look, but decided against saying any more, he moved towards the stairs. Oh John, Chloe thought, what had happened to the nice evening she had planned, she had ruined it now.

CHAPTER 11

Charles was amazed at the change in Jennifer when he came home that evening. She bounced up to him, and gave him a huge hug. She'd not been like this for a long time, and he picked her up, twirling her around. Dragging him into the sitting room, she had poured him a large whisky.

"Fancy a swim before dinner then?" she teased "skinny dipping?"

"Wow, good idea darling" he threw down his briefcase and chucked his suit jacket on the sofa. She looked really good tonight, in a shell pink camisole top, her perky nipples just showing through the fine fabric, and a floral skirt. It was more than that though, she was positively glowing and happy. Perhaps she was excited about the party next weekend, although frankly he was dreading it himself. Stuck up lot they could be. For him, it didn't matter - he was used to their judgemental attitudes and just ignored it, but they'd been horrid to Jennifer, and he minded very much about that. She pulled at his hand and taking his whisky with him they walked together across the lawn to the pool. She teasingly started to undo the buttons of his shirt and he smiled down at her – God she was sexy! He threw off his clothes as she slid out of hers, and laughing they jumped into the pool. Bobbing to the surface clutching on to each other spluttering and gasping, she kissed him and he kissed her right back.

The noise of their frolicking drifted through the open kitchen window. Mrs Fuller looked up from the sauce she was making, took it off the hot ring and putting it to simmer, she went to investigate. In her slippers, she ambled quietly around the back of the house, and could hear the shouts of hilarity coming from the pool. It had been a long time since she had heard them laughing like that, and popped her head around the trellis that screened the pool from the house. Both Charles and Jennifer were stark naked, chasing each other around the side of the pool, shrieking and trying to push each other in. Mrs Fuller felt her shocked face redden, - she had never seen the like and hastily backed away. Jennifer and Charles totally oblivious to her, fell gasping onto a sun lounger exhausted.

At dinner that night, Mrs Fuller banged the plates onto the dining room table, the candles wobbling dangerously in the candelabra, she was still outraged and indignant at their behaviour. Mr Charles should know better - he was obviously led astray by that hussy. She scowled at Jennifer in dislike, who in turn pretended not to notice. Charles shot Jennifer a look, and smiled slightly.

"It's one of your favourites Mr Charles" Mrs Fuller informed "Sole Meniere, with new potatoes and salad"

"It is indeed one of my favourites, thank you Mrs Fuller" complimented Charles. Mrs Fuller inclined her head in acknowledgement. Jennifer was famished, for once eating with gusto, rather than just pushing the food around her plate. Mrs Fuller glared at her with malice, willing Jennifer to choke on a bone.

Jennifer glanced up, the look of dislike on the older woman's face astonishing her, but she merely remarked "Thank you Mrs Fuller, this is absolutely delicious." She was determined not to let this old bag spoil their evening. Mrs Fuller ignored her pointedly and shuffled out of the room.

"Oh my God Charles, do you think she heard us in the pool?" whispered Jennifer giggling.

"I don't care if she did, it's no business of hers what we do" scoffed Charles, "and I have to say it was the perfect home coming."

Mrs Fuller who was listening at the door was furious. How dare they behave like that, what would Celia have had to say about their antics! What if someone had called round, or one of the other staff had seen them, it was a damned disgrace and no mistake.

Pete had decided to follow Lucy down to the pub that night. He gave her a head start, and then made his way down the footpath. It was still very warm, the sun casting long shadows from the trees across the field, but in the spinney it was much cooler, where only shafts of light, like lasers could beam down through the branches of the trees. Suddenly he stopped, standing absolutely still. He thought he could hear a voice and he strained to listen - had he been mistaken? His dark eyes darted around, flicking quickly from side to side, expecting to see someone lurking in the trees, but there was no-one there. He listened again, cocking his head to one side like a dog, when he heard the voice again, whispering to him. He shrugged - those voices, he had heard them once before when he was ill, he would just ignore them, it must be his imagination, and he carried on out of the spinney into the sunshine. He paused at the kissing gate into the churchyard, the tombstones lay crouching like sinister creatures waiting to leap out on him and he was afraid. He only had to cross the graves and he would be out onto the green and into the sanctuary of the pub. He steeled himself, and ran at full tilt along the path, until he reached the lynch gate, and leant back gasping against the old oak supports.

Happy hour was in full swing at the Fox. Lucy had met up with Oli and Tom and as usual they were enjoying their drinks in the garden. The air was laden and sultry, perhaps the weather was going to break after all and Lucy was maliciously voicing her thoughts that she hoped it would rain for Jennifer's party. From their vantage point in the garden, Lucy saw the familiar ungainly figure of Pete crossing the green, and hesitate before coming into the pub garden, and she nudged Oli to look at him. What's he doing here she wondered? She didn't fancy the walk back across the footpath to Nantes with him a few yards behind - he gave her the willies! Pete shuffled into the garden, his head down, not looking at anyone and stepped into the snug, emerging moments later with what looked like an orange juice. He looked around, found a small unoccupied table and took his drink and sat down. He took a clean handkerchief from his pocket and carefully wiped it around the rim of the glass, before taking a sip. He was really creepy, Lucy thought and pointedly turned her back, so that he couldn't see her, but she felt his eyes boring into her. He made her feel really uncomfortable that was for sure. The boys had noticed nothing but Lucy was conscious of Pete sitting all alone with his drink staring at her back.

Patrick was working late, he always was at this time of the year. He still had two more calls to make before he could pack up and go home. He whistled as he drove along, passing the Fox and tooting, waving to Lucy and the lads sitting in the garden. He swung on down the lane, heading towards the Pillsworthy's place where Rachael had called him to ask if he could tack on a lost shoe. He passed the vet's office, and their two Toyotas were side by side in the little car park, they were obviously working late too - good he wasn't the only one then. He was just outside the village, driving on auto pilot, miles away in thought, when an old Landrover, travelling at speed, hurtled around the corner.

"Fuck me, get over you nutter" he spluttered, wrenching his van over in the nick of time to avoid a collision. He put two fingers up, but the Landrover had already gone. Bloody people drove too fast around these little lanes, probably going to the pub he thought. He negotiated the tiny track down to Rachael's place, bumping up and down over the ruts, to the old farmhouse at the end – relieved he only had one more call to go after this.

The Landrover slowed its pace as it entered the village, and drove sedately past the Fox and out onto the Cosham Road. Laura craned her neck to look in the pub garden, scrutinising the drinkers. Typical fucking horsey lot she thought. Then a lone man in the garden caught her eye. She had seen him before, when they had done that recce last week. Her heart leapt, progress at last!

"Turn round Jonty, I'm sure that's the gardener bloke, you know the one that we saw in the grounds?" she said excitedly. Jonty swerved round in the road, and drove back, pulling into the car park. "Now we don't want to appear too conspicuous, okay? We'll just have a drink and suss it all out."

Jonty nodded his head "Whatever babe." He rubbed his eyes, he was bloody tired, having been up half the night, but still it had been a good haul. Now he was down here on some hare brained scheme of Laura's. Oh well.

Frankly it was hard for them not to look out of place and Laura was very conscious of their clothes, if the plan were to succeed then they may have to get some stuff to blend in with this lot. They walked into the garden and a few people looked up at them, a youngish girl with blonde hair had her back to them, chatting to a couple of lanky lads. Laura turned her face away ostensibly to admire the hanging baskets. They slipped into the snug, which thankfully on this fine night was more or less empty, just two old codgers in flat caps sat at the bar.

Angie appraised them before asking "what can I get you both then?"

"Two halves of lager please" again Laura turned her head away pretending to look around the room.

"Nice pub" remarked Jonty

"I don't think I've seen you in here before" said Angie, looking at them.

"Nah, we're just passing through and fancied a drink" replied Jonty. "Your garden looked nice" he smiled.

"Always busy, you've just caught us at the end of Happy Hour, popular with the locals you know" said Angie, losing interest in the strangers.

They took their drinks to a small table inside the snug, but where they could look out through the window and have a good vantage point of the garden. Sitting close, their heads together, they watched Pete, as he sat muttering to himself, and repeatedly wiping the rim of his glass.

"Odd bloke" Laura said "look at the way he keeps looking at that girl over there, the one sitting with those two lads."

"What gives with all that wiping the glass stuff then?" Jonty smirked "He must be a nutter, and he keeps talking to himself."

"If he's a bit disturbed, that could work in our favour y'know" she replied. Their eyes glued as they watched the dynamics of the people in the garden. "I think we should follow him when he goes, see where he lives?" she clamoured excitedly.

"Laura, you're talking to the man who knows about sussing out jobs" he laughed quietly, "You have seen him, you know who he is, now leave it, we can come down again. Besides," he added, "I am fucking knackered." They finished their drinks and left, not looking at anyone, nor glancing behind.

Lucy felt very uncomfortable, why had Pete come to the pub, he never did. She had a nasty feeling about this, and for once perhaps she had gone too far. After all he wasn't right in the head, and you read terrible stories about this sort of thing. She smiled engagingly at the two lads.

"How much do you love me?" She cooed at them both. "Don't suppose you want to give me a lift back do you?"

"'Course we will" they replied, looking at each other knowingly, "let's go!"

Patrick was finished at last and was on his way home, idling along the road, he was dog tired and hungry. Bloody hell, he thought, there's that Landrover again. He had a good old look at the driver this time, a shaven headed bloke, and a pretty blonde girl sitting next to him. He didn't know them - strangers, no wonder they didn't know how treacherous these lanes were. He slowed down to let them pass. Just ahead was the vet's surgery, only one car now, someone had been called out he thought – poor buggers, they worked hard. He wouldn't want to be on call through the night! A car turned into the surgery car park, a small Peugeot, it looked like Caitlin's car, must be picking something up for the horses. He wondered once again who this bloke Ace might be, it was hard to think of her having it off with a married man, there had not been a hint of it despite all his fishing in the local yards. No, to all intents and purposes she was a thoroughly respectable girl and everyone still thought she was going out with old ginger nut, but he knew he hadn't made a mistake, it was there as clear as anything on her phone. Mind you it might have been a wind up perhaps. Ah well, time would tell. Meantime, she was a nice girl, a good client, made a great cup of coffee too, and always had a good selection of biscuits! At the thought of the biscuits, his stomach rumbled, he put his foot down anxious to get home for his dinner.

CHAPTER 12

In the morning Jennifer stretched luxuriously in bed, Charles had kissed her goodbye and left much earlier. She smiled to herself, memories of the night before came flooding back, it had been just like old times. Happily, she looked at the clock, she had better get going if she were to be up at Chloe's! She leapt into the shower and shoved on the same light dress she had worn yesterday and grabbing her hand bag and phone dashed down the stairs, almost colliding with Mrs Fuller in the hallway.

"Morning Mrs Fuller" she gasped "sorry about that!"

"Will you require any breakfast?" Mrs Fuller retuned stonily.

"Yes, but just a bit of toast and butter and a coffee, if you don't mind, and I'll have it in my study" adding "also too Mrs Fuller, if you have a minute this afternoon, can we go through the acceptances for the party? I'm going out this morning, but say about half past three, would that suit you?"

Mrs Fuller sniffed "That would suit me perfectly, meanwhile I'll bring in your breakfast." Where was that madam going in such a hurry, she thought, and in the same dress too. Normally, she had nothing better to do all day than dress herself up like a Barbie doll.

Jennifer dashed into her study and sat down in the chair and spun round to face her desk. It was well positioned looking out over the lawn and even the sight of Pete dawdling about near the pool didn't spoil her mood. She glanced at the stack of invitation replies on her desk, she would have to deal with them later, and right now it didn't seem half so important anymore. More pressing was her need to get herself some suitable clothes for her sorties to Mileoak. She turned on her lap top, Googled 'riding breeches' and it came up with a host of information. Mmmm - where to start she thought. She flicked through a few sites, and there was a brief knock and Mrs Fuller pushed in with her breakfast on a tray. Jennifer hastily shut down the computer away from her prying eyes - she was a nosy old bat was Freda Fuller.

"Thank you very much, I'll see you then later" she smiled and Mrs Fuller had no alternative but to go. Jennifer turned back to the computer, it was hopeless, she had no idea what to get. I'll ask Chloe she thought. She drank the coffee, leaving half the toast uneaten on the plate, picked up her handbag and was gone.

Chloe was pleased to see her. "We're going to ride first thing, so as to avoid seeing anyone in the yard. Go down and get Rufus in and Susie will help you, okay?" Jennifer looked delighted and she and Susie strolled off down the fields, with headcollars and this time a bucket of nuts for the recalcitrant Rufus.

"She's not so bad" remarked Beebs, as they watched them go.

"No, I don't think she is either" said Chloe, "She hasn't had an easy time of it really. It must have been a hard call to step into Celia's shoes, and you know how snobby people are."

Horses tacked up, Chloe set off with Jennifer on the lead rein, she was much more relaxed this time, her obvious happiness relieving the tension in her body. They ambled around the fields, Rufus snatching at the odd leaf from a branch when he had the opportunity. The stillness of the air was punctuated by the occasional birdsong and a heat haze shimmered off the land. They chatted amiably about the horses, and Jennifer said how much she'd admired the way the Chloe and the girls had ridden yesterday, and how she wished she could be like that.

"You will be one day" reassured Chloe "they've been doing it a long time."

"My dream" said Jennifer "Would be to pitch up out hunting one day and surprise Charles! Can you imagine his face!"

"I like people to set themselves targets, gives them a goal. Why don't we aim to get you out on board by ... Mmm, let's say Autumn

Hunting"

"Oh, Chloe, do you really think I could?" Jennifer said excitedly. "How amazing would that be!"

"I don't see why not, but remember it's up to you in the long run. Riding is about practising as much as you can, and you'll be as good as your dedication. You may not be up to the jumping, but you could certainly go with the non-jumpers, I think that's perfectly feasible, and there's not much anyway at that time of year" Chloe laughed. "Come on we're going to have a little trot now, don't think about it, just do it and feel the rhythm of the horse's gait underneath you." They started off, tentatively at first, Chloe allowing Rufus enough off the lead rein for Jennifer to have to kick him on a bit. To begin with she rocked and lost her balance a little and then for a few strides, she got the hang of rising to the trot. Chloe smiled at the delight on Jennifer's face. "You're going great, just keep relaxing into him, and enjoy it!" Rufus enthusiastically started a little canter, which of course was much easier to ride, although beginners were always nervous of the speed, but not Jennifer it seemed, as Ben began to canter alongside too. Chloe glanced at Jennifer, the smile on her face telling her all she needed to know. Jennifer was unperturbed and sitting well into him, and had a good natural balance and loped along easily at Ben's side. That was what Chloe loved about her job; it gave her enormous satisfaction to see people progress. Onwards and upwards she thought.

Whilst Jennifer had been talking to Chloe about suitable clothes for her clandestine riding, Laura was busy thinking about clandestine clothes too. She knew that if they were to mingle in with the locals, then they would have to alter their image. She knew just the right stuff to wear, these bloody people - with them it was like they wore a uniform! Jonty had been good about this, although at first he'd thought she should forget all about it. He listened to her ranting and raving about what had happened. She had gone on and on about how all the time he was abusing her, forcibly pushing her face down on the desk, she was looking at photos of his wife and children! What sort of man was he? Some rich bastard who had too much money and a lovely family back at home, who abused girls like her for fun! When she mentioned the wealth and his family, Jonty had suddenly become much more interested, he asked her about the photographs, and what sort of bloke this Charles was. Encouraged by his sudden interest, she had gone on to tell him all she had found out, and it was then that he had agreed to go along with her plan, telling her that she would have her revenge and he would have a nice bonus. Who was it who said that revenge was a dish best served cold?

Caitlin had disappeared, saying she was nipping into the feed merchants to see her friend Jude who had told her there were some good offers on in their sale for winter jackets. Lucy watched her drive off, and immediately downed tools and put the kettle on, lighting a fag. She sat down in the yard, her back against the warm brick of the stables with the Horse & Hound in her hand and flicked to the classifieds, although it was a bit too early to be starting looking for jobs. The hunting season began at the end of August, or early September with cubbing, euphemistically called Autumn Hunting since the ban. Hunting proper, with the opening meet, started on the last weekend of October, or depending on the day, the first week of November. Ideally, from her point of view, she would leave at the end of November, so she had plenty of time. She put her face up to the sun, enjoying the heat, flies buzzing on the horse shit left in her barrow. Had Caitlin really gone to the feed merchants she wondered? She had loads of winter coats, as they all did, it was a necessity of the job, and she was sure she didn't really need one, or was she going to meet Tony? Thinking about it, she realised she hadn't seen him for ages either, although that in itself was not surprising at this time of year. Tony was a copper who went out regularly with the Fittlebury Hunt, on a hireling from Chloe Coombe's place, and bearing in mind there was no hunting at the moment, she supposed he wouldn't be hanging around the horses so much. She really couldn't see why Caitlin was attracted to him. He was a nice enough bloke but fucking hell he was he dull. Still Caitlin was too, so perhaps they were made for each other! She smirked to herself, drifting back to the events of last evening. Tom and Oli had given her a lift alright, and she had certainly given them one too! She had been glad of the ride home from the Fox, that Pete was a strange one, what had possessed him to go there last night? As far as she knew, he never went out anywhere. He gave her the right creeps he did, always appearing out of the blue like he did. She would make sure she didn't give him any sort of encouragement in the future that's for sure.

Caitlin pulled her car into High Ridge Woods, she had bought a great jacket at the feed merchants, reduced to half price and her friend Jude had knocked off another 10%, so it was a bargain. She was really pleased although it was hard to think of wearing it, especially when the weather was so glorious. She turned off the ignition, and checked her face in the mirror, delved around in her bag and found some lip gloss. She was a pretty girl, with long dark hair, that hung in glossy locks down her back, her blue eyes were very blue indeed. She was tall, with endless legs, and a slim but curvy figure, with ample breasts. More than her pretty looks though, Caitlin was funny, intelligent and kind, with that sexy Irish voice, she could have had men eating out of her hand, and although she could flirt with the best of them, she was very choosy. She often wondered how she had got herself into this situation, it wasn't like her at all, but in the good old fashioned sense, her heart had ruled her head, and now she was in too deep to turn back. If she had been talking to one of her friends she would have told them to steer clear, advising you could only end up getting hurt. Despite all his promises, she had a horrible deep down feeling that their affair could go no-where, but for the time being she was in love and there was no logic that could deter her.

She locked her car, hiding her handbag and her new coat, and for safety put her purse in her back pocket, along with her phone. This was an isolated spot, that's why they chose it but there had been a lot of thefts from these car parks lately and you couldn't be too careful. She turned at the sound of an engine approaching; the vehicle swung into the car park and drove around behind the shelter of the trees. Caitlin smiled to herself and walked into the dark shadows of the woods.

It had been another fantastic day for Jennifer, she had returned from the ride with Chloe euphoric with her progress and motivated with their plan, chattering non-stop. She seemed so less awkward today, and Beebs and Susie nudged each other.

"Wow, you're so much better and it's only been a day" smiled Beebs. Jennifer clambered off patting Rufus, while Susie held him.

"You're a little darling" and with that she threw her arms around the sweaty little horse's neck! The others laughed.

"Well you certainly don't seem afraid of him now!"

"No! I don't" said a surprised Jennifer, "you're right! How did that happen?"

"Don't think about" advised Chloe, "just go with it eh?" They washed the horses off together, and Jennifer even managed to untack him herself, fumbling a bit with the buckles. She and Beebs took the horses back to the fields, nattering away like old pals. Chloe smiled, thinking - so far so good.

The morning wore on, and they all worked hard, Jennifer doing the easier stuff, like washing the feed buckets, and picking up the droppings, as one by one the horses were exercised. She helped the girls deal with each horse, and gradually she got the hang of the awkward straps on the tack, and the knack of picking up hooves. The sun was so hot and punishing today, and it was with relief, when they all fell into the shade of the tack room. Coffee on the go and biscuit tin open, debating the best place for Jennifer to get some togs.

"I suppose I could get stuff off the internet, but I don't want anyone knowing what I'm doing, and my every move is watched by Mrs Fuller" she complained.

"Anyway, breeches are quite difficult to fit, but once you find a style that suits you, then you can order off the net. Beside you need boots too, so you'll have to try everything on. "

"Go to Cuckfield, they've a great tack shop there called Penfolds, a fantastic place and loads of selection too, and you could hide the stuff in the boot of your car when you buy it, then leave it here when you come up" offered Chloe.

"Great, if you don't mind, I will! I'll try and nip over there after we are done here. I could do with some shorts and stuff too, and a pair of those boots you've got on Chloe."

"You know, it won't be too long before people find out you are coming here, you're in the country now, and things get around like a dose of clap!" Susie said "but not from us of course" she added hastily.

"She's right" said Beebs "like Katherine or Sandy for instance, they are in an out of here all the time. You've been lucky not to see them so far, and they'll put two and two together, they aren't stupid!"

"Mmmm" Chloe murmured "they're right Jennifer, I don't know how we'll get round that one if they were to see you. We could confide in them, I suppose that might work. I think they'd quite enjoy being allies, and you know they'd give you lots of useful advice, would be good for you to have them on board. After all it wasn't so long ago that Katherine took up riding again."

"Oh God, I'm not very good at meeting new people. Not exactly top of the popularity polls am I, especially around here, I've made a good job of ballsing it up so far!"

"Come on, you've met us." said Susie, "You've fitted in fine here!"

"That's lovely of you to say that Susie, and you've no idea what that means to me!"

"Yep you have fitted in fine" agreed Beebs laughing "who would have thought it, that deep down you were …." She guffawed with laughter "a woman who actually enjoys shovelling shit!"

"Whaaaat! Take that you cow!" Jennifer launched her wet sponge at Beebs and it landed with a satisfying splat on her arm. Beebs responded like lightening, and with glee hurled her sponge catching Jennifer smack bang on her face! Suddenly a full blown water fight had started, sponges being lobbed everywhere, with Susie and Chloe joining in, until they were all wet through and gasping with laughter.

"What's going on here then" came a voice from the door, and they all looked up to see Katherine watching them in amusement.

"You sound like policeman plod, 'ere, 'ere, what's going on then" returned Beebs.

"Oh Katherine" gasped Chloe "your lesson this afternoon, is that the time!"

Katherine laughed "No I'm very early chick, you know me can't keep away!" She turned to Jennifer "I don't think we've met have we?"

"This is Jen" Chloe intercepted quickly "she's here to learn the ropes."

"Hi Jen" said Katherine easily, "Nice to meet you."

"Hi" stammered Jennifer. She hated being called Jen, it reminded her of her old London days, but somehow with Katherine and Chloe the name had seemed okay. "Nice to meet you too." She flushed, thinking I must look a right sight with my hair all wet and plastered round my sweaty face.

"Your boy is in" diverted Beebs, "been off the grass, what there is of it, for about an hour." Chloe shepherded Katherine out of the tack room, and away from Jennifer. The others all looked at each and grinned guiltily. "Don't worry" she continued looking at Jennifer's worried faced "Chloe will deal with it. Katherine's lovely, it'll be fine."

"God, I hope so" murmured Jennifer, "look I had better get going if I am going to Cuckfield, is there anything that you need?"

"Nothing we can afford" laughed Susie, "Go on, off you go Jen, whilst the coast is clear, and see you in the morning eh?"

Caitlin's pretty face was flushed with an afterglow of sex. She tingled all over, and could still feel the imprint of his hands and mouth on her body. She felt wonderful. Driving back towards Nantes Place, all she could do was think of him, what he'd said, how he'd felt when she held him. He was so strong, his upper arms muscled and tanned and the lovely feel of his toned body, she supposed it was because of his work that made him so fit. She loved the way he smelt, a faint musky cologne mingled with a tinge of horse she grinned to herself. A tiny gloom descended though, how long could they go on meeting like this without someone seeing them and finding out, then what would happen? She dismissed it - carpe diem that was all she could do.

The car sped along the road, rattling the umbrella heads of the cow parsley, mingling with the speckles of red Campion on the verge. It was such a beautiful time of year, she had never felt so happy. She drove carefully through the village, past the pub and the green, and pulled over just outside the village shop. She would get her and Lucy an ice cream, it might just not melt before she got back. As she got out of the car, another vehicle pulled up behind her. Oh sweet Mother of Mary, she recognised it immediately - b' Jesus it was the boss' wife. Caitlin smiled weakly at Jennifer.

"Hi Caitlin" Jennifer called "what're you up to?"

Caitlin looked guilty and felt herself flush. "Hello Mrs Parker-Smythe, I've been to the feed merchants and just stopped for ice creams for myself and Lucy" she explained. "I'm going straight back now."

"Caitlin" Jennifer exclaimed, "It's time you called me Jennifer, no need for all that Mrs Parker-Smythe stuff." Caitlin was astonished, she had thought she was in for a right bollocking, she would've been if Celia had spotted her!

"Why, yes for sure, if you don't mind ... Jennifer. I really was only out for a minute."

"Look, I don't mind what you're doing, I'm not here to check up on you, Okay? It's a lovely day, and I don't blame you if you make the most of the quiet time of year in the yard"

They walked into the shop, Mrs Gupta looked up from her book and beamed at them from behind her counter. They both smiled at her, Jennifer heading for the biscuit section, selecting the most expensive sort in cellophane boxes, cherry shortbread, oat and sultana crumbles, chocolate dipped ginger nuts and a few others, and then bought some instant coffee, teabags and squash and went back to the counter. Caitlin had selected her ice creams and was searching frantically in her pockets.

"I just can't find my purse" she exclaimed "I had it in my back pocket, I know I did!"

"Where did you last have it dear" asked Fatima. Caitlin paused, of course she knew exactly where it must be. Bugger.

"I must have left it at the feed merchants" she lied "I'm so sorry Mrs G, can I pay you later?"

Jennifer stepped in "really no need Caitlin, I can pay for those, no trouble. Can you put all this together Mrs Gupta please?"

Mrs Gupta looking from one to the other said "of course I can m' dear."

Caitlin looked up embarrassed from her searching "Mrs Par... Jennifer, thank you so much, I'm so grateful so I am now. I'll ring the feed merchants to check it's there and drop the money in to you, so I will."

Jennifer grinned, "No need, if I can't buy you a couple of ice creams, it's a sad old day. Just hope you find the purse." She paid for her goods and handed Caitlin her ice creams. "Excuse me though, I'm in a bit of hurry. Goodbye both of you."

Caitlin looked after her as she hurried out of the shop, and watched her throw the things into the boot, jump into the driver's seat and negotiating a quick three point turn, drove back towards the green. She didn't know Jennifer at all really, and she'd been really kind back then, perhaps she's not the bitch everyone says she is? Mind you, she's in a hurry thought Caitlin, I wonder where she's dashing off to, and what was she doing buying all those things, surely Mrs Fuller took care of all that? Why would Jennifer be buying them? Still in that brief encounter Caitlin had seen Jennifer in a new light, and she thought, actually, it's none of my business what she does. More importantly, she would have to go up to High Ridge Woods later when she had finished to find her purse. She left the shop and got into her car, pulling out her phone, which luckily she still had, and started texting, the melting ice creams momentarily forgotten on the passenger seat.

Jennifer drove off, unaware of Caitlin watching her, she was miles away. She was pleased that she had thought to stop at the shop and buy those bit and pieces, the least she could do for the girls. She was going to have to talk to Chloe about money and paying for the riding lessons, but it was a tricky one, she didn't want to offend her but neither did she want to be a free loader. She'd have to do it carefully. She took the road off to Cuckfield, mentally going over in her mind the things that she needed. The car swept along the lanes, scattering magpies quarrelling in the road, and passing a few locals out with their dogs and little children. The lane meandered on, round tight little corners and as she slowed down, she could smell the sweet scent of the tiny pink dog roses and the honeysuckle that tumbled through the hedges. Ahead silhouetted on the hillside, stood the ruins of the old Abbey, just an old shell now really, with ivy crawling up its sides, gaping holes like watching eyes peppered the walls as it stood guard over the small hamlet of Prior's Cross below. This is wonderful she thought and for the first time she really felt at one with the country side.

The village of Cuckfield was large, almost a small town, hosting a plethora of quaint little shops with white painted bow front windows selling exclusive goods. Nearly two centuries ago, it had been situated on an ancient turnpike, and had been an important coaching stop for weary travellers, and to accommodate the visitors, the village had grown and the shops had sprung up. When the horse drawn coaches were replaced with steam trains, the village had suffered as the railway was eventually built through the neighbouring town of Haywards Heath. The final nail in its commercial coffin was when the village was by passed by the A272 and since that time, most of the little shops had become very select, catering for luxuries, rather than necessities. Snuggled into the heart of the main street was Penfolds, with its dark green livery, rather like Harrods.

Jennifer parked the Mercedes in a neat little car park, and strolled along the sunny pavement admiring the shops. She had never bothered to stop in the village before. She found the saddlers easily and pushed open the door, an old fashioned bell clanged and the girl on the counter looked up and smiled at her. The shop was on two levels, and from what she could see it was crammed from top to bottom with all sorts of riding gear. It smelt pungently of leather, and she realised that this was coming from the stacks and stacks of saddles all piled on top of one another. The clothing was on the ground level, with racks of jodhpurs, fleeces, coats and shirts. It was a veritable equestrian Aladdin's cave – but where to start?

"I wonder if you can help me" she called to the assistant.

"Of course, what are you looking for?"

"I need some breeches, and a pair of long riding boots, and a crash hat. Oh yes and a pair of those little rubber boots, ones that you muck out in?"

"You mean muckers" laughed the assistant. "No problem at all! Breeches - what size are you – about an 8 or a 10? Let me show you what we have."

About an hour later, two pairs of Pikeur breeches purchased, some Muckers, a riding hat, and some smart Ariat Grasmere boots, she was satisfied. She looked briefly around, wishing she had more time to browse and tossed some gloves onto the counter, and spotting some tee shirts, picked up half a dozen in various sizes added those as well.

"I think that's all for today, I haven't got a lot time, although I could spend hours in here!" she laughed, fishing out her credit card to pay. The assistant gave it a small glance, when she spotted the name but said nothing. Laden with plastic bags, she made her way back to the car, and put the whole lot in the boot. Mission accomplished she thought, and now for Mrs Fuller.

"That's it, just a little more flexion, really ask him to soften his poll and his jaw" Chloe coached to Katherine, as she and Alfie cantered around the ménage "that's much better, well done, just like that, remember, 'flexion and bend are your friend', especially when he's spooking!" Chloe had on her trade mark big floppy hat and sunglasses, which shaded her eyes from the glare of the sun, and naturally the proverbial shorts and strappy singlet, no wonder she was always so tanned. "That's probably enough for today Katherine" she called "It's bloody hot and he's gone well"

"Too right! I'm worn out, don't know how he must be feeling!" grinned Katherine, as she brought the big horse down to trot, and allowed him to lower his head and stretch on a large circle.

"Okay. Just put him on the other rein Katherine and we'll finish" instructed Chloe, watching, her head slightly tilted to one side, as they changed direction. Alfie's coat was shiny with sweat and he had a thick layer of froth between his back legs as he rolled into walk.

Katherine leant down patting him, then sat up and wiped her face with the back of her hand.

"God I'm gasping for a drink, pass up my water will you?"

Chloe called Beebs over to take Alfie and wash him down, as Katherine dismounted.

"Katherine" Chloe began, "I need to talk to you about something"

"What have I done? You're not annoyed with me are you?" Katherine, like everyone else at Mileoak had a healthy respect for Chloe, and the last thing she would want is to have upset her.

"No course not, nothing like that, I just need your help with something." As Beebs led Alfie away, she and Chloe walked over to the tack room, where Chloe made a couple of glasses of Ribena, and passed one to Katherine. She knew she had to put this just right to her, to get her on side.

"Katherine" Chloe started "that girl who you saw earlier, Jen?"

"What about her, who is she, I thought she looked familiar, although everyone looks different when they are soaking wet! You looked as though you were having a right laugh!"

"That was Jennifer Parker-Smythe - Charles' wife. She has come to me to learn something about horse management and riding. The thing is that she is doing it as a surprise for Charles, and doesn't want anyone to know, so can you keep it a secret? Actually, I had thought that you may even help her a bit yourself. She's quite a laugh once she relaxes with you."

"Chloe, you know me better than that, 'course I won't say anything to anyone, why would I, especially as you've asked me not to, although I am interested in your horse management training with that water fight going on!"

"You're a star Hun, thanks so much, I knew I could rely on you ...but as for the water fight" and with that she picked up a sponge heavy from cold water in the sink and caught Katherine straight on the chest, and they both fell about laughing.

CHAPTER 13

Charles picked up the phone, took a deep breath and punched out a number. He had a brief moment in his day and he wanted this call to be uninterrupted. The seconds ticked by as he waited, four rings, six rings and then the answer phone clicked in "Hello, this is Celia Parker-Smythe, I can't take your call at the moment, please leave a message after the tone and I'll get back to you'. Good thought Charles, relieved that she hadn't answered, he would just leave a message for her, he wouldn't bother to call her mobile.

"Celia, hi, it's Charles, just to ask if it was okay if I have the children for the weekend, the one after next, that's 16th June. I can pick them up on the Friday afternoon and bring them back on Sunday after lunch" he drawled "that's if the date suits you of course. Get back to me can you? Hope you're all okay" he added hastily and replaced the receiver.

He sat back in his chair, glad that he hadn't had to have any dialogue with her. She always found something to moan at him about, if it wasn't the kids it was something else. He hadn't regretted the divorce once, although he did miss the children. He'd felt obliged to be married and have a family, it was *'the done thing'*, they'd never really been suited, other than Celia rode to hounds like a demon and initially that had been good enough. Once he had gone along the expected route it had been impossible to go back. His affair with Jennifer started with lust and desire but grew into something much deeper and stronger, and he had just loved being with her when they were in London, it was only since she had come to live at Nantes she'd changed. What was it about the place he wondered? He could understand that Jennifer had found it difficult to adapt to the lifestyle there, bearing in mind where she had been brought up. Whereas Celia, should have found it easy, but Christ she was boring to live with and moreover she was a first rate bitch. You could never say that about Jennifer he contemplated, thinking back over the skinny dipping incident last night, she was really good fun when she was like

134

that! The look on Mrs Fuller's face had been priceless; of course the old bag had heard them, probably seen them too, knowing how nosy she was - well tough.

The phone rang briskly beside him. "Charles Parker-Smythe" he barked.

"Charles, its Celia" her clipped upper class voice irritating him immediately "it's fine for you to have the children for that weekend. Although you will have to make sure they do their homework, they need stability you know. Whilst I am on the subject..." Here we go thought Charles, and held the receiver at arm's length.

"Can you make sure that when they come home, you ensure that all their belongings come with them? Last time Rupert had left an important text book behind and Jessica one of her dolls. It simply isn't good enough, Jennifer should make sure they are well supervised and pack their things properly." Charles was pissed off, poor kids and poor Jennifer - Celia couldn't resist sniping about her all the time. He could understand that Celia was the woman he had slighted, but he often wondered if she had ever thought that she might have to take a bit of the blame?

"Of course Celia, I'll make sure that this time they don't leave anything behind." He soothed, "I'm sure it wasn't done on purpose you know."

"So you say Charles, so you say. I'm sure that Jennifer just wants to make my life difficult. Rupert told me when he came home last time Mrs Fuller was remarking to him how very difficult she could be. I suppose that is what you get when you marry out of your class." Charles was furious, what a bloody snob Celia was and how dare Mrs Fuller make remarks like that about Jennifer to his son! He swallowed his rage, he didn't want a fight and had learned by now how to deal with Celia, it had taken him long enough!

"I think you are being unfair actually Celia, but I'll make sure that all the children's things are returned as I said I would. You've caught me at a tricky time at the moment, so I have to go now" and before she could respond, he ended the call. He thought about what Celia had said. It was true in a way - he had just left Jennifer to deal with the house and the staff on her own. He had just expected her to be able to cope. It was at times like this, when talking to Celia, stuck up cow that she was, that he felt very guilty indeed. After all he had rescued Jennifer from the misery of the council estate, just to plonk her into the misery of a country estate. Fundamentally he wanted his marriage to succeed, he loved her, even though he went off the rails occasionally. Okay he was going to make more effort. The first thing he could do was to have some input into this bloody party, and secondly he may well have a gentle word in Freda Fuller's ear.

Whilst Charles was musing about Jennifer, she was thinking about the impending meeting with Mrs Fuller. She was sitting in her study at her desk by the window, empty envelopes strewn on the floor and a stack of reply cards in two piles in front of her. She had carefully listed on her lap top, the acceptances and so far very few people had declined which surprised her, expecting the usual snub from the snobby lot around here. She supposed it had got round that it was to be a bit of a swanky bash, so she doubted whether they were coming for anything other than a chance to get dolled up and a free meal, rather than as a chance to get to know her better. Don't delude yourself she thought. She glanced around the room with its dark walls, and heavy curtains. The Rockingham ornaments and figurines, its austere spoon backed chairs and orderly tidiness, this didn't reflect her, but the person she thought she wanted to be, she felt more at home in Chloe's tack room she grimaced. The only part of it she really liked was the old oak pedestal desk with its green leather top and her antique leather office chair. I'm going to revamp this room, make it much more mine, it can be my little sanctuary she decided.

A sharp knock at the door and Freda Fuller came in, with her 'bible' clutched in her hand, it was spot on three thirty pm.

"Ah, thank you very much Mrs Fuller" said Jennifer "you are right on time. Do sit down." She gestured to one of the small hard chairs which placed Mrs Fuller slightly lower than she was at her desk, the small psychological advantage making her smile inwardly.

"I am always on time" came the icy reply, as Mrs Fuller sat down. Jennifer swivelled round on her office chair to her desk, taking the pile of acceptances. "I've had quite a few acceptances so far, and I need to be thinking of a seating plan."

"You can leave that to me." said Mrs Fuller rudely.

"Ah, I know that I can Mrs Fuller, you are very competent, but I should like to have some input, and actually I've invited some other people who are not on your list of guests" Jennifer added, wondering how Mrs Fuller would accept this piece of information.

"And who might that be?" enquired Mrs Fuller, "perhaps you should have consulted me first, they may not be…. suitable." Jennifer ignored her - she would not let her get to her, she just wouldn't!

"What I should like you to do, if you would be so kind, is to look at the acceptances so far, and decide who would be best to seat with whom. I think tables of eight or ten would be good don't you?" Jennifer said, forcing a smile and looking her straight in the eye. Mrs Fuller gazed back stonily, her face tight with anger. "Now I know that you've everything we discussed last week in hand, but I should like you to give me a detailed plan of where the marquee, loos etc are to be situated. Also too how the tables will be laid out, and where the Jazz Band will be? Have you had a time confirmed for when the marquees are to be erected yet?"

"I'll be happy to look at the seating arrangements, although personally I think tables of ten would be more preferable myself. Naturally, I do have an idea where I'll be placing the tables on the evening, and the marquee people when they confirmed to me did send a plan."

Jennifer noted that she used the first person singular. Cheeky old bat, but she knew that she had to do this the diplomatic way, the old girl clearly thought that she wanted to usurp her.

"Mrs Fuller, look, I know you don't approve of me, but I'm doing my best here, and I'm extremely grateful to you for all your help and advice, which I certainly do take on board, but I should like us to be able to try to do more of the organising together. I don't want to take over, but I do want to have some input and I'm really relying on you to meet me half way" Jennifer coaxed, smiling directly at Mrs Fuller, who this time couldn't meet her eye.

"Of course Mrs Parker-Smythe, let me take the invitations and look over them tonight and perhaps we could meet up again tomorrow and we can make the final decision." It was a breakthrough, albeit a small one, and for the first time Mrs Fuller had used her name!

"That would be lovely Mrs Fuller, I'm so grateful, shall we say three thirty again?"

Caitlin was anxious about her missing purse, it would a while before she could go back and retrieve it, how stupid to have left it there. She was really worried, it had all her cards in it, her driving licence and all sorts of other personal stuff which she certainly didn't want to lose or to be found by anyone else either. She arrived back at Nantes, feeling tense and preoccupied, to find the yard in much the same state as it had been when she left, with Lucy dawdling about with a broom. Christ what had she been doing all morning?

"You've been gone ages Caitlin, I'm fed up here on my own" whined Lucy

"Well for sure, if that's the case why haven't you done more Lucy, this yard looks a right mess, what have you actually been doing? Feet up, coffee, reading the nag and dog I suspect now?" snapped Caitlin. "I even stopped to get you an ice cream, although why I bothered when you are so bloody lazy beats me!"

Caitlin had hit home with her assessment of Lucy's morning. "Whatdya mean lazy, you're the nutter who works herself to the bone all winter, and what for, a poxy groom's pay. You should back off a bit in the summer, do what everyone else does or are you too busy shagging your man!" Lucy bit back at her.

Caitlin reeled at the spiteful remarks "I don't know what you're talking about" she stammered, her face flushing , "but what I do know is that you have real attitude!"

Lucy's vindictive little eyes glared at her, who did she think she was? "You can stuff your fucking ice cream Caitlin, and you can stuff your fucking job too!" she yelled, throwing her broom on the ground, and stamping hard on the handle, splintering it into two pieces. She spun round and marched up the stairs to her flat.

Caitlin could hear her banging about in anger. Oh b' Jesus she sighed, now what was she going to do. She was going to make a bloody coffee that's what, she thought. She sat down with her head in her hands, whilst she waited for the kettle to boil. If Lucy were to walk out, she would have to tell Mr Parker- Smythe what had happened, luckily it was the summer, and she could cope without her for a while. Caitlin was never normally snappy, but frankly what she had said was nothing but the truth. Charles was a decent enough boss, she had worked for him for a long time, and he knew she ran the yard like clockwork, but he wasn't going to be pleased. Perhaps Lucy would change her mind, although it would only really be delaying her eventual departure. Lucy had never fitted in here, and was hard to work with. Caitlin would just wait and see what happened in the next hour or two. She went outside and picked up the splintered broom wearily throwing it into the dustbin, listening to the crashes and bangs coming from the flat upstairs.

Lucy was in a terrible rage, ripping her posters off the wall, and throwing open her cupboards and tossing stuff into her cases. She's a fucking bitch she thought, in her irrational outburst conveniently forgetting all the times that Caitlin had covered for her. Lucy raged on, she'd had enough of it here; she could get a job stacking shelves in Tesco's and earn more money!   Stuck up fucking bunch of toffs. She picked up her mobile and dialled Tom's number.

"Hi Tom, it's me Lucy, something's happened here at Nantes, and I need to get out right now. I've had a row with Caitlin and walked out, can you pick me up straight away?"

Tom was in the middle of mowing the grass at his parents' place and was pleased to have a chance to escape "Bloody hell! What's happened? I can be there in about 15 minutes, shall I come round to the yard?"

"Tom, you're a fucking life saver, yeah come to the flat." Thank you, thank you God she muttered as she flew about shoving the last bits and pieces into her bags.

Caitlin heard the growl of the Landrover before she saw it. Her heart sank as it rumbled into the yard, and she saw Tom driving. He looked a bit sheepish when he saw her.

"I've come to pick up Lucy, I hear you two have had a row."

"Well you might call it that" sighed Caitlin, looking up as she heard the flat door open and saw Lucy bumping down the stairs with her cases.

"Just these two Tom, and I've got a couple of bags to bring down, and I'll take my hat and boots from the tack room" Lucy said, not glancing once at Caitlin "I've had it with this stinking place."

Tom was aghast, Lucy's tone coupled with the look on Caitlin's face said it all. "Look Lucy, don't you think you're being a bit hasty here?" he pleaded, "It can't be that bad!"

"It fucking is, you don't have to work here do you?" shouted Lucy "with that fucking cow!" Tom looked at Caitlin, he'd known her for years, she was the last person you could call a cow. "Look, you're either gonna give me a lift or you're not Tom?" she demanded, "one thing's for sure, I'm outta here okay!"

"Okay" Tom shook his head but picked up her stuff and shoved it into the back of the Landrover, Lucy cast a scornful look around, careful not to meet Caitlin's eye, and took great delight in gobbing on the ground. She jumped into the passenger seat, and was gone.

Resignedly, Caitlin took out her phone, she'd better start explaining what had happened. She rang Charles' mobile, but it went straight to voicemail. She had the number of the direct line to his PA, but dreaded speaking to the tight lipped Cynthia. What to do, what to do, she pondered. She knew that Jennifer was back, as she'd heard her car come down the drive when she was in the yard listening to Lucy's irate packing. She supposed the next port of call would be to tell her, not that there was much she could do, she didn't have anything to do with the horses. Caitlin felt tears coming, it was just one thing on top of another, and the day had started so well too.

Laura had spent her day rummaging around in the charity shops. She had gone through racks and racks of musty clothes but couldn't find what she wanted, it was just not the sort of thing people in this part of London bought, wore and subsequently threw out. It had been a fruitless search, though she doggedly carried on, but at last had to admit defeat. She trailed back to the flat dispiritedly, to find Jonty had got up at last.

"Hey kidda, what you been up to? You look right pissed off"

"I fucking am, can't find anything that's right, y'know?"

"You're looking in the wrong part of town, why you just can't buy the stuff beats me?"

"Two reasons, first it needs to look used, and second we don't have the money, that sort of gear costs." she sighed. Jonty put his arm around her, he'd gone along with this revenge scene of Laura's and was cool about it, but she knew jack shit about planning.

"To pull off a job babe, every angle needs to be taken care of. That takes a lotta planning. Don't sweat, we'll go off to Horsham, that's the kinda town that'll have it and we can do another recce after – okay?" Laura looked up at him gratefully, she was so lucky to have him.

"Do you really think it will work Jonty" she whispered "I so want to teach that guy a lesson and if I can get these Hunt Sabs on my side …"

"Oh, it'll work all right, 'specially if I've anything to do with it" he laughed. "But you gotta be patient, you know the timing's gotta be just right."

Caitlin rang the bell, waiting agitatedly for Mrs Fuller to bumble out of the kitchen and down the passage to the back door. Mrs Fuller was surprised to see her, dusting her floury hands on her apron.

"Oh Mrs Fuller, so sorry to be disturbing you now" Caitlin faltered "I wonder, is Mrs PS in?"

"Caitlin, what's the matter, you look right upset?"

Tears sprang again to Caitlin's eyes, and she wiped them away angrily "Oh Mrs F, that wretched Lucy has walked out, and it's my fault!"

"Now, now Caitlin, I'm sure it isn't, she was a right flighty piece and make no mistake, good riddance. Look come in to the kitchen and we can decide what to do."

Caitlin followed her down the corridor to the kitchen, and they sat down together at the table. Caitlin explained what had happened, and that she had tried to get hold of Mr Charles but no luck, and she now she had come up to report to Mrs PS.

"I'll come with you" said Mrs Fuller, not altogether wanting to be kept out of the loop, "she's in her study - I've just left her".

They stood up, and walked down the corridor towards the big hall, their feet tapping on the floor boards. Mrs Fuller didn't hesitate, striding on through the house with Caitlin trailing reluctantly along behind her, until they stood outside Jennifer's study. Freda knocked on the door and went straight in, Jennifer was still at her desk, and hastily stuffed '*The Manual of Horsemanship*' into her desk draw, surprise registering on her face as she noticed Caitlin fidgeting behind the bulk of Mrs Fuller.

"Do come in both of you" she invited as she swung round on her chair "Sit down please". Clearly something was up she panicked, had they come to ask her where she'd been?

"There's been some trouble at the stables and Lucy the groom has walked out" informed Mrs Fuller bluntly "Caitlin's not to be blamed, she was a proper little madam that one."

Jennifer sighed in relief, and turned to Caitlin, whose eyes were full of tears, with her hands fiddling in her lap. She looked totally wretched, a far cry from earlier in the afternoon.

"Oh Caitlin, don't worry, we can soon sort this out. Now Mrs Fuller would you be kind enough to bring a pot of coffee and some of your delicious cakes for us all and we can decide what to do." She had said the right thing. Mrs Fuller was full of grandiose to be included, and Caitlin sighed and looked a bit more reassured.

As Mrs Fuller bustled out, Caitlin blurted "It really wasn't my entire fault, really it 't wasn't."

"Tell me what happened Caitlin." By the time Mrs Fuller had come back with the coffee, and poured them all a cup Jennifer knew the whole story, handing the weeping Caitlin a tissue.

"Look Caitlin, I don't think you've anything to reproach yourself for at all. From what I gather Lucy is no loss to any of us, and I know Charles has every faith in you, so we'll just have to find a replacement in time for the hunting season. Not a problem, I'll tell him and we can deal with it ourselves, okay?"

"Oh Mrs Parker- Smythe, thank you so much" whispered Caitlin.

"Just one thing though, please don't call me that, call me Jennifer, and it's high time you did too Mrs Fuller."

CHAPTER 14

Andrew had organised an informal meeting with their accountant Gary on the Friday lunchtime in the surgery. He had managed to clear his diary for a couple of hours, but would probably have to work late to catch up. He was excited about this new project, he just hoped that Gary thought the figures would stack up financially. It had always been his dream to build the practice up into a fully-fledged equine centre, and now he had Oliver on board, it looked like it just might happen. They were expanding rapidly and if they were going to develop the practice now was the time. He wasn't quite sure about how big they could be initially, but let's get this first hurdle over with he thought. He ran his hands through his thick black hair, slightly going grey now, his handsome tanned face was a little lined with the sun, he squinted down at the paperwork on his desk, wondering how much longer would it be before he needed reading glasses.

Gary Rutherford popped his head round the door "Okay to come in?" he asked and edged past Paulene hovering behind him. He had been Andrew's accountant for a long time now, and was no stranger to being here. He was a short guy, going slightly bald, but hey Karen loved him. The important thing was he was bloody good at his job.

"What's all the urgency Andrew? Not like you to need me so quickly, Tax man after you?" He laughed.

"No nothing like that, that's what I pay you for, to keep me out of trouble!"

"Okay, okay, just joking! What up then mate?"

"I need to run something past you" said Andrew, and started to outline the plan.

Gary listened making notes and asking the odd questions and finally sat back in his chair rubbing his pate "Phew, that'll be big money we're talking about y' know."

"Well, I know it's not going to be cheap, but is it feasible? Could we do it?" pleaded Andrew anxiously.

"Look, I'll need to look at the figures, and if you're serious, I'll put together a business plan for you to take to the bank, but I'll need to know more, what sort of money would the premises be, and some costings for staff and equipment." He scrawled down some more notes on his pad. "Get back to me with some ideas, but for Christ's sake be realistic". He picked up his diary, "Let's meet up in a week, see what you can come up with, but if you want the quick answer, I would say yes, done the right way, it could be a runner."

Andrew walked him through to the front reception and the door. Turning and punching the air with his fist "Yes!!" he yelled. Paulene looked up curiously.

"Paulene can you come through to my office, I need to talk to you about something important" smiled Andrew.

Grace Allington sat on her loo seat, desperately trying to pee into a jug. The directions on the packet had said to catch the flow midstream. Easier said than done she thought - as she whipped the jug out balancing it on the nearby window sill. She crossed her fingers and dipped the little white stick into the jug. She waited, praying and hoping, she hardly dared look. She knew before she opened her eyes that the test would be negative. The disappointment was overwhelming, even though she had known deep down that she was not pregnant, but it still hit her just the same. She so longed to be able to give Colin a baby, it would make them complete. She loved him so much and he her, and they were happy, but to have a child would be the icing on the cake for them both and for her parents too, they would adore to have a grandchild. Still, it wasn't to be, not this time anyway, thank goodness she hadn't mentioned anything to Colin, at least she could bear the brunt of yet another frustrated test alone. Her emotional ache for a child was so intense, it was like a physical pain. She sighed deeply rubbing her temples with her fingertips. From their bedroom she could hear the soft burring of the phone, whipping up her knickers, almost tripping in her haste, she dashed to picked up the extension.

"Grace, its Lavinia Appleton- Lacey here, just wondered if we could ask you to make some cakes for the Puppy Show. Hate asking as you do so much, but we're a bit short of good cake makers this year, since George's wife died".

Oh God this is what her life had become, a good cake maker thought Grace gloomily, but she politely agreed "Of course Lavinia, just let me know how many you think, and I can bring them up on the morning of the show"

"Grace you are a dear, thank you, I knew we could rely on you, Amanda said you were the one to ask. How are you by the way and your parents?"

"Oh, we're all fine" she lied, all fine except me she thought, "Mummy and Daddy are in good health and will be coming to the Puppy Show."

"Jolly good.We have to look after our farmers after all, haw haw!" she brayed "Oh and by the way, if you hear of any young thing wanting a job as a groom, I heard that they have a vacancy at Nantes." Before Grace could ask any more she had rung off. A vacancy at the Parker-Smythe's, she had only seen Lucy last week, and she'd said nothing, it must have been quick. Blimey, has Caitlin left, saints preserve us if Lucy was head groom there. She was trouble that girl.

She made her way down the old reclaimed oak stairs into the lofty space of the converted barn, and started to tidy up. Picking up the strewn cushions from over the floor, and the discarded crumpled newspapers, that Colin had let slip from his hand when he fell asleep on the sofa the night before. She hated doing housework, much preferring to be outside in the open air with her animals. Gloomily she tugged out the vacuum cleaner, but again and again she was overwhelmed by disappointment, trouble was, she was on her own a lot, it gave her too much time to think. Perhaps I should get a job, keep my mind occupied, and her thoughts returned to the conversation with Lavinia, should she apply for the job at Nantes?

Caitlin was feeling brighter and had worked hard this morning - not that Lucy had ever done much, but she was still another pair of hands. Jennifer had been really sweet about what happened yesterday, and actually the yard felt a much nicer place since Lucy had stormed out. Last evening Mr PS had caught an early train home for once, and had come over to the stables with Jennifer to see her. They had been holding hands and walked with their heads close together, just like they used to do when Jennifer had first come here. It was good to see and Caitlin was pleased that they seemed much happier, but in that moment the poignancy of their affection only served to highlight her own covert situation. She could weep with the unfairness of life, but quickly managed to shrug off the feeling. Charles had been great about Lucy, telling her not to worry, and that he was sure that between her and Jennifer they would find someone else who was probably much more suitable. Jennifer said they would get together once the party was over, as she had a lot on at the minute. Caitlin was relieved, it seemed it would all work out after all, about Lucy's replacement that was anyway.

Once they had gone, she knew she had one last thing to do that night, and had climbed into her car and made her way back to High Ridge Woods. It had been really creepy, as the sun was just going down by the time she got to the car park which was totally deserted. As she locked the car, she had heard the soft hoot of a barn owl and the screams of the vixens on the night. Each rustle and movement was magnified tenfold as she crept towards the darkening woods. She knew the way by heart, but had a flashlight with her just in case. Stumbling over the odd hidden root and her hair catching in overhead branches, she inched her way off the path, down the little track they had made into the dense woodland, until she found the little clearing with the soft springy grass. She dropped to her hands and knees and started to grope around for the purse, she was just about to turn on the torch, when her fingers touched it, just waiting for her on the grass. She grasped it gratefully, and started to retrace her steps back towards the car park. The night had set in now but her eyes had become more accustomed to the gloom and she took her time, there was no hurry. As she found the path, she stopped, very still for a moment, her head slightly to one side, she had thought that she'd heard the sound of voices on the air, she listened again. Nothing, so she crept on, edging her way back, and unexpectedly, there it was again, definitely a voice, coming from the direction of the car park. She stopped, standing very still and listened. Yes, two people from the sound of it and she felt

147

suddenly afraid and vulnerable. Her car was probably less than a hundred yards away, but it could have been a hundred miles for the isolation she felt. She waited, creeping forward, taking the odd step now and then. She could see the car park, as the trees thinned out, her car was hidden around the corner as usual, but in the main part she could make out an old Landrover with blacked out windows, and two people standing beside it, one was smoking and they seemed to be deep in quiet conversation. She paused suddenly having an irrational desire to pee. She crossed her legs, her heart beating faster. The man moved away from the Landrover, and crushed his cigarette underfoot, his shaved head almost translucent in this eerie light. Please let them go she thought, don't let them come over here. The man moved back to their vehicle and to her intense relief they climbed in, switched on the engine and the lights and started to pull away. She'd waited until she saw the lights disappear along the lane, and then run as fast she could to her car. Now on this bright sunny day her silly fear of last night all seemed ridiculous, her over reacting imagination working overtime after a tough emotional day. It was probably just a couple out for a snog and a cuddle, after all it wouldn't be the first time that had happened in High Ridge Woods she thought happily.

"Hi Jen" called Katherine, as she pulled up her car beside the horse walker. "Look, Chloe has told me, so don't worry your secret is safe with me, and you know if you'd let me, I can brief Sandy, she's a barrister and great with secrets, then you won't have to worry about bumping into her."

Jennifer blushed "You're very kind Katherine, I know it's silly really and of course pretty soon Charles will find out, but I want to be a bit more competent before he does. I'm not sure about Sandy, what do you think she'd say?"

"Oh Sandy's cool, and she's coming up later, so you could meet her if you like?"

"Well - okay if you're sure you think it'll be alright." They walked over towards the tack room chatting amiably, Katherine helping Jennifer with her carrier bags. Chloe and the girls were going over the feed list and looked up as they came in.

"Wow" said Beebs "you certainly did go on a shopping spree, Whatdya buy?" Jennifer pulled out her new breeches, and held them up.

"Perfect – just what you needed" admired Chloe.

"I got these for you, as a sort of 'thank you' for you all being so lovely!" grinned Jennifer "I hope they fit, I wasn't sure what to get" she handed over one of the bags. "I bought some supplies for coffee time too" she laughed "since I seem to be drinking and eating so much here!"

"These are just amazing Jen" screeched Susie, "Kyra K too, you really pushed the boat out!" The girls dived into the carrier bags, holding up the tee shirts and dancing round the tack room. "You're a star!"

Jennifer was pleased, it had been such a small gesture after how much they had done for her.

"Now ladies calm down" Chloe switched on the kettle, "Jen, do you think that you could go and get Rufus yourself today, while I tack up Seamus? Sandy's coming up and she doesn't always have a lot of time, so I want him to be ready for her. Katherine you okay doing Alfie?"

"Sure, of course Chloe, Sandy and I are going out on the gallop track before it gets too hot, I know she has to get back on time."

"Jen, Beebs is taking you out, whilst I do some lessons here, that okay with you?"

"Yes, thanks Beebs, hope you don't get fed up with me, I can't even rise to the trot properly yet."

"You're doing really well Jen, I said yesterday, it's just about practice, and the more you do, the better you get."

"Susie, the vet is coming today, to do Jimma's teeth, so he needs to be brought in, and whilst he's here I thought he could have a look at that cut on Ksar's leg, it's healing well after the antibiotics, but I just want to make sure, that okay?"

"Yep, boss no problem, which vet. Hope it's the dishy Oliver!"

grinned Susie, "Mind you Andy Pandy's not bad, but a bit too old for me!"

"Hey watch it, he's probably still in his 30s!"

"They're both pretty tasty" agreed Beebs, "wait till you see them Jennifer!

"They are indeed, but ladies, they are both very married, so you're out of luck there!" Jennifer looked from one to the other, it was all so normal here she thought, everyone bantering together, really enjoying themselves, she loved it. They just accepted her into their fold without any bitching or motive and for the first time in her life she felt included and wanted. She had always yearned for this kind of camaraderie. At school, she had been a loner, working hard with her head down, whilst the others all mucked about, even in her work she hadn't made friends. Her greatest fun had been when she met Charles, but she was so afraid of losing him and doing the wrong thing when she came to Nantes, she knew she had become a misery, and now these lovely people had turned her life around, even after a few days.

"Okay, let's get going girls."

Caitlin was waiting for Patrick to arrive. She had lugged the hunters up from the water meadow where they were spending their summer break after a long season, and they were now dozing patiently in their stables waiting to have their feet trimmed. The horses looked really well, fat and round and rested. It had been a right palaver though bringing them up single handed, and once again she thought about Lucy's replacement. She couldn't have been more surprised when Charles had delegated the task of recruiting a new groom to her and Jennifer alone, normally he wanted to have a big input into who was employed. Actually Caitlin thought, she wasn't even certain if Jennifer knew anything about horses, she'd never shown any interest in them before. Ah well, it would work out now, she was sure. She wondered why Mrs Fuller was always moaning about Jennifer, she had been very sweet to Caitlin yesterday, and that Pete, when he did say anything at all, he did nothing but grumble. She was deep in thought, when she heard Patrick's van trundle up the drive over the gravel. She liked Patrick, he was like a Cadbury's crème egg, naughty but nice! Radio Two blaring from his open window, the door swung open and Patrick climbed out, his dogs tumbling after him. Love your farrier, love their dogs!

"Good day to you Caitlin, my beautiful Irish Colleen" he laughed "How are you this bright and lovely morning?"

"Hi Patrick, I'm very well to be sure and how are you?"

"Keep talking in that sexy voice of yours my lovely and I'll be even better" he laughed, "Where's that naughty Lucy today?"

"Ah well now, there's a tale that needs a cuppa over the telling. Kettle's already boiling." She went back into the tack room to make the tea, whilst Patrick donned his leather apron, and slid open the side door of the van to get out his tool trolley. He arched his back and shoulders, swinging his arms to meet over the top of his head, thinking, if little Lucy isn't here, perhaps Caitlin might spill the beans over Ace He was just pondering the question, when she appeared back with two steaming mugs of tea, a packet of biscuits tucked under her arm.

"Now come and be sitting down and I'll tell you the whole torrid tale! He looked up surprised, was she talking about Lucy or Ace?

They sat side by side on the wooden bench outside the tack room, Caitlin's long legs stretched out in front of her, as she laid her head back against the brickwork. Patrick sipped his tea, and listened whilst she regaled the whole stormy episode of Lucy's departure.

"So that was it, she just slammed up to the flat, packed her bags and left" she recounted, "Young Tom Snowhill picked her up and I haven't heard from her since."

"Blimey, what a to do. Still she never really fitted here did she? You're probably best rid of her, she was a bit of a slapper you know."

"You'd know, would you now Patrick?" She laughed, leaning forwards, crinkling her freckled nose at him, her eyes sparkling, "What is it now that you're not telling me!"

Patrick laughed "Just what I thought, though never had it confirmed, sadly!"

"Ah Patrick you're a naughty one to be sure, and that's why we love you!"

"What about you Caitlin, how's your love life, still going out with that young copper, what's his name – Tony?"

Caitlin hesitated for a nanosecond, "Well I haven't seen much of him lately. We had a great time last winter, and 't was fun with him riding to hounds. We really enjoyed going to the Hunt Ball together too, but you know, it's a busy time for him, but now the hunting's finished, he's no call to come to this neck of the woods much." Patrick glanced at her, taking in her garbled excuse - just too much information.

"Got someone else?"

"No - so you could still be lucky, if you play your cards right!" teased Caitlin, winking at him. Only if I play an Ace thought Patrick!

Oliver bumped the Toyota into the yard at Mileoak, talking on his hands free, Christ he was busy today, and another visit to do. Chloe was teaching in the school and he waved to her, and parked the car alongside the stables, ending the call, and jumping out. His long tanned legs in shorts, and a navy blue polo shirt, with the vet logo emblazoned on the front. His pushed his mop of hair out of his eyes, he liked coming here, they were a good bunch, friendly and mega efficient and knew their stuff.

"Hi Oliver" greeted Susie, "you've got to put up with me today, Chloe's teaching and Bibi is taking a client out."

"Hi Susie, you're a beaut, so that suits me fine. What have we got to do?"

"Not that much, I've brought the old boy Jimma in, he needs his teeth doing, as he's quidding a lot, but Chloe said to go easy, as his teeth are pretty loose, and he can't afford to lose any. He's 31 now you know!" Oliver opened the tailgate of his car, and pulled out a worn holdall, full of different kinds of floats, which he used to rasp the teeth, and a stainless steel bucket. She led Oliver over to one of the stables, where a woolly dun horse was waiting crossly, banging his legs on the door, and whinnying at the top of his voice."

"He's pretty annoyed about coming in" laughed Susie "he's been calling ever since I brought him up. He lives out the whole time now and as you know he has a touch of Cushings, hence the shaggy coat, but he's well enough in himself, other than going a bit feral!"

"Come on old fella" crooned Oliver, "this won't take long and then you can go back out to your mates! Can you fill up my bucket with some water Susie?" He opened the holdall, pulling out the instruments and found the speculum, a sort of gag which fitted over the horse's head, and which once fitted made his and the horse's life a lot simpler and kinder.

It was bloody hard work rasping teeth, if you did them properly, but he would have to be careful with this old boy. Susie returned with the bucket and clipped on a lead-rope, and they moved into the stable, Jimma's eyes looking suspiciously at them both. Oliver moved quietly but quickly, fitting the gag before the old chap knew what had happened, and started to work, feverishly filing off all the sharp edges, stopping now and then to clean his floats. Eventually he was satisfied. He took off the gag and patted the old horse "job done old boy!"

"Fantastic" said Susie making a fuss of Jimma, "not too bad was it now." She turned to Oliver, "Chloe just asked if you could check that cut on Ksar's leg, we've finished the antibiotics now and it looks okay, but just wondered if you thought he might need another course just to make sure of no infection?"

"Sure" said Oliver, "Lead the way." Ksar was in the next block, and was one of the most beautiful horses, his fine black head looking out over the stable. Susie took him out of the box into the daylight and Oliver squatted down, the tops of his thighs hardening, and his broad shoulders almost close enough for Susie to run her hand along. He was very hunky was our Oliver!

"It's fine" he said "just keep it clean and try and avoid the flies if you can, I don't think it needs any more work, but just keep an eye on it, and call me if you need to." He stood up, unaware of the effect his body had made on Susie, whose tongue was only just managing not to hang out. She put Ksar away and walked with him back to his car, watching as he washed the rasps, just as Chloe had finished her teaching.

"Hi Oliver, how are you?" Chloe came over and Oliver kissed her on either cheek, "Everything okay?"

"Yep fine thanks, Jimma's teeth are done, and none fell out – Praise the Lord, and Ksar is fine. How are you Chloe, looking as lovely as ever. Are you going to the do up at Nantes Place next week, Andrew and I have both been invited."

"Yes, I think I'm going, but John isn't keen, I'm doing my best to persuade him though!"

"Oh he's gotta come, it should be good I think, although I know what you mean, Suse, is dragging her feet too! Tell you what, if John doesn't want to come and neither does Suse, we could go together. That'd set the tongues wagging!"

"It would indeed, can you imagine the gossip" she laughed, but actually she was secretly quite enamoured with the idea of going with the gorgeous Oliver Travers. "I'll keep you posted!"

CHAPTER 15

The weekend disappeared quickly, Jennifer had gone up to London and joined Charles in the flat. It was like old times, they visited their favourite restaurant in Holland Park and had an early supper. Charles managed to get some tickets for War Horse, and Jennifer had cried all the way through. He glanced at her during the performance, surprised to see the tears rolling down her cheeks, and he reached over and took her hand, whispering

"I didn't realise you liked horses so much."

She took out her handkerchief and dabbed at her face "you'd be amazed" she whispered back to him.

That night they had gone back to the flat and opened a bottle of champagne, chilled from the fridge, eating huge pacific prawns dipped in hollandaise with their fingers. Slightly tipsy, they had fallen into bed hungry for each other, finally falling asleep wrapped up together.

On the Sunday, Charles had woken first, he edged himself up on one elbow, looking down at her as she slept, she really was very beautiful he thought. He leaned over and stroked his finger down the length of her belly, circling her tummy button and leaned over and kissed her gently on each breast. She opened her eyes and put her hands out to stroke his hair. His mouth moved down and then he sat back, she edged her legs apart and with both hands he spread them out further, so that he could look at her. She felt a quiver of excitement, but still he did not touch her. She looked up at his handsome face trembling with anticipation, as slowly he bent his head downwards, and she arched her back up to meet him, pushing herself into him as he licked and probed with his tongue. Slipping his hands underneath her, he flipped her over and parting the cheeks of her bottom, explored her with his fingertips, until she was gasping with pleasure. Only then did he pull her upwards on her knees and enter her from behind, his hands on both of her hips as he moved rhythmically backwards and forwards reaching his own climax moments later.

They had breakfasted late. She put a snowy white cloth on the small table on the balcony which overlooked the private garden at the back. Charles nipped out for the papers, whilst she cooked scrambled eggs with smoked salmon, coffee and toast. They sat reading in companionable silence in the sunshine, the only sound between them was the rustle of the newspaper as one or other of them turned a page. In the afternoon, they had strolled over to Hyde Park, embracing on the grass, like all the other lovers, surrounded by tourists snapping away with their cameras, and the vendors selling hotdogs and balloons.

Out of the blue, he asked "Are you worried about the party next week? Is there anything that I can do to help?"

Jennifer looked back at him in astonishment "I think Mrs Fuller and I have everything under control, this next week is going to be a bit hectic though, what with the marquee and everything, but I think we'll manage."

"I've been meaning to say this to you for a while. Don't take any nonsense from Mrs Fuller will you, she'll try and boss you around. I've been thinking I might have a word with her about her attitude. Trouble is she's never forgiven me for divorcing Celia, and you my darling have had to bear the brunt of her displeasure, and I'm really sorry about that."

"Oh Charles" sighed Jennifer, "I can't pretend it hasn't been difficult, but I may have turned the corner with Mrs Fuller. I think I've been as much to blame as her really, it's taken me a long time to get used to living in such a different environment you know, but we may have reached an understanding now. Let's just see how this week pans out shall we? By the way, I want to thank you darling, for entrusting me with replacing Lucy. That meant a lot to me, Caitlin is a sweet girl and I'm sure you'll be able to rely on us to find someone suitable."

Charles looked at her, she made him realise what a bastard he'd been, leaving her high and dry at Nantes all week, while the bloody staff ran rings around her. He was glad that he'd made the effort and suggested this weekend in London together - he realised too just how much he had missed and loved her "Darling, of course you can be relied upon to do it, and the party too! You were ace at organising when you worked for me at the office. You've just lost a bit of confidence that's all, it'll be fine!" He leant over and kissed her on the lips, "Come on sweetie, time we got back home to Nantes."

Andrew picked his way carefully through the cobweb of brambles, which had invaded the path from either side of the overgrown verge. The drive was once probably quite wide but the encroaching weeds had reduced it almost by half, barely enough to get a small car down now. It was made of cinder and probably about a hundred yards long from the start of the lane to where it swept up behind a bank of trees. He had left his car about half way down and decided to walk the rest. A bubbling stream that ran along the edge of the main road fed into the old mill pond on his left and up ahead, around the curve of the trees hid the watermill. It was a creepy place even at this early hour in the morning with the sun just breaking. The pond still had an eerie look, dense reeds surrounded the banks, and the odd moorhen slid silently across the water. From this point on the drive, he could see the watermill on the far side as the roadway curled around the edge of the pond, its rotting wooden wheel encrusted with moss. It was an amazing place he marvelled, tucked away quite out of sight from the road. No-one would know it was here. He walked on along the drive until he saw several old barns housed on the opposite side of the drive to the mill. Attached to the mill but not as tall, was the cottage, of the same blackened weatherboard as the rest of the buildings. He tried the handle of the cottage door, but it was locked, and he peered in through the grimy windows. As he had guessed, just a small place, probably a two up two down. Alongside and attached to one side of the cottage were old out houses in a dreadful state with missing windows and broken doors. What a place he thought! His ideas running ahead of him, imagining what it could be like if it were to be restored, but what a helluva lot of money it would take! He heard the sound of footsteps behind him, and spun round to see Mark Templeton.

"Sorry I'm late Andrew. It's a bit early for me!"

"No problem, I've only just got here myself, and sorry to make it so early. I don't want people to know I'm interested. You know what a nosy lot they are round here."

Mark laughed "Tell me about it! Don't worry the place isn't on the market yet, and not likely to be for a while, you know what Lady V is like about making decisions. It's a pity to let the old place go to rack and ruin though, but it's not viable for us to renovate, and the estate could do with an input of cash."

"Could be just what I'm looking for though" sighed Andrew, "but I've a feeling that it's going to be well out of my price range"

"Well she's a funny old stick is Lady V, you never know. Obviously we want the best price for it, but we've also got to be realistic. The chances are if it went to auction, some townies would buy it and convert the whole thing, but you know what she's like about that! So I suspect she would rather you had it, provided the price is right. Shall I show you round?"

"Please, I'm keen to look" replied Andrew, "lead on McDuff!"

"I'll show you the cottage first then, it's the least worst." Mark got out a couple of enormous old keys from his pocket. "It hasn't been lived in for a while now, but it does have some services, water of course, and electric was put in too. It has private drainage for the sewage." He clanked open the door, pushing aside some cobwebs, "I've not been in here for quite a while as you can see!" he laughed.

They went in, ducking their heads under the low beams. It wasn't a bad sized room, with a fireplace on one side and a set of open stairs leading up to the first floor on the other. Through the door at the back was the kitchen, again much larger than he had thought, with an old Rayburn on one side. Off the kitchen was a small pantry and a back door. Creaking their way up the stairs, there were three rooms, a small bathroom with an antiquated bath and a lavatory with a high cistern and chain flush. The first bedroom was quite small, but with a fireplace, the second bedroom was much bigger, again with a fireplace and quite a large window which looked out over the drive.

"Mmmm, it's not as small as I thought" said Andrew "and at least there's a bathroom, even if it is out of the dark ages."

"Old Ted thought it was the height of luxury! That was done

before my time of course- they decided to split one of the bedrooms into two to put it in. I did try and have a new suite put in here, but he wouldn't hear of it."

They went down the stairs, and moved outside, Mark carefully locking the door behind him, and gestured for Andrew to follow him into the Mill itself.

"Watch your step, there's a load of old bits and pieces littered about, and it's not all that sound on the upper floors, and what with their weight, the old grinding stones have long since gone."

The whole place smelt damp and musty, although Andrew could see the enormous potential. The ground floor was huge, still having the bones of the original workings in place, the chutes and chains used for hoisting the grain were still there but the mechanical sluice gate had long since rusted and there was little left of any of the gearing system. They gingerly made their way up the open stairs to the first floor. Again the space was large, you could see where the old mill stones had been and high windows allowed the sunlight to beam down through the large round hole where the driveshaft of the mill yawned a gaping hole to the ground floor. There was another identical storey above, even the old hopper used for pouring the grain down to the stone floor below was still in situ.

"God they must have had to work hard. Must have been backbreaking."

"Yes" said Mark, "It was a tough trade, and this mill probably served the whole village community at one time, but it hasn't been operational for about a hundred years. The structure considering, is not in bad nick, but it would have to be totally gutted inside. Come on, I'll show you the rest of the outbuildings."

They came out into the brightening sunshine, and the promise of another blistering day ahead. Andrew was becoming more and more excited, it would be a huge undertaking but it was just what they were looking for, and after a tour of the barns, he was more convinced than ever.

"Look Mark, I'm seriously interested" he said "where do we go from here? Should I approach Lady Veronica? I'd really like to show Oliver the place too, he obviously has to agree, but I can't see that being a problem." His thoughts were tumbling out one after the other.

"Whoa! Let me talk to Lady V, and you can bring Oliver up any time you like, just let me know and you can pick up the keys, you don't need me, but just be bloody careful in the mill, it could be quite dangerous."

"Thanks mate, please keep me posted, when do you think you can speak to her?"

"Andrew, don't be so impatient, I know you're keen, but you have to pick your moment with Lady V and I also need to prepare, she's a wily old bird."

The two men shook hands and Andrew made his way back down the track to the car. Christ it was more than he had hoped for in a million years, and he couldn't wait to show Oli.

Chloe had had a rotten weekend. The children had been fun, ebullient and their normal selves, but John had been withdrawn and the situation between them was worse - if that was possible. She had begged him to come to Jennifer's party the following Saturday but his response had been that he couldn't imagine anything worse. Well he could bloody well babysit then! The atmosphere was frosty to say the least, luckily though the children didn't seem to notice. The innocence of youth she thought. For once she was glad it was Monday! She took the children to the bus for their last week before they broke up for half term, and she'd cleared her diary of lessons then, so that at least she could spend the time with them.

She let the dogs out and walked down to the yard. The girls had been busy and were waiting for her, Jennifer had arrived early too and had gone down to get Rufus. She had already pre-warned Chloe that this week might be a bit awkward for her with all the final party arrangements, but she was still determined to come every day. Chloe had come to really quite like her, she had a wacky sense of humour and they enjoyed their hacks around the fields together. Next week, Chloe had planned to add more structure to the sessions, now Jennifer had seemed to be more confident around the horses, doing some work in the school, and that should fit in well with the kids being at home too. All in all, Jen had slotted in well, finding a good ally in Katherine, and even Sandy liked her, and they had all been invited to the party on Saturday. Jen had even asked Beebs and Susie and they were terribly excited, never having been invited to such a do before. They discussed it endlessly, planning what to wear and had asked to leave early on Saturday. Chloe could hardly say no, but that meant that she would have to finish up, and it would leave her little time to get ready herself, and she was bloody determined to go she thought doggedly, Sod John! Perhaps he could finish up – some hope! She wondered if Oliver had been serious about accompanying her, perhaps she should ring him, but that could wait, the day loomed ahead, busy as always.

Lucy sat on the edge of her bed. She had been forced to go home to her parents' house in Horsham and she was seriously pissed off. After Tom had picked her up, she had hoped she could go back and stay at his place, but he had put her firmly in her place - there was no way his parents would have her. Fucking snobs! It wasn't Tom's fault though and he had been good enough to bring her back here. Her mother's disapproving face when she saw Lucy said it all. Yes, it was true, the door was always open for her, but it was accompanied with a set of chains. She hated it here, her parents were deeply religious people and had been very strict with her when she was growing up. She had learned to be devious in what she told them and invented plausible excuses for any excursions to her less savoury friends. She had not worked at school, despite her parents watching over her whilst she did her homework, and she became deliberately obtuse. She sailed close to the wind, being caught smoking, playing truant and scrawling obscenities in the lavatories. Her parents were at their wits end, their only solution being to ground her at every opportunity. So, on the pretence of going to school, she bunked off, nicking stuff from shops, finally being caught taking a mascara from Boots. Her parents had been called by the store detective, and the police too. She remembered only too well sitting in the manager's office waiting for them to arrive. The police had come first, a WPC, who looked like something out of horror movie. She took all the details, Lucy answering in insolent monosyllables, but she was frightened nonetheless and all her bravado was well acted. Finally her parents had arrived, and she had burst into tears when she saw them. She promised to mend her ways, said that she would never do it again. Her parents were horrified, she remembered well her mother's thin lipped smile, and her father's sad eyes when they spoke to the authorities. Finally she was let off with a warning and a ban from Boots. Her parents had marched her back home to discuss her future. Actually the answer had been okay in the end, she had agreed to stay on at school and finish her GCSEs and go as a working pupil to a riding school down in Somerset to get her BHSAI qualification. She had agreed, as it meant she could leave home. Now here she was four years later back where she had started. She had been stupid to walk out of Nantes, but that fucking Caitlin had not even tried to stop her, it was all her fault, and she had been having a great summer too! Bitch! She couldn't hope for a reference either, now what was she going to fucking do?

Nantes was a hive of activity that week. Mrs Fuller and Jennifer had gone over the seating plan together, Jennifer adding her extra guests from Mileoak, although Mrs Fuller had sniffed disapprovingly several times especially when she heard that Chloe would be accompanied by her grooms! She had never heard the like! Jennifer decided that a '*no comment*' stance was best and breezily went on to ask if she knew what time the marquee people would be arriving.

"They said as close to ten o'clock as possible, although they are bound to be late" denounced Mrs Fuller, "However, it's all fairly straightforward, I have the plan here, I hope you approve?"

Jennifer glanced at the plan, "Yes that looks great Mrs F", slipping into the vernacular. Mrs Fuller gave her a horrified sideways look.

The menu had been finalised, and was an inspiration. A light salmon mousse topped with tempura prawns, and a rocket salad with chive and dill dressing to start. The main course was to be Scotch beef fillet with Jerusalem artichoke puree, asparagus and seeded mustard jus, sauté potatoes & Vine Tomatoes, followed by a trio of desserts in tiny glass dishes of white chocolate mousse, crème brulee, and fresh chopped strawberries in a champagne jelly. Of course cheese and fruit to finish. Mrs Fuller had assured her this would be perfect and she had to say it did sound good. Of course Mrs Fuller had catered for vegetarians, so that was okay.

"Well done Mrs F, it's fantastic" she smiled at her "What about the canapés with the champagne to start?"

"All taken care of, a selection of appetisers, the caterers are quite inventive, so I've left it to them, but suggested not too much garlic" she gave a rare laugh, "We don't want the guests to asphyxiate each other before they sit down."

"You are a marvel, thank you! You've thought of everything." She just hoped it would all go as smoothly on the night.

Jennifer had timed her week like a military operation. She would be back from Mileoak, after an early ride on Thursday morning so as to be here for the marquee people. She wanted to make sure that everything was put in the right place, and the same again on Friday. She had booked a hair appointment and manicure for the Saturday after lunch and that would give her plenty of time to be ready to receive her guests at 7pm. Charles had promised to be home early on the Friday afternoon to give her a hand. Meanwhile, she had ample time to write out the place names for the tables. She had spent the afternoon confirming the musicians, and been on the phone to the caterers with final numbers. The florist had confirmed too, and Mrs Fuller was finalising the extra help needed. At long last, she was actually starting to look forward to the evening.

"You just won't believe it Oli!" exclaimed Andrew, "It's perfect for us! I can't wait for you to see it!"

"Hang on mate, it sounds great, but also expensive. Mark Templeton is no fool - he knows how much it's worth. Don't let's get our hopes up until we know for sure we can afford it!"

"I've just gotta good feeling about it, can we try and go and see it next week sometime?"

"Oh okay sure, but as I said don't let's hold our breath eh?" Their conversation was interrupted by Oliver's mobile, he glanced at the number, "Oh fuck - it's Suse, I just don't wanna have this conversation" he said gloomily.

"Oliver, I've been trying to get you all day, what have you been up to?" Suse yelled at him down the other end of the phone.

"I've been working Suse, what else do I do all day?"

"Don't get smart with me, who am I after all, only your bloody wife! Well, I just want you to know that I've absolutely no intention of going with you to that stuck up party on Saturday. All those bloody toffs and making daft small talk all night, bloody bunch of snobs, you can stick it!"

"Well thanks for that Suse, perhaps you might consider what part of me wants to go with you eh? " Oh God, he shouldn't have said that! Andrew squirmed in his chair, trying not to listen, but honestly Oliver was a great bloke, hardworking and decent, how he put up with Suse he had no idea.

"What did you say Oliver? I've had it with you, don't be surprised to find me gone when you finally decide to come home!"

"Yeah, yeah Suse, change the record will you, why don't you just make an effort to fit in around here for a change, instead of expecting everyone …." he looked at the phone, she had cut him off. He looked at Andrew embarrassed.

"Sorry about that mate, I really have tried, and she did know what it entailed being a vet's wife before we came over, it was no different back home. If she'd wanted a nine to five man she should have married one. In truth it was probably all going wrong long before, but you shouldn't have to listen to it all!"

"Forget it, are you sure you know what you're doing though? If Suse goes home, wouldn't you be tempted to go with her?"

"Wild horses wouldn't make me, not even those mad ones of Lady Veronica's! I have to face facts Andrew, it's all over, and frankly I'll be relieved in many ways to have it sorted out. If she did just pack up and go, it would make the parting all the easier. I know that's the coward's way out, but I can't carry on like this."

"Well you'll always have my support, you know that, whatever happens." Andrew thought of his own loveless marriage, but at least Julia didn't carry on like this, as long he kept earning the money, she was happy to spend it. He didn't ask her what she got up to and frankly he would rather not know, but to be fair when forced to make an appearance with him she was always there with her best smile on her face. Poor Oliver, he wasn't surprised he didn't want to go home.

CHAPTER 16

Pete was talking to himself when Jennifer came up behind him, he started when she spoke and glared at her.

"Hi Pete, I just wanted to say how lovely the garden is looking and to thank you so much for all your hard work." That's the right way to handle him she thought, be very nice, just like Celia would have been. He was probably just as fragile as she felt at times.

"Thank you Mrs Parker -Smythe" he said in a strangled grimace. Bloody bitch he thought, bloody, bloody bitch, who did she think she was. Jennifer smiled at him, but he refused to look at her. It was her fault that Celia had gone and now Lucy too. The voices had returned daily now and strangely he found them comforting, they told him it was her fault. He missed Lucy, he wondered what had become of her. He had tried to ask Caitlin, but she had gently said she didn't know and that he was not to worry about it - but he did worry.

Jennifer looked at him, he was really acting in a peculiar way, okay she'd been stupid with him sometimes, but she was trying now. There was little else she could say or do. Pete rudely turned his back on her muttering under his breath, and short of grabbing him by his shoulder she was forced to turn away and walk back across the lawn. Fucking woman he spat after her.

Beebs and Susie were terribly excited about the party. Jen had turned out to be good fun, not at all like they had thought she would be and they liked her coming down to help. She didn't mind getting her hands dirty and was more than willing to learn and she was doing that fast. Just shows how wrong you could be about someone they decided. Chloe on the other hand was pre-occupied and although not exactly snappy with them was definitely not her normal self. The girls had discussed this too and put it down to the day of Borde Hill, when John had gone off and left the kids with Beebs. What was going on there they had no idea but it had affected Chloe that was for sure. They knew that John had refused to go to the party, as they had been there when Chloe had made his excuses for him.

More pressing for the girls though was what to wear? It was going to be a posh affair, and neither had anything in their wardrobes which would do. It was tricky, they knew that if they asked Chloe she would just say, oh don't worry about it, wear anything, but half the fun was choosing. Trouble was a groom's salary didn't extend to buying expensive clobber that was never going to see the light of day again. The only answer was the charity shops, they often had some good stuff in Horsham and if you were selective you could get a bargain. It would be much better if they could go together, but their days off never coincided, and Chloe was already letting them finish early on Saturday so they could get ready and they didn't like to ask her for more time off.

Chloe was on the way down to the yard when her phone rang, it was Oliver Travers.

"Hi Chloe, it's Oliver. Look you may say no about this, but I just wondered if you were serious about wanting to go to the Parker-Smythe's party with me, no strings, it's just that Suse doesn't want to go, and I know you had mentioned that John didn't either, so perhaps we could go together, it would make sense." Chloe was taken by surprise, it had been a bit of a joke as far as she was concerned, but she was angry with John for letting her go on her own, and if Oliver was serious, why shouldn't she go with him?

"Won't Suse mind?"

"No, it's not her thing at all" he improvised, "How about John would he mind?"

It was on the tip of her tongue to say, he won't have to, but hesitated, she didn't want to be disloyal. "No, it's not his thing either. Okay why not? Thanks for thinking of me, it's much nicer to go with a partner, even of the no strings variety!" Chloe laughed. Indeed why not? Crikey though she had nothing much to wear, and whereas before it hadn't seemed important, somehow it did now. She marched into the tack room.

"Ladies" she spoke to Beebs and Susie, I'm going to pop out for a bit this afternoon, I'm going into Horsham to get something to wear for the party."

The girls looked at her "lucky you" said Beebs. Chloe caught their expression, it was an insensitive thing to have said, she had not thought about the girls at all.

"If you want to come too, you're welcome, but we'll all have to work a bit later tonight to finish up."

"Chloe, thank you, thank you!" they chorused!

Chloe looked at their delighted faces and felt mean, this party meant a lot to them, "I'll just make a couple of phone calls to make sure I can get someone to pick the kids up, now steam on you two, the more we get done this morning, the sooner we can go."

Laura and Jonty, having woken up late thought it would be a good afternoon to pay a visit to the charity shops too. They had decided that Jonty should remove his studs when they were doing their recces, and for good measure he had shaved off his goatee. Laura put on a plain cotton summer dress, no scarves or beads - very ordinary she thought gloomily, still she had to play the part too. Jonty had just worn his jeans and a tee shirt, she thought he looked very odd without his beard and looked him up and down and he did the same to her. They had both grinned thinking the same. They went down to the Landrover, which Jonty had managed to park quite close by for a change and climbed in. It was a bloody long way to Horsham and this old tank drank up the juice. They drove along in silence.

Her plans were coming together nicely, she was going to be a real pain in the arse to Charles and his hunting mates, the unintentional pun of what had happened to her, made her wince at the memory. Now Jonty was taking her more seriously it was all much more realistic, he was a master at organising these things and he covered every detail carefully. Her initial idea about cultivating the Sabs was coming along nicely but he was pushing her much harder about them and she had a funny feeling he also had another motive, but couldn't for the life of her think what it could be. She didn't want to ask as he got really annoyed about stuff like that, so she dared not question him. When he got angry he flew into a terrible rage, smashing things up and she had seen him be really violent not caring about who got in his way in the process. His reputation as a hard man was well deserved and normally she basked in his protection, she certainly didn't ever provoke him. He had never hit her, but she was never sure he wouldn't. He was always sorry afterwards and she always forgave him, but she was careful not to antagonise him. What was he up to she wondered, still as long as it didn't affect her payback he could do what he liked. Her need to avenge had become an obsession and she was determined that Charles Parker-Smythe would not get away with what he had done to her.

Jonty, his eyes ahead on the road, was deep in thought too. Laura had got onto a good thing here and there was money to be made, much more than she thought, but he was not going to tell her the whole plan otherwise she would never go through with it. He never told her what he got up to anyway, he could probably trust her but the less she knew the better. He could use this obsession of hers to his own ends, but he would need to manipulate her carefully.

"You know, you'll need to see a bit more of Linda and her buddies."

"Don't remind me!" She dreaded the thought, but he was right it had to be done. "I'll go over sometime next week, when I have a bit of spare time, I've got an assignment due in. I'm short of dosh too, you got any to spare?"

"Fuck me, I'm always giving you money" he didn't see why he should support her all the time. It irritated him the way she whined.

They pulled off the A24 towards Horsham town and took the signposts for the town centre looking for somewhere to park.

"Fuck" said Jonty, "All the poxy car parks are too low to park the Landrover, there must be somewhere that caters for them, all this lot have big 4 x 4s." They drove round and round trying to find somewhere, Jonty getting more and more irate, and then they spotted a filthy Discovery with three women passengers.

"Follow it" demanded Laura at the fuming Jonty "It might be going to park somewhere." Jonty put his foot down, catching up with the car and tailgating it round the one way system. They stopped at a traffic light and he saw the driver of the Discovery look at him through her rear view mirror. Bloody women drivers he thought. The Discovery moved off as the lights went green and then it indicated and turned right towards a car park - Pirie's Place. Jonty hurled the Landrover round the corner to follow it.

"You had better be fucking right Laura!" said Jonty, and he held his breath involuntarily ducking his head, as they went under the roof of the car park. They followed the other car around the small multi storey, it was bloody tight in there. The Discovery found a car parking space and Jonty drove past it, looking for another. He pulled into the tight space after several attempts and sat back his hands taut on the wheel. "Thank fuck for that!" he laughed.

Beebs leapt out of the car, and went over to the Pay and Display, putting in enough money for a couple of hours, and came back waving the ticket.

"Right" said Chloe, "now shall we stick together or do we need to split up? I want to go to that little shop in the square by Waitrose."

"We could come with you and have a mosey around but it will be too dear for us, we thought we would go up to the Cancer Research Shop, they have a designer rail there."

"Okay, let's meet back here then in ... say an hour?" They slammed the car doors and made their way down the ramp of the multi storey, Chloe glanced back, she was sure she'd seen that Landrover, the one that had been sitting on her rear bumper all the time round the one way system, somewhere before. She couldn't see the driver though as it had pulled in engine first, and she may be wrong of course – oh well. The girls shouted at her to hurry up and they all went in their respective directions; Chloe diving into a small dress shop, and the girls nipped down a little cobbled alley way.

Chloe knew the girls in the shop, not by name, but enough to say a '*hi, how are you*'. Although it was quite a tiny place, it was crammed full of frocks and outfits and upstairs had racks of ball gowns, and catered for smart and uber smart functions. The assistants were savvy enough to make sure that their customers left with an outfit that was entirely appropriate for the function and really suited the client, so their repeat business was good, as was the recommendation of their clients to their friends. On the plus side too, they always asked where they were going, and kept a little book of who had bought what, so that there could be no embarrassment of identical or similar dresses - everyone's nightmare.

Chloe browsed through the rails, thinking she would prefer something shorter, rather than full length, and summery rather than dark. The assistant came over to help, and showed her a couple of things that might fit the bill. One was a floaty just below the knee dress with a gypsy hem line. Another was a straighter cut number, coming a little way above the knee, much more fitted, very chic in a deep shade of summer blue. Totally different styles and Chloe liked them both. She carried on looking, finding a deep lavender knee length dress in silk with a fitted ruched bodice, that might do she considered. She made her way to the changing rooms where the assistant had hung the other dresses. She tried them all on, pirouetting this way and that in the clever mirrors, what a hard choice, they all looked good. Finally, taking the assistant's advice, she went for the fitted blue one, it was totally understated and less fussy than the others and with her tousled hair it looked great. She paid for the dress, thanked the girls and looked at her watch, she'd only been 30 minutes – miracle or what! She might just have time to find some shoes, but then decided to see if she could catch up with the girls first. She retraced her steps and darted down the cobbled alley.

Laura and Jonty meanwhile had been perusing the plethora of charity shops and had bought a few bits and pieces, a weathered old Barbour wax jacket, and a Puffa waistcoat, and some almost new Hunter wellies. They had also found some fleeces emblazoned with the Toggi logo, which seemed to fit the bill. They were just going to have a coffee, when down a little side street, Laura spotted the Cancer Research shop.

"Hey look babes, there's another one. Let's give it a go eh?"

"I could do with a cuppa" moaned Jonty "Do we have to?

Haven't we got enough?"

"Yes, we bloody do, then you can have a drink, this is important." Jonty decided to humour her, as she dragged him along the road, full of little curio shops selling gemstones and jewellery, alongside an Aga shop, the window full of gleaming cookers with heavy cast iron pans.

The Cancer Research shop had two bow fronted windows with enticing displays, and seemed to be crammed with stuff. They hesitated briefly and walked in, it was quite busy. Customers looking at the books and DVDs, some mums with buggies looking at the children's clothing. The lady serving the customers was quite elderly, with almost white permed hair and glasses, and was showing someone an item of jewellery from the locked glass display beneath the counter. They headed quietly, neither speaking, towards the coats lined up on a rail on the far side of the shop. Laura took down a long waterproof coat, in good condition, with the label *Drizabone* tacked inside, she put it over her arm. Jonty found a flat tweed cap, quite shabby but perfect for what they wanted, and a worn waxed hat for Laura. A loud laugh came from the changing room beside them and then a lot of giggling, followed by another shriek of laughter. Jonty and Laura looked swiftly at each other and moved away as surreptitiously as they could, the last thing they wanted was any attention drawn to them. They hurried over to the counter and paid for their items, the old lady seemed to take forever, folding and wrapping everything up, and painstakingly counting the money. At that moment, the shop doorbell rang, and Chloe walked in, Jonty and Laura looked towards the door and their eyes met Chloe's. She recognised them immediately, suddenly twigging where she'd seen them before. They did not smile and neither did she, who were they Chloe thought? At that moment Beebs and Susie bounded out of the changing room, and Chloe's attention was diverted for an instant, and when she looked again they had gone.

Grace was still feeling gloomy after her disappointment of the negative pregnancy test. She knew that it was stupid to feel like this, she had so much to be thankful for in her life. She hadn't told Colin about it and tried to be bright and breezy when he had come in, and bless him, he was tired after a long hard day, and didn't really notice anyway. The weekend had gone by, and every now and then she would have a fit of the miseries, the anguish flooding in like a rushing tide. She had woken up this Tuesday morning feeling as though she had a large weight on her shoulders, and morosely stirred her coffee. At least the hunting season would be upon them soon, and only another month or so and she could start getting the horses fit. Oh heavens I need to pull myself together she thought, I'm wishing my life away, she could be like her aging parents, who were struggling with the farm these days; she had to snap out of it, she really did. Life was too short to be unhappy, especially when she had so much to be grateful for. She drank down the coffee, called Monty and Daisy, her two black Labradors, who looked up expectantly from their bean bags and thumped their tails at her, and set off to walk up to her parents' farm.

It was a glorious morning, the sun was warm, caressing her bare arms and legs, the quarrelling tree sparrows chattering in the hedgerows, mingled with the blackbird's alarm call as she approached. The oaks had come out now, always the last to get their leaves and were so majestic in stature, the odd squirrel dashing from branch to branch their tails whizzing vertically at the sound of the foraging dogs. She bent down, chucking a stick for Daisy, who dashed after it and obediently brought it back, dropping it at her feet and waiting expectantly. She ambled along the path alongside one of her parents' barley fields, it was disappointingly slow, a dismal growth for this time of the year, this early drought was not helping. How much longer could it stay dry?

Her parents' farmhouse was at the top of a small rise in the land, and the views from it were magnificent. The farmhouse itself was really pretty being part tile hung and dated back to the 16th century, and Grace's family had lived there for four generations. She approached via the farm yard and through the hotchpotch of buildings ranging from an ancient granary supported on staddle stones, to modern implement sheds housing tractors and farm equipment. She passed by the old cow sheds and milking parlour, long since disused when her parents had gone out of dairy after the BSE crisis. Although they had not had any infected cattle themselves, the knock on effect to the British beef market was catastrophic, so they had sold the herd and turned the farm over to arable. On the whole it had been a good decision, but she knew they still missed the cows, just as she did. The empty byres always gave a tug at her heart strings. She whistled to the dogs who were ferreting about in the buildings and wandered up to the farmhouse, through the white picket gate in the stone wall that surrounded the house, and led up to the back door. Her mother was in the kitchen, her apron on as always, rolling pastry.

"Morning Mum, got the kettle on?"

"Darling, how lovely to see you so early, yes of course, I'll make tea and I've just got some scones out of the Aga."

"I'd love a cup of tea Mum thanks, but no scones for me, a bit early, although I'll take one home for Colin to have with his tea when he comes in. Where's Dad?"

"Oh, he's out with the dogs, walking the crops. He's worried sick about the lack of growth."

"Oh Mum, it's always the same every year, too wet or too dry, whatever, it'll work out, it always does. Has he thought any more about what Colin said?"

"Turn the old buildings into industrial units you mean?"

"Well, it would make good economic sense Mum and alleviate a lot of worry for you and Dad."

"And have a lot of intruders around here too Grace, it would drive us mad."

Grace sighed, they were very set in their ways. Losing the herd had been hard for them and although a lot of the day to day slog had gone it gave them more time to worry about things. She sipped her tea and looked at her mother, her brown curly hair so like Grace's, had now gone silver, and her spectacles balanced on the end of her nose, emphasised her brown eyes. Her once smooth skin was quite lined now, a consequence of the hard years of farming in all weathers.

"You look a bit peaky dear, are you alright" her mother asked "you are eating properly aren't you?"

"Oh, I'm fine Mum, really I am and eating like a horse. It's just I think I should be doing more with my life you know. I heard that the Parker-Smythe's groom has left, I was thinking of applying."

"What on earth for Grace? You're busy all the time, what with Colin, your animals and the way you fuss over your Dad and me. Look love, I know that you'd like to have a baby and that just hasn't happened for you and Colin, but what good would getting a job as a groom do to help? It would drive you nuts and how would you find the time to do your own horses?"

"It was just an idea that's all, just seems I could be doing more with my life. Lavinia Appleton-Lacy rang and asked me to make cakes for the Puppy Show, and I couldn't help but wonder if that's all I was good for." Her mother came and put an arm around her shoulders, stroking her curly hair.

"Grace" she said gently, "don't be so silly, of course you have more in your life, it's because you're so capable that they ask you, everyone knows how much you do and how busy you are. You know what they say, if you want something done, ask a busy person! Where would Dad and I be without you?"

"Oh Mum" sighed Grace, "I know, it's just I feel kinda useless at the moment."

Andrew waited for Oliver to answer his phone. He drummed his pen up and down on the desk as he waited. Bugger - voicemail. He didn't bother to leave a message, he would try him again later. He got up from his desk and walked out to the front office. "Paulene, have you got a minute?" Paulene looked up from her computer, pushing her glasses up on to the top of her head, "can you come into the office for a mo'?"

"What's up boss?"

"Just wondered if you'd had any time to get those quotes for me yet? I know it's only been a day or so, but I need to cobble something together for Gary and want to get on with it!" He laughed as she gave him a withering look, "I know, I know, but I'm quite excited about this!"

"Andrew, as it happens I'm excited too." she grinned back at him "and actually I've got most of the information you need and don't worry I've been discreet."

"You're a bloody marvel! I'm busting to tell people too, but we can't risk it getting around yet just in case some developer gets in before we do."

"It's okay Andrew they won't hear anything from me and it's in my interest to keep it quiet. I'll just pop out to my computer and print out the information – okay? Have you heard anything from Mark yet?"

"No, I'm going to ring him later, but I want to take another look at the place and I'm trying to track down Oli, so that he can meet me there."

Paulene pulled a face "Do you know that's funny, I've been trying to get hold of him for about an hour, his phone keeps going to voice mail, it's not like him, he must be in a bad area." She went back to her office and Andrew heard the whirr of the printer. She was a good girl was Paulene, and it would give him great pleasure to promote her to Practice Manager, she deserved it. God he could hardly contain himself, how exciting would this be for them all - if it came off.

"Thanks doll," he said, scanning the pages of quotes that Paulene had researched. "By the way, sometime soon we must do a drug stocktake, you okay for a couple of hours overtime?"

"Bring it on boss, I could do with the money!"

Andrew tried Oli's mobile again, waiting impatiently for him to pick up, still going to voice mail. Oh well, he would see Andrew's missed calls and ring back when he could, sometimes it was just that you couldn't answer if it was a difficult case. He took a deep breath, and picked up the phone again and dialled Mark Templeton's number.

"Hi Mark, Andrew here. Any luck with Lady V? Sorry if you think I'm hassling you, but I'm keen to get on with this?"

"It's no hassle Andrew, I'm keen too, the old place needs to be sold before another winter, otherwise it'll depreciate all the more. As it happens I've spoken to Lady V and she says would you pop in and have tea with her sometime this week? How about Friday, if I can sort it?"

"That'd be great, I'll keep the afternoon free, I'm sure Oliver can handle the emergencies. Speaking of Oliver, I'm going to try and take him over to see the mill later, that's if I can find the bugger, he's not answering his mobile!"

"I just passed him coming along the lane, up by High Ridge Woods - on his way back to you I should think, and yes that's fine, go up when it suits you. I'll leave the keys under that old milk churn outside the barn door, put them back when you've finished, and I'll pick them up in the morning."

"Thanks Mark, that's perfect, I'll make sure I put them back, and let me know about Friday. Bye" he replaced the receiver. It was all going well so far, he just hoped Lady V would not be too greedy. Once they had the price, they could approach the bank. He heard the sound of Oliver's car turning into the car park, and the beep of the lock. Good, he could see if he had time to come up to the mill today.

Oliver strode into the office, his tanned face looking a bit flushed, "Bloody car, I had a flat tyre, took me ages to fix it, sorry I missed your calls, thought I'd better drop back to see what's so urgent."

"Just wanted to know if you had time to come up and see the Mill today, I can see Lady V on Friday, if you agree it's the right place for us."

"Coolio with me! Can't wait to see it mate. Paulene did you need me for anything urgent, I missed a call from you too?"

"Not urgent no, just wondered if you had time to pop in today to Alice Grant's at Smoke House Cottage, she wants you to have a look at one of their hunters, got a bit of a runny nose she says."

"No problem, I can do it when I go up that way later, can you tell her, I'll call her when I'm about half an hour away"

"Sure, you two off now then to the Mill?" They looked at each other and like a couple of overgrown kids with a new toy, they grabbed their car keys and dashed out the door.

CHAPTER 17

Oliver got home that night to find Suse snoring quietly on the sofa, her mouth hanging slightly open, a thin trickle of saliva coming out of the corner, and an empty wine bottle overturned on the floor. He looked at her gloomily, this is what it had all come to, and he felt very sad. He went into the kitchen, and looked in the oven, there was nothing to eat, she had obviously had a liquid supper. He yanked open the fridge, pulling out the cheese and cut himself off a large hunk. How long could they go on like this he wondered? Sitting down at the kitchen table, he thought we must talk, see if we can get over this and find a solution, although he knew in his heart that it was hopeless. He sighed running his hand through his mop of hair, and rubbed his eyes. Christ he was tired. He thought back about the visit to the mill with Andrew that afternoon. What a perfect place it was, - Andrew was so right. They could expand and spread the work load and it would be amazing to build a first rate diagnostic centre, but it would take some capital outlay. He had loved the little cottage too, it was very quaint and unlike the mill, it wouldn't take too much to renovate.

"So you've finally bloody come home" slurred Suse, her eyes red, and her bitterness making her face ugly "'bout fucking time."

"Suse love, it's only just on 8.30 and I've had a really hard day, I hate seeing you like this, can't we talk?"

"It's too fucking late to be talking Oliver, and I've had a hard day too, or d' you forget that I work as well? It's always all about you isn't it?"

"Suse, please, I've a lot to tell you which might change things for us, things I need to talk to you about."

"I said it's too fucking late to talk, didn't you hear me? Too fucking late, I don't want to hear anything that you've got to say anymore. Just looking at you makes me cringe."

Oliver reeled from the venom of her words, he looked her up and down sadly "you're drunk Suse, why don't you go to bed and sleep it off?"

"Whaaaat!" She lunged at him, clawing his face with her nails, and he took both her hands and tried to fend her off. "Don't touch me, don't touch me, I hate you, I hate you!" she yelled.

"Calm down, calm down" he spluttered, "Just calm down and pull yourself together Suse" and with that she just crumpled into a heap on the floor. Oliver knelt down and put his hands on her trembling shoulders.

"Just leave me alone" she spat angrily, "It's over, we both know it's over. Just leave me alone."

Caitlin heard the beep of a message coming through on her phone and whipped it out of her pocket. She read it twice, smiling to herself. He always made her smile. She tapped out a reply and put the phone away carefully, what would they have done without mobiles. It wouldn't have happened she thought, or would that have been a good or a bad thing? She had never been happier, but she was not proud of herself, she hadn't planned this, it had just happened, and all she could do was think of him, and how she loved him, loved the way he loved her too. The way they chatted, the laughs they had, the love making they had, she had never felt like this about anyone before. Oh Holy Mary she prayed, forgive me, I know he's married, and I know it's wrong but I can't find the strength to stop myself.

"Caitlin!"

Caitlin leapt up in the air, and put her hands to her heart "Oh Mrs ... Jennifer, you frightened the life out of me, so you did!"

"I'm so sorry Caitlin, I didn't mean to make you jump! You okay?"

"Just in a day dream" Caitlin laughed recovering, "how are you today, what can I do to help?"

"Well I thought we ought to have a chat, do you fancy putting the kettle on?"

"Of course now, come on in to the tack room." They walked into the shade of the old bricks, Jennifer pulling out a stool, whilst Caitlin plugged in the kettle.

"Look Caitlin" Jennifer began, "I wanted to know about the set up here really, how many horses we have, what types, what sort of work they do, so we can work out a plan well before the hunting starts." Jennifer was drawing on her new found education from *The Manual of Horsemanship*.

Caitlin looked surprised, she didn't think that Jennifer was interested at all in the horses, let alone the hunting, or the logistics of it either. Still Jennifer had been very kind to her and she genuinely seemed to be interested.

"Well, Mr Charles has two hunters, Dandy and Beano!" she smiled at the joke, "Jessica has a pony - Queenie, as does Rupert - Scooter . We have a couple of old retired hunters, Nellie and Bumble, which are not in work. The first Mrs Parker-Smythe sold her hunters , except for Snowdrop, who was lame at the time when she left, she's fine and sound now but has remained here ever since, and I hunt her when I have the opportunity."

"Okay, so that makes seven in all?"

"Yes, that's right, but the two olds live out all the time, and they've a good field shelter, which I deep litter, that means ..."

Jennifer smiled "Yes, I know what that means" thinking she did too – first hand! "Right, so five in boxes then? What about exercise?"

"I do Mr Charles' hunters every day and Snowdrop too, but lighter work for her, and the children's ponies, get ridden about three times a week, we don't want them too fit and bucking the kids off when they ride." Caitlin was surprised at her questions, wondering quite where they were going with this conversation.

It was as though Jennifer had read her mind, "the reason for my asking, is that it's obviously too much for you to do on your own, that goes without saying really, but perhaps it might be a good idea to consider two part timers to help you, rather than a full time girl. That way, they could cover if you wanted to go hunting and if Charles needs you to go with him. Also too they could cover days off and sick, that sort of thing. I know I'm not experienced with horses but it was just a thought." Caitlin considered for minute or two, as they sipped their coffee, it was quite a good idea, she'd even thought about it herself.

"Yes, I can see the advantages for sure now, but we'd have to work it out carefully."

"Well perhaps we can talk about it some more next week, after I have got this bloody party out of the way!" Jennifer laughed adding "by the way Caitlin, Chloe Coombe is bringing her grooms with her to the party, would you like to join their table?"

Caitlin was astonished, she was staff, not supposed to be invited! You could have knocked her down with a feather so you could, "Well Jennifer … thank you, that's very kind of you" but why not thought Caitlin, why not, "I'd love to join them."

"That's settled then Caitlin, it'll be nice to have you. I'd better go, Mrs Fuller will be after me otherwise. See you!"

"Bye and thank you" called Caitlin after Jennifer. Well, well, what a turn up, being invited to the party! Jennifer was alright, not at all stuck up actually, fancy Chloe asking to bring her grooms along! Blimey! She pulled out her mobile and started to send a text.

Beebs and Susie were pleased with their purchases, the charity shop had come up trumps, they had bought two really good frocks, both short, one black, and one black and white, both were sexy but not tarty. Chloe thought they were great as the girls twirled round in them. They admired Chloe's dress too, it was really classy. Lily sat on Chloe's bed whilst watching the fashion parade, Rory was on the floor playing with his trains, oblivious to them all.

"Why can't I come?" she wheedled "and don't say I'm too young."

"Lily my sweet thing, you would be bored stiff, no balloons or jelly or party games, just a lot of boring old grown-ups talking to each other" Chloe sat down on the bed next to her, and gave her a hug, "You will have lots of fun at home with Daddy, and the next day we are all going out together. I thought we could go to Arundel Castle, you'd all love that."

"Yes that does sound fun, although I still wish I was coming Mummy."

"Darling, it'll be your birthday soon and you can dress up then." compromised Chloe.

"I'd like to go to the castle Mummy, I think the party sounds silly." piped up Rory.

"You bloody would." said Lily "you're just a boy!"

"Enough now Lily, let's all go down to the yard and get the ponies out, we could have a ride round the woods." She took each of them by the hand, leaving her dress on the bed to put away later. "Toby," she called, padding down the corridor to his room, "Come on we're going for a ride."

"Do I have to Mum, I'm just in the middle of something" Toby wailed.

"Yes you do, you can do that later." Chloe said, "Come on, it's too nice a day to stay indoors." Toby turned off the computer reluctantly, and stomped off down the stairs, followed closely behind by the others.

The house was dead quiet when John came home, even the dogs had gone, and bugger it all he was early for a change, he had made a real effort and they weren't even here. He put his briefcase down on the kitchen table, and flicked on the kettle, glancing at his post on the table, turning the envelopes over but not bothering to open them. The kitchen was in its usual messy state. Chloe and the kids had obviously been baking cakes, their multi coloured efforts cooling on a tray, waiting to be iced, the three mixing bowls piled in the sink, and flour still all over the working surface. Sod it all, he would have a beer, and went over to the fridge, tripping over one of Rory's trains on the floor. He bent down and picked it up, he had loved trains when he was his age, his little boy was fixated by them, that was for sure. Where had all the years gone, he felt so old, it only felt like five minutes ago that he and Chloe had run round this house in its dilapidated state, full of excitement and their plans for the future. My God they had worked hard the pair of them and now here he was, years later, older, greyer, and changed. Mileoak was a wild dream then and together they had made it work, but now it felt like just another bloody great millstone around his neck. He took a long draught of his beer, and picked up his jacket, which he had slung over a chair, and went upstairs, ducking his head automatically on the low beams, and picking up more debris from the kids en route. He opened the door to their bedroom, for once the bed was made, and on it was Chloe's new dress. He just couldn't face going to the party with her, making a lot of small talk when his mind was a million miles away. He hadn't been a bit concerned when she said she was going with Oliver, in fact he was relieved. He dropped the toys and his jacket, put his beer down, and picked up the dress, holding the silky fabric close to his cheek. He closed his eyes and he could smell Chloe's perfume where she had tried it on earlier. Oh God, why did this have to happen, he didn't want to hurt her or the children. He had no idea what to do.

Chloe oblivious to John's early arrival at Mileoak, was chattering away to the kids on the ride. Rory bobbing along on the leading rein, on his tiny old pony, Lily, her ringlets dancing down her back under her crash hat, and Toby, wearing a cloak and carrying a sword, was heavily into Camelot role play.

"Rory, keep your heels down like me" Lily instructed, "that's better, now keep your hands still, oh for goodness sake, not like that!"

"Lily love, leave him alone, just let him enjoy himself."

"Mummy, can I have a sword? One like Toby's" asked Rory, his crash hat falling down a little over his eyes, his thick blonde fringe sticking out.

"Darling, when you are a little bit older, it's tricky to ride with a sword and hang on too, but next time I can find you a cloak if you like?" Rory grinned his approval. "Okay, every one ready for a trot then?" It was so perfect Chloe thought, a wonderful warm afternoon, the dogs running along beside them, occasionally zooming in and out of the bushes, chasing a particularly juicy scent. Her and the children, she felt really happy for the first time in a while, forgetting in that moment to be worrying about John.

Sean lay back on the couch his legs apart, watching as Linda licked her lips and went down on him. She was good at giving head and she loved doing it too, he shut his eyes and enjoyed her teasing and licking his cock, her mouth lingering just above the nerve endings at the top. God that felt good, he moaned a little and she moved down over the shaft, taking as much of it as she could in her mouth. There was a sharp rap at the door, and then another.

"Fuck me!" shouted Sean

"Mmmm, I would have liked to babe! Bad timing!" she eased off her knees and wiped her mouth, he sat up wriggling back into his boxers.

"Coming!" she laughed at Sean struggling on the sofa, and walked over to the door, yanking it open. "Why Laura, you're a surprise!" She held the door open and called out to Sean "hey babe, we have a visitor!"

"No kidding" he grumbled.

"Sorry, am I interrupting you?" Laura took in the situation, Sean sitting in his pants, a fed up look on his face. "I can come back another time eh?"

"Don't be silly Laura, we're really pleased to see you, aren't we Sean?" she said daring him to disagree.

"Course, come on in Laura" he said resignedly.

The room was its usually filthy state, old coffee cups with fag butts floating in the dregs, and plates with bits of crusts half eaten all over the place and the overpowering smell of dope lingering in the air. Sean leaned over and lit a spliff, inhaling deeply, "Want a toke?"

he offered the joint to Laura.

"Not for me ta, still got that cold."

"Oh, this'd do it good!"

"Nah, thanks anyway" she sniffed. "Just thought I'd drop by and see how you guys are?"

"Well existing on Job Seekers Allowance, which is rubbish" said Sean, "but I've gotta little job in a bookies that pays cash, so that's handy."

"What about you Linda?" Laura asked "Definitely not going back to college then?"

"I'm through with that shit and I meant it. Living off the benefit too, we can earn a bit of cash now and then and we're happy. How's it going with you then, still slogging away at it?"

Laura looked at the pair of them, hardly containing her contempt, at their dishevelled and dirty way of life, living off coffee, toast and dope, and thought, Christ I don't want to end up like you two. "Yep still there, I really want to try and get through it, though sometimes I feel just like you do." Liar she thought, especially about the last part, nothing could be further from the truth.

"Yea, I know what you mean, we've a great lifestyle, don't we babe?" said Linda glancing at Sean, waiting for him to agree. "There's more to life than slogging your guts out for nothing at the end, and d' ya know, it sickens me, why shouldn't we cash in on the benefits all the other spongers get?"

"Yeah, too right, but this college lark I'm gonna give it a shot." Laura added "Y' never know might get a job at the end of it."

"Why bother to try, there aren't any jobs, the rich stay rich, the poor stay poor, it'll never change no matter how much y' might think it will" said Sean gloomily. "What do the fucking government do about it, nothing, sweet fuck all, that's what! The hunting bill's a classic example, passed legally and fairly, but those rich fuckers still do it, and the pigs do nothing to enforce it. Why? 'Cos they're stinking rich, the Government's a puppet to those people, I tell you it makes me fucking seethe!" he ranted.

"There's a lot in what you say Sean, but I thought you were anti-hunting cos of the foxes and cruelty and all that?"

"Course I don't like that, but I don't like those fuckers that do it either! Ignorant, upper class arseholes, chasing dumb animals like that, but at least us Sabs won in the end, we beat 'em legally." He triumphed.

"But they still carry on, just like you said" sighed Laura, slyly looking at him from under her lashes "they need teaching a lesson I think."

"You said that before Laura, but what can we do now? We're well outnumbered and there's no press about it anymore."

"What we need to do is make a real statement" said Laura, "make the fuckers sit up and listen. Actually, after I saw you last, I've been thinking about it a lot. It's so unfair and those poor animals, it makes my heart bleed to think about what happens to them. We need to act in a drastic way and d' ya know I might have a bit of a plan."

"Go on" said Sean intrigued, he sat forward, leaning towards her, his arms resting on his hairy legs, "Go on then, what is it, I'm all ears."

Jennifer, had been flat out all week, getting up really early, and once Charles had gone off to London dashing down to Mileoak, and then coming back to help Mrs Fuller with the preparations. She had apologised to Chloe and the girls, explaining that it would only be for this week, whilst she was needed at Nantes.

Chloe had totally understood, and in truth was still reeling with amazement at the way Jennifer seemed to have changed her whole attitude towards life - underneath that sad, lonely woman, was a lovely person struggling to get out. Horses had the strangest effect on people - put all sorts of life experiences into a new perspective somehow when you were near them. You only had to look at Riding for the Disabled, and the fantastic work being done by organisations such as the Emile Faurie Foundation, taking children from inner cities and introducing them to horses. She was so pleased that she had been able to help Jennifer, even though she was so privileged in many ways, money didn't make happiness. Chloe just wished she could sort out her own life.

On Thursday morning two large and laden flatbed trucks rolled down the drive at Nantes Place, pulling up at the front of the house. Four burly chaps jumped out, in shorts and Doc Martin's calling to one another and dropping the tail gate on one of lorries.

Mrs Fuller had been watching from the hallway and bustled out of the front door, calling up the stairs to Jennifer as she went. Jennifer looked at her watch, it was just gone ten o'clock, they were spot on time. She quickly towelled herself dry from her shower, and pulled on some shorts and a top, dashing down the stairs to the front door. Mrs Fuller was already out there, with the plan in her hand consulting with what looked like the foreman, a great big guy, going bald, and with a bit of a pot belly.

"Now, this is where we need you to put it up" she was saying, indicating the back of the lawn on the drawing, "do you want to come round and have a look first? Oh here's Mrs Parker-Smythe" she turned to look at Jennifer like she was a piece of dog shit on her shoe.

"Morning, what a lovely day" remarked Jennifer, "You are very prompt, excellent! Mrs Fuller and I can show you where everything has to go." The foreman looked at her appreciatively, beautiful woman he thought appraisingly, good legs too!

"I'm Terry, we'll try and have this little lot up before teatime" he laughed, "the boys are pretty quick!" he was about to say 'with erections', but changed his mind when he saw Mrs Fuller's stony face. He followed them around to the back lawns, "lovely house" he remarked.

Jennifer beamed at him, "Yes isn't it! Been in my husband's family for generations." The lawns were looking lovely, Pete had done a good job she thought, I must remember to thank him again, although she doubted he would acknowledge her. The back of the house with its mellow stone walls and lofty windows looked glorious in the warmth of the sunshine. The marquee was to be situated just off the drawing room terrace and there was to be a covered walk way leading from the terrace itself directly into the main marquee. They all consulted the plan and Terry said it was all pretty straight forward. He marched back around the side of the house to organise his team. Jennifer looked at Mrs Fuller, whose face had softened a bit.

"I think it seems pretty clear, don't you? We'll have to keep an eye on them though." She prattled on, "I've checked the weather forecast and it's looking as though it will stay fine, a low coming in maybe on Sunday, let's keep our fingers crossed it doesn't arrive too soon."

She was excited - she just hoped there were no last minute hitches. They both moved back to Jennifer's study to go through last minute arrangements. Jennifer had decided that if the weather looked good, the string quartet could play on the terrace, and they could serve the champagne and canapés there, moving into the main marquee for the sit down meal. People would arrive through the front door, their coats taken there and then on through the drawing room onto the terrace at the back. Mrs Fuller and Jennifer worked together for the rest of the morning, ringing the caterers with last minute details and confirming the other arrangements, periodically one or other of them would pop out onto the lawn to check that Terry and his gang were okay.

The morning shot past, and finally Mrs Fuller looked up, "I'll go and make them some tea and sandwiches, is there anything that you would like Madam?" she asked. Mrs Fuller had surprised herself, and Jennifer more so - where had the madam come from?

"No, thank you Mrs Fuller, although I wouldn't mind some fruit, I'll come down to the kitchen and give you a hand." At long last thought Jennifer, I think we've reached a mutual understanding. They had worked side by side in complete harmony for the whole morning and there had not been one snide remark, the label 'madam' said it all, although Jennifer didn't want to be called that, but now was not the right time to say. They stood up and walked towards the kitchen, "Mrs Fuller, I want to thank you very much, I couldn't have put this party on without you, and I want you to know how very much I appreciate you and all you do for us."

Mrs Fuller sniffed, but her face softened "it's my pleasure

Madam" she said.

Pete watched the comings and goings of the men erecting the marquee - a coarse common lot that they were, making lewd remarks and jokes all the time. Treading all over the grass with their dirty great boots, and no doubt she would blame him for that too just like she blamed him for everything else. He turned away in disgust and went back to his cottage for his lunch. He rubbed his arms, he couldn't wait to wash his hands and face - he felt so dirty. Why had that woman come here, why had Celia gone? It was her fault, sometimes he thought, if he had a knife in his hand, he would stick it right in her. He scrubbed himself clean in his mad obsessional way and sat down at his kitchen table. The room was quite gloomy after the bright sunshine outside, and his eyes were taking a while to focus - what was that? He listened carefully, yes he had definitely heard it, the voice again, but where was it coming from? He listened again, it was clearer this time. "Pete, you could stick the knife in and twist it right round, she is the devil that woman. Pete, Pete, are you listening? You know what you need to do." The voices were right, she was the devil, everything had been all right until she came he ruminated, churning angry thoughts over and over in his head. Now Lucy had gone too, then it would be him, he wouldn't let it happen, the voices were telling him what to do, he must listen to them.

CHAPTER 18

Katherine and Sandy were out for a hack together, they did not have another event planned until Rackham at the end of June. So whilst they had to keep the horses fit enough, there was time for some lazy rides where they could just chat. Sandy had been busy at work, preparing for some pretty salacious cases but was not due for a court appearance until Tuesday, so had taken the opportunity to enjoy some time off for a ride with Katherine. They ambled along the little lanes, the horses on a long rein and enjoying the sunshine as much as the riders.

"I'm looking forward to Jen's party, it should be a good laugh, especially now, since she appears to have invited the whole yard!"

"Yeah, me too, she's much nicer than I thought, she must have been bloody unhappy before, not surprised though married to that arrogant tosser." Sandy laughed "Bloody men, I'm much better off being single!"

"Come on! He's probably okay, just has a reputation as being a bad boy, we don't really know him, do we? Let's see how he is with her on Saturday. You know not all men are bad, look at Jeremy, he's very good to me and I know he loves me and the kids."

"You're one of the lucky ones then, and I thought Chloe was too, but you can't help but notice how things are between her and John can you? I can smell infidelity a mile off, goes with my job."

"Oh Sandy, you don't know that do you, they've always appeared so happy together, it's hard to believe it of him."

"The plausible ones are always the worst." said Sandy, "Look how I was with my ex." Katherine and Chloe were probably the only two people who really knew what had happened with Sandy's marriage, and neither of them was particularly surprised that it had put Sandy off men, but it had coloured her judgement of the whole male species nonetheless. "Anyway, I think there's more to it than meets the eye, look how she was talking to Patrick the other day, they shut up the moment they saw us."

"Might have been nothing to do with it all" laughed Katherine, "You know what a gossip Patrick is!"

"Mmmm, but what gossip though? Curious eh? Another thing - is Chloe really going to the party with the dishy Oliver? Wouldn't mind a crack at him myself!"

"You're totally incorrigible! They're going together because John won't go and neither will his wife, but you're right it will make tongues wag.

"Too right it will, and there's no smoke without fire! Okay I'm joking!"

They turned off the lane onto the bridleway and kicked the horses into an easy canter up towards the hill, the ruins of the old Abbey looming at the top.

"God that's a creepy old place" gasped Katherine, loosening her rein when they came to a halt up alongside it. The Abbey was bathed in the sunshine, although even with the light streaming through the paneless windows it still looked a bit sinister even on this bright day. "They say its haunted by some monk y' know."

Sandy scoffed, "load of bloody rubbish! It's just a ruin, one day I might have a look round though, all we ever do is ride past it."

"Well not with me and not today!"

"Scaredy cat" laughed Sandy, "Come on race you down the hill!" She kicked Seamus on and he responded immediately, game on for a contest, his grey flanks gleaming as he sped off. Alfie took up the challenge and Katherine found herself tearing after them, hanging on like a limpet whilst she took up her reins.

Oliver should have been looking forward to the party tomorrow and to hearing the outcome of Andrew's meeting with Lady V, but he was too preoccupied. First and foremost was Suse, how much longer could he struggle on like this. The morning after her drunken outburst, they had made up in a frosty way. Each of them avoiding what she had said the night before. He was sad about it all, and for the millionth time wondered nostalgically if he shouldn't just try one last time to make a go of it? They had been good together once, and okay he wasn't a saint especially lately, but could he rekindle something of what he had once felt for her? If he was brutally honest, he didn't believe that he could – but the alternative was so radical. He was deep in thought, turning over and over in his mind how he truly felt and where his future might lie and with whom. He knew that Suse was unfulfilled but not prepared to make a go of any kind of career, she seemed to be spiralling further down into her own pit of misery and didn't want to make any attempt to meet him halfway. He was ambitious it was true, and he loved his work, but she had never found his kind of job satisfaction in anything that she'd done. Perhaps if she had, she might see his career in a different light.

His phone rang – it was Andrew, "Oli mate, I'm going on a call, then straight up to Fittlebury Hall for tea with Lady V at three o'clock, any chance you and I could meet, say about five ish, so I can fill you in on what she says?"

"Sure" responded Oliver, "I've got a shed load of calls, but I can crack on this morning and get as much done as I can, then anything that's left I can do afterwards. See you back at the surgery at 5.30 then - .Ciao." Bugger he thought, he might have had a bit of spare time, but not now, he pulled over, taking his mobile out of the hands free to send a text.

Andrew replaced his phone, good that was settled then, he glanced at the clock on the dashboard of his car, he would have plenty of time now and still be at Lady V's easily. It had meant a really early start for him, luckily most horse owners were early birds he reflected, he had got loads done, and had managed his day well considering. He smiled to himself, he'd never felt happier.

Katherine and Sandy were on their way back homewards, the horses ambling along in a lazy walk. They had cantered up towards

Grace Allington's parents' place, and then skirted back along the bridleway alongside the crop fields, walking the last mile or so to cool the horses off.

"What're you wearing to the party then?" asked Sandy

"Oh, I've got a couple of things that might do and that I've only ever worn to Jeremy's business functions, so no-one round here will have seen them. How about you? Not coming in a wig and gown are you?"

"Hey don't' joke, I just might!" Sandy grinned, "No, actually I'm quite well off for that sort of cocktail frock, I have to have a few for the Chambers and Bar functions, I'll drag one of those out."

"Jeremy has offered to drive too, makes a change! Do you want picking up, no sense in you having to drive too."

"That'd be great, if you don't mind coming to the cottage, or I could drive to you if that's easier and pick my car up on Sunday?"

"It's no problem to collect you en route, I asked the girls if they wanted a lift, so we have to swing past Mileoak to pick them up anyway. Oliver can only get one extra person in that car of his, the rest of it is crammed full of his vet gear. He's got to drive anyway, he's on call apparently, so he can't drink."

"Poor old Oliver, he always draws the short straw! I suppose Andrew is going then, with that snotty wife of his?"

"Well they must be I suppose, otherwise Oli could've swapped." They rode down the lane and pulled into Mileoak, clattering down the drive. Beebs having heard them coming was waiting to greet them.

"Don't worry Beebs, we're not in any hurry, we can do them ourselves" called Katherine.

Bibi looked up gratefully, "thanks Katherine, we've loads to do today, so we've more time to get ready for tomorrow." Katherine looked fondly at her, it was such fun at that age to go to a posh do.

"So glad you're looking forward to it. I'm sure we'll all have a great time!"

Andrew checked his tie in the car mirror, adjusting the Windsor knot. He had dressed carefully today, normally favouring a polo shirt and shorts in this hot weather. He was wearing some khaki corduroy trousers, checked shirt with a tie and a jacket. Lady V was a bit of a stickler for correct dress, although not for herself ironically! It was vital that he got off on the right foot, and present the right image. He drove down the lane, his mind racing ahead to the meeting. He knew he would just be so disappointed if this did not come off, it was a wonderful chance for the practice. Okay, even if they did not get the Old Mill, they would still have to expand, they just couldn't carry on this workload anymore, but how much better if they had their sights on new premises and it would be a real lure to any potential assistants they might employ. Oh God he thought - please let it go well!

He swung into Fittlebury Hall, with its tall stone entrance pillars, topped with moss covered snarling lions. The ornate iron gates were fixed open, and he pulled up the long drive with the old park railings on either side, Lady V's glossy brood mares and foals frolicking about in the paddocks. The drive wound round in a long smooth curve, and the house was easily visible in the distance, a large red brick Tudor house with tall chimneys, and stone ledged latticed windows. It was huge and rambling with myriads of ivy and creepers clinging to the walls. Andrew turned to the right of the drive as it swept on to the front of the house and parked the car in the stable courtyard at the back. Mark Templeton's vehicle was already there, and he got out when he saw Andrew arrive. The two men shook hands and both turned simultaneously at the sound of footsteps, to find Lady Veronica Hartwell stomping across the courtyard towards them from the stables, four dogs running at her heels. She was a tall woman, with white hair, and sharp periwinkle blue eyes, her skin was smooth and fair and she must have been a real beauty in her day, although now she must have been in her mid-seventies at least. She walked with the air of a young woman, and marched over to them.

"Andrew my dear chap, come in, come in, good to see you. Mark, you too."

"Lady Veronica, thank you so much for seeing me, I really appreciate this."

"No problem at all, let's go inside, it's damned hot out here on

194

these cobbles." She strode ahead of them to the back of the vast house, the dogs dashing in the door before her "you blighters, don't be so bloody rude!" she roared at them.

Andrew had only been inside the house once before, it was an astonishing place, with its huge studded oak doors and massive iron handles. The flagstones on the floor in this, what was the old servants' hall, were old and well worn, and he wondered about all of the pairs of feet that had trodden that way over the years. He followed behind Lady Veronica's wake as she swept through to the kitchen, the dogs charging ahead of her. Andrew and Mark followed behind into the vast room, hardly a kitchen at all, with cavernous open fireplaces, and very few modern appliances, dominated in the centre by the biggest kitchen table Andrew had ever seen. A slim young woman was standing at the table, efficiently cutting bread.

"Ah Nina, my guests have arrived, can we have tea in the drawing room now please?"

"Of course your Ladyship, it will be ready in about ten minutes."

"Thank you my dear, can you bring it in when it's ready." She gestured for the others to follow and she strode through the servants quarters to the main part of the house. It was very similar, with the same massive doors, but in stark contrast was panelled in expensive dark oak and the flags had been replaced with oak boards and topped with red Axminster rugs. The furniture was all of the same period and mainly dark oak, and in the centre of the hall was a long refectory table with a sweeping arrangement of enormous white hydrangeas. They followed her into a large room, with the same tiny lattice panes of glass in the windows, but these windows were tall and long and opened onto the garden, and the sun beamed through them, spreading great pools of light onto the floor. She plonked herself down into a feather armchair, covered in a William Morris print. The two men, sat down opposite her on a sofa.

"Now let's get down to it" she barked at them.

Mark began, "Well as you know your Ladyship, I have been talking to you about the possibility of selling the Old Mill House, owing to its dreadful state of repair, and the cost of renovations."

"Yes, yes, we have talked all this through before. Now," she turned impatiently to Andrew, "I gather from Mark that you might be interested in buying the old place, is that right?"

"Yes your ladyship, I'm very interested. I'd like to renovate it and turn it into a specialist equine diagnostic unit, and use the cottage for the staff. The Mill would become administrative offices and an in-house laboratory, with the outbuildings used for x-rays, theatre, that sort of thing." He tailed off, looking at her to gauge her reaction.

She gazed back at him, looking at him hard before replying. "The thing is Andrew, I applaud that idea, certainly far more so than if some townies were to buy it and do one of those awful modern conversions and split the place up, but of course it has a good resale value should I put it up for auction, so no matter how altruistic the reasons, it has to be financially viable for me, and of course for you too."

Mark leant forward, "I have some figures here for you both, and you can see that I have had three independent valuations on the property, all of which vary considerably."

Lady Veronica, pulled out a pair of ancient spectacles from her pocket, held together with a paper clip, and studied the information. Andrew quickly did the same astonished by the disparities in the opinions - from the outrageous, to the downright ridiculous - the middle one was probably the most realistic. He gulped, scanning the figures again, surreptitiously watching Lady V's reaction as she peered through her glasses. Andrew could hardly bear the silent waiting – she was certainly taking her time as she slowly read the reports, wrinkling her nose every now and then. The only sound in the room was the rhythmic tick of the grandfather clock as the time trickled past. At last there was a creak outside the door, and then a rattle as Nina rolled in the tea trolley

"Ah Nina, thank you my dear, I can pour, that will be all." Lady Veronica irritatingly put down her sheath of papers, and Andrew had never felt more frustrated, willing her to read on. "Now, tea Andrew, milk or lemon? I cannot stand it with milk myself."

She handed him a cup, not waiting for a reply and another cup to Mark. On the tray was a tiered plate, on the bottom one small triangles of sandwiches, and on the top small pink and yellow cupcakes. "Sandwich?" she asked. Andrew could do nothing but acquiesce, and wait irritatingly for tea to be over. He bit into the sandwich, expecting something like cheese or ham or even salmon, but to his surprise it was crunchy peanut butter! Lady Veronica saw his expression and said "I just love peanut butter, don't you?" He had to laugh, she really was eccentric!

After what seemed an agonising age, she took up the paperwork again, and studied it. "Yes, yes, I see, quite a difference in the valuations, what do you think Mark?"

"Well, I think that they are certainly diverse if nothing else, the highest seems to me to be quite unreasonable bearing in mind the state of the market at the moment and the cost of the renovation work involved getting the place anywhere near up to scratch. The lowest would indicate an agent just wanting a fast sale and a quick commission, so too cheap and not viable for us your Ladyship. So my gut feeling would be to go for the middle one, based on a fair price for the estate and a realistic one for Andrew."

"That seems sound to me, what say you Andrew?"

"Yes, I think that figure is more reasonable certainly, but would there be any room for negotiation on that price? I don't want to haggle, but the cost of renovations would be high after all?" God he hoped he had not antagonised her. He felt like he was treading on eggshells here!

"Mmmm, I see your predicament, but of course you must see mine too, it is my duty to the estate to ensure we get the best possible price and the best possible outcome in terms of the environment, I don't want to see the place split up. Make me an offer!"

"Well ..." he was taken aback, mentally calculating desperately, "How about fifty thousand off the middle price" he offered tentatively.

"Twenty five" she countered. He saw the gleam in her eye, she was certainly savvy.

"Factoring in your marketing costs, how about we split that and take a figure of thirty six off the valuation price, plus throwing in that five acre paddock alongside." he bargained.

"Hmm. You mean Henry's five? What are we currently doing with that Mark?"

Mark scratched his chin, "At this present time, not a lot. It is too small and too far away from the main arable land for us to make a special journey to drill any form of crop, and as it is cut off from the haylage fields by the stream, and can get quite wet, we don't tend to use it much. Generally, we run some sheep in there to keep it clean, and at this time of year use it as a bit of a paddock for the brood mares before they come further upland for the winter and that's it. Although of course we do get RPA payments for it, but on that small a hectare the sum is negligible."

Lady Veronica, thought for a while, "So, not much value to us in terms of production then and we shouldn't miss it much in the big scheme of things?"

"No, not in the big scheme of things – we wouldn't." Mark agreed.

"Thirty six thousand off and the five acres you say?" She consulted the paperwork again and thoughtfully took another bite of her cake, "Very well. Done!" Andrew couldn't believe it, she had agreed, he swallowed hard "but" she continued, "I would put certain conditions onto the sale, limitations as to use and making any renovations aesthetically pleasing, that sort of thing."

Andrew felt like jumping up and down, the first hurdle was over, but restrained himself, "Of course, that goes without saying and our solicitors would have to draw those up, but if in principal you are agreed, and subject to my bank agreeing our loan, then all I can say is thank you!"

"My pleasure dear boy, it will be nice to see the old place put to good use, and nice for the estate to have an injection of cash, eh Mark?"

In no time at all she briskly concluded the meeting, wolfed down another sandwich, and he was dismissed. As he drove back down the drive, he was ecstatic, he couldn't wait to tell Oli. He picked up his phone, and pressed speed dial, listening to the ringing on his hands free. Voice mail, bugger he would have to try again later.

The day had passed in a flurry of activity, Jennifer whizzing backwards and forwards, taking charge of the siting of 'Chic Loos' watched over by an eagled-eyed Mrs Fuller. Crikey thought Jennifer, they really were posh loos! Bowls of pot pourri, and Moulton Brown Rose Granati hand wash and cream, luxury tissues, and a large bouquet of flowers in the Ladies, with pretty Cath Kidston paper on the walls. The Gents by comparison, had brown regency stripe walls, with the same Moulton Brown products but in a manly Amber fragrance. Better than a lot of people had in their own bathrooms thought Jennifer guiltily. The loos were hidden by their very own ready-made hedge, which came in long troughs and was about five feet high – discreet indeed.

"These are excellent Mrs Fuller, what a good choice you made here!"

"They are good aren't they Madam? I knew you'd approve."

Terry and his men had been as good as their word and the marquee had been erected by tea time the day before. It looked splendid, the interior had long arched windows along two long sides and the round tables, with their gold chairs had been clustered in groups, with the raised dais and the dance floor at the back. The ceiling and walls were lined with swathes of white chiffon material, and small fairy lights had been strung across the domed roof and the supports and would give the appearance of a twinkling sky as it got dark. Around the garden similar lights had been put in the trees, with larger spotlights, to enhance the features of the garden, especially around the lake. She sighed happily, it was all going so well, she turned to Mrs Fuller "It looks great, don't you think?"

"Yes, it certainly does, but I'll be happier when we have the tablecloths on, and the silver has arrived. Have you done the name cards for the table placings yet?"

"They're all ready, it took me ages to write them out."

"It is only proper Madam that they're written by hand" Mrs Fuller replied huffily.

"Well, I bow to your better judgement Mrs Fuller, although the table plan has been done by computer." Luckily she was saved from further explanations by the tooting of a car horn.

"That'll be Fletchers, I'll go and see to them." Mrs Fuller shot out of the marquee as fast as she could, and Jennifer was glad to be left on her own for a bit. She hugged herself, it all looked splendid, and please God don't let anything go wrong.

The rest of the afternoon was spent with Doris and her cleaning team, whizzing about with vacuum cleaners and dusters. Mrs Fuller orchestrating the whole operation, the small snug had been emptied and rails had been brought up from storage in the garages ready for any coats, although it was difficult to think they would be needed in this sweltering heat. Doris' husband, Fred, busied himself roping off a car parking area at the back of the Granary, and had strung some more fairy lights in the trees at the back. They'd got as far as they could today, and tomorrow would see all the final touches.

Jennifer sat down in her study with relief, looking over the check list on her desk, thinking she just hoped it was all worth it. She added a final note here and there to the list in red pen, crossing out things that had been done, deep in thought. She turned her head and glanced over to the computer screen, and was unexpectedly aware of a shadow at the window. She looked up, suddenly crying out in alarm - her hands flew to her face, as there standing at the window watching her was the great hulk of Pete. She gasped, he looked so sinister and evil, just standing there staring at her like that! In that instant the study door swung open and she spun round as Charles breezed into the room.

"Darling, I'm home early as promised. You've done a great job, it all looks splendid, and you've been so busy!" He took in her stricken face, "Whatever is the matter darling, you're as white as a ghost and you're trembling?" She could not speak, and just pointed to the open window, he ran over looking out, and helplessly turned back towards her shrugging. She reluctantly went over to join him, but when she finally looked again Pete had gone.

Andrew, Oliver and Paulene all huddled into the back office like naughty children. Andrew had told them all about the meeting with Lady V, and that provided Gary agreed and could come up with a good business plan for the bank, he felt that they had good chance to buy the mill. Paulene had whooped and hugged him! Oliver grinned, it was a huge step, and had been little more than a pipe dream until now. Andrew said he would get on the blower to Gary this evening, and on Monday, make an appointment at the bank for next week. Hopefully that would be enough time, as he wanted to make a formal offer as soon as he could. He didn't think Lady V would change her mind, but the sooner it was in writing the better.

"Now remember you two, not a word to anyone. Especially tomorrow night Oli."

"Don't worry buddy, I won't say a word. Anyway remember I'm the one on call and not drinking, so you just make sure you don't open your mouth and insert your size 10s!"

"I was thinking about that, why don't I do the on call? You could do with a bit of fun, if you don't mind doing mine tonight, then I'll do the weekend, okay?"

"Blimey, mate, there's an offer I won't refuse! You sure?"

"Yep, do you good!" Oliver looked at him, Andrew wasn't stupid, he knew how things were at home for him at the moment with Suse. He was a great bloke was Andrew and he was right, it would do him good.

CHAPTER 19

At last, the morning of the party had arrived and everyone at Nantes, except for Charles, was busy. Mrs Fuller was at her most officious, running around with her clipboard in her hand, directing the caterers, instructing them how to set the tables correctly, and ensuring that each serviette was shaped exactly into uniform fans. Jennifer watched, concealing her amusement, Mrs Fuller was in her element! She herself, consulting her seating plan, was adding the name cards onto the tables, the flowers had not yet arrived, and she hoped they would not wilt in the heat. It was another baking hot day, with a fierce sun in a cloudless blue sky. Thank you God, she prayed that for today at least, it would stay that way. She knew how badly they needed the rain, she only had to look at Chloe's parched hay fields, but not tonight, please not tonight! She looked around, everything seemed to be going well, but she was still feeling a bit worried, she had been badly frightened by Pete the day before, he seemed to hate her beyond all rational explanation. Okay, she had been stupid in the way she handled him at times, but surely not enough to warrant such creepy behaviour. Charles had not been overtly worried, saying she was over-reacting and Pete probably didn't realise she was in the study and had just been looking through the window, whilst pruning the roses. Jennifer had calmed down, but she was not totally convinced about Pete. Ah well, she had more pressing things on her mind at the moment. She had booked to go into Horsham this afternoon, to have her hair washed and blow dried, encouraged by Mrs Fuller, although she felt that her keenness was not for totally altruistic reasons, she just didn't want her interfering! Well, let her get on with it, Jennifer thought, it was just a matter of dotting the I's and crossing the T's, and once the florist had been and gone, she felt she could relax more.

Charles breezed into the marquee, he looked very handsome this morning, in his light blue jeans and white polo shirt. He came over to her and gave her hug, and kissed her cheek "Mmmm, you smell gorgeous" he said, running his hand along her cheek. "Looking forward to this evening?"

"Yes and no, in equal parts!" She grinned at him, "I think the arrangements are all in hand, but I'm terrified something'll go wrong!"

"Don't be silly sweetie, it'll be fine. Let Mrs Fuller take the strain now and you enjoy yourself tonight."

"Oh Charles, I really want to, but I feel so guilty about not doing my bit."

"But you have done your bit! Mrs Fuller told me this morning, that you had been marvellous this week."

"Did she?" Jennifer was amazed. "Did she really say that?"

"Course she did my darling, because it's true."

"Oh Charles, how sweet of her, I didn't know she had it in her. She always looks at me in such a disapproving way."

"You are silly, of course she doesn't. It was bound to take time for her to adjust to having you here, but it's all fine now." Charles looked down at her, poor Jennifer, she had had a rough ride over the last 18 months, and he knew that he hadn't helped, and was pleased that he'd managed to have a quiet word with Mrs Fuller this week. She was a bit of a battle axe, but fundamentally her heart was in the right place, and her bark was certainly worse than her bite. It hadn't just taken Mrs Fuller time to adjust he thought wryly, but him too, but he really was going to change and try and be more considerate. The last week or so the magic seemed to have returned in their relationship, and he realised how much she meant to him. "Now come on darling, let's have a coffee and take it by the pool, you might even have time for a dip before you go off to have your hair done." He slipped his hand around her waist, and kissed the tip of her ear. Jennifer shivered at his touch, and they walked off together arm in arm, all thoughts of Pete gone.

Mileoak Farm was equally busy this Saturday morning too. Chloe was teaching back to back in the school but was finishing at lunch time. John had taken the children into Horsham to Sainsbury's to get some bits and pieces for their picnic at Arundel tomorrow. Katherine and Sandy had already been up and ridden early, before the sun got too hot, promising to pick up Beebs and Susie promptly at a quarter past seven that evening. The girls were going like bats out of hell to make sure that all the jobs were done, so that they could finish early. They were very excited, chattering and laughing. Their mood affected the other liveries and every now and then Chloe, teaching in her old shorts, tee shirt and floppy hat, could hear shouts of laughter from the yard. She smiled, she was glad that the girls were to have a good night out, it had been sweet of Jennifer to invite them too, although she was beginning to have second thoughts about going with Oliver, but it was too late to back out now, even though John was not in the least bit worried it seemed. He was so distracted, she really hoped that their day out tomorrow as a family, away from Mileoak, would help. Meanwhile, she would try to have a good night, and must see if she could summon up some enthusiasm. She mustn't be a wet blanket and spoil everyone else's fun. She heard the clopping of hooves coming across the yard, she looked up plastering a smile on her face, her next client was riding into the school. "Morning Polly!" she said brightly.

Beebs and Susie were doing well, everything was mucked out, the field horses had been checked and the tack was clean. "Phew" said Beebs leaning heavily on her broom, "What a morning! It had better be worth it after all this!"

"It should be fantastic! By the way, I had a call from Caitlin. Jen's invited her too, she's gonna be on our table."

"Who else is on it, do you know?"

"Well us, Chloe, Oliver, Caitlin, Katherine, Sandy and Jeremy that makes seven, and Jen said they were tables of eight or ten, but no idea who the others are."

"I'm sure she'll put us with some okay people."

"Imagine if she put us with Lady V!" They both shrieked with laughter at the thought.

"Look, I'm just going to nip into the cottage, and boost up the emersion, don't want us running out of hot water." Beebs leant the broom against the side of the stable wall. She and Susie lived together in a cosy cottage attached to the end of the old beef barn. It was a sweet house and was comfortably furnished. Chloe had made sure they had all mod cons, based on the premise that happy staff worked hard. When Susie had first come to Mileoak, she had been offered accommodation in the mobile home, but when she and Beebs had hit it off so well, they had decided that it would more fun to move in together, and they loved it. They were great company for each other and rarely argued, which was amazing since living and working together was never a recipe for success. Luckily the cottage although not large, was big enough that the girls had a double bedroom each, shared a bathroom, and had a good sized kitchen, and sitting room. They even had a tiny secluded garden at the back. At first Chloe had had reservations about them sharing, but now was pleased that they had each other for company.

"Okay! You can go in and have the first bath tonight if you like, while I finish up, as you have to work tomorrow morning."

"Don't remind me!" Beebs grimaced, "Still you did last Sunday, so I suppose it's fair. Back in a minute." Susie carried on sweeping where Beebs had left off, her pony tail swing madly with the effort. She hummed as she worked, it was gonna be a great night.

Grace and Colin were walking up to Grace' parents' place, hand in hand and deep in conversation. The dogs charging ahead of them, dashing in and out of the hedgerows excitedly sniffing out the mice, their fat black tails wagging madly as they rooted about. It was a glorious morning, purple Foxgloves just bursting into flower and white dog daisies were dotted all along the headland, with the odd glossy head of an early buttercup, and the air was filled with birdsong, punctuated occasionally with a bark from the dogs.

"Ah, it's so beautiful this walk Gracie, what a superb day. I so love this time of year, everything has burst into life, the smells, the colours, the sounds, so perfect!"

"I know, I do it most mornings, and I still never tire of it. How lucky we are." she took a deep breath of the wonderful air.

"Yes my darling we are lucky" he glanced at her "we always need to hold onto that y' know?" Grace was surprised, Colin wasn't usually so expansive or sensitive.

"Oh Colin" stammered Grace, and her eyes filled with tears, she fumbled for a tissue out of her pocket.

"There, there old thing," and he put his arm around her "don't get upset, I just mean we have so much, compared to other people, and we must make the most of every moment of life."

"I know, I know." Grace managed a wobbly smile. He was such a good man. She carefully changed the subject. "Are you looking forward to this evening?"

"Well not much to be honest. I think it'll be a lot of dull small talk, and I just hope we don't have to sit with a load of old bores."

Grace laughed, "I know exactly what you mean! It'll be good to see Charles though, we don't seem to have seen him for ages. It was different when he was married to Celia, I hardly know Jennifer, other than to nod 'hello' to her."

"Do you think he's happy?"

"I don't see why he wouldn't be, she certainly is a beautiful creature, but is she as beautiful inside? D' y' know, I feel a bit sorry for her, it can't have been easy taking over from Celia, can it?"

"No, don't suppose it was, she's a bit of a fish out of water, even if she is the best looking fish in the tank!"

"Well, let's not judge her until we know her eh? I hate all this bitching! The oldies have had a field day with her."

"You must be the only woman I know who doesn't like bitching! Must be the reason I married you."

"You cheeky sod, is that the only reason?"

He turned and looked at her seriously, "You know why I married you Grace, because you are simply the loveliest person I know, and am ever likely to meet, and without you my life is nothing."

"Blimey Colin" exclaimed Grace "Whilst you are telling me how much you love me, I want to run something past you? Do you think I should get a job?"

Colin looked astonished "What on earth for? "

"Well, because I think it would take my mind off, you know … the other thing."

"Look love, if you think that'd help, then I'm right behind you, but I don't want you tiring yourself out, trying to do the dogs, the horses, and run the house, notwithstanding looking out for your parents. Pretty soon, when the hunting starts again you are going to be even busier, keeping the horses fit, where'd you find the time?"

"Ah yes, I know it's not practical really, but it might take my mind off things for a while"

"Well it's your call love, as I said. If you think it'll help, you'll have my support all the way." They linked arms, and walked through the farmyard to the picket gate, the tantalising smell of baking oozing out of the open kitchen door.

Lucy had been for an interview. It was not her idea, but her parents had more or less forced her to apply for the job. They had made it quite clear that she wasn't going to doss about in bed all day and that they expected her, as her mother had put it, to pull her weight around the house. The thought of having to be supervised in her mother's company all day was the catalyst, so she leafed through the County times and saw an advertisement for a waitress at a little bistro in the centre of Horsham. It wasn't ideal but at least it got her out from under her mother's feet, and she would only have do it for a short while until she could find something else with accommodation thrown in. The bistro was really just a smart little coffee-cum-sandwich house, run by a young Italian family. It was in a good location, facing out into the middle of the pedestrianised cobbled square, and was always packed with people. It had a great reputation for its excellent food, which was quite reasonably priced, so made a good watering hole for weary shoppers. Gino the owner, baked his own pastries and they made up baguettes and rolls with a huge variety of fillings to the individual customer's orders, and you could eat there or take away. Lucy was to work the expresso machine and wait at the tables, half of which were outside in the square under bright parasols. Gino offered her the job on a probationary basis, although he thought she was a bit surly, and quite evasive as to why she had left her last job, but he needed staff fast and she could start next week. He watched her go as she left the shop, he just hoped he had done the right thing. Resignedly Lucy got the bus back home as per her mother's instructions. She was so fed up - living at home was boring and not for the first time did she regret leaving Nantes under such a cloud.

The flowers had arrived and their pungent scent now filled the marquee, Jennifer was delighted, Mrs Fuller had made an excellent choice. The centrepieces on the tables where made up of really long tall tubes of glass, filled with clear cellophane and water, mixed flowers cascading over the top, and surrounding the entire base was a low cushion of white roses. They were spectacular. The other arrangements were more traditional, but large and imposing, they certainly added the finishing touches to the décor perfectly. She glanced at her watch, she had better get going if she were to get into Horsham in time for her hair appointment. She called over to Mrs Fuller, "I'm just off now, I shan't be long."

Mrs Fuller looked up, she was very pleased with herself, if she said so herself, she had done a good job. "That's fine Madam, don't worry or hurry back, everything's under control here." Jennifer sped off, and burst into Charles' study, "Darling, I'm just off to the hairdresser, I'll see you in a bit."

He swung round in his chair, "Okay sweetie, drive carefully."

Jennifer ran round to the garages, and pulled the remote control out of her bag, the garage door rumbled up and she jumped into her car, her tyres spinning on the gravel. She did not see Pete watching her from the shrubbery.

The silver Mercedes drove quickly through the lanes, although she slowed carefully on the narrow bits and the bends, much more aware these days of horses on the road. Her head was spinning with things that had to be done, but by this time tomorrow it would all be over, and it would either be a success or it wouldn't, but she was damned sure she was going to do her level best to ensure it was. She put her foot down when she got onto the dual carriageway and the powerful car ate up the miles. She had made good time as she pulled off the main road towards the town centre, and luckily she found a parking space straight away. Grabbing her handbag, she rushed out of the car park and headed towards the town square. It was crowded today in the pretty market town, shoppers idling along, and she found herself darting in and out of them. She didn't want to be late, today of all days. As she pelted on, she hesitated for a moment, she recognised that girl coming out of the little coffee shop. Was that Lucy? She looked awful, her face was pasty and her hair greasy, she slowed a little more, yes it was her. She wondered for a moment how she was, where she was living and what had prompted the row? There was no time to say or do anything, anyway, it was all too late, and she didn't even really know her, so she hurried on towards the hair salon.

Oliver was struggling, he was bent double, a horse's foreleg between his legs as he pared away at its hoof, looking for an abscess. He could feel the sun beating down on the back of his neck, and this horse was leaning on him like a bugger, and the poor thing was in pain and not appreciating Oliver's efforts to make him feel better, fidgeting and dancing about on three legs whilst his owner, Libby, tried to soothe him. Oliver held on gamely and continued to scrape away carefully, and with relief spotted the tell-tale pinprick of the site of an abscess. He cut away a little more of the hoof, and with a satisfying POP, it burst, a shot of gunge exploding out from being trapped within the box of the hoof, which alleviated the pain almost immediately. He cut a little more away exposing the site, and then gently put the horse's leg down, and stood up, stretching and arching his back. The sweat running down his back between his shoulder blades, he ran his hand across his brow, Libby looked at him, pushing her cleavage together in the low cut top.

"Phew, that's got it, well done old fellah, you were very brave!" he stroked the horse's neck, who gave him a grateful nip. "We'll just clean that out, and then put on a poultice. You'll need to replace that every day for a few days Libby, then some dry poulticing, and he should be fine. I'll give him a shot of anti-biotics now and some pain relief, then we'll continue with that for about five days, Okay?" he glanced at Libby, who was exaggeratedly listening to every word he said.

"Thanks Oliver, you are a marvel, and a handsome one too. How can I repay you?" she flirted. Oliver smiled but was totally oblivious to her innuendoes, this was the part of his job that he loved, not the digging out of abscesses but the ability to make things better. If only he could do that in his personal life. He slapped on a hot Animalintex poultice, wrapping it carefully with reams of cotton wool and vet wrap, Libby rubbing against him as often as she could manage, and Oliver gave the horse a couple of injections. "That'll do him then, now Libby you okay doing the redressing yourself, and giving the medication, you can always call me if you are concerned?"

"Yes, that fine Oliver, it's a relief, although I'll need you to come out again, I'll want to make sure he's okay won't I Topper? " she added to the horse. Then batting her eyelashes seductively at Oliver asked "You going to the party tonight at the Parker-Smythes'?"

"Yes, I'll be there, and not on call either. So I can let my hair down for a change!"

"Great, see you later then! I'll expect a dance." She smiled at him invitingly. Oliver thought, yes and when you see me later with Chloe, you'll get a right shock, and he wondered if it was a good idea after all, it was the last thing he needed. Everyone knew though that Chloe was very firmly married, but it was equally common knowledge that his own marriage was on the rocks. Libby lounged against the side of the car playing with her hair and Oliver ignoring the come on, moved around to the back, shutting the tailgate of the Toyota firmly, and checked his phone for text messages, there were none and he felt vaguely disappointed, shrugging he jumped into the driving seat and waved goodbye to Libby and went onto his next call. She looked after him, he was gorgeous and the irony was he had no idea!

Beebs was in the bath, the foamy water steaming, and she just hoped she had left enough for Susie, who would be coming in at any minute from finishing up. She dunked her head under the water, rinsing off the conditioner, and coming up to the surface gasping. She was really looking forward to tonight, it was lovely to have an opportunity to get dolled up, and she was pleased with the dress she had bought. Chloe had lent her a pair of high sandals too, and she had bought some bling from Accessorize, which set it all off a treat. Good old Jen asking her and Susie and Caitlin too. It was funny how you can misjudge a person she thought, when she had come for those couple of riding lessons the first time, she had thought her such a snooty bitch, and Susie and she had laughed like drains when she had fallen off. Beebs felt guilty when she thought about it, especially when here she was getting all dressed up to go to her party.

She heard the click of the door, as Susie blundered in, "Hey you! It's my turn, we'd better get a move on, it's gone six and they are picking us up in an hour."

"Okay, okay, I'm getting out!" She pulled the plug and the water gurgled down the plughole, she draped a towel around her and slopped off to her room.

"I'm gonna open a bottle of Cava, d' you fancy a glass?" yelled Susie from the kitchen, "might as well start as we mean to go on!"

"Great idea" she yelled back. It was going to be a great night.

Chloe was in her bedroom, a towel draped round her head and she was smoothing body lotion onto her legs. Oliver had rung to say he would be there as near to 7.30 as he could be and had organised a taxi, but he was a bit delayed on one last call. Suited her she thought, she could spend a bit more time with John and the children. She hastily blow dried her hair, luckily it was one of those styles, and she had the kind of hair, that just needed roughing up to look good. Squinting into the mirror she carefully applied some eye shadow, liner and mascara, adding some pale lipstick. Mmmm not bad, she thought she should make the effort more often. She slid into the dress, and dug around for some shoes. She wished she had bought some now. She found a pair of strappy silver sandals, and added a single silver chain around her neck. Rummaging around in her drawer she found a silver clutch bag and threw in some perfume, a lipstick, and a few pounds for the cab. There, that should do it she thought. A quick squirt of deodorant and she tottered towards the door, Christ she was not too good in heels, always took her a while to get used to wearing them.

John wolf whistled when she came into the kitchen. "Honestly Daddy" admonished Lily, "but you do look bloody lovely Mummy!" Chloe smiled at them all, not bothering to correct Lily for swearing.

"Thank you darlings!" she laughed, turning her smile up full beam to John "Don't you wish you were coming too?"

"Look Chloe," he said wearily, "I've already said, I'm happy to stay here and look after the children, I really don't want to make small talk with a lot of people I hardly know." He looked really tired and she thought for the first time, had lost some weight, not that he needed to with his slim frame, "I'm really happy for you to go and I know that Oliver'll be a good escort, and I'm just not in the mood. You look really beautiful and he'll be proud to have you on his arm, just as long as he brings you home safely!"

Chloe smiled at him "If you're sure, I'm sort of obliged to go really, and the girls are looking forward to it so much."

"I know, it's fine with me honestly it is, and we have our day out tomorrow, so go and enjoy it. Here why don't you let me pour you a drink before you go?"

"Okay, that'd be lovely, I could do with one, I don't seem to have stopped all day. I quite fancy the evening at home really, watching a movie with you lot!" She looked at the children fondly, they were absorbed at the kitchen table making a Lego village, each making their own houses. "I hope you have a nice time."

"Yes, we will Mummy, Daddy has got us Shrek to watch, it's supposed to be really brilliant!" said Toby looking up from his model, "You go and have a lovely time, and don't worry about us." Again that pang of guilt assailed Chloe, this was where she should be really.

John smiled at her, reading her mind, "Stop it, go and have a good time, you'll really enjoy it and we're going to be fine." She smiled back at him reassured, suddenly seeing the old John again. The one that was considerate and kind, loving his family and not always preoccupied all the time. He let his hand linger on hers as he gave her the glass of wine and their eyes locked as she took a sip. It is going to be all right she thought.

Grace was still wet from the bath, when Colin came up the stairs and into the bedroom. He looked very handsome in his DJ, it really suited him. He had been wearing it when she first met him all those years ago, and he brought it out for occasions such as these and it still fitted him well.

"Darling, you're still not dressed! Come on we're going to be late at this rate."

"Oh I know, just can't seem to muster much enthusiasm." Grace plopped down on the bed, inspecting her toes.

"Come on love, get cracking." She gave a huge sigh and dropped the towel, totally naked underneath, "Phew, don't do things like that to me!" Colin spluttered, looking at his wife appraisingly, she was very lovely, her lithe body glistening with droplets from the bath.

"Colin you are incorrigible! You just said we're late!"

"Not that late!" he replied, taking off his jacket.

Jennifer was ready in good time, the cream silk of the dress making her skin tone almost translucent. She twirled around, taking in her appearance in the huge mirror in their bedroom. The dress was quite beautiful and she had put on her make up carefully and gone for a very natural look, her eyes lightly mascaraed and a faint eye-shadow, with a soft peach lipstick.

Charles came up behind her kissing the back of her neck. "You look good enough to eat."

"No snacking please!" She slapped his arm playfully and turned to look at his relaxed and handsome face, "Come on, I'd better go down and make sure everything is going smoothly."

"Spoilsport!" he laughed

CHAPTER 20

It was a perfect evening, the white hot sun slowly metamorphosing into a golden orb sinking low in the sky, and the breath of a breeze took the edge off the heat. Nantes Place was lit with barely seen lanterns all along the drive, and towards the car park where Fred was already on duty to supervise the parking. Charles and Jennifer had cast a look around the marquee and it looked stunning. Mrs Fuller assured them that the caterers and their staff were all on schedule, and the string quartet had set up on the terrace and were tuning up their instruments. It was nearly seven o'clock. Jennifer's heart was thumping as she held Charles' hand. The uniformed waitresses were pouring the champagne into long flutes, and Charles reached over and offered one to her.

"I'd better not darling, I haven't had time to eat, and I don't want it to go to my head." For the thousandth time she pushed her hair back and smoothed down her dress.

"Well, I'm going to have one! Here have some elderflower pressé instead, it looks just like champagne." They toasted each other "Here's to a perfect evening my lovely!" They clinked their glasses together as they heard the sound of the first cars arriving.

Caitlin waited in her cottage in the granary and heard the cars too. Normally she would have been excited about going to a party but now things were different. She had chosen her outfit carefully selecting a simple little black dress, which hugged her body seductively and came a few inches above her knee showing off her long legs. The top was fitted too and had a V neck which was just off the shoulders. She put a simple rope of pearls around her neck and added pearl studs. Her tumbling dark curls were glossy, and she had added a deep shade of red lipstick for drama. The girls from Mileoak were going to give her a knock when they arrived, so that they could all go in together. She stood anxiously looking out of the window watching the cars rolling down the drive. Crikey there were going to be a lot of people coming, and she was glad that she knew quite a lot of them. One of the first to arrive was Amanda Lewington-Granger and her husband William - she was Chairman of the Hunt Supporters, arriving with Ian and Alice Grant, he was the Master of Fox Hounds for the Fittlebury. Just after her, picking their way towards the house, carefully lifting their long dresses were Rachel Pillsbury and Felicity Coleridge, with Giles, Rachel's husband and Michael Gainsborough, all of whom were bigwigs in the hunt. A screech of laughter caught her attention and Angus and Victoria Ferrers arrived by taxi, she was clinging on to his arm, shrieking out to the Pillsbury's - bloody social climbers! They lived in London most of the week, only coming down to their house at the weekend and for the odd social function. Caitlin couldn't stand them. She played with her pearls, and continued contemplating the guests arriving, her heart thudding in her chest. Then she saw Jeremy Gordon's Range Rover Sport coming down the drive, she knew that they were bringing Susie and Beebs, so she picked up her evening bag, checked her make-up and made her way out to meet them.

Charles and Jennifer were greeting their guests and she was starting to relax, everyone so far had been charming, complimenting her on her dress, and saying how marvellous the house was looking. Waitresses glided discreetly amongst the throngs with trays of champagne and canapés. The terrace was humming with the murmurings of guests and the black clad string quartet played sonorously in the background. Jennifer glanced around taking in the scene, the ladies in their cocktail dresses like a dazzling collection of exotic birds in a rainbow of colours; the men in their traditional dinner jackets, although there were quite a few seams straining from the weight the older men had put on since they had last worn them. Mrs Fuller hovering in the wings was organising the caterers and the waitresses. She heard a clamour of chatter and turned to see the Mileoak brigade being escorted out to the terrace. Jeremy and Katherine, her hand in the crook of his arm, Caitlin and Sandy following, with Beebs and Susie looking a little over-awed behind her. She had never been more delighted to see them, and made their introductions to Charles who knew Jeremy from the City, and Sandy a familiar face out hunting, but he was a little surprised to see the girls. How did Jennifer know them he wondered, he must ask her later. Although Jennifer longed to spend more time with them, they moved off along the terrace, as more guests arrived.

Jeremy hailed a passing waitress and took a glass of champagne, handing it to Katherine, and then one to Sandy and the girls. "Cheers! Here's to a lovely evening, and to a lucky man with five beautiful women to escort!"

"Bottoms up and down the hatch!" laughed Sandy tossing back her drink.

Jonty and Laura were rattling away in the Landrover. Jonty was in a black mood, swearing at the other motorists, and banging his hand on the steering wheel in rage, gesticulating rudely at anyone who was in his way. Laura sat quietly and said nothing, she knew better than to irritate him when he was in a temper. Huddled on the far side of the passenger bench seat, inwardly flinching at every expletive, she occasionally glanced across at him, his brows knitted together and his face contorted with anger. He had been like this all day long, and she knew it was not owing to tonight's outing - something else must have happened, but she knew better than to ask. The miles rolled past and soon they were approaching Fittlebury, the Landrover hurtling around the narrow lanes, the dust smoking up in plumes when it hit the verge as they veered to avoid oncoming vehicles. There seemed to be a lot of cars on the road tonight, heading away from the village, swanky Range Rovers, BMWs, Mercedes and the like.

"Fucking nobs, trouble is these wankers can't drive" muttered Jonty, as he pulled over for another 4x4. "Don't buy it, if you can't drive it mate!" he yelled.

"Jonty for fuck's sake! We are s'posed to be keeping a fucking low profile."

"Shut your mouth Laura, or I'll shut if for you. Wankers, they piss me off!"

"Listen babe, they piss me off too," she began gingerly," but you don't want to scupper the plan before we've even begun. If you carry on like this, we'll never pull it off y' know, they'd recognise us a mile off."

"Laura d' ya want me to punch your lights out? Eh? Is that what y're fucking asking for?" he grabbed her leg squeezing it hard between his fingers, making her wince, "So just shut the fuck up." Laura backed off straight away gasping, and cringed further away from him in her seat, snaking away from his vicious grasp.

"Jonty, please don't hurt me like that, I'm really sorry, very sorry, I won't say anything else, I mean it."

"Poor little Laura" he mocked "have I frightened you, well good if I have, perhaps I need to teach ya a lesson or two" He grabbed her hair, yanking it hard, so her head twisted awkwardly, and then pushed her away violently.

"Jonty, no please, I mean it, I won't say another word." She was frightened, his anger had never been so explosive, especially towards her. She silently shrank into her seat, not daring to look at him. He drove on angrily, swerving into the car park at the Fox, and pulling the Landrover up with a scrunch of the gravel. He leant forward, rocking his head onto the steering wheel. Then he turned slowly and looked at her, his eyes full of remorse.

"Babe, I'm sorry, so sorry." He put his hand out and took a tendril of her hair in his hand, gently winding it through his fingers, she braced herself instantly, "I dunno what comes over me sometimes." She didn't believe him, he was sorry now for his viciousness towards her, but something else was wrong, something which had prompted it, and for the life of her she couldn't think what that could be.

"S' okay Jonty." She was careful and frightened. "Shall we go in then?"

"Okay." He leant over and touched her leg, "Sorry babe. Forgiven?"

"Of course, come on, let's go in." She handed him his flat cap from her hand bag, "Here put this on." He jammed the cap on over his glistening skull, adjusting it over his eyes.

"Yeah, let's go in."

The slight breeze had blown some clouds across the sky, tiny scudding little fluffs of white, momentarily blotting out the sprinkle of stars. People were leaving the terrace and filtering into the marquee and having consulted the plan were now busy seating themselves at their tables, laughing and chattering. Bottles of red and white wine were opened on the table, the glasses and silver sparkling under the twinkling lights overhead. Jennifer glanced across her own table to Charles, who was deep in conversation with Duncan Worthington-Barnes, MFH of the hunt and a wealthy landowner, and with whom Charles had been friends for years. Deirdre his wife, had been one of those women who had snubbed her previously and she was making a supreme effort to engage Jennifer in conversation, in fact all of the women on the table were. It was almost as though they had made some secret pact before they came and were determined to be pleasant. She could see right through them of course, but she played their game, and was equally charming, smiling and listening in apparent fascination at the inane conversation. Charles, looked at her momentarily, raising his eyes slightly, and she smiled reassuringly at him.

Chloe and Oliver had arrived quite late, and had managed to slip into the throng of guests on the terrace without causing too much of a stir, grabbing a couple of glasses of champagne as they slid up to the others. They joined the snake of people moving towards the marquee.

"Who are we sitting with, have you looked on the plan?" asked Chloe.

"Yep, there's the seven of us, plus Grace and Colin Allington, and Harry James, the whipper in, so it should be a good crowd." said Susie, "I'm so glad that we're on a table where we all know each other."

"God yes, it makes such a difference."

"Christ, what Lady V is wearing, it's so old, it's vintage! Just look at Libby Newsome, she's dressed to kill, you could scrape her make up off with a knife!" They laughed and moved to their table, checking their name places, "This is us."

Colin and Grace were already at the table and Colin stood up as they approached hailing them heartily, pulling out chairs exaggeratedly for the ladies to sit down.

"The age of chivalry and all that" laughed Grace, "Hi everyone, how lovely to see you all."

Jeremy leant forward and kissed Grace on each cheek, "Gracie, you look wonderful!"

The women were all talking at once, complimenting each other on their dresses, when they were interrupted by a trio of girls, who had sprung onto the stage, taking up the microphone, all kitted up in spotted 1950s swirly skirted frocks and white sunglasses, their hair in pony tails, they looked amazing!

"How fabulous! What a great idea." said Katherine, as they started to sing, "I think it's going to be a real fun evening." Waiters and waitresses whisked round with the starters, and soon everyone was tucking in. Chloe glanced over at Caitlin, she looked very pale and tense, hardly looking at her and Oliver, and she thought briefly about what Patrick had told her, perhaps Ace was here tonight? Beebs and Susie were stuffing their mouths full, eating as though they had been starved for weeks, and Sandy and Oliver were toying with theirs, but knocking back the wine, engrossed in conversation. Harry James was animatedly talking to Grace and Colin, who were responding in between forkfuls of food. Chloe had not thought she was hungry, but the food was delicious, Jennifer had certainly done a good job, it must have all cost a fortune.

The Fox was very quiet, just the two terrier men propping up the bar, and a smattering of people in the garden. "Not many people here for a Saturday night" said Laura conversationally to Dick Macey, who was manning the bar. Dick looked them up and down, his copper's nose twitched suspiciously, these two were not from round here, and they didn't seem, well... quite right.

"No, I knew it was going to be quiet tonight, big bash on up at the Nantes Place, loads of people going. I haven't seen you around here before though have I?"

"Oh we come in quite a bit when we're passing," Laura lied, "but your barmaid usually serves us." Laura brushed off his enquiry vaguely and she and Jonty hastily picked up their glasses and went outside.

"Nosy old bastard, I didn't like the way he looked at us" whispered Laura

"Don't be paranoid babe, you always feel like that when you are doing a recce." They sat down at a bench in a corner of the garden catching the last rays of the fading sun, from their vantage point they had a good view of everyone coming in and going out. "No-one very interesting in here tonight - although it's still quite early. We'll see how it pans out and then take a mosey up to Charlie boy's place."

They drank in silence, Laura being cautious about what she said as Jonty was in a strange mood, his eyes glittering and spiteful. They heard the rumble of a van coming into the car park, a tall blonde-haired man jumped out. They watched him walk through the little gate and saw him take in who was sitting in the garden, hardly noticing the couple in the corner and went directly into the snug.

"Wonder who he is?" ventured Laura, "he looked like a local, he saw us y' know!"

Jonty sucked though his teeth exasperatedly, "Laura for fuck's sake, what have I just said, he probably is a local, but he won't think twice about us, unless you give him summat to look at! You are becoming a right pain in the arse, it's time I took over now, and if you can't deal with it, piss off!"

"Whatdya mean, you're taking over? Laura hissed at him urgently, "this is about me not you!"

"Shut it, you've just opened my eyes to some possibilities that's all, and you'll have your revenge don't worry, but I'll make some dosh in the meantime, so fucking keep it down."

She looked at him aghast "I don't like it Jonty, what are you talking about?"

He tapped the side of his nose, "You started this ball rolling babe, but I'm gonna finish it, you just do as you're told eh."

The party was in full swing, the main course had been cleared away and the desserts were being brought out to a series of delighted approval. The spotty clad singers had announced their last number, and Chloe could see the Jazz band waiting to set up in the wings. Sandy and Oliver were a bit pissed, and Katherine and Jeremy were deep in conversation with the Allingtons, only Caitlin seemed to be pre-occupied and uncomfortable, whilst Beebs and Susie were chatting up a delighted Harry. She missed John, okay it wasn't his thing much, but it would have been nice to do something together, without the kids for a change. She put her head close to Caitlin's, "I'm just popping out to the loo, want to come?" The girl looked so miserable. Caitlin stiffened as Chloe spoke and looked terrified for a moment, which was odd she thought, but Caitlin inclined her head and they pushed back their chairs and went out together. "You all right?" asked Chloe, she hardly thought that Caitlin would open up to her, but it was surprising how sometimes it was easier to talk to someone you didn't know so well.

Caitlin looked down at her shoes, avoiding Chloe's eyes "Ah, affairs of the heart, you know, life is not always straight forward, so it isn't."

"Anything you want to talk about? You're going out with Tony the copper aren't you?"

"That was over a long time ago, he's a nice guy to be sure, and we're still friends, but y' know we weren't really suited."

"Someone new then?" coaxed Chloe,

"Yes, but to be sure it's complicated." Caitlin looked wretched, wringing her hands together and still not able to face Chloe "Most of the time I cope with it you know, but tonight is hard."

"Who is it then, is he here? Why is it so hard?" Of course Chloe could not let on that she knew he was married, and any further chances of discovering who the mystery man was evaporated, as a gush of excited laughter heralded the arrival of Beebs and Susie clattering up the steps to the loos.

"Hey, you two, enjoying yourselves?"

"Whoa Chloe, what a do, must have cost a shed load of money, and we are having a great time!" Chloe looked at them fondly, it wasn't often they had a fancy treat like tonight. Caitlin disappeared into the loo and locked the door. Beebs made a silent '*what's up with her?*' face to the others, and Chloe shrugged her shoulders, poor Caitlin.

Jennifer was having a good time, Charles could not have tried harder she thought. She was even warming a little to their companions, shoving the bitter thoughts to the back of her mind with fierce determination. Sophie had been right, this was a perfect dress and her understated make up made the others seem a bit raddled somehow. She felt confident about herself; she had lost that brittle appearance when she had tried so hard to fit in, this all felt natural now, and she liked it. The girl singers had been her idea, although Mrs Fuller had sniffed her mighty disapproval, not the *done* thing at all, but Jennifer had been adamant, and wow they had been a real success! The food had been exquisite, and the wine was flowing freely, and as she looked around the marquee, the lights sparkling jauntily, giving a soft glow to the women's faces, she knew it was going well. Only another few hours to go she thought, and realised with surprise that she didn't want the party to end after all. The jazz band was just starting up, and Charles was cradling a brandy, putting it down, he motioned to her to stand and took her hand, leading her to the dance floor. Amidst applause, and admiring glances from their guests, they kicked off the dancing to Glenn Miller's '*In the Mood*'. They laughed and twirled around and were soon joined by others, the band swung into '*One O'Clock Jump*', the infectious beat encouraging more and more people to the floor. Jennifer was gasping with laughter, "Oh Charles, it's going so well, I'm so happy!"

"You deserve it darling, you're the most beautiful woman here tonight, this is the best party at Nantes for many years." Jennifer flushed with pleasure, at long last the ghost of Celia was being laid.

Celia however, was not the only one being laid, lying on the lawn at the back of the shrubbery, her short dress around her waist and an exploring hand inside her knickers, was Libby Newsome, she had given up with Oliver, he was just too pre-occupied. He hadn't even really noticed her, well fuck him she thought. Angus was getting a bit keen, she pushed him away, "Not so fast sweetie, supposing your wife comes out?"

"Victoria, she's too busy hobnobbing her way into social circles, to notice where I am", Angus whispered urgently, his drunken breath smelt sour, and his advances becoming a bit agitated. "Come on Libby, y' know I've always fancied you, and you got such great tits!" His hand was trying to pull down the straps of her dress. Oh well, thought Libby, she was a bit tipsy and would probably regret this in the morning, but why not? He sprang her breasts free and he plunged down onto them like a hungry wolf. It was better than nothing, and she mused she was a 21st century girl - her motto was use men, like they had used women for years, and she began to fumble with his trousers. It was a loveless and unsatisfying fuck for her though, and all over in a flash.

"Sweetie, you city boys are all the same." she admonished. Angus was hastily dressing himself, looking around anxiously, obviously not too confident now that he wouldn't be found out. Libby was pulling her dress straight, "Although Charles seems to have mended his ways, he looked very loved up this evening."

"Well Charles ended up marrying his mistress, fatal mistake."

"Didn't look too fatal tonight" Libby said wistfully, her modern ethos momentarily disappearing, "In fact I've never seen him enjoying himself so much, certainly more so than he ever was with Celia!" They separated and walked independently back into the party, Libby returning via the loos, so as not to draw attention to them, confident that no-one had seen them leave.

Beebs nudged Chloe, "They're back then, look one of Libby's false eyelashes has come adrift!" They both laughed, "She's a real man eater that Libby! Oh, and there goes Angus, he's going to get a right ear bashing from Victoria later." In fact Victoria was not stupid, and she knew her husband too well, in fact she was relieved, thinking she wouldn't have to put up with his sweaty advances tonight now, adultery had its advantages!

The party thrashed on. Oliver felt a hand on his arm, he was just sitting out this dance, having boogied with Sandy through a medley of swinging tunes, and he turned to see Caitlin, her face concerned.

"You okay?" he asked, "Coping?" his eyes held hers, her soft lovely face gazing into his.

"Why shouldn't she be coping?" piped up Susie, coming up behind them.

They both looked up in surprise, "Hmmm, I meant about Lucy leaving so suddenly an' all?"

"Oh that, you're better off without her Caitlin, she was a lazy cow and a right trollop! I've a friend who's looking for a job, I'll give 'em your number shall I?"

"That'd be grand Susie, give me a ring tomorrow and you can tell me more, although Jennifer says she is going to be doing the interviews with me, so I'd have to run it past her."

"Good for Jen!" Susie grinned, momentarily forgetting herself.

"For the love of God, don't let her hear you call her that" laughed Caitlin, she'd be furious, so she would!"

"Yep, she would!" countered Susie quickly covering up her mistake "Still can't quite believe she invited us tonight y' know!"

Caitlin considered, "No, nor why she asked me either come to think on it! Still it's a grand party, although, I'm just going to pop back to the yard , Queenie was a bit stiff tonight, and I brought her in, just thinking she might be in for a touch of laminitis, all I can do with. So I am just going to check her."

Oliver jumped up immediately, almost knocking over a glass, "I'll come with you Caitlin, I know I'm not on call, but just in case you need a hand." Susie watched them go, she was a nice girl was Caitlin, really cared about the horses, there wouldn't have been many grooms who would have left a party like this to check up on a horse. That was real dedication for you.

Jonty and Laura, had spent an uneasy evening in the Fox, Laura hardly trusting herself to speak, her thoughts running wildly in her head. Jonty on the other hand was excited, he still didn't let on what he was planning, but she knew it had to be pretty big, and she was worried. Her thoughts of revenge had run along the lines of getting the Hunt Sabs interested, letting down tyres, spray paint, that kind of thing, she wished she had never involved him, but it was too late now.

"Cheer up babe, stop worrying" he said interrupting and guessing her thoughts, "old matey will have his just desserts like you want but there is a nice spin off for me and the boys!" Jonty looked hard at her, he didn't want her panicking at the last minute, so he added "Besides we haven't done anything yet, and won't for a month or two until the plans are made, so relax and enjoy yourself, worry when you have to." Laura just nodded feebly, she did not trust herself to speak, lest he go overboard again, and in a way he was right, sitting here in the pub, they were not doing anything illegal, and perhaps not knowing was better.

Jonty glanced at the church clock it was 10.30pm, "Come on, you and I are going for a little walk, but I'm going to move the Landrover first, just in case we are a little while." They finished up their drinks and went out to the car park. Dick Macey who had been keeping an eye on them through the little windows of the snug, walked out to collect the empties, watching them drive off as he did so. Bloody townies he thought, locals would have brought their glasses back, and there was something odd about those two.

Jonty pulled the Landrover into the small parking space in the lane opposite the church. They got out and tentatively went into the churchyard edging along the path with a flash light which Jonty had on his key ring. Laura clutched hold of his arm, it was really spooky, she could feel the hairs on her arms standing on end and her fingertips tingling, and she felt a desperate urge to pee. The tombstones loomed up on either side of them and the grass rustled lightly in the little breeze, compared to the street lights and constant bustle of London, it was eerily silent. They crept onwards, stumbling occasionally until they felt the kissing gate. The meadow opened out ahead of them but it was almost impossible to see the way to the spinney, the night had become quite dark and the little clouds of earlier were building up to cover the sky. Jonty decided that rather than follow the path across the field, they would be better to keep to the hedge, that way they would have to eventually come to the stile into the spinney. They seemed to be stumbling on for ever, until they saw the treeline etched darker against the sky and clambered over the stile. From within the spinney, the sound of music drifting on the air and the glow of the marquee lights in the distance made it easier to find their way. At last they came to the final stile from the field into the bottom of the drive itself, with its jaunty lanterns and concealed spotlights all the way along to the house.

"Keep on the grass, behind the lights" Jonty ordered in a whisper, "or they may see us or hear our feet on the gravel." Creeping down the drive, keeping well back behind the shrubs they suddenly jolted to an abrupt halt, as they saw two figures coming towards them. Jonty dragged Laura down to the ground, crouching like vermin and ready to make a run for it. The voices although hushed were clear on the stillness of the night.

"It's all coming to a head now, I know that. It's madness to stay together, our marriage is a farce, but of course you know that. I just have to make sure that the timing is right, for both our sakes."

"I don't know what to say."

"Nothing you can say, I have to deal with it that's all, before I can move on properly."

"I can totally understand that, it must be so difficult ."

The figures moved on, then took a turning off from the main drive, and Laura and Jonty squatted absolutely still until they could hear them no longer. Gingerly they stood up, and started to walk on, the beat of the music was louder now, and they kept close to the shelter of the rhododendrons. A car came from the direction of the house, making its way slowly up the drive and once again they held their breath lest they should be seen, but the car moved on unaware of them. Keeping as hidden as they could, they came round the last bend of the drive and there was the house, its mellow walls glowing golden from the spotlights at the front, and the cascading water tumbling from the fountain.

Laura clutched Jonty's arm, "Fuck me, what a place!" she whispered.

"Bloody lucky bastards, still they can afford to lose a few bob can't they?"

Fred Windrush, no longer needed to park the cars, had disappeared into the kitchen to have a glass or two with his wife, and so they made their way unimpeded around the granary towards the garages, and the back of the house, carefully listening for the tell-tale scrunch of anyone walking on the gravel.

"But what are we doing here?" Laura urged, beginning to feel quite faint at the thought of being caught.

"We're just looking - casing the place. Tonight is not the night, but we need to know the layout, and find out more about these people, and this is the perfect opportunity, so shut the fuck up and keep your eyes open."

The kitchen garden lay to one side and there were lights blazing out of the windows. They peeked in, two old biddies were sitting in the kitchen drinking what looked like sherry from small glasses and an old boy was in a rocking chair, with a bottle of beer. Jonty nudged Laura to move and they slid around the corner, the light from the house and the garden now making it easy to see the way. A number of older folk were leaving, and they could hear them chorusing their thanks for a good evening and their goodbyes, but there were still quite a lot of the stuck up wankers lounging on the terrace smoking and drinking, and the shadows of dancers in the marquee, silhouetted against the thin canvas. Periodically people were disappearing behind a tall hedge - obviously going to the bog. Jonty and Laura edged their way into the centre of a large shrub and waited quietly, Laura crossing her legs, she wanted to pee so badly, but she was too afraid of being challenged. They watched a couple snogging behind the marquee, and the waiters and waitresses drinking the dregs from the left over bottles of wine, before dashing back to replenish the stocks for the revellers. They overheard snatches of conversation, talking about the coming hunting season, the puppy show - whatever that was, and someone called Libby Newsome's behaviour. It was all mundane talk, and they started to get a bit fidgety and cold despite the sultry night. From behind them, they heard the sound of footsteps and a soft Irish voice murmuring, but they couldn't distinguish what was being said, nor the reply either, but they saw two people arm in arm coming around the corner from the kitchen absorbed in earnest conversation. The man, tall and blonde, leant down and kissed the girl on the cheek and gave her a hug, parting before they walked on towards the terrace.

"Jonty, I'm frightened and it's getting cold now" hissed Laura, "there's nothing much to see here, 'cept a load of nobs!"

"Know the enemy, know the enemy Laura, that's the first rule, so watch and listen." They heard the distance sound of the church clock chiming midnight, along with a deep rumble of thunder.

Inside the marquee, the party was going full pelt. The jazz band were belting out popular tunes and Katherine and Jeremy were rock and rolling, doing exaggerated lifts and turns to the approving shouts of the onlookers. Charles and Jennifer were whirling around with different partners, occasionally catching each other's eye conspiratorially and laughing. Jennifer was really happy, it was a huge success, and most of the stiff upper lip brigade had gone home, leaving the hard core revellers. Beebs was well stuck into Harry the Whip, and Susie was in deep conversation with Tom Snowhill. Sandy was dancing with Mark Templeton who was clearly very smitten with her.

Chloe was sitting at the edge of the dance floor talking to Julia and Andrew. He was such a nice chap, although she more often than not saw Oliver these days at the yard, she knew him well, and he was a good vet. He had been a real catch when she first knew him, he was good looking, hardworking, and successful, building up his practice from nothing. Everybody liked Andrew. Julia was a beautiful woman, with chic bobbed dark hair and one of those perfectly made up faces which never seemed to have a crease or line in it. She was wearing a simple black dress which must have cost a fortune with diamond studs in her ears. Even though she was talking to Chloe, she was constantly looking over her shoulder and round the marquee to see if there was someone better or more interesting to whom she could talk. Chloe couldn't help it but she didn't like her much, she was always talking about herself and her tennis and her bridge and her clothes, and Chloe didn't think she'd ever heard her once ask about anyone or anything else. Poor Andrew she thought, he was a gorgeous looking guy and they made a handsome couple but you could see that Julia wasn't interested in him either.

There was a brief respite in the music, and the band leader announced that they'd be playing the last two numbers. At that moment Oliver and Caitlin appeared, and Oliver sat down a little unsteadily, a tad bit drunk.

"How's the horse?" asked Chloe, watching as Julia used their arrival in obvious relief excusing herself, having spotted Rachael Pillsworthy.

"Oh, 't will be fine till tomorrow now" breathed Caitlin "I'm probably just over-reacting."

"What's this, did you have a problem Caitlin?" asked Andrew, "You only had to ask."

"No probs buddie, we only took a quick look, didn't we Caitlin, and if we'd needed you, one or other of us could easily have popped back. Don't worry I've had a bit too much to drink, so I wouldn't have done anything anyway."

"Glad to hear it!" There was a tiny pause, whilst Andrew took them both in with a long look. Caitlin blushed and looked away but Oliver roared with laughter!

"Come on Chloe, let's have this dance, our cab'll be here soon!" He dragged Chloe onto the dance floor and they were soon boogying away.

"Do you want to dance Caitlin?" asked Andrew, "Although I warn you, I'm no Fred Astaire" He leant over and grabbed Caitlin by the hand and joined the others on the dance floor. The music had changed to a slow number and couples were clamped around each other swaying to the soft lilt of *Summertime*. The evocative beat of the music was a perfect closing number, Charles was nuzzling Jennifer's neck, and as Andrew hand circled Caitlin's waist he watched Oliver whispering in Chloe's ear. Grace and Colin, his face flushed from all the exertion, were dancing cheek to cheek, it had been a good evening he mused, he glanced over and saw Julia, deep in conversation with Rachael and smiled at her, but she looked away.

The music came to an end, and everyone drifted reluctantly apart, when Charles suddenly threw his hands up in the air "Who's for swimming then!"

Jonty and Laura from outside, heard the roar go up, and watched open mouthed as a crowd of a dozen or so people stampeded out of the marquee and off across the lawn.

"What the fuck!!" exclaimed Jonty.

There were shrieks of laughter, women throwing off their shoes, men tearing off their bow ties and shirts. After the initial pandemonium, Jonty and Laura gingerly slunk out, under cover of the shadows, staying well behind the lights, and crept over the lawn towards the excited voices echoing in the night. The turquoise water of the pool was lit and sparkling under the night sky, and men were stripping off into their underpants and the ladies in their underwear, great spouts of water flying everywhere as they plunged into the pool, gasping and yelling. Jennifer went into the pool house and brought out baskets of swimwear for those ladies who were too modest to swim in the buff and had no underwear. She stepped out of her own dress and laid it carefully over the back of a lounger standing momentarily in her white Janet Reger bra and lace French knickers, took a run and plunged in to join the others.

Jonty and Laura stood peering through the trellis at the top of the outer fence taking in the scene, but unbeknown to them, they were not the only witnesses. Pete stood motionless, his black hooded eyes dark with malice was also watching from the shadows.

Mrs Fuller too, had heard the shout go up and bustled outside, immediately seeing what was going on, oh dear God, she thought, this is going to be a long night! She turned on her heel, and stomped back to the kitchen.

"What's going on then?" asked Doris yawning, "What's all the ruddy noise?"

"Doris, look sharp, go to the laundry room and bring out more large towels and robes, they're only bloody swimming! Fred can you go down to the cellar and fetch up some brandy and I'll make some coffee, they'll surely need it." She was smiling though, she knew the party had gone well, all thanks to her of course she preened, even if she had to admit that those spotty singers had been a good idea. The food had been excellent too, and she must remember to tip the waiting staff, they had worked hard.

Doris clumped back into the kitchen, her eyes only just visible over the armful of towels. "Right, we'll take those over then, and Fred - keep an eye on the water." She relieved Doris of the robes and they both struggled back over the lawn towards the pool just as a great fork of lightening came down in the fields momentarily lighting up the whole lawn.

"Here who are they?" Doris shouted, pointing to Jonty and Laura, "They're not guests! Where did they come from?"

231

"Hey you!" shouted Mrs Fuller, "What're you doing?"

Jonty and Laura, turned around seeing the two women bundling towards them, the towels tumbling to the ground as they came.

"Quick Laura!" Jonty grabbed Laura by the hand and they sped past the women, knocking them aside, running as fast as they could around the kitchen garden, towards the granary and the drive.

"Pah, who were they?" grunted Mrs Fuller righting herself, "You okay Doris?"

"Yer, I am, but no thanks to them! What're they up to I wonder?"

"No good, that's for sure. Come on let's get these over to the pool, and I'll go to the house and check the silver." Overhead another rumble of thunder growled, and Mrs Fuller said "better hurry, it's gonna rain for sure!"

They arrived at the poolside, just as the revellers were getting out, shivering in the colder air and another streak of lightening split the sky, wet hands gratefully receiving the towels being doled out by Mrs Fuller and Doris. Jennifer put on a robe, her hair wet against her face and grinned at Charles.

"What a great idea darling, but it's freezing now, come on let's get inside, I think we're in for a big storm!" The last stragglers gathered up their clothes and they all made a run for the marquee as the first fat drops of rain started.

Mrs Fuller marched back into the house, instructing Doris to make the coffee and take it out, and Fred to bring the brandy. Hardly pausing she stalked around the rooms, checking all the valuables, but nothing seemed to have been touched, she would tell Mr Charles in the morning, no point in disturbing him now she thought.

CHAPTER 21

The storm raged for most of the night, hefty claps of thunder grumbling away for hours, and the rain drove down persistently. Jennifer lay snug and warm wrapped around Charles, who was gently snoring. She was content - it had been such a success, the last guests drifting away at about 2am, after much coffee and brandy in the marquee. It had been a great idea to go swimming, everyone really let their hair down, and Mrs Fuller was a treasure arriving with all those towels and robes. She gave a start - her dress! She had left it on the back of the sun lounger and it would be drenched! Oh well, it can be cleaned she thought, nothing she could do now, and finally she fell into a dreamless sleep.

Chloe too had crept in quietly in the early hours, glad to nestle up to John, who put his arm around her and she snuggled up under the crook of his arm. She had enjoyed the evening, it had been a really good bash, but she had missed him, and she hoped that they'd all had a good time too watching Shrek. Again she felt the twinges of torn loyalties, still it was half term now and she would really make it up to the kids, pity if the weather was breaking just before their outing to Arundel Castle. Oliver was sweet and had been good company, making sure he escorted her from the taxi right up to the front door, and the girls had been delivered back safely. Sandy had seemed to hit it off with Mark Templeton, and he had driven her home. In that half state before sleeping, she mused about Caitlin and Oliver, they had been gone a long time when they went to check that horse hadn't they? Still Ace couldn't be Oliver could he?

Beebs and Susie were busy chattering having a last coffee before turning in, even though it was 2.30am.

Beebs clutched her head "Oh God, I've gotta be up in four and a half hours!" she moaned. "Still what a great night that was, Jen certainly knows how to put on a party, and that food was fantastic!"

"You looked like you were having Harry the Whip for dessert!" laughed Susie, "He's quite dishy isn't he?"

"Yes, amazing what a DJ can do for a man. He's a good kisser!"

"That all! Looked a bit more than that to me!"

"You're a fine one to talk, you were all wrapped around that Tom!" countered Beebs.

"Yep, he's kinda cute, not really my type but I said I'd meet him at the Fox later."

"Good on you, but I've gotta go to bed, I'm knackered!"

Oliver grappled noisily with the lock of the door, willing himself to be quiet in the way that only drunk people do, when they know they are making a hell of a racket. He drank a couple of glasses of water down at a gulp and took two Paracetamol. He groaned he knew was going to be sorry in the morning. Trying desperately to be quiet, he felt his way up the stairs to the bedroom, not turning on the lights, and expecting at any minute to hear Suse shouting at him, but to his surprise she was totally silent. In fact he mused, he couldn't even hear her breathing. Tentatively he felt over to her side of the bed, it was empty. Clumsily switching on the light, he saw that the bed was undisturbed, and the doors of the wardrobe were half open. He lurched over pulling open the cupboard, all of her clothes had gone; he looked under the bed, and their suitcases as well. He hurried into the bathroom, her things were missing from in there too.
Dangerously leaping down the stairs, two at a time, he went into the sitting room, nothing - all of the photographs had gone, and the little knick knacks she had collected over the years. Propped on the mantel shelf was a note addressed to him, he ripped it open, read the contents and sank down onto the sofa, his head in his hands. She had left him.

Mark drove Sandy home, pulling his Discovery into the drive of her cottage behind her car. It was a quaint house nestling just outside the village, and not small either, traditionally tile hung with quaint little windows and rambling roses. They had sat in the car for a moment listening to the pounding rain and Sandy invited Mark in for a nightcap, and now they were tangled up on the sofa together, snogging like teenagers. Mmmm, where had this man been she thought! He was quite delicious! She was not quite so abandoned that she hadn't sneakily gone up to the bathroom to quickly brush her teeth, and now she could enjoy herself uninhibited by the thought of any dog's breath! Mark was stroking her face as he kissed her, running his fingertip along her collar bone down to her cleavage, and cupping her breast with his hand. Her hands were running through his hair, and tracing his cheek as she kissed him. They parted sitting back, both unexpectedly surprised at the frisson of electricity between them.

"God you're gorgeous Sandy, I'm sorry if you think I'm a bit forward." he stammered, "but I just can't help myself!"

"Mark, sweetie, you're gorgeous too - don't apologise." and she leant forward and kissed him again, taking his hand she led him up the stairs.

Jonty and Laura had scarpered from the party, tearing down the gravel, skipping in and out of the shrubs when the odd car head lights from departing guests came along the drive. Laura was in a real state, she knew now exactly what the expression '*your heart is in your mouth*' meant. Jonty urged her on, tugging hard on her hand, and she was stumbling and falling as they ran across the field towards the spinney, the thunder rumbled overhead and big rain drops started to fall. Once there, Jonty cocked his head to one side and listened. Nothing, no-one had followed, silly old cows he thought. He looked at Laura who was panting beside him, bent double trying to catch her breath.

"You a'right babe? That was a laugh eh?"

"Jonty, it may have been a laugh to you but it scared the shit out of me" she countered angrily. "What the fuck were you thinking of?

We were nearly caught!"

"Aw, don't make such a fuss, you're always moaning these days. Anyways you didn't get caught did you? Come'n - home time." He caught hold of her hand again, lugging her along behind him as they floundered across the meadow trying to find the kissing gate. They fell against it in relief, and Jonty shook her by the shoulders, "now pull yourself together, walk normally, there may be people about."

She took a deep breath, and threw him off, and they walked sedately through the churchyard. The tombstones loomed up creepily on either side of them, and the rain drummed down hard and persistent soaking them to the core. When they finally found the Landrover they were both cold and dripping wet and she had never been so relieved. Laura slunk miserably into the passenger seat. A real old storm was raging overhead, the lightening flashing periodically and the thunder was almost ear-splitting. She was tired, cold and fed up, and was beginning to wonder what she had gotten herself into with Jonty.

The storm died away overnight and the morning dawned dry, but misty and damp at Nantes. The overnight deluge had left the garden refreshed with that peculiar smell of '*just rained*' after a long dry spell, the droplets on the grass and the shrubs sparkling like little gems. The low wall around the terrace was strewn with wine glasses and cigarette ends which had missed the discreetly placed sand pots and instead littered the flagstones; wrought iron chairs were long abandoned upturned and askew against the tables. The marquee too, had a '*tent*' smell, enhanced by the damp, and the tables were peppered with empty wine bottles, bits of cutlery, coffee cups, and brandy glasses. The ornate table decorations looked quite incongruous against the debris surrounding them.

Mrs Fuller stood at the entrance, surveying the wreckage from last evening, luckily she had organised an army of help to clear up this morning and hopefully, it should be done by the time those two got up. She glanced up at the windows on the upper floor, and the small balcony to the master bedroom. She huffed in satisfaction, she was pleased with herself. She heard the quiet chatter of voices as

Doris came round the corner with another two women, the same pair that had been on duty in the lower snug last night.

"Righto, we're here. Where shall we start Freda?"

"If I give you black sacks can you go round and pick up the rubbish Doris, don't forget to do the terrace will you, there's cigarette ends all over the place. Gwen, can you clear any glasses, the ordinary plain ones belong to the caterers and use their crates, which are at the back of the stage, to stack them in, we don't have to wash 'em. The cut glass ones belong in the house so can go into the kitchen. Eva, can you put the table decorations on the terrace outside and clear the table cloths and napkins and put them in sacks to give back to the caterers too?"

The women grabbed the sacks, and Mrs Fuller started picking up the towels and robes that were thrown over the back of the chairs, they would all have to go to the laundry this lot! They worked methodically for some while, finding a stray silk scarf and a pearl earring, a small clutch bag with no name, and just some perfume and lipstick in it, no doubt there would a phone call about those later. They laboriously stacked the tables to one side, and the chairs one on top of each other, the rest would be cleared by the marquee people on Monday, including the lights.

"Come on let's go make ourselves a cuppa in the kitchen, we deserve it." They gladly abandoned the work, and trooped out of the marquee and Mrs Fuller turned to Doris, "Be a duck and nip over and see if there are any robes or towels left by the pool and bring 'em in, and I'll get that cuppa on the go. Although I'd better get some coffee and toast ready for them upstairs. There are some puds for us, left over from last night." She shuffled off to the kitchen, Gwen and Eva in tow.

Doris grumbled her way across the lawn, dragging some black sacks with her, why was she sent over to get the bloody towels! Why couldn't Eva or Gwen have gone? She was dog tired, still at least she would get a good bonus for all the extra work she and Fred had put in, there was never a problem about the money anyway. This grass was soaking, she looked gloomily at her slip ons, her feet would be sopping at this rate.

The pool area was wet and glistening too, the water looked cold as it lapped gently against the sides. Towels and robes were all over the place, just left in heaps, and sodden with rain, waiting for some skivvy like me to pick them up she thought. She stooped down crossly gathering them up and stuffed them in the sack, looking at all the glasses and bottles littered about, she had better pick them up too she thought, otherwise Freda would only moan at her. What a bloody mess! Painstakingly collecting everything up, she glanced around wearily. Job done - now for a mug of tea! Then, her eye caught sight of another robe thrown over the back of the sun lounger on the other side of the pool, sighing she traipsed around the edge to fetch it. Bending over to reach, she realised that it wasn't a robe at all, but a dress, saturated from the rain. A gorgeous cream silk, it must be the one the missus was wearing and she must have left it here last night. She started to fold it up, and then gasped out loud - to her horror she realised that the beautiful dress had been slashed to ribbons.

Charles and Jennifer were in the small breakfast room, just off the terrace. Mrs Fuller had delivered a tray of tea and coffee with toast and preserves, when they saw Doris Windrush through the casement windows tearing across the lawn heading back to the kitchen, trailing a large black sack.

"She's in a hurry" remarked Charles, turning back to the Sunday paper.

"Yes, wonder why?" mused Jennifer, "She was as white as sheet, looked as though she had seen a ghost." She began toying with her toast, sipping her tea, she wished Charles would put down the paper, she wanted to talk to him about last night, to analyse the evening. She was so pleased with the way it had all gone, even those old bags were nice to her, she smiled to herself grimly. There was a sudden sharp rap at the door and Mrs Fuller barged in, her normal efficient appearance had evaporated and she looked really flustered, and had a rubbish sack in her hand.

"Mr Charles, Madam, I really must speak with you both."

"Mrs Fuller" said Charles lazily, not looking up from his paper, "Can't it wait until we've had our breakfast?"

"I'm afraid it can't Mr Charles, it's very important." The tone of her voice was agitated and urgent, and her large bulky frame was heaving.

"Very well" Charles shook out the paper, folded it and gave her his full attention. Jennifer looked at her quizzically, she looked in a real state, what on earth could be the matter.

"I don't quite know how to say this Mr Charles, but ..."

"Just get on with it please Mrs Fuller, I've a bit of a headache this morning" yawned Charles. Not surprised thought Jennifer, the amount of alcohol you had last night, but she refrained from saying anything, she just hoped Mrs Fuller was not giving in her notice.

"Mrs Fuller, are you all right, do you need to sit down?" she said anxiously.

"No thank you Madam, I'll be fine, but something dreadful has happened, and I suppose I should have alerted you last night, but I didn't want to spoil the party."

Charles, clearly exasperated snapped "Look Mrs F for God's sake, just get on with it please."

"Well, we've found this by the poolside!" She dramatically opened the sack pulled out the ruined dress holding it up for them to see.

Jennifer's hands flew to her face, "But that's my dress, I left it by the pool last night, what on earth has happened to it?"

"My God, how did this happen Mrs Fuller?" ranted Charles, "Who's responsible?"

"Doris Windrush was just clearing up the pool area and she found it like this, draped over the back of the sun lounger! We've absolutely no idea how it happened, but Mr Charles, ...there is something else I have to tell you" she continued meekly and went on to describe how the intruders had been seen in the garden last night.

"Why the hell didn't you tell me about this when you saw them" stormed Charles, "is anything missing from the house that you can see?"

"I didn't tell you Mr Charles, because they ran off, and when I checked the house, nothing was missing. I'd believed them to be just passing and having heard the party decided to see if they could gate crash. This morning when I saw Madam's dress, I realised their intentions must have been more sinister. I'm terribly sorry."

"Mrs Fuller, you weren't to know of course" said Jennifer gently, "You were so busy last evening organising our wonderful party, and I can quite understand your train of thought. Can't you Charles?"

"Well I suppose so, but what to do now, too late to ring the police of course. Are you sure nothing else was damaged or taken Mrs Fuller?"

"Not that I can see Mr Charles, and I'm so dreadfully sorry." She looked at Jennifer gratefully, "I'm afraid the dress is beyond repair Madam."

"Well, that can't be helped, as long as nothing is missing and everyone is safe, that's what matters more. Leave the dress here, and go and have a sit down Mrs Fuller and have a cup of tea, you look as though you could do with one, and Charles and I will discuss this and decide what to do."

"Thank you Madam, I do feel very shocked I have to admit." She turned around and went out of the door, her shoulders stooped and looking very old.

Sandy woke stretching like a cat in the white cotton sheets, their heavy quality pleasing her and she leant on her elbow and turned to face Mark, who was still sleeping. Thank heavens for a man who doesn't snore she thought naughtily. Mark had a good body, which had not run to fat and he had no beer belly, and even though he was so relaxed in sleep he was really well toned. He was an attractive man, not too tall either, which was always a bonus as Sandy was so tiny. He had light brown hair cut short, with flecks of grey, and a strong angular face. One of the things Sandy liked was his hands, long tapering fingers but strong and clean nails, another bonus she considered, her own natural fastidiousness extending to her partners.

He must have felt her watching him, as he slowly opened his eyes and smiled at her. She smiled right back.

"Morning, sleep well?"

"Mmm, yes I did thank you, and you?" He rolled over to face her, and wrapped his arms around her, "You're still gorgeous, you know that?"

She kissed the top of his head, and he kissed her neck, moving his mouth down to her breasts, "Keep telling me!" she murmured.

"You're gorgeous, you're gorgeous, and you're gorgeous" he laughed looking up at her. "Coming in the shower with me?"

Sandy thought, he gets better and better. "You bet!" They threw back the sheets and clambered out of the bed, stopping to admire each other, "and you know, I've said it before but you're pretty gorgeous yourself!" She walked into the bathroom, her feet padding on the painted white floorboards. He followed her, placing both his hands on her hips, and kissing her shoulder.

"Wow! This is nice!"

"Yes, I like nice things." she laughed.

The bathroom was all white except for pale blue painted woodwork, with a blue and white striped blind half drawn at the window. A huge shower was in the corner, with two sparkling chromium shower heads, and a free standing hip bath in the other.

"I converted one of the bedrooms to have this." She pulled him into the shower and switched on the taps, they both gave a gasp as the cold jets shot all over them, and as the water gradually flowed hotter, the glass panels started to steam up. She took the shower gel, her favourite Jo Malone Grapefruit fragrance and began to soap him all over.

"Good enough to eat" she murmured.

"Try me" he looked down, at her spiky hair, her intelligent blue eyes, thinking, I really like this woman.

The initial shock was huge, Suse had always threatened she would go, but Oliver had never truly believed her. His senses dulled by alcohol and then the shock of finding Suse had gone had made him maudlin, he sipped a coffee, and tried to make some sense of it all - he was so tired, not just because of the booze but emotionally and physically. He could no longer deal with this he thought, I must sleep, I may wake up and find a solution. He fell into bed, fitfully tossing and turning, only to waken early, and pace around the house, pulling open drawers and cupboards. Everything of hers had gone, and there was no trace that she had ever been here at all. He slumped down on a chair in the kitchen, sitting in his boxers, the house felt empty, her presence, even if at times it had been a pernicious one, was better than this dreadful cavernous silence. Of course he considered, in a way she had forced his hand, made a difficult decision easy for him, but not like this, surely not like this.

There was a ring at the doorbell, he glanced at the kitchen clock, it was 11am on a Sunday morning, who on earth could that be? He must look terrible, he looked in the mirror, his face was haggard, with a definite growth of beard, and his eyes were bloodshot. The doorbell rang again, more insistently this time, and he knew he'd have to answer. He wrenched it open, to find Andrew standing on the doorstep. Andrew took one look at Oliver, clearly shocked at his appearance.

"Blimey! You okay mate? What's up?"

"Suse has left me" said Oliver flatly, "I came back last night and she'd gone, she must have been planning it for days."

"Oh fuck me, I'm sorry, what a bloody shock! Look can I come in?"

"Sorry, course you can." Oliver stood aside and Andrew followed him into the kitchen "Coffee?"

"Yes, great. Look Oliver, I know it's been a terrible shock, but let's face it mate, you haven't been happy together for ages."

"I bloody know that, but it doesn't make it any easier y' know" Oliver said bitterly, running his hand through his hair in despair. "It was just so out of the blue, just to come back and find she'd done a

242

bunk. I know she'd threatened it but actually I'd thought we might just try again."

"Did she say she would then?"

"Well no, she didn't actually, but I thought she might. I was just trying to find the time to talk it through."

"What was stopping you then, with the time thing I mean?"

"Oh God, I don't know, it's my fault, I just didn't make the time, and now she's gone and it's too late."

"Look Oli, you will probably see things differently in a day or so, see that maybe it's for the best, for both of you." Andrew looked at him closely, he looked awful, but in a funny sort of way almost relieved too, and from what he was saying he certainly felt guilty about it all. He thought about Oli disappearing with Caitlin last night, and was desperate to ask him about it, but clearly now wasn't the right time, but he felt sure something had been going on.

"It's hard to see that right now frankly." Oliver interrupted Andrew's thoughts, "I've made a right mess of things."

"Don't be so hard on yourself, or Suse either, sometimes these things just don't work out, at least you don't have any children and the house is only rented, so you can start again. You're a young guy and have your whole life ahead of you."

"Oh mate, it doesn't feel like that right now, I've been so preoccupied with other stuff …" Oliver's phone beeped an incoming text message, he picked it up, glancing at the screen.

"Suse?" queried Andrew.

"No, just a mate" said Oliver quickly, "I'll reply later. Now did you want me for something?"

"Nope not really, just fancied talking about the Mill, I haven't mentioned it to Julia, not that she'd be particularly interested" he added wryly, "not unless it affected her bloody lifestyle. I just can't stop thinking about it – that's all. Nothing compared to the shit you're going through. Come on, I'm going make you some scrambled eggs, helps the hangover, if nothing else."

"I wonder who they were darling, it's not the dress that upsets me, just that someone was here with such malicious intent." Charles and Jennifer, were lounging in the bath together, sitting at opposite ends, he was soaping her toes.

"Well it's too late to do anything about it now, just a couple of spiteful people with nothing better to do. Try and forget about it my love, we could debate this for hours."

"I know, but it's horrible! I can't see how they managed to do it either, unless they didn't run away but lurked about until we'd left the pool and that gives me the creeps."

"Darling, Mrs Fuller is hardly a marathon runner is she? They probably just ran away and hid, and came back later. Changing the subject Jennifer, why on earth did Chloe Coombe bring her grooms last night and why in heaven's name did you ask Caitlin?"

Jennifer thought quickly, she couldn't let on she had asked them herself and said airily "Oh, I bumped into Chloe and she asked me if they could come." Sorry Chloe she thought, and added "not much I could say really, and I asked Caitlin so that she could keep them company" she improvised.

"Oh, okay, funny though, not like Chloe to do something like that, and what was she doing coming with Oliver Travers? Are they having a thing? I always thought that she was firmly married to John?"

"Oh I don't know them well darling, no idea what gives between Oliver and Chloe, but they were hardly all over each other, he seemed more interested in Caitlin."

"Yes, I noticed that, they went off for a long time together."

"Good for Caitlin, he'd be quite a catch, although I thought he was married."

"He is my love but that has never bothered you."

The barb hurt, and she looked at him coldly. "Nor you either."

Charles was immediately sorry, knowing his remark was below the belt, "I'm sorry darling that was out of order." He changed the subject, "I see Libby Newsome was up to her old tricks last night!"

"What do you mean? I did see her trying it on with Oliver but he didn't even seem to notice her."

"Oh, nothing she hasn't done before, she disappeared with Angus Ferrers, and they came back looking a bit worse for wear. Not surprised he's a real philanderer. Mind you, she has quite a reputation too, tried it on with me a few times!"

"No! You are not serious?" Jennifer wondered if Charles had succumbed, and when that had been, but decided not to pursue it, deftly diverting the conversation. "By the way, when are the children coming?"

"I'm going to pick them up on Friday and am taking them back on Sunday afternoon, - that okay with you? I know it's not easy darling."

"Of course, I'm looking forward to having them" she lied.

Chloe was nursing a hangover and trying not to show it. Although the weather had turned she was looking forward to a family day out, and just hoped this bloody headache would go. She had struggled to get up early, and dragged herself down to the yard to help Beebs, who looked terrible, and was wearing dark glasses, despite the grey day. They had wordlessly done the mucking and chucking out in record time, Beebs having a momentary break to puke up on the muck heap. Chloe looked on sympathetically and advised her to try and have a quiet day, saying anything not done today, could be done tomorrow. When she got back to the house, the children were all up, and clamouring to make the picnic together. She managed to boil some eggs for the sandwiches without throwing up herself, and stuffed the basket with all sorts of goodies that they'd bought at Sainsbury's the day before. In high spirits, with lots of noise, arguing and shouting the children were all ready and raring to go, dashing out to the car, where John was waiting in the driving seat. Chloe downed some last minute Alka Seltzer and shot out of the door, apologising as always to her dogs for leaving them behind.

John was almost like his old self as they drove over the downs towards Arundel, she reached over and took his hand and kissed it, he looked at her fondly, when his phone beeped a message. She looked at him questioningly, but he just shrugged his shoulders and ignored it, putting his hand carefully back on the steering wheel.

The castle was a splendid affair dating back to the 11th century with many later additions. It was like something out of a fairy tale, with an elaborate gatehouse and proper castle walls and a moat, even though it had been dry for years. The children were in their element, tearing up the narrow stone steps and racing around the battlements, although Toby looked a bit sick as he looked down at the dry moat far below. Chloe held him tightly by the shoulders and kissed the top of his head, overwhelming protection engulfing her. They clambered back down the steep steps carefully, and went into the main furnished part of the castle, with Chloe nervously clutching Rory firmly by the hand as they browsed through the extravagant old living apartments. The children spoke in hushed voices for a change, in awe of the surroundings.

"It's bloody amazing Mummy!" gasped Lily, "Did they really live like this?"

"Don't be stupid Lily, of course they did." snarled Toby

"Well, I was only asking Mr Grumpy!" retorted Lily

"Ask sensible questions then, don't be such a girl."

"Mummy, tell him not to be so horrid to me!" hissed Lily.

Chloe looked at them both, and gave them one of those '*stop it right now, or I am going to be very very angry looks*'. "Enough!"

The tour of the castle over, they went back to the car, the children skipping along hand in hand, for the moment not quarrelling. John laughed to Chloe, and he gave her a wink and a conspiratorial look. They clambered into the car and John drove along slowly beside the fast running River Arun, its tide sweeping in dangerously, the children watching the swans being carried along in the racing water. John stopped by Swanbourne Lake, and they locked the car and walked over to the trout farm, stopping to buy some pellets to feed the fish. The children laughed with glee as the greedy trout came to the surface gulping up the food. Chloe looked at them all standing there, John enjoying himself as much as the children, and felt content, they were all so good together. The trout disappeared as soon as the food had gone and the children begged them to buy more, but with a promise of taking a boat out on the lake the fish were soon forgotten.

Ambling back to the lake, the children running on ahead, John went over to the kiosk, and they were soon all dangerously trying to balance as they stepped into the rocking boat. John took the oars, and Chloe looked at his strong familiar arms and felt a surge of love waft over her. What would her life be without him, she just couldn't bear the thought, whatever he was preoccupied with, she was going to make it right between them. In the end they all had a go at rowing, the little dinghy swerving madly going round and round in circles, they collapsed with giggles, urging John to take over again. Suddenly, with their usual quick about turn of boredom, the children decided they were very hungry indeed and dumping the boat, Chloe and the kids raced over and found a good place to picnic beside the lake, whilst John was despatched to the car, struggling back with the laden picnic basket. Lily dived in, and set out the plastic beakers and bottles of Coke, everyone wolfing down the sandwiches and they saved their crusts to chuck to the clamouring ducks. Toby had taken a bat and ball and they started playing games, Rory struggling to keep up with the bigger ones, until they all fell sprawling onto the rug for a rest and played eye spy. Eventually they sauntered back to the car, stopping en route to buy an ice cream.

It was an idyllic family afternoon, and for the first time in months she felt things were on the up. John looked happy and relaxed and she didn't see him check his phone once. By early evening the children were tired, but as it was half term and they didn't have to get up for school the next day, they drove up to a nice pub along the river, The Black Rabbit, an old favourite of theirs from years ago. The children ran screaming into the little playground and Chloe and John took their drinks outside to watch them.

"Things are okay between us aren't they?" Chloe asked.

"Of course they are! Don't be silly" he replied, but he had turned his head away, so Chloe could not see the despair in his eyes.

CHAPTER 22

It was Monday morning and Susie was struggling with water buckets in the yard, Chloe was coming down later this morning, as the children were on half term, and she looked up with relief to see Jen's Mercedes creeping down the drive. Jennifer parked up by the horse walker as usual, and picking up a carrier bag she had plonked on her passenger seat, she joined Susie in the yard.

"Morning Susie, how are you?" she called brightly, "It's very quiet today, where's everyone?"

"Chloe's up at the house with the children, Beebs is on a day off and Katherine and Sandy are due in about an hour, and boy, am I glad to see you!"

Sorry for Susie, but glad to be wanted, Jennifer donned her rubber gloves. "Right. Where do you want me to start?"

Susie looked relieved, "You're a bloody marvel Jen! I've done most of the mucking out, just a couple left to do, can you start with that? I'll turn the last lot out."

"Who needs doing then?"

"Ksar and Maisie, both in the back yard, that okay?" Jennifer grinned, grabbed a wheelbarrow, shavings fork, and broom and set off. There was something remarkably cathartic about mucking out she thought. Chloe had the children at home, and her mind ran ahead to Charles' kids coming. She had found it difficult to be a stepmother. and knew she was stiff and awkward with them, and they with her, perhaps Chloe could give her some tips. Of course it didn't help that she couldn't ride as Charles always took them out on the ponies, and it would've been something that they all had in common - still she was sorting that out now, hopefully soon she would be able to surprise them all. Digging in with gusto with the fork, she shook the clean shavings through the tines and she tossed the muck into the wheelbarrow - she was getting quite adept at it now. Fluffing up the banks around the stable edges, she swept the front clean, and moved onto the next stable to start the whole process all over again. God that Ksar was a messy bugger, he looked as though he had had a party of his own in here. She turned her thoughts again to her party and moreover to the ruined dress – who would have done such a thing and why? It hardly seemed the act of a random passer-by, and yet who else could it have been? It was a real worry, and made her feel uncomfortable at such a malicious and personal act. Did they do it because it was her dress, or because it was just anyone's dress, it was hard to know. The thought that someone did it as a deliberate act against her personally was hard to fathom, who could have such a grudge against her? Only Celia and she had been miles away. Charles didn't seem concerned though, so she supposed she shouldn't be either. Suddenly a cacophony of noise and the sound of barking, as the dogs hurtled into the yard, made her look up from the mucking out, and heralded the arrival of Chloe, and today she had the children in tow.

"Morning Chloe! Have you recovered yet?"

"Morning Jen! Yes, only just though. Great party, we all had the most fabulous time. Everyone did!"

"I'm so glad, I was dreading it, but do you know it went off really well, and as you say everyone seemed to have a good time, even me! I must tell you though that something very strange happened which has really upset me." Jennifer leant on her fork and explained the business of the intruders and the destruction of her dress.

"Noooooo! Jen, that's terrible, what a ghastly thing to have happened! Who could they have been those people, and what was their motive for doing that? Surely they ran off after Mrs Fuller discovered them, why would they have come back?"

"Christ knows Chloe, that was what I thought, but Charles says to just forget it now, but it's left a really nasty taste in my mouth you know?"

"Blimey, it would mine too, still you'll probably never get to the bottom of it, so he's right, just try and forget it. Look when you have finished that stable, come on round to the tack room, I'm going to put the kettle on for poor Susie, she's been going flat sticks and could do with a cuppa, and I've the children home on half term, so the routine is a bit up in the air this week."

"Great! Just what I could do with. Be round in a bit." Jennifer looked after her, the dogs whirling round and round Chloe's feet, and she could hear the chattering of the children, she felt so at home here, and again marvelled at the difference it had made to her life.

Fatima Gupta leaned wearily against the counter, she felt very tired, she was sweating, and had a pain in her chest. She had only been helping Ravi stack the shelves when the attack came on. She gulped for air, and he came over to her putting his hand on her shoulder.

"Dear you are needing a rest, go upstairs now" he said anxiously in his soft voice.

"No Ravi, I'll be fine, I'll just be sitting down for a minute or two, and I'll be alright, you carry on, and I'll do the serving." She moved round behind the counter with an effort and plonked her heavy frame down on the stool, easing her legs up onto a box. Phew, that was better, she turned and smiled at Ravi who was watching her intently. Her heart was beating fast but now she was sitting down she was breathing more easily. She put two of the pills the doctor had given her under her tongue and waited for them to dissolve, trying to stay calm.

"You cannot be carrying on like this anymore dear, you have to go back to see Dr Corbett"

"I know, I know Ravi" she gulped "but I'm so afraid." Just as quickly as it had started, the pain was easing now, and her heart had stopped beating so fast, and she smiled at him "it's passing now, please dear don't worry." The mild mannered Ravi shrugged his shoulders, Fatima was a rule unto herself and she would not be pushed, but he was determined to get her back to the surgery.

The shop door rattled open, the bell clanging and Caitlin came in wearing old jeans and a sweatshirt, she looked very drawn and pale.

Fatima plastered a smile on her face, and Ravi walked away sadly shaking his head.

"Good morning dear, did you find your purse the other day?"

"Yes thank you Mrs Gupta, I did find it luckily, I'd dropped it." Caitlin picked up a basket and moved into the shop browsing the shelves, she desperately needed a sugar fix. She tossed packets of biscuits into the basket, and added some sugar coated cereal. She moved round to the little bakery and spotted a tray of Danish pastries calling to Ravi "Is it okay if I take a couple of these?" Ravi popped his head out of his little kitchen, and put two in a cellophane wrapper. "Thanks so much Mr Gupta, they look great." Ravi inclined his head and smiled, he rarely spoke. Caitlin moved backed to the counter, and plonked down the basket, "That's all for today, thank you."

"Are you all right dear, you are looking a bit peaky?" asked Fatima.

"Oh I'm fine Mrs Gupta, just a bit tired after a long weekend y' know." She was tired it was true, she was miserable and she felt helpless. What a weekend, and Saturday night had been so awkward, she had never felt so lonely or isolated, and he hadn't answered any of her texts yesterday. "Thanks very much."

Well thought Mrs Gupta, young Caitlin was certainly not her usual bubbling self, what was wrong there she wondered, momentarily forgetting her own worries. Caitlin packed the shopping into a plastic bag, paid for it and with her head down left the shop. Once outside, Fatima watched her as she pulled her phone out of her pocket, looked at it for an instant, saw her smile and start texting.

Jonty was busy planning. Laura had gone off to college and some of his mates had come round and they were sitting drinking beer, the room was clouded with smoke. Jonty had outlined the plan to them, and they all seemed keen but it would need intricate planning to the last detail, plus a lot of inside info.

"Now timing is the most important thing, it's got to be done when they least expect it, and I've already done quite a bit as far as casing the place is concerned. Laura is gonna be in on it to an extent, but she doesn't know the whole story – got it, so keep schtum to her? Now are you lot in?" He looked around the serious hard faces, and one by one they nodded their heads in assent, "this is probably the most dangerous job we've ever done, but'll be the most lucrative if we get it right." Jonty grinned, "Good!" They cracked open some more cans, Jonty spread an ordnance survey map of the area on the table, marking it at strategic points. "Here is Nantes Place, where he lives. This is the local pub, the Fox, where all the toffs drink. This" he drew a large circle in red around the area "is the location, and we need to know the area real well, so we are gonna doff some boots and do some walking. Weasel, and you Tubby, are gonna come with me tomorrow - okay?" Weasel, who was well named as he had a sharp pointy little face and small darting eyes, with a slight sinewy body, nodded his head. Tubby, who was not fat, but just enormous, a real hard faced con, just grunted. "That's settled then, we meet here at 10.30. Remember not a word to Laura, or anyone else come to that."

Sandy and Katherine were gently hacking out with Jen. They were enjoying their new found responsibility of teaching her, and Chloe had given them strict instructions on how to go about things, as she herself was going to be pre-occupied with the children this week. Jen had mastered the rising trot, and Seamus and Alfie were trotting quietly beside him around the fields. She was still quite wobbly, but Rufus, old master that he was, was careful with her, welding himself to the other horses, and trotting soberly in between them.

"That's it Jen, you are going great guns, just keep the rhythm up, and you'll be great" encouraged Sandy, "You are doing really well for a beginner." Jennifer just grinned her acknowledgement to Sandy, she was having enough trouble concentrating on staying in balance to say anything. "Okay, shall we have a little canter now? Just nice and steady and Katherine and I will stay right beside you, so that if you have a problem we'll be there to help. Ready?"

Sandy and Katherine struck off into a slow canter, and Rufus taking their lead did the same, Jennifer gasped, and clung on to begin with, then as Sandy urged her to just relax and enjoy him, she felt her body ease into the easy three beat of the canter.

"This is so much easier than the trot!" she laughed. It was too, she didn't wobble nearly so much, although it was much faster. "Ah this is great!" Katherine glanced at Sandy, and they kept the pace very steady, the last thing now was for Rufus to piss off if he felt he was in a race. They cantered up to the top of a small slope, and they pulled up to admire the view down over Chloe's land. It was breathtaking, the fields had greened up overnight it seemed after the rain, and refreshed everything. They could see the little dots of the horses in the fields and Susie in the yard way in the distance.

"It just makes you feel lucky to be alive." said Katherine, "We're all so fortunate you know." She turned mischievously to Sandy, "Okay now tell us all about Mark Templeton!" The horses ambled off, quietly walking along the top of the ridge, towards the woods, the three riders relaxing, Katherine and Jennifer agog to hear what happened.

"Ah, yes the lovely Mark!" mused Sandy "Well not much to tell really."

"Go on, that's not what it looked like to me. He's very good looking though, so I don't blame you." Katherine teased "What's he like in bed then?" Jennifer squirmed but glanced over at Sandy to see her reaction.

"Pretty good as it happens! Good body!"

"Sandy! You are incorrigible! You didn't?"

"Why not? I am free, single and over 21! Actually I'm rather smitten with him, he's a really nice guy!" she winked at them both.

"Are you going to see him again?" asked Jennifer.

"Well tonight actually. I've got a busy day tomorrow in court and the case is likely to go on all week, so seemed like a good idea to strike while the iron is hot, or he is to be more precise."

"Good for you, where are you going?"

"Dunno out for a meal I think, he's booking somewhere local, then who knows!" she laughed.

"Ah, I'm pleased, it's time you settled down."

"Whoa, don't go buying a hat Katherine! We're only going out for a meal. Come on, let's trot on a bit, I need to do a bit of work at home before I go out tonight, ready for tomorrow's case."

Sandy clicked her horse into a trot and Katherine followed, Jennifer bumbling along between the two of them. They rode on for some way, it was the longest that Jennifer had been out, and she was getting tired, but she didn't like to say anything to the others, she was surely going to ache tomorrow. They slowed up at the next rise, it was turning into a lovely day again, not the scorching weather of the past few weeks but a bright sun with great fluffy clouds like the heads of giant cauliflowers high in the blue sky. In the distance, they could see the ruins of the old Abbey.

"What is that place?" asked Jennifer, "I've seen it loads of times before but don't really know what it is."

"Oh, it always really gives me the creeps when you ride past it." smiled Katherine, "It's the ruins of an old Abbey dating back to the 1100s but was abandoned when good old King Henry VIII destroyed all the Monasteries. It's supposed to be haunted!"

"Jesus Christ Katherine, not that old tale again." scoffed Sandy, "you always tell that story!"

"I know, but it still gives me the creeps."

"Crikey" said Jennifer, "have you ever been in it?"

"Nope, but one day we will, just to prove to Katherine that there are no ghosts." The Abbey loomed on the horizon, it was menacing, and its gruesome history made it all the more so.

"Hey! Look, can you see something standing by the Abbey walls?"

"Not that old chestnut!" laughed Sandy, but they all looked into the distance, and could just make out a black figure against the backdrop of the Abbey, "Blimey, what the fuck is that?" They strained to see, shading their eyes against the sun, yes, it was definitely the figure of a person, although who it was, they couldn't tell from this far away.

"Hold on. Isn't that someone else? Look, there are two people aren't there?"

"You're right Jennifer , there are two of them, it's probably just some walkers. Blimey that gave me a fright!"

"Pretty good friends those walkers! They were in a clinch if ever I saw one!" Sandy laughed.

"You've got sex on the brain at the moment Sandy. It's impossible to see from here."

"At least I haven't got spooks on the brain!" Sandy grinned, "Come on, we'd better head back, I've got work to do, not like you two ladies of leisure!"

Patrick stopped at the village shop for a pie for his lunch. The door opened with its customary clang, and he greeted Mrs Gupta who sitting behind the counter.

"Hi there Mrs G, you okay? You look a bit tired today if you don't mind my saying so."

"Hello dear, no I've not been feeling too well, but the doctor has given me some pills to help."

"Oh, I'm sorry to hear that, glad you are seeing the doc though, he's a good bloke. Now can I have a steak pie please?

"Yes, he is a very nice man" she replied guiltily, thinking how she had refused Dr Corbett's advice to go to the hospital. "Now a steak pie is what you are wanting is it? Ravi has just made them." She took a golden pastry out of the heated display counter with the tongs and put it into a bag. "Anything else you are wanting today?" Patrick glanced around resisting the temptation to buy some cigarettes and opted for a bar of chocolate. The shop door chimed again and Oliver walked in, he looked terrible, as though he had been up half the night. Well, that was the lot for the 'on call' vet Patrick thought.

"Hi buddy, what's new? You look wrecked."

Oliver sighed "I may as well tell you mate, as it'll be all round the village soon, Suse has left me."

"Christ, Oliver, that's terrible. I'm so sorry, when did this happen?"

"Came home from the party early hours of Sunday morning and she had just up sticks and gone. I know we've had our ups and downs but it's still a shock. I've not heard anything from her since. I've rung of course, but her phone keeps going to voice mail."

"Oh mate, I'm sorry, do you think she'll be back?"

"No, I think she'll have got on a plane home, I've rung them of course, but they said they hadn't heard from her, but I don't know what to believe." He looked so miserable, Patrick didn't know what else to say. What could he say after all? The normally big framed Oliver looked small and totally dejected.

"Look, fancy meeting me down the Fox tonight for a pint, nothing worse than going home to an empty house."

Oliver looked at him, why not, Patrick was right, the silence of the cottage was deafening. "That'd be ace, thanks buddy, see you there about six, if I get called out I'll ring you."

Patrick picked up his pie and his chocolate, "Good, see you later then, bye Mrs G, keep taking the tablets now!" and he clanged out through the shop door.

Poor old Oliver, thought Patrick as he jumped into his van, what a bummer. Mind you, she had never fitted in that Suse, and from the few occasions he'd met her, she was actually pretty rude. He put the keys in the ignition and started the engine, unwrapping the pie as he went along, and taking great bites, chucking the odd bits of pastry to his Jack Russell Terrier. He was bloody starving, and the only trouble was that eating and then bending down to shoe always gave him raging indigestion. Ah well, too late now, he groped on the dashboard for his Rennies. Plenty, that was good. He checked in his mirror and indicated, pulling into Nantes drive. Caitlin had rung him to say she had a problem with Queenie, so he was making an unscheduled detour before going up to Chloe's.

Caitlin was in the tack room when he pulled up, she looked terrible too! What was the matter with everyone today.

"Patrick, thanks for coming now, sorry to call you out but I just wanted you to take a look at Queenie, she's had a touch of laminitis, and thought there might be something you can do?"

"No trouble chick, where is she? Have you had the vet?"

"Yes Oliver had a quick look on Saturday night, and I've given her Bute so I have, and she's not too bad but I thought you could perhaps see her and maybe some heart bar shoes?"

"Course I'll look, but best to make sure the vet agrees before I do any surgical shoeing, but I can certainly put the hoof testers on and trim her back a bit, make sure there is plenty of frog pressure." He followed her into the stable, the little white pony was standing like a china ornament. Gently Patrick felt down her legs and stood back looking at her carefully, "not the usual laminitis stance, she's not taking too much weight off the front legs" he bent down feeling for the palmar artery, "and she's not throbbing, so that's good news."

"I think I may've caught it in time, she's been out on grass, even with the drought 'twas probably too sweet and rich for her, you know what these ponies are like now."

"Well, seems you've got her off it in time, and the bute will have helped of course" he picked up one of the front legs, "I'll just trim these up a bit, that might help, and I'm meeting Oliver for a pint tonight at the Fox, so I can ask him about it then if you like? Poor old Oli, don't expect you've heard, his wife has left him!" Patrick put the horses hoof down and looked up at Caitlin - she had gone as white as a sheet, "You all right Caitlin?"

"Yes, yes, sorry just felt a bit dizzy for a moment then, I've not been feeling too well. Poor Oliver, how awful for him."

"Yes, poor bugger looked wiped out, that's why I said I'd meet him, you ought to come, he might need a woman's perspective."

Caitlin thought for a moment "I'd love to Patrick, if you think I'd be of any help."

"Well it might cheer him up a bit eh?" He bent back down again, lifting the other leg, and began to trim the hoof.

Mark Templeton had thought long and hard where he should take Sandy that evening, and in the end settled for a small Bistro in Cuckfield, not too far away but not too close to the village. He booked it for half past eight, and they could stop for a drink if they fancied at the Fox before they went. To have met Sandy was the last thing he had expected to happen. Mark had been married before, ending in a relatively amicable divorce quite a few years earlier and he'd been on his own ever since. Of course he'd had affairs, but nothing serious and when they started getting keen, he had run a mile. He lived in a tied cottage on the Fittlebury Hall estate, but had bought his own house in Horsham which he rented out, with the money he had left over after his divorce. His life he considered had been quite content, he was a self-sufficient, successful man, with fairly simple needs, and he liked it that way too. That was until he met Sandy. She had taken him by storm, a feisty dynamic woman of independent means and no baggage, in fact a lot like him. She was funny, sexy and as afraid of commitment as he was, and he found that fascinating. There was more though, there was a kind of frisson between them that he hadn't felt in a long long time.

Now with the decision of which restaurant sorted he brought his attention back to the papers on his desk. The Old Mill - he was pleased to be getting rid of the burden of renovation, which the estate could ill afford, especially as there were all sorts of restrictions involved. Lady V had struck a good deal, and so had Andrew, all in all, it should prove a good outcome for all of them. He picked up the telephone and dialled the number of the estate solicitors, the sooner this conveyance was underway the better. Tomorrow he would go down and measure out the plot to be sold, and draw up the plans ready for the sale. Andrew had said that he would be seeing his bank this week to make sure the funds were available, so he wanted everything to be ready, and once Andrew got the go ahead, so much the better.

Susie ended the call, she had been on the phone to Tom, she had seen him on the night after the party, and they had got on really well, funny how things happened she mused. If she hadn't been invited to

259

Jen's she might never have met him. Okay it was not a love affair, but it was great to have met some local talent and make new friends. Beebs had got on quite well with Harry the Whip too, and they were all going down to the Fox tonight for a drink. Should be fun she thought. She looked up as the sound of hooves came down the drive and she saw Katherine, Sandy and Jen coming back – they'd been out for ages. Jen looked pretty comfortable, and this was just what she needed to gain her confidence, lots of gentle hacks, so that she could just begin to enjoy riding. Once you enjoyed it, then you could start learning the finesse.

"Hey ladies, did you have a great ride?" she called, moving over to hold Rufus as Jen clambered off.

"Absolutely marvellous Susie, I had such a good time. Thank you all so much for your help and support today!"

"Chloe would have our guts for garter if we didn't." grinned Sandy.

"We genuinely want to help Jen, I think it's such a good idea, I can't wait to see Charles' face when he sees you can ride!" encouraged Katherine, "Chloe says you are aiming for one of the early meets at the start of the season. Fantastic!"

"Well, that's the target. Chloe says it is doable! More though, I want to know how to tack up and stuff as well, so I can be really hands on."

"You can tack up yourself now though Jen, you have already got the hang of it all. We are all really proud of you!"

Jennifer glowed with happiness, the ruined dress was completely forgotten.

CHAPTER 23

The Fox was crowded that evening, the air was cooler tonight though, and the women drew their cardigans around them as they sat in the garden. Oliver and Patrick were sitting at one of the benches nursing their drinks, their heads bents closely together as they talked quietly. Patrick sat back and took a slurp from his pint, and Oliver sipped his juice - he was on call from 7.30pm.

"The thing is that she just upped and went, made it her decision, like I had nothing to do with it. I just feel that there is no real closure for me, y' know?"

"I can understand that, but y' know Oli mate your marriage was washed up, there was probably not much you could've done to stop her, she'd made up her mind."

"I know, I know, but there I was, going to that do up at Nantes, and all the while she was packing."

"But y' said she encouraged you to go, and that she didn't want to go herself, face it, she'd probably been planning this for a while, and you going out to the party gave her a golden opportunity to do a disappearing act."

"But there might've been something I could've said - even if it was just goodbye."

"Have you heard anything?"

"Nope not a word, and I've rung her mobile a million bloody times, and it just goes straight to voicemail. I've rung the folks back home and they aren't saying anything. It's like some fucking conspiracy."

"Yep, I can see you'd think that" said Patrick sensibly, "but has it occurred to you that she might be on a plane and can't use her phone, and that she wouldn't have arrived back yet, so her parents don't actually know where she is?"

"Yes, of course it has, but it's so inconsiderate of them and her, I'm worried sick that something might have happened to her." Oliver twirled his glass round and round in his hands anxiously. "It's just so frustrating, I feel helpless, sad, angry, and guilty all at the same time."

"I can see the frustration, anger and sadness but guilty? Why? What've you done to be guilty, other than work hard and try to make a good career and future for yourself and her come to that? "

"Guilty for many reasons mate."

"Such as?"

"Well, there is plenty of stuff you don't know of course" stammered Oliver "some things I haven't told you about..." His imminent confession was loudly interrupted by Susie plonking herself heavily down beside him, the bench seat on the opposite side jumping Patrick up in the air, spilling his pint all over the table.

"Whoops, sorry about that Patrick! Budge up Oliver, room for more. What are you two talking about? You look bloody serious!"

They were joined by Beebs, Tom and Harry, bringing their drinks over to the table. Oliver clammed up immediately and Patrick wondered what it was he'd been about to tell him. He was not to find out though, as their moment for confidences had disapparated as fast as Harry Potter. Oliver continued to fiddle gloomily with his glass and the others laughed on raucously and aimlessly, totally oblivious to his awkwardness.

"Blimey, how did you lot get invitations to the party then?" asked Patrick sulkily, "thought they were like gold dust?"

"Chloe managed to wangle us one." improvised Beebs, "We were as astonished as you! But it was really fab do, no expense spared."

"Well, I wasn't invited." said Patrick peevishly, "don't know what they were missing and you know you lovely girls could've had a dance with me!" It was true that Patrick was a great dancer, he went to local lessons for rock 'n roll, Salsa, Zumba and all sorts and it was his favourite thing to whirl the girls around the yard practising his new moves.

"Well we were disappointed you weren't there too honey. I'd like to have seen you strut your stuff on the dance floor. How about you Oliver, did you enjoy it?"

"Well, I did at the time but not since." Oliver said evasively and the girls looked at him sideways and then at each other.

"You certainly seemed to be enjoying yourself - you and Caitlin were gone a long time looking at that pony!" said Susie mischievously, "We thought you were never coming back!"

"Talking of Caitlin," interjected Patrick diverting the conversation, "She's supposed to be meeting us here for a drink tonight, I said we're all coming down, wonder where she's got to? Mind you I thought she looked quite poorly this morning, not her usual self at all."

"Shall I call her?" asked Susie, "find out what she's up to?"

"Nah, I'd leave it, it was pretty open ended. Talking of people looking ill, have any of you noticed how ill Mrs Gupta looks lately? When we were in there this morning she looked dreadful, didn't she Oli?"

Oliver looked up, startled "What?"

"Wake up mate, Mrs Gupta, I was saying she looked terrible this morning."

"Yer right, she did that's true. Although, she'd never admit it." The sound of a car arriving in the car park made them all look up - expecting to see Caitlin pulling in, but instead it was Grace and Colin.

"We'll come over and join you" shouted Colin, "anyone wanna drink?"

"Can't mate, I'm on call, I owe Andrew big time as he did the weekend for me, but thanks anyway" Oliver called back.

"I'll come over Col and give you a hand," yelled Patrick to Colin, "what d'you all want to drink?" He took their orders and stood up, the bench seat tilting madly, so that the others almost fell off,

"Sorry!" he laughed, "just getting my own back!"

Patrick strode over the garden to meet Colin and they disappeared into the snug with Grace. It was busy tonight and they had to wait for a while before Dick came over to serve them. Balancing the drinks on a tray, they walked back out to the garden.

"Hi you lot" said Grace, "Recovered from Saturday night?"

"Don't you start Grace" remonstrated Patrick, "they've all just rubbed it in that I wasn't invited. Where's Oli gone by the way?"

"He got a text message and he had to go, told us to say goodbye and see you soon" said Beebs, "Went off in quite a hurry, didn't say where he was going, but I assume it must be some emergency, he's on call isn't he?"

"I thought he looked bloody miserable and away with the fairies tonight" remarked Harry.

"Well, I suppose you're all gonna find out sooner than later, his wife left him on Saturday night, whilst he was at the party" gossiped Patrick, "been a right shock."

"Noooo, I don't believe it, how simply dreadful for him. Poor poor Oli." sympathised Grace.

"Come on Grace, she was a right cow, he'll be better off without her in the long run."

"Well, I still think it's terrible even if they hadn't been getting on."

"I think it was terrible the way she did it, he just came home and found out she had done a bunk!"

"She must have been damned unhappy then, that's all I can say. You never know what goes on in people's marriages do you?"

"No, you don't" said Patrick, thinking had there been more to it though? What was it that Oliver felt guilty about and what was he going to say when the others interrupted?

Caitlin was sitting in her Peugeot in the car park at High Ridge Woods, she had parked right at the back, sheltered from the road. She looked at her watch, they'd only have a little while together, but she was just desperate to see him. She'd hardly heard anything from him since Saturday, and she'd begun to resent that more and more. She knew it was wrong to feel like that and she knew that he had been more than preoccupied, but she missed him so dreadfully. She heard the sound of an engine coming along the lane, and quickly put on a squirt of perfume, checking her reflection in the mirror. She got out of the car and made her way into the woods, she knew the way so well, it was their place. They couldn't risk being seen and her heart was thumping. Behind her, was the sound of footsteps, and turning around she saw him coming along the path. He looked so tired, and she simply put her arms out and he fell into them, and they stood like that with her caressing his hair, he stroking hers.

"God, I've missed you baby" he whispered, "It's becoming harder and harder. I've had a really tricky few days, I don't need to tell you and I'm so sorry."

"I know Hun, I know, it's the same for me too." He pushed back taking a tendril of her hair in his hands, and kissed her so gently on the lips, she felt her heart would break.

"I know things are coming to a head now, but I just have to be so cautious, despite everything, still so very careful. It's killing me. We'll need to talk about the future you know, but right now all I want to do is kiss you." He ran his fingers along her cheek and took her once more into his arms. The future could wait, the present was what they both wanted.

Chloe was with the children, their day had been exhausting, but she loved being with them, and they had all had great fun. Rory looked up from his drawing, craning over to look at Lily's.

"Stop copying me Rory do your own picture!" she squeaked.

"Don't be nasty Lily, he's only interested not copying you." said Chloe, "here Rory, let me look at what you've done." Rory, leant back in his chair so that she could see, "That's good darling, you've a real flair for colour." Rory beamed at her, "Lily let me look at yours."

"Well it'll be better than Rory's anyway, he's only five after all." sulked Lily, handing over her picture.

"Why that's really good Lily, well done, I love the way you've drawn and painted the petals." Oh, the jealousy of sibling rivalry, you had to be so careful to make sure the praise was always equal. Actually Rory's picture had been excellent and she was really impressed, she turned to Toby, "What have you been drawing darling?"

"I'm doing a cartoon series, with Disney characters."

"Wow, that sounds amazing, let me look." Toby pushed the sketch over to her, "Hey Toby, that is excellent, what a clever idea." She looked at them all fondly, as they sat there at the table, Lily with the tip of the paintbrush in her mouth, as she contemplated the next colour to use, Rory yawning, his mop of blonde hair flopping in his eyes and Toby concentrating hard, his tongue poking out between his teeth whilst he worked. For once she did not feel guilty about not spending enough time with them, they'd all had a brilliant day. She pushed her chair away, time was ticking on a bit, they'd gone out for a McDonalds this afternoon, so had already eaten, but she would still have to cook for John. She rummaged about in the fridge, there was a piece of salmon which would be good with some new potatoes, or even pasta she mused.

"Mummy" Lily looked at her with an angelic face, "can I have some ice-cream?"

"Yes please Mummy, that would be lovely" agreed Rory.

"Rory will you please stop copying me, I've told you before." shouted Lily. "I said I wanted ice-cream first!"

"Lily, Lily, does that really matter, he was just agreeing with you, and the answer is yes, of course you may. How about you Toby?"

"Great Mummy, yes please" Toby replied, still working hard on his cartoon.

"Okay, you can have vanilla, strawberry or chocolate, what's it to be?"

"All three" shouted Lily

"Okay Okay!" Chloe laughed jumping in before Rory could agree with Lily, "a little bit of each for everyone." She doled out the ice-cream in bowls, and topped it with a bit of squirty cream and a cherry. "Voila!"

Plonking the dishes on the table, the kids dived in, quiet for a moment or two, and Chloe turned her attention to John's supper. He should be in soon, she would make a nice mushroom and wine sauce, and some tagliatelle, that would tempt him. She busied herself, chopping onions, the acrid fumes making her eyes water, she picked up a tissue. Bloody things! At that moment her phone beeped a message, it was from John, saying he wouldn't be home for another couple of hours. Oh no she couldn't believe it, she read the text again - they had been so good together yesterday. She felt her eyes running with tears.

"Mummy, are you crying? You are - why are you crying?" asked Toby.

"No darling, it's just the onions" she lied, wishing that were true.

Sandy was scrutinising herself from every angle in the long mirror in her bedroom, she had dressed with unusual care tonight she mused, and was looking forward to seeing Mark again despite her insouciance with the girls on the ride today. She'd deliberated about what to wear and finally chosen a khaki green cap sleeved linen dress, with large buttons down the front - the colour suited her, with her blonde hair, and the length was perfect with these shoes. She smoothed down the bed covers, and straightened the pillows – just in case she thought. Grabbing her cardigan, she shut the bedroom door behind her and sped down the stairs. She waited in the sitting room, which looked out onto the drive, watching for him to arrive. She wondered if he would be punctual, she always was herself, another one of her obsessional traits.

It was a lovely room, with a traditional inglenook fireplace and a frame work of oak beams which had been carefully sand- blasted when she bought the cottage. The whole room was painted a pristine white, but she had resisted covering the oak floor boards with her favourite Farrow and Ball paint, but only just, and had instead laid a large white rug as a compromise. There were two squashy feather filled white sofas, strewn with blue cushions. On the only large space on the wall not crisscrossed with beams, hung a stark abstract painting in a variety of blue and white hues. The room was minimalist mixed with traditional and it worked. She moved to the window when she heard the sound of a car arriving, she glanced at her watch - he was bang on time. Better and better she thought.

Mark pulled into the driveway, glanced at his watch, - just right, he hated being late. He walked up to the front door rapping hard on the big iron hooped knocker, and must have waited for about 45 seconds, but to him it felt like 5 minutes until Sandy pulled appeared. He smiled at her, she looked stunning, he loved her simple chic style.

"Hi, hope I've not kept you waiting?"

"Not a bit. I'm ready, shall we go, or would you like a drink first?"

"Let's have a drink first shall we?"

She held open the door and he followed her into the hall and through to the kitchen. "This is lovely" he said admiringly as he took in the lofty vaulted glass ceilings of the room, obviously an extension but the supporting beams exactly matched the rest of the house. The cupboards were all white oak and quite modern with a lot of stainless steel appliances, and a large central unit housed a massive butchers cutting block. At the far end, two whole sides of the room were glass and led onto the garden, with a small sofa and a farmhouse kitchen table and chairs.

"Yes I like it, this is probably the room I use most - I love cooking." she said looking at him over her shoulder, "What do you want to drink?"

"Well I'd love a whisky, but as I've got to drive, I'd better have a soft drink."

"No probs, it's a bugger but there you go. Lemonade okay?"

"Fine thanks" Sandy poured his drink, added some large chunks of ice and handed it to him, and then poured herself a whisky. She turned to face him and smiled, he really was a most attractive man. They clinked their glasses together, "Here's to a wonderful evening!"

Celia was having supper with the children. Rupert was eleven now and growing into a tall handsome lad, just like his father. He was an intelligent boy, and doing well at his prep school, but the divorce had scarred him, and paradoxically rather than being insecure and lacking in confidence, he had grown into an arrogant and cynical young man, who shrugged his shoulders in a superior way, as though life revolved entirely around him. Jessica was eight, a pretty doll-like little girl, with long blonde hair and she was bubbly and effervescent, and constantly chattering.

When the divorce came through Celia had at first been shocked - in her social circle, mistresses were accepted but divorces were not. Her parents were old fashioned in their values and whilst of course they had naturally stood by her, they had considered that she should have tried harder, and weathered the storm. If she was honest, she and Charles had only ever gone along with their marriage to please her parents. Celia though, was made of sterner stuff and her initial astonishment that Charles had intended to marry his mistress turned to a stoical resignation of the situation, and left her with a bitter residue of realisation that she actually disliked Charles and frankly hated Jennifer. However, she was determined that her children should not suffer because of it, but even so, whilst she had never denied Charles access to them, she hated it when they went to see him and the woman, and she never missed a trick to put their father and his new wife down when talking about them to her children.

Charles was going to pick them up on Friday, but this week it didn't seem quite so bad, as Celia actually had a new man in her life. She smiled to herself, perhaps her life was going to change. Of course though, the children must come first, and they had met Anthony a couple of times, and it had all gone well as far she could tell. She had met him at the Easter Ball at Rupert's school. She hadn't wanted to go, everyone had partners and she felt very de trop, but she had been bulldozed into going with a group of married friends and they had invited Anthony to make up the numbers on the table. She had been cross at the time, as they were always trying to match make her with one suitable chap after another, but this time it had been different. She had struck up a laid-back conversation with him and liked his undemanding, easy going attitude, but didn't really think he was quite top draw enough for her. Anthony too was divorced but had no children. He was a corporate lawyer and a partner in a Surrey law firm. They had danced the night away and he made no overtures to her and at the end of the evening she had said goodnight, neither of them exchanging phone numbers. Her concerned friends, who'd thought they made an ideal couple, then arranged a dinner party, inviting them both and it had just gone on from there. It had been a slow courtship, they became friends before they became lovers, and it was far removed from her relationship with Charles. He was coming to dinner on Friday night and they had planned to spend the weekend together, so the long hours when the children were gone this time seemed much more bearable.

"Mummy, what time is Daddy picking us up?" asked Jessica, "I'm looking forward to seeing Queenie again, I love her so much!"

"I'm glad you do darling, and you'll have a lovely time. Daddy is coming on Friday afternoon."

"Do we have to go?" Rupert drawled, "I get so bored, and Jennifer is very trying."

"Yes, you do have to go Rupert, and boredom is all in the mind." Celia was pleased with her son's loyalty to her, making life as difficult as he could for Jennifer, "Jennifer is common but there is nothing we can do about that I'm afraid."

"She's such a pleb."

"That's quite enough now Rupert."

"Well she is, she can't ride and Mrs Fuller and the staff absolutely loathe her."

"Do they indeed." said Celia angrily "well you should not encourage the staff to gossip. When I was at Nantes they certainly wouldn't have done so."

"Mrs Fuller didn't actually say that, but I know it's what she thinks."

"I'm pleased to hear that Rupert - and that you understand not to fraternise with them in that way."

"Mother" scorned Rupert "please don't be anal."

"Rupert, that's enough I said. You are not to speak to me like that, do I make myself clear?"

"Perfectly" he said coldly, "Now if you will excuse me" he pushed back his chair, "I've some prep I should do." He stalked out of the room, and banged up the stairs.

Celia pulled herself together and smiled at Jessica.

"Don't take any notice of him mummy, I certainly don't" she said sagely, busy trying to manage her spaghetti, which kept falling off her fork.

"You are quite right Jessica, but he should not be so rude nonetheless" she answered, but thinking - what Rupert needs is a man about the house, and a proper family life, he's getting quite out of hand, and it would be another two years before he sat his common entrance to Sherbourne. Was Anthony the right man she wondered, or would it just make matters worse? She sighed, just for once, should she allow her heart to rule her head.

Mark and Sandy were finishing off their meal. It had been a delightful evening. They found they had a lot in common, their love of the countryside, and their passion for their work, even though their jobs were poles apart. Mark did not ride but was genuinely interested in hearing about Seamus and how much Sandy enjoyed her eventing, saying he'd like to come along one day and watch them compete. She listened to him talking about the estate, and the various enterprises he supervised, about his days of being a land agent at a big company before he took the job at Fittlebury Hall. She told him about her days at University and then her pupillage and her journey to becoming a successful barrister. The evening had sped past, and the waiters were hovering in the background, anxious for them to leave. Mark and Sandy had hardly noticed them, and it was only when the head waiter came up behind Mark, saying they were waiting to close, that they realised the time. Guiltily Mark apologised and asked for the bill, which was promptly proffered. Sandy bent down for her hand bag to grab her purse.

Mark put his hand on her arm. "Let me, please."

"I couldn't possibly, at least let me pay half?"

"I wouldn't dream of it. If it makes you feel better, you can buy the wine next time."

"Next time?" She put her head to one side and smiled at him, "I'd love to."

They walked out of the restaurant arm in arm, and when they reached the car, he opened the passenger door for her, and for a moment held her to him, their bodies very close and their faces almost touching.

"Sandy I've so enjoyed tonight, it's been great" he murmured.

"Me too Mark, it's been lovely." He kissed her gently under the sodium lights of the car park, running his forefinger along the side of her cheek, and she kissed him right back. "Let's go back to my place for a nightcap" she whispered

CHAPTER 24

The weather had changed, the bruised sky was still full of rain despite lashing down all morning on the window panes and it was chilly after all the sunshine of the previous weeks. Mrs Fuller was grumbling about her arthritis playing up with the damp weather.

"Plays havoc with my knees" she complained to Doris rubbing her legs gingerly.

"My 'ands too, look at my swollen knuckles."

"Good job they got that marquee down yesterday, would've been murder in this weather."

"Where's her ladyship this morning then?"

"Don't ask me, she goes out every morning these last few weeks, no idea where. Could be doing anything for all I know. Still not ours to reason why eh? At least she leaves us in peace!"

"Odd though, do you think she's got a bit on the side?"

"No, not her, she's very lovey dovey with Mr Charles, and she's never dressed up. This morning she had on a pair of those track suit thingy's. She's always back just after lunch and always goes straight upstairs and has a shower too."

"Well, that's it then! She's going to one of those gyms or something – tho' there's a gym here – so why she'd go out, gawd only knows! Maybe she goes off to play tennis, I know the veterinary's wife's keen on playing."

"Pah, her! She is a snotty bitch an' no mistake. Right social climber that one!"

"Perhaps they'd get on well together then." sneered Doris.

"Actually Doris, the missus has been much better lately, seems to have turned a corner, she's not as bad as I thought. She was right nice over Caitlin, and tried to help with the party as best she could."

"You've changed your tune then Freda!"

"Credit where credit is due Doris - credit where credit is due. Anyway, we can't sit about gossiping, we've got to get the children's rooms ready, they'll be here Friday afternoon, staying til Sunday night. Let's get on with it shall we?" She stood up stiffly, and Doris followed her wearily up the passage towards the stairs.

Pete was sheltering in the old greenhouse in the kitchen garden, avoiding the downpour, engrossed with pricking out seedlings into pots. He meticulously separated all the little shoots, and gently placed them into the compost, watering them carefully. It was very cosy standing in here he mused, the steady rattle of the rain on the glass roof made him feel safe, like he felt when his mother was with him, or Celia. He removed another seedling carefully cradling it in the palm of his hand stroking it with the forefinger of his other hand, and then suddenly crushed it, rubbing it together between his two hands until it was a mangled green mess. His face clouded with anger, as black as the skies overhead and his lips contorted into a malicious smile. He picked up his shears, staring at the tangle of cream silk caught between the blades and smiled with satisfaction, that would learn her he thought. The voices had been right, she had no business being here, it was just a pity that she hadn't been in the dress when he had shredded it up.

The girls too, were sheltering from the rain in the tack room cradling cups of tea, as they looked gloomily out of the door at the deluge. The horses that had been kept in were only putting the tips of their noses out of the stable doors to avoid the torrent driving into their faces, and were obviously glad to be in their loose boxes. Chloe had been down earlier and said that there was no need to exercise any of the horses other than Seamus and Alfie, as those were the ones that needed to be kept super fit. The other horses had all been turned out, with their lightweight waterproof rugs on, and Jennifer could see them, heads down in the paddocks, oblivious to the rain. Beebs and Susie, who had been really soaked earlier had nipped back into the cottage and were now at least in dry clothes. They moved back inside the tack room and sat down on the chairs.

"What a bloody day, I seriously don't fancy riding in this. At least we've only got the two to do!" wailed Beebs.

"Shall we wait and see if it clears up a bit later? After all, the horses are in and we can go anytime if there looks like a break in the weather."

"Don't suppose I'll get a ride today now" sighed Jennifer, "I've got to be back after lunch, as I'm going to see Caitlin about advertising for another groom."

"You must be nuts wanting to ride in this" exclaimed Susie, "Oh and by the way, I have a friend looking for a job, I did mention it to Caitlin on Saturday, and she said she would have to ask you. You'd better not let on to her you know about him though."

"I know you think I'm mad, but I'm just so keen to keep riding, the more I do, the better I'll get, that's what Chloe says! Who is this person then Susie, did you say he?"

"Yes, his name is Felix, lovely guy, good with the horses, knows his job and a hard worker too. I met him when I started training at Hartpury, he's a few years older than me though. He left the year after I started, and since then has been working in quite a variety of places. We've kept in contact and when you meet him you'll know why!"

"How intriguing! But it's good to have a personal recommendation for the job, especially after the way Lucy turned out. Why don't you give Caitlin a ring now and tell her, so when I see her later, she can tell me all about it. Obviously, we don't want her to know I've been here."

"One of these days Jen, you are gonna have to come clean, someone is bound to say something!" said Susie picking up her mobile.

"I know but I just need a bit more time."

About an hour passed and the rain didn't seem like relenting, so Jennifer decided to call it a day and go home early. She asked the girls if there was anything else that she could do, and they assured her that there wasn't. She changed out of her breeches and put on her track suit. Bugger she thought, I really wanted to ride today, she would just go back and try and see Caitlin earlier.

Susie and Beebs watched her jump into the car and waved as she drove out.

"Okay, this rain is not going to stop, let's tack up and head out - we can go for a fast hack, now that Jennifer is not coming and be back within the hour."

"Yep, Okay, might as well get it over" sighed Susie. They each grabbed the horses' respective saddles and bridles and made a dash for the stables. "Bloody hell! I'm soaked again." she moaned.

The horses didn't look very impressed either at the sight of the tack, Seamus turned round in the stable and put his bum to Beebs in disapproval. They tacked up in record time and went to find waterproofs and crash hats. They brought out the horses simultaneously and jumped on awkwardly with all the wet weather gear hampering them.

"Right, let's get cracking, the sooner we go, the sooner we'll be back."

"Where do you fancy going?" asked Susie

"Let's go via the old Abbey, there's loads of cantering." With that, they clicked the horses on to a smart trot and disappeared up the drive.

Jonty, Weasel and Tubby had motored down in the Landrover, the pathetic windscreen wipers hardly able to contain the deluge. The roads were awash with the flash flooding and they splashed through the puddles delighting in soaking anyone who happened to be on the side of the road. Jonty was pleased that Laura had found him that old Barbour in the charity shop and the wellies, at least he would stay dry, even if he did look a right prick in all that gear. Weasel and Tubby had on stout boots and dark coats, although probably not waterproof - well he mused that was not his fucking problem. Mind you, this weather would work for them, there wouldn't be many people out in this today. Before they had arrived at the flat this morning he had scanned the ordnance survey map, looking for landmarks, he had to find just the right place and had earmarked two spots in red pen which might just be worth a gander. He was concentrating on the road, swinging through the village and took the turn at the pump, onto the Cuckfield Road, past the garage and the doctor's surgery, and then on into the countryside along the twisty lanes. Up ahead on the skyline, looming out of the sheets of rain, he saw a tall, murky building half hidden in mist. He pulled over, and took out the map, spreading it out over the steering wheel.

"This is it mates". He parked the Landrover, pulling it off the road, onto the verge, crushing the grass. They hauled on their coats and got out, walking a little way down the lane. Just ahead on the left hand side was a public bridleway sign, its wooden finger pointing up the hill towards the ruin. They opened the gate and began to trudge up the hill, the rain stinging their faces.

"Fucking hell Jonty, you could've picked a better day, you old tosser!" moaned Weasel, "This is fucking hard work." His hard pinched little face screwed up in annoyance.

"Stop being such a girl Weasel." Jonty snorted, wiping his eyes.

Tubby said nothing, just grunted in his usual way, head down against the rain. Jonty glanced at both of them, they were hard geezers and in a tight spot he would have them around him any time. Anyway, they knew the spoils would be worth it. They followed the trail of the bridleway as it passed right beside the Abbey and the ruins emerged in the gloom, its great ramparts standing menacingly, high above them. They skirted around the edges of the remaining outer walls and wound into the inner rubble core, where the sketchy remains of the cloisters stood. A myriad of rocks, glass and lead had been pillaged over the years, and all that remained were the toothy stumps of the old pillars which had supported the roofs of the inner sanctum, and their walls were partially gone.

"This is perfect, lots of places to hide." Jonty exclaimed. They explored the remains fully, and found a footpath at the back, at right angles to the bridleway. "Look at this lads, it gets better and better"

"Sshhh, I can hear summat." muttered Weasel and he clutched at Jonty's arm.

They all stood and listened. He was right there were voices. In the distance being carried on the air through the rain and they hid behind one of the rubble walls, peering out onto the bridleway. There was the sound of laughter too and into view came some riders cantering up the hill, pulling up short outside the ruins. Two girls, very pretty and quite young, their faces wet with the rain were catching their breath after their exertions of the pull up the hill, the horses nostrils flared, their flanks glistening with the rain. Weasel held Jonty's arm and motioned to him with his forefinger to his lips, whatever happened they must not be found here. One of the riders pulled out a blue packet from their pockets, cigarettes - she gestured to the other girl, who shook her head. Then the riders moved on, the rain still teeming down, and they were soon lost in the mist, as they trotted down the hill. Jonty, Weasel and Tubby stood up, watching them go - that had been close.

"Let's just get on with it!" Jonty took a small notebook and began sketching as best he could in the downpour, a plan of the ruins and its relation to the bridleway and the footpath. He looked at his watch and noted the time, and then they set off, not back down the track to the Landrover, but took the footpath, trudging through the rain. The path seemed to go on forever, slightly downhill, meandering across fields, and through some woodland, eventually coming out on a lane. Jonty pulled out the mangled map from his pocket. He glanced over it, before shoving it back in his coat again, and signalled the lads to follow. About 25 yards down the lane, was another footpath sign, the path threaded its way through some woodland, and they followed the track which came out adjacent to a pond flanked with rushes and reeds. Jonty looked at his watch, noting the ten minutes it had taken them to get here.

"This is the place." Jonty turned to the others and smiled.

Jennifer came down the drive, but instead of going back to the house, veered left towards the stables. She pulled on her raincoat over her track suit and went off in search of Caitlin. She tracked her down, following the sound of the radio playing in the tack room. Caitlin was taking the opportunity of the rainy day to sort out the rugs, the room was piled high with them, in a variety of heaps.

Caitlin wheeled round when she heard Jennifer "Oh b'Jesus, you startled me!"

"I'm so sorry Caitlin, I always seem to be doing that. I didn't mean to, you look like you've been busy!"

"Oh that I am, sorting the rugs out to take to the cleaners, ready for when we clip the horses out. 'Tis a filthy job, but has to be done." Jennifer looked at Caitlin, and noticed the dark circles under her red rimmed eyes.

"You okay Caitlin, you look a bit tired."

"No, no, I'm fine to be sure, just a bit of an allergy."

Jennifer didn't think that for a moment, but didn't like to take it any further, "Is there any chance you might spare a minute earlier than we planned, to talk?"

"Why to be sure if you like, just give me a few moments to have a wash."

"Tell you what, why not have a wash and come over to the house and have an early lunch with me. I could make us a sandwich, and we could have a think about what we want to do?"

"That'd be lovely, are you sure?" Caitlin was surprised, being asked over to the house for lunch was unheard of in the hierarchy of Nantes!

"Of course, see you in about twenty minutes, okay?"

Jennifer turned around and walked out of the tack room, leaving Caitlin with her mouth open. She parked her car in the garage and ran into the house, kicking off her boots at the back door, she ran soundlessly straight down the passage into the kitchen. Mrs Fuller and Doris were sitting at the table with some cutlery and untouched cleaning rags, in reality doing the crossword in the Daily Mail. They leapt up as she came in momentarily nonplussed.

Mrs Fuller managed to stammer "Madam, you gave me a shock, I didn't hear you coming."

"Oh dear it seems to be my day for giving people shocks, I've just done the same to Caitlin!" she laughed. "Mrs Fuller, Caitlin is coming over and we're going to talk about Lucy's replacement, is there any chance you could make us some sandwiches and bring them into the study for me?" It was stupid really Jennifer thought, she was quite capable of making sandwiches, but the kitchen was Mrs Fuller's domain, and she didn't want to tread on her toes.

"Of course Madam, I'll bring them along as soon as they're ready."

"Thank you so much, that would be excellent!" She smiled at Doris, who was trying to hide the paper and pretended to be polishing the silver "How're you Mrs Windrush, thank you for all your help on Saturday."

"I'm fine thank you, no problem at all about Saturday, Fred and I enjoyed ourselves"

"Glad to hear it! Thanks Mrs Fuller." Jennifer breezed out of the kitchen, leaving both women gaping after her. She ran up the stairs to her bedroom, throwing off the damp clothes and put on a pair of linen trousers and a cotton jumper, brushed her hair and went down to her study.

Caitlin knocked on the back door, waiting nervously on the doorstep, luckily sheltered from the rain by the porch. Doris ambled her way down the passage, standing back as she let her in.

"Come in, come in m' dear, it's terrible out there. The Missus is in her study, I'll show you the way, shall I?"

"No need Doris, I know the way now, shall I just go straight there do you think?"

"Come into the kitchen first, Freda is making y' lunch. What's up with her then" she gesticulated towards the hallway, "she's in a good mood."

Caitlin didn't like to gossip, Jennifer had been very good to her "We're going to sort out about the replacement groom." They walked into the kitchen where Mrs Fuller was busy making the sandwiches.

"Hello duck, goodness you look tired. Chicken mayonnaise sarnies okay?"

"T' would be lovely for sure Mrs Fuller, thank you" Caitlin replied neatly avoiding her enquiry.

"They're all ready, I'll just put them on a tray, coffee is done, let's take it through shall we?" She piled up the tray and Caitlin followed her down the hallway to the study.

Jennifer who had heard them coming, shoved the *Manual of Horsemanship* back into her desk drawer and greeted them both smiling, "Wow, they look great, I'm starving, sit down do Caitlin, good I see you've brought the Horse and Hound with you. Thank you Mrs Fuller." Freda who was dying to be involved had no alternative but to leave them to it. Caitlin sat down awkwardly and Jennifer grinned at her, "Tuck in, help yourself to coffee."

Caitlin was not hungry, she was full of misery, but she did as she was asked, and put a couple of the delicate little triangles on her plate. Jennifer poured some coffee from the jug into her mug and heaped up her plate with sandwiches.

"Now Caitlin, tell me what you think we should do about Lucy's replacement?"

Caitlin took a nibble of her sandwich, "I've thought about what you said before, and to be sure it may well work with two grooms, but I think I'd prefer one full timer, if that's okay with you now?"

"Of course it is, you must have what suits you best" encouraged Jennifer, "You run the yard after all."

"Actually, Susie from Chloe Coombe's yard has been on the phone to me this morning, she mentioned she might know someone who'd fit the bill."

"Really, that sounds interesting, do tell me more."

Caitlin went onto explain about Susie's friend. "He sounds quite suitable and 'tis always better to have a personal recommendation."

"If you think he might do, but we should set up an interview first, don't you think?"

"Of course Jennifer, shall I arrange it then?"

"Great, not for Friday though as I have my step children coming then and they're staying until Sunday. Next week would be better for me, just let me know when, okay? These sandwiches are fab aren't they? More coffee? Tell me how is poor little Queenie and her laminitis?"

Caitlin looked at Jennifer astonished that she should even know about Queenie, let alone the laminitis. "She's well on the road to recovery, I think we caught it in time."

"YOU caught it in time you mean, clever girl. Do you think that Jessica will be able to ride her at the weekend?"

"Yes, she'll be fine by then."

"Brilliant – I'm sure that Charles and the children will want to go out for a ride, would you mind awfully making yourself available over the weekend?"

"Of course, 'tis no problem at all". They finished their lunch, Jennifer asking all sorts of bizarre questions, about rugs, clips, feeding and the like and Caitlin tried to hide her surprise at her interest, eventually saying, "I'd better be getting back to work now Jennifer, I need to finish sorting the tack room out." She stood up and tidied up the tray, "I'll drop this into the kitchen on my way out."

"Excellent Caitlin, fingers crossed this lad works out, let me know as soon as you can when we can interview him. Thanks for your help." When she had gone Jennifer spun round in her chair, fished the *Manual of Horsemanship* out of her desk drawer and cranked up her computer.

Jonty and his mates skirted around the edge of the mill pond, close to the woodland at the side and crept up towards the buildings.

Stepping cautiously over the old mill race, the water tumbling fast and furiously owing to the rain, they edged their way around to the back, and peered in through the window. There was a wide wooden door, with a rusty iron handle, but when Jonty tried to open it, he found it was firmly locked. He cupped his hands across his eyes and stared in through the grimy panes of glass. It looked totally deserted inside, just cluttered with bits of old rubbish and machinery covered in white dust. He moved stealthily along the back of the mill, and discovered the small attached cottage and with it some dilapidated sheds. He tried the handle of the cottage door, and again it was locked. Weasel was moving ahead of him around to the front, and tried that door, but again no joy. Tubby had forged on exploring the barns opposite, managing to get in through a tiny door at the side and had squeezed his huge hulk through and disappeared. Jonty and Weasel hurried to join him. The barn was old and cavernous with huge oak beams and rafters as its main supports. There were two towering doors at the front, fastened from the inside with a long iron bar, and a set of open tread oak steps led up to a loft above covering a third of the roof space. They glanced around, and walked towards an opening on the right, which led them to two smaller barns, not nearly so grand or high. Jonty took out his phone put it into camera mode and started taking photos. They did not speak, as they took it all in. Nodding to them Jonty made his way out through the small door again and the others followed. He photographed the front of the mill and the cottage, then walked around the back, the way they had come, pausing now and then to take more pictures. They jumped the mill race over the tumbling water and edged back into the cover of the woodland.

"It's perfect" Jonty said.

Patrick was soaked through and fed up. He had been shoeing all morning and even though most of the horses had been indoors and he'd been able to pull his van up pretty close to the stables, the constant drip drip from the tailgate barely gave him any shelter. He was on his way into Haywards Heath on another call, and took the Cuckfield Road out of Fittlebury. His damp clothes making the windscreen steam up as he drove along the twisty road. He was just coming into Priors Cross when his phone rang and he pulled over and took the call, booking an appointment in his diary, and was just moving off when he noticed that same Landrover that had nearly run him off the road last week. It was parked up on the verge side ahead of him - so, they had been from round here then, he thought triumphantly, well - they should've known better! He was curious, and as he drove past he slowed right down to peer inside, no-one was inside, but what kind of loony would want to be out on a day like this? The Landrover had been parked quite close to the bridleway up to the Abbey and being nosy, he glanced up the path and saw three figures coming down the hillside, half obliterated with the relentless rain. Bloody idiots he thought and drove on.

Oliver had heard from Suse, just a text to say that she was safe and had arrived back home now, and would not be coming back. He read it over and over again. The initial shock of finding her gone and the remorse he'd felt then had now developed into anger at her cowardice in running away. She had made a real fool of him, as the news by now would be all over the area - people loved a bit of spiteful gossip he knew only too well. Still in a way, it put her in a bad light and portrayed her as the guilty party and not him, so he considered it was probably best to have the pitying looks from people and their sympathy, rather than thinking he was a callous bastard who had left his wife. He convinced himself that it was not really his fault, that she had never fully understood him. He had texted her back, thanking her for letting him know she was safe but decided against saying any more than that. Looking at things in a rational way, her taking control of the situation had in fact made everything a lot easier. He didn't need to make any immediate plans - he wanted to be clear in his mind, just to take each day as it came, and for the time being at least his life could stay exactly as it was. Meanwhile he would sink himself into his work, and there would be no-one to moan about his long hours, that in itself was a relief.

CHAPTER 25

Paulene looked up as Andrew came into the surgery, she was trying to make out Oliver's spiky hand writing from the previous day.

"Morning boss" she greeted, returning to the papers on her desk, "what does this say, any ideas?"

Andrew picked up the work sheet, "Mmmm, well it's a call out to the kennels, so must be for that young hunter who has thrown a splint, Oli told me about it, so I am guessing that word is Metacarpal."

"Thanks Andrew, I know he has a lot on his plate, but his writing is getting worse." She sighed in frustration and began typing.

"Don't be too hard on him Paulene, he's had a shock, and we need to be supporting him right now." Andrew put his hand on her shoulder, "he's having a rough ride, we all know it's not unexpected but it's tough just the same."

"Okay boss, you're right, I know that, but it's just so exasperating and this wastes so much of my time."

"Now, I need to talk to you about something else, have you got a minute?"

"Of course, what's up?"

"I'm going to see the bank in Horsham this morning about the Old Mill, Gary has rushed the figures and business plan through, and I want to get this moving as soon as possible. I've decided though, that whatever happens today, we're going to have to get some more help in here, another assistant vet and some office help for you."

"Well if you take on another vet, then I'll definitely need help. Have you run this by Oliver?"

"Someone taking my name in vain?" Oliver said over Andrew's shoulder, leaning over the desk, "Sorry Paulene, I knew you wouldn't be able to read my writing, I was trying to do this in the rain!"

"It's okay Oli, although if you had been here two minutes earlier, I might have thumped you!" she laughed up at him and Andrew, God they were both so good looking, the blonde and the dark heads towering over her.

"Oli, I was just saying to Paulene, that no matter how the meeting goes with the bank today, we need to take on an assistant vet, and that means an extra pair of hands in the office too."

"I agree, but let's just see how the meeting goes first shall we?"

"I think Paulene should draft an advertisement for an assistant vet anyway; it'll be a while before anyone could start, by the time the ad is accepted and we sift through the applicants and hold interviews. The office assistant post can be advertised once we have a shortlist drawn up."

"Yes, you do have a point mate, it's not a quick process, and regardless of whether we get the mill or not, one thing for sure is we do need an assistant."

"Why don't I draft it this morning then, and you two can see what you think of it this afternoon?"

"Great idea Paulene. Right, time for a coffee before I go, who wants one?" He moved towards the door, he felt really elated, everything seemed to be fitting into place.

Oliver groaned, "I can't buddy, I gotta go, loads of stuff on, I just needed to stock up the truck with some drugs, I had a run on gear yesterday."

"I'll have one though Andrew" called Paulene to them as they walked through to the back office.

Andrew went over to the coffee machine, whilst Oli went over to the locked drug store. "Sure you haven't got time for one Oli" Andrew shouted from the other side of the room "It's all ready!" He pulled some mugs out from under the shelf, pushing the little capsules into the machine.

"Nope, I'd better get cracking" Oli shouted back, "By the way we need to do a re-order today in here, we're running short of quite a few things."

"I'll do it when I get back" Andrew took Paulene's coffee out to her, "We might need that office assistant sooner rather than later."

Andrew went back, picked up his own coffee and looked again at the business plan. He knew it inside out by now, but it was important to be well briefed, borrowing money was not as easy as it used to be, and he wanted to impress the bank guy. Oliver came out of the drug cupboard, his arms piled high with boxes. Andrew watched him as he marked them out in the inventory ledger, he looked tired, although of course that was not surprising, not just because of his personal difficulties but the immense work load they both had.

"You really okay buddy?" he said

"Well I would be lying if I said I was, but I'm coping and that's different eh?" Oliver grimaced, "Anyway keeping busy is a good tonic."

"Yes, it is, but you know I'm always here if you want to talk about anything."

"Thanks, I know you are, and I really appreciate it, but I just have to get on with things, and working hard seems to be the best option, you know that, you're a workaholic yourself." He heaved up the boxes, bade Andrew farewell and good luck with the appointment and was gone.

Andrew picked up his briefcase and stuffed in the papers, slurped the rest of his coffee, picked up his keys and made for the outer office.

"Bye Paulene, wish me luck, I'll be back as soon as – okay."

"Good luck boss" said Paulene looking up, "I really mean it you know?" She watched him go out of the door, looking very smart in his suit; he looked fantastic, Julia was a lucky woman, a pity she didn't seem to appreciate him.

Charles drew a deep breath and picked up the phone dialling Celia's number, praying to get the answer phone, but after a couple of rings she picked up.

"Celia - Charles here, just want to confirm what time I'll be collecting the children on Friday. I thought about two, if that's okay with you?"

"Hello Charles, yes that should be fine. What are you planning to do with them, so I can make sure that they pack the right things?"

"Oh, the usual, probably go out for a ride, and maybe a trip out on the Saturday, but not sure where yet."

"How are the horses?" Celia always had a pang when she thought about them, she really regretted not riding, much more than she missed Charles. Of course, she could still have a horse at her parents' place but their disappointment in her was always irksome, so she hadn't ridden for a long time now.

"They're fine, Caitlin is still with us and she runs a pretty tight ship, very efficient, although we're a groom down, but plenty of time before the season starts to replace her."

Celia felt her hackles rising at the '*we*' reference, "Ah well, I'm sure you'll cope" she said pointedly, hardly disguising the bitterness in her voice, "Charles, please don't be late on Friday will you, the children get fed up when they are sitting waiting about for you."

"Celia, I'll be there at two, how often am I ever late for them?" he replied patiently, determined to keep his temper and not let her wind him up.

"I only said don't be late that's all. By the way, Rupert is becoming quite difficult, he's been really recalcitrant lately, see if you can talk to him about his behaviour."

"He's just growing up Celia, having his own opinions, it's a difficult age. Just bear with him, he'll grow out of it."

"Like you did, I don't think so. Anyway what the hell do you know about it Charles, it's difficult enough being a single parent without your amateur psychology."

"Okay okay Celia, I'll have a word with him. See you at two on Friday. Ciao." Charles replaced the receiver firmly, yet again Celia had to moan about something and whatever he did would be wrong. He was glad that he had not risen to her bait. Actually, the prospect of the children coming over was really appealing to him, as for the first time, Jennifer was actually totally on board and had planned a day out for them all on the Saturday. Arundel Castle so she had said, oh well he would go along with whatever she had organised. Whatever though he must not be late on Friday.

Lucy got off the bus, at least it wasn't pissing with rain, like it had been yesterday. She marched across the town square to the bistro, knocked on the glass door, and Gino smiling at her came over with his keys unlocking it to let her in. Lucy did not smile back but looked around gloomily, there was a delicious smell of baking and she could hear the sounds of chatter coming from the kitchen. Gino gesticulated for her to follow him wondering to himself if it had been a mistake to hire this girl with her miserable face, but Maria was pregnant and he didn't want her working herself to the bone. Lucy followed him into the kitchen where two women were working and talking at the same time.

"Lucy, this is Maria my wife and this is Francesca my niece, they will show you what to do" Gino said as he made the introductions.

"Welcome Lucy" said the woman who was Gino's wife. She was pretty with dark hair and keen chocolate brown eyes, her slim body very obviously pregnant, "I will show you the ropes but pretty soon, you will be on your own I think." She patted her bump affectionately.

"And I am Francesca, but people usually call me Cesca" added the other girl frostily, who was without doubt one of the ugliest girls Lucy had ever seen. Cesca, was not tall, and was bordering on obese, with thick dark glasses and short brown hair.

"Hello" said Lucy adding hastily "Nice to meet you both."

Maria, moved away from the work surface, "Now Lucy, let me find you an apron, and you can start by making the fillings for the baguettes and baps. We always make this up fresh every morning."

Lucy took the apron, put it on, and followed Maria over to the work surface. There was a vast selection of salads and vegetables, all washed and ready to chop. A stack of white polythene containers were on the side.

"Now Lucy, here is a list of all the fillings we do, and we make up one container of each, which goes into the chiller cabinet in the shop so that the customers can see what's on offer. There are strict hygiene conditions, you must wear latex gloves," she pointed to a bright yellow box, "and every chopping board and knife is coloured coded. Look the codes are displayed here" she indicated a laminated sign on the wall "and you must remember to wash your hands each time you touch different meats, in that little sink over there. That sink is only to be used for hand washing, not cleaning food – okay?"

Fuck me thought Lucy what a palaver, but she said meekly, "yes, I understand Maria."

Lucy toiled away all morning in the kitchen, but at least the time passed quickly. At lunch time she waited at the tables, and by the afternoon she realised she had not sat down all day and her feet were killing her. Maria was very nice to her, as was Gino, but Cesca made it clear from the outset that she didn't think much of Lucy, and kept her piggy eyes on her the whole day long, never missing an opportunity to criticise her. Lucy muttered to herself to keep thinking of the money and that she wouldn't be here for long. Once again she cursed herself for being so hot headed and walking out of her job at Nantes, but on the other hand, she fumed that they had not even bothered to try and find her and change her mind. Dastards.

Jennifer was having a lunge lesson on Ksar in the school from Beebs, concentrating madly on her balance and keeping her hands still. It was such hard work, she had never dreamt how much effort it would be, to do what everyone else found so easy. At first she had been very apprehensive at the thought of the lunge lesson especially as Ksar was much bigger than Rufus and it alarmed her not having any control of the reins. Chloe had assured her that she would be fine, Beebs would make sure she was safe, and all she need worry about was her position in the saddle. They had started cautiously until Jennifer had relaxed, and Chloe had been right, she didn't feel unsafe, but she didn't feel very tidy either, bobbing about all over the place.

"You're going great Jen, don't forget to keep breathing, and feeling the way the horse goes underneath you." urged Beebs, "Now take your arms away from the balancing strap and put them both out straight in front of you."

"Are you sure?"

"Okay, if you are nervous about that, just do one hand at a time."

"I'm trusting you Beebs." sighed Jennifer, but she did as she was asked and sure enough it was okay, "Right now I'm going to do the other one." She wobbled a bit, and clutched back at the strap, then once she had righted herself tried again. After a few goes she was putting both hands out. "I can do it!" she laughed.

"Okay, now try putting them out to each side, like an aeroplane."

Jennifer did as she was asked "It's like balancing on a tight rope." she called, "But hey it's not so bad!" They worked on, Jennifer moving her arms about, whilst still maintaining the balance in the saddle. At the end of half an hour she was exhausted and Beebs had finally allowed her to stop.

"Well done, you did really well, I'm very proud of you." laughed Beebs. Patting Jennifer on the back, "You have a natural seat and have made such amazing progress!"

"Thanks Beebs, but I couldn't do any of it without all of you, you've been fantastic with me." Jennifer beamed. She felt great! They led Ksar back to his stable and Jennifer started to un-tack him just as they had shown her. The big noble head nuzzled in her pockets, looking for a treat. Jennifer now stocked up with Polos, gave him the rest of the packet. Then she led him outside to wash him off.

Chloe had come down to the yard, and she looked on approvingly. "Beebs says you were fine. Lunge lessons are really good for you Jen, helps you to balance on your bum, rather than relying on the reins to support yourself. You'll feel the difference when you ride Rufus next."

"Chloe, I can't tell you how grateful I am to you, I'm so enjoying it all, I can't thank you enough."

"Our pleasure. It gives us all a lot of satisfaction to see you progressing so well."

"By the way, thanks for telling me about Arundel Castle, I thought it'd be a good idea to take Jessica and Rupert there on Saturday with Charles."

"That's a good idea, it's a great day out for everyone, including you."

Jennifer finished washing Ksar off and put him back in his box, joining the others in the tack room for a coffee. She plonked herself down on a chair, rubbing her aching legs, and Beebs handed her a mug, and the biscuit tin.

"Thanks Beebs, I'm starving! Chloe, there's something I need to talk to you about."

"Oh, what's that then?"

"Well, I can't just go on having riding lessons in return for the odd bit of help in the yard, I'd like to pay my way." Jennifer stammered not wanting to give any offence at the mention of money.

"But you do! You have helped the girls enormously, and me too" Chloe added, "you really don't need to do that."

"Look how would it be then if I paid for Rufus' keep, at least that way I'd feel I'm not taking you for granted?"

"Look there's really no need, you do your fair share." expostulated Chloe, "But if it would make you feel better, why not pay for his shoes and stuff?"

"Well if you're sure, then okay, but if at any time you feel you want more, then please, please tell me."

"It's a deal!" laughed Chloe. "Now I had better get back to the house, I'm taking the kids to the cinema this afternoon. Everything under control here ladies?" she asked the girls.

"Sure boss, go and have a great time."

Laura was worried. She knew that Jonty was planning something big but he wouldn't talk to her about it at all. His horrible friends had been coming round to the flat a lot, leaving empty lager cans and fag ends all over the place, but any evidence of what they were plotting was cleared away before she had a chance to see it. Obviously she knew that it concerned that bastard Charles but what could Jonty be interested in that would make him a shed load of money as he put it? She had racked her brains to think, but could come up with no sensible answer. He'd asked her to go back again to chat up Linda and Sean, which she was dreading. He'd given her some dope for them, to sweeten them up, it sickened her, but she'd agreed. His instructions were to fire them up about hunting, and inflame them to do something radical at one of the meets with her. It would not be hard to do, as they were already dedicated Hunt Sabs, but they weren't villains. How was he going to use them to fit in with his plans she wondered? Whatever her misgivings though, she was afraid of Jonty, and what he would do if she defied him. So she had no alternative but to comply, and she picked up her bag and put in the gear, and clambered down the stairs out into the normal life of the street below.

Andrew left the bank, swinging through the glass doors with a spring in his step. He couldn't quite believe it, but he had pulled it off! Thank God for Gary and his amazing mind, he'd drummed up that business plan in record time, put all the salient points and their financial position. It was a really cohesive document and had clearly impressed the bank. They had agreed in principle to a mortgage on the mill subject to all the usual legal stuff and also agreed to the extra finances needed to employ a new veterinary assistant and another office member. The bottom line was that they could go ahead with plans to buy, but that also had the downside that they would have to work their butts off to pay for it! Ah well, no gain without pain he mused. Andrew crossed the Carfax skirting around the chairs and tables at the Bistro heading for the car park at Piries Place. He stopped in at Waitrose on the way past and bought a bottle of Champagne and some buns – they would have to celebrate! Going through the checkout into the square, he took out his phone and rang Oliver, the phone rang and then his voice mail cut in – bugger. Then he rang Mark Templeton to give him the good news.

"Mark, its Andrew, we're on, I've secured the finances. Obviously subject to surveys etc."

"Fantastic news Andrew! I'm really pleased and I know Lady V will be too."

"Can you keep it under your hat though Mark, just for a while, as I don't want someone else making a higher offer."

"I don't think Lady V would do that to you mate, but of course, just between us, until it's all signed and sealed."

"Great, I appreciate it. I'll ring our solicitors when I get back to the office and get the ball rolling."

"Let me know how it goes. Anyway well done! See you later."

Andrew ended the call, and tried Oliver again, but still it went to voice mail, he must be busy. Still good for him, probably the best tonic at the moment. He found his car and with his head full of plans drove out of the car park towards Fittlebury.

Chloe parked the Discovery in the car park, noticing Andrew Napier pulling out in his Toyota, she waved but he didn't see her. She turned around to the kids in the back, who were excited at the thought of going to the cinema. Toby was in the front this time and offered to go and get the car park ticket, she gave him some money and looking very grown up he marched over to the pay machine. She looked at him fondly, they were all growing up, where had those little babies gone, and she suddenly felt quite gloomy, thinking of all the hours she must have wasted working and being away from them.

Toby came back with the ticket and stuck it on the windscreen and they clambered out , Chloe carefully took the little ones, one in each hand and they walked across the car park.

"I think we have time for a milkshake before the film if you like?"

"Yeah, I want a strawberry one!" shouted Lily, her eyes glittering, "and can I have a cake too?"

"You are so greedy Lily, you'll end up looking like Miss Piggy!" snarled Toby.

"Don't be so horrid Toby! At least I won't end up looking like you!" yelled Lily "with your big head!"

"Mummy, tell her to shut up!"

"Now you two, you can stay in the car and squabble on your own, if you don't behave yourselves. It's your choice, so what's it to be?"

"Okay, but I hate him" sulked Lily, "I really do hate him."

"Lily" warned Chloe, "What about you Toby?"

"I hate her too."

"Now this is your last chance - either make up or sit in the car." The looks on their faces said it all, "come on then, let's go."

They ambled towards the Carfax, Toby wanted to go to MacDonalds. Chloe patiently explained they didn't have time to walk all the way to the end of the town, and how about the little Bistro, which did lovely cakes. The thought of the cakes won them over and the children took ages to choose what they wanted. After a lot of deliberation about what flavour milkshakes were on offer, they finally ordered and sat at a little table out in the square, waiting for the goodies to be brought out. Chloe was deep in conversation with the children, when the shadow of the waitress loomed over the table and she looked up, her mouth almost dropping open in surprise.

"Lucy! What on earth are you doing here?"

"Hello Chloe, what does it look like? I'm working." she replied rudely.

"Well good for you, I had heard you had left Nantes."

"Did you indeed, I suppose that bitch Caitlin told you."

"That's not a very nice word, is it Mummy?" said Lily looking up surprised.

"Sorry, you're right, it isn't" muttered Lucy, fuming at being put in her place by a seven year old, fuck them all!

"Actually Lucy, Caitlin didn't say a word to me, Susie told me you'd left. You know how things get round in the village."

"Whatever - anyway, I'm best out of there, this is a much better job." she lied.

"I'm glad for you, I truly am. Well, see you around." Chloe turned away to help Rory cut up his cake, clearly terminating the conversation with the bad tempered girl. God, she thought Caitlin was well rid of her.

Lucy turned on her heel. Who the hell did Chloe Coombe think she was turning her back on her like that! She was furious - they were all the same, stuck up wankers. She wished she had spat on their food before she brought it out!

Chloe thought, what a nasty piece of work, talk about bitter. Still she was not going to let the petulant Lucy spoil her afternoon with the kids.

CHAPTER 26

It was Thursday morning and Jennifer was aching all down the inside of her thighs, and her stomach muscles were killing her after the lunge lesson. When Charles had made love to her last night, she had secretly winced with pain as he pumped away between her legs. Still she was just relieved that they seemed to be back on course again, he was really making an effort, but she knew she had changed too. Going to Chloe's had given her a real purpose in life and the thought of surprising Charles was a delicious secret. She sat in her study and pulled out her cheque book, she was going to leave an envelope for Chloe in her letter box, so she couldn't object - although she had no idea how much even a set of shoes for a horse would cost. She Googled livery yards in West Sussex and discovered that to keep a horse at livery alone would cost in the region of £120 per week. Crikey, and she had been having lessons too. She put her fountain pen to her lips and thought - then wrote a cheque out for five hundred pounds, there that should be enough, she put the cheque into the envelope and sealed it, writing Chloe's name on the front with a flourish. She opened her desk draw and took out two little notelets, one for Beebs and one for Susie, dropped a £50 note into each and wrote a simple thank you note. Good, she was pleased - she wouldn't leave them in the tack room, but put them through their cottage door.

She popped down to the kitchen with her breakfast tray. Mrs Fuller heard her coming and had turned to the door - for once a smile on her face.

"Morning! Thanks for breakfast. Just wanted to ask if we were all ready for the children tomorrow? I'm sure you are, but is there anything you want me to do, or get when I go out?"

"We're all sorted thank you Madam. Doris and I've done their rooms ready, and I've ordered all the things they like from Waitrose on-line"

"Why Mrs Fuller how good you are, did you do it on the internet then ? I'd no idea! How cool!"

Mrs Fuller looked pleased with herself, and added mischievously, "Celia showed me how to do it and she got me a little lap top for myself."

Jennifer felt foolish, of course, how did Mrs Fuller manage to do all she did, and shop too. She had been stupid not to have realised. Bloody marvellous *WC* strikes again she thought bitterly. She managed to pull herself together and remarked, "Well that's excellent Mrs Fuller, and if there is nothing you want me to do then, I'm popping out for a couple of hours."

Before she left for Chloe's, Jennifer walked to the stable yard. Caitlin was busy lugging shavings into the boxes, and putting down thick snowy beds for the horses.

"Morning Caitlin, just checking on Queenie?"

"Oh she's fine now Jennifer, seems as right as rain, sound as a pound so she is."

"That's really good news. So she'll be alright for Jessica tomorrow then?"

"Yes, she should be fine, and I'm bringing up Dandy and Scooter, so that they'll be ready should the children want to ride with Mr Charles. Of course they're not fit, but they're quiet enough, and the children won't want to do much."

"Well done Caitlin, do you need me to do anything?"

Caitlin looked at Jennifer strangely "No 'tis not a problem, I can manage."

"Well if you're sure? Just let me know if there is anything though." She moved out of the stable, "Oh and by the way, did you manage to contact Felix?"

"Yes, I did and he's interested, he's going to call me tomorrow to let me know his day off next week and when he can come for the interview."

"Excellent, okay Caitlin, see you later" She turned and left

Caitlin to it. Caitlin watched her go, how did she know that the boy's name was Felix she wondered - she was sure she hadn't mentioned it?

Jennifer walked out of the yard, unaware of her slip, and saw a car coming down the drive. Who on earth could that be? The car drew level with her, and she bent down to talk to the driver, it was Grace Allington.

"Hi Jennifer, I was just dropping in a note to say thank you for such a great party at the weekend. We really enjoyed it!"

"I'm so glad Grace, it was fun wasn't it?"

"Look do you mind if I ask you something?"

"Go ahead, do you want to do it over a coffee?" Jennifer desperately hoped she would decline, as she was anxious to get up to up to Mileoak.

"I'm so sorry Jennifer, it'll have to be another time, as I have to get up to mum and dad's. I was just wondering if, well I know that... are you looking for another groom?"

"Well yes we are, Caitlin and I are interviewing next week as it happens." Jennifer was surprised, this was the last thing she thought Grace had wanted to talk about.

"I was just wondering if you might consider me, I could only do part-time I'm afraid."

"Oh Grace, I'm so sorry but Caitlin wants a full timer, but I'll mention your interest to her naturally."

"No – please don't" said Grace disappointed, it had been a stupid idea anyway, "Look I have to go, perhaps we can have that coffee another time?"

"Love to. Bye." Jennifer watched her turn the car around, and was sorry, she seemed very low. Why did Grace want a job, surely they weren't short of money were they?

Sandy was exhausted, it had been a difficult case, always so harrowing when children were involved. There had been a lot of evidence on both sides to wade through, allegations of abuse and drugs but finally it had gone her way and the mother was given custody. Okay it was satisfying to win but the price was high - she felt wasted. The mess people made of their lives never ceased to amaze her. She hadn't ridden since Monday, and riding was her salvation. Monday - she smiled to herself, Mark had been good company, and they got on so well together. Since then, they'd only communicated by texts, but every day nonetheless. She rang Simon saying she would come back to Chambers in the morning to wrap things up, but she was going home straight from the Court. Now she stood in her shower, the hot water pumping over her, and she put her head up so that it coursed over her face. Reluctantly, she turned off the taps, and stepped out, wrapping herself in a towel. She moved over to the mirror above the basin, steamed up from the hot water and rubbed a little hole, so that she could see her reflection, pulling faces at herself. There was a distant beep beep from her phone in the bedroom and she padded out of the bathroom, and picked it up from the bed. She smiled, the text was from Mark, suggesting they meet for a drink at the Fox this evening. She tapped her answer straight away, she was not into game playing and making him wait for the response. '*Great*', she typed. There was definitely something different about him. When she had married her artist, it was just a lot of lust really, and looking back she knew that he had seen her as an easy meal ticket, he was a waster and she was a successful barrister and a stupid sucker. The scars still ran deep, and she hid behind her tough shell exterior, but this was different somehow - she genuinely liked him. He was a good laugh for sure, a great fuck, but he was also a decent man, but he had set alarm bells ringing in her head, although instead of running away like she normally would, she found that she was really quite excited about seeing him again. Oh well, she sighed, don't wear your heart on your sleeve kidda, it might get broken and that was the last thing she wanted when her life was on an even keel. She couldn't bear the thought of all that upset and trying to put a lonely brave face on it all. She pulled off the towel and oiled her body all over, glanced at the bedside clock, it was only 5.30pm, she would go down and see what she could throw together in the fridge and suggest he came back for some supper.

Jonty ran his finger down Laura's cheek, cupping his other hand under her chin, then swiftly took hold of her hair and pulled it back.

"Jonty, please, don't be so rough!" She cried out, but the more she tried to wriggle free, the more he held her fast. A moment of fear coursed through her and she knew he had seen it by the expression on his face.

He released her not taking his eyes from hers, and started to unbutton her jeans, yanking them down over her snaky hips, and they fell around her ankles. She stood in her knickers, like a rabbit trapped in the headlights, and his hands roamed up to her tee shirt and pulled it up over her face and head, so that she couldn't see.

"Don't move babe"

"Jonty I can't see!" She suddenly felt terribly vulnerable, her breasts exposed and blindfolded by her own tee shirt.

"All the more of a surprise for you." Deftly he circled his fingers around her nipples, making them stand pert and erect, and he took each one in turn in his mouth sucking hard. Despite herself she moaned with pleasure, and he sucked harder, letting his fingers roam down to her tummy button, and then down towards the edge of her knickers. He slipped his fingers inside, pushing her open as far as her trapped legs would allow. Jonty knelt down, sliding the knickers down and licking her with his tongue -he could feel how wet she was with wanting him. Without looking down, he groped for her ankles and she stepped obligingly out of her jeans and opened her legs wider, and he pushed his fingers up inside her.

"Oh fuck me now please!" She begged, and made to pull the tee shirt off from her face, but he slapped her hard on the top of her leg. She shrieked in shock. "Jonty!"

He slapped her again "Leave the tee shirt alone Laura, you'll spoil the surprise!" He pulled at the back of her knees and she collapsed onto the floor, he drew her legs together and pushed them up towards her face, so that her bottom was totally exposed to him, and he carried on stroking between her legs with one hand, and with his other pulled out a tube from his pocket. Flipping the lid off with his thumb he shook out two large white tablets.

"Jonty, Jonty, that's so wonderful, but please let me take off the tee shirt"

"Hush hush Laura, be a good little girl. Stay with your legs just like that and don't move, you'll love it, you will honest!" He stood up, went over to the drawer and pulled out a large syringe, filling it with water from a bottle, and went back over to her. She was obediently quite still, her knees bent right up to her chin and her little pink clitoris peeping out. "Lay still sweetie, it's coming!" He pushed the tablets deep inside her vagina, and he heard her gasp, inserting the syringe as far as he could, he plunged in the water.

She screamed out "that's so fuckin' awesome!" She bucked and writhed about, as he held up her legs fascinated with the frothy water gushing out. "Amazing, amazing" she panted, her convulsions subsiding. He leant forward and pulled the tee shirt off her face watching her closely.

"Good or good?" he laughed.

"Brilliant, brilliant!" She smiled up at him."Just fucking brilliant, what was it?"

"Alka Seltzer! My turn now eh?" She sat up, as he lay back and she started to unzip his trousers, when he was like this she would do anything for him.

John was late coming home again. Chloe had put the kids to bed hours ago, and she was bloody tired herself but was sitting in her office distractedly tapping away at her computer. She dimly heard the hall clock chime eleven, and she leant back in her chair, running her hand through her hair, not able to concentrate - where the bloody hell was he? She had called his mobile so many times she had lost count and it always went to voice mail. He had sent a text earlier to say he was going to be delayed, but Christ there was late and there was late! What was going on? Their day at Arundel had been good and he'd seemed to be okay, but since then it all had all gone wrong again. She tried to make some sense of her jumbled thoughts. She knew that he'd been having a tough time at work, but surely he could talk to her about it? Over the years he'd become disenchanted with his company, he had worked hard and they took advantage of him, but surely that couldn't be the reason? Was he ill? That wouldn't explain the late evenings though would it? The only other thing it could be, and this had been nagging at her for a while now, and she had not dared think about it seriously before, was that he was having an affair. All these late nights, his reluctance to leave his phone unguarded, his perfunctory love making, all seemed to add up to another woman. Surely not though? Not her John? He had always been so totally reliable - such a home man she would have trusted him no matter what. What else could it be? Oh God, not John, not John. It was impossible to work, she just couldn't focus on anything. Sam laid his head in her lap and she fondled his ears, leaning down and kissing the top of his head, and he nuzzled into her. "Oh Sam, what am I going to do?"

Jennifer stoked Charles' back, kissing each shoulder blade as he stood at the basin brushing his teeth, he turned to look at her, his mouth still frothy from the toothpaste.

"I know I'm a shit a lot of the time, but I do really love you, you know?"

"I know you do, and I love you, it's been a difficult year for us both."

"It has, but it's coming right now. I want to thank you too my darling for being so lovely about the children coming tomorrow."

"Oh Charles, I'm looking forward to it, really I am, we're going to have a super time. I just hope they enjoy it too." He leant forward and kissed her, his breath minty and clean. She took his hand and pulled him into the bedroom "Shall we go to bed darling?"

From the garden, watching their silhouettes against the window Pete stood watching them embrace, his face contorting with anger.

The next morning, when the dew was still on the grass, Cailtin was rudely woken by the shriek of her alarm - she rolled over in bed and hugged herself. It had been a lovely evening, she could still feel the imprint of his arms around her and the touch of his lips on hers. It had been a bonus to see him last night and he had said he would try and see her today, but she knew it would be difficult, more for her than him. Jessica and Rupert were coming this afternoon, and she wanted to make sure that the yard was spotless when they came to ride. She had a million things to do. The thought of it made her toss back the duvet and dash into the bathroom. Washing and dressing in break neck speed, she shoved on her muckers and scrunched out across the gravel to the stables. She had brought in Dandy and Scooter the night before to join Queenie, and they whinnied quietly as she walked into the yard.

"Good morning my beauties, are you hungry for your breakfast then?" Tugging open the feed room door, Dandy started banging on the door impatiently "Hey you bad boy, don't be so greedy!" she laughed. She slopped a scoop of mix into a bucket, and took out two handfuls for the ponies, fat little buggers they don't want much. Horses fed, she made herself a coffee in the tack room, nibbling a biscuit for her own breakfast. It was true what they said, you lost your appetite when you were in love. Come 'n Caitlin, she chided herself, get a bloody move on!

Katherine thought Chloe looked dreadful, bags under her eyes and if she didn't know any different she would have thought she'd been crying. Beebs and Susie gave Katherine a look, and none of them said anything. Chloe stomped around the yard, checking and nit-picking about everything, it was so unlike her, she took up a broom and started sweeping so violently that the broom head snapped off, she threw down the handle in disgust. The others whispered together in the tack room, as they watched Chloe pick up the broom and lob it in the bin. Katherine took a deep sigh, wiped her hands on the back of her breeches and went outside, walking up to Chloe and putting her arm around her shoulders. Beebs and Susie watched in admiration, as Katherine talked to Chloe and led her back towards the tack room. The girls made excuses and scarpered for the safety of the yard.

"Come on Chloe, what's up, this is not like you, what's happened?" said Katherine gently, watching Chloe as her face crumpled.

"Oh Katherine, you'll think I'm being so stupid and please, please don't let this go any further" pleaded Chloe.

"Of course it won't Chloe, you know that, and you know, it is trite but it's true, a problem shared is a problem halved."

"I just don't know what to think Katherine, I'm just at a loss" snivelled Chloe, and suddenly out came tumbling all the worries about John. Katherine let her talk on without interrupting, and finally Chloe stopped and just sat silently wringing her hands together in anxiety.

"Look Chloe, you don't *know* anything at all do you? Why don't you talk to him, come straight out with it and see what he says. I don't know John very well, but I expect he's in as much turmoil as you are. Try and make some time that you can be together, and talk about this, much better now than later."

"I really have tried Katherine, but he just brushes me off with one excuse after another and it's always difficult when the children are around. You know what I mean, and I certainly don't want them to witness a row, or listen to us talking about affairs."

"Oh Chloe, of course you don't, the age of innocence is so short lived at the best of times. Can't you try and find some time and space for just you and John? I'm more than willing to babysit if you need?"

"Thank you Katherine, I'll certainly give it some thought and you're right talking about things has helped. I'll see how things go now, but I can't thank you enough for listening."

"Oh Chloe, it was the least I can do, and I really mean it, if there's anything that I can do at all, any time, just let me know, even if it's only just to talk about it, okay?"

"Katherine, I can't tell you how much that means to me, I've been going through hell keeping it all to myself." Chloe looked into Katherine's sweet face and felt better, it seemed unreal now, all those stupid fears, she was just over-reacting.

They both looked up hearing the sound of a car arriving in the yard, it was Jennifer. Chloe wiped her eyes, and ran her fingers through her hair. Katherine stood up and gave her hug and went out to meet Jennifer, so that Chloe would have time to compose herself. Jennifer was lovely but right now Chloe was in no state to see anyone. She strode over to Jennifer's car, headcollars slung over her shoulder, she bent down to speak to Jennifer and they ambled off together towards the fields. Chloe watched them go, heaving a sigh of relief, good old Katherine.

Charles had not gone to work that day, he wanted to make sure he was spot on the dot to pick up Jessica and Rupert, he couldn't bear the thought of Celia moaning at him, it would give her great pleasure to spoil the weekend. He took his time with his breakfast, rifling through the FT as he idly chewed on his toast. He put the paper down, Jennifer had gone off in a hurry this morning, saying she had wanted to get some last minute bits and pieces for the children's visit. He smiled fondly, he had asked a lot of her, coming down here to Nantes. She seemed to be so much happier lately, and he was glad. He wanted the weekend to go well, and he picked up the brochures of Arundel Castle that she had left for him. It certainly looked as though they would have a good day, he just hoped the children thought so too. Jessica was okay, but Rupert was a different kettle of fish. Well this time he was not going to put up with his nonsense, and if he was rude to Jennifer again, he would have to deal with him. He sighed, he couldn't be bothered with the paper and decided to go over to the stables to check how the horses were, he had precious little enough time at home and he wanted to make the most of it. He went out through the drawing room and over the terrace, skirting around the orchard, and wandered around to the back of the yard, via the paddock. As he strolled into the yard, he noticed that the vet's car was there, and thinking it was odd he walked quietly over to the tack room, his loafered feet making no sound as he approached. The door was open and to his amazement he saw Oliver and Caitlin were embracing, and she was stroking his hair.

"Hmm" he coughed discreetly. Oliver and Caitlin whirled round, totally shocked.

Very red in the face Caitlin spluttered "Oh good morning Mr Charles, I ... We didn't hear you coming!"

"Clearly" remarked Charles dryly.

"It is not quite what it seems Charles, Caitlin was just consoling me, I had some bad news at the weekend" muttered Oliver.

"Look Oliver, Caitlin, it really is none of my business at all, let's forget it shall we?"

"Mr Charles, it really wasn't what you think, Oliver's wife has left him" blurted Caitlin.

"I'm sorry to hear that Oliver, a difficult time for you naturally. Whatever is between you and Caitlin is not my business – okay?"

"But really that's all we were doing, wasn't it Oliver?" Caitlin turned to Oliver for his affirmation.

"Yes, it was, but I can see what it must look like to you Charles, but I can assure you it was innocent." Oliver looked beseechingly at Charles, who smiled at him, with a knowing look.

"As I said let's forget it. Now Oliver, why are you here?"

"Just checking Queenie and her suspected laminitis, I saw Patrick last night and he said you were asking about surgical shoeing?"

With the conversation on a professional footing now, Oliver gained his normal confident manner and they discussed the merits of heart bar shoes. Caitlin could hardly bring herself to look at either of them - what a mess, she thought.

CHAPTER 27

Charles slung the children's bags into the back of the Range Rover. Jessica was in the back with an army of dolls and he jumped in beside Rupert who was sitting in the front passenger seat. The children waved to Celia as she stood at the front door and he gave her a perfunctory nod of his head put on his seat belt and swept off down the drive. Rupert was sullen and silent giving a lot of sighs whilst Charles drove. Jessica was chattering away in the back to her dolls.

Charles tried to make conversation with Rupert "How's school going then old chum?"

"Finc" replied Rupert stonily, not offering any more information and gazing straight ahead.

Charles sighed inwardly and tried again, "Been playing much sport? Cricket?"

"Cricket, playing for the first team this year" Rupert replied, and then after a pause he asked "How are the horses?"

Charles was relieved, at last something to talk about he thought. "Caitlin has brought up Scooter and he's fine, Queenie's had a spot of laminitis but thankfully it was caught in time. Thought we'd ride later if you'd like?"

"Good that means she won't come" Rupert said nastily, "definitely I want to ride."

Charles was immediately on the defensive "Now look here Rupert, let's get one thing straight young man, I will not have you being rude to Jennifer. I know the divorce has been hard for you to deal with, but these things happen and you have got to make an effort you know."

Rupert snapped back at him with venom "She doesn't make any

effort with us"

"Well it's hard for Jennifer too, don't forget that, perhaps if you tried to meet her half way things might be different" Charles bargained, thinking, little sod, but knew that he had to handle this carefully, if he wasn't going make things worse. He tried again, "Look, let's all try and make an effort this weekend and see how it goes, do it for me please?"

"Mrs Fuller and everyone hates her you know" Rupert stared at his father, his eyes blazing with defiance.

Charles was shocked at the look and blustered, "Actually that's not true, Mrs Fuller has been getting on very well with Jennifer and so have the rest of the staff, so don't start causing trouble there."

"You just always take her side Dad, and we are your children, it's just not fair!"

"Rupert, I don't always take sides, there are no sides, and I try to be fair with you all. You know one day your Mum will meet someone else, are you going to be like this with him?"

Rupert shouted, "Mum does have a boyfriend, his name is Anthony, and I don't like him either." Charles looked at him in surprise as he went on "She's spending this weekend with him, she thinks we don't know."

Charles was momentarily lost for words. He wasn't sure how he felt about Celia having a boyfriend. Why not though, after all, he had been the one to be unfaithful to her, and she was entitled to a life, but what would this change mean to the children, better or worse, and what was this guy like? Finally he spoke "Well your mother needs a boyfriend too, and I hope that she'll be really happy with him. I'm very pleased for her."

"Are you really Dad, I was kind of hoping, that it might make you feel a bit, well you know ... jealous I suppose."

Charles glanced at his son, so that was what he was hoping for, reconciliation between him and Celia, poor kid - it just wasn't going to happen. "Well, it doesn't, your Mum deserves happiness, just like we all do, you should be pleased for her Rupert."

"I'm not pleased, I don't like you living with Jennifer and I don't like Mum having Anthony" he said his voice strangled; he twisted his hands together, his little face pinched and white with misery, and his eyes moist with tears.

"Rupert" said Charles gently, "sometimes we all just have to move on in life y' know and you need too as well. You can't just keep hoping that Mummy and I will get back together, because it just isn't going to happen. Think about it in a positive way, you get the best of both worlds this way after all." Rupert did not answer but looked ahead. Charles put his hand on his shoulder saying "It's okay you know, change is always hard, but sometimes it can be for the better, let's make the most of this weekend together and have a great time."

"Okay Dad, I'll try, but only because you asked me to."

"Good enough for me" and with that Charles put his foot down anxious to get home to Nantes.

Jennifer meanwhile was in a state of agitation, she had stopped off at the village shop to buy some goodies for the children, and was now waiting in the hall for them to arrive. They should be here any moment, and it was really important to her that she give this weekend her best shot, and that for once Rupert might just be prepared to speak to her civilly. She danced anxiously from leg to leg and finally hurried into the cloakroom for a high speed pee, dashing back to her post at the window. She sank down into one of the armchairs at the window, a bowl of roses was on the small table in front of her, their musty perfume was glorious and she took a deep breath and tried to stay calm. Gazing out of window she watched Pete, his great shape ambling across the drive, she was sure that he was talking to himself, as his thin lips moved soundlessly. He was a strange one, she had made no headway in trying to make friends with him, and half of the time he just stared at her and more often than not did not reply when she tried to speak to him. Ah well, she thought she would just have to go on trying, although he did give her the creeps.

Suddenly Charles' Range Rover swept down the drive pulling up at the front porch, with Rupert in the front and she could see Jessica's

310

little fair head in the back. Jennifer leapt up from the armchair and rushed forward, wrenching open the front door and spilling out onto the drive to greet them, her face lit up with smiles. Rupert glared at her from the front passenger seat, his face tense and hard. Jessica on the other hand beamed at her from the back, waving as the car slid to a halt. Charles opened his door and walked around the front of the car and kissed Jennifer on the cheek. She flushed with pleasure, and they both went over to help the children out of the car.

"Hello Rupert, Jessica" exclaimed Jennifer, "how lovely to see you both, I'm so looking forward to our weekend together."

"Hello" was all that Rupert could muster, and he barely looked at Jennifer, walking to the back of the car to take his bag from Charles.

"Hello Jennifer, it's nice to see you too" said Jessica very politely, clutching her dolls in her hands.

"Are those your dolls? Aren't they lovely, what are their names?" Jennifer bent down to look, admiring them.

"This is Pansy and this is Polly" Jessica smiled at her, "aren't they pretty? I've brought lots of clothes for them, do you want to see?"

"Yes, I'd love to, shall we take them into the house together?" Jennifer took Jessica's hand and she turned to Rupert, "do you need help with your stuff?"

"I can do it myself" he said shortly. Charles looked at Rupert arching his eyebrows, and Rupert added hastily "thank you Jennifer."

"Good chap" muttered Charles quietly to Rupert, and they picked up the cases and followed the others into the house.

Mrs Fuller had rushed up the passage from the kitchen, wiping her floury hands on her apron and greeted them in the hall. "Jessica, Rupert my little lovelies, how are you?" The children ran over to give her a big hug, clearly delighted to see her. Jennifer looked on gloomily, thinking, why don't they do that to me? Well she was determined this weekend would go well, so that next time she would get a hug too.

Mrs Fuller grinned, "I've made those lovely little cupcakes, I know you're so fond of, and your favourite supper tonight."

"Hooray, hooray" shouted Jessica as she danced around the hall, "it's so lovely to be here!"

"Mrs Fuller, why don't you nip down to the kitchen and put the kettle on, and I'll help the children up to their rooms, and perhaps we can all join you there for our tea?" Jennifer said brightly. Charles looked at her surprised, and then smiled, she was really making an effort he thought and was pleased. Jennifer called to Jessica and Rupert, "Come on darlings, shall we go up?" Rupert reluctantly untangled himself from Mrs Fuller and Jessica grabbed Jennifer by the hand, as Charles picked up the cases and they disappeared upstairs.

As soon as they had unpacked their things, they joined Mrs Fuller in the kitchen, she had laid the table for tea, with some little sandwiches and a mountain of fancy cupcakes. She was standing at the Aga pouring boiling water into the teapot and turned to greet them, "sit down do, I'm just making the tea, and children there's juice in the jug on the table." They all sat down, Rupert and Jessica eyeing up the cakes, Mrs Fuller brought over the teapot, and sat down with them. "Tuck in!"

"Now, I thought we'd go out for a ride this afternoon" said Charles, his mouth full of sandwich, "Caitlin has brought the horses up and I've said we'll go over about 4ish, after we've had our tea"

"Oooo," squealed Jessica, "I can't wait to see Queenie again!"

"That'll be cool Dad" said Rupert, a smile for once breaking over his face, and then settling again into a scowl. He helped himself to a cupcake.

"Good, I thought you'd like that, and then tomorrow Jennifer and I are taking you out for the day, so we're planning a visit to Arundel Castle." He smiled at them both, he'd really missed them, and it was only when they sat down all together like this that he realised just how much.

"What all of us?" Rupert said sulkily, fixing his father with a stony stare.

"Yes, Jennifer, you and me, we should have a great time." Charles said brightly, ignoring the inference in his voice, hopefully Rupert might thaw out a bit as time went on.

"Oh okay", the disappointment in Rupert's voice was clear. "I'm not sure about going to a castle, that's for babies, I might be bored."

"'Course you won't it'll be great fun. So eat up, and we'll get changed and go over to the stables."

Jennifer started chatting to Jessica about her dolls, and what she had been doing at school, and the little girl replied animatedly. She was such a little sweetie Jennifer thought. She tried to talk to Rupert, but all of her questions were answered with either a plain yes or a no. She tried another tack, and changed the subject to the horses, and said she had a surprise for them when they went out on their ride. Jessica clamoured to know what it was, but Rupert didn't even respond. God thought Jennifer, he was going to be a tough nut to crack, but come hell or high water she was going to do it. The tea consumed, she turned to Mrs Fuller, "that was really lovely Mrs F, a tea fit for royalty."

Mrs Fuller beamed, "Thank you so much, but it's no trouble at all, it's so lovely to have the children back home."

Charles stood up, pushing his chair back, "Yes a wonderful tea, thank you, now come on let's get our breeches on". The children pushed back their chairs, Jessica grabbed another cupcake as she went, before dashing out of the kitchen with Rupert hot on her heels. Jennifer pushed her own chair back, smiled at Mrs Fuller and went after them. She followed Charles up the stairs and into their room, watching him peel off his chinos and put on his breeches. She sat down heavily on the bed, he glanced up at her "You okay?"

"Yes thank you darling I'll walk over to the stables with you all, and look" she pulled out a carrier bag from under the bed, "I bought these for the children, I thought it might make their ride more exciting" She rummaged in the bag and brought out a cloak and a sword for Rupert, and a cloak and a wand for Jessica, "What do you think?"

Charles looked at her with admiration, "What a fantastic idea, they'll love them, did you buy me one?" he joked.

Jennifer laughed, thinking good old Chloe – it had been her idea, as had the trip to Arundel tomorrow. Inclining her head slightly on one side she said huskily "I can just see you in a cloak, but I'd rather see you in nothing at all!" Charles moved over to her, pulling her to her feet, and kissed her hard on the lips, his hand squeezing underneath her bottom.

"Hey not now, not whilst the children are about!" He pulled away reluctantly, sighing as he did so. "Tonight" she whispered.

"Can't wait" and he kissed her again, lightly this time. Jennifer picked up the carrier bag and they fetched the children from their rooms and together they walked over to the stables.

Grace had gone up to her mother's earlier in the day, they had been planning to have lunch out together as a treat, so she had taken the car rather than walking, leaving two very disgruntled dogs behind at home. Her mother was in the kitchen as usual, but for once had on a floral skirt and blouse, and some delicate pumps, all in a soft shell pink, which really suited her silver hair. Grace was glad that she too had made an effort, rather than just drag on jeans and a tee shirt, she had put on a sleeveless daisy printed cotton dress, with a large belt, and flat sandals. A smidgeon of make-up, and she looked quite different from her usual careless style.

"You look nice love, I'm really looking forward to our lunch out, such a treat."

"You look lovely too Mum, it's fun to have something to dress up for isn't it, and I'm so glad it isn't raining. They didn't hang about and picked up their handbags and walked out to the car, and were soon speeding along the road. "I thought we'd drop in at the Garden Centre first and have a quick look round, you might like to choose something for your birthday?" Grace reached over and took her mother's hand, "I love you Mum and I don't tell you often enough."

"I know you do darling, and I love you right back." She smiled fondly at her daughter, watching her striking profile as she drove along. Grace was such a lovely girl and she so wished that she could have a family of her own, but she knew it only added to Grace's anguish if she kept talking about babies, so instead said "Great idea about going to the Garden Centre, I could do with a few roses for that new bed I'm planting up, and they always have some lovely ones there."

"Well, we'll have a look round and see if you fancy anything, but there is so much more there than just plants now, and they even have a really good craft section."

"I haven't been for ages, so it'll be nice to see what they've done with the old place since it was taken over."

"They've opened a restaurant, I suppose we could always see what the menu is like instead of going to the pub?" Grace pushed her hair out of her eyes, and groped about for her sunglasses.

"Whatever you like dear, I'm in your hands." She laughed, "I'm just going to look forward to a nice day out."

"Good, so am I, y' know we should make time to do this more often."

The Garden Centre was a big sprawling place, on the other side of Cuckfield and was like one enormous greenhouse. Outside was a riot of colour and smells, huge stone pots, and little paved paths wove around the displays. They ambled between the aisles, every now and then stooping down to inspect something unusual. There was even a large ornamental pond, full of koi carp and dramatic aquatic plants, it was very peaceful and they stood watching the graceful fish for a moment.

"I've got to say dear, they've made a lovely job of this, so much more to see than when old Mr Rogers ran it."

"Yes, I think his heart had gone out of the business really and you're right, they have made a good job of sprucing the place up. Shall we go and have a look inside?"

"Good idea!" They walked inside through large glass doors, "My goodness, it's huge." It was huge too, aisle upon aisle of gardening tools, weed killer and the like, and even down to dog food. "Shall we have a coffee, before we go any further, we can size up their menu." They made their way towards the café, through tempting displays of books, and crafts, pausing to look at a display of garden furniture.

Grace clutched her mother's arm, "Look! Isn't that Julia Napier?" She was sure it was, she recognised her voice straight away and now peering over, she could see the back of Julia's shiny black bobbed head.

"God preserve us from that woman" sighed her mum "she's such a parvenu!"

"I agree, but what is she doing?" She poked her mum in the ribs, her mother followed her gaze, and they both peered behind a particularly large fronded fern. It was definitely Julia Napier, and she was with a really hunky young man and was looking adoringly up at him. Julia reached up on tiptoe and lightly brushed her lips against his, and he put both of his arms around her, his hands fondling her bottom. He was a good looking guy, tall and tanned, with a well-toned body, and shaggy blonde hair. He had the look of an athlete and was clearly at least ten years younger than she was! Grace and her mother clutched each other and giggled.

"Oh I can see what she's doing! Who is he I wonder, never seen him before!"

Julia looked around her quickly, brushed down her clothes and pushed the young Adonis away from her. Grace pulled back hastily, catching her mother's arm, and they held their sides to stop themselves from snorting with laughter. They immediately pretended to be looking at the garden furniture as they watched Julia and her young man disappear towards the exit.

"Well, what do you think of that?"

Grace's mother laughed, "You don't need a degree to know what they were up to!"

"You don't really think so do you? Why on earth would they meet here?" Grace looked incredulous.

"Of course I think so Grace, she was all over him, and he was all over her. As for meeting here, why not?" her mother said sensibly. "Sometimes you are so naïve!"

"Oh poor Andrew" sighed Grace.

Jonty had decided it was time to make another trip down to Fittlebury. He had commandeered Weasel to come with him. Although the original idea itself was germinating nicely, timing was going to be crucial and the more homework they did the better. It was a daring plan, and they couldn't afford to make a mistake about anything. They decided to stop off in Horsham, local information would be useful, and the town might be a good place to start. Jonty parked the Landrover in Piries Place, just like a local he thought. He and Weasel made their way out towards the Carfax stopping off in a café for a drink - there was a nice little place with tables outside and they sat down, looking about them. Horsham was busy on this Friday with people milling about, and they watched the world go by, saying very little. The waitress came out to take their order, she looked vaguely familiar to Jonty and both he and Weasel sized her up and down. She was a pretty thing, with long blonde hair, tied back in a ponytail, she had big tits and good legs in her short black skirt and white waiters apron. She gave them a knowing flirty look, and they returned it.

"What can I get you gents" she asked bending over to show her cleavage.

"Do you sell beer?" asked Weasel ogling at her tits.

"No, sorry we don't. It's coffee, tea, or cold drinks and some great cakes." she smiled at them, following Weasel's gaze "They're very tasty!"

"So are you darlin'" Weasel leered. He looked her up and down and she stared straight back at him.

"What do you fancy then?" Lucy winked at him.

"Well how about you on toast!" said Jonty, his eyes mischievous.

"Keep cool big boy, not when I'm working, Come on what do you want, I've got other customers y' know." she chided.

"Okay, two white coffees and a couple of doughnuts"

She scribbled on her pad, "Fine, I'll bring it over."

They watched her wiggle her way back to the café, Jonty licked his lips, "she's cute eh – think she fancies a threesome?"

"I bet she's a right dirty cow." sneered Weasel, "I'd give her one. Better keep it in our trousers and back to business, how we gonna find out more about this geezer?"

"I think we need to try and get some insider information, y' know, chat up the locals, find out what he gets up to and when. Trouble is we need to mingle in more, and right now we stick out like fucking sore thumbs."

"I don't want to look like those wankers." Weasel moaned.

"Well you might have to, this is worth a lot of money to us." Jonty snapped, "Just do what you have to fucking do." He stopped talking abruptly as the feisty blonde waitress sashayed across to them carrying a tray.

"Here you are chaps" she said doling out their coffees and doughnuts, and plonking down the bill. "Enjoy."

"Rather enjoy you!" countered Weasel.

"You local round here?" asked Jonty, he was sure he had seen her before somewhere.

"Might be?" she teased, then added "Well I was living in Fittlebury, a little village near here, but I've come back to stay in Horsham for a while."

Jonty perked up "Fittlebury, I know it. I know someone who lives there, bloke called Parker-Smythe, d' ya know him?"

"Know him!" she exploded, "I bloody do! He's a bastard!"

"You may be just the person I need to talk to then darlin'. Wanna meet us for a drink when you've finished here? Jonty couldn't believe his luck. A chance stop at a café and to find someone who knew the arsehole.

She eyed him carefully, "Okay, why not, meet me for a drink in B52, in Piries Place, d' ya know it?"

"Yeah I do" Jonty didn't know it, but he would find it, he wasn't going to let a small detail like that stop him. "We can talk more then eh? Wassya name?"

"I'll be there at six. I'm Lucy" she said.

The children rushed up to Caitlin and gave her a hug, "Oh we've missed you Caitlin and the horses too" prattled Jessica, skipping happily up and down, "Look what Jennifer has bought us to wear when we're riding, it'll be such fun." She twirled around in her cloak, brandishing her wand. "She bought Rupert a cloak too and a sword."

"And I've missed you too for sure. What a wonderful idea Jennifer" murmured Caitlin, looking surprised.

Jennifer blushed slightly, feeling a bit guilty having cribbed the idea from Chloe, but she couldn't let on, instead she led Jessica by the hand across the stable yard to the loose boxes where the ponies were craning out over the stable doors.

"Oh Queenie, I love you so much." Jessica crooned and the little pony nuzzled into her hand "I've brought you lots of Polos, and we are going to have such fun this weekend."

Rupert was busy stroking Scooter "he looks great Caitlin, really well." Rupert's whole face had softened, and his eyes seemed wet with tears as he hugged Scooter's neck.

"Now he's not too fit Rupert, as he had a break after the hunting, and I've not started the fitness work yet now. He'll be fine for you for today though. Come on let's get the tack."

Charles squeezed Jennifer's hand, "You don't have to stay sweetie, I know horses aren't your thing." He looked down at her, taking a strand of her hair and brushing it away from her face.

"Oh, I don't mind staying at all Charles, I'm interested to learn more. The children seem to really like their cloaks." she smiled up at him, her face alight with pleasure.

"They love them and it was a great idea! You sure you want to stay? I know you're frightened of the horses, and there's no need with Caitlin and me here?"

"Quite sure darling, I want to stay" she said firmly and walked over to the tack room, and offered to help Caitlin with the tack, coming out moments later carrying Queenie's saddle and bridle, with Jessica skipping after her. Caitlin appeared with Dandy's tack and Rupert carrying Scooter's.

Charles was astonished, "Caitlin, don't worry I can tack up Dandy myself, you help Jennifer and Jessica and then we can both help Rupert." Caitlin looked over at Jennifer, she seemed to be more than capable of saddling up the pony, but she handed over the tack to Charles and made her way over to Queenie.

"There now Jennifer let me be doing that for you now."

Jennifer desperately wanted to show off her new skills, but if she did then the cat would definitely be out of the bag, so meekly she replied "thank you Caitlin, that'd be wonderful." She watched Caitlin carefully tack up the pony, thinking I could have done that and hugged herself with glee at the thought.

The horses were soon ready, and the children donned their crash hats, and swirling their cloaks clambered aboard. Charles swung easily into the saddle, and Caitlin handed him Queenie's lead rein, "Oh Daddy, do I have to be on the lead rein?" Jessica complained, "I can ride perfectly well without one." She looked very angelic with her cloak on the snowy white pony.

"I know darling but Queenie might be a bit fresh, so best to be on the safe side, especially to start with. If she's good, I'll take you off, okay?"

"All right" said Jessica "but I want to come off it as soon as possible." Rupert sat on his pony saying nothing, throwing his cloak over his shoulder, but clearly anxious to be gone.

"Have a good ride now" called Caitlin.

"Be careful" said Jennifer.

"Of course we will" snapped Rupert, and with that he kicked his pony on and they clattered out of the yard. Caitlin and Jennifer watched them until they were gone.

"That was a grand idea to give them the cloaks Jennifer" smiled Caitlin "such fun for them."

"Thanks Caitlin, I'm trying to win Rupert round, he's a bit hostile towards me." She stopped suddenly and bit her lip, "Oh, I shouldn't really be saying that, forget it will you."

Caitlin stared at Jennifer surprised by her confession, and felt sorry for her. "Look Jennifer, it's not my business of course, but he'll come round, he's at such a difficult age and it has been a rocky time for him."

Jennifer looked at her gratefully her face crinkled with worry, "Oh I know, and I know too that he thinks I'm to blame, and to him I'm the wicked stepmother, but he won't give me a chance and I so badly want him to like me."

Caitlin felt sorry for her, it wasn't her fault really, Celia and Charles' marriage was a sham long before she arrived, and it was only a matter of time before they divorced. She wasn't in a position to say that though so instead she said "Jennifer, perhaps you should not be trying so hard now, for sure, just be yourself, and take things slowly."

Jennifer flushed, she knew that she had said too much, she shouldn't have voiced her personal feelings to Caitlin, it wasn't fair. "You're right of course Caitlin." Embarrassed, she quickly changed the subject, "Now how long do you think they'll be out?"

"Only about 45 minutes I should think now. The ponies aren't fit and Jessica will get bored after a while. Why don't you wait in the house, and I'll ring you when they're back?"

Jennifer thought for a moment before replying, "Thank you but no, I'll just skip the stables out while I am waiting for them – d' you have any rubber gloves?"

Caitlin could hardly contain her amazement, Jennifer – what did she know about skipping out! Gussus, what was she thinking.

CHAPTER 28

Jonty and Weasel located the B52 bar in the corner of the square at Piries Place, and made their way back to the car park, deciding to take a quick trip down to Fittlebury before they met up with the blonde tart later that evening. Jonty glanced at his watch, it was just getting on four, and they'd have plenty of time. He'd have to play this carefully with the bimbo tonight, get her to do the talking and see what she could offer them. It was important that they didn't let on to her anything about them. In the meantime, they'd do a run to the village, you never know they might turn up something useful while they were waiting. Weasel was a randy sod though, he'd have to watch him, although on the other hand a bit of a shag and she might open up all the more. He smiled to himself at the pun, and she was a tasty bit of skirt, although there'd have been plenty more there before him. He briefly thought about Laura, and promptly dismissed her, she was beginning to give him right ball ache, but she was useful and he could put up with her for the time being leastways. In fact, he had to give it to her, if she hadn't kicked up such a fuss about a bit of rough sex up the arse, and brought him down to this godforsaken place he would never have thought of this stunt. Silly cow, she hadn't realised just what a can of worms she'd opened. He glanced over at Weasel, he was a mean bugger, but no doubt that his bollocks ruled his brains, and he'd have to watch him tonight.

They made their way across the square towards the small multi storey car park, and found the Landrover. Jumping in, Jonty switched on the ignition, awkwardly negotiating his way out and made his way onto the main road towards Fittlebury. The traffic was not busy yet, it was half term and the usual hordes of mums in posh cars picking up their precious kids were absent, and soon they were wheeling their way onto the Horsham by pass. Jonty wasn't sure what they were likely to find, but he just had a feeling about today. Weasel lit up a fag and passed it to him, and he took a long deep drag.

Charles was hacking down the quiet lane towards the village, towing Jessica along on his inside and Rupert following behind brandishing his sword at imaginary villains in the hedge. Jessica was chattering away to Charles, her long blonde ringlets bobbing up and down with her cloak flowing out as they trotted along.

"I just love this pretty cloak, look it's got all sparkly bits on it" Jessica squeaked, her face animated, "and I love Queenie too" she sighed patting her pony. "I really miss her when I'm living at Mummy's house, I wish I could have her there." Her little face suddenly looked dejected, crinkling up, "It's all right though Daddy, I know I can't."

Charles looked at her sadly, it wasn't just Rupert who had been affected by the divorce, but it was no good – he was sure that in time to come the children would settle and things would improve. His mind wandered to Celia, could he ever go back to her? The answer was an emphatic no, and yet when he was with the children he realised just how much he missed them. Perhaps he and Jennifer should have children of their own? No, not yet anyway, the time wasn't right, it could only make matters more difficult and over the last few weeks, things had been brilliant between them. The sound of a vehicle coming up behind brought him sharply back into focus, and he slowed the horses to a walk, so that the car could pass. He looked down and saw Grace Allington and her mother driving slowly past and waving to them. She was a nice woman, he had quite fancied her once, but she was almost too sweet to be wholesome for him, he liked a feistier woman, he smiled at the memory, that was in his wilder days, long gone now.

"Dad" Rupert shouted "where're we going?"

"I thought we'd just go up to the village and back - we could stop at the shop and buy some sweets if you like? Charles answered "Caitlin said that the horses aren't that fit so we shouldn't go too far, that okay?"

His son smiled back at him, clearly enjoying the ride and the thought of stopping at the Guptas' shop for sweets was tempting. They carried on towards the village.

Jennifer was busy with the skip bucket and rubber gloves, she quickly picked up the droppings and had put the beds back to rights, fluffing up the banks with a flourish. Caitlin was busy hanging hay nets and was watching Jennifer out of the corner of her eye. She was frankly astonished, she had no idea that Jennifer knew anything about mucking out, let alone doing a good job of it. Really, thinking about Jennifer, she realised that she knew nothing about her at all; every one of them had labelled her as a total bitch before she had even arrived at Nantes, and none of them had bothered to give her a chance or get to know her. There was no doubt in her mind now that she had misjudged her. She felt guilty about that, but there again she felt guilty about so much lately. What happened to being worry free in life eh?

Jennifer glanced up "You okay Caitlin? You look a bit worried."

"Well fine to be sure, just a bit on my mind you know."

Jennifer stood up, knocking the shavings off her gloves and pulling them off, "shall we have a cuppa whilst we wait for them to come back?" Poor Caitlin did look really pale with dark shadows under her pretty eyes - she didn't want to pry, but perhaps it might be something she could help with. She picked up the skip bucket and pushed open the stable door, chucking it in the wheelbarrow. "Come on, I'll put the kettle on."

Caitlin had no option but to follow her into the tack room, she sat down on a stool, whilst Jennifer made the tea. This was awkward, the last thing she wanted was the third degree from Jennifer, but she supposed she was only trying to be kind, but there was no way she could open up to her.

Jennifer sat down on the other stool and handed Caitlin a mug looking at her carefully, but Caitlin could not meet her eye. "Look Caitlin, you seem really down in the dumps, like you've the weight of the world on your shoulders, d' you fancy talking about it?" Poor girl she looked so bloody miserable.

"Oh 'tis nothing now, I'm just fine really" she looked down wringing her hands together, "just a lot of nothing."

Jennifer reached over and touched her hand, "Come 'n Caitlin, it doesn't look like nothing, and maybe I can help you, whatever you tell me, I swear will go no further." To Jennifer's surprise Caitlin started to sob, her shoulders shaking with emotion. "Hush now, it can't be that bad whatever it is. Let me see if I can help."

Caitlin look up at her, tears streaming down her face, "Oh Jennifer, if only 't were that simple. "I can't talk about you know, I just can't."

"Okay, okay, but y' know I'm always here if you do." Jennifer knew there was nothing else that she could say, but she also recognised that look, and she was pretty certain that there was a man at the bottom of Caitlin's trouble and that would explain her prolonged absence with Oliver the night of the party after all. She knew exactly how that felt, her mind wandering back to the agonies of when she had fallen in love with Charles. Right now though, unless Caitlin wanted to talk about her problems then all she could do was ensure that she was there for her when she did. She put her hand on her shoulder patting it gently to reassure her. Poor Caitlin.

Jonty and Weasel chugged into Fittlebury in the Landrover, pulling up near the green. They sat and watched the comings and goings of the village; the vicar hurrying out of the vicarage and making his way towards the church, the mums their cars crammed with children and dogs drove past, Dick Macey was dead heading his hanging baskets, a couple of old codgers gossiping by the pump. Jonty lit a cigarette letting the smoke drift out through his nose, idly drumming his fingers on the steering wheel watching them all.

"I don't know why the fuck we 'ave to linger about here?" moaned Weasel picking his nose.

Jonty looked at him angrily, this cunt had no idea about anything. "Look you wanker, the more we prepare the territory, the easier the lift, fuck me do I 'ave to explain everything to you?" His fuse was short, Weasel had no fucking brains at all. "Y' never know what we might find useful when the time comes."

Weasel, who started raking his other nostril glared at him, "don't bite my fucking head off, I only asked you." Jonty could be a serious arsehole at times, and what they would find out sitting here in full view of everyone beat him. "Don't you think we look a bit odd sitting here?"

Jonty considered him for a moment or two, a Landrover was hardly out of place, but sitting loitering about in it might draw attention to them. He started the engine and drove further down the road parking outside the village shop. "Okay I'm going in, you wanna come, or gonna sit here? But just to let you know, the place is run by Pakis so no crap remarks – right."

Weasel snorted, "Fucking even out here in the country the place is taken over by them, no thanks mate, I'll stay here.

Jonty slid out of the Landrover, pulled up his jeans a bit, and yanked the cap Laura had bought from the charity shop onto his shaven head. He saw Weasel smirking at him from the front seat, -he felt a right dick in this get up, fucking waistcoat an' all. He gave him the finger and walked into the shop. The fat old Paki woman was at the counter and she smiled at him, he strangled a smile back at her and pulled the cap further over his face, and he marched straight past her and started wandering around the aisles looking at the goods. Christ all a bit up market in here, no value lines to be seen. He smiled, well if that wanker could pay these prices, then he would cough up all the more.

Mrs Gupta watched the young man in the security mirrors, as he loitered around the aisles, she was sure she had seen him before, but with that cap pulled down over his face it was hard to tell, and he could just be a local with that green waistcoat. Still he looked shifty and her many years as a shopkeeper had given her an inbuilt sense of legitimate trade and he made her suspicious, although down here in the country they rarely had any trouble with shoplifters.

She heard the clatter of hooves outside on the road and looked out through the window and saw three riders had stopped outside. She smiled, ah, it was that Mr Parker-Smythe with his children, they were such nice little kids, although he was a stuck up man whom she had never really liked much. It had been the talk of the village when he had divorced his wife - such an unpleasant woman, still she should not be judging, although his new wife seemed much nicer when she had popped in for bits and pieces. She watched as the children slid off their ponies, handing their reins to their father as they dashed into the shop.

"Mrs Gupta hello!" gushed Jessica, "We've been out for a ride with Daddy and he's given us each £10 to spend on sweets!" Her sweet little face was flushed with smiles as she beamed at Mrs Gupta.

"Well m' dears, how lovely it is to be seeing you both, are you staying with your Daddy?"

"Yes we are and we're having a lovely time! Jennifer bought us these super cloaks," she spun around, so that the pink frothy material billowed out, "aren't they lovely? Tomorrow we're all going out to spend the day at Arundel Castle too. Mrs Fuller is going to do a super picnic for us!"

"How lovely dear, you should be having a wonderful time, and I'm liking these cloaks very much indeed! Let me be seeing yours now Rupert" she turned to him adding "My my now you have grown so very much, very tall indeed – like your daddy!"

Rupert grinned at her, "Yes, I have grown Mrs Gupta, I will be as tall as Daddy soon. These cloaks are for cissies really, but I've promised Daddy that I'll try and be nice to Jennifer, so I'm wearing it to please him"

"Well that's a good boy then, you should always be wanting to please your parents." said Mrs Gupta seriously, thinking of how her own twins had gone to University despite her and Ravi's wishes.

"Jennifer is not my parent" Rupert snapped, "and never will be." His eyes narrowed in hatred, and then as his face crumpled he turned away.

Mrs Gupta smiled at him, poor little chap, it was always the children that fared worst in a divorce, "No of course not, but she will be trying hard all the same, and your Daddy is right everyone in this life should try and be nice. How is your mother though m' dear?"

Jessica piped up, "Oh she's very well thank you, she has a boyfriend now - although she thinks we don't know!"

"Well, I am glad that she is being happy, you should be pleased for her. Now what will you be wanting to spend that money on?" She smiled fondly at the children, watching them hovering over the sweet counter deliberating on what to buy.

"I'm going to choose something for Jennifer, and something for Daddy and some polos for Queenie" squeaked Jessica, "and then something for me."

"What do you want to buy her anything for?" moaned Rupert, "She doesn't deserve anything."

Jessica looked at her brother, her eyes solemn, "Just because you don't think so, I do, she's really quite nice, if you only gave her a chance, but of course you're a boy so you couldn't do that. Why not surprise her yourself and see!" She turned on her heel angrily and started to walk up the aisle her curls bobbing as she walked towards the back of the shop, pausing to look at some pretty hair slides. "These are very nice, I think she might like one of those!"

Rupert walked over to her, picking up the hair slides, "they're very girlie."

"Well perhaps you haven't noticed Rupert but I am a girl and so is Jennifer!" she shot back at him, "if you can't be nice leave me alone."

"Okay, okay, I'm sorry, all right, why don't we buy one between us then?" he compromised, he really didn't want to upset his sister, she could be irritating but underneath he loved her very much, and right now she was the closest person he had in his life and he didn't want to lose her too. "Or we could buy two in different colours?"

Jessica stared at him "Do you mean it? Are you really going to try and be nice?"

"I do mean it" he said firmly, smiling at her "I'm sorry and I don't want to quarrel with you. Now come on what colours shall we get?"

Jonty from behind the aisle was watching them carefully, what a stroke of fucking luck! The girl was a dainty little thing and a real innocent, but the boy was an angry stuck up little bastard and that was worth knowing. It might alter things a bit. Interesting too their conversation, he ducked back behind the shelf as he heard them moving round the shop, he definitely didn't want to be seen. He shot off in the other direction and dived out the door, muttering a hasty goodbye to the fat woman. As he came out into the daylight, his eyes adjusted and there was a tall man on a huge horse, skilfully holding two ponies, a white one and a brown one. So this was the bloke then. He clocked him carefully from under his cap, he had a snobby arrogant look about him, and was wearing a green waistcoat –how funny he thought, Laura had been right about the blending in thing. The man looked up and caught his eye for a fraction of a second and Jonty touched his cap and walked on. Christ he thought where did that fucking gesture come from? Swinging into the Landrover, he pulled off carefully past the horses, just as would have been expected, whereas normally he would have roared off tooting the horn at the wankers.

The children clattered out of the shop, holding a plastic carrier bag, and Charles dismounted and helped Jessica up on Queenie, whilst Rupert scrambled onto Scooter. "Everything okay?" he asked, "What did you buy?" He put his foot into his stirrup and swung back onto his horse, good old Dandy he thought, he didn't bat an eyelid at the flapping plastic bag, most horses would have skittered about!

"We bought sweets and stuff, and a nice present for Jennifer" chorused Jessica happily, "Some hair slides, I really hope she likes them, Rupert and I bought one each for her."

Charles looked at Rupert who was fiddling with his reins, "Well done, she'll be delighted. That was really thoughtful." Rupert didn't reply, his handsome young face hard with emotion. Charles decided not to pursue the matter, but perhaps Rupert at long last was starting to thaw out. Thank God for that he thought.

Jonty and Weasel headed off towards Horsham. Jonty had a huge grin on his face, "Fuck me, that was lucky! Fancy seeing them. Did you get a good look?"

Weasel who was thoroughly bored and had no idea what he was supposed to have seen said "What you mean that wanker and the kids on those nags?"

"Course I mean them dumb arse, that was the very git and his snotty kids" Even Weasel's lack of enthusiasm could not curb Jonty's elation. "that was only Charlie boy himself. Got a good look at the kids too when they came in the shop. The girl's easy prey, but the boy will be trouble. All very useful."

"Blimey, I'd no idea, would've paid more attention if I had. All seems a bit more real now."

"Don't get too excited, there's a long way to go, but very interesting." He put his foot down, the old Landrover's engine screamed into action, and they hurtled down the lane. "Roll a spliff will you – I need it!"

CHAPTER 29

Jonty and Weasel were at B52, the town clock had struck six already, and they were starting to get restless. This bloody no smoking thing was a fucking pain in the neck, they took their drinks and found an empty table outside. Horsham was a dump, who on earth would put that stupid statue in the middle of this square, a life size donkey and cart with a fat ugly man – Christ it was an eyesore. Jonty drummed his fingers on the table whilst they waited, hoping it was gonna be worth it.

Lucy had tarted herself up in the loo at the Bistro, she didn't have any decent clothes with her, but decided to undo the top buttons on her shirt, so that her tits were tantalisingly on view. It would have to do, and she strolled off towards Piries Place, she was looking forward to meeting these guys again, they seemed very different from the usual run of the mill geeks around here. She turned the corner out of the old alley and clocked them sitting at one of the aluminium tables outside, they caught sight of her and beckoned her over.

"Hi!" she called, "Sorry I got off a bit late, you been waiting long?"

"No not a bit darlin'. D' you want a drink?" Weasel sprang to his feet, and she sat down next to Jonty.

"I'll have a Becks please." Weasel sauntered back into the bar, and she smiled at Jonty "What you boys been up to then, you're obviously not from around here?"

Jonty was a bit taken aback by the direct question, blimey what could he say? He fiddled with his lighter, racking his brains, "just taking a look around the town, I run a market stall in London, and thought there might be an opening around here." He thought that was pretty good - off the cuff as it were. "What about you? Pretty girl working as a waitress in this dump."

Lucy bristled, "it's not for long, I'm using the job as a stopgap, I used to work for the Parker-Smythes, but I left a few weeks ago, but I was planning to move on anyway. You said you knew him, how's that then?"

Jonty eyed her carefully, where'd he seen her before, fucked if he could remember? He would have to play this just the right way, what was it she had said earlier - she thought the bloke was a bastard. He replied casually, "Oh some mates of mine in London know him really, say he's a right arsehole. Could do with being given a slap or two!" He laughed at Lucy, as he saw the glee in her face. "What happened when you worked for him?"

Lucy was only too glad to tell the whole sorry tale, embroidering it well with her own additions. Embellishing what a philanderer Charles was and what a bitch Jennifer was too. Adding in with a flourish all about the pious Caitlin and their final showdown, making herself out to be really hard done by - after she had been such a good worker. It made a good story and Jonty listened carefully, taking in every detail. "So you've had a right rough ride eh? This Charles, what happened to the first wife and the children then?"

"Oh he paid them off I think, although they'd left before I started at Nantes, but the children came and visited every now and then. Right spoilt brats too."

"Poor old you" he feigned sympathy, "sounds as though you had a rotten time. Didn't you have anyone to help you, what about other staff" he asked curiously. This silly cow had no idea he was pumping her for all the information he could.

"Well there was me and Caitlin in the yard, and a weird bloke who lives in the cottage called Pete, he does the garden. There's the housekeeper Mrs Fuller, been there for years and she lives in an apartment in the house, and a couple who come in every day to help." She said carelessly, enjoying the attention he was giving her. "That Pete though he was really strange."

Jonty was interested, this was the guy that he and Laura had seen that night in the pub, and then it clicked into place, Lucy had been in the garden too! He fished for more, "Why was he strange, in what way?"

"Well, I think he was mental, he was always watching me in a really dirty way" she said shivering remembering Pete and his weird behaviour.

"Well that's not strange is it, not mental to fancy a gorgeous girl like you!" Jonty buttered her up and she was loving it.

"Ahhh, go on!" she preened, "No I mean he was sinister. He was always watching me, he'd creep up on me when I wasn't looking, y' know the sort of thing. He was funny too about the new wife Jennifer, he really hated her, y' should've seen the way he looked at her sometimes, you'd have thought if he could, he would have attacked her. It was really nasty!"

"Perhaps he resented her, but you say he lives in the cottage, doesn't he ever go out?" Jonty was very interested in this guy maybe he could be useful to them.

"Well I did see him once at Happy Hour at The Fox, but he just sat in the corner on his own, other than that I think he's just a real loner. I'm glad to be out of it." This wasn't true of course, she was now working three times as hard for half the pay and living with her parents, looking back she'd had it cushy then. "Anyway, why are you so interested?"

Jonty smiled "Just interested in you sweetheart, and you obviously needed to talk. Now tell me more about yourself, not that bastard you worked for." Jonty was spared the boredom of listening to her, as Weasel arrived with the drinks, and immediately started to chat up Lucy, there was no doubt she would put out tonight. Oh well, he'd let Weasel have his way, he was cool with a threesome and she was loving it, there was plenty of room in the back of the Landrover. Jonty sat back sipping his beer letting them do all the work, and thinking hard about what he'd learned today.

Charles and Jennifer were in bed at last after a long day, he had forgotten what hard work children could be! He reached over to her, pulling her towards him, cupping her breast in his hand, God he felt randy tonight, and she looked very tempting in her nightdress. He allowed his hand to wander down between her legs and pulled the nightie up, pushing open her legs and lightly stroking the inside of her thighs, moving his lips onto hers in a blistering kiss that melted any resistance on her part. He moved her underneath him and sat astride her, pulling her nightdress up over her breasts, gently stroking her nipples. She had her eyes shut and was moaning quietly.

"Jennifer I have brought you a little present, I thought you'd love this!" He reached down under the bed, and pulled out a box.

She snapped her eyes open, pulling herself up on her elbows "What do you mean Charles, what is it?" Her eyes had a wary look, she knew Charles, and sometimes his idea of what she would love could be translated as more what he would love to do to her.

Charles opened the box and pulled out a large dildo and a bottle of oil. "Look darling, the main part has a fun rotating head with these two extra bits either side! You'll love it!"

"Charles, I'm not sure darling. It looks kinda large!"

"Sweetie, let's give it a try!" He kissed her nose and pushed her back on the pillow and sat to one side, and gently moved her legs apart. He bent over and kissed her again, licking along her lips with his tongue and he felt her starting to relax, "Now darling just lay quietly while I play with you and I promise you'll enjoy this" Deftly he took the oil, drizzling it over her breasts and started to massage it in lightly. She moaned and he traced a delicious cold trail down over her stomach, softly he caressed her, his hands moving further and further down her body and between her legs, until she was shivering with anticipation. Her body jerked upwards as he pushed the vibrator up inside her, with one of the smaller ends, shaped like a long tapering finger edging its way up into her anus and the other flatter one paddling on her clitoris, he switched it on, watching her expression. Her face registered shock and pleasure equally, and he smiled and turned up the speed, enjoying himself visibly as his cock grew harder. Turning up the speed again, she was begging him to stop, but then spluttering - no don't stop. Her whole body was bucking and rearing, just like one of his horses he thought! Her hands clenching hard on the bed sheets as she shuddered to a huge orgasm, Charles pulled out the vibrator out and moved up the bed, pushing his cock into her waiting mouth.

Charles and Jennifer were not the only ones to be enjoying themselves in bed, Sandy and Mark were cuddled together in a post coital embrace, his hand stroking her head as she nestled into him. It had only been a week but things were obviously getting serious between them, much more than just a drunken fuck. He was such an easy person to be with reflected Sandy, and he worked as hard as she did, but that made it all the easier to really enjoy their leisure time together, and they were certainly doing that. Tonight she had cooked for him, or rather they had cooked together, fooling about chucking stuff around the kitchen and then collapsing on the sofa laughing. This time when he accepted a drink he didn't say anything about driving and it was obvious without either of them saying anything that he would be staying the night. For once Sandy was glad of the company, normally she would be pleased to usher any guest out of the door so that she could be on her own again, but with Mark she didn't want him to go. What was happening she asked herself, as she snuggled into him and he kissed her ear nuzzling her neck. She had only known the man for a week for Christ's sake and there he was sharing her bed again, and her cosmos moreover. She hadn't allowed anyone into her space since the arsehole of a husband, and she had vowed no-one would ever do so again. Somehow though life without Mark, even after this short time would seem very empty indeed, and that was a dangerous place for her to be in, she liked to call the shots. She felt like a teenager and suddenly very vulnerable.

"What you thinking about?" he murmured sleepily

"You" she replied quietly.

He jerked his eyes open, "Me? Why? You okay?"

"I'm very okay" she turned towards him, stroking his cheek, "very very okay."

He looked down at her tiny frame, "That's good, 'cos I'm more than okay with you too. I know what you are thinking."

"Oh yeah, and what's that then?" she laughed.

"You're thinking this is all going too fast and you feel a bit out of control." He said seriously, "and I know that feeling, because it's what I've been thinking too, but I just can't help myself, you're bloody addictive!"

"That's just what I've been thinking, what are you some kind of bloody mind reader! You're right though, I can't seem to help myself either."

"Look Sandy, at the start we both said about neither of us wanting any form of commitment, and perhaps we don't, but right now we both enjoy each other's company, have fun in bed, and perhaps it will lead to more, but maybe it won't. Why don't we just take each day or week as it comes, and just enjoy ourselves and see where it leads? Time will tell but meanwhile don't let's run away in opposite directions and not give us a chance. Why not just go with it and not question the whys and wherefores?" It was a long speech but one that needed to be said, and he looked at her anxiously, watching her face carefully.

She smiled up at him, hugging him "Mark you are such a sweetie, that's exactly what I think." she laughed changing the subject quickly "Now tell me more about the sale of the Old Mill, in confidence of course!"

Chloe on the other hand lay awake troubled, as John breathed lightly beside her. She had never felt so low. She moved over on her side and looked at him through the silvery moonlight as it slithered in through a gap in the curtains, watching his chest rise and fall with every breath and longed to touch him. She couldn't go on much longer like this, she had to be realistic, the only reason he was becoming so distant must be because of another woman. She found it so hard to believe it of him, they still made love, although it was with less ardour then it had been, and true he was often too tired when he came home from work. She thought about the secretive way he guarded his mobile phone, the day he went missing when she was at Borde Hill and she had never got a satisfactory answer from him about where he had gone. He blamed it all on work and had even hinted that he may have to go away for a few days in the coming weeks, that in itself was unusual. She had a good mind to ring his office and check but was too afraid of what they might say. Oh God, what would she do if he left her, how would she ever manage without him, the poor children how would they cope, it was just too awful to contemplate. She should have tried harder to be a better wife and mother, she had failed them all. She must have sighed out loud, as John stirred and put his hand out to touch her, pulling her towards him and onto his shoulder. She could hear the dull thud of his heart as she melded into him, how would she ever live without this strong wonderful man whom she loved so very dearly. She must be wrong surely, but it was no good hiding from the truth, this would not go away by desperately hoping all the problems of the past few months would just disappear. No, she needed to pin him down and have it out with him, but there just never seemed to be the right opportunity. She thought about what Katherine had said, she must make time.

The next morning dawned bright and fresh, everywhere was revitalised after the rain of the previous week, the grass had started to grow and the flowers had all perked up. The sun was already warm with the promise of a fine early summer day. The turquoise water was gently rippling in the pool with the merest hint of a breeze, and the garden was filled with the musky scent of honeysuckle and roses. All around the birds were singing and there was the hum of bees as they rummaged in the petals of the flowers.

Charles rolled over in bed, to find that Jennifer was already in the shower, he could hear it running and her moving around in the bathroom. He gazed up at the ceiling, on the whole he thought, so far things had gone well with the children, and he was pleased that Jennifer had come up with the idea of going to Arundel. The cloaks had been inspired as well, and Jessica had even gone to bed in hers. Their evening together had been spent happily playing board games, with them all lounging around after a splendid supper from Mrs Fuller. Jennifer had been delighted with the hair slides and even Rupert seemed to be thawing. Yes, things all seemed to be fitting into place at long last, he was actually looking forward to the day ahead. He pulled off the duvet, nearly treading on the vibrator which he had tossed on the floor after last night's antics, hastily pushing it back into its box and stowing it in the bedside drawer, he wouldn't want Doris to find it! Jennifer strolled out of the bathroom, her hair wrapped in a turban and a white fluffy towel around her, fresh from the shower and not a scrap of make up in sight. Most women would have looked awful but she looked absolutely stunning and he looked at her in admiration, she was radiant, and he felt an overwhelming love for her.

He was a lucky man.

"What is it darling?" She looked at him questioningly.

"Just thinking how wonderful you look and how much I love you" he said quietly.

Jennifer felt herself glow with pleasure, "What a lovely thing to say, and I love you right back too." She moved over towards him, and kissed him gently, "We are going to have a fabulous day." They were interrupted by whoops of laughter and noise which sounded like a herd of elephants charging down from the nursery floor. "Looks like they're up! We'd better get dressed darling!"

The children burst into the kitchen to find Mrs Fuller bringing out fresh rolls from the Aga. She stood up balancing the tray carefully and putting the bread on a cooling rack. "Good morning my little lovelies, how are you? Did you sleep well?" She beamed at them, watching their little faces, they seemed to be very excited and happy, and it was a long time since she'd seen them like that. Well, well the tide was on the turn. "Do you want some breakfast?"

We'd love some in a minute but we're going over to stables to say good morning to the horses." grinned Rupert, "We won't be long."

"Okay my little darlings. I thought I'd do scrambled eggs and crispy bacon for breakfast, but I won't start it till you're back" she called as they dashed out of the kitchen and out down the passage to the back door. She leant back on the Aga and picked up her tea, it was lovely to have the little ones back in the house, made her feel quite young again. She would pack a really good picnic for them all to enjoy, and bless 'em, the day looked as though it was going to be lovely.

CHAPTER 30

Oliver was busy, even though it was Saturday morning and things were usually quieter, but it seemed the world and his wife had some catastrophe or another. He had already been out to a foaling, a colic, and now he was busy stitching up a bad cut. These things always took longer than you thought, and this was nasty, poor bloody thing had got caught up in some half concealed barbed wire which had rusted in the corner of a field. The sobbing owner was a decent woman, and she was beside herself with remorse, anxiously hovering around him. He methodically cleaned the cut, luckily it had not gone so deep that it had torn anything vital, it was just untidy and these things were always prone to infection. He had already sedated the horse and was now cutting away the jagged edges of the cut ready for stitching. You just had to take your time he thought and do a thorough job. Actually he was pretty good at suturing even though he did say it himself, the precision of it appealed to him in a perverse sort of way. Slowly and carefully he pulled the edges of the wound back together and neatly sewed it all back into place.

He stood up, his back aching, and smiled at the distressed owner saying "Don't worry, he'll be fine. The only trouble with this type of cut and suture, is that it may well break down and the possibility of infection, but we can only try, because of that we need to bandage the leg well, and change it regularly. I'm going to give him a shot of antibiotics and some pain relief, but he will need a whole course of jabs for five days, and some Bute in his feed for four days. I'll come back tomorrow and see how he is – okay?"

She could not reply just nodded and he felt sorry for her, it was a rotten thing to have happened. He heard the beep beep of a text message, but decided to ignore it, he would finish here and deal with that later. He went to the back of the Toyota and fished out the vet-wrap and cotton wool, loaded up the syringes, and went back to work.

Bugger thought Caitlin looking gloomily at her phone, she had hoped for a reply, but nothing so far. She would just have to try again in a while, meanwhile there was the mucking out to do, the kids had been here early and she had spent time chatting to them and playing with the ponies and had gotten behindhand with the day. She had kept Queenie in because of the possibility of laminitis not wanting to put her out on the lush grass, but the others she'd turfed out directly they'd gone. She put Queenie on the horse walker and grabbed the wheelbarrow. Just better get on with it she thought, this was when she needed help, she'd a million and one things to do today, and this was the quiet time of the year. Trouble was she was more than just a groom, she did all the forage ordering, including the haylage, made sure all the repairs were done for the tack, kept all the stable accounts, including the insurance on the horses, the shoeing and vet bills, field and yard maintenance and much of her work was administrative these days. She hoped this Felix would come up trumps and be the person they were looking for to replace Lucy to do the routine stuff. Mind you now, he couldn't be worse than her! She wondered what had happed to Lucy, she'd heard nothing at all about her since she'd stormed out, even Tom had no news. She needed to get her replacement soon, so that she could show the new person the ropes and be ready to get the horses up and beginning walk work by the end of July, so that she could have them fit enough for the season. Hound exercise started so much earlier now and the children loved to go out on these days, which doubled the work, as she had to keep the ponies all fit and running, and babysit the kids too. Felix sounded as though he would be more than able to do the work, but perhaps he was a bit too qualified, he might want more responsibility. She was protective of her own job which she loved, she was well paid for what she did, especially bearing in mind the terrible pay and conditions normally associated with yard work, and she wouldn't want anyone overstepping the mark. It was hard to see why he would want to take the job, but hey now until she met him she shouldn't make judgements. Throwing a shavings fork and broom into the barrow, she marched off towards Queenie's stable, but stopped in her tracks as she heard a car crunching up the gravel. Jennifer, Charles and the children had long since gone for their day out, and no deliveries were expected, it must be going to the house, but her face creased into a grin, as she glanced up to see a car pulling into the yard. Without another thought, she abandoned the mucking out, just like she had abandoned herself.

Laura was sitting on the floor, her arms hugging her knees protectively, shiny blonde hair cascading over her bare shoulders, her smoky eyes fixed on Linda, who was practically comatose and hardly able to hold herself up - she was doped up to the eyeballs. Sean was sitting with his back propped against the sofa, a can of coke in his hand. The room had its customary fug of smoke choking the room and today the window was barely open.

"Well what do you think?" she asked him, "could we rally some troops, I've got some insider info on this mob."

"I dunno Laura, I'd have to see what the others think. Howdya know anyway?" Sean was curious, all this talk was making him suspicious, or was it the dope making him paranoid?

"I've a friend who used to work for them, she told me she can get the dates of when they go out. They don't publish the meets but to have a mole on the inside is pretty useful, you've got to admit." She was luring him down the path as Jonty had instructed, "Anyway, we could go once and see, it makes me sick to think that they just get away with their antics and no-one makes a stand against them." She was warming to this now, "You said that they needed teaching a lesson didn't ya, or have you got cold feet now!"

Sean eyed her, she certainly seemed to be on the level, "Okay, I'll speak to Annie and Ewan, see what they say, but the hunting season doesn't start for ages yet y' must know that surely?"

Laura stared at him "'Course I do, but they do these things called Hound Exercise or Autumn hunting now and they start at the end of August time. Took the place of cubbing, but of course that's not true, we all know that - so we could really campaign against this mob for the whole of their lousy season. Really target them!" She hoped she sounded as though she knew what she was talking about, and that she was deadly serious. She glanced over at Linda, who had her eyes shut and was snoring gently, and Laura shifted herself over towards Sean, "Come 'n it'll be fun!" Her smoky grey eyes met his knowingly, and he reached over and took up a lock of her hair, letting it trail through his fingers. She had to stop herself shuddering, fuck the things she had to do to please Jonty, but his instructions had been very specific. She smiled up at Sean, touching his knee lightly with her fingertips, "I'd better be going, speak to the others, and let me know what they think eh?" Tantalisingly, she levered herself up, touched his arm, "Bye then."

He watched her go, she was a sexy sort and it would be easy to fuck her, he would ask Ewan what he thought and anyway it would be a way to get closer to her. He wondered how she had got her info, it seemed funny, but actually it could be a good crack, so why not, a bit of disruption never did any harm after all. He looked down at Linda, she had not stirred, he was feeling horny, and getting down on the floor beside her he began to lift up her T shirt, and then stopped in surprise as he took in the track marks on her arm.

Chloe had been busy all morning giving lessons in the school to her regular clients and a few extras that were keen now that the eventing season was in full swing. At long last these riders were beginning to appreciate how important the dressage phase was to the competition and understand if you could balance and engage the horse enough how much easier it made the jumping. Sometimes though she felt as though she was bashing her head against a brick wall, they would come for a lesson or two and think that you could wave some magic wand and dramatically improve the horse's way of going, never grasping that it was sheer hard work and practice that made you better at the job.

She had just finished a particularly gruelling session with a brat of a teenager who had been bought a seriously expensive horse with a good track record, but had no conception that she had to be more than just a passenger on its back. Ah well, it brought in the cash and the day to day running of the yard sure ate that up. Sandy was her next client and she was just finishing tacking up and Beebs had brought her a coffee, so she was sitting down for a moment's respite when all the worries about John came flooding back. Tonight, she was going to speak to him - definitely. The good thing about working was it did make you forget for a while, but when you stopped it hit you like a double whammy. She sighed as Sandy walked into the arena, Seamus looked amazing, his coat gleaming, and his muscles rippled all along his toned frame. Looking at Sandy too, she had a bit of a spring in her step, her face looked radiant, and her eyes were sparkling. She parked Seamus at the mounting block and for once he stood obediently whilst Sandy jumped on grinning.

"You look like the cat that got the cream, and would that cream be in the form of the delicious Mark?" asked Chloe smiling at her, she would be delighted if Sandy had a regular man in her life, she deserved one.

Sandy's face creased into a naughty twinkle as she winked at Chloe "Well it just might be!"

"Whoa Sandy, that's fab news, he's a great guy. Serious?"

Sandy considered for a moment, "Well I'm not wearing my heart on my sleeve and neither 's he, we're just having fun, who knows what'll come of it, but meanwhile I'm walking like a chicken – all that sex!" she burst out laughing.

"Sandy! You're incorrigible but good for you! Now I'm gonna make you work so hard, you'll wonder what's hit you!" Chloe laughed back at her, "if we want to improve those scores at Rackham."

"Bring it on boss!" Sandy grinned and adjusted her stirrup leathers, "I can tell you've been riding Seamus, look at the length of these."

"Sorry I forgot to put them back to your length. I did school him a couple of times this week for you. He's a tense bugger at times, but I think you've improved him hugely but it's gonna be even better. Onwards and upwards now." This was what Chloe loved about her job, it was great to see the partnerships improving all the time.

"Okay we are going to work a bit on the lateral work today, I did a bit with him this week, and he's getting the hang of it now. I know it's not in the test, but it does make the quality of the ordinary work so much better and gets Seamus listening to you."

Sandy grimaced "Oh God, I've got a feeling you're on a roll today."

"You bet!" Chloe replied but she was not thinking of Sandy and Seamus at that moment.

Lucy was thinking about the antics of last night. It had proved to be a good evening, nice to meet people from out of this bloody area, at least they were more interesting. That Jonty, he'd even bothered to listen to her wittering on about bloody Nantes and all that shit! She must've bored him silly, but she didn't think she had afterwards. Weasel was a laugh, and despite his slight frame had as much staying power as a steam train. After a fair few drinks at B52 she was really squiffy, and they'd driven off in the Landrover. Jonty had pulled over into a field entrance, parking behind the hedge, all the while she and Weasel had been snogging with his hands running all over her, whilst she writhed and moaned. When they stopped, he'd pulled her out of the door, and they'd tumbled onto the grass, tearing each other's clothes off. She'd been conscious of Jonty who'd stood watching them, taking pictures on his phone, he'd been stone cold sober, only drinking coke after his initial beer, but she hadn't cared, it just added to the pleasure for her. Afterwards they'd stopped to get fish and chips and eaten them in the front of the car tossing the paper out of the window on their way to dropping her off a few streets away from where she lived. Jonty had taken her mobile number and said they'd call her in a day or two. She was pleased, it was something to look forward to, anything was better than this fucking job, even though she was on the late shift today and had managed a lie in. She got off the bus at the Carfax and walked slowly over to the Bistro. She didn't know how much longer she could stand it, there had to be an easier way of making money.

Katherine drove into the yard late that afternoon, she was coming for a quick fix of riding before dashing home. She and Jeremy had enjoyed having the children for the half term break and were taking them out for a meal that night before driving them back to school tomorrow. They'd all gone to Horsham this morning to stock up with treats for their tuck boxes and she knew that she indulged them terribly, but it was nice to send them back laden with goodies. She loved having them at home, but she missed her riding, she had hardly seen Alfie all week and was starting to get restless. She parked her car by the walker and was greeted by a cheery Susie, who was tidying up the muck heap.

"Hi Susie!" she called out to her "How's my boy, I've neglected him this week. I've got withdrawals."

Susie planted her fork and wheeled her barrow down the muck heap, she was hot and sweaty from all her exertions, "Hi Katherine! He's just fine, such a gentleman always, a real sweetie. Don't worry we've kept him nice and fit for you. I brought him in about an hour ago, so he won't be full of grass." She knew that Katherine would be in a hurry today, the last full day with the kids at home "I'll grab your tack for you shall I?"

"You doll, that would be great, I haven't got a lot of time, but Jeremy is doing stuff with the kids this afternoon, so I have a short window and who better to fill it than Alfie!" On her way towards the stable she spotted Chloe in the feed room, so she made a quick detour. "Hi Chloe, how's you?" She looked at her questioningly, Chloe looked really tired although still gorgeous in that sexy rumpled way she had about her.

Chloe looked up, she had obviously been miles away, "Oh Katherine, you gave me a start! Oh, I'm okay, not much change y' know." After breaking down to Katherine last week, there'd be no hiding anything from her, so she added, "I'm going to try and talk to him tonight, I'm dreading it."

Katherine put her hand on her shoulder, "Good, you'll feel much better when you do, I'm sure it's nothing that can't be sorted, but until you know what's up with him you can't deal with it. So make sure you have that talk."

Chloe knew she was right and there was to be no excuses or putting it off any more, she had to take her head out of the sand and confront John before she went bloody mad. "I will don't worry."

Katherine smiled "It'll be okay, and when you need to talk, y' know I'm always here. I have to take the children back to school tomorrow, so I won't be up but how about we make time for a coffee together on Monday morning?"

Chloe smiled gratefully at her, "thanks that'll be great. Stop off at the house before coming down to the yard, I'll be back from the school run by about quarter past eight and will just pop down to sort out the chores and be back up by nine – that okay?"

"Perfect – be strong Chloe!" Katherine gave her hug and disappeared to her stable and the lovely Alfie. If only men were as simple as horses thought Chloe as she watched her go. Still Katherine was right, she was strong and once she knew what she was dealing with she'd be much better off.

Katherine hugged Alfie, and he nuzzled into her pockets for Polos, his gentle kind eyes following her as she reached for his bridle. He edged his nose under her elbow, and gently picked at her shirt with his teeth. Katherine pushed him away lightly, catching his ears with her spare hand, he really was so affectionate and loving, the bond between them grew stronger each time she saw him, the wonderful thing about riding was that it was so therapeutic, to be at one with your horse just made you forget all your troubles. Not that she had any, but her mind wandered back to Chloe. She felt so sorry for her, the agony which she was going through. God she hoped she saw it through and actually confronted John tonight. It was hard to credit that he could be having an affair, he had always appeared to be such a devoted husband and father. Okay he was away at work all day, but he was always seemed so supportive to Chloe and the children. She desperately hoped that there was a simple explanation for the way he was behaving. It had occurred to Katherine that perhaps he might be seriously ill, and that he was not telling Chloe to spare her the worry, but even so this was much worse in the long run. Her mind wandered to Jeremy, she was so lucky, he was such a good man, he worked hard and she never wanted for anything and she had never seen him admire another woman. Sometimes he could be a bit lack lustre but he was safe and kind and that was surely better than living out of control on a roller coaster like so many marriages were. Perhaps she should ask Jeremy to have a word with John – man to man as it were, over a pint in the pub. Maybe he could find out what was going on, or she could ask them over for a meal? Although perhaps she should wait and see what happened after tonight. Yes that was what she would do. If nothing was resolved, then she could put Plan B into action.

Down at the hunt kennels work was going at full tilt. The stables and kennels had all been freshly painted, and the hanging baskets and tubs were stuffed full of bedding plants, Petunias, Pansies, Geraniums in a rainbow of colours with sapphire blue Lobelia tumbling over the edges. The cobbled yard had been weeded and swept, and the grass surrounding the yard and the lawn, where the marquee would be, was mowed to perfect stripes. Old George pulled his cap down further over his eyes and surveyed their handiwork, those lads Tom and Oliver had done a good job – most of the hard work was done, and now it was just keeping it a bit tidy till next Sunday. Bloody hell, where had the year gone he thought, seems only yesterday we were getting ready for last year's show. He was pleased with the hounds this season, he had some right beauties and they seemed to be shaping up well too, although you could never tell until you got 'em out. He'd had some damned good walkers though, and that made such a difference. Took the job right serious they did, as they should. The Hunt Committee had all the arrangements in hand, all he had to do was make sure the place was shipshape, and as he looked about appreciatively, he knew he had done his bit. His Mary would have been proud of him, keeping up all the traditions, but by God he missed her. Her death had been so sudden, such a terrible shock, and it was still a shock when he allowed himself to think back, one minute she was there, the next she was crumpled up on the floor - gone. He had not known what to do, just stood there helpless. Luckily young Jay was with him and he had acted quickly trying to resuscitate her and yelling at him to call an ambulance. It was too late, a massive heart attack, and her still in her apron. Everyone had been very kind, offering all the usual platitudes, *'she wouldn't have known anything about it'*, *'the way she would have wanted to go'*, these trite little phrases that pop out, all meant nothing at all really. He had put a brave face on it outwardly, and the Masters and the Hunt Committee had made sure that he had lots of visitors bringing casseroles and cakes, keeping him busy, but his bed felt very empty and the long comfortable companionship which he had taken so much for granted all those years had been lost forever. There were so many things that wished he had said to her, but it was too late now. Jay Potter, who was the Assistant Huntsman and kennel man, had moved into the cottage to keep him company and had still not gone and that was a comfort to him, although he must be bored silly with an old man like him. Their own children had long since left home, one to Australia and the other to the Midlands and apart from the funeral and the phone calls he did not hear much from them. Jay had become like a son to him, he was a good lad and had the makings of a fine Huntsman. George was proud of the way he had turned out, but now it had become a nagging fear in the back of his mind that one day he would move on. He sighed, and walked on round to the flesh house, where Jay was busy dealing with a casualty cow he had picked up earlier. He looked up as George approached, then bent down back to his job.

"How long you going to be lad?" he asked

"Oh, nearly done George, be about thirty minutes, then we'll take the hounds out eh?"

"Righto - I'll just walk down and check the horses, and we'll have a cuppa tea before we go." He turned, whistling up the Jack Russells which were sniffing around the shed and tramped off towards the fields.

CHAPTER 31

Mileoak had never looked more beautiful or surreal as it nestled in the warmth of the early evening. The sinking sun beamed its last fingers of light onto the house and even the walls felt warm to the touch. The dogs were snoring out on the porch, and apart from the warble of a blackbird the place was eerily silent without the chatter of the children. They had gone out for the afternoon and a sleep over with their Aunt and Uncle and their children who were of a similar age, and were not due back until tomorrow morning. Chloe was making herself busy in the kitchen putting off the dreaded conversation, whilst John sat with a beer on the little terrace reading the paper. She knew it had to be now or never, it was a rare golden opportunity with the evening stretching ahead of them and the children away for the night, but she was nervous nonetheless. She had always tried to avoid confrontations if she could, but had never been afraid of them either and this was not going to be an exception. She marched over to the fridge, and pulled out a bottle of white wine, and glugged a large measure into her glass, she was going to need it. Taking a swig she stepped out onto the terrace forcing a smile on her face and sat down in one of the chairs. John looked at her over the top of his newspaper, and before he could say anything she stiffly began her rehearsed speech.

"John, I want to talk to you and it's important, so can you put down the paper and hear me out?" He looked surprised, and folded the newspaper slowly before he looked up into her eyes. She gulped down another slug of wine and blundered on, "Thank you. Now I just want you to listen before you say anything. You and I both know that things haven't been good with us for a while, and I've tried to broach this before, but you always seem to be fobbing me off. I know something is wrong, I'm not stupid. Now I want you to be really honest and tell me what is going on." There she had said it, and she had his full attention now. He looked like a rabbit caught in the headlights.

He responded almost immediately, too immediately for Chloe's liking, "I don't know what you mean Chlo'? Everything's fine."

Chloe felt her anger rising and struggled to remain composed. "Don't fob me off John. You've been quiet for weeks now, months even. Coming home late, a lot of the time saying you've been working, guarding your phone like it's some precious jewel!" She was in her stride now, all pretence of calm gone "Pre-occupied, hardly paying any attention to me or the children. I want to know what is going on, - I can't carry on like this anymore!" She felt her cheeks flushing and her heart beating faster, now was the moment, surely he must respond. She looked at him as he computed her allegations and formulated his response. John was not a good liar, they had been together for long enough for her to know that, and she watched his eyes carefully to see which way he looked as he answered her, remembering the old psychology, eyes to your right they were constructing a lie, to your left and it was the truth. Blimey, John's were darting about from one side to the other - so much for psychology.

Finally he looked at her directly, his face very sad. "Chlo', I know that I'm being unfair to you and the children, and things have been happening in my life that will affect you all but right now, I just don't know how much I can tell you – because I'm not sure myself. I don't want you to worry, I'm worried enough on my own, and it may amount to nothing at all. So I'm not prepared to speak about it yet."

Chloe was aghast, his admission that something was wrong was a given, but that he wouldn't talk about it was just bloody unacceptable. "That's just not fucking good enough!" she yelled at him, "How dare you behave like this, you have a bloody duty and fucking moral responsibility to us! I'm your wife for Christ's sake, I've a right to know!"

"And I take that moral responsibility very seriously, which is exactly why I don't want to talk about things. Suffice it to say, that when the times comes, you'll be the first person I come to, but right now I just can't – and I'm not being bloody awkward, and in the fullness of time you'll see why."

"Are you having an affair John? Is that what the problem is? If so why can't you tell me now about it, we can be adult about things. I'm fully aware that sometimes life at home can be pretty fucking dull, and sure you may have been attracted to someone else and even slept with them for all I know, but we could work it out, I know we could."

His eyes hardened and looked definitely to her right, "No, I'm not, okay - satisfied?"

She didn't believe him, "Are you sure, why've you been so late coming home then, and so funny about your phone?"

"Christ, it's like living with the Gestapo. I was working, I told you that, and bloody hell, you often get held up with your work, and I don't complain do I? You're always dumping the kids with me when it suits your job." He glared at her, "And the reason I don't leave the phone around is because I am fed up with the kids fiddling with it."

Chloe took a deep breath, "You swear you're not having an affair John? You promise me?" Her voice was thick with pleading and hope.

He softened, took her hand, and without hesitation said, "Yes Chloe. I know I'm being difficult at the moment, and I know that you find it hard to believe me, but I ask you to trust me. I've told you I can't give you the answers yet, but I will when the time is right. Please darling, if you really love me, as I love you, don't ask and just bear with me."

"Oh John, I just don't know, I can't go on like this, and I don't know why you have to be so mysterious about everything. You say that what's going on will affect me, the children and our home – so don't you think it's only fair that you tell me? You're expecting me to just accept what you say, and not ask any questions at all?"

John ran his fingers though his hair, his face looked white and drawn, "Yes that's exactly what I'm asking of you Chlo'. It's a lot and I know that, but I don't want to involve you just yet, I need to work things out on my own just for a little while. We've been married a long time and I wouldn't want to jeopardise what we have."

Chloe looked at him disbelieving "You wouldn't want to jeopardise what we have? Are you joking? Your silence does just that, don't you see? You say we've been married a long time, yes we have, and I can't believe that whatever you are up to you can't talk to me about." She wrung her hands together, shaking his own away,

"Have you ever thought how I'll be able to function until you deign to tell me?"

He looked deflated and weary "I'm sorry Chlo' that's all I can give you at the moment. I know it's lame but that's all I can and want to say, and I'm not going to talk about this again – okay."

"No it's not fucking okay!" She was so angry she could hardly respond "No it's not! You owe it to me and the kids to explain!"

"There's nothing to explain, nothing to say at the moment, so you're just going to have to deal with it, I'm sorry but that's just the way it is, and if you love me, you'll leave it, because right now that's all I can offer." He looked awful, his normal relaxed bonhomie gone, he looked ill. "I beg you Chlo', just leave it, for me and for everything we have together."

Chloe stared hard at him, her wonderful John, so strong, so dependable, looked a wreck a shell of the man she thought she knew. She saw though when she was beaten and her anger evaporated, she didn't want to lose him, she loved him and she thought he loved her. She also knew of his stubborn streak, and that she wouldn't shift him on this, so her only alternative was to try and do as he asked and wait. Bloody hell, could she do it though? "Okay John, I'll wait because I hope that whatever is wrong will sort itself out and that you haven't betrayed my trust, but I won't wait forever, do you understand that? If I find that you've been having an affair, when we could have possibly worked this out, then I'll take you to the cleaners, you got that?"

Andrew Napier was sitting in the surgery, it was getting quite late, and he had put on his desk light. He was pouring over the ordnance survey plans of the Old Mill which Mark had dropped through the door that morning. It was his first opportunity to sit down, they had been going flat sticks all day, both him and Oliver, and he was itching to have a look and this was his first chance. Mark had also enclosed a letter, telling him that the land indicated in red was the parcel that Lady V was prepared to sell him and that there was an additional small field behind the barns that could either be bought separately or rented. Andrew would love to be in a position to buy it, but he didn't think they could stretch to it, so perhaps renting might be an option, with some sort of clause that it could be purchased at a later date. He moved his coffee cup out of the way and spread the plans out in front of him, checking exactly what was being included in the sale. It all seemed straightforward enough and exactly the package that he and Mark had walked around that day, and he had actually forgotten to ask about the mill pond itself, but that was included too. He sighed happily, it was no longer a pipe dream, seeing the plans themselves brought home the reality of what he was prepared to take on – correction they were taking on. Of course this was just the tip of the iceberg in terms of hurdles, there was the planning consent and all the other massive legalities to go through, and once they did that it would be public knowledge. He got up and poured himself another cup of coffee pondering what would be the best way to handle this? The outlay in terms of expense was huge and a risk. He needed to discuss this with Oliver in detail as to how much they could feasibly do initially without overstretching themselves and landing up in trouble financially especially if they were taking on extra staff. He folded the plans up carefully putting them back in their brown envelope stowing them safely in his desk draw, and picked up the draft advertisement that Paulene had left for him to see. He would run it by Oliver when he came back from his call, but it seemed fine. She had made up two ads, one for the assistant veterinary post and one for a part time office assistant. He scanned them, and she had left a post it note to say she had promoted herself to Practice Manager – he grinned to himself, good for her!

Equine Position, in the heart of the Sussex countryside A busy 2 vet practice, looking to expand owing to heavy work load which includes a varied case load from competition & sport horses, to hunters, and stud work. Ambulatory role initially, and must be a motivated team player with excellent client skills to join our dynamic and highly qualified partners. Would be willing to consider a new graduate and full support would be given. 1:3 rota, with flexible salary package. Apply in writing with CV in the first instance to Paulene Godwin, Practice Manager, Napier and Travers Equine Veterinary Practice, Fittlebury, Near Horsham, West Sussex RH13 4RN.

Office Assistant required to support Practice Manager in busy Equine Veterinary Practice in the village of Fittlebury. Must be a motivated team player with excellent client skills and able to work under pressure, be competent with Word and Excel, and flexible in range of duties required. Initially a flexible 20 hpw, but some overtime may be required during busy periods. Apply in writing with CV to Paulene Godwin, Practice Manager, Napier and Travers Equine Veterinary Practice, Fittlebury, Near Horsham, West Sussex RH13 4RN.

He reread the advertisements – yes they were fine, he would run them past Oli and get his okay and then they could advertise, whatever happened with the Old Mill, they definitely needed extra help. He heard the outer door lock being opened and the familiar thump of feet across the reception floor, when Oliver barged in balancing his briefcase and some boxes in his arms. Andrew thought he was looking much better today, less of that weary droop he'd had of the last week, and more like his old dynamic self.

"Hey – you're late buddy, but I do need to talk to you, if you've got time to spare?"

Oliver dumped the boxes on his desk, "Yes, plenty of time mate, it's great not having to go home cowering like a dog with my tail between my legs, apologising for what I do all the time. I'm busting for a coffee though, I could have stayed on and had one up at Libby Newsome's but I thought the better of it. She's a man eater that one!" he laughed and shoved a pod into the coffee machine, "Want one?"

"No, I'm all coffee-ed out thanks. Got some interesting stuff from Mark Templeton about the Mill though, he's sent the Ordnance Survey plans, I thought you'd want to take a look. Also Paulene has drafted out some good ads for extra staff, which I think we need to get cracking on with straight away, otherwise we'll all go under."

The steam hissed in the coffee machine and Oliver pulled his cup out – "I just love this machine it's magic! Great about the plans, let's have a gander then." Andrew spread them out once again over the desk and Oliver scanned them and the accompanying letter exclaiming"Wow, mate! This is gonna be bloody excellent if we can pull it off." He sounded excited, "Where are these ads then?"

Andrew pushed them over, and they both laughed about Paulene's new job title. "I think they look good, other than adding an email address is there anything else you think we need to say?"

"Nah," Oliver's eyes skimmed over them again, "they look good, and although it would be easier to have someone with a bit more experience, but we can mould a graduate the way we want, and I'm more than happy to be supportive in that role – we all started out somewhere after all."

"Yep, we're both agreed on that. It's coming up to the right time of year too, just doing their finals, bit of a summer break and looking for a job around September time, would fit in with us perfectly. Also it would be a cheaper option too, especially as we'll have to order another wagon and extra gear to equip it. I'll get Paulene onto the job for some quotes from Mayfairs." Andrew hesitated "And I've had second thoughts about the office assistant post, we could do with someone a bit sooner than that, get them used to the job and stuff before the extra load of another vet – what do you think?"

Oliver ran his fingers through his hair, "It's certainly a thought, I suppose anyone with a job now would have to give a month's notice – let's go with that then. The other thing I've been thinking is that we should give Paulene a raise, she's bloody invaluable to us and it'll be extra work for her after all, as she'd have to train this new bod."

"Okay, I'm game on with that, she will have extra responsibilities, and I certainly don't want her nose put out of joint with someone new coming in, and I think she'll have to be in on both interviews too, she needs to be happy with whoever we choose too." Andrew smiled – he was very fond of Paulene, she had been with him since the day he started the practice.

"What about accommodation for the new vet?" Oliver asked "they could always bunk in with me I suppose, till we know more about the Mill project, and that would save some money too."

Andrew glanced naughtily at him "Won't that cramp your style a bit? Now you're foot loose and fancy free?"

"Two lads together – not a chance, could spice things up a bit you never know!"

Charles and Jennifer sat down in the drawing room, large drinks
in their hands, they were exhausted. It had been a wonderful day at
Arundel and the kids had really enjoyed themselves, it had even
seemed to break down Rupert's determination to hate every second of
the weekend and by the time they had come out of the castle, he was
as animated and talkative as Jessica. They'd followed the same route
suggested by Chloe and luckily the weather was fine, so the awesome
picnic Mrs Fuller had prepared was greedily wolfed down by them
all.

They had not got back until late, and Charles had rung ahead and
told Mrs Fuller to have an evening off, and they had stopped off for
fish and chips eating them in the car – something that would never
have happened under Celia's regime. They sang songs all the way
back and had two very sleepy, yawning children in the back of the
Range Rover, and Jennifer had ushered them up to bed, not bothering
to make them have a bath. Now sitting down in the squashy feather
sofa she felt totally happy, it had gone so much better than she had
planned and she hoped it was just one of many great days ahead of
them. She thought back to the unhappy miserable woman of a month
or so ago, and wondered what had happened to her? It was all since
she had taken up riding and found some friends down here, she was
beginning to feel she really belonged. Her scheme to continue riding
secretly until she could surprise Charles was going well, but deep
down she knew that she would have to tell him fairly soon. Perhaps
now would be the right moment, after such a perfect day. "Charles…"
She began tentatively.

"Hmmm," he said sleepily "What a lovely day, you were clever
to plan it, I'm very proud of you darling."

Jennifer considered, should she tell him or shouldn't she? "Yes,
it was fabulous day, I really enjoyed it and I'm sure the children did
too. But Charles, there is something that I need to tell you."

He sat up from where he had been lolling on the sofa and turned
to look at her, "That sounds worrying. You're not ill or anything are
you?"

She laughed "No, nothing like that, but well. You need to know
that I've been taking riding lessons, and helping out in Chloe
Coombe's yard, as I really want to be more involved with you and the
hunting and taking the children out…." she tailed off, not knowing

quite what else to say.

Charles' face visibly relaxed, he was clearly thinking it was going to be much more of an earth shattering announcement "Darling that's wonderful news, how exciting for you! How are you getting on?"

Jennifer beamed at him "Oh quite well I think, I was going to keep it as a surprise for you and just come out one day, but I don't like having secrets from you."

"I'm simply thrilled, it'll be great fun, and" he thought for a moment, "that of course explains why Chloe and her grooms came to the party, I've been wondering about that."

Chloe - Jennifer thought had been her salvation, as had the girls at the yard, they'd all helped her so much. "Chloe's been brilliant, as have her girls, become more like friends and they've been very patient with me. I've been riding a little old horse of Chloe's called Rufus and he's given me a lot of confidence."

"Ah" Charles grinned "I know Rufus, a great little sort in his day, perfect for you to start on. Can I come up one day and watch?"

"Of course, but I'll be very nervous with you there you know! I'm quite self-conscious!" she stammered.

"That's only natural to start with, and I can understand that darling, it's a big thing to be doing, how about you tell me when you feel ready?"

"You're a love, you understand perfectly how I'm feeling – but I'm getting better all the time, then come and see. I've also been helping Chloe round the yard too, tacking up, mucking out, cleaning tack, so that I get a really broad picture of the way a yard runs. I'm really enjoying it."

Hmmm thought Charles, that'd explain the transformation from the pupae trapped here with no friends or real country interests, to the happy exotic butterfly she seemed to be lately, well good for her and good on Chloe too. "Excellent, that's just as important as being able to ride, when I was a kid we all had to muck in and know the inside of a wheelbarrow! Of course now, I simply wouldn't have time, but I still remember the days of Pony Club and going to camp. You know though darling, Rufus, is a lovely little type, but he's quite old, it may be that you have to think of having a horse of your own one day?"

She blushed and laughed nervously, "Oh oh, don't go getting any ideas, I don't think I'm quite ready for that yet. Meanwhile you're quite happy with me going there every day? It means a lot to me, but for the time being I want to keep it a secret, don't mention it to anyone will you, especially the children or the staff."

"Of course I am, whatever makes you happy, makes me happy too! I want to thank you too darling for making such a big effort with the children this weekend, and that means a lot to me. I have to take them back tomorrow afternoon, - will you come with me?"

This was a big thing for Jennifer, she had never gone to meet Celia when Charles had the children, but she felt more confident now and seemed to be on a better footing with the kids too, although she would hate going there, "Okay, of course I will."

"Thank you darling, that's excellent, come on I'm knackered, let's go to bed."

CHAPTER 32

Grace and Colin were woken by the sound of the church bells that Sunday morning, the sun was streaming in though the long windows of the barn conversion and filtering onto the oak floor.

"Christ!" said Colin "Look at the bloody time! We have well and truly slept in this morning."

"Colin, it's Sunday, we can have a lie in if we like" Grace muttered sleepily, "Nothing's spoiling. You don't have to go to work today, so just enjoy being at home for a change."

"I hate sleeping in Grace, you know I do. Let's make the most of the day. I thought we could nip up to Kennels before lunch and see how old George has got the place looking."

"You want to eye up the other hounds you mean, see what competition our two have." laughed Grace, sitting up and stretching, "God what a glorious day! You are right, don't let's waste it." She pulled back the duvet and Colin admired her long legs and pert bum as she ambled into the bathroom. She squatted on the loo, shouting, "come on lazy bones, and get up then!" She heard the bed groan as Colin scrambled out of bed, fishing around for his slippers and otherwise bollock naked slopped into the bathroom, Grace was already brushing her teeth and mumbling to him, her mouth foaming with toothpaste.

"Gracie, I cannot understand a word you are saying!" he laughed at her, coming up behind her and kissing her shoulder his hands straying to her breasts, she squeaked in surprise and started to wriggle he said "sorry no good can't understand you at all." His hands ran down the front of her tummy to her hips and slipped in between her legs, and she spun round him and gave him a sloppy toothpasty kiss. "Bloody hell, yum yum!" he spluttered.

They were finally sitting over breakfast, the big glass doors open and the dogs wandering in and out of the kitchen, the view was wonderful, beyond their stable yard and manège, the hills undulated in the distance painting a thousand different shades of green. Their horses were sunning themselves in the meadow, standing end to end flicking off unwanted flies with their tails. It was so tranquil, only the sound of birdsong and bees to be heard. Colin put his hand over Grace's, echoing her thoughts "we are so lucky you know, we should make the most of every moment."

She looked pensive, "I know darling."

Sean had been speaking to the others about Laura, outlining what she had said about targeting a particular hunt this season, rather than just causing trouble at random ones. They had been interested, especially when Sean had told them that Laura had some insider gen on the Fittlebury and Cosham, about the dates for their meets and any functions that they would be putting on. Hunts rarely advertised those details, and were fiercely protective about who was told what, usually by telephone or direct posting to members - even avoiding emails, so that was indeed golden information. They could really plan a strategy of disruption and maybe even catch the buggers out when they overstepped the law. How she had got this, he didn't know and he hadn't asked. He wasn't quite sure he trusted her motives yet, although Linda had said he was just being paranoid.

"What sort of thing is she talking about" mumbled Ewan, "We could rally quite a few troops for this if it's not too risky."

"Usual stuff, just heckling. Perhaps a bit of letting down of tyres, car scratching, horn blowing that kind of thing, but she reckons that it we target one hunt continuously, then it would seriously piss them off more than just doing the odd day or two." Sean repeated what Laura had said, "We'd know exactly where they are meeting and where they are going – it would be much more organised than before, less haphazard. He liked the idea, those rich upper class bastards needed a run for their money.

"Sounds good. You say more organised – whatdya mean by that?" asked Annie.

"Well, some of us create diversions, whilst the others do the damage, that kinda stuff, but plan it beforehand. Obviously the usual stuff of taking photos and videos as well, but perhaps a bit more troublesome behind the scenes." As he was talking he was warming to the idea, it could be very satisfying as well as a good laugh. "So what do we all think then? Shall I tell her it's a goer? Shall I can get her over here to meet the hard core to sort it out?"

"Let's do it!" Ewan's normally dull eyes glittered with excitement.

The children had gotten up later this morning, they had been exhausted after a long day yesterday and were sitting in the kitchen chatting and eating their breakfast. Charles had somewhat surprisingly sat down with them eschewing his normal insistence at eating in the breakfast room. Mrs Fuller was in her element, bustling about after them all, doling out more toast and coffee. Jennifer asked if she wanted any help but she'd declined, so she too sat at the table listening to the others.

"What do you want to do this morning?" she asked Jessica, "Do you want to go for a ride again? It's a lovely day."

"I'd love that, but can you come too?" Jessica took Jennifer's hand, "it'd be so nice."

"Jessica," said Rupert in a matter of fact tone, "Jennifer doesn't ride, you know that."

At least Rupert wasn't being spiteful about it like he normally was thought Jennifer which was definitely step in the right direction. She glanced at Charles who smiled at her with a ghost of a wink, but said nothing and she turned to Jessica saying "I could walk along with you though sweetie, if you'd like me to come?"

"Yes definitely" laughed Jessica, "I promise I won't trot, so you won't have to run."

"Thank you" said Jennifer solemnly, "How about you Rupert, are you coming too?"

He hesitated for a moment and then said slowly "Yes, please I'd like that, and Dad as well?"

"Of course. You're not going without me!" laughed Charles, "I'll let Caitlin know. Let's finish up here then, or it'll be lunch time before we know it."

When they got over to the stable yard, Caitlin had been going like a demon to be ready on time having brushed all the horses and was already halfway through tacking them up when they arrived. Jessica rushed over to Queenie, patting her and stroking her long silvery mane, and Rupert went over to finish tacking up Scooter.

"We won't be able to be out long Caitlin, as I have to take the children back later this afternoon, so it'll just be a quickie. Jennifer is going to walk with us today, so she can take Jessica on the leading rein. When we come back, we'll have to leave you to it I'm afraid as we'll be in a bit of a rush. Mrs Fuller is doing lunch for one o'clock prompt so she tells me and I don't want to get on her bad side!" Charles laughed and winked at Caitlin.

"No problem to be sure" Caitlin smiled back at him, he was in a good mood today. They must have had a good crack yesterday as even Rupert looked happy, his face no longer looking like a slapped arse. Saints be praised. She herded the children onto the ponies and handed Jennifer the leading rein, and they were off, to all intents and purposes the ideal 2.2 family.

Charles and Rupert rode side by side ahead of Jennifer leading Queenie, the lane was shaded by the big oaks and the lazy Sunday traffic ambled past. Jessica had worn her cloak again and was twirling her wand about in her hand. Rupert was chatting to Charles who was nodding his head and making the odd reply. They turned up into a bridleway track, and Charles called back to Jennifer that he and Rupert were going to have a canter up the hill and would she be okay holding onto Queenie, she waved her assent and with that they loped off around a corner and into the distance. Queenie shot her head up in the air, and was furious at being left behind, she started dancing about on the end of the lead rein, with Jessica clinging on, looking a bit white and afraid on top. Jennifer started to croon to Queenie, offering her Polos and calming her down and the little old pony responded, feeling her sore feet, and content once more to amble on at her own pace.

Jessica relaxed "I was really frightened just then you know, you did really well holding her Jennifer, especially since you don't know anything about horses. She really likes you I think."

Jennifer stroked the pony's neck, "She just wanted to join in, but she's been a good girl for you and was very well behaved considering. Perhaps it's because you have that magic wand!"

"Do you really think so?" Jessica held the wand up and examined the end, "you could be right."

"I'm sure I am, you've put a spell on Queenie to behave and she did, well done you!" They had started to climb up the hill now and could see Rupert and Charles waiting for them at the top, she was puffing a bit, it was quite a climb, but it was worth it, the view was startling - you could see for miles.

"Jennifer was marvellous Daddy, she held onto Queenie really well, kept her totally under control, until I could put a spell on her to behave." Jessica said earnestly to Charles. "I didn't feel at all afraid."

"Clever girls indeed." grinned Charles, "Aren't they Rupert?" He turned to his son, who grinned back and nodded his head, "Better walk back home otherwise Caitlin will tell us all off for sweating up the horses when they are supposed to be walking and then we mustn't be late for lunch, or we'll be in trouble with Mrs Fuller too!"

Lucy was sweating her guts out in the Bistro, it was bloody hot and although it was Sunday the town was busy with shoppers, all stopping by for coffee and lunch. She had been rushed off her feet trying to keep up with the orders, running backwards and forwards waiting on the tables, having spent all morning preparing the fillings. There must be more than to life than this she thought. Francesca was giving her the evils again, she was a bloody pain in the neck, always moaning about her to Gino and Maria - she didn't give a fuck though. Tomorrow was her day off and she couldn't bloody wait, she was going to comb the Horse & Hound for another horsey job so that she could get out of this dump. Problem was she needed a reference and she wondered if she dared ask Caitlin for one, probably not - given the circumstances of her departure – God she regretted it now.

Another thing she regretted was meeting up with that Jonty and his Weasel, they hadn't phoned her or even texted, although she was so sure that they would've done. Bastards. She had a break in an hour, and might text Tom though and see what he was up to tonight, it'd be nice to have a drink in the Fox and find out what everyone was up to.

Gino yelled at her from the kitchen, and she hurried to pick up the orders he'd made up, bloody slave driver. She stomped out to one of the little tables outside and plonked the plates down, grudgingly turning to serve any new customers. Unbeknown to Lucy, Jonty was watching her from the edge of the Swan Centre, and smiled to himself as he watched her take the order and march back into the café. He and Weasel moved out into view, sitting at an empty table, and waited for her to come out again. Time they cultivated the luscious Lucy some more.

The atmosphere at Mileoak was strained. After their heart to heart of the previous evening, John and Chloe had been extremely and falsely polite to each other, having now acknowledged that there was a problem, it was hard for Chloe to act normally, she was still furious at his refusal to talk to her. John on the other hand had tried to shrug it off and was trying to make a big fuss of her and especially the children when they came back. The yard itself was quiet, Katherine was not coming up today, and Sandy had made a brief flying visit and the other liveries had been and gone and Chloe did not teach on a Sunday, it was Beebs day to work and she was well on schedule, and the family were all in the house. Chloe was organising the school things ready for the morning, and John had offered to cook the meal. The children made it easier for them, they were always interrupting and so there were not many opportunities for John and Chloe to be on their own. John was banging pots about, whilst Chloe did the ironing, they had put the TV on, so they didn't have to talk. The children were busy at the table doing last minute homework projects. Chloe glanced over at him, as he was peeling potatoes at the sink, she was so angry with him, why wouldn't he confide in her, what could be the matter? She banged the iron down on the board with venom and everyone jumped.

"You all right Mummy?" asked Lily, "your face looks all

screwed up. You need to be careful you know you'll stay like that if you aren't careful."

Chloe rearranged her face immediately, it was what her mother had always told her and she had said the same to her children too. She looked at them busy cutting out and sticking things into their project books, and her heart melted, it wasn't their fault, and she was going to make sure they didn't suffer no matter what was going on. She put down the iron and went and sat with them at the table, admiring their work, stroking Rory's fair hair as he struggled to cut out a picture from a magazine.

"That's really good darling, you've made a super job of this, let me see yours Toby." Toby pushed his book over towards Chloe and she flicked through the pages, "This is really interesting Toby, I'm very proud of you, you've worked hard." Toby smirked to himself, basking in her admiration. Lily looked furious and came and sat on Chloe's lap. John put down his peeler and came over to see, pulling out a chair beside his son. He looked up into Chloe's eyes and smiled at her, really smiled at her and she suddenly thought – it'll be all right, I know it, and she smiled right back at him.

Mrs Fuller had surpassed herself with roast beef and all the trimmings, followed by lemon meringue pie. It had been delicious, and the children had eaten well, as had Charles and Jennifer, they were all starving after their busy morning. Now they were loading up the car with the children's bags whilst Jennifer did a last minute check around their rooms to make sure they hadn't forgotten anything. She stood looking out of the window in Rupert's room down onto the drive at the Range Rover. It had been a successful weekend, more than she could have hoped for, and now the last hurdle was the journey back and her seeing Celia. She was dreading it.

Her eye was caught by a movement in the garden, she looked again and saw the shadow of Pete watching Charles and the children, his face was softer than she had ever seen it as he gazed at them. He walked slowly over to Charles, and the children ran up to him and his big hands patted them on their backs and he was speaking to them and smiling. The whole scene was over in a matter of a minute. Pete nodded to Charles and walked away from them back towards his cottage, but then quite suddenly he turned around and waved to them once more, his eyes roaming upwards to the window and locked with hers, and his whole face contorted with hate. Jennifer shivered and turned away, he was just so weird and she was sure he was getting worse, although by the looks of things he was quite capable of being nice when he wanted to be, his spite seemed to be only directed at her.

The Range Rover sped along the lanes, the miles being eaten up far too fast for Jennifer's liking. She was only half listening to the conversation as they drove along, deep in thought about the meeting ahead with Celia. It was only natural that Celia had no reason to like or even be civil to Jennifer, so she had no idea about how she would react when she saw her. Jennifer had made up her mind to be totally charming and sweet, no matter what Celia said or did. After all she had won Charles and although he was very generous in every way towards Celia and the children, it was she Jennifer, who now lived in Celia's old home and had effectively booted Celia out. No, Celia had no reason to be nice to Jennifer, why would she, if Jennifer were in her shoes she would be pretty shitty, but she was not going to retaliate. Charles was chatting away to Rupert, oblivious to her inner worries, discussing where they might like to go for a holiday this year.

"I thought we could go on a safari? We could do some of it on horseback and some in a Landrover, should be great fun, I was thinking Botswana – everyone says it's superb. I think you'd love it, and I know I would, but we'll have to have a chat with your mother first to check she agrees."

"Wow Dad sounds fantastic, I'd love it, how about you Jess?" enthused Rupert.

"I agree it'd be great fun Daddy, but I'm a bit concerned about Jennifer, how'd she do the horseback bit? I wouldn't want to leave her out, that wouldn't be very fair would it?" sighed Jessica. Jennifer tuning in, listening in surprise, what a lovely little girl Jessica was, to be concerned about her, she was a real sweetie.

"Oh I'm sure we'd get round it darling, but would you quite like to go, that's the point?" asked Charles, "because I'll have to talk to

Mummy and arrange the dates, but I can't do that if you're not sure."

"Definitely sure, but if Jennifer doesn't do the riding part, then I'd want to stay and keep her company if that's okay?"

"All settled then, but don't mention anything to Mummy just yet, I'll telephone her to discuss it, okay?" Charles had no intention of Celia kicking up a fuss in front of the children and Jennifer and she almost certainly would - just to be awkward. It'd be better to ring and ask her. "We're nearly back, only another 5 minutes." Jennifer went quite pale, and felt her heart start to thud, Charles leant over and took her hand, "It'll be fine" he whispered.

"Did I tell you that I saw Julia Napier wrapped around a chap when Mum and I went into the garden centre?" Grace announced as they walked up to the kennels. "It was quite amusing. You should've seen her!"

"You're joking!" Colin was astounded "Mind you that woman is ghastly, I never knew what Andrew saw in her, she is such a social climber."

"Well she was certainly climbing all over this chap! Good looking he was too, quite a bit younger than her I should say, sporty type and pretty fit looking." Grace teased, "I could've quite fancied him myself."

"Oi Grace! You don't mean that!"

Poor Colin Grace thought he was so easy to wind up. "No of course I didn't, don't be silly. But it was curious nonetheless and a strange place to see her. Wonder who he was and what she was up to eh?"

"Frankly darling, I don't really care two hoots about her, but I do about Andrew, - poor guy, there he is working all the hours God sends and she is fooling around with someone else." Colin was dismayed "Do you think I ought to tell him?"

"No I bloody don't!" Grace was cross, "Keep out of it Colin, I wouldn't have told you if I thought you'd blab. It could have been quite innocent and you could just make trouble!"

"Okay, I won't but it's a disgrace nonetheless." Grace looked at him, dear Colin so proper and correct, at least they had a solid marriage, it seemed as though few people did these days.

They walked on hand in hand until they came to the kennels. It was a wonderful old place, the huntsman George lived in one of the cottages with young Jay, but the hounds themselves were housed in a gutted 16th century cottage that had been left to the hunt by some landed gentry about a hundred years earlier. In the scheme of things it would have been restored and would by now have had a family living there, but it had been the home of the Fittlebury and Cosham hounds for many years. The whole place was looking very dapper, as they walked into the cobbled yard. George greeted them like old friends, as indeed they were, ushering them over to the kennels, where the two hound puppies they had walked were now integrated into the pack. He fished them out, and they made a huge fuss when they saw them, launching themselves with glee at Colin and Grace, and leaving great trails of slobber all over their jeans.

"How do you think they'll do George? Have they settled in well? They were a mettlesome couple."

George scratched his chin and pulled his cap down, "They'll do well enough, once we start taking them out proper, hound exercise on bikes is no fun, but we've coupled them up with Archie and Remus, they're good old boys and they'll soon show 'em the ropes."

"Ah, what good boys you are, you take notice of the older boys and you'll do well" she crooned at the bouncing hounds, "Now get down , get down!" as she was nearly knocked flying "They are certainly enthusiastic George!"

"Aye, well that's good, we need them to be full of stamina for the job, nowt worse than a dull, miserable hound." He cracked his hunt whip, and they immediately stopped leaping about and were calmer, "Now Nettle, Nimrod, you two back with the others." He ushered them back into the main kennels, the hounds were lounging about on tiered straw beds, the older ones grumbling at the younger ones to put them in their place.

"The kennels are looking as neat as a pin George. As long as we have a nice afternoon, it should be good for the show next week. I've been roped in for cakes as usual."

"Well, I'm sure they'll be very tasty Gracie! Yes hoping for fine weather - makes such a difference." George looked up at the sky, "threatening to be unsettled though, we'll have to wait and see."

"Now George, don't be offended, but would you like me to take home your white dust coats for the show to give them a good laundering, I know it's not easy for you now without Mary?" she asked tentatively.

"Why thank you, that'd be right kind, you sure you wouldn't mind?" George's weathered brown face crinkled into a smile "I'd be so grateful."

"That's settled then" said Grace, "Why not go and get them for me now and I'll have them spick and span for you and Jay." George touched his cap and marched off into the offices, bringing back with him a plastic bag stuffed full with dirty white coats. Grace grimaced, they'd obviously not been laundered since the last show, now to see if those washing powders did all they claimed. She took the bag, "I'll bring them back as soon as I've done them – okay?" She turned to Colin, "We'd better get back sweetie. See you later George."

"Bye George, see you next week. Show our boys well!" boomed Colin, and he took the bag from Grace and they wandered out into the lane. "Hmm, I don't envy you Gracie, washing this lot – they're bloody filthy!"

"Oh I don't mind, keeps me busy, plus making the cakes I promised. The boys looked well didn't they, they've grown so much, I'm really looking forward to next week."

"Good darling, we'll have a super day, and you never know we might win a prize."

Pete was sitting ramrod straight in his armchair, it was Sunday, so he didn't have to work, but he'd enjoyed seeing the children again, they were bonny and of course they would be, after all Celia was their mother. He missed them around the place, their constant chatter brought the house to life and made him feel important and wanted again. But she had been looking down at him – he'd felt her presence like a festering sore. The voices kept telling him, that if it wasn't for her, Celia and the children would still be here and he'd be safe again. He knew he was going to have to do something about it, she couldn't be allowed to stay here. He got up and paced about the room agitatedly straightening things here and there, flicking imaginary dust from the window sill. He must wash his hands he thought and went back through to the kitchen ducking his head under the low beam, scrupulously he scrubbed his hands again and again at the sink and went through his ritual of rinsing the bowl. The voices would send a miracle to help him, they'd told him so, and he would have to be vigilant and wait for their signal to act.

CHAPTER 33

Katherine knocked on the door, even though it was half open, and breezed into the kitchen just as Chloe shouted hello and was plonking the kettle on the Aga. The kitchen table looked a nightmare of cereal bowls, cups and uneaten bits of toast, she picked up the dirty crockery stowing it in the dishwasher, and made a space for them to sit down.

Blimey what a mess, Chloe could really do with some help Katherine thought, picturing her own neat and ordered lifestyle and sighed, "Come on Chloe I can help you tidy up while we talk." She moved over to the sink and ran some hot water into the bowl, rinsing a dish cloth and wiping down the work surfaces.

"You don't have to do this Katherine, it's like it every morning. Just some mornings are worse than others!" Chloe grimaced as a piece of toast and honey stuck to her hand, she shook it off, "I try not to let it get to me."

Katherine stopped "Chloe don't give it another thought, I've had kids too remember. Now come on, what happened on Saturday night? Did you manage to speak to John?"

Chloe pulled a face, and leant against the kitchen table, "yes, I did, but you're not going to like this, because I don't either."

Katherine chucked the cloth into the washing up bowl and sat down at the table, "What happened, what did you say, or rather what did he say?"

"Well, he refused to talk about it - point blank, just refused." Chloe put her head in her hands and poured out the whole story. "I just don't know what to think, I really don't."

Katherine didn't know what to say, what was there to say "Didn't he give any reason at all? No excuse, not even a clue?"

"Nope, he was totally adamant, just said it would affect all of our lives, but until he was sure he wasn't saying anything and that I'd have to trust him. I know John, he's bloody stubborn, there was no way he was shifting, what could I do? But I did say I would bloody kill him if I found he was having an affair."

Katherine looked frustrated, "So you're no nearer the truth then?"

"In a nutshell no, but there was something in the way he looked at me yesterday and the way he was to me and the kids, I actually don't think it's an affair. I don't know what it is, I'll just have to wait, but I'm hoping that he'll confide in me pretty bloody soon, otherwise I'm going to go mad."

Oh God thought Katherine, this was terrible, how could Chloe be so stupidly naïve, and how could John be so senseless, surely now was the time to be talking, not later when things may have gone too far. There was nothing she could do though, she saw the light and hope in Chloe's eyes, how could she be the one to disillusion her, even though privately she thought he was up to no good. All she could do was support her as much as she could and be around to pick up the pieces when and if things went belly up. Poor Chloe, she reached over and touched her hand, "Okay, well we'll just have to get on with things then, if that's how he wants it - but just be on your guard, in case he lets anything slip. I thought you both may like to come over for supper one night, I could ask Sandy and Mark too, what do you think?"

"You are super Katherine." Chloe squeezed her hand back, "That'd be lovely."

"Right – how about Friday night?" Plan B thought Katherine, rapidly scheming ahead.

"Perfect, thank you." sighed Chloe. "it would give me something to look forward to, and something we can do together." They both look up simultaneously to see a silver car gliding down the drive, "that'll be Jen, I wonder how her weekend turned out?"

"Oh, I'm sure it was fine, she seems to be so much more relaxed these days, and that will rub off on the children" mused Katherine. "They've had a tough time with the divorce and it can't have been easy for any of them having to adjust, but it was a good idea of yours

Chloe to suggest they went to Arundel, just hope that Charles played ball."

Chloe slurped at her coffee, toying with some pens strewn on the table, "Bloody divorce, I just hope it doesn't come to that for me."

Katherine smiled sympathetically, thinking, not if I have anything to do with it!

Caitlin was busy tidying up the stables after the horses had been brought in for the weekend. She had turned them back out now into the lower meadow, all except Queenie, she wanted to keep an eye on her and had put her on the walker, and then into a small paddock, carefully fenced and almost bald of grass. Queenie had been glad to go out again, it was so difficult to find the right balance between allowing her to let off steam, so she wasn't too fizzy for Jessica, and the danger of her getting laminitis on the rich grass. Hopefully half a day out on the '*starvation paddock*' and then a strict regime of reduced protein intake, with regular visits from Patrick and she should be fine.

She stood up from bending over in the stable, where she had been picking up the droppings, Christ she was tired, she'd not had a day off since Lucy walked out, and although there was not that much going on at this time of year, it would be nice to have a lie in for a change, and she really would need a holiday before the season started, when the work load would be trebled. That guy Felix had not rung her back yet, and if he didn't by this afternoon, she supposed she would have to ring him again, although she didn't want to appear as though she were chasing him. Perhaps they would have to draft an ad for the Horse & Hound after all.

She thought back to the weekend, the children seemed to have a good time and Jennifer coped surprisingly well with handling Queenie, Caitlin had been a bit worried about that, she knew how mad Charles and Rupert could be once the responsibility of Jessica was put onto someone else, but it seemed to be okay, they had all come back smiling. She felt her phone vibrate in her pocket, and then a cacophony of electronic beeps as her phone rang, her heart leapt into her mouth, "Good morning!" she said brightly, feeling the colour rise in her face.

"A top of the morning to you my beautiful Irish girl, how are you today?"

"I'm grand and even grander now that you've called! What are you up to now?" Her eyes were shining, it was still a wonder when he rang her. His voice so deep and sexy, she could picture him now - naked in her arms.

"Oh working hard, as I always do!" he laughed, "I desperately want to meet you today, but it can't be tonight, could you snatch off a few hours later do you think?"

Caitlin didn't think twice, she had worked all weekend after all, "I'd love too, what sort of time?"

"Well it depends on how the day goes but about three ish? It's good weather, so usual place?"

"See you then, if it changes – ring or text me, I just ..." but her conversation was stopped mid flow, with a lot of crackle and static and then the phone went dead. Bloody signals, he must be in a bad area, she slipped the phone back into her pocket smiling to herself, she was looking forward to seeing him. Was it love or lust - whatever she couldn't help herself. The phone vibrated and chorused out again, she answered immediately "Darling, I just ..." Again she was interrupted, but this time by a totally unfamiliar voice.

"I'm not your darling ... yet! Is that you Caitlin, it's Felix here. I promised to ring and let you know when I could pop over for the interview."

"Oh Felix, I'm sorry, I thought it was someone else. That's great, what day suits you?" Caitlin said embarrassed, thank the Lord she hadn't said anything else.

"Ah pity, I thought you were pleased to hear from me! I was thinking Wednesday this week?"

Caitlin laughed "You don't know how pleased I am to hear from you actually, and Wednesday should be dandy, but I've to clear that with Mrs Parker -Smythe first, as she wants to meet you. So take it that's fine, unless you hear from me – what time?"

"Blimey, what's she like? Hope she's not some old battle axe?" he sounded concerned, "Oh and about three o'clock would be good!"

Hmm, how could she describe Jennifer, she compromised "No, she's very nice to be sure, not horsey at all, but wants to be involved y' know, and three in the afternoon is a good time for me." She said goodbye to Felix. All happening at three for me these days she thought happily, and started to daydream about the afternoon ahead.

Jennifer eased into her breeches, tugging them up over her narrow hips, she smoothed down her polo shirt, God it felt good to be in them again. How she had changed, before she would have died a thousand deaths before being seen in this get up. The only drawback were these bloody long boots, they felt so cumbersome, but Beebs has assured her that Ariats were the most comfortable for everyday riding and she should try Konigs if you wanted pain, it was like your legs were encased in concrete. Sighing, she reached down for them grimacing as she pulled them on. No sign of Chloe this morning, although her car was here and so was Katherine's but she was not around either. She was going to take Rufus into the school this morning, and Beebs was going to give her a hand again. She would quite like to have had two rides a day, it always seemed to be time to get off before she had gotten into her stride, but Rufus was older now and the last thing she would want to do was break him! What would I do then she reasoned. He was a dear old thing, and she could easily tack him up on her own now, although she knew that either Chloe or one of the others gave him a surreptitious glance over to check everything was okay before she got on. She was so pleased that she had told Charles about what she was doing, although it would have been a great surprise for him, it was better to have him onside, and he had seemed genuinely pleased. She stomped out in the boots to the yard where Rufus was waiting patiently for her, and she called out to Beebs that she was ready when it suited her. I'll just get on she thought and have a little walk around the school while I'm waiting. She put her hand into her breeches pocket and pulled out the obligatory Polos, she never went anywhere near a horse without them now. Rufus nuzzled into her, and she walked him over to the school, positioning him at the mounting block whilst she clambered on. He was such a dear, not moving a muscle until she was settled, taking up

375

her reins, and squaring up her shoulders she pushed him into a walk, practising the turns and circles like she had been shown. She was becoming quite adept at it now, but of course Rufus knew his job and helped her lot, how these people managed on tricky horses she couldn't fathom!

Beebs was watching her from the tack room, it was really satisfying to see how much Jen had progressed in a matter of weeks, and moreover how keen she was, it was a pity really that Rufus was not a bit younger. She picked up her coffee and strolled over to the school, ducking under the post and rail fence careful not to spill her drink. She shouted a hello to Jennifer, who looked up a bit embarrassed, "I was just doing a bit of practising Beebs, hope that was okay?"

"Course it is. The more you do the more skilled you'll get, and your position is so much better even after this short time." Beebs complimented, "and today we are going to work more on you keeping your balance both in and out of the transitions. Your body will naturally want to work one way, and that is to fall forward as the impact of the horse's hind legs pushes you there, and then that pushes the horse onto the shoulders and both you and he then lose balance. So we need to alter your muscle memory to react in a different way, so that you can stay in balance and make a better and safer transition. Just come onto a 20m circle round me, and stay in walk for the moment whilst I explain what I want you to do – okay?"

Jennifer manoeuvred Rufus onto the circle and walked around her, sitting up as straight as she could, keeping her hands down and her elbows into her ribcage. "Okay ready!"

"Now your basic position like that is fine, in a perfect world you need to keep your earlobe, your shoulder , your hip and your heel in a straight line down towards the ground, and that is straight forward to do in the walk, but when the gait changes to a faster one, it's not so easy. The rising trot means that you have to sit a little more forward, but in the canter it is easier to stay up straight. So, what I want you to do now is go into rising trot and see how straight you can sit, without flopping so far forward onto the horse's withers. Try and keep your hands still as you do it, so that your body becomes independent of your hands – remember how you could balance yourself when we did that lunge lesson, now see if you can manage that without the balancing strap - okay let's do it!"

Jennifer urged Rufus forward concentrating hard not to fall forward and keep her hands still at the same time, not as easy as it sounded! "Whoooa – it's really hard!" she gasped with the effort.

"Keep concentrating and now prepare to walk, but take your time so that your body can absorb the movement and not be cannoned forward by the change in pace." Beebs instructed, "That's it, right sit into the saddle and feel yourself relax into walk. Well done. Good!"

Again and again they went through this exercise, changing the rein periodically so that she could do it either way, until it started to feel more natural for Jennifer to remain in balance. She could feel the sweat running down her back, and her muscles aching from the isometric control she was constantly having to use to keep herself still.

"Well done Jen, that is very good work, now let's have a go in the canter, this is harder. The canter is a much bigger pace as you know and because of that there is a huge amount of energy shoving you forward when you want to trot, and that makes keeping the balance really hard. When you are beginning this is the hardest transition you will make, but just do the same as you did before – prepare yourself for the movement and concentrate on not pitching forward. Okay canter when you are ready then."

Over and over they repeated the transition work, Jennifer felt exhausted not just physically but mentally too, she really had no idea that riding needed such mental stamina. She was determined to get it right though, and gritted her teeth and carried on until she was satisfied that she was getting the hang of it. "That felt better!" she shouted with elation after a particularly successful transition.

"Yes, it certainly was! I know we always say it, but it is just practice, over and over again, and then you won't have to think it through so much, it will become automatic, just like driving the car! I think too, on that good note you should leave it now and do it again tomorrow. Practise every day, even when you are out hacking."

"Oh I don't want to stop Beebs, I'm just getting the hang of it." Jennifer was astonished, where had the time gone!

"Nope that's enough, Rufus is an old boy, and you've both done quite a lot for today, so come back to it fresh tomorrow" Beebs insisted. She walked over to Rufus and gave him a Polo, "Come on old fellah, let's wash you off."

"Oh I feel terrible now, poor Rufus, that was really selfish of me, it's just I can't get enough, you know." Jennifer slipped off and threw her arms around him, "You are such a special horse Rufus, you've taught me so much already." They walked into the yard together and took off his tack, Jennifer put him in the wash down box and started hosing him off, carefully avoiding his eyes and face. He was loving it, she scraped all the excess water off his body, and sponged his face gently. "I really love you little Rufus" she whispered.

It was past lunch time as Jonty and Weasel walked into B52, they'd arranged to meet Lucy but she was not here yet and they sauntered over to the bar, a few people were sitting down, but took little notice of them. Weasel ordering a beer and a coke for Jonty - he wanted to keep his head clear for today. They walked outside to the covered area and found a spare table, more or less at the same spot they'd been last time. The square was quiet, the odd person popping into Waitrose, the shops here were quite posh and pretty empty - how do they make a living Jonty thought, still he supposed it was Monday and it was bound to be quiet. Weasel took a slug of his beer, belching loudly, and laughed, he really was disgusting!

"You fucker!" Jonty scorned, "You're like an animal sometimes."

"Yer and I love it mate!" he farted, "how's that then!" Weasel's little face looked peeved, he had a short fuse and was always spoiling for a row.

Jonty twisted his face up "Phew you stinky bastard! Now stop fooling about, we're here for a reason remember?"

"I know, I know! We gonna get Luscious Lucy on our side, stir her up about that git Parker-Smythe and get her to spill the beans about the hunt. That right?"

"Yep, but we're gonna be careful how we do it, so leave that side to me. You chat her up and flirt with her a bit, she enjoyed it last time, and you got a good screw out of it. Here look at this." He got out his phone and showed him the photos he'd taken of them rolling about in the fields, "She's got great tits!"

Weasel grabbed the phone, his ferrety eyes leering over the photos, "good shots – could sell these y' know!"

Jonty snatched the phone back, and put it in his pocket "No we're not, they may come in useful later if we need something on her, so shut your gob and keep quiet about them. Use a bit of bloody sense for a change."

"Okay, okay you wanker, just joking." snapped Weasel, his face angry and tense, "don't get so fucking uptight."

Lucy leaned over them, her tits spilling out of a strappy T shirt, in the heat of the impending argument, they hadn't heard her arrive, she glanced at the phone, "having a fight boys? Not over me I hope?" She straightened up, and as the shirt rode up it exposed her midriff and her pierced belly button, "Buy you a drink – it's my turn I think!" She smiled, as always running the pink tip of her tongue over her lips.

"Hi darlin', Nah sorry to disappoint ya, just talking about football! I'll have a beer though, d' ya wanna hand?" Weasel leered at her as he stood up, he clamped his hand on her bottom and they shimmied off to the bar.

Christ that Weasel could be a bleeding liability thought Jonty as he watched them go. He seemed to think this was some kinda fucking game. There was no way he was going to let this opportunity slip through his fingers, he needed this girl to talk and he was going to make sure she did, even if it was the hard way. He heard them clattering back, Lucy tottering on her stacked heels, Weasel supporting her on his arm. They plonked themselves down on the chairs, and crashed down the bottles on the aluminium table, making the other customers look up in surprise. Jonty pulled himself together and started to join in their banter, laughing and joking with them, chatting up Lucy, and plying her with drink. She was clearly enjoying the attention and getting quite pissed as Weasel trooped into the bar to get more drinks. Weasel was pretty tanked up too, but Jonty stayed on the Coke and played the game with them.

A couple of hours past in flirty conversation with Lucy getting more loose tongued, and vulgar as the time went on. The other tables filled and emptied around them, but they continued to sit laughing raucously and getting more and more pissed, all that was except Jonty. He had gradually steered the conversation round to Fittlebury and her friends there and she complained loudly and bitterly that none of them had rung her, admitting that she had considered texting her friend Tom, to see what was going on there. Jonty said she should do it, and that it was crazy to lose touch with friends just because of a row with someone else! He kept insisting that she must get back in touch with them and that he was sure that they would be pleased to hear from her. She had fixed him through alcohol glazed eyes, affirming he was right and she wasn't going to let Caitlin be the reason for her losing friends. Jonty had smiled to himself, stupid pathetic bitch, still she was going to be very handy with her contacts, and he was certainly going to extract every bit of information out of her, come what may.

Jennifer was still aching, her ribcage and tummy muscles felt like they were on fire with the effort of keeping her balance and the lesson had only been 40 minutes. She started to wash over the tack, scrubbing the bit clean. She and Beebs sat in companionable silence as they cleaned the bridles and saddles, for once the radio was silent and apart from the slosh of the water in the buckets, the only sound was the stamping and snorting of the horses as they swished the flies. She couldn't remember when she'd felt so happy and contented, how ridiculous she thought, to feel like that with her beautifully manicured hands elbow deep in greasy water!

Beebs considered her, watching Jennifer's face as she was smiling to herself. "What you smiling about Jen? Come on give?"

Jennifer felt herself go red, unaware that Beebs had been watching her, but responded like lightening, "Oh! I'm caught out! Just thought of the sexy guy with the huge cock I shagged till he was begging for more last night!"

Beeb's mouth gaped open "You what!"

"Joke!" Jennifer giggled at Beebs "Ha ha, your face! You should see it! It's a picture!" She started to really laugh, holding her aching ribcage.

"Blimey! I hope you enjoyed it! Did you ask his name!" She too started to laugh, Jen was really becoming one of them now, she would never have made a comment like that before. They bantered on, lewdly exchanging stupid remarks and were still laughing when Katherine came back from her hack with Chloe, struggling into the tack room laden with her saddle, a bridle balanced on her shoulder and Alfie's brushing boots under the other arm. "Here let me help you with that lot" Beebs slipped off her stool to take the saddle, throwing it over the saddle horse.

Katherine hung the bridle on the cleaning rack, and shoved the brushing boots into her box, "What's so funny then you two? You look as though you're having a right old laugh."

Beebs winked at Jennifer, "Oh just Jennifer being filthy you know!"

"I was not!" Jennifer protested, "it was your dirty mind! Oh …okay, so I was really!"

Chloe walked in, it was good to see everyone laughing and happy, and she just wished she could feel like that. When would it be before she could genuinely smile again, everything she did these days seemed to be a façade of how she really felt. Beebs looked full of mischief and her eyes were dancing as she took Chloe's tack from her. "Just whiling away the time tack cleaning! How's your ride ladies?" Boys behave themselves?

"They did indeed thanks Beebs and talking of behaving, have you seen that Harry again – you were all over him at the party."

"The delicious Harry, yep I've seen him, but you know, treat 'em mean, keep 'em keen!" Beebs laughed "He's a nice guy, but I'm letting him do the chasing, much more fun."

"Jennifer," Katherine touched her arm, "I'm having a small dinner party on Friday night, I wondered if you and Charles wanted to come – only John, Chloe, Mark and Sandy if they're able, and you two, - how are you fixed?"

Jennifer was really taken aback, it was the first time that they'd been properly invited out like this, by real friends since she came to Nantes. "That'll be wonderful!" she stammered, "but of course I'd better just check with Charles - in case he has to work late" she added quickly.

"Of course – just let me know, nothing posh." Katherine watched Jennifer's animated face, it'd only been a spur of the moment invite, but it had clearly meant a great deal to her. Poor girl she thought, she'd been pretty much ostracised since she came down here, it was time that changed.

CHAPTER 34

It was well after two when Jennifer got home, sweeping down the drive spraying up gravel as she pulled up by the garages, surprised to see Caitlin running down the steps of the granary to meet her.

Caitlin gasped as Jennifer opened the car door, "Oh Jennifer – I'm so glad you're back, sorry to be jumping on you the moment you arrive now, but I need to ask you if you'd mind awfully if I had a couple of hours off this afternoon. I've not had time off since Lucy left, and I'd like to meet a friend later today" she gabbled, looking flustered and anxious.

"Of course that's okay Caitlin, I hadn't thought, I'm so sorry, but you know you don't need to ask me, just take any time you want." Jennifer felt guilty, she hadn't even thought about poor Caitlin not having a day off. She wondered for a moment who she was meeting, but decided against asking, probably better not to know, that was if she would tell her anyway.

"Just one other thing Jennifer, before I go, I've heard from Felix, and he can come for an interview on Wednesday at three. Will that be okay with you, you don't have to see him if you're busy, I can do it if it's easier?"

"No" Jennifer said firmly, "I want to meet him, and Wednesday's fine with me, I'll make sure I'm back in good time. You get off, and I'll talk to you about it tomorrow."

"Thanks, I'll be off then, and I'll text Felix and say that's okay. See you tomorrow." She turned and dashed back up the stairs on her long Bambi legs, her dark hair bobbing about in her hurry.

Jennifer eased her aching stomach out of the car and walked thoughtfully towards the back door. The smell of new mown grass lingered in the air with the pungent perfume of summer jasmine and honeysuckle, she breathed in deeply, the intoxicating scent of summer arousing a huge sensation of contentment. She was thrilled to have been asked to Katherine's dinner party, she just hoped Charles would be as pleased. She was really glad that she had told him about going to Chloe's, it would make it much easier with the small talk, as then the girls didn't have to hide it from him, she must remember to tell them it was okay. Ducking under the back porch, she pushed a stray strand of a frothy wisteria away from her face, its heavy purple blooms dancing on their stems, the distinctive vanilla scent making her sneeze. It was so exquisitely pretty, she wished she could paint and capture their fragile beauty. This was such a glorious time of year, and they had the Puppy show to look forward to on Sunday. Last year, they hadn't gone, although they'd been invited, she had been too worried by the snubs that she might encounter. This year would be different, she had her own friends now, and after the success of the party she felt she could handle anything. She had even managed to carry off returning the children with Charles, even though Celia's ice cold stare had been glacial, followed by some seriously chilly remarks. She herself had remained polite and sweet, and it was Celia that had let herself down. It was a small personal achievement that she had been able not to fall to pieces, stuttering and losing control of herself.

Taking off her shoes, she walked quietly down the passage towards the kitchen in her socks pushing open the door, she was desperate for a cup of tea and a biscuit. The kitchen smelt wonderful, Mrs Fuller had obviously been baking and there were a stack of cookies cooling on a wire tray on the table, but she herself was nowhere to be seen. Jennifer picked up the bright blue Aga kettle and moved it onto the hot ring, taking down a mug and chucking in a teabag, she turned leaning against the stove whilst she waited for it to boil. The kitchen looked spic and span as usual and there was a colourful arrangement of sweet peas on the table, her eyes strayed to the cookies, they did look good. Slightly hesitating, she reached over and stole one, they were still a little warm from the oven, she took a bite, yum yum, choc-chip her favourite! She was just taking her second bite when Mrs Fuller appeared from her little sitting room, Jennifer started with surprise, almost dropping it on the floor.

"Oh you gave me a fright, I hope you didn't mind me having one." she spluttered, her mouth half full with the stolen cookie.

Mrs Fuller gave her a rare smile, "Of course not, it's a new recipe, hope you like them?"

"They're fab! I was just going to make a cup of tea, do you fancy one? I'll make it, you sit down." Jennifer prattled, swinging round to get another mug.

"Don't mind if I do madam, it was a busy weekend with the children an' all, I'm feeling my age." she sighed and sat down rubbing her knees, "I'm not as young as I was."

Jennifer put the boiling water into the mugs, Mrs Fuller would probably want a pot made she mused, ah well, too late now. She fished out the teabags, putting the mugs on the table and sat down opposite her.

"I think I'll have another of these" she said taking another cookie and adding milk from the jug to her tea. "Mrs Fuller there's something I want to ask you, it's about Pete."

"Oh yes Madam, what's he done now?"

Jennifer watched her carefully, "Nothing at all, but I wondered if you could tell me more about him?"

"Well it's a long tale and a sad one really, and perhaps I shouldn't be talking about it" she hesitated, "but I think you've a right to know really, because he can be a tricky one."

"I would appreciate it Mrs Fuller, I don't want to pry but he looks at me with such dislike, he can be quite disconcerting at times, and quite truthfully he frightens me a bit." She looked at her questioningly - willing her to carry on, "if you could tell me anything that may help me to understand, I'd be grateful.

Mrs Fuller rubbed her knees again and took a drink of her tea before she continued, "Pete's mother worked for Mr Charles' family for years, started as a young girl, obviously that was well before I came here. She got herself pregnant and had Pete. No-one knew who the father was, of course there were all sorts of rumours - but she never let on. Apparently she was a hard woman and brought him up very strict so she did, according to the gossip he was a nice little boy, but she was always on at him and very religious, I think he must've had a dog's life. They lived together in the cottage, minding their own business for quite a few years."

Jennifer interrupted, "Poor little boy if she wasn't very kind to him, it must've been awful. But you have been here for a long time Mrs Fuller, how old is Pete now?"

"Well, Pete must be well turned forty now I should think, although I don't know that for sure."

"Over forty!" Jennifer exclaimed, "I can hardly believe it."

"If you look at him carefully you can see his age, but his hair's so long it's difficult to see his face clearly, and he's kept himself pretty fit working in the garden all these years. No he must be well gone forty if he's a day."

"Anyway, sorry I interrupted - go on with the story."

Mrs Fuller took another mouthful of tea and carried on "Well to cut a long story short, one day his mother didn't turn up for work, Pete said she wasn't well. After a few days went past, she still hadn't appeared and Mr Charles' mother went down to the cottage, and found her dead in bed, a heart attack apparently. It was all a bit queer as Pete said he had thought she was just sleeping. When they took her away he collapsed completely, as he would, terrible shock it must have been for the him and you've to bear in mind, she was the only family he had ever known, even though she was supposed to have been quite cruel to him at times. He had a total breakdown and was admitted to a psychiatric hospital. Mr Charles' mother was a very kind woman, and kept in touch with him and told the authorities she would always make sure he was taken care of and eventually he came back here and worked in the gardens. She was always very good to him, but he never really recovered, he lived in the cottage just the same, refusing any offers of modernisation. He went in and out of hospital quite a lot over the years, but he always had a home here. Mr and Mrs Parker-Smythe senior decided to move to their house in Devon when Mr Charles became engaged to Celia, so that they could live at Nantes, naturally Mr Charles kept Pete on here and looked out for him. Celia made sure that he took his tablets and was actually very kind to him. He adored her and the children."

Jennifer was really shocked by this revelation. "No wonder he hates me so much, I suppose when I married Charles and Celia left, it must have been the end of his world."

Mrs Fuller looked at her sadly, "To tell the truth Madam, it was a shock to us all, but Pete took it worst."

"Thank you for telling me this, it's really helped me see the reasoning behind his attitude towards me. I think the divorce has been a hard time for us all, there're many casualties in this situation, and we've all had to adjust."

"Yes Madam, but I'd like to think that things are improving. We've all had to learn to live in the present not the past - me included, and it made my heart glad to see the children so happy this weekend" she looked at Jennifer steadily "and we're getting to know one another much better now I think."

Jennifer held her gaze, this was quite an admission from the old girl, "Yes, I think that's very true. I've been pretty gauche, it has taken a while, but I'm starting to get used to my life here now, and I love it" she added emphatically.

"I should tell you though Madam, that I'm worried about Pete, it makes me think he's not taking his medication, and is slipping back into his old ways, I'm sure he's talking to himself again, but I don't know what can be done about it?" she wrung her hands together, looking agitated. Her face suddenly looked old and tired.

"I'll speak to Charles and see what he thinks. One thing you can do for me though please Mrs Fuller?"

"Yes, of course, what?" she looked at Jennifer quizzically waiting for her to continue.

"Please, please, can you call me Jennifer?"

Caitlin brushed the grass off her T shirt, shaking her hair out to free it from any twigs, and made her way back to her car. Her face was glowing with the flush of blistering and illicit sex, he was a red hot lover and she was tingling all over from a marathon shag. She could still feel the touch of his hands exploring every part of her body, and her responses exploring his. They had tumbled and rolled in the grass, exhausting each other, and afterwards had laid in each other's arms, only to begin all over again – their sexual appetites insatiable. They had both carefully skirted around any mention of his marriage, it was dangerous territory. She knew that he wouldn't do anything more at the moment, it was a waiting game and one in which she had to play her part. Of course she knew it was difficult for him, but he had assured her many times that he was in too deep and loved her, they would definitely be together, and begged her to be patient. She shrugged off these unwelcome thoughts, instead dreamed of the life they would lead – she trusted him and she believed in what he said. She trudged along the path, pushing away the over-hanging tendrils of small branches, jumping the small dips in the ground, so well-known to her now. What would happen she thought when the weather changed to autumn, where would they meet then, they could hardly have their trysts in the pouring rain could they? They wouldn't be able to go to her place or his either for sure. She was so tired of these snatched meetings. She desperately hoped that it would be settled soon, after all his wife had made the first move now, at least that was a step in the right direction – her face flushed again, but this time is was with guilt.

In her car driving back towards Nantes, she realised she was starving, she hadn't eaten since this morning, and all that sexual frisson had given her an appetite, so she indicated and pulled over at the village shop. She'd snatch a bun now and get something more substantial for her dinner later. As she grabbed her handbag, she glanced up to see Pete ambling along the footpath, his great lumbering frame and bizarre appearance unmistakable in the distance. He must be coming down to get his shopping, she could offer him a lift back to Nantes, that might cheer him up, she thought kindly. She waved to him, but he didn't see her, his dark head fixed down on the pavement. Oh well, she would meet him in the shop, she checked her watch, it was nearly half past five, Mrs G would be closing soon, she'd better get a move on.

It wasn't Mrs Gupta who was sitting at the counter but one of her daughters, either Selinda or Ayeesha, she could never tell the difference between the twins, they were both equally beautiful, with their enormous dark brown doe eyes, and slick black bobs. She called out a cheery greeting and made her way to the back of the shop to find some pasta. Ravi Gupta was stacking the shelves, and in his polite quiet way he nodded his head to her, and she smiled over at him.

"Don't suppose you've got any buns left have you Mr G?"

"Now my dear, we may have sold out I am thinking, but I had a bit of a disaster with one I was making this morning, an odd shape, I couldn't be selling it like that! You're welcome to it. I'll be fetching it for you."

She watched him disappear into the kitchen, thinking how on earth did such a fragile little man end up with Mrs G who was so enormous! "That'll be grand now Mr G." she called after him, and then delved into the shelves rummaging for the fettuccini. She heard footsteps coming into the shop behind her, the trudge of heavy boots and looked up to see Pete looming along the aisles. "Hi Pete" she called, "Just finished work?"

Pete glared at Caitlin, apparently in a world of his own, and not seeming to register her for a moment, he frowned and then spoke in his usual careful and precise way, "Yes, I've walked down after work, Mr Gupta has kept me a small loaf back and I need some cheese. It's for my tea."

"Is that all you're having Pete, you should eat more than that you know now, you need to keep your strength up" returned Caitlin, she felt sorry for him, he was a pathetic creature really, for all his huge hulk. She looked at his large hands and feet, his lank hair and felt an enormous sympathy for him, he was a real misfit of a man. "When you've finished, I'm going straight back to Nantes, if you want a lift?"

"Why yes, thank you, that'd be right kind. I'm feeling tired today" he looked gloomily at his hands which were red and chaffed, "I've been clearing the orchard, the weeds in there are terrible since the rain." His face looked troubled as though he was having difficulty concentrating on the words and stringing a sentence together. Caitlin's kind heart went out to him in compassion, poor bloke she thought, he could do with looking after.

Mr Gupta returned with Caitlin's bun, and a brown loaf wrapped in paper for Pete. "I saw you coming" he said "I was baking first thing this morning, so it should be more than fresh for you, and my dear, so sorry about this bun, but it will still be tasting just as good!" He laughed as he handed it to her, "Don't go telling people I baked it, I will be a laughing stock." This was a rare joke for Ravi, who was such an intense and serious man, and chuckling, Caitlin assured him that she wouldn't let on. She put some pasta in her basket and chucked in a jar of ready-made sauce. Pete headed for the cheese cabinet, selecting some strong farmhouse cheddar and she joined him, putting in some pre packed mozzarella.

Pete looked at her basket, and said very slowly, "You shouldn't be buying that pre-packed muck y' know, you don't know what they put in it. You need plain and healthy food. Good bread and cheese – much better for you."

Caitlin suitably admonished decided to humour him, "Well, it's only just this once, I've been busy what with Lucy going so suddenly, and the children coming back this weekend, never enough hours in the day, you know how it is." She smiled at him and was astonished to see his features change, scowling and his eyes blazed black and hard.

"The children should be back at Nantes and Mrs Celia too, it was that witch of a woman. It was her fault, without her they would never have had to leave. They should be at Nantes, where they belong!" he spat with venom, his features contorted and evil.

Caitlin recoiled in shock, the malice in his tone was dreadful, he'd made the hairs on her arms stand on end and she said cautiously, "Now Pete, these things happen y' know now, 'tis a sad fact of life, and Jennifer is not so bad once you get to know her. Mr Charles and Celia were unhappy and that would not have been good for the little ones either. They've had a grand weekend together now." She added gently "I know tis not been easy, but we mustn't judge them, but try and make it as easy as we can for everyone to make the best of it."

Pete's eyes became wild, darting madly from side to side like a quick game of ping pong, "No, it's her fault, she's a bad woman, none of you can see it, and she should pay for her wickedness!" He dropped his basket, running his hands through his lank hair, his face twitching, "I just don't know what to do."

Caitlin put down her own basket, and touched his arm, "Aw, c'mon Pete, tis not as bad as that now, we just have to deal with it as they have for sure, let's try and stay calm" she added anxiously.

He shook her off madly, shouting at her, "Caitlin, you can't understand, you're a good woman, but she's evil and needs teaching a lesson, and I've been told that I should be the one to do just that!"

"What d' you mean Pete, who told you to do what?" she

demanded watching his manic face with alarm, "What're you talking about?" By now Ravi had come round to see what all the noise was about, they were creating quite a rumpus and the twin at the counter had her hand on the phone ready to call the police for help.

Pete suddenly changed, "Forget what I said" he muttered, "I'm sorry Caitlin, Mr Gupta, I'm just very very tired, and I lost my temper." He hung his head, looking at his massive boots, "I've not been feeling too well lately."

Caitlin felt a huge wave of pity for him, she reached down and picked up his basket, "Com' on Pete, let's pay for this and go home now." She steered him towards the till, where the twin looked at him warily, and without speaking rang up his items, and then passed onto Caitlin's basket. Nothing more was said inside the shop and they walked out to her car, stowing the shopping on the back seat. Pete sat mute in the passenger seat and wouldn't look at her, just sat with his hands twisting together in anguish.

Just as they were about to move off, Caitlin spotted a car drawing up behind them, and saw Grace Allington jump out and hurry into the shop before it closed. She turned to Pete, "Hey fellah, I've just gotta see Grace for a moment, you okay if I just pop and have a word with her? Won't be a minute." She barely heard Pete's mumbled response, patted him on his shoulder and stepped out of the car to wait for Grace. She stood resting one leg and then another, contemplating what Pete had said and how he'd behaved, he was certainly not right in the head that was for sure - as mad as a box of frogs, but what could she do about it? His threats against Jennifer had certainly seemed real enough and then just as suddenly he'd become lucid again, and with it apparently normal. Without a doubt it was very weird and disconcerting, the problem was though - should she tell someone?

Grace came tumbling out of the shop at high speed with a large bottle of tonic water and bumped into Caitlin, who was still deliberating about what she should do about Pete.

"Christ Caitlin, I'm sorry, didn't see you there!" Grace gasped, "didn't hurt you did I? Just wanted to catch the shop before it closed, ran out of tonic, Colin and no G&T after work is not a good combination!" she laughed, then stopped, "You okay? You look a bit upset."

"No, Grace, thanks for asking now, just something on my mind that's all, but I did want to see you, that's why I waited."

Grace was curious, "Heavens Caitlin, what about?"

Caitlin liked Grace, she was a thoroughly nice woman and she began falteringly, "Look Grace, Jennifer mentioned you had asked about a job with me at Nantes, and told you that we needed a full timer really. We did consider two part timers, and decided against that idea, but I just wanted you to know that this was the one and only reason and to say that I think we'd get on brilliantly otherwise." She blushed, her lovely face full of concern.

"Oh that's so sweet of you Caitlin, I totally understand, it's not a problem at all, just thought I'd ask. To tell the truth, I'm not that fussed, it'd just do me good to have something extra to fill my days. That probably sounds strange to you, but I think it'd be good for me at the moment" she looked wistful and sad, "ah well, not to be and as I said to Jennifer - no problem."

Caitlin looked at Grace, her pretty face framed with bonny brown curls and her dark eyes warm and genuine. She knew that she was talking about wanting children, and that must be the reason she wanted a job, to fill the hours of longing. In that moment Caitlin felt such empathy with her, she knew exactly what it was to long for something that seemed unattainable, what the hell she thought and said "Well, here's a thing, and you must swear not to let on how you found this out - but a little bird told me that they'll be looking for a part timer to work with Paulene in the office at Oliver and Andrews' place fairly soon. Why not ask them before they advertise?" Caitlin could have bitten her tongue out directly she said it, but too late - it was said now. Grace would be perfect at the vet's, and why shouldn't she tell her, but cautiously added, "Promise me though, if you do ask, you must never let on it was me who told you – okay?"

Grace spluttered excitedly, "But that's a fantastic idea Caitlin, I'd love to do it, it would be right up my street and if they could be pretty flexible about working hours, that would be even better! I promise you I won't say a word about how I found out, but I'm pretty curious to know who the little bird is nonetheless. Do you know when they are likely to put the ad in?"

"No, but soon I think, as I said good luck with it, but don't drop me in it whatever you do – look I'd better rush now, I'm giving Pete a lift back and he's not feeling too well" she turned to go, adding "Let me know what happens."

"I will" called Grace, "and thank you!"

Caitlin got back in the car, "Sorry about that Pete, we'll be off now." She looked across at him, he seemed to have recovered himself a bit and was just sitting staring ahead seemingly in a world of his own. Holy Mother she thought, what was she going to do about him, and moreover, had she spoken out of turn to Grace? She pulled out, moving along the road, trying to make small talk to a withdrawn Pete who, just like her computer, was not responding.

CHAPTER 35

Lucy had a banging hangover, her mouth felt like the bottom of
a bird cage, and she could hardly walk after all that shagging
yesterday. She had been pretty pissed at B52, and when Jonty had
suggested they get a room in the Travel Lodge she had easily agreed.
That Weasel was a fucking lunatic, putting her in all sorts of positions
- her back was killing her. Jonty had just sat in the arm chair, he was a
strange one – not drinking either just eating crisps and fiddling with
his phone, whilst she and Weasel bonked each other's brains out. It
had been fun, and she had enjoyed herself. She liked the way they
were interested in her, and Jonty had been insistent that she not lose
touch with the Fittlebury mob - well they were not worth the effort in
her opinion, but he'd been keen for her to see them again and she
promised she would text Tom today. She wasn't that bothered but she
would do it to please him. She rolled over in bed, feeling sick, as her
mother shouted up the stairs for her to get up. Fuck that, she felt
awful she wasn't going to work today, she could holler all she
fucking liked, she pulled the duvet up over her head to shut her
mother out. In fact, she never wanted to go back to that dump, she
was sick of sandwich fillings, the very thought of them, and she
gulped and shot out to the bathroom puking all over the lavatory lid.
Why oh why had she drunk so much? Lucy rinsed her mouth under
the basin tap when the bathroom door burst open and her mother
stormed in fuming, and yelled at her so loudly that she thought her
head would explode. Lucy could hardly lift her head from the sink,
she turned her head sideways, spittle running down her chin, gazing
stupidly at her mother's wild eyes and tuned herself out from the
angry shouting. She watched her mother blearily, not caring about
what she thought or what she was saying. Right now, she felt lousy
and once again she felt an overwhelming desire to vomit and did - all
over her mother's feet.

Grace looked at herself in the mirror, she'd taken a lot of care with her appearance this morning, brushing her shiny hair, and even bothering to put on a smidgeon of mascara. She looked deeply at her reflection and was pleased - she looked okay, and taking a deep breath, turned away, to pad down the stairs. After she had seen Caitlin yesterday she could scarcely think of anything else, a part time job at the vets, fantastic, it was just what she was looking for; although how Caitlin had heard about it was mysterious, but she wasn't going to let that be an obstacle for her. She had discussed it at length with Colin last night, dissecting the problem from every angle. If she just breezed into the office and asked about the job, then that would drop Caitlin in the shit, and the same if she asked the vets direct. She could just drop massive hints to any of them that she was looking for a job and see what they said? It was difficult to know what would be the best way to handle things. Colin, bless him, had not been all that keen about the job anyway, his old fashioned virtues baulked about having a wife who worked, but his love for his wife and her needs overcame what he personally would have preferred, and he had taken her in his arms, kissing the tip of her nose and running his hands along her back, saying he would go along with whatever she wanted, if it made her happy. So finally they had come to no firm conclusion and she decided that she would just pop into the surgery on the pretext of wanting some wormers, and play it by ear.

She was tense though, she breathed deeply trying to steady her nerves and she wasn't even there yet! She shut the dogs in the kitchen, picked up her keys and ran out to her car. She had timed her visit hopefully to coincide with coffee time and with any luck she would be offered one, which would be an ideal opportunity to make small talk. She had no idea how to make an opening gambit, being underhand was not something that came naturally to her, and she was sure that it would be better to be straightforward about the job. After all, it wasn't as though she didn't know them pretty well, but thinking about it perhaps that might be a drawback, they might not want someone they knew working with them for all sorts of reasons. Hey ho, she could only give it her best shot and see what happened.

Caitlin had not had a good night, she had dropped the mute Pete back at his cottage and then gone home to the Granary to cook a solitary supper. She switched on the TV automatically and poured herself a large glass of wine, trying to concentrate on the programme but her mind kept wandering back to the events in the shop. Pete's strange behaviour this afternoon was a real worry, she was concerned about him - his thinking was so irrational and bizarre. It was almost as though he had transformed into another person, it was horrible, and she was at a loss to know what to do. His venom towards Jennifer was totally crazy and she genuinely thought that he could be dangerous. What could she do – warn Jennifer - hardly a good idea, how would she begin? Mr Charles? He would probably shrug it off thinking she was over reacting and although she got on well with him, she hardly saw him anyway. There was one person with whom she really wanted to talk things through, he would take her seriously and be able to give an objective view, but when she had texted him, she had just received a kind but firm response, *'sorry babe, can't talk till tomorrow morning'*. Bugger, bugger, bugger! She contemplated what she should do now, and then it came to her in a flash, Mrs Fuller was her best option. She knew Pete better than anybody and she would surely know how to handle the situation?

All the through the long night she tossed and turned, catching only the odd snatch of sleep which was disturbed by bizarre dreams of Ace, Pete and a dying Jennifer calling out to her for help. This damp morning she had woken up feeling groggy and wasted. She ran her hand through her dishevelled hair, miserably eating her Frosties. In the cold light of day it seemed as though she was the one over reacting and that it was her own thinking which was so disordered, but when she replayed the scene in the shop over again, she knew that she would never forgive herself if anything happened to Jennifer and she'd said nothing at all. She would tell Mrs Fuller, that's what she'd do.

When Paulene arrived at the surgery that morning, she was surprised to smell the coffee already on the go, and she popped her head around the door to see Andrew at his desk deeply engrossed in paperwork.

"Morning Boss! You're here bright and early" she called out to him, and going back to switch the phones and computer on. Strolling back into the office to get herself some coffee she asked "want another cup?"

He looked up, his dark hair flopping in his tired eyes, "You're an angel Paulene, just what I need, I've been up half the night with a foaling, didn't seem much point in going back home, when I've got this lot stacked up here." He indicated the pile of stuff on his desk, I can't expect you to do it all The sooner we can get some extra help the better."

"Well, I'll second that!" Paulene laughed, "but what about Julia doesn't she get fed up with you not getting home at night?"

"Oh she doesn't notice whether I'm there or not!" he laughed, "It was her bridge night last night, so she was out anyway, she won't be surprised that I didn't come back. I did leave her a voicemail, in case you're thinking I'm an uncaring bastard." He grinned at her, looking at her with his seriously sexy eyes, and his face crinkling with the smile. "Truly, she was fine."

"Good, we don't want an *Oliver* situation on our hands, two foot loose and fancy free men would be too much to deal with in the morning." The coffee machine started to hiss and spit that it was finished and she passed the cup to him, turning back to make her own, "Mind you, once Oliver is over the shock of Suse going I think he'll realise it's for the best, after all they were always rowing, and led each other a dog's life. Not much pleasure in that."

"Hmmm, I don't know what's better someone who cares too much or someone who cares too little – like Julia" Andrew said ruefully, "but I'm sure you're right and pretty soon, once the dust has settled, Oli will have every available woman in the county after him, and probably every unavailable one too!"

"You're spot on there, give them a month and they'll be flocking like flies on shite!" Paulene's eyes sparkled, "Now Boss, whilst we have a moment, have you and Oliver had a chance to look at those ads I left for you on Friday? We need to get cracking you know."

Andrew shuffled about with the papers on his desk, finding the drafts for the ads under a mountain of other stuff that had accumulated since the weekend, "Sorry they got lost in this lot, but the good news is that Oli and I looked at them on Saturday, let's run with the office assistant first, I don't know how much longer we can all cope with this lot." he gestured to his desk and Oli's. "Run it in the local paper as soon as possible, would be better for us if we have someone from around here who knows the area." He sighed again, "I'll get onto Gary and ask him to come up with a salary package."

"Fan-bloody-tastic!" Paulene said taking the drafts of the ads from him, "What about the Vet Assistant?" Just as Andrew was about to reply the sound of the outer door opening and the bell ringing stopped them both in their tracks. "I'll just see who that is eh? We'll talk about this more when they've gone." She went back through the door to see Grace Allington waiting in the reception. "Hiya Grace, how's you this morning? What can we do for you?"

Grace opened her mouth to respond but got no further as the outer door clanged opened again and Oliver breezed in, looking his usual handsome self, his tousled tawny blonde hair damp from the drizzle, he looked in surprise to see Grace standing apparently in conversation with Paulene. He immediately reached over and gave her a perfunctory kiss on either cheek, "Gracie, Paulene, good morning little beauts! Horrible bloody morning out there! Is the coffee on Paulene?"

Paulene cuffed him around the shoulder, "it's always on you great lummox, as well you know! How about you Grace, have you time to stop for one too?"

Grace couldn't believe her luck, "Well, if you're sure Paulene, don't want to hold you up."

"No, you won't although believe me I could do with some extra hours in the day around here sometimes." Paulene grinned, opening the inner door, and calling to Andrew "It's only Oli and Grace, gonna make them a cuppa – okay?"

"Course it is, but I must get on with this lot, so don't think I'm being rude." Andrew kept his head down engrossed in what he was doing.

Paulene took the steaming mugs out to the little waiting area, and put one down beside Oli and Grace who were busy chatting. "Now Grace, what was it you wanted – not that it isn't lovely to see you of course!"

Grace flushed, it was now or never, "Well, I don't quite know how to ask this, as there's no easy way, and of course you can say no and I shan't be offended at all – okay?" Paulene and Oli looked at each other quickly, wondering what on earth she was going to say. Grace went on, "I've been looking for a part time job and I just wondered if you needed any help here?" she blurted, "Not on the vet side of course, but office work, that sort of thing?"

"Phew," spluttered Oli, "I thought you were going to say something awful!" He laughed his big hands clapping her on the back, "Grace, we may have just what you are looking for, whatdya say Paulene?"

Paulene grinned at them both, "How soon can you start?"

Mrs Fuller was sitting in the kitchen, having cleared away the breakfast things and was waiting for a delivery from Waitrose. She looked up at the old fashioned servants' bell system as it chimed to announce that someone was at the back door and wiping her hands on her pinny bustled down the corridor to take in her delivery. To her surprise it was a rather damp Caitlin who sheltered under the porch and not the Ocado man as she had expected, she stood back straight away to let her in. My my, she thought, she does look bedraggled. It was true, tired from her sleepless night, Caitlin's eyes were dull and her hair hung in damp tendrils and was plastered to her face, her jacket was soaked.

"Come in, come in m' dear, you're wet through, let's go and get dry by the Aga." Not waiting for a response she waddled back down towards the kitchen, leaving Caitlin to kick off her boots and follow her. Mrs Fuller was filling the kettle when she got to the kitchen and without turning round invited Caitlin to sit down. "Come on now duck," she said, "let's have that wet coat, I'll hang it up for you."

As soon as Caitlin had a cup of tea and a biscuit in her hands, with Mrs Fuller sitting at the end of the table, she blurted out the whole tale about Pete. For once Freda Fuller sat there without any form of interruption, listening keenly to what had happened. Her mouth set in a grim line and her eyes heavy with anxiety, nodding her head here and there. Poor Caitlin had obviously been distressed by the incident, and it was all she could do to get Pete home safely without panicking that he would start ranting again. No wonder Caitlin looked in such a state, not surprising, poor kid. She should've come straight in yesterday afternoon, but there, what was done was done - but what now had to be done, remained to be seen.

"You did quite right by telling me Caitlin, it must've been very upsetting for you indeed. Truth to tell, I've noticed the way he's looked at Jennifer, and mind you so has she, he quite frightens her and we talked about it only yesterday. She's going to speak to Mr Charles herself about it, and I'll mention to him what happened in the shop, but maybe not to her, it might only make her more worried." Mrs Fuller said kindly, "Now you're not to fret any more my dear, so try and forget it now and let Mr Charles deal with the situation."

Caitlin's blue eyes brimmed with tears, "you don't know what a relief that is Mrs Fuller, it's hard to credit how he changed in that split second, back to his usual self." She gulped "I thought you might think I was being stupid you know now."

"No m' dear, I don't think that at all, we've all noticed a change in him. As I said I'm sure Mr Charles will sort it out. He's probably not been taking his pills."

"Well, I hope that's all 'tis to be sure. By the way Mrs F, just to tell you that I'm interviewing for a replacement for Lucy tomorrow afternoon. It's a young lad called Felix, comes recommended by one of the grooms at Chloe Coombe's yard."

Mrs Fuller sniffed, "Well, I hope you make a better choice of it than before, with that tarty young madam Lucy. She was a right one she was!"

Caitlin sighed, "Well I'd have to be agreeing with you – but that wasn't altogether my fault, Mr Charles interviewed her too, but this time Jennifer is going to be in on it instead. Although I don't know what she'll be able to contribute, as she knows nothing about horses. Ah though, she means well and she's been very kind to me."

Mrs Fuller fixed a beady eye on Caitlin, who turned away under her scrutiny, "I think Jennifer has been misunderstood here for a long time, but she may just be settling in now. Mark you, it's taken time, and let's face it none of us, me included, has made it easy for her. So if she wants to be involved that's got to be a good thing, even if she doesn't know the head from the arse of a horse or much about the job, the least you can do is involve her."

Caitlin was astonished, she'd always thought that Mrs Fuller and Jennifer were arch enemies, it'd always seemed that way. Mrs F never had a good word to say about her before, and here she was calling her Jennifer, and supporting her, even down to Jennifer telling her about her fear of Pete. Extraordinary! She was pleased nonetheless, Mrs F was better to have as a friend than an enemy and Caitlin had always tried to stay on the right side of her. "Well, this lad is coming at three tomorrow, shall I bring him over for a cup of tea when I've shown him round? You can tell me what you think of him too? I'd value your opinion" she added tactfully.

Mrs Fuller visibly preened, "What a good idea Caitlin, I'll make some cakes, and expect you about four then."

"Perfect" Caitlin purred

Jennifer herself was totally unaware of the goings on that morning either at Nantes or the vets', and was too busy enjoying herself, despite the drizzle. She had been for a good ride with Chloe and Susie, and Chloe had said how much she'd improved. It was like getting a gold star! They were walking home on the horses, little Rufus although he was getting fitter now, was lagging behind as he was tired, and the others had to keep waiting for him. Jennifer was talking to him and encouraging him gently, and Chloe looking back at them struggling to catch up thought that it was probably time that Jen rode another horse as well, to take the burden off Rufus and to improve on horses that were younger and more supple. She called to her "Jen, what time do you have to go home today?"

"Not fussed Chloe, why is there something you want me to do?"

"No, it's just I thought that if you had time, you might like to actually ride Ksar in the school today. He's a lovely horse, as you know from your lunge lesson of course, he's beautifully trained and you could really benefit from riding a horse that's more supple on the flat." Chloe tempted her, "So much easier for you, as Rufus is getting a bit stiff in his joints now and doesn't find the work as easy as he did, like us all!" she laughed.

"Oh Chloe, d'you mean it, gosh I'd love to, but do you think I'm ready? I wouldn't want to spoil him." Jennifer gushed, going quite pink in the face at the idea. "Won't Flora mind?"

Flora who owned Ksar, was a student away at University in Durham and the horse was at Chloe's at full livery, so they rarely saw her other than in the holidays, and she was studying at the moment for exams, so had no time to ride herself. "No, it'll be fine, we have to exercise him for Flora anyway, and she won't mind as long as I'm there to supervise. He's a nice horse with lovely manners and a bit like driving a Ferrari in the dressage arena, so it'll give you a good chance to practise some of the more refined movements, good for you and good for him, he doesn't need to be doing the high school stuff all the time."

"Okay, if you're sure, I'd love to" she beamed at Chloe, and bent down to pat Rufus, "don't worry Rufus, you'll always be my favourite!"

Lucy was feeling better, she had been sick several times and had slept for most of the morning. Her mother had telephoned the Bistro to say she had a stomach bug. Gino had been surprisingly sympathetic and said that under no circumstances could she come back until she'd had three clear days without being ill, owing to the risk of an e-coli infection, and the problem of working with food. He said he'd rather she have more days away and be sure she was well before she came back. *Result* thought Lucy hiding under her duvet, she'd get bladdered more often, if it meant legitimate days off work! Her mother was scathing, she scowled at Lucy festering in her bed, knowing her daughter only too well, seriously doubting this was a bug, but more than likely an excess of something or another and stomped down the stairs muttering to herself. Lucy poked her head over the duvet, sitting up and taking a long draught of water. Hair of the dog, that's what she needed, but the likelihood of her escaping from the house today was doubtful. It fucking pissed her off, she was like a bleedin' prisoner, perhaps she could ask Jonty for a job on his market stall, she'd like to live in London. Almost on queue her phone beeped a text, she reached out to pick it up from the floor by the bed, her head felt like someone was splitting it with an axe as she bent

down. She read the text, well think of the randy old devil it was
Weasel, she squinted to read it through bloodshot eyes, '*GR8 shag.
Again?*'. How tempting, she contemplated for a bit and typed back
'*when?*' The reply came back almost immediately, "*Thursday?*" and
then quickly another one "*J says contact those old M8s*". Fucking hell
he was persistent but what did it matter, "*Ok*", she texted back. She
lay back on the pillow and hugged herself, who knew where this
would lead, but hopefully out of this dump

CHAPTER 36

The sun had come out by the time Charles came home, the ground was steaming after the persistent drizzle of the day. The rain had brought down some of the clematis from the walled garden, and the wisteria needed hooking back up, but there was a pungent smell of fragrant summer flowers in the air from the honeysuckle and roses. He pulled the car around to the garages and stood outside for a moment soaking in the beauty of the early evening. Ambling into the house past the kitchen he called good evening to Mrs Fuller and on towards the hall, where he shouted to Jennifer that he was home.

"In the drawing room darling!" she responded, leaping up from the floor where she had been sitting absorbed in *The Manual of Horsemanship*, thinking of what sort of questions she should ask Felix tomorrow.

Charles walked in and gave her a hug, tossing his briefcase and jacket down as usual over the sofa, "So good to be home sweetie, I need a stiff drink, it's been a tough old day." His handsome face looked strained, but his eyes were soft when he looked at her. "I could do with a holiday." Jennifer had poured him a large drink, and brought it over to him smiling and he bent his head and kissed her gently on the lips as she passed it to him, "thank you angel, I do love you."

"I love you too darling, come on sit down, let me rub your shoulders, ease away the pressures of the day."

"Mmm, that would be wonderful, just what I need." He slid down on the sofa, and she sat on the arm gently trailing her fingers and hands through his hair and then along the back of his neck, "Oh sweetie, that's heaven" he murmured. She moved on down to his shoulders, deeply kneading the tight knot of muscles, and he squirmed and moaned beneath her touch. She worked away until she felt his neck and back start to relax, and then she stroked his hair again. "God Jennifer that is wonderful, I feel so much more chilled, thank you darling."

"To do it properly you need to take your shirt off, but hey let's save that for later" she teased, kissing the top of his head and plopping down next to him on the sofa. He picked up her hand and kissed it lightly, "And there are some things I need to talk to you about."

"Oh God" he groaned pulling his hand away, "I can't bear it, what's gone wrong?"

"Nothing too ghastly – don't panic!" she laughed, "firstly we've been invited to Katherine and Jeremy's for supper on Friday evening, I'd quite like to go, is that okay with you?"

"Is that all, yes splendid, love to, nothing formal though?" he pleaded, the thought of having to come home from a long day and then put on a penguin suit didn't appeal.

"Not posh she said, so I suppose that means chinos and a shirt. Honestly Charles you are hopeless, you used to love dressing up!"

"That was before I was a happily married man, who wanted to put on his slippers and snuggle up to his gorgeous wife" he breathed on her neck, "Okay what else?"

"Mmmm you can snuggle up to me all night" she whispered, "but I'm looking forward to going, showing off my handsome husband. Now the next thing, is that Caitlin has arranged for this lad Felix to come tomorrow for an interview as Lucy's replacement, do you want any input?"

"No, I bloody don't, I made a big enough mistake with Lucy, I'll just leave it to you eh? That okay? Usual conditions five and half day week, flat provided, don't really want their own horse here if it can be avoided, and speak to Caitlin about the wages and other stuff. Just make sure he's not too good looking." He pouted "don't want him making eyes at my sexy wife!" His hand strayed down between her legs, "I can't be bothered with supper, let's get an early night."

"Behave! Mrs Fuller will go mad if we don't eat supper. Now the third thing, and don't moan, is that I'm seriously worried about Pete."

"Christ Jennifer, not again!" He sat forward annoyed, "Look the man isn't quite the ticket, we know that, just ignore his silences, it's what I do. He's had a hard and strange life and the family have always looked after him and I will too so if you're going to ask me to sack him, the answer is no."

Jennifer knew when to back off, he hated being pushed into corners, "I don't want to sack him either but I do think we could maybe help him." she pleaded, "Charles you don't see it but he looks at me so strangely, even Mrs Fuller has noticed it."

"You haven't been gossiping to her about this have you!" he exploded, "For God's sake Jennifer!"

"No I haven't been gossiping, I just said that he looked at me with such intense dislike that at times it frightened me, and she agreed that she'd noticed him too. That was all we said and she advised I talk to you about it. So stop getting stroppy with me, I don't know why you are so testy about it!" She put her head in her hands and started to cry.

Charles was instantly sorry, it had been a bitch of a day at work, and perhaps he was just used to Pete's bizarre behaviour, after all he had grown up with it, but Mrs Fuller too! Really what a pain women could be. "Sorry darling, please don't cry, this has all got blown out of proportion in your head, he's pretty harmless, I'm sure you've nothing to worry about, but look, why don't I keep an eye on him when you're around and see what I think? Meanwhile you steer clear of him – okay?"

Slightly mollified, she sat up, wiping her tears on her hanky, "would you darling, that would make me feel better, and I'm not making it up Charles. He's definitely weird around me."

"Well, let me watch for it myself and see what I think. Come on, I'm sorry, don't cry please." He reached over and pulled her back into his arms, kissing all over her face gently, and stroking her hair, until he felt her sobs subsiding. "Don't worry, it's all a storm in a teacup, really it is."

That night confined to her room, Lucy sent a text message to Tom, asking if he fancied meeting tomorrow night. He didn't respond immediately and in the meantime she caught up with things on Facebook, lots of the hunting folk used it, although they never revealed their private information on the public wall, but they'd befriended her when she was working at Nantes and hadn't bothered to block her when she left. She was just surfing to see what they'd been up to, when her phone beeped a text, it was Tom replying. '*ok 4 2mro. Pick u up carfax at 7. Lol*'. Good, she texted back '*ok lol*' and thought that would keep Jonty quiet and it would be nice to see Tom again, even though he was a bit straight laced, coming from his snooty family. She wondered where they would go, hopefully to the Fox, she could catch up on all the goss properly! Perhaps he would bring Oli too, although they had no hope of a shag, and serve them right, they could just dream of what they were missing instead! She texted Weasel '*tell J doing what he wanted 2moro. Lol*' She waited for a response but none came.

Grace had prepared Colin his favourite meal – cottage pie, bloody ridiculous really, but he loved it! He always said he had to go to so many business lunches that he just wanted good plain cooking at home, although frankly she would have liked to be more adventurous herself. Nothing though could dampen her spirits this evening, she couldn't believe how lucky she had been today! Everything had fallen into place like clockwork, she hadn't had to mention a word that she already knew about the vacancy. Good old Caitlin, she had a lot to thank her for. Of course she'd telephoned Colin straight away, but he was with clients and made bland cursory and unsatisfactory replies to her exuberant gushing down the phone at him. She'd put the phone down and felt deflated, she really needed to talk about it. She had shot into her car and speedily driven up to her Mum and Dad's to tell them the good news. Her mother had been in the kitchen, and had peered at her over her specs looking doubtful when Grace blurted out the story, but when she saw how happy she was her face wrinkled up in smiles. They had sat down together, cups of tea in their hands and talked about it endlessly. Grace though was still busting to talk to Colin about it. Trust him to be late tonight! She dotted some butter on top of the mash and shoved the pie into the Aga, so that it would crisp up the top, just the way he liked it, and poured herself a large glass of Rioja.

She flopped down onto the kitchen chair savouring the wine, stroking the dogs absently, as she waited for Colin to come in. Restless and impatient she picked up the remote and put on the TV, flicking idly through the channels. What a lot of tosh she thought, finally selecting ITV 3 which was doing yet another re-run of Midsomer Murders; ah a good old murder mystery – perfect, although she had probably seen them all before, but it was easy watching, as she tried to take her mind off things. She was almost at the denouement, when she heard the sound of Colin's car in the drive, she glanced at the kitchen clock, Christ! She had been sitting there for ages, what about the fucking cottage pie! She rarely swore but this was an exceptional circumstance, she raced to the Aga and pulled out the pie, plonking it down and trying to snip off the burned bits when Colin walked into the kitchen.

"Hi, sorry about earlier, was with some important clients, tell me all about what happened …" he began, "Blimey what's happened to the pie?" He looked at the dish, crispy was an understatement and then he started to laugh. "You do look funny trying to cut off those burnt bits with a pair of scissors! What happened, not like you doll, hope this isn't a sign of things to come?".

"Just shut up Colin," she shouted crossly, "if you weren't always so bloody late, I wouldn't have got bored and watched some crap on the TV and forgotten all about it! Bloody hell, it's cremated!" She looked at the pie, then at him rolling up with laughter, and started to giggle. "What a mess, although I think if we scrape the top off we should be okay."

"Why don't we go down to the Fox sweetie, give this to the dogs?"

"Definitely not, I've been waiting all day to talk to you, if we go out we're bound to meet people and then I'd never have an opportunity to tell you my news. Anyway the dogs are too fat!" She pulled out some plates from the bottom oven and started to dissect the pie into edible parts.

Colin sloshed some wine in a glass, "Perhaps we should be drinking champagne, to celebrate your job." He picked up her glass of wine, topped it up and handed it to her, "Cheers darling and congratulations! Now tell me all about it."

Grace abandoned the pie, clinking her glass with his, "I just couldn't believe it - it all just fell into place." Her eyes were dancing, and she gabbled on excitedly, "It'll just be a few hours a week to begin with, then maybe increasing depending on the work load. I get holiday too, and not a bad rate of pay, and they're more than prepared to be flexible to fit in round the hunting and my parents! How good is that?"

Colin looked at her fondly, it had been a long time since he had seen her so animated, "I think it sounds perfect darling, as long as you think you can manage to juggle everything around here?" What would happen if she got pregnant he wondered, but this wasn't the time to dampen her spirits, nor to think of something that might never happen.

"Of course I can Colin, hardly rushed off my feet am I? I'll just have to manage my time better, and it'll do me good you know" she added quietly, "I need something to keep my mind occupied instead of pining for a baby." There, it was said, for the first time she'd really voiced out loud how she felt about not getting pregnant, it was all right for him, he went off every day to his busy agency, and she just brooded, well there would not be so much time for that self-indulgence any longer. "I'm so looking forward to starting, and we all sat down and thought next Monday would be good for a trial period to see how I got on. Suited me fine - gives me a chance to make all those cakes for the bloody puppy show on Sunday."

Colin smiled at her, deciding to say nothing about her reference to a baby, "Well just don't burn the bloody things, otherwise I'll have to make a mercy dash to Sainsbury's so you can pretend to everyone you made them."

Charles had blearily crept out of bed early, carefully disentangling himself from the sleeping Jennifer, she did not stir. He looked down on her, her face looked so young and carefree in sleep, he smiled, no doubt dreaming about horses. He found her secret enthusiasm to learn to ride rather enchanting, but he doubted that she would stick it, but as long as she was happy and she clearly was, then that made his life content too. It had made him smile to see her mugging up on *the Manual of Horsemanship* ready for the interview later today. God he hadn't opened a page of it since he was in the Pony Club. He wondered if he was doing the right thing leaving her to see this lad, but he wanted her to feel she had more input into the way things were run, and Christ knew he'd made a fudgy Horlicks of employing Lucy. Still Caitlin was bloody sensible and he trusted her completely, she knew her stuff and so as long as she was there that'd be fine. He dragged on an old sweater and some jeans and crept out of the bedroom, leaving Jennifer to her dreams.

The house was sleeping too, weak shafts of sunlight slanted through the gaps in the closed curtains, and other than the ticking of the grandfather clock in the hallway, it was very quiet. He loved this house, he had lived here all his life and despite its vastness he always felt it was homely and snug. He tiptoed towards the kitchen corridor padding silently on his bare feet, past the laundry room and the scullery, and the stairs to the cellar, opening the door to the kitchen and the warmth of the Aga. He'd just started to make himself a cup of tea when he heard steps outside on the gravel, and looking out of the window, saw it was Caitlin going over to the yard to start her day, and then behind him he heard the unmistakable shuffle of Mrs Fuller herself coming out from her apartment adjacent to the kitchen. Bugger he was hoping to see Pete before he saw her – oh well! She pushed open the kitchen door, humming to herself, pulling on her apron, then visibly jumping in fright when she saw him.

"Mr Charles, you gave me a turn! Whatever are you doing up so early?" She clutched her chest and sank down on a chair, "I'm too old for shocks like that!" she had gone quite white, and was shaking.

Charles was immediately sorry, thinking poor old dear - last thing he wanted to do was give her a heart attack. "I'm so sorry Mrs F, I didn't mean to scare you. I just wanted a cup of tea, and moreover an opportunity to speak to you on our own. Look let me make you some tea." he said pulling down another mug from the dresser.

"Really Mr Charles , there's no need, I can do it, you sit down now." she staggered up from the chair, "I'm fine now, really I am."

"Now Mrs Fuller, you sit down and let me do it." he ordered, "It's the least I can do." He rummaged about for teabags and milk, and brought the tea over to the table, sitting down opposite her. "I wanted to speak to you, I gather that Jennifer has been talking to you about Pete? She's very worried, tell me have you noticed him behaving in a peculiar way?"

His eyes didn't leave her face, and he saw her hesitate, and look down at her feet, pausing before she spoke. "Yes I have, I thought at first he was just having a bad day, you know like he does. But I think it's getting worse and there's something else that I need to tell you, which happened on Monday afternoon." She hesitated, not knowing where to start and then with a sigh told him about the incident in the shop. "I don't think Caitlin would be exaggerating, she found the whole incident very upsetting and came to tell me about it yesterday morning, I told her I'd inform you, but I haven't told Jennifer, I didn't want to worry her all the more." She wrung her hands in her apron, her face glum.

"I see" said Charles "it would certainly seem as though nobody is exaggerating if you've all noticed it." He ran his hands through his unruly bed hair, his blue eyes hard, "Well, I'll have to do something. Do you know if he's been taking his pills?"

"No, I don't, but it was my first thought too."

"Right, I'll make a point of talking to him myself first." He glanced at his watch, "he should be starting work soon, and then if I think the same as the rest of you, I'll give Dr Corbett a ring to ask his advice. Meanwhile I'm asking for your discretion here Mrs Fuller, don't tell Jennifer about what happened in the shop, and I'll ask Caitlin to do the same. If anything else happens you must tell me straight away." He tipped up his mug and finished his tea, "Right, I'll have a quiet saunter along to the yard and then around the garden." He stood up adding, "Sorry about frightening you Mrs Fuller, entirely unintentional."

"Of course Mr Charles, let me know if I can help in any way." She watched him go, his footsteps muffled on the flagstone floor. Well, well, she thought, he must be pretty concerned to get up so early. She hoped it would all just be one of those little things that would blow over, like a shower of rain on a sunny day, but she had an awful feeling this may well prove to be a full blown storm.

It was the usual melee at Mileoak with Toby still glued to his computer even though the others were waiting in the car. Chloe raced up the stairs, taking two steps at a time, ducking with skilled practice under the low beams, and stampeding along the landing, bursting into Toby's room like a torpedo "Toby!" she yelled, "Come on, we're all waiting in the car for you!"

"I'm not going, I don't feel well" he snapped at her, "I told you that last night but you took no notice of me." He didn't look ill, just cross, his little face screwed up with anger.

"What is it darling?" She moved over to him, looking carefully at his face, "where do you feel ill? Tummy?" She was concerned now, guilt sweeping over her, she hadn't taken any notice of him he was right, she was too wrapped up with her own worries.

"No, I've got a headache, and it's making me feel sick." he complained bitterly "and if you and Daddy would stop arguing, you might have noticed!"

Chloe watched his face carefully, this wasn't about him feeling ill, this was about her and John. She stroked his hair off his face, "Look darling, you really don't have to worry about Dad and me, everything's okay - really it is."

"You're not going to get a divorce then, Lily said you were" his worried expression made Chloe's heart lurch, "I don't want you to, but you're always cross with each other."

"Lily shouldn't be saying things like that" Chloe fought to contain her irritation, "of course we're not getting divorced, it's total nonsense." Oh God she thought, she certainly hoped that was true, but there was no way that she was going to say anything about their problems to the children, not until she knew what she was dealing with anyway.

"I hate Lily, she's always winding me up." growled Toby, then he reasoned, "Why would she say it then?"

His expression was so serious, again her fury at John threatened to boil over, how dare he put them all through this, it simply wasn't fair. She took his little hand, the smallness of it clutched in hers brought about a huge protectiveness, she wouldn't let them suffer because of them. "I've no idea darling, but it's simply not true, so

come on now, let's get in the car and forget all this nonsense."
Together they bundled up his school bag and ran down the stairs to
the car.

They only just caught the bus, Chloe had seen it disappearing
along the lane from over the top of the hedgerow already having
passed their stop, and she careered after it, tooting and flashing her
lights until Bert pulled over.

"Sorry Bert, we got behind today" she panted as she carried
Rory to the steps of the bus, the others already scampering to the back
seats, "thanks for stopping, see you this afternoon." She called to
them all.

Jumping down, she watched the doors hiss shut and the old bus
rumble away on its journey to school. For a moment or two she just
stood there, the only sounds were of a blackbird and the rat tat of a
woodpecker, the awfulness of what Toby had said suddenly hit her
and she felt like weeping. Would it have been better not to have said
anything to John, rather than this terrible stalemate she had found
herself in now? He was still trying hard to be more than solicitous as
far as she was concerned, but things had changed between them, was
it for good or could they ever retrieve their hitherto happy lives
together, and if they couldn't – what would happen to her and the
children? The sudden rattle of a car shooting around the corner and
tooting for her to get out of the road, made her start and she ran back
to the Discovery, which she had shoved askew into a field gateway.
She got in and put her head in her hands, how much longer could she
stand it?

Back at the yard, the day had begun, the horses stamping and
calling impatiently, as Beebs and Susie were putting in their feeds.
The day was promising to be fine after yesterday's drizzle, and there
was a lot to get through. Katherine was coming up early to ride with
Sandy and they were going out in the trailer to take the horses for a
work out on the gallops, so at least that was two less to exercise. Jen
was coming up as usual and Chloe was going to give her a lesson on
Ksar, whilst the girls got on with the chore of mucking and chucking.
Susie had collected the empty haynets from the stables and sauntered
down to the hay barn to refill them ready for tonight, and Beebs had
jumped onto the quad bike and was steaming off across the fields to

check the horses that were out at night now, making sure that the water troughs were okay and that none of them had got into trouble and injured themselves. It was a familiar routine and they worked in happy harmony and relative silence to get the work done before Chloe came into the yard after the school run to go through the programme for the day, and enjoy a well-deserved cup of coffee. Susie was still in the barn finishing off when she heard Beebs roar back, and they loaded the daytime hay onto the trailer and drove more sedately into the yard, distributing the nets to those horses that were staying in for the morning.

Finished at least for the time being, horses settled, they opened up the tack room and put the kettle on, Susie was rummaging about in the biscuit tin, "Blimey, there's been a raid on this, only rubbish ones left!" She stared gloomily inside the tin, "who's had all the custard creams?"

Beebs looked guilty, "Oh, okay, I own up, it was me! I'll get some more at the village shop when I go down. Here's your coffee!"

"Not the same without a biscuit" Susie grumbled good naturedly, "Joking! Hey, I've got a bit of gossip for you."

"Go on! What?" Beebs eyes gleamed mischievously,

"Tom had a text from Lucy!" Susie delivered the titbit with relish, making a face at Beebs.

"Nooo, she's got some neck though! What's she up to? Did he say?" Beebs, her curiosity aroused immediately, egged Susie to tell her more.

"Well, he's gonna meet her tonight and find out. So we'll know more tomorrow!"

"Aren't you a bit pissed off, after all you and Tom 've been seeing a bit of each other." asked Beebs cautiously. She wouldn't want her friend to be hurt because of that slag.

"No, I'm fine about it, he's only going to get the goss, besides Tom and I are just mates, I don't feel like that about him and he knows it. He did have a bit of thing with Lucy a couple of times, but it was just a shag, she was the one doing the offering, and he took her up on it." Her eyes glittered, "But she puts out to anyone!"

"Well, it'll be interesting to see what she has to say for herself."

CHAPTER 37

It was quite late in the morning and when Charles finally got into his office, and was sitting nursing a cup of coffee, wondering what to do next. Sighing he picked up the phone and dialled Alex Corbett's surgery, asking to be put through to him, only to be told he was out doing his rounds. Frustrated, he made an appointment for tomorrow afternoon, and put the phone down. This was going to be tricky as he knew that Alex would not discuss Pete's illness with him, owing to patient confidentiality but he was not sure if Pete was sound enough in his mind to be making any decisions for himself and he had no family, so what else could Charles do?

His mind wandered back to his visit to the stables this morning and his conversation with Caitlin. She had been reticent at first, but after some prompting had reluctantly described the whole scene in the shop. Charles had reassured her, privately thinking at the time that they were all prone to exaggerating, and said she was not to mention this to Jennifer or to anyone else come to that, and that he would deal with the matter. He marched out of the yard across the lawn looking for Pete and had come upon him in the kitchen garden, digging up some potatoes and picking the salad for Mrs Fuller. At first Charles had thought he seemed alright. He had his usual dishevelled and unkempt appearance, there again this was not new - Pete had always looked like that, but not the vacant expression in his far-away eyes. He'd tried to talk to him and at first Pete had answered him fairly mechanically and then Charles had steered the conversation around to the children. Suddenly Pete's whole face changed - he seemed to lose control and become totally irrational and incoherent. Charles had to admit that it had shocked him to the core, the man was obviously in some form of delusional state and wasn't able to think clearly. So now he was considering what he should do? He could of course ring his own mother and get her advice, she knew Pete better than anyone, but he didn't want her worried either. No Alex Corbett was the right route to take he felt sure. Pete should be getting his medication from

416

him and the tiny dispensary in the surgery, so he more than anyone would be able to help. God he hoped so anyway.

The morning had sped past for Jennifer, who was exhilarated after her lesson on Ksar, he was the perfect gentleman, ignoring any mistakes she made and politely waiting for her to get it right before he responded to her aids. It had been an awesome experience and then she had ridden Rufus, and it was like slipping into a comfortable old pair of slippers as she hacked him around the fields with Susie. Today she had felt she had made real progress. She was also delighted to be able to tell Katherine that they would be able to come on Friday evening. All in all a very good day she pondered, as she stopped off at the village store for some biscuits – some for Mileoak and some for Caitlin. She had come to realise how important biscuits were in the scheme of yard life! She'd asked Chloe and the girls about the sort of questions she should ask Felix this afternoon and they'd given her some helpful hints, but she was nervous about it, supposing she looked a complete idiot. She swung into the stables, the top down on the Mercedes and her hair flying about all over the place, and spotted Caitlin, pulling up weeds that had sprung up in the yard.

"Hi Caitlin!" she called, "Have you got a minute?"

Caitlin stood up, arching her back, "Sure Jennifer, what can I do for you?" she asked, thinking it was the life of Riley that the other half led.

"Just wondered what the plan was for this afternoon? Do you want me to come over here for three or will you bring Felix over to the house, we could have a coffee first and then show him around?

"If I bring him over when he arrives, we can talk to him about what the job entails and then show him around the yard after. Mrs Fuller has offered to make us a cup of tea too. I think she wants to vet him after the problems we had with Lucy, and I wouldn't want to be offending her now!" She laughed ruefully at the thought of Mrs Fuller's displeasure.

"Me neither, the thought of it makes me quake!" Jennifer said wryly, "okay that's a plan then, I'll expect you at three in my study."

She turned away leaving Caitlin to get back to her weeding, "Oh by the way, I forgot, I bought you some provisions for the tack room." She leant over to the passenger seat of her car, and pulled out a plastic bag, "just some biscuits , teabags and stuff."

"Well, that's grand, thank you very much. Staple food for grooms." She took the bag, delving inside, and wondered what had prompted this - nobody thought of replenishing the tack room stocks usually. Jennifer was certainly full of surprises.

Jennifer herself, thinking no more about it, stopped in at the kitchen and made herself a chicken and mayo sandwich, and was chatting away to Mrs Fuller, who was only mildly disgruntled at being told to put her feet up, whilst Jennifer made her own lunch. The Grandfather clock in the hall chimed the half hour, Jennifer stuffed the last of the sandwich in her mouth and beat a hasty retreat to her study. She dragged out the trusty *Manual of Horsemanship* and had a quick scan at the stable management chapter. She threw the book back in her desk drawer, God she was more nervous than if she were going for the job herself! Mrs Fuller had said she would bring in some coffee when she heard Caitlin come through the back door with Felix, so all Jennifer had to do was wait.

It seemed ages before she heard footsteps coming across the hall towards her study and the lilting Irish tone of Caitlin murmuring and then another voice, followed by a knock on her door and they came in. Jennifer swivelled around in her chair to face them and stood up to see Caitlin and the most extraordinarily divine looking young man. He was like an Adonis, tall, blonde and lean, with a fine angular face, square cut jaw, and the biggest blue eyes. He had the kind of looks that you see in a book on the classics, except he was not sporting a fig leaf! Blimey she thought, what was it Charles had said about not employing anyone too good looking! She pulled herself together, managing to turn her dropping jaw into a smile, and walked over extending her hand, "Hi, you must be Felix, I'm Jennifer Parker-Smythe."

Felix turned the full beam of his startling eyes onto her, "Hello, I'm Felix Stephenson, nice to meet you Mrs Parker-Smythe." He shook her hand, smiling at her, showing very straight, even white teeth.

"Please, Felix, call me Jennifer, sit down do. You too Caitlin"

she indicated to some chairs, "Now Felix tell me all about yourself."
She swivelled round in her chair to give him her rapt attention, and he
was definitely worth looking at. No wonder Susie had kept in touch
with him!

Felix began to speak, and his voice was as lovely as his face,
deep and rich without appearing affected, mesmerising both her and
Caitlin. They discovered that he was twenty four, had ridden since he
was a little boy, and had been brought up with horses, and been an
active member of the Pony Club, enjoying all the disciplines,
including eventing. He had gone to Hartpury College to do a degree
in Equine Studies and had passed with hons. Since then he had
worked in a variety of equine based work environments, but wanted
to spend the next season in a hunting yard to broaden his experience,
before deciding on a final career path.

"Before you ask" he said, "I can't put my hand on my heart and
say I expect to be here for more than the season, as one day I want my
own yard – but I'm just not sure what I want to specialise in yet."

"Well that's honest enough. Tell me have you hunted before?"
asked Caitlin, "It can be a hard slog in the winter and the hours are
long."

"Only in the Pony Club and those meets are specially designed
for kids really, so grown up hunting – the answer has to be no" he
said frankly, his face looking momentarily anxious "but that doesn't
mean to say I don't want to." He was interrupted by a brisk knock on
the door heralding Mrs Fuller with a tray of coffee. She stopped in her
tracks as she saw Felix, Jennifer was amused to see that even she had
the same reaction as the rest of them when she saw him. Felix to be
fair must have been used to this , she couldn't think of one woman
who would have reacted differently to his film star looks. He leapt to
his feet, "here let me take that from you." Taking the tray and setting
it carefully down on the little side table, he offered her his hand, "Hi,
I'm Felix." Mrs Fuller gawped, she was as hooked as the rest of them.

The remainder of the interview passed well, Felix answering all
of the questions that Jennifer had dreamed up, and actually she felt
quite foolish asking them, and Caitlin had looked mildly surprised at
her and then asked "Well now, shall I show you the yard?" she
beamed at him finally, making to stand up and move to the door.

"Great!" said Felix enthusiastically, "would you like to see me ride?"

"Definitely, as you'll have to be helping me with keeping the hunters fit, so that'd be grand, and you'll be wanting to see the accommodation too. Of course, it's pretty much the way the last groom left it, and that was an unholy mess now!" Caitlin laughed, "Are you coming along Jennifer?"

"Absolutely" said Jennifer firmly, and they all stood up, Felix picked up the empty tray and dropped it back into the kitchen as they passed, thanking Mrs Fuller profusely.

Caitlin had brought in Beano for Felix to show off his riding prowess. Jennifer had never really taken much notice of Beano before and was impressed by the obvious quality of the horse. She knew enough now to know that this was not some woolly old hunter but a very smart, well-bred animal. His summer coat was sleek and glossy, and even though he had been summering out since the end of hunting he still looked as fit as when he had finished, he was rippling with muscle, but he did have a bit of a wild look in his eye.

"Now, Felix," said Caitlin, "this is Beano, he's Mr Parker-Smythe's favourite horse, a lovely ride but a bit sharp sometimes, so watch him as he's not been ridden since the last meet. You don't have to do anything fancy, just a bit of walk, trot and canter will be fine, as despite his appearance he's not fit, but 10 minutes won't hurt him. Here, let me give you his tack." Jennifer realised that Caitlin had selected Beano as part of the test, to see if Felix really could ride, rather than giving him the safer option of Dandy, and by asking him to tack him up she could see how dextrous and familiar he was at handling the horses.

Felix carried the saddle and bridle over and expertly put it on, patting the nervous horse and talking to him all the time, Beano's wild eye calmed a little, and Jennifer could see that Caitlin was impressed. "Hang on" Felix said, "Just need my crash hat."

"At least he's half sensible" Caitlin muttered to Jennifer, "doesn't want to show off and not wear one." Felix shot back, buckled up his skull cap, and led the dancing Beano out of the stable. "The mounting block's over there" she said pointing to the far end of the yard.

"Oh, I'm fine, don't need one." in one swift move he vaulted onto Beano before the horse could object and was adjusting his stirrups. "Where's the school?"

"Follow me" called Caitlin, leading the way out to the arena. Felix followed, Beano's eyes were rolling around in his head, he was prancing about and humping his back in objection to being ridden. "Holy Mary, hope I've done the right thing now in getting out Beano!" she whispered to Jennifer, who looked aghast as rider and horse clattered past them.

She needn't have worried, as after just a few moments Felix's skill was evident. The normally fiery horse was like putty in his hands, as he bent him this way and that, making deft fluent transitions from canter to walk. You didn't need to know anything about horses to know that this lad could really ride. They watched in him in awed silence for a while, neither able to speak, but gazed on the spectacle of horse and man at one and both as beautiful as each other.

"Blimey!" said Caitlin.

They showed him around the flat, although neither Jennifer nor Caitlin could quite believe the state it was in following Lucy's hasty departure.

"Don't worry" Jennifer was embarrassed, "I'll make sure it's all cleaned up before you come."

"Don't worry about it Jennifer" Felix said easily, "It's a super little place and will be a paradise after the shared accommodation I've got now." He grinned at her, "I'll soon have it looking a lot different to this!"

They made a tour of the rest of the yard, walking Beano in hand back down to the meadow, where he galloped off with gusto to join the other horses, who were lazily flicking flies off each other under the shade of the oak trees. Ambling back, Caitlin talked of the work that would be expected of him here and hoped he wouldn't find it dull after working in a big yard as he would definitely find it a lot quieter. They walked through the fields towards the yard, skirting around the horse walker and Queenie trapped in her starvation paddock. She whinnied to them pathetically as they passed. Jennifer told him about her step children and how important it was that they had fun when they came and hoped he liked kids. Felix grinned saying he was quite a kid himself in a lot of ways, and his disarming smile melted away any doubts.

"Well now, I think we've more or less covered everything Felix, is there anything else that you want to see or know?" Caitlin enthused, Jennifer noticed that she had become quite animated since Felix had arrived. Good, she could do with cheering up!

Felix looked around, taking in the yard, and the set up, "No, I think we've just about covered everything. Oh one thing though, could I bring my own horse?"

Jennifer looked glum, it was the one thing Charles had specified last night that he wasn't keen on "Well we may consider it …" She tailed off, as Caitlin interrupted her.

"It's not something we usually do" she said, "and it would depend on what sort of horse it is, how big, temperament and stuff. Of course, you would only be able to do your horse after the others had been finished, and the cost of its keep would reflect in your wages."

"Okay," Felix said amiably, "just asking. He's a big fellah about 16.3, quite young - only six and I've been doing a bit of low key eventing, but don't have a lot of time, he'd be a good hunter I'm sure, and it would be great to have the opportunity to take him out whilst I'm here. But it's not a problem, I'm sure I could find a DIY yard locally."

"Well, we'll see now, Mr Parker-Smythe might not be keen, and we can discuss that with him later. Oh, and one other thing, can you drive a horsebox?" Caitlin asked, "it's just a small hunting box, takes three horses, with a little bit of living? But you need to have your HGV licence."

"No problem, I did my HGV a couple of years ago, I've driven plenty of different trucks. Give me a Yorkie bar and I'm away!" He laughed, enjoying his joke. God he was sexy thought Jennifer.

The humid heat in London was starting to make Laura feel quite sick, and she'd elected to take the bus rather than the tube to Linda's gaff. She rode along on the top of the bus, looking down at all the people in the street going about their daily lives and thought morbidly about the job ahead. Even though it was stifling, there seemed to be a grey saucer over her world and one in which the sun could not break through. She wished she had never met Charles Parker-Smythe, yet when she said his name, it brought back a lot of the anger and hate she felt towards him, and memories of that sick incident in his office when he had abused her. Things had taken a bit of a different turn now and in a funny kind of way she was relieved that Jonty had taken over, even if she had no idea what he was up to. She knew that whatever he was planning involved that fucker and his demise and she was all for that, but she also knew that Jonty was unscrupulous and had a wicked streak in him. All she had to do was play Linda and Sean along and get them to invoke the help of the Sabs to disrupt the hunt, but she had no idea what Jonty's ulterior motive was. Oh well, today she was going to meet with the other members of the group and persuade them it was a good plan and that she had information from the inside that would help them do their job.

The bus was lurching around, stopping and starting in the traffic and the journey seemed to take forever, the filthy grime on the bus windows and old grease on the seats coupled with the fetid air of other people's sweat added to her depressed mood. Just one more stop to go. She was going directly to Linda's flat and then they were going on somewhere else to meet the others .Fuck me what am I doing she thought. At last the bus creaked to a halt and she sprang down the stairs and marched up the pavement, towards the blue door, narrowly avoiding a pile of puke someone had thoughtfully sicked up in the entrance. Christ! Dragging herself up the steps to the flat, picking her way over the rubbish, she pushed open the door to the flat.

"Yo, Linda, Sean, I'm here!" she called, walking in to the sitting room.

They were no-where to be seen, fucking hell, they'd better not have forgotten, she'd be bloody livid. Tentatively pushing open the door to bathroom, she found it was empty, as was the kitchen, and then opened the bedroom door, to see Sean's little white arse pumping away between Linda's legs.

She made a hasty backtrack, mumbling, "Sorry, sorry."

"Hey Laura, don't go, come and join us!" shouted Sean, "we'd love it!"

"No thanks Sean, not my scene y' know" the very thought made her want to vomit, "I'll make a drink and wait."

She edged into the kitchen and leaned against the sink, which was not unexpectedly piled high with dirty plates and mugs. Finding what resembled a clean glass she poured herself some water, at least that couldn't be contaminated, and waited impatiently for them to come out.

In fact she didn't have to wait long before Linda wandered out, her goth make up smudged even more than usual and great streaks of black were streaming all down the side of her nose. She had shoved on a baggy sweaty T shirt and some pants and she looked stoned as she always seemed to these days. Laura looked at her skinny arms, poking out like brittle sticks from the sleeves and saw the tell-tale sign of track marks. She was using the hard stuff, what a fucking idiot. She felt a pang of guilt, she had never thought to ask Jonty exactly what was in those little packages he sent over for her to give to Linda but she was pretty sure she knew now.

Sean came up behind Linda, cupping her breasts with his hands, "you should've come in Laura, no need to be shy."

Laura was immediately angry, she wasn't shy but wasn't desperate either - was what she wanted to reply, but instead she sighed and just smiled coyly at him, thinking wanker! Whatever her gut feeling she must not alienate them now, but for two pins she would just walk away, but the wrath of Jonty would be heavy and not worth taking the risk.

"Come on" she said, "I'm keen to meet the others."

CHAPTER 38

Tom pulled the Landrover into the bus stop at the Carfax, it was just on seven, but Lucy was no-where to be seen. It was okay at this time of night as it was not busy , so he could loiter about here without fear of being moved on. He was curious to see her, her text had given no information about what she was up to now and frankly he had been amazed to hear from her at all. She was a funny girl, his mind thought back to those salacious nights with Oli and he felt embarrassed in a way, it was not like him to be a slut himself but she had really given them the come on. Ironically it made him pity her, that she felt the need to cheapen herself so openly to invite attention and, he felt that her hard exterior was a bit of an act for someone really craving to be loved. This is what reading Psychology at Uni does for you he thought grimly.

"Hey Tom!" he jumped as there was a rap on the window and he saw her standing on the pavement. She opened the passenger door and climbed in her short skirt riding up to give him a good view of her knickers. She leaned over and kissed him on the cheek, "Where shall we go then?"

"I don't mind at all - you say. You look great!" he spluttered.

"Okay, shall we go to the Fox, it's as good as anywhere, and I might see some old friends." she suggested innocuously. "That's if you don't mind dropping me back to Horsham after?"

"No, of course not, but are you sure you want to go to the Fox though, after what happened?" he privately thought that she wouldn't be terribly welcome after the way she'd behaved, but it would be hard to say that directly to her. He felt uneasy, he didn't want to be a party to a slanging match.

"Especially after what happened" she countered, she wasn't afraid of any confrontation, but in fact she had decided to play the '*I behaved very stupidly and it was a rash spur of the moment thing and I'm sorry'* role and in parts she thought that was true. She should've waited and dropped them in it, as was her plan, but her hot temper had ruled her brain. She continued "I'm so sorry about what happened, I just lost my temper, I don't want any hard feelings."

Tom breathed a sigh of relief, if she was really sorry and said so, then things would probably be fine. Most people would just accept that – okay, she would never be bosom buddies with any of the hunting folk again, but she wouldn't be ostracised either. "Great, the Fox it is then." he said, ramming the car into gear and lurching out of the town towards Fittlebury.

Whilst they drove, Lucy filled him on what she'd been doing, saying she had the job in the Bistro as a stop gap, but that she really wanted to get another job with horses, and was actively looking. She asked what the gossip was and had they replaced her yet at Nantes.

Tom who was concentrating on the driving and refusing to let his eyes be drawn to Lucy's legs said distractedly "No, I don't think they have, after all it's the summer time and there's no hurry. I've been busy too, been up at the Hunt Kennels most of the last few weeks getting ready for the Puppy Show. You should see the place it looks really smart, we've done a good job, not a weed in sight."

"When is it then?" Lucy considered whether or not she could gate crash, oh well, she thought, I'll see what happens tonight.

"Sunday. Just hope we have a nice afternoon weather-wise, it'd be a disaster if it rained." he laughed, "all those ladies in their frocks they'll bloody freeze to death!"

The Landrover rumbled down the narrow lanes, the cow parsley in the hedgerows swirling madly as they passed, and Lucy thought, actually she'd missed this, so much nicer than the town. The view across the valley as they approached the village was lovely in this evening light and up on the hilltop she could see Grace Allington's parents' place. The patchwork of fields and hedges with the odd splash of brilliant yellow as the rape flowers coloured the landscape, it looked like a scene from toy town. They slowed down to pass some horses on the road ambling out for an evening jolly, their riders gossiping as they thanked Tom for slowing down. The smell of horse drifted in through the window and Lucy felt suddenly hungry to be back with them again, and she said as much to Tom.

"Do you think they might take me back at Nantes?" she asked him, "I miss it all so much, being with the horses and everything."

"Oh Lucy, I don't know, it wouldn't be easy for you to go back and eat humble pie would it, and apologise for walking out. You could try I suppose. Have you spoken to Caitlin since you left?"

"No, I haven't, as the days went by it seemed more and more difficult, so in the end I just didn't, and now the moment's passed. Too late to do it now." She sighed, "Do you think I should send Caitlin a text apologising?"

Tom didn't need to think about his reply, "Yes, I do, even if it isn't about going back there to work, it'd make you feel better about how you left." He couldn't be sure if she was serious - was she really sorry? He knew one of his own weaknesses was to be pretty gullible and perhaps that was what he was being now. Surely not? "Yes, I would definitely do it, send the text Lucy" he said firmly.

The car park at the Fox was quite busy and Tom expertly squeezed the Landrover into a corner. He glanced around to see if he could recognise any of the other cars; Patrick's van was here and Colin's Landcruiser too. He hoped Caitlin wasn't here, he looked at his watch it was just seven thirty with any luck she wouldn't be.

Caitlin was in fact in the arms of her lover and the last thing on her mind was Lucy. They were both naked and lying on a blanket in the woods, he was propped up on one elbow, stroking the space between her breasts after making love. He leant down and kissed the tip of her nose, even after all these months he still made her insides feel like jelly. Their love making was wonderful, sometimes tender and slow and sometimes mad, falling upon each other tearing each other's clothes off. Tonight had been the gentle type and she felt lazy and relaxed and satiated, stretching her long legs and wiggling her toes off the edge of the blanket into the grass.

"Do you know I'm starving, I could eat a horse." he laughed.

"Not one of mine you couldn't!" She twirled over and fished in her bag, "here, I've got some chocolate, and surprise - some crisps, don't say I don't spoil you!"

He tore open a packet of crisps and sprinkled some on her tummy, eating them with slow deliberation, whilst she wriggled and squirmed underneath him. "Yum yum! Hmmm, Caitlin flavour, delicious!" He looked up at her sideways serious for a moment, "I love you Caitlin, and I always want to be with you."

"I love you too my darling" she whispered, "I want to be with you too, but I don't understand what we're waiting for?

"Oh honey, you just have to trust me on this, I just can't do anything yet, the timing's not quite right, although I can see why you think it doesn't matter anymore, but believe me it will make a difference if we act in haste. We have to wait a bit longer, but I promise you that we'll be together." He leant over and kissed her with such tenderness and passion that she thought she would melt with the love of him, "together for always, I promise" and gently he started to make love to her all over again.

The sun had started to go down, and finally they parted, sitting up on the blanket and pulling on their clothes, she broke off a piece of chocolate and handed it to him, "I never did tell you the whole story about the lad we interviewed this afternoon – Felix."

"Go on then" he mumbled his mouth full of chocolate, "what did you think of him?"

"Well now, he's certainly a looker and can ride for sure!" she watched his face carefully as he digested the good looking part, "I think we're going to offer him the job, that's if he wants it of course. He even had Mrs Fuller eating out of his hand with his charming manners, and you know how awkward she can be!"

"Hmmm, good looking you say! Do I have competition then?" he rolled her over backwards, pinning her down playfully, "You'd better not fancy him!"

She pushed him off laughing, "Course not, but there is one drawback, he wants to bring his own horse."

"Well, is that a difficulty, you've got loads of room haven't you?

After all as long as he does his job what does that matter? Seriously if it takes the load off you, and gives us more time together, that's got to be good surely?"

Caitlin considered what he said for a moment before replying, "Yes that's true, but in my experience, they always start off okay and gradually their own horse starts to take precedence, and that can lead to all sorts of trouble."

"Darling, you're in charge, you just have to make it clear to him right from the outset where the boundaries are and stick to them. If he's hard working and a good rider then he's probably just what you're looking for, as long as he doesn't have designs on you!"

"Don't be daft!" she laughed "anyway nothing is certain yet, Jennifer has to talk to Charles and see what he thinks, but we were both quite impressed with him – he might not even take the job."

"How could he pass up the opportunity of working with someone as gorgeous as you my darling!"

He held out his hand and helped her up, and bent down to fold up the rug, tucking it under his arm, and holding her hand with the other, and they moved off down the path together, whispering and laughing. At the edge of the car park they separated, Caitlin going first and he watched her from the long shadows of the trees, making sure she got into her car safely and watched her drive away. Cautiously, he moved towards his own vehicle, parked further around the corner between the trees, chucking the rug in the back, and drove home.

In the garden at the Fox, Grace, Colin and Patrick were sitting enjoying a drink. It was really pleasant with the longer days and the mild evenings, although it was not as hot as it had been during May, but at least the hay and crops had started to grow with the rain, and weren't top of the agenda of conversation. Patrick was busy regaling them about his afternoon, with a tale of how at Libby Newsome's place whilst he'd been shoeing, she had been riding, clearly without her bra in a skimpy little vest top, her boobs bobbing about all over the place.

Grace and Colin were falling about laughing, as he gave a good imitation of Libby, the table rocking madly about as he threw himself around. "You should have seen it! It's a wonder she didn't give herself a black eye!" He grinned wickedly, his naughty eyes sparkling.

"I bet they're not real. She must have had a boob job." exclaimed Grace "They're enormous!"

"No doll, they are, if they're fake they don't swing about, they stay in one place and don't move." sniggered Colin, the thought of Libby's knockers making him go hot under the collar.

"I'm bloody glad you qualified that remark Colin, I'd have wondered how you knew they were real otherwise." remarked Patrick, "Mind you, I bet Libby doesn't mind who has a feel!" he roared with laughter and the others joined in. "No, I mustn't be a bitch!" he said soberly and they fell about again.

"Well, well, look who's just waltzed in with Tom!" Grace's eyes were popping out longer than the stalks in a corn field. "She's got a bloody nerve!"

Colin and Patrick who had their backs to the garden gate swivelled round to have a look. "Bloody hell!" said Patrick, "Our Juicy Lucy!"

"Blimey, so it is! I'm surprised she's got the neck to come here after the way she behaved." Colin admonished, he was a stickler for old fashioned principles and the gossip about Lucy's mode of departure had made village headlines at the time. "You'd think she'd steer clear wouldn't you?"

"I hope they don't come and sit with us." moaned Grace, who'd been enjoying her evening and certainly didn't want it spoiled by Lucy.

"Too late!" Colin sighed as Tom waved to them, signalling if they wanted a drink. "They will, you wait and see." He turned back and steeled himself to be pleasant.

On cue, Tom and Lucy came over with their drinks asking if they could join them, the others replied in frosty tones, after all they liked Tom but he obviously had poor taste in women. What on earth was he doing with her?

"Hi everyone" said Lucy brazenly, "How are you all?" Her antennae had immediately picked up on the thin layer of ice but she was buggered if she would react in anything other than pleasantries. She thought of Jonty and what he'd said about making an effort.

"Hi Lucy, Tom" said Colin, sounding as though he had eaten a bag of lemons, "nice evening."

"Hello" was all Grace could muster, looking at Lucy with distaste.

Only Patrick greeted her with any vestige of enthusiasm but it was tinged with a heavy sarcasm, "Hi Lucy, I'm surprised to see you here? Thought you had flounced off in high dudgeon."

Lucy flushed despite her initial bravado, inwardly seething - these fucking wankers, she didn't know why she'd bothered, but instead said replied woodenly "I know I was stupid and if I could turn back the clock I would. I acted in haste and with anger and without thinking, and I bitterly regret that now." There, she thought, that should stop them in their tracks, now what could they say?

"Yes you were stupid, you had a good job at Nantes and Caitlin is a decent person and didn't deserve to be treated like that" Grace muttered indignantly, this bloody girl thought that she could come back here and just be accepted again, well she could have another think as far as she was concerned, but her natural good manners would not permit her to be as crass as Lucy, so she added, "but we can all act in haste and repent at leisure."

The others listened with embarrassment, squirming at Grace's remarks which they'd all thought, but none of them had the courage to say. Colin was proud of his wife, secretly thinking good old Gracie, say it like it is. There was a yawning silence you could have driven a horse and cart through and nobody quite knew what to say, looking at their drinks awkwardly.

"I'm going to text Caitlin to apologise. I was entirely in the wrong and as I said I'm sorry, not much else I can do is there Grace?" Lucy muttered, "Surely everyone is entitled to a second chance?" She held her gaze directly at Grace, who eventually looked away.

"I suppose, but if you're thinking of your old job back, you're out of luck, I heard that they appointed someone new today. Still an apology won't go amiss."

"How's the Kennels looking then Tom?" said Patrick, with his silver skill at changing the subject, "All set for Sunday, must say I'm looking forward to it."

Tom shot a relieved and grateful look at him, "Oh fine, spruced up a treat, old George is well made up. An important day for him, and tough without Mary, he still misses her dreadfully."

"Yes, we were up there at the weekend" Colin said, "Christ knows what he'd do without Jay and the beloved hounds. Poor bloke, I don't know what I'd do without you darling." He laid his hand over Grace's and gave it a little squeeze, and she knew that this was in support of what she'd said to Lucy. She smiled at him, good old Colin, he was her rock, and more to the point what would she do without him.

"I loved the puppy show last year" added Lucy, "such a fun afternoon" she was rather hoping that she might wangle an invite.

"Yes I remember" said Grace acidly, "you were totally pissed on the champagne. Just as well you won't be going this year then."

Lucy rallied, her fighting spirit incensed by the bitchy remark, "Oh but I'm going with Tom, didn't he tell you?" She turned to Tom, giving him a knowing smile and the tiniest wink, "We're looking forward to it aren't we?"

Tom opened his mouth and promptly shut it again, looked at Grace and then looked at Lucy, "Well..."he began, "I don't ..."

Colin decided it was time to intercede, "How lovely for you both, you should have fun then, Jennifer and Charles are going, and I'm sure it will be nice for you to see them again Lucy. Patrick old mate, shall we have a top up then?"

Tom flashed him a grateful look, "I'll get them Col, Lucy can you give me a hand?" He shot up from the table relieved to be away, "for Christ's sake" he hissed to her as they crossed the garden, "What the hell are you playing at?"

"She pissed me off" Lucy said huffily, "she's a bitch!"

Finally the normally gullible and delightful Tom had blown a fuse, and was seriously pissed off, "Well thanks a bunch, you put me in a bloody awkward position. They're my friends and just because you don't know how to behave, don't let your inadequacies rub off on me."

Lucy looked momentarily shocked, "it was only a joke, you know it was, but she was being a cow." then more soberly she added "sorry Tom, I wasn't thinking."

Tom sighed, "That's your trouble Lucy – you don't think do you?"

Jennifer was once again massaging Charles, but this time it wasn't his shoulders. He'd arrived home and gone immediately upstairs to change out of his suit and she'd followed him up, sitting on the bed, watching whilst he took off his shirt and trousers, carelessly tossing them over his chair. Tantalisingly, she'd sprawled back against the pillows spreading her legs a little, and smiled at him.

He had glanced over at her, "You're not wearing knickers" he said breathily, and in answer she pulled up her dress and spread her legs further. It had been too much for Charles, who immediately started to feel his cock growing stiff as he had watched her playing with herself. Now she was taking him in her mouth and massaging his balls with the cup of her hand, and he was groaning in pleasure. "Hmmm, more darling more, squeeze a little more. Oh yes, just like that!!" He squirmed beneath her, and her mouth full with his cock still managed a tiny smile.

Later after dinner, as they were lounging around in the drawing room, she brought up the interview with Felix. Charles had forgotten all about it, "Darling I'm so sorry, I didn't remember – how did it go with the interview?"

"Very well actually. He was a nice lad, not a lad really though - twenty four. Very competent on a horse, Caitlin was impressed, and not that I know anything but even to me it was evident he knew what he was doing. He had good references but he made it clear it would probably be for the one season, which was the only blow really as he wanted to add it to his CV before settling into a career path, but at least he was up front about that. Caitlin was great, she made him ride Beano, he even tacked him up, and all in all I think he should do very well." She skirted around the issue of his horse, waiting for Charles to ask more.

"So, did you offer him the job?" he yawned clearly rather tired and bored and not really caring about the details.

"Of course not darling, I'm not that stupid, I said we'd let him know after I'd spoken to you. He came for tea afterwards and even dear old Mrs Fuller approved!" Jennifer knew the next part would be the make or break, but she was beginning to know how to handle Charles, to make him think everything was his idea.

"Well if Mrs Fuller approved, then he must be okay. If you and Caitlin like him, why not offer him a three month temporary contract to see how he gets on? Frankly darling, I'm pooped and I'd like to get an early night if you don't mind?"

Jennifer's heart starting beating a little faster, "Well there's just one thing, he has his own horse, although he did say he would put it in DIY livery locally, if we weren't keen? What do you think darling?"

Charles was mildly pissed off, not just with the fact that the lad wanted to bring his own horse, but that he was finished with the conversation. "Look, as I said give him the trial period, let him bring his horse, make sure that Caitlin keeps him in check and that he doesn't neglect my horses in favour of his own- that's all. If he's no good get rid of him after the contract is up. I leave it all up to you – okay? Call Cynthia in the office and get a contract drawn up, and make sure she checks out the references, now I'm knackered – shall we go up?"

Jennifer smiled to herself, "Okay sweetie, all fine with me" she took his hand and led him up the stairs, I handled that perfectly she thought.

CHAPTER 39

The next morning after Charles had gone to work, Jennifer tore out of the back door the gravel skidding under her shoes and over to the stables to see Caitlin who was scrubbing buckets outside the feed shed.

"We're on!" she exclaimed delightedly, a gleam in her eye. "Charles was fine about it, said we need to have a three month trial contract drawn up, and that as long as you make sure our horses come first he's fine about Felix bringing his own. Isn't that good news!"

Caitlin was astonished that Charles had agreed so easily, she thought he might've had a protest or two at least, she didn't like to think how or why he was being so amiable, but just that he was.

"Grand news Jennifer! Shall I ring Felix and tell him now? To be sure, I'm amazed Mr Charles agreed about the horse, 'twas something he'd never consider before."

Jennifer winked at her, "Just a bit of careful handling even though I say so myself. Seriously though, I'm really pleased, will be good for you Caitlin, you won't have to lug heavy stuff around anymore, someone one else to drive the truck and above all someone who smiles!" She laughed, "I didn't get to know Lucy much but she certainly seemed to have a chip on her shoulder."

"You're so right, Lucy did get me down and you don't realise how much hard work someone is till they've gone. Felix certainly seemed a happy go lucky sort, 'tis a pity though that he will only do a season, but I can't say I blame him, it would be a dead end job for him for ever." Caitlin agreed.

"Go on ring him, the sooner he comes, the sooner you'll be able to have some proper time off." urged Jennifer, "Look I've got to go, but I'll call Cynthia this morning, and organise the contract and get her to check the references. Have a good day, see you later." she

435

called and dashed helter-skelter back to the house.

Pete watched her from the garden chatting to Caitlin, he was tying up the straggling roses with some string. She was laughing and happy, it made him so angry to see her, she was an evil woman, his disordered mind ruminating wildly. She had to be stopped, he would have to be the one to do it. He wrung his hands together, the voices in his head egging him on - not even noticing that the penknife in his hands had cut his fingers to ribbons.

For once Paulene had made coffee before the others had got to the surgery, the delicious aroma was filtering through the office as Oli walked in, "Hmmm – I smell coffee. Wonderful just what I need, I've had a bitch of an 'on call' last night!" He walked into his office and Paulene trailed in behind him with a sheath of papers. "Oh no!" he groaned "what can't you read now?"

Paulene tutted, "I just hope that Grace can decipher your writing better than me. What the hell does this say?" she waved a piece of paper in front of him.

He took it, squinting at it closely, "Buggered if I know? Wait let me see, it was the visit to the Grant's, I sewed up a cut, so it must be ... suture, or is it rupture, anyway doesn't matter, the outcome is the same!"

"Oli!" Paulene was exasperated, "stop mucking about, suture it is. Here - coffee's ready. I must say," she added conversationally, "I'm looking forward to Grace coming, it will make a huge difference to me, you never know I might just catch up with myself."

"Yep, I bet you will - well we all will, I just hope she turns out okay. When did you arrange for her to start?"

"Next Monday, the day after the Puppy Show, she's coming in at 9.30, thought that would give me time to get rid of you lot on your rounds and us some time to sit quietly whilst I give her an idea of what the job entails. I don't want you to put her off before she even begins. She'd be out of this door like a shot!"

"Don't say that, I couldn't bear it! Oli groaned, "have you managed to put the ad in for the Vet Assistant yet?"

436

"Did it yesterday, going on line today and out in the various journals at their next publication, so we'll have to wait and see. You never know you might end up with some pretty young thing, that you'll enjoy initiating in every sense!" She laughed, "Just what you need."

"Not me, I've enough on my plate as it is, I'm not looking for another woman." he smiled grimly.

Grace was up to her elbows in cake mixture, she'd promised to make three for Sunday, and thought she had better get cracking, she could make them and put them in the freezer and ice them on the morning of the show. Her mind was darting all over the place, she was very excited about starting the job next week, but terrified too. What if she couldn't manage the work, what if she made a right Horlicks of everything? She licked some cake mixture off her thumb, running her finger along the bowl for some more. It was so strange how things had happened, not for the first time she wondered how Caitlin had found out about the vacancy - as far she could tell they had only just decided. Still, she had promised Caitlin she wouldn't say a word and as far as the vets and Paulene knew it all had just come up in conversation that morning. She didn't like being deceitful but in this instance she didn't really have a choice, but it was intriguing nonetheless. As far as the job was concerned, Paulene had confidently assured her that she would be given full training, the vets said so too and that the most important thing to them was that they knew she was totally trustworthy; not a good start really as far as she was concerned, but of course they didn't know that.

Oh to hell with it she thought, this cake mixture tasted strange. Oh Christ, she had forgotten to put in the bloody eggs, they were still there waiting on the table. She sighed and wondered if she would get away with adding them now, probably worth a shot, after all she'd always deny it was her cake if anyone said anything on Sunday – Oh No! Deceit again, what was the matter with her? Her mind was certainly not on the job, not on cake making that was! A brisk rap at the kitchen door made her look up quickly, she rubbed her hands on her jeans - more mess.

It was Patrick at the door, "Morning Gracie! Have you forgotten I was coming? "He started to laugh, "By the way do you know you've something on your nose!"

She quickly rubbed her nose - damned cake mixture. "Oh Patrick! I'm sorry, yes, it had completely slipped my mind." Christ, what was the matter with her, she'd only seen him last night. How could she think she could hold down a job when she couldn't even remember what happened yesterday!

"Put the kettle on, I'm gasping, been a long morning already and it's only ten thirty." He plonked himself down on a chair, pinching a bit of the cake mixture, "this tastes a bit odd, if you don't mind me saying so!"

"I know I forgot to put the wretched eggs in. I don't know what's up with me this morning." She laughed and put the kettle on. "Talking of eggs, the hens are laying well, would you like half a dozen?"

"Thanks, I'd love 'em, nothing like your eggs, especially when you forget to put them in cakes."

She cuffed him playfully around the ear, "You cheeky sod!"

"Tell you what though, in return I can give you a juicy bit of gossip! Guess who I've just seen pulling into Chloe's?"

"Surprise me?"

"Jennifer Parker-Smythe. Well, I was just leaving Chloe's, went there first thing to put a shoe on Katherine's horse, I was getting in the van and she drove past down the yard. I waited around a bit, fiddling with my phone, to see what she was up to, but she lingered too long in her car, almost as though she was waiting for me to go. Very odd I thought, she's not that friendly with Chloe that I know of?" He took another dip of the cake mixture, "Do you know I could get used to cake mix without eggs!"

"I didn't think she knew Chloe that well either, but she did invite her to the party, so perhaps they're matey after that?" Grace considered, "Oh, I know, I bet she's gone up to see Susie, I gather it was a friend of hers who went for the job at Nantes."

"Maybe, but it was a bit strange all the same, she's not horsey is she?" Patrick asked, "As far as I know she's terrified of them, or so

Caitlin said."

"Well I expect that's it, must be about the job" declared Grace, Can't think what else it would be."

Patrick scratched his nose, taking his tea from Grace, "What else indeed?"

"Talking of gossip, what about that Lucy last night! She's got some neck hasn't she?" Grace said indignantly, "After all the trouble she caused walking out like she did."

Patrick laughed, "She certainly has, and I pity poor old Tom, if she's got her claws into him. He didn't look very happy to me. She's a right tart!"

"It's not funny, she's trouble that one, I just hope she doesn't turn up on Sunday, would create a really bad atmosphere." Grace sipped her tea, and dipped into the mixture, "Can you imagine?"

"Add a bit of sport Grace, liven the show up a bit that's definite. You mark my words we haven't seen the last of juicy Lucy yet.

Laura was reporting back to Jonty about her meeting with the Sabs. She hadn't had a good time, she was upset too that it seemed pretty certain that Linda was now using and was out of it most of the time and that she was responsible. The Sabs themselves were a pretty fanatical bunch, and she reported that they were very interested in her ideas about targeting a specific hunt and that she knew someone who could be a mole for them.

"So you think you convinced them you're genuine then?" Jonty asked, "Sure? We don't want any fuck ups if they think you're a plant."

"No, it was alright, easier because Ewan and Sean introduced me, I don't think it would've been if they hadn't been there. They were dead cagey, didn't commit themselves one way or another, and I think it'll take a few more meetings till they trust me. All I've got to do now is feed them the information they want, so you'd better come good with that Jonty, I think they could be an ugly bunch if crossed."

Jonty laughed, "Ugly, don't make me laugh. They're just a load of do gooders, off their heads on dope, living like hippies. I'm glad Linda is using, you can keep pushing stuff her way, keep her sweet. Same with the others too, I don't mind making a bit of an investment."

"Jonty, that's a terrible thing to do and say, I know Linda is skanky but I don't want to be a party to making it worse. I won't do it."

Jonty grabbed her arm, wrenching her wrist right round, until she cried out in pain, "You'll do what I say Laura, or you will see how ugly I can get eh?" He dropped her arm, and she whimpered, and rubbed her wrist. "No fucking arguments, you do as you're told."

"Okay, okay, no need to get rough, but I don't like it Jonty, I really don't, it scares me."

"I'll scare you more than that if you don't do as I say Laura. Anyway you like a bit of pain now don't you?" He took hold of a cheek pinching it quite hard, "You're my little victim, look how you were with that Charlie boy, led him on, then got all high and mighty with the consequences. Lucky for me though."

"That's not how it was, he more or less raped me!" she screamed at him, "I'm not a bloody victim!"

"Now don't get all distraught, just do as you're told and things are fine – okay?"

Laura swallowed hard, "Okay, I'll do it, but what are you planning Jonty, why won't you tell me?"

Jonty stared at her with hard eyes, "You don't want to know Laura, so just shut it – don't push me any further, you're making me seriously angry, and you know what happens when I get angry." Laura did know and she had the sense to shut up. Jonty got up and found his mobile, "You did well Laura, now I need to speak to the lads, so when they come I want you to bugger off."

Laura was afraid, she wanted to know what was going on, but she didn't dare cross him further and knew when to back down. "Okay Jonty" she said meekly, the tears starting in her eyes.

Celia was furious, Charles had telephoned to ask her which three weeks during the school holidays he could have the children, so that they could all go away together. She had been very frosty with him, it was bad enough for her that the children had come back full of eager enthusiasm about what a great time they'd had staying with their Dad and Jennifer, and then that bloody woman had the gall to accompany them back with Charles on the Sunday. Like they were playing Sylvanian families! She had been fuming when she saw Jennifer, whom she'd had to admit was extremely pleasant and charming to her, as well she might be. Celia could hardly bring herself to speak to her, let alone look at her. When they had gone, Jessica had prattled on about what they had done, playing board games, the trip to Arundel Castle and the riding, and how marvellous Jennifer had been with Queenie when she got a bit excited. Celia became more and more angry. How dare Charles - that woman knew nothing about horses, how could he leave his daughter in her useless hands whilst she was riding. Celia was answering Jessica in monosyllables, when Jessica announced that they had even had tea in the kitchen with Mrs Fuller. Celia had whorled round, demanding to know who had been there, and was astonished to find out that it had not only been the children and Jennifer but Charles too. That would never have happened in her day! Tea was always taken in the morning room! Even Rupert who was usually so sour and surly was full of what they had done, and saying what fun they had together. Celia was livid. She knew she was being unreasonable and that it was good that when the children went to Nantes they had a fun time, but she felt usurped, moody and irrational.

Now Charles was asking to take them on holiday – on a safari of all things. She could hardly refuse could she, but it irked her nonetheless. At least Jessica and Rupert were back at school now and things seemed to have settled down, and then this phone call to upset the apple cart again, well she was not going to tell them. In her temper she screamed at her au pair, Eva, who was ironing in the kitchen, and then again at the gardener and then stomped upstairs to have a bath, which always calmed her down. Tonight Anthony was coming again and she hoped that the children would be on their best behaviour, she was getting on well with him, and she didn't want the children to spoil things. Trust Charles to put her in a bad mood, it was all his fault.

Lucy's phone beeped a text message, she was still off work, as it was not yet the obligatory three days before she could return to the Bistro. Although it was great not to have to go, her mother was driving her insane in the house. She looked at her phone excitedly – Weasel. She went into the bog and read the text '*B52, 6pm*', she sent a message back immediately, '*GR8*'. She sat down on the toilet, considering, it would be good to see them, she hoped that Jonty would come, she quite fancied him, although he had made no move on her at all. They were so much fun compared to Tom, who was a sweet guy but so fucking straight laced it wasn't true. Her mind wandered back to the evening in the Fox and that snooty fucking bitch Grace and her husband and realised what snobs they were and had spent the whole evening looking down on her. She had sent the text to Caitlin, prompted again by Tom on the way home, just a simple little message, saying she was sorry, she had acted rashly and no hard feelings. Caitlin, the good little Irish soul that she was had texted back, '*Thanks for the apology, no hard feelings at all, forget it.*' Lucy had been fuming, trust her to be so fucking forgiving, well what they didn't know was that Lucy wasn't really sorry at all. One day she'd pay them all back, every last one of them. She had a funny feeling that Jonty had another reason for wanting her to remain friends with them anyway, and if it involved a bit of trouble so much the better. Tonight she may well find out why. Roll on six pm. She ran herself a bath and began to shave her legs.

Charles had finished early and was catching the three thirty fast train home from London, he was bloody weary. Work was a bitch at the moment, and although he was very good at what he did, it took its toll every day. He would be glad to be home, how strange he thought, he had certainly changed, always been such a city boy, drinking and shagging till all hours and often staying in the flat and not bothering to come home - yet now it was like an oasis and he couldn't wait to get there. But one thing to do before he did, was to keep the appointment with Alex Corbett, and he was not looking forward to it one bit. The last thing he wanted to do was stir up trouble, but the thought of Pete losing control and hurting Jennifer was too much, he knew he had to act, it was in everyone's interest, however distasteful.

The train thrummed and rattled along the tracks, diving under tunnels and zooming through stations and he watched everything flashing past. He gazed in at the council blocks and scrub land by the side of the tracks, and the old Victorian houses terraced in rows with washing hanging out of windows and dusty tired trees battling to survive the ravages of the city, and he thought how fortunate he was to have what he did have and to live where he lived. His mind wandered back to the conversation earlier in the day with Celia. God she could be a pain in the arse! He was doomed if he didn't spent time with the kids and doomed if he did. Last weekend had been fun, they had all enjoyed it and the idea of going on a safari really appealed to him, and he was sure the children would love it. Okay so Jennifer might not be ready to do the riding part, but in a way that was good, because she could spend time with Jessica, whilst he and Rupert went and did 'boy' things. It would be really great, one thing about Jennifer was she was willing to give something a go and had a good laugh when she was doing it. As usual though Celia was putting all sorts of obstacles in their way, moaning about money, and how little help she had with the children and then in the next breath, moaning about the au pair and her gardener. In the end he had shut his ears to it and asked her just to get back to him with some dates and abruptly ended the call - sick of her. How had he lived with her all those years - had she always been like this, was that stiff snobbery inbred into her he wondered? Okay he could be an arse and he wasn't afraid to admit it, but she could be damned supercilious, just for once why couldn't she be nice? Deep in black thoughts of Celia, the train started to slow down, and he picked up his briefcase and paper and waited for the announcement. '*Horsham, the next stop is Horsham*' and the train slithered to an abrupt stop and he clambered out, clunking the carriage door closed after him.

Driving along the roads towards Fittlebury, he rehearsed what he was going to say to Alex. It was not an easy subject to discuss, Alex would no doubt plead that he had patient confidentiality to consider, but at least if he could alert him to a problem, they could go from there. He supposed that Alex could ask Pete to pop in and see him, or wondered if Pete still attended the hospital outpatients - after all it had been a few years since he had been an in-patient; how long did they follow them up for, Charles had no idea. He drove slowly as he approached the village, and drew up outside the village shop, he would buy Jennifer a bunch of flowers - they usually had a pretty good selection. He walked over to see what they had displayed outside under the awning and he picked up the biggest one and walked in to pay for it. Mrs Gupta was sitting like a huge Buddha behind the counter, her great brown eyes reading a magazine but she looked up smiling when he came in. Charles fished into his pocket for his wallet handing over the bouquet, smiling back at her.

"Afternoon Mrs Gupta, how are you today?"

"Good afternoon Mr Parker-Smythe, oh not so bad, and what about you?"

"Yes I'm fine thank you. Thought I'd buy Jennifer some flowers, these look nice." He flashed his charming smile at her, "and perhaps a box of those Belgian Truffles too." She turned around to get the chocolates wobbling, momentarily giddy and then steadied herself.

"Are you all right?" Charles called out in alarm, "I thought you were going to fall then."

"No, no thank you sir, just a bit dizzy for a moment I'm thinking. I'm fine now." She said breathlessly, supporting herself on the counter. "Are these the ones you were wanting?"

"If you're sure you're okay?" he hesitated, but she said no more casting her eyes down, "Yes, those are fine, thanks." He paid for the flowers and the truffles and bid her a hasty good afternoon. She had looked dreadful, mind you she was pretty overweight, and sitting behind that counter all day long she couldn't get much exercise.

Charles left the shop and turned left at the pub, past the little garage, and then stopped in the little surgery car park, he glanced at his watch, he was fine for time. Fittlebury was lucky to have its own small doctors' practice, although it had grown a lot since he was a little boy. He remembered originally it had been at old Dr Shipton's own house, with a consulting room off the hallway, where you waited to be seen in uncomfortable stiff wooden chairs with leather seats with big dips in the middle. God that had been eons ago, Dr Shipton had long gone and Alex Corbett was the senior GP along with another couple of doctors and they were now housed in this purpose built surgery, with modern consulting rooms, a treatment room, and its own little dispensing pharmacy. They even had their own nurse - Alex's wife, Diana; it was all very sophisticated from the old days. God, I am getting more like my mother every day he mused.

He sat down in the waiting room, glancing through an old copy of Horse & Hound, and waited to be called. He was deeply engrossed in a piece about the repeal of the Hunting Act. The Act had been passed in 2004 and became law in 2005 but it was considered unlawful in the opinion of many in that the bill had gone before the Lords and been rebuffed twice. A dodgy bit of legislation under the act of 1949 stated that the Commons could make anything law despite being twice rebuffed by the Lords. What sort of democracy was that he pondered - in other words it made the Lords obsolete. Of course it had been a Labour Party in power in 2004; although in the Tory election manifesto they had promised that Parliament would be given a free vote to repeal the Act. The Coalition Government now in power planned to honour that commitment by putting forward a motion on the issue - at an appropriate time apparently. There was a lot of lobbying as to when they would find the time. Meanwhile hunting still went on after a fashion where false trails were laid, but all in all it was a ridiculous Act, ill thought out and almost impossible to enforce. The article quoted Jim Paice last December, just before the traditional Boxing Day meets all over the country, as saying '*the hunting bill simply doesn't work*' and this was reinforced by the quarter of a million people who turned out on Boxing Day. Charles tutted quietly to himself, this was an issue that would wage on for a long time he knew. Alex Corbett appeared in the waiting room calling his name. At last Charles sighed, and replaced the magazine on the table and stood up to meet him.

CHAPTER 40

The weak sun had not long risen when Charles kissed Jennifer goodbye, and she mumbled a muffled response to him, he was already leaving for work to make up for skiving off early yesterday. Rolling over she glanced at the clock it was just after six in the morning, fighting the desire to go back to sleep she sat up in bed. It was really sweet of him to bring her the flowers and chocolates last night and they seemed to be drawing closer and closer these days. She was so looking forward to dinner at Katherine's this evening. What to wear though, that was a bit of a problem, should she ask Chloe what she was wearing, or ring Sophie and get her advice. She had masses of clothes in her wardrobe, but she wanted to get it just right. She was wide awake now, and slipped out of bed, putting on her slippers and disappeared into the bathroom turning on the shower and shoving her hair in a shower cap, she would wash it tonight before they went out. She hummed as she walked into the steaming water, thinking how good life her was.

Caitlin was awake early too, she couldn't sleep, tossing and turning in fitful dreams of Ace, and bizarrely Felix. The dream had left her feeling uneasy, she just hoped Felix's coming to Nantes would work out, she couldn't face another Lucy disaster. She thought grimly of Lucy and the text she had sent yesterday, ironically on the day that they had interviewed for her replacement. Caitlin had waited before she replied carefully composing her answer, and satisfied that is was as bland as boiled rice, sent it the same night. She hoped she would never see her again.

Felix aroused her curiosity though, why did he want to spend a season at Nantes? Not that it wasn't a nice cushy job, but he was hardly going to set the world on fire here was he, it would be awfully quiet for him, and him bringing his own horse was a bit of a worry. He'd been delighted when she rang him offering the job, and said he would give his notice in straight way, and that he could start at the end of the month. Ah well she thought it was done now.

Her mind drifted on to Charles' hasty visit yesterday when he had surprised her and dropped into the yard. She had thought it was about Felix, but he didn't mention him, other than to say he was pleased they'd found a new groom. No, he'd come to say that he'd seen Dr Corbett about Pete's erratic behaviour, and forewarned him that something was not quite right. As far as the doctor was concerned Pete was still taking his pills, but he'd make a medication review appointment for him. Charles had said that it was all that could be done under the circumstances but Caitlin must tell him straight away at the first sign of any more bizarre behaviour, and definitely not mention it to anyone else. Alex Corbett had promised Charles that he would let him know his findings. It all seemed as airy fairy as a dandelion clock to Caitlin, with a lot of ifs and buts, but she agreed she would keep an eye out.

She rolled over in bed, contemplating whether or not to get up yet, it was still early and she was tired and worried about her future. She longed for the day that she and Ace could be open about their relationship, go out for dinner together, or to the cinema, or to the pub – like a normal couple. It couldn't be much longer surely?

There was another person who was lying in bed wide awake long before the shrill beep of the alarm. Chloe couldn't remember the last time she had slept well, she either couldn't go to sleep, or she would waken in the early hours worrying, and fall into an unsatisfactory fitful doze after hours of agitation and anxiety. John, on the other hand, was dead to the world and she wondered how on earth he could sleep like he did when their marriage was seemingly in such crisis. Perhaps he didn't think it was, he might perceive that it was already over, she tortured herself again with the thought.

Tonight was Katherine's dinner party, she desperately hoped that it would be an opportunity for her and John to have some 'together' time and enjoy an informal meal with friends. He got on well with

Jeremy, and although he only knew Mark slightly, Charles and he had
known each other for years - ever since they moved to Mileoak. He
may well open up a bit more - she could drive so that he could have a
drink - a bit of the old amber nectar might make him relax and realise
what he was throwing away. There, she had thought it again, the
worst. John grunted and rolled over to hug her, nuzzling into her
neck, and wrapping his legs over her, she snuggled subconsciously
back into his familiar warmth and smell wanting to weep. He stirred
and started to run his hand over her breast, and she felt the old
familiar burn of desire tingle through her body. She felt her nipple
stiffen and respond to him, he reached up and kissed her, moving his
hand down to her hip and circling her tummy, already aroused, he
pushed against her leg allowing his hand to stray down further. She
tried to lose herself in the moment, concentrate on the feeling but she
could only wonder if he had been doing this to someone else, and the
thought sickened her. She couldn't help herself, her body stiffened
and she felt suffocated, gasping she pushed him away. John
misinterpreting, intensified his caress and started nibbling at her ear.
She felt like screaming, but managed to pull herself together,
swallowed hard and forced herself to relax. It was like being in bed
with a total stranger.

Sandy sat in her chair in her office, skimming files and making
notes on a yellow legal pad. The case was due to be heard next week,
but she'd a sneaky feeling that it would not get that far, the option of
settling out of court was becoming more attractive to the other side.
She would nail them to the wall otherwise in her normal ballsy
fashion, and she was pretty certain that this piece of aristocratic shit
would not want his dirty washing laundered so publically and boy she
had enough on him to make him cry. She was itching to get him, the
trouble with some of these toffs was they thought they were above the
law, well tough they weren't, and it was at times like this that she
loved her job supremely. She sighed putting down her pen, looking
out of the window, it was so inviting outside and she wished she
could be cantering on the downs on Seamus. Still it was work that
paid for him and his keep, so nose to the grindstone, she got back on
with her notes. She worked steadily on, her pen scratching page after
page, highlighting one thing then another in her usual meticulous
way, smiling to herself with satisfaction as she made more headway

into the case. The mobile rang and interrupted her train of thought, she groaned and put down her pen, seizing it up in irritation and then smiled, it was Mark.

"Hi, how are you this afternoon?" he asked in his deep brown sexy voice which made her insides squirm, "not interrupting you am I?"

"No, I'm just wrapping up some stuff for a case next week, anyway always lovely to hear from you sexy."

"You smooth talker! Bet you say that to all your callers." he scoffed, thinking of how he had last seen her, naked and tousled in bed this morning.

"It's my job!" She laughed, "You know me, always a silver tongue!"

"Hmmm yes, you do have a lovely tongue it's true." he flirted lazily, "Just wondered what time tonight? I've got a meeting with the estate solicitor at four, which should be fairly straight forward, it's only about the Old Mill discussing some covenants Lady V wants to put in, so shall I come round about six ish?"

"Perfect, that'll give me time to wind up here, and then I'm going straight home, the girls have done Seamus for me today. So see you later, that'll give us plenty of time."

"Good, I like to take my time." he said softly, "lots of time!"

"I know sweetie - me too!"

She ended the call, and sat quite still for a while thinking of Mark, their relationship was going so well, and that in itself was frightening, she felt she was wearing her heart on her sleeve and was sure something would go wrong at any minute, like finding out he had a double life and whole hidden family in Scotland for example, just like the bastard in the case she was working on.

It had been such a short time they had been seeing each other, but in another way it felt like a lifetime. They fitted together like two perfectly matching gloves, mutual physical desire when they wanted to tear each other's clothes off, but each equally respecting their professional and personal lives, but nonetheless interested in it too. It was a rare combination, and she wanted to throw herself whole heartedly into the crackle and firework fizz of these initial exciting days, where you looked at your phone every five minutes to see if he had texted, and you could feel the touch of him on your body long after you had left him, and the pure delight of exploration of each other. It was a seemingly idyllic relationship, but underneath her confident patina she was anxious about being hurt. All a bit late to be worrying about that now though, because whatever the future was for her and Mark, if she lost him now emotionally she would be up a gum tree. Why couldn't she just enjoy him and take off the hand brake of her feelings and stop judging Mark against her other disastrous relationships. She must pull herself together she thought determinedly, stop destructive bloody ruminating and start constructive romancing.

Katherine was whizzing around her super-duper new age kitchen, half listening to the afternoon play on Radio Four. For the hundredth time she wondered why she organised these things, it had all seemed like a good idea at the time, and what was going to be a small intimate evening with John and Chloe, she now had a full blown supper party to organise. Although actually she did enjoy cooking and it was nice to making something more exciting than the meal for two she did for her and Jeremy every evening. She had ridden early this morning and then afterwards had dashed around Marks and Sparks for the grub, stopping off on the way back at the farm shop for the meat. Luckily none of them were bloody vegetarians. She had decided on slow roast belly of pork - Jamie Oliver style, Jersey new potatoes, baby courgettes and new season carrots, It was a great recipe and the pork was always succulent. A light starter of langoustines and rocket and a strawberry tart to follow – should be fine and not too taxing.

She had decided against having too formal an affair in the dining room preferring to eat in the orangery, which was light and cool and gave a Mediterranean feel with all the aromatic climbers which filled the room with their heady scent in the evenings. She hoped that the relaxed atmosphere would make John unwind and give an invitation for him to open up, which after all, was the purpose of the evening. She wondered again what was the matter with him, it had to be another woman, all her instincts told her that, the secrecy about his phone, the late nights back home, the distraction with the Chloe and the kids, although to be fair she didn't think the children had noticed. They were so ebullient and confident, their wild and carefree childhood appeared so far to be untroubled by their parents' problems. No, she couldn't think of what else it could be, other than he may possibly be ill, but he certainly looked well enough, if anything he looked more attractive than he had ever been. She had always slightly envied Chloe her fairy tale handsome husband. Jeremy, bless him, was getting a bit thin on top and in the thatch at the sides she had noticed grey streaks starting to become more prominent, so whilst he was not classically striking, he was the kindest most generous man and this shone through in his face. Handsome is as handsome does she thought grimly. She started to hull the strawberries, popping one in her mouth every so often. God they were gorgeous at this time of year!

Her mind wandered on to the next affiliated horse trials at Rackham in a couple of weeks, she was excited and looking forward to it, she couldn't believe how far she had come in such a short while, thanks to Chloe and of course to her lovely first horse Polly. She reminisced fondly of the mare, she had been a wonderful start for her to come back to riding, and she wondered how she was getting on now with her new owner. They had kept in touch to start with and she heard news from Chloe, who taught the lady, but she knew it would break her heart to see her again, and of course she now had the lovely Alfie and he had proven such a good choice, even if he had been bloody expensive. Jeremy hadn't minded though, and that was another thing she loved about him, he certainly wasn't mean. She finished the strawberries, snaffling another before putting them in the fridge and went to lay the table in the Orangery, she just hoped for Chloe's sake, that it wasn't John who was doing the laying.

For Jennifer the day had sped past, riding first of course and then she had dashed over to Penfolds the saddlers in Cuckfield for some other bits and bobs. She had become fascinated with the shop and was forever pouring over internet sites of things she needed. She stopped off at the florist in Cuckfield to buy some flowers for Katherine, and the girl in the shop had been so helpful and the heady scent of them was filling the car as she drove home. It was a lovely day, not too hot with a breath of warm breeze taking the fierceness out of the sun, and she drove slowly, always on the lookout these days for horses on the road. She passed Prior's Cross and looked up at the old abbey lurking like a sinister skull on the hillside, thinking of the day they had seen those two people up there, when they had been out hacking, it was a great meeting place for lovers. The hedgerows were overgrown now, stuffed full of wild flowers making the roads seem even narrower than they really were, and she carefully negotiated the bend. Up ahead she saw an old Landrover squeezed onto the verge on the other side of the lane, making it almost impossible to pass without slowing right down. The two people in the Landrover stared at her as she passed and then, at the last minute as her eyes met those of the driver, he waved to her and she waved back wondering who they were. Oh well - no idea probably some hunting cronies of Charles' she had met at some point or another. She quickly forgot about them, thinking of the evening ahead and what she was going to wear.

Jonty watched the silver Mercedes slow down to pass them, the blonde haired woman driving had stared at them hard, she was certainly a looker, with her sunglasses perched on her head. He knew it was Jennifer, recognising the car and at the last minute had decided to wave and she had smiled and acknowledged him back – silly tart, she didn't know what she had coming.

"Our lucky day mate! That's her" he said to Weasel, "stuck up cunt."

Weasel screwed himself around to look at the back of the Mercedes as it pulled past them. "Fuck me she's a class bit of skirt. You sure it's her?"

"Yeah Lucy said she had a silver Mercedes and I saw one just like it in the garage when Laura and I gate crashed their fucking party. Gotta be her. Nice to get a good eyeball of the target."

"Why d' ya wave for then, we don't want her to know us and this old bus aint especially discreet."

Jonty snarled. "Oh but we do wanna be seen you fucker, we do. This car needs to be conspicuous." He licked his lips, the sweat on his forehead forming into tight beads, "fuck me I'm hot, let's get going."

They fell out of the Landrover, and started walking towards the

Abbey. "Christ it's a pull up here" he panted as they climbed up the hill surveying the view as they walked. The vista was stunning stretching far away cross the bosky downs with a heat haze rising over the fields, the different shades of green edging into the sandy yellow of the hills in the distance.

"You can see for fucking miles here mate."

"That's not good is it? I don't get you, the more cover the better." Weasel moaned, "don't see how we can do it mate."

Jonty grinned to himself, "You will, you will, let me take you through it 'cos this is the crucial part."

He led Weasel over to the ruins and towards the footpath they had taken before, the one leading to the Old Mill, gesturing with his hand this way and that, back towards the Abbey and beyond and then down to the speck of the Landrover on the road.

Weasel started to laugh "Fuck me mate, it could seriously come off, I can see it all now, but it'll take careful planning and a lot of back up, who you gonna use?"

"No worries back up is all arranged and best you don't know, but we're in no hurry – it'll be a few fucking months to set it up." He punched Weasel in his side, "it's a steal mate – in more ways than one!"

Jennifer, oblivious to Weasel and Jonty, sped home towards Nantes, she might just have time for a swim before she went upstairs to get ready, it was such a glorious day and the thought of the crystal water of the pool was very tempting. She swooped down the drive, to find Caitlin just pulling out in her Peugeot. She looked a bit red-faced thought Jennifer, and slowed down to speak to her, but Caitlin jumped in first.

"Oh Jennifer, I'm just popping out to the shop, hope that's okay now, I won't be long? What a grand day it's turned out to be."

Jennifer looked at her carefully, she looked guilty, although she may just be imagining things and for the life of her she couldn't think why she should be - she'd told Caitlin often enough she was her own boss as far as she was concerned and if she needed to go out it was fine with her. She laughed, "No problem, I was just going to say if you fancy coming over for a swim, that's absolutely fine, make use of the pool whilst the weather is so lovely. Just help yourself, there's towels and stuff in the pool house. Gotta dash, have a good afternoon!" and with that she carried on down towards the garages.

Caitlin was open mouthed, to be told she could swim in the pool was unheard of - Celia had never permitted the staff that kind of luxury, but Jennifer was happily inviting her to help herself. Blimey!

Jennifer parked the car, picking up the flowers and her handbag and sped down the corridor towards the scullery, calling to Mrs Fuller that she was home. She plonked the flower arrangement in a vase till later, not bothering to stop off in the kitchen for anything to eat, and sprinted back to the hall and up the stairs two at a time. She ran into her room, throwing off her clothes onto the bed and rummaging about found a bikini in her draw and snatching up her cotton robe from the back of the door, padded barefoot back down the stairs to the pool.

It was simply lovely, the glittering water lapped gently against the pool sides and the smell of the summer jasmine and honeysuckle filled the air mingling with the sound of the bees buzzing in and out of the flowers and the shrill birdsong. She sighed, this was just perfect, so serene, she was lucky she reflected, to be able to enjoy all this. Throwing off her robe, she sat on the pool edge dangling her feet in the water, and throwing back her carefully sun screened face to the sky, the warmth of the rays kissed her cheeks.

She pushed her hair back and slid into the pool allowing herself to sink right under its sparkling depth and the whole sound of the world was instantly shut out. Blissful she thought as she felt the velvety water encase her. She allowed herself to sink right down and as soon as her feet touched the bottom she pushed herself gently back up - but as she floated upwards to the surface she was suddenly aware of a dark shadow cast across the water, momentarily blotting out the sun. Seemingly from nowhere - something forced her head back under the water and in that instant she felt a rising panic. A powerful hand was aggressively holding her down under the water and she felt herself struggling to try to get away, but whoever it was clutched her by her hair, so that she couldn't escape their vicious grasp. She writhed and twisted, fighting with all her strength until her lungs were bursting, they were very strong and the more she struggled the further her head was forced under. A red hot fire raged in her chest as she burned to breathe the air, she knew that she couldn't hold her breath for much longer, already she felt as though she would explode. As she grew weaker her arms flailing uselessly, the urge to breath became too much and she started to take in water. Her thoughts were racing, - desperately thrashing hopelessly as her lungs filled with the water, and just as suddenly she just gave up fighting, feeling her body going limp and relaxed - almost weightless and absurdly thinking that this was not a bad way to die.

As she stopped struggling and her body went floppy, she felt the hand momentarily release its pressure, her mind snapped into refocus and in a last desperate attempt she plunged away and into the centre of the pool and bobbed up to the surface spluttering and coughing, gasping for breath. Her head felt huge and swollen - the pain in her chest was so intense that for a moment she sunk again, but this time revitalised by the tantalising gasp of air, her survival instincts forced her to struggle to the surface, choking and wheezing. Rubbing her eyes desperately with her hands she tried to make out through the blur of water just whose hand it had been, but when she finally managed to see clearly - whoever it was had gone.

Instinctively, she knew that she had to get back to the side, she felt so weak stuck out in the middle of the pool just treading water, but the terror that whoever it had been might just come back made her stay where she was, and then her heart raced all the more as she heard the sound of footsteps padding along the side of the terrace, and she started to panic. She tried to think but her brain didn't seem to be working properly, she was exhausted and gasping for breath, and didn't know how long she could stay afloat. Even if she got to the edge and tried to make a run for it, she knew she just wouldn't have the energy to escape. Her heart was hammering desperately having only nanoseconds to make a decision, and then to her enormous relief, a bikini clad Caitlin came round the edge of the trellis, carrying a towel.

She tried to scream but her voice came out croaking and faint, "Caitlin, help me! Help me. Please - help me, someone's just tried to drown me!"

Caitlin didn't hesitate and launched into the pool swimming

fiercely towards Jennifer, grabbing her, and dragging her to the shallow end, where they could both stand up.

"What happened Jennifer" Caitlin asked urgently, holding the hysterical Jennifer by both shoulders, "What d' you mean?"

Jennifer was trembling, her breath rasping, "Oh Caitlin someone tried to drown me, I didn't see who it was, I was terrified! They held my head under the water, grabbing my hair so I couldn't get away!" She began to cry and shake. Caitlin just stared at her open mouthed before ushering her out of the pool, and wrapping her in a towel, "Who would do such a thing?" she sobbed.

Caitlin was in shock herself, she wrapped her arms around the terrified Jennifer to comfort her. Holy Mary it was just pure chance that she had decided to take Jennifer up on her offer of the swim and came when she did, deciding to make the best of the afternoon, but moments before, as she had come down the path around the back of the garden, she had seen Pete slink away across the lawn from the pool.

Charles was sweating on the stuffy train, coming home early to avoid the Friday night commuters. He huffed exasperatedly when his phone rang and glanced around him, he always hated people who spoke loudly into their mobiles, especially on the train where you knew everyone was listening. He was surprised to see the caller was Caitlin and he answered immediately, knowing it must be urgent. Caitlin was almost incoherent, stammering and blustering, and finally breathlessly told him what had happened. Charles, keeping his voice as low as possible asked her to repeat it all again calmly, confirming that Jennifer was fine and was in the kitchen with Mrs Fuller, recovering from her ordeal with a cup of tea.

Charles could hardly take it all in, he felt physically sick. Christ, he thought, that fucking lunatic Pete was dangerous, and moreover he felt responsible, Mrs Fuller and Caitlin had warned him about his mental state, and all he had done was make an appointment to see bloody Alex Corbett. Thank God Jennifer was safe for the time being, how would he have felt if the outcome had been different, he would never have lived with himself. Meanwhile he had to take some action, he had to do something but he felt pretty helpless trapped in the train.

He told Caitlin to stay with Jennifer and Mrs Fuller in the kitchen and that he would be home within the hour. Neither she nor Mrs Fuller was to mention about Pete, nor leave Jennifer alone until he was back.

Angrily he dialled Alex Corbett's number and was lucky enough to find him in the surgery, once he got past the defensive receptionist, what a fucking obstructive woman she was - didn't she realise this was serious. Alex listened to Charles whilst he recounted what had happened, with Charles getting really worked up the more he thought and talked about it. He irately insisted that Alex do something immediately and that once he was home he was going to call the police, who would act even if he didn't. Directly Alex had made sure that Jennifer was okay, he tried to calm Charles down, saying that he would go straight away to Nantes with a psychiatric social worker and that they would section Pete under the Mental Health Act if necessary. Charles was only marginally mollified and still seething as he ended the call, and then seeing the astonishment of the other passengers who had been listening agog, resisted the urge to tell them all to fuck off and turned his head to gaze agitatedly out of the window. He couldn't wait to get back home.

Meanwhile, Jennifer was looking pale and traumatised, sitting drinking sweet tea with Mrs Fuller in the kitchen when Caitlin came back, she smiled weakly at her and bleakly thanked her for her help. Mrs Fuller glanced at Caitlin, who shot back a warning look.

"I've rung Mr Charles and he's on his way home now and shouldn't be long, in the meantime he says we're all to stay here till he gets back."

Caitlin put her hand on Jennifer's shoulders which were still wrapped in the towel, and Jennifer reached up and took her hand. She looked dreadful, as well she might thought Caitlin, another few minutes and it didn't bear thinking about what might have happened. Thank the Lord that she had gone over when she did. They waited in silence, the ticking clock seemed so loud and the minutes dragged past.

Jennifer was perking up a bit after the tea, saying she was fine now and perhaps it was not as sinister as she'd thought, expecting Mrs Fuller and Caitlin to agree with her, but instead they said nothing, just looked anxiously at each other - neither of them knowing quite what to say. Both looked mightily relieved when they heard the sound of a screeching car on the drive, the gravel spraying up as it came to a lightening stop, the slam of a door and running footsteps down the passage to the kitchen. Charles charged through the door took one look at Jennifer and gathered her up in his arms, kissing her damp hair and stroking her face. Jennifer took one look at him and burst into tears, clinging onto him sobbing for all she was worth.

It was not long afterwards that two more cars came down the drive. Charles disentangled himself from Jennifer and asked Caitlin to come with him. "Darling, Caitlin and I have something to do, Mrs Fuller will take care of you for a while, and I promise I'll be back directly."

Jennifer looked pleadingly at him, "Please don't leave me" she said weakly, tears threatening to come again, "I'm okay but I really need you to stay with me."

Charles held her close, "I promise darling, I'll only be gone a little while and be straight back. Be a good girl and let Mrs Fuller take care of you." Jennifer was too fragile and shocked to argue, and Charles hurried out of the door with Caitlin.

Alex Corbett was getting his bag out from the passenger seat and introduced the woman in the other car. "Charles, you made good time, nasty business? This is Susan Marsh, she's a psychiatric social worker and she knows Pete. Now where is he now - do we know?"

They looked at Caitlin who gestured helplessly, "last I saw of him he was crossing the lawn heading towards his cottage, but obviously I didn't follow him, I was helping Mrs Parker-Smythe."

"Let's try the cottage" Charles urged, "Jennifer is safe and in the kitchen with Mrs Fuller." They walked across the formal lawn, around the rose arbour towards the wild flower garden taking the quickest route to the cottage. Caitlin's heart was slugging hard against her ribs, she had seen Pete in one of his incoherent psychotic rages and she didn't want to be on the receiving end of one.

The cottage lay sleeping in the sunshine, masked with rambling roses and seemed eerily silent. They tiptoed up to the back door, which was wide open and gingerly stepped inside.

Charles called out "Pete, Pete, are you at home?" There was no answer, his voice echoed around the empty scrubbed kitchen, and looking cautiously at one another, they moved through to the sitting room. No-one was there, the place was as usual, spotless and Susan looked around assessing the room, taking in the obsessional and sparse belongings. "He must be upstairs" said Charles, making to go up the rickety stair case.

Susan motioned him to stop. "Let me go" she said "we have to deal carefully with this and I know him when he's psychotic."

Charles was not about to disagree and Caitlin who had been lurking in the sitting room door was mightily relieved. Susan trod carefully up the creaking steps, calling out all the time and then disappeared. The others waited silently and it was only moments later when she reappeared "he's not here" she said in a worried tone, "let's search the gardens."

They all trudged back out into the blinding sunlight, splitting into pairs and systematically combed the grounds. They searched for a long time, scouring the bushes and every conceivable hiding place, fully aware that he could just be watching them, but eventually and reluctantly they called a halt. Nothing, Pete had disappeared without a trace.

CHAPTER 41

Sandy had just got home, she tossed her keys and briefcase onto the kitchen table and opened the fridge taking out some ice cold water and poured herself a large glass. Wandering over to the casement windows and throwing them open she stepped out onto the terrace - it was a glorious afternoon, the candy striped pink and white clematis was running riot over the loggia, the enormous flower heads nodding in a gentle breeze. She put down her glass for a moment, slipped off her shoes and wriggled out of her tights, throwing them with her jacket over one of the chairs and walked barefoot onto the lawn to inspect her garden. The soft grass was cool against her feet as she padded across towards the flower beds which were a passion of colour at this time of year. The herbaceous border was really spectacular, crammed with elegant spiky delphiniums in a variety of striking shades of blue, big fat peony heads heavy with petals were like exquisite jewels, in a mass of pinks ranging from the most delicate shell to a dramatic cerise. Stuffed in between were bushy green Phlox yet to burst into white flowers and the whole bed was sprinkled with the dancing ballerina heads of Aquilegia. Her gardener had done a good job - it was certainly impressive. Sandy had wanted to make little pockets of interest in the garden, and there was a small wooden love seat, painted blue under the shade of an enormous old fashioned Rugosa rose in the deepest purple, its lofty old branches were smothered with blooms, and beside it several yellow and orange Azaleas of varying heights, combined to make the most pungent and evocative scent.

She sat down in the seat and lifted her legs up to inspect them – she could do with a bit of tan, they were pretty anaemic encased in stockings all day, perhaps she should consider one of those quick tan booths. She closed her eyes, allowing herself a moment of pure relaxation for the first time that day, her face embracing the sun. She felt truly content, and that was how Mark saw her as he walked around the side of the house - he stopped and watched her for a moment.

"Hi" he called out to her, hoping he hadn't made her jump, "you look like you're really relaxed – sorry to spoil it." He walked over as she opened her eyes and sat up, and he kissed her slowly and gently on the lips, his hands cupping her face.

"Hmm, my day just got better" she murmured, "It's Friday night, the weekend ahead, the sun is shining and I've just been kissed by the most sexy man, nothing could spoil it."

He laughed and sat down beside her on the other side of the seat, wrenching off his tie and tossing his jacket on the lawn before taking a swig of her water on the little table between them, and then reaching over to take her hand in the other. "This is heaven, the garden looks fabulous. I haven't really taken much notice of it before."

"Too interested in upstairs!" she laughed "No, I'm not serious. We've just never had any time to be out here much, but it is lovely, perhaps we could do a barbie this weekend, if the weather holds?" She could have bitten her tongue out - she was just assuming that he wanted to spend the weekend here, "that's if you've no other plans" she added tentatively.

"Sandy, I can think of nothing I'd like better than to spend the weekend with you." Mark turned towards her, "I know you think this is all going a bit fast, but I've never been happier, and I hope you are too, I don't want to scare you off."

Sandy grinned thinking of her earlier misgivings – romance not ruminate, "You certainly haven't done that, I'm enjoying every minute. The only trouble is I'll need to go food shopping at some point, as the cupboard is bare, and I haven't had a spare minute to do an online order – luckily we're out tonight."

"Ah, we can go shopping together like an old married couple What could be nicer?"

Sandy contemplated the couple remark, and decided she liked it, laughingly responded "Nothing could be nicer." She picked up his hand still clasped in hers and kissed it, "Waitrose, it's a date, you old romantic you! Come on, I need to get out of my work clothes and into the shower, and that's an invitation!" She smiled at him twinkling her eyes, and got up. Mark didn't need asking again.

Later, they were both sprawled naked on her bed, a soft breeze rippling the curtains at the open window, both relaxed and sleepy, Sandy stroking his belly, and Mark resting with eyes closed. "I meant to ask you darling, how did your meeting go about the Old Mill?"

Mark opened his eyes and rolled over to face her, circling his arm around her, "Oh well, it may not be as easy as I thought, I think there'll be some opposition to the conversion, as the mill will fall under the category of listed buildings by English Heritage, and because of its age they will be notified of any planning application and will take an interest in any proposed development. They can get mighty shirty if they think it'll be changed for anything not in keeping with the environment."

"I suppose you can understand that, after all, it must have been an integral part of village life and as such would have enormous historical importance. Do you think there will much opposition?"

"Well depends on what sort of plans Andrew has for the old place. If he does it up in keeping it should be okay, obviously they will keep a careful eye on all the work, and of course, it has to be in his favour that he is prepared to do it up, after all it is only going to rack and ruin now. It just makes the whole process much longer. It could be months before any plans can be drawn up, let alone passed. Bloody headache for me and everyone else." he moaned, "Still, if he's keen it'll be worth it, and it would be a great asset to the area, and would guarantee the mill's survival" He sighed "He may even be entitled to all sorts of grants to help which could be a bonus, but what should've been an easy transaction will be a lot more complicated, but d' you know, I don't want to think about that now." He kissed the top of her head, "roll over and I'll give your back a massage." Sandy squirmed onto her front, and allowed his delicious hands to work their magic and ease away the tensions of the day.

Katherine was putting the final touches to the table, she was pleased with the effect, it looked fabulous. She had bought some new rattan furniture at the beginning of the summer and it made for informal yet chic dining, with its huge glass covered table and pacific chairs, with their squashy striped cushions. The glass orangery was one of her most favourite places in the house - except for her kitchen. It was a stunning room, built in Georgian style and the wide double doors opened directly onto a paved pool area surrounded by a miniature boxed hedge, and at the far end was the pool house, similarly glassed and domed to match the orangery. It had been baking hot earlier in the day, and Katherine had flung open the doors and windows, a slight breeze wafted in, which, with the huge colonial fans whirring overhead had made it much more bearable. The dense green leaves cascading along the eaves were thriving in the tropical atmosphere, and were dotted with fairy lights. She had also added some discreet candles in huge glass domes around the room giving just the right amount of intimacy for a relaxed supper with friends. Perfect.

She gave one last look around and went back through to the kitchen to check on the food. Mmmm, it smelt very good, and she opened the oven door to check on the pork - yummy! The tart was already made and the starters assembled and in the fridge, so she could leave the rest of it all for a bit and go upstairs to have a bath before Jeremy got home. He could sort out the wine, but she had already chilled some champagne ready so there was not much for him to do - just as well, he would be knackered after the Friday night journey home on the train. She hummed to herself as she went up the stairs and into her room, running a bath and slipping off her clothes. The bath was almost filled - the bubbles frothy and foaming enticingly, when she heard the phone ringing. Bugger she thought – bloody bad timing.

Turning off the taps she slipped on a bath robe and padded back into the bedroom. "Hello, 679487" she answered, it was probably one of those damned cold callers, so she got ready to put the phone down.

"Katherine, it's Charles speaking" a deep drawling voice replied, "I'm so sorry but I need to talk to you about tonight. Something's happened to Jennifer today and I don't think we'll be able to come."

"Oh Charles, what on earth do you mean? What's happened, is she all right?" Katherine gasped, slumping down on the bed, "She was so looking forward to coming."

"I know Katherine, we both were" he said bleakly, "she's fine now but has had an awful shock, and at the moment I don't think she is in a fit state to do anything much."

463

"What do you mean? Is there anything that I can do? What in heaven's name happened?" Katherine had only seen Jennifer briefly this morning and she had looked absolutely radiant.

"Well, I don't know where to begin really, but of course you must know, and naturally tell the others too, but if you could all keep this under your hats for the time being, we'd be very grateful. It's not the sort of thing that I'd want bandied about, Jennifer has had to endure enough gossip in the past, and I don't want to make it any worse." Charles sighed and took a deep breath and told Katherine the whole story, including Pete's strange behaviour leading up to his attack on Jennifer, and ending with his disappearance. "Naturally, it's been a dreadful ordeal for her and whilst physically she's okay, she's in a bit of state."

"My God, I can hardly believe it, poor poor Jennifer, what a simply dreadful thing to have happened. She must've been terrified poor love. Is there anything that I can do?" Katherine was so shocked she fired the questions out one after the other, "Do you want me to come over? Would that help? So you've no idea where Pete is now?" she rattled on, "Thank God Caitlin arrived, it beggar's belief what might have happened!"

Charles agreed, "Yes, thank the Lord for Caitlin, and no, no need to come over, she's actually bearing up extremely well now, but I'm really concerned about her especially now Pete has disappeared." Charles gritted his teeth, bloody bloke he would kill him if he found him.

"Look Charles, you might think this is the wrong thing, but it could be a good idea to come along tonight, take your minds of it all - after all there's nothing that you can do now about Pete, the authorities will find him soon enough, and you need to live your life as normally as possible and put it behind you." She added, "There's no pressure here, I can tell everyone what's happened so that you don't have to talk about it if you don't want to, but it would stop Jennifer brooding, and you never know she may enjoy herself – you too."

"Ah that's really kind of you Katherine but I don't think so, we wouldn't be much company."

"Why not ask Jennifer and see what she thinks? You might be

surprised - she's more resilient than we give her credit for. Give me a ring back and let me know"

Charles hesitated, he was not sure it would be a good idea, but he owed it to Jennifer to ask her at least, "Okay, I'll call you back."

Katherine was shocked, she replaced the receiver and looked at the phone, staggered by the news. She barely knew Pete, but it was hard to credit someone could be that mad, and moreover where had he gone? Until he was found Jennifer would be on a knife edge and who could blame her, in fact they all would be.

Jennifer was lying on the bed in their room when Charles returned. He sat beside her and stroked her hair, "How're you feeling darling?" he looked at her, his eyes worried and anxious.

She sat up "I'm okay you know, I truly feel a lot brighter now you're home; I feel safe again. It's been like a nasty dream but I've woken up." She took his hand, cradling it to her face, "I still find it hard to believe it of Pete, I knew he didn't like me, but never dreamt he do something like that."

"None of us did, although I should have taken more notice, I blame myself totally, you kept telling me how difficult he was being. Of course, the man is mentally ill, and once they find him he'll have treatment, but I swear I'll never have him back here again. The thought of losing you my darling, I couldn't bear it." He began to tremble at the enormity of it all suddenly sinking in, "Thank God you're all right."

Jennifer seized him by the shoulders and made him look her squarely in the face, "I'm made of much tougher stuff! Don't forget where I was brought up - the East End is much worse, it was just unexpected! Now come on don't treat me like an invalid." She slid off the bed marching determinedly towards their dressing room, "Now what time is it, we had better get a shove on, if we're going to Katherine's."

Charles looked awkward, "Well I rang and said we weren't going, I explained about this afternoon and cancelled, although

Katherine did say we ought to come and not sit at home and brood. Are you sure you want to?" He looked a bit embarrassed, "I did say I would call her back and let her know."

Jennifer picked up his phone and handed it to him, "Call her, and say we're definitely coming, I've been looking forward to this and I'm not letting that nutter spoil my evening or anything else in my life for that matter!"

Lily was sitting at the kitchen table arduously learning her spellings, she poured over her book, writing them down laboriously and then chanting them out loud. "Bugger, I can never remember the difference between necessary and successful!" she moaned.

Chloe turned around from cooking their supper, "Remember – to be successful, you need two 'c's and two 's's, but it's only necessary to have one 'c'! Chloe laughed at her, "It's tricky but remember that rhyme and it makes all the difference."

Lily looked delighted "That makes it a whole lot easier! What's for tea?"

"Spag Bol, and don't forget Daddy and I are going out tonight to Katherine's, so Susie is going to look after you, so be good for her eh?" Chloe chucked the mince into the pan, "Go to bed when she asks you and don't be naughty."

"I'm never badly behaved." said Lily seriously, "only other people are." She looked pointedly at Toby and Rory. "The boys on the other hand are very naughty! They never want to go to bed."

"Oooh Lily, how can you say that!" squealed Toby, looking up from his homework, "you always argue."

"No I don't!" shouted Lily crossly, glaring at her brother, who stuck out his tongue.

"There you go" said Toby, "Arguing again!"

"Mummy tell him to stop!" shouted Lily, hurling a rubber a Toby, just missing Rory who was making a Lego model.

"Stop it the lot of you - I won't have you being naughty for Susie, she's doing me a favour tonight, so don't let me down." She bent down to give Rory a hug, "That's lovely darling, you've made a super job of that."

Rory rewarded her with his lovely smile, saying "they always argue Mummy, what a waste of time." Toby and Lily rounded on him both shrieking out and squabbling, Chloe sighed, Rory ignored them and carried on with his Lego. She wondered for the hundredth time how Rory had become so philosophical at his tender age. She stroked his hair, and went back to the stove, the mince sizzling and hissing. She stirred it thoughtfully, she hoped John would be back on time, she didn't want to be late at Katherine's. Despite her own gloom of late she was looking forward to this evening. John didn't want to go much but he was trying hard to be nice to her so had agreed, she looked fondly at the sad bunch of flowers drooping in their vase on the window sill. He had bought them for her from the garage yesterday and they were already dying - like their marriage she sighed. She must pull herself together she thought angrily, she was no fun to be with when she was like this, no wonder he was fed up with her, she was fed up with herself. She slung in a can of tomatoes to the mince, hastily chopping up some basil, and made herself a cup of tea and sat down at the table with the children, testing Lily on her spellings waiting for John to come home.

Jeremy leant up against the kitchen work top, admiring Katherine as she decanted some cream into a jug. She looked lovely, her burnished chestnut hair cut in a smart bob was shining, and her pretty heart shaped face needed the minimum of make-up to enhance her jade green eyes. Her figure looked svelte in cream linen trousers and a pink silk camisole, a single pearl on a fine silver chain around her neck. She put the jug back into the fridge and turned to him continuing what she had been saying , "Poor Jen, what a ghastly thing, she's certainly plucky though, Charles said she was quite definite about coming tonight."

Jeremy took a sip of his gin and tonic, his blue eyes fixed on her, he looked very dapper tonight in his chinos and blue striped shirt, "I'm surprised they're coming quite frankly. I've always thought Pete was a weirdo. Obviously a total screwball, his mother was no better, I remember her when Charles and I were kids, we were terrified of her, and she was damned cruel to her son." He nibbled on an olive, "No wonder Pete turned out so crazy, I wonder why he targeted Jennifer though?"

Katherine snorted, "God knows, poor old Jen, don't suppose she knows either, did he have to have a proper reason? He's clearly deluded. Frightening to think he's just disappeared, where d' you think he'll have gone?"

Jeremy groaned, "No bloody idea, but he'll turn up, after all where can he go, he's only ever known Nantes and the village, and the hospital of course. Did Charles say any more?"

"No he didn't, he was too worried about Jen, but Alex has notified the police and they must be searching. After all he could hurt someone else or even himself couldn't he?" Katherine reasoned, "They can't just leave it, can they? One thing though Charles didn't want to make a big thing of it tonight, doesn't want to frighten Jen all the more."

"Presumably the others know? Otherwise it'll be difficult to keep it out of the conversation tonight?" Jeremy asked, "and going to make it damned awkward if they don't."

"Yes, I've rung and warned them, so ..." There was a ring on the door bell, Jeremy put down his drink and went to answer it.

Sandy and Mark were the first to arrive, Jeremy brought them both through to the drawing room and Katherine joined them from the kitchen. She smiled at Sandy, she certainly had a bloom that was nothing to do with the sunshine, she saw the way Mark looked at her, and was pleased - perhaps this might just come to something.

"Hi you two, good to see you. You look fab Sandy!" She did indeed look amazing, her gamine looks and short spiky blonde hair really suited her, her petite frame hugged in a short pale green linen dress and bejewelled sandals. She went over and hugged her, it was great to see her looking so happy. She turned to Mark, who looked equally blooming and kissed him on the cheek, "Now drinks you two? Who's driving tonight?"

"We walked down, so we both can" Sandy laughed, realising

immediately that they would cotton on that Mark would be staying at hers that night. "Lovely evening for it!"

"Champagne all round then!" laughed Jeremy giving Mark the faintest wink, "I'll get them."

"Terrible business with Jen" remarked Sandy, "she always said that bloke was odd. I assume they've got the police looking for him?"

"Apparently Alex Corbett notified them straight away but so far no luck in finding him, but he can't have gone far, after all he was on foot" said Katherine, "it must have been so frightening for Jen, though according to Charles she's determined to come tonight. Mind you he's in a right state about it all, says he blames himself."

"Well of course that's bloody nonsense, but I think she's right to try and carry on as normal, at least with all of us around she's perfectly safe."

They heard the doorbell ring again, and the sound of Jeremy's feet padding across the hall, moments later he was back carrying a tray laden with an icy bottle of champagne and crystal flutes, John and Chloe in tow. They were such a strikingly handsome couple, John was so good looking and Chloe too, although she looked a little tired, her normal dancing eyes dulled with concern.

"Hi doll, you looked lovely" welcomed Katherine to Chloe, kissing her on the cheek, and stood back admiring her short blue striped shirt tied at the waist over white pedal pushers, her tawny hair tousled around her face "we were just talking about poor Jen, what a nightmare."

"Hi guys, yes hardly able to believe it, from what I hear though it was a damned good job that Caitlin came when she did." Chloe moved over to Sandy, giving her a hug and kissing Mark. "Are they still coming tonight?"

"Yes definitely, so Charles said, anyway no doubt we'll know more when they arrive. Top up Mark?" Katherine picked up the bottle and refilled the glass. "Anyone else?"

Mark laughed and thanked her, "That went down very well – perfect evening for champagne!" He slipped his hand around Sandy's waist and she leaned against him holding out her glass to Katherine and smiled at her impishly.

"How are you John, haven't seen you for ages." Jeremy asked, having been previously primed by Katherine to find out what was going on, "How's business these days?"

John didn't falter, wryly smiling at Jeremy, "Oh y' know, not a good time for any of us, but we're just managing to keep our head above water, but it's tough out there." He took a slug of his champagne, "How about you, things good in the city?"

"Surviving too, but as you say it's not so easy these days, and with so many overheads." He glanced over at Katherine who was in animated conversation with the others, "but you're pretty lucky with Chloe in that respect, she's always been such a worker. You make a great team."

"Yes we do, Chloe works damned hard and I probably don't give her enough credit for that, but you know what it's like, coming home late after a hard day, all you want to do is crash." John said easily, "I don't know how she does it really, running the yard and managing the house and the kids with not much help, especially from me lately." he added ruefully.

"She's always been a grafter John, and she's more gorgeous than ever, you're a lucky man. Not that I don't mean Katherine isn't!"

"No, I know what you meant. Chloe is a worker, but she loves her job and I don't think she wants it any other way" John looked at Chloe, and his face frowned in worry, "I should make more effort really, but I've got a lot on my plate at the moment."

"She's worth it John, she looks lovely tonight. Nothing serious though on your plate I mean...." Jeremy was interrupted by the doorbell again, "Better get that, excuse me."

John drifted over to the others, Chloe did look wonderful tonight, although he knew her outwardly animated sparkle masked the way she was really feeling. The others were deep in discussion about the forthcoming Rackham Horse Trials, he felt himself start to tune out - frankly it was a subject in which he was not interested in one bit. He could have done with an early night - he felt worn out, but Chloe had been so anxious to come. Ah well he must make the best of it he sighed, and tried to get into the spirit of the conversation. Jeremy bustled in with Jennifer and Charles, and there was an awkward moment when no-one quite knew what to say.

Jennifer amazed them all, Charles included by immediately saying, "Look - you all know what happened this afternoon, I'm fine luckily, thanks to Caitlin, and frankly Pete is a pussycat compared to the hoodies and gangs where I come from. So please can we not let it spoil our evening because I've been so looking forward to it!" She laughed, "So pour me a glass of that Taittinger Jeremy and let's have a great night!"

"Good on you Jen!" exclaimed Sandy, as Jeremy topped up their glasses and handed two to Charles and Jennifer, "I knew you were made of tougher stuff, let's party!" She laughed hugging Jennifer, "A toast, to good friends!"

"Good friends!" they all chorused, and the difficult moment passed.

CHAPTER 42

Pete was burrowing in what seemed to him a bottomless ditch behind a tall hawthorn hedge flanking the lane. He felt safe in the dark, the long grasses on the field side cascading over him, so that he was almost covered. His arms were stung by the nettles but he didn't notice as he clutched his bag tightly in his hand. In the moments that he was now capable of rational thought he knew he was in trouble, and that was why he had gone on the run, he just couldn't face going back to the hospital again. He blamed Jennifer for his illness, blamed her for the voices that popped into his head telling him that if only he was able to get rid of her, then all would be well again. If it wasn't for her, then there would be no voices and he would be safe. When he watched her go into the pool and slide under the water he'd seized his chance, pushing her head down, tearing at her hair so that she could not swim away. He'd thought she was dead when he felt her body go limp and relaxed his hold, but she had tricked him, and got away. He couldn't swim so when he heard someone coming he had made his escape, knowing instinctively that he must not be caught. In a blind panic he had dashed back to the cottage, thrown some of his belongings and as much food as he could find into a plastic bag, and all of the money that he had. It was quite a lot really as other than food he never spent any of his wages, and it would tide him over until he could decide what to do.

His thoughts were jumbled as he churned the events over, but one thing was clear that because of Jennifer he had now lost his home. He felt his chest heaving with the emotion and unfairness of it all, and every pulse seemed to be beating like a series of bass drums in his body, the loudest in his head. Now and then the odd car slowly crawled along the lane and he felt sure that every one that passed was on the lookout for him but he would wait until the darkness of the night had settled around him before he made his move. The voices were leading him to a place of safety where he could hide until they told him what else they wanted him to do. He closed his eyes, he just

472

wanted peace, wanted to be able to sleep without the worry of it all.

Katherine brought in the main course, it was turning into a really good party, everyone chatting and laughing and getting rather drunk. The last of the evening sun beamed its low gentle rays through the open doors and twinkled invitingly on the pool outside. The pungent scent of heavy bloomed syringa wafted in, mixing deliciously with the sweet fragrance of waxy white Stephanotis stars weaving their way through the orangery.

She had been so concerned about Jen but she was incredible really, appearing relaxed and at ease. Jeremy was handing around plates with the steaming pork and Katherine plonked the vegetable dishes on the table, telling everyone to help themselves. She had carefully planned the seating, putting herself at the head of the table, with Charles on her right and Mark on her left. Sandy was at the far end, Jeremy on one side and John on the other, leaving Chloe and Jen opposite each other in the middle. She was hoping that Jeremy could talk to John for most of the dinner with Sandy keeping an eye on things. So far so good, John by now had drunk quite a lot and was joking and laughing with Sandy, with Jeremy joining in, although from where she was it was difficult to know exactly what they were saying. Charles too had relaxed and was talking animatedly to Chloe. After Jen's confession to him about her riding he was keen to know how she was getting on and he seemed to be pretty impressed with Chloe's glowing report. Jen was looking a bit embarrassed as Charles declared he must come and see for himself. Mark - on her left was listening in on the conversation, saying he felt left out being the only non-rider of the group, which Jeremy with half an ear on their chatter, staunchly defended, as he was one of the non-riding sector himself.

The laughter and the wine flowed on, as Jeremy bobbed up and down opening more and more bottles. Chloe switched to water as she was driving, and watched John unwind with the others looking more like his old self than he had in months. Charles who was also driving and wanted his wits about him tonight caught Chloe looking at John and whispered quietly, "Perhaps I can have a word with you later Chloe – about Jennifer?"

Chloe looked startled, "Of course, you're not cross about the riding are you?" she said anxiously realising how implicit she had been in the deceit.

"No, far from it. Can I ring you?" he said quietly "It's about the riding and about this business with Pete. I know I can trust you to be discreet." He glanced quickly at Jennifer who was chatting to Mark, "I can't talk here, I don't want her worrying."

"Okay, Call me" Chloe turned quickly to Katherine, "This meal is scrumptious!"

"Yes it is!" agreed Mark, who was thoroughly enjoying himself. "I won't be able to move if I eat anymore."

"Thank you! Save room for the pud and cheese though." laughed Katherine to Mark. She really liked this man - she hadn't seen Sandy so happy for a long time and she could quite see why. He was charming, very easy on the eye, and had a great sense of humour.

"If you're stuffed, I can drop you both off later, if you like?" offered Chloe, "I go right past your door."

"That'd be lovely, in that case – bring on the dessert."

Patrick and Sharon were coming home from seeing her mum in Cuckfield, it was not quite dark, although it was almost ten o'clock. Patrick yawned as Sharon drove carefully down the lanes through Priors Cross, he was tired and rather bored, visiting Sharon's mum was a duty thing which he did for her, but was tedious in the extreme. He had drunk a few beers too which always made him sleepy and he felt his eyes closing, only to jerk himself awake when Sharon braked, which she did often - he thought just to annoy him. He had just felt his eyes droop again when she violently stopped the car, he shot forward in his seat, the seat belt jerking him awake.

"Patrick, did you see that?" she shrieked agitatedly, "Was it a man?"

"Whaaat? I didn't see anything, I had my eyes closed." he said irritated "for Christ's sake Sharon, you're driving like a retard! Braking all the bloody time!"

Sharon clenched her hands on the steering wheel, "I'm sure that was someone, a dark figure just ran across the road, I nearly hit them!"

"Probably a deer or summat. Who'd be walking along the lane at this time of night? Or you imagined it. Come on, I am knackered, I've had a hard day, plus an evening at your mothers and could do with my bed." He yawned again, "I've got another long day tomorrow."

"I didn't imagine it and I'm sure it was a person. And, if you don't like the way I drive, try doing it yourself for a bloody change." Sharon was annoyed, she always had to do the driving. To annoy him she did a wheel spin and hurtled off down the road.

Pete's heart was thumping, as he stumbled awkwardly and hid in the trees, that car had nearly hit him, luckily he had jumped out of the way. His limbs were stiff and awkward from being cramped in the ditch, his head ached and he was hungry. He didn't have far to go now, but he wouldn't go back onto the road and he crept warily deeper into the woodland that fringed the lane.

It had been a very successful evening Katherine agreed with Jeremy as they stood at their front door and watched the tail lights of the two cars moving away down the drive. They turned and went back indoors to begin the clearing up, stacking the crockery on trays and collecting the glasses.

"The food was spectacular darling" complimented Jeremy, "You did us proud, mind you that lot have drunk us out of house and home." he laughed as he collected up all the empty bottles and put them out for recycling.

"Thanks sweetie, it did go rather well didn't it?" She bent over and started to stack the plates into the dishwasher, "Mark and Sandy look very loved up don't you think?"

"Yes, they seem to be very well matched and she looked really cute tonight, she's a striking woman, and bloody clever too." He started to fill a bowl with hot soapy water for the glasses, "I thought Jen looked amazing too, especially considering the terrible day she's had."

"She did look good, and very gutsy you'd have thought nothing had happened. She's really great fun when you get to know her, much less stuffy than Celia. I can see why Charles married her." Katherine added, "I'm so pleased too that she has told him about her riding now, he was bound to find out sooner or later and much better coming from her. I think he seemed rather pleased about it, didn't you?"

"Don't ask me, I like watching but wouldn't want to do it myself, I think you're all bloody nuts jumping those fences. But, yes he did seem pleased, but he looked worried too, must have been one helluva shock for him with the Pete business."

"I wonder if they have found him yet? It's quite disconcerting to think he's lurking about somewhere."

"I wouldn't worry sweetie, they've probably found him by now and he's safely in hospital which is where he belongs. I'm glad it's the weekend though and at least Charles will be at home with Jen, just in case you know?"

"You don't seriously think he'd try it again do you?" Katherine looked worried, "Surely he's been frightened off and wouldn't dare go back?"

"Well you never know with these nutters do you? They get so single minded, can't get thoughts out of their head, but I'm pretty sure he'll have been found, after all he's hardly inconspicuous is he, he's a hulking great bloke!"

"Yes, I suppose so." Katherine passed him some more glasses, "I thought Chloe looked stunning tonight."

"She's a very sexy lady is our Chloe, although she doesn't know it, which makes her all the more attractive. It's just a way she has about her, one thing though, she only has eyes for John. He's a lucky bloke."

"More to the point though, did you manage to find out anything from John?" Katherine dried up the glasses whilst he washed, "After all that was why we arranged this evening."

Jeremy considered, a soap sud on the end of his nose, "Well, he was full of admiration for Chloe and how hard she works and said he should do more to help her but he was bone tired after work every night."

"Do you think he was telling the truth, not just tired and late home 'cos he's got someone else?"

"Christ Katherine, who do you think I am, Hercule Poirot, how do I know?" exclaimed Jeremy, "I'm just repeating what he said. Even when he'd had a bit to drink, he didn't say anymore to me, so sorry, I did my best."

Katherine put the tea towel around his neck and pulled him over to her, kissing off the bubble from his nose, "I know you did darling, I know. You were a perfect host as always."

Jeremy mollified, put his arms around her waist, "Come on let's leave this lot and go to bed."

Pete trod warily up the cinder track keeping well into the side of the trees, he could hear the water cascading through the mill race and the eerie screech of a barn owl. The mill loomed up in the gloom across the pond, the moon casting silvery threads on the water. He stood for long while just watching from the trees, his head ached fiercely and he felt his belly groan with hunger, but still he waited his eyes fixed ahead, listening intently. Cautiously he made his way further towards the buildings protected by the darkness of the overgrown foliage. The barns came into view, and he edged his way towards them, and slipped around the side, pushing open the small door into the largest one. It was inky dark, there was no light filtering in from the outside and he fumbled his way around the walls to find the stairs to the loft above. With one hand he groped his way upwards, and then like an animal, on his hands and knees crawled along the floor, finally settling down on some old sacks. The sound of rats scuttling away made him shiver, it smelt damp and musty in here, but the voices had told him he would be safe. He rummaged around in his bag, pulling some bread off the loaf and blindly cutting a chunk of cheese with his penknife, crammed the food into his mouth. He ate methodically just as he always did, taking comfort in the chewing, he just wished could have washed his hands first, he felt dirty, but that couldn't be helped. She had brought him to this filthy state, it was her fault. His head throbbed as he yanked a jumper out of the bag and pulled it on, and settled down to a restless sleep.

Chloe and John crept into the house, they could hear the sound of the TV in the sitting room and whilst John put the kettle on Chloe went to find Susie to tell her they were back.

"Thanks so much Susie, I'm really grateful, I hope they weren't too naughty?" Chloe hugged Susie as she pulled on her coat yawning, "I'll pay you in the morning, if that's okay?"

"Oh Chloe, there's no need, you do enough for me, I'm happy to be able to help." Susie smiled, "They were really good - made me laugh. Hope you both had fun?"

John got down some mugs, "We had a great time, a really lovely evening. We should try and go out more often – eh Chloe?" He smiled over at her, "Do you want a cuppa Susie?"

"No thanks John, I'm bushed, I'll be off now. Glad you had a good time, you're right – you should do it more often, you only have to ask, I'll always babysit." she pulled open the back door, patting the dogs as she went.

Chloe sat down and took her mug of tea from John, "Thanks darling, I'm so glad you came, Susie's right we should make more effort to go out." She sipped her tea, reaching out across the table to take his hand in hers, "it was like old times."

John looked a bit uneasy, "Chloe..."

"Don't John please, don't say anything, let's just enjoy this moment and not think about anything else. You have asked me to trust you and I do." She held his eyes for a moment until he looked away. "We're very lucky, we have three wonderful children, good jobs and a lovely home, I don't want to lose that, and I'm sure you don't either. What happened to Jennifer today puts it all into perspective. Life is very precious and we have one chance at getting it right, and I'm not going to spoil that and I hope you aren't either." She stood up putting her mug in the sink, and took his hand and they went up to bed.

Mark and Sandy were laughing till their sides ached, they were both tipsy and had poured themselves a nightcap to finish off the evening. Mark was lounging on the sofa and Sandy laid along its length her head in his lap. He stroked her face, and she threw her head back and looked up at him, "It was a lovely evening, I hope you had a good time too?"

He looked down at her and his voice was suddenly solemn, "It was the best Sandy, just the best."

"Wow, you sound serious." she started to sit up surprised, her heart skipping a beat.

"That's because I am serious, about you I mean. I know we were just going to see how it panned out and enjoy the moment, but I'm in too deep Sandy." He looked at her, his eyes holding hers, "I know I might risk losing you, frightening you off, but I need to tell you how I feel, I can't keep it to myself any longer. I watched you at dinner tonight, you're so beautiful, and witty and intelligent, and I was so proud to be with you, and I've never felt like this about anyone before." She started to interrupt him, but he carried on, "These last few weeks have been amazing, I've never been so happy."

"Mark – it's been the same for me too" she looked up at him, her eyes shining, "I've been afraid to say anything for fear of losing you." She laughed, "I keep having to stop myself from thinking too far ahead because I keep thinking the bubble will burst."

They both started to laugh, rolling off the sofa onto the floor, he kissed her face and her shoulders, his hands straying up the inside of her thighs. He slipped her dress over her shoulders bending his head again to kiss down to her breasts, his hands inching off her knickers, and his head moved further down over her tummy. She groaned with pleasure, stroking his hair with her hands urging him on down further, he parted her legs and sat back looking at her naked body admiringly. Slowly parting her legs with his fingertips, he bent his head and started to lick gently, then more urgently, sucking at her clitoris until he could feel it stiffen and harden in his mouth. She was almost climaxing when he stopped, unzipping his trousers and throwing them off, she moaned, taking him in her mouth whilst he stood above her, and then he pulled out, opening her legs again he plunged into her, they both gasped with pleasure, rolling from one position to another, finally when she could resist no longer allowing herself to come, only then did he relax and reached his orgasm almost simultaneously with hers.

Charles pulled up outside the garages and stopped the car walking round to open Jennifer's door for her. Helping her out, he put his arm around her shoulders and they hurried into the house. Charles locked the door behind them and set the alarms. They walked down the corridor towards the sitting room where Mrs Fuller had drawn the curtains. It felt snug and cosy, Charles poured them stiff drinks, handing Jennifer hers as she sat on the sofa.

"I'm glad we're home, it was good evening and you were right about going tonight - took our mind off things."

Jennifer sipped at her brandy, the heat burning her throat, "Yes, I had a great time. They're all lovely people." She plucked an imaginary hair from the sofa, "I'm so glad you don't mind about the riding, I'm having such a good time at Chloe's."

"I can see you are. I can't wait to see how you're getting on, when will you let me watch you?" Charles grinned at her, "I won't believe it till I see it."

"No – not yet." she teased, "You'll just have to be patient. Don't tell the children will you, I want it to be a surprise for them. Especially if we go off on this safari, Jessica and I will be able to ride with you."

"Okay, I won't say a word, but before I let you loose on the plains of Botswana, I want to make sure you're safe on a horse." He sat down beside her, "I can't risk anything happening to you darling, today has been a big wake up call for me."

"Look sweetie, I'm okay, and hopefully Pete is now sectioned and in hospital and we can just put it all behind us. I'm pretty resilient you know, and it explains so much, I thought that I was just imagining things, being paranoid and not coping. It's actually quite a relief that it's come to a head, even if it was a nasty one. I know that sounds stupid to you probably."

"No it doesn't. You did try to tell me but I ignored you and I'm truly sorry." He pulled her close to him "You never realise how precious something is, till you nearly lose it. I'm going to call Alex in the morning and find out what's happening. I won't rest until he's found. Until we know for sure, I want you to be really vigilant – okay?"

"I don't need telling twice." she shivered, "Surely he can't just have vanished into thin air?"

"Probably not, but until we are certain, we're taking no bloody chances."

CHAPTER 43

Grace was awake early and was already in the kitchen. The air was very still outside as the sun crawled up the sky and she'd flung open the doors and the dogs were rooting around in the garden. She sat at the table sipping her tea, thinking about next week and starting the job at the vet's. After her initial euphoria, she was becoming rather nervous, worrying whether or not she would be able to cope with the work, after all it had been a long time since she had done an office job. Years ago she had worked as a secretary to a firm in Horsham, but when she had married, and her parents needed her more, she had given it up, encouraged by Colin who said they didn't need the money – and that was when they had decided to try to start the family that had never happened. Now here she was going to work again. She knew that deep down her mum thought she was mad, both Colin and her dad said she should do what she thought was best for her, but Grace knew she had to fill her days, to stop her having so much time to think about a baby. Anyway she thought, it was only a trial period for both sides and only part time, so if it didn't work out she could always quit.

The most pressing part of her day today though was these bloody cakes, she sighed, -they had to be high on her agenda, God what a thought. Colin was going into work this morning but coming home after lunch to help out at the kennels to get ready for the big day tomorrow; she hoped the weather would be nice, nothing worse than sheltering inside a dripping tent. She reluctantly stood up and opened the fridge taking out the ingredients for the final cake she was going to make and do the icing for the ones in the freezer, when Colin stomped down the stairs. He was in his usual work clothes, and was fixing his tie and absent-mindedly came over to give her a kiss. She smiled, "Cup of tea?" she asked him, putting the butter on the table.

"Yes please love, I won't have time for any breakfast, I want to do as much as I can in the office before I slope off this afternoon. You on cake making duties this morning?"

She filled the kettle, "Yes, bloody things! I should finish them this morning, so I'll come up with you to help set up and I can take them then, they won't hurt overnight in the marquee, I'll put them in tins, to make sure no bloody rodents are tempted to have a nibble."

"Good idea, I expect a lot of the ladies will do that, it's only the sarnies that will have to be done tomorrow. You involved with that?"

She laughed, "No thank God! Lavinia is supervising this year, so I managed to avoid it."

"Good for you!" He gulped down the rest of his tea, "Gonna dash, see you later." He leaned over and kissed her on the cheek, and was gone.

Grace looked gloomily at the fridge, she supposed she had better get on with these damned cakes.

Lucy was back at the Bistro having skived off with her bogus tummy bug, and fuck me she was having to make up for it today. The town was busy being Saturday morning, and the market always attracted loads of people. The world and his wife seemed to want coffee, sandwiches and cakes, and she was rushed off her feet. Gino had been pleased to see her, but was quite adamant that she must be completely well before she came back. Of course he had to be careful - but he hadn't paid her either, she was not entitled to sick pay, she hadn't been there long enough he explained, so reluctantly she had come back but only because she needed the money.

The tables were packed outside and she hurried backwards and forwards taking and delivering orders, she was exhausted, still only another quarter of an hour before her break. She fucking needed it. She was standing outside taking an order from four customers who were being a right pain in the arse deliberating about what they wanted, chopping and changing their minds whilst she waited, barely disguising her irritation, when she saw Colin hurrying across the square from his office. By chance he looked up and saw her, their eyes met, his face uncertain at first then he smiled and came over.

"Hi Lucy. So this is where you're working." Colin looked around the crowded tables, "Gosh, it's really busy!"

Hi Colin, yes it is," Lucy pushed up her tits in her blouse, "are you looking for a seat?"

"No, can't stop, dashing back home, I've got to be at the hunt kennels this afternoon to help set up for tomorrow."

"Oh yes, I'm going." Lucy laughed, enjoying the look of surprise on his face, "I'm going with Tom, and just because I don't work at Nantes any more, doesn't mean I'm not interested in the hunting."

"No, of course not" stammered Colin embarrassed, "Well ...look forward to seeing you then."

"Waitress" whined the waiting customer, "Are you taking our order or not?"

"I'd better go Colin, see you tomorrow," she forced an obsequious smile onto her face and turned to the lady, "Of course madam, what can I get you?" She took the order and watched Colin as he walked away, that should put the fuel on the fire she thought with glee.

She strode back into the Bistro, she was looking forward to tomorrow, Tom was a mug she had easily persuaded him to take her, and Jonty would be pleased with her – wait till she told him. When she had seen Weasel and Jonty on Thursday they had admitted they were Sabs and would be very grateful if she could pass on any information about the hunt. She liked the idea of being a mole, and any disruption caused by them would serve those upper crust fuckers right for being so gross to her. Jonty's idea of being grateful was a line of coke and he said if she came across with anything good it might be worth a quid or two. She was going to show him just how resourceful she could be and earn some money in the process!

Charles had left Jennifer in the kitchen having tea with Mrs Fuller, he didn't want to let her out of his sight. There had been no news of Pete, he had totally disappeared, and the police seemed to think he had scarpered right out of the area, but Charles knew him and thought it highly unlikely. Alex Corbett had no news either and there seemed to be little else he could do. Charles decided he would go over to the cottage and search for any clues as to where he might have gone. He marched across the lawn, deep in thought. What was he going to do if Monday came and they still hadn't found him – God only knew. He didn't want to leave Jennifer here at Nantes on her own, but he couldn't see her wanting to come up to London with him either, she was just starting to integrate down here now, and he didn't want to spoil that for her.

He crept slowly up the flagstone path to the cottage and around to the back door and walked in - Christ it was creepy in here he thought, for all he knew Pete could have come back. He started to search the kitchen and opened the fridge, it was empty, not even a carton of milk. He moved through to the sitting room, it was just how they had last seen it, nothing had been moved and from the sparseness of the room, it looked as though it hadn't been lived in for years except that there was not a speck of dust to be seen. He climbed the stairs and went into the bedroom, opening drawers and cupboards. There were a few neatly folded clothes but it was difficult to see if any of them were missing. The wardrobe was the same, a single coat on a hanger, and a pair of shoes precisely placed side by side in the bottom. The only decoration of sorts was a faded sepia photograph of Pete's mother standing outside the front door at Nantes, and Charles knew that it was one his own mother had taken years ago and given to Pete. He looked under the bed - again nothing. The other bedroom was the same, except in one of the bedside drawers he found Pete's payslips, going back for years. He had always arranged for Pete to be paid in cash, in fact he wasn't even sure he had a bank account. It was how he wanted it, but there was no money in any of the envelopes, it had all gone. He moved to the bathroom which again was immaculate, none of the detritus and mess you would expect from a gardener living on his own. He pulled open the medicine chest and took out dozens of packets of pills, stacked one on top of the other, branded Largactil, all prescribed by Alex and all full. Obviously Pete had not been taking his medication for a long time. He rifled through the rest of the contents discovering more unopened boxes of pills. There was a stack of carbolic soap and a nail brush, but no toothbrush, so it could be that he had no intention of coming back here. He chucked the contents back into the cabinet and closed it firmly, glancing around him to see if he had missed anything. It was as though Pete had never lived here. Charles left the cottage, closing the door carefully and locking it behind him and walked back towards the house, pondering where he could have gone. He would have to ring up and get the locks changed and also he would have to find another gardener at some point, meantime he would get a contractor in to do the lawns. He had one more thought and before he went inside, he dialled Chloe's number waiting impatiently for her to answer.

He walked around in circles on the grass listening to the burr burr of the ring tone and finally she picked up, "Chloe, it's Charles here, hope it's not a bad time to call?"

"Hi Charles, no I'm just taking a break from teaching. What a lovely evening last night!"

"Yes, yes it was" he said distractedly, "listen Chloe, I'm really worried about Jennifer. They haven't found Pete yet and I'm concerned about her being here on her own when I go back to town on Monday."

"Surely they'll find him, he can't have gone far" said Chloe "after all he's pretty hard to miss."

"Well that's as may be, but supposing he's still at large. I've just been over to the cottage and found a pile of unused medication, he's obviously not been taking it for some while and if he's still lurking around, he may well come back here." He was really agitated. "I know Jennifer loves coming over to you, is there any chance that you could, well you know, take care of her at least for the morning and then I can ask either Caitlin or Mrs Fuller to keep their eyes open?"

"Of course I will, she comes most days anyway, so that's not a problem and I could always increase the lessons to take up more of the day, God knows she's keen enough."

"That'd be a real weight off my mind Chloe, it's very good of you." Charles breathed a sigh of relief, "Whilst we're on the subject of her riding, seriously how's she getting on? You can be quite honest with me, I won't tell her what you say."

"I would say the same to her Charles, she's doing really well, and that's the total truth. You'll be amazed when you see her." Chloe laughed, "She's been a wonderful asset and we've all become good friends."

"Yes I saw that last night. I want to thank you, it's been a difficult year for her here, not easy to adjust y' know."

"There's no need to thank me really."

486

Charles hesitated, "Chloe, one more thing, if this riding thing is really serious perhaps it might be a good idea to look out for a horse for her? What do you think? Rufus is getting on a bit now after all."

Chloe sighed, "He is old, and he has done her a good turn, given her confidence just when she needed it, and types like that are hard to find, but I'll keep my eyes open and let you know if I hear of anything. See what comes along eh?"

Charles smiled, if anyone could find the right horse it would be Chloe, she had a gift for matching suitable riders and horses together. "I'll leave it to you then, don't say anything yet to her though, she loves that little Rufus, but we both know he won't stand up to a lot of work."

"Okay Charles, look, I'd better crack on, but keep me posted about Pete and don't worry Jen can stay here all day if she wants." Chloe ended the call and Charles looked surprised, he had noticed the same thing last night, they all called her Jen – extraordinary! He shoved the phone back in his pocket and marched into the house.

Grace and Colin were driving up to the kennels with several cake tins stacked in the back of the Landcruiser. The forecast for tomorrow was good, and this afternoon it was just the finishing touches that were required before the main event. Colin negotiated cautiously into the driveway conscious of the trouble he would find himself in from Grace, should the cakes shoot all over the place, especially if they ended up on the dust coats she had lovingly laundered for George. There were already quite a few cars there, the troops all arriving to help. People were dashing about with hammers and ropes, others setting up trestle tables in the main marquee and pinning on tablecloths. Oli and Tom were perched precariously on ladders hanging up yards of coloured bunting. It was a hive of industry, Colin walked around and opened Grace's door helping her out, and taking out the cake tins and laundry and they carried them over to the tent.

Lavinia Appleton-Lacey was most definitely in charge, in a pinstriped butcher's apron and carrying a clip board, regimentally ticking off jobs as they were done. Several women behind her were setting up a large chrome tea urn on one of the tables and had crates of cups and saucers stacked up beside them.

"Don't put those out till the morning dear" called Lavinia, waving her biro at them, "it can all be done tomorrow, and then we can just wipe them over with a tea towel."

"Hi Lavinia" Grace said, "cakes as promised."

"Ah well done my dear, shall I just have a little peek?" She drew the lid of one tin, and the delicious smell of fresh cake wafted out, "Delightful! They're not all the same though are they?" she asked doubtfully.

"No, all different, you've got a lemon drizzle, chocolate and orange sponge, and a coffee and walnut, that okay?"

"Thank you my dear, that's perfect. You can put them over there with the others" she fluttered her hand in the direction of a pile of containers already on the table, "Everyone has been very good, we've got sausage rolls, cheese straws, mini quiches, scotch eggs, an embarrassment of savouries and an army of cakes. Still more to come too, and then there'll be the sandwiches to be made tomorrow, shall I count you in on that?" Lavinia fixed her with a beady eye, "we'll be starting at about 11am."

Grace groaned, thinking bugger, but answered, "Of course, glad to help, anything you need me to bring?" Why had she allowed herself to be commandeered again.

"I think we have the fillings in hand, it's just hands on we need." Lavinia brayed loudly at her joke, "Well done my dear!" She turned away for a moment, calling to some other poor unfortunate who was in her firing line, and Grace and Colin took their opportunity to escape and find George.

A little gaggle of men were crowding around the kennels, watching Jay wash the hounds which would be shown tomorrow, with old George holding court and laughing as water gushed in every direction. Jay was soaked but was grinning as he struggled to hold on to a slippery resisting hound, slithering and sliding on the wet concrete. Grace clutched Colin's arm laughing, whispering that it was their puppy that was causing all the grief to poor Jay, who now resembled the old man of the sea! They were such a naughty pair, and whilst she had loved them when they walked them, she had been glad when they returned to kennels. The fun over, George took a look around to see what else needed doing, and issued jobs reverently to

488

the helpers. Grace handed him his freshly laundered white dust coats and he thanked her profusely and asked if they could take over more bunting that needed to be strung up. They carried their bundles over to Oli and Tom, dumping it on the grass.

"Got some more here lads!" grinned Colin, "Where d' you want it?"

"Well I could tell you Col," laughed Oli "but I won't!"

"I think we could do with some more over here" called Grace gesturing to the other side of the grass rings, "even it up a bit."

"Woman's touch!" scoffed Colin, then said playfully to Grace "Coming dear!"

Grace thumped him playfully, "Cheeky bugger!"

Colin looked at Tom as he stooped down to pick up the bunting, "What's this I hear about you bringing Lucy tomorrow? Thought she was joking when she mentioned it last week."

Tom went red, and the others all stared at him, "Well, she just kind of talked me into it, and before I knew it, I'd said yes. I've been trying to think of an excuse to get me out of it."

"You are kidding right?" Grace demanded, "You idiot, what did you do that for? Everyone from Nantes is going to be here, and you know what a reactionary little cow she can be, we don't want any trouble."

Tom looked sheepish, "She sent a text to Caitlin apologising, and got a nice reply apparently, so it should be all right. After all Grace she can be pretty persuasive, and I think she's genuinely sorry. Can't you just give her a chance?"

"Genuinely sorry! What banana boat did you fall off? She's out to cause trouble mark my words." said Grace sharply, and then regretted being so nasty Poor Tom he was a nice kid, and he had been in a difficult position after all. "Oh well, never mind, I suppose we'll just have to put up with her, but don't expect much."

"Ah Grace, I'm sorry and I promise she'll cause no trouble, if she does I'll take her home." Tom looked relieved and turned to Oli,

"You'll help me with her won't you mate?"

"I suppose I'll have to." grumbled Oli, "but she's a right tart, why on earth didn't you just ignore her when she got back in touch."

"Come on lads, let's just get this lot up, and we can go and have an early pint and talk about it later." Colin marshalled them all along, and clambered up the ladder, "I'm not going to let her spoil my day."

Pete had spent all day hiding in the barn, peering out of tiny holes in the wooden cladding to see if anyone was around. He was filthy and he hated it, but he was afraid to go out during the daytime to wash in the pond. He had eaten all of the bread and cheese and was down to the end of his water. The night time had been terrible with the scurrying of rats and the unfamiliar creaking of the barn. He had hardly slept as the voices kept talking to him telling him he was safe and not to be frightened. The events of the previous day whirled around in his head, and made no sense to him.

When the daylight finally broke and the inky blackness turned to a cold grey, he looked around. The old pile of hessian sacks he had lain on were musty but dry, and he dragged them out and shook them, clouds of dust billowing through the loft making him cough, the sound of his own voice echoing around the huge empty space. If he were to stay here, he'd have to make it more comfortable. He cleared a space for himself in the corner, shaking out an old broken bale of straw which had been discarded, and then laid the sacks on top for a bed. He ventured down the stairs, warily testing each tread and stepped down onto the main grain floor. It was vast and completely empty as far as he could see in the gloom, huge doors at the front spanned from floor to rafters, and a heavy iron bar clamped them shut. On one side was the small door leading outside, on the opposite side another door leading onto an adjoining barn. He shuffled over pulling it back on its rollers so that he could slip through the gap. The other barn was much smaller than the first with a system of pulleys and hoists with hooks and chains and large rings bolted into the floor, but other than that it was as empty as the first. On the far side was a sturdy door and he cautiously walked over and drew back the latch to find a small room which must have served as an office and workshop. Grey light streamed through a tiny window and he could make out some odd sticks of furniture and an old milk bottle, with a battered tin kettle and a chipped enamel mug. Thinking they might be useful he picked them up and rummaging about discovered an ancient bucket and stowed them away, together with a ball of string. There was a bench fixed to the floor, groping underneath he found an old hammer and chisel and he added them to his other finds. Hanging on the walls was a rusty bow saw and some wire, and an ancient bill hook with a broken handle.

There was nothing much else of value to him, and he moved back quietly to the main barn again. His footsteps seemed so loud as they echoed in the cavernous space, despite his efforts to be as quiet as he could, his senses were heightened to such a pitch that once back in the loft he threw himself down on his makeshift bed and covered his ears. Pete had no idea how long he stayed like that, only that he was becoming hungry and thirsty and knew that he would have to go in search of food and water. His belly rumbling, and his spittle thick and dry in his mouth, he waited till the silver streaks of light gradually faded. Reluctantly he dragged himself up, taking one of the sacks with him, examining it for holes, it would have to do.

CHAPTER 44

Oliver had been busy during the night, he had been called out previously to a bad colic in the late afternoon and they had called him again at midnight. He decided that the horse needed to be sent to the specialist veterinary hospital for an operation. He had just gotten home and had another call out to a tricky foaling, a healthy colt in the end but now he was bushed. He rubbed his eyes wearily, he would be glad when they had a bit of help, more because of the demands of the night work. Still the ad had gone in now, and hopefully the applications would soon come flooding in, and they'd got lucky in recruiting Grace, she would be a real asset.

In retrospect, he thought it must have been miserable for Suse, if you didn't have a job where you understood the rigours of being on call, it must have been pretty irritating. Soon he reflected, if they got the Old Mill, then they would have their own hospital and that too would make things easier, but a fully staffed operating theatre was probably a long way off, it would break them financially at first to buy the place, let alone do it up and equip it. He took a slurp of his coffee, glancing at the clock and wearily went up the stairs to his bed, taking his phone with him. He could get his head down for a couple of hours if he was lucky and then he'd have to go to the kennels. In truth it would be easier not to, but he would be expected - it was part of the protocol. He threw off his clothes chucking them in a heap on the floor, and slid under the duvet. Heaven - it just felt like heaven, the cool sheets embraced him, he wondered how long it would be before he had a partner to share it with. He picked up the phone and started texting.

Charles had lain awake sleeping poorly in spits and spats, his mind churning with worry. Pete had still not been found, where could he have gone? In his deranged state he could come back, he knew Nantes and the local area as well as he did, he would have to arrange for some sort of security for Jennifer. He couldn't expect Chloe to do it indefinitely, but on the other hand he didn't want to make a big thing of it, on the whole Jennifer was pretty stoical and had recovered from her ordeal well. He didn't think she realised the full implications of what Pete was like, but he had seen him in his psychotic phases and he was capable of anything and cunning too. Bloody hell, why hadn't he done more, what was he thinking - visiting the doctor thinking he could sort it out. He was so angry with himself. He forced himself to calm down, he must think logically. Pete could only be on the run for a short period of time, he surely must be caught before long. Of course they had Felix arriving soon too, so that would be another member of staff to keep their eyes open for anything sinister going on, he must make certain he spoke to him directly he arrived. At least today he felt he had taken some action, the locksmith had come out and the cottage was now secure, as if that mattered really he thought helplessly, talk about bolting the stable door. That was part of it too, he felt powerless, and never in all of his life had he not been in control of a situation, and he didn't like it one bit. He rolled over and stroked Jennifer's arm, she murmured in her sleep but he didn't want to waken her, but just to have her with him was enough. He was bloody sure he wasn't going to lose her.

"Oh my God!" spluttered Grace into her mobile, "I don't believe it! What can I do to help?"

Colin looked up from his tea, mouthing 'Who is it?' and Grace waved her hand at him willing him to be quiet. Colin could only sit and listen to her half of the conversation,

"Of course, yes, yes I will. Leave it to me, I'll be with you as soon as I can, call if you need anything else." She put the phone down, her face shocked, "You'll never believe it Col, Sabs have raided the marquee in the night, and taken most of the food!"

"Christ! When did it happen?" Colin's jaw had dropped in surprise, "Much damage?"

"No idea, in the night they think, and only the inside of the marquee has been touched, everything else is fine, but Lavinia says nearly all of the food has gone, and the drink too!" Grace could hardly believe it, what were they going to do, their hunt was hosting one of its most important functions and this was a catastrophe!

"What all that champagne? They'll be as drunk as skunks! What are they going to do about replacing the stuff?"

"No, ironically it seems the booze was untouched but the juice and water has gone, and the grub, they must have been disturbed or something, as I can't think of another reason they'd leave cases of fizz behind. Anyway, come on Col, we'd better get our skates on we're needed up there right away." She dashed up the stairs shouting back to him, "I said we'd call at Mrs Gupta's and see what stocks she's got. Probably one of us will have to make a trip to Horsham to the supermarket."

Colin pulled on his loafers, and grabbed his wallet and his keys and was waiting in the car when she thundered back down the stairs, skittering into the drive, showering gravel like a spray gun. He tore off up the road, making it to the kennels in record time. It was bedlam, cars parked askew all over the place. Outwardly the jolly bunting was all still intact, as were the parade rings and flowers swinging gaily in their baskets. They strode urgently over to the marquee, it was full of people milling about all open mouthed and muttering in shock. There was not a Tupperware box or a tin to be seen.

Lavinia stood in the middle of them shouting for them all to be quiet, and finally a hush fell about the tent. "Right!" she ordered, "Now this can be rectified but we have to work as a cohesive team. A great deal of the food has gone, plus the water, fruit drinks and ironically the teabags. Luckily we were making the sandwiches this morning, so the team of ladies that were planning to do that job can start as planned." She smiled ruefully and continued, "Except for you dear Grace, I want you to make a comprehensive list of the things that we need and take a party of people and do a run to the shop. I'll give you a list of what was donated and you can check what has been taken and replace it. I know it'll be shop bought but it will just have to do. Colin, you check the drink and see if we need to get anything in that line, but I believe that has been untouched. This is obviously the work of Saboteurs and I am damned if we are going to let those hooligans spoil our day. Right get to it everyone!"

Grace took the list from Lavinia, "This is frightful, are you sure it's the Sabs?"

Lavinia scoffed, her eyes rolling, "Of course it is, who else would it be? We won't let them beat us, this reminds me of the war, Dunkirk spirit and all that."

Blimey thought Grace, she actually thought the old girl was enjoying this! To Grace it was reminiscent of '*Sixty Minute Makeover*' not bloody Dunkirk! Still you had to hand it to her, she had the situation under control, and with luck they would turn it round. She called to a couple of the other women and together they made a list of what they would need. She couldn't believe they had taken so much, it would mean a trip to Horsham for sure, the village shop would not have the quantities they would need. This was going to be a mammoth sprint to get it all ready in time for two o'clock.

Lucy had skived the day off work, saying she felt ill again. Gino was not pleased but grudgingly decided he couldn't risk insisting that she came in, the Foods Standards Agency were hot on this sort of thing and if anyone should fall ill and blame the restaurant, then he would be in serious trouble. Reluctantly he agreed and Lucy replaced the receiver checking that her mother had not been listening. It was not worth her wrath to say where she was going and she had told her that Gino had given her the day off. She crept back up the stairs, closing her bedroom door managing to be back in bed just as her mother put her head round the door to tell her that she and her father were going off to church and would be back soon. Lucy grunted and rolled over feigning sleep, silly old cow she thought. She waited until she heard the front door slam and got up again, watching them leave through her window. Picking up her phone she texted Weasel, and then Tom. She loved the idea of this under cover role and couldn't wait to see the faces of all those snotty fuckers today when she arrived! She trembled in delight, stretching her arms above her head and wriggling in anticipation of the day, and even more how she would report back to Jonty. Life was suddenly going to become interesting again!

The jungle drums were beating all over Fittlebury and before eleven o'clock most of the stalwart hunt supporters knew of the catastrophe. A steady stream of cars drove up to the kennels with offerings of food and Lavinia orchestrated the proceedings with an astonishing efficiency and had the situation well under control. By twelve thirty, there were platters and platters of sandwiches tightly wrapped in cling film, and more than twenty cakes made hastily that morning by supporters. Grace had returned with the Landcruiser stuffed to the roof with bags of goodies, which she and her team were now laying out on dishes, the tables were staggering under the weight of it all. She leaned back wiping her face with the back of her hand, surveying their efforts. They were going to pull it off, no-one would ever have known. Thank God though, the antis had not trashed the marquee - which on reflection she thought was odd, why take just the food? It could have been so much worse than this. Oh well, that was their gain, it was funny too, since the Act had been passed this kind of thing just hadn't happened, okay they had the odd troublemaker when they went out hunting, but gone were the days when they had to be on their guard. She remembered back to a few years ago, two days before the point to point, the Sabs had burned all the fences on the course in the night, and they had found nothing but smouldering wrecks the next morning. After that, volunteers had manned a 24 hour guard, but that was ages ago, surely this sort of disruption was not going to start again?

She glanced over at Colin who was setting out cups and saucers, having filled the tea urn with water, and a bunch of ladies were teasing him; he was taking it all in good heart, flirting and joking with them. The glasses were marshalled in regimented rows on the table all polished and gleaming, with the champagne standing in great tubs of cold water to keep cool. Lavinia was darting around checking and rechecking on her clip board, ticking off items with a flourish of her biro, she seemed satisfied - they may even have time to go home and get changed.

Lavinia clapped her hands above her head shouting "Okay everyone, well done, great team work! Those of you who want to go home and freshen up, that's fine, but we need volunteers to stay here until the Masters arrive at one o'clock, after which they can stand guard and greet the judges. Guests will start arriving at two, the first class is at two thirty. So volunteers please?" she looked enquiringly about the room. Grace thinking, please don't volunteer Colin, please don't!

Colin immediately put his hand up, "I don't mind staying, and I'm sure Grace will too, if you want to get off now." Grace smiled weakly, she could have killed him!

496

"Good show Colin, Grace. Well done everyone, marvellous job, now off you all go and see you later this afternoon. At least it's not raining!" she cackled out the joke, and people started to disappear until only Colin and Grace were left.

"What did you do that for Colin, I need a bath and to get changed. I've done more than my fair bloody share." moaned Grace, "It's always us."

"Stop complaining Grace, this is an important day and we can't risk those bloody little fuckers darting in here when they think the coast is clear and wrecking it all again. It makes me seethe!"

Grace looked quite shocked - Colin rarely swore which meant he must be seriously pissed off. She put her hand on his arm, "I know sweetie but we've all managed to retrieve the situation, it'll be fine now. Wasn't Lavinia marvellous, I bet she was a formidable old bag in the war, ordering everyone about being super-efficient and taking command. I was surprised she didn't have us girls in the land army uniform. I pity any Sab that she encounters!"

Tom picked up Lucy just outside Horsham, she didn't want to risk being seen near the Carfax when she was supposed to be sick in bed. She had dolled herself up, wearing a short pink summer dress with no bra, her nipples sticking out perkily beneath the flimsy fabric and high wedge heeled strappy sandals. She had washed and blow dried her hair into a windswept look, and wore fairly sensible make up - for her anyway. The Landrover chugged up beside the pavement and she got in showing a good deal of fake tanned legs, and promptly lit a cigarette, opening the sliding windows so that she could blow out the smoke.

"You look nice Lucy" remarked Tom, as he leaned over to kiss her on the cheek, "Pretty dress."

"Thanks Tom, you're sweet, yes I'm really looking forward to this." She had decided to adopt a sweet submissive attitude today, she wanted to get them all on side and was prepared to keep her opinions to herself for a change. "It'll be great to see everyone again, I hope Caitlin will be okay with me."

Tom looked embarrassed, "Well don't be surprised if she isn't your bosom buddy, after all you did walk out and leave her in the shit. You can't expect her to greet you like a long lost friend" Lucy's lack of sensitivity amazed him and he added "at least you did text her and the ice may have been broken a bit."

Lucy was annoyed, stupid fucking Caitlin and her pious wholesome ways, she could slap her, but instead she said, "Well I'm hoping she's forgiven me, she did reply after all, so that must be a good sign." She crossed her legs again, bugger she had a bit of an orange streak on her knee, oh well she doubted anyone would notice.

"We're lucky it's still on actually" said Tom, "there was a raid on the kennels last night by the Sabs."

Lucy screwed her head around to stare at him, feeling a guilty flush creep up her face, "NO! I don't believe it, what happened? Tell me!" She couldn't see how Jonty and his pals could've been responsible; she hadn't spoken to them since Thursday.

Luckily for Lucy, Tom was concentrating on driving and didn't see her blush, and he went on to recount the events of last evening and the melee of trying to sort it out this morning. "Right old state they were in, I can tell you" he finished.

"How dreadful, was there much mess?" Lucy asked, thinking delightedly how she could imagine them all running round like headless chickens.

"No luckily, only the food got nicked. It's okay now, Old Lavinia Appleton-Lacey got everyone rallied round, and you wouldn't even really know."

Lucy could picture the scene and hugged herself with glee, how bloody funny, shame they discovered the damage so early! "That's good" she said, "I can imagine it would have been awful though."

Tom had driven through Fittlebury now and the jolly bunting flags could be seen ahead at the entrance to the kennels, he joined the queue of cars waiting to park in the adjacent paddock, and Lucy checked her lipstick in the mirror. He looked at her sideways; he was dreading this - why oh why had he agreed to take her. They parked and got out, making their way towards the festivities, Lucy tottering precariously in her high shoes on the grass.

It was already packed and the judging had not even begun. People were milling around chatting and laughing, the ladies were like a herbaceous border of elegant flowers in a dazzlingly colourful array of summer dresses and hats. The men in contrast were sporting a variety of tweed jackets and caps, blazers and chinos with panamas or smart suits with bowlers. Just outside the marquee white tables and chairs had been set up and were already filling up, people bagging their places for prime position. Around the parade rings, behind the freshly painted railings, chairs had been placed for the ringside spectators. Old George was holding court, in a smart black bowler hat with his startlingly white dust coat talking earnestly to Grace and Colin. She looked pretty, in a mid-length floaty floral dress in subtle shades of yellows and greens which matched her tawny complexion. Colin as usual looked the country gent in a smart linen jacket, with a crisp shirt and Countryside Alliance tie, topped with a panama hat. They looked more as though they should have been going to a day at the races. Talking to Sandy and Mark, were Jennifer and Charles, and they had all dressed up for the occasion too, Sandy so petite in her usual elfin style and Jennifer, taller and very elegant in a fitted linen dress with a wide brimmed hat showered with roses. Chloe and Katherine were chatting to one of the masters, and looked equally chic smart, it was definitely an occasion for dressing up. The main topic of conversation amongst the guests was the damage from last night; and speculation was rife as to whether this was sign of things to come.

Lucy held onto Tom's arm for support, he wished he could shrug her off without being too rude, but it was impossible, she was clinging on to him like a leech. They made their way over to Oli who was talking to Jay; he too was in the traditional dress of the hunt servant, with a borrowed bowler and white coat, they glanced up when they saw Lucy and Tom approaching, nudging each other in the ribs.

"Hi lads" smiled Lucy pushing her tits out in front of her, "good to see you all again."

Oli could not take his eyes off her chest, watching her breasts swinging provocatively under her dress, "Hi Lucy, nice to see you too" he said pointedly.

She leaned over and kissed him on the cheek, "How've you been? It's so great to be here. Tom's such a darling for bringing me!"

Tom squirmed, "Well you kinda insisted" he stammered.

Oli grinned, poor old Tom, too nice for his own good, "Well you certainly look perky enough." staring openly at her tits again, "What've you been up to?"

"Not much really – I miss the hunting world, didn't realise I would so much." She flirted, "We had some fun didn't we!"

Oli looked at her remembering the sex crazed demonic Lucy when she had worked at Nantes, and felt slightly awkward. It'd just been sex for him he'd thought - and for her too, and here she was saying she missed them all with a wistful look on her face! Was it because she missed the sex or genuinely their company, he was sceptical that it was the latter. "We did have some fun" he said reluctantly. "I'm surprised though after everything, that you wanted to come here today."

"Oh, I want to carry on and be a hunt supporter, even if I'm not working at Nantes anymore" she added smiling naughtily "I love hunting, you definitely haven't seen the last of me."

"Good for you!" said Jay, eyeing Lucy up and down "We need all the supporters we can get, if my job's to stay safe."

"You…" she winked at him slowly, "can always have my support! Come on let's mingle and grab some champagne."

"Well…we have to help with the food and stuff, so unless you want to work for your tea, you'll have to socialise on your own." Tom interrupted, he didn't want to be seen with Lucy too much, although he was fully entitled to bring a guest today - just not this guest.

"Okay! I'll be fine   don't worry about me" Lucy said sweetly, "off you go and do your bit!" She sashayed away, smiling to people she knew, making a bee line for Giles Pillsworthy one of the masters who'd always had a roving eye for a bit of skirt. Perfect opportunity whilst his old battle axe of a wife was helping in the tea tent, he was talking to Michael Gainsborough, and these were exactly the people Lucy wanted to impress.

In a quiet corner slightly offset from the main throng of people, Caitlin and Oliver were deeply engrossed in conversation, she was looking at him anxiously, his hand touching her shoulders and he was obviously trying to calm her down. He leant forward and gave her a hug, and when they pulled away Caitlin had a tear in her eye, Oliver took her hand and led her off to get a cup of tea. She looked very upset.

Jennifer and Sandy exchanged glances at each other, "What's going on there then?" enquired Sandy, "Caitlin looked a bit fraught. Oli is so sweet."

Jennifer considered, "Yes she did look upset didn't she. It could be of course that she's worried about Pete, after all he's not been found."

Sandy studied Jennifer, "Aren't you afraid?" she added anxiously

Jennifer smiled, "No Sandy, I'll be on my guard don't worry. I've taken care of myself in some tough situations when I was a kid and living in London - you know the old saying, 'What doesn't kill you makes you stronger', and I know that everyone is looking out for me too -so that helps."

"You're a remarkable woman. I don't think I'd be quite so cool!"

"Yes you would be, besides I've fought hard to be with Charles and I'm just starting to live my life, no-one is going to take that away from me." Jennifer said defiantly, "Especially Pete!"

"Good on you kidda!" laughed Sandy, they both turned as the hunting horn sounded, "Look they're starting with the judging, let's catch the others and try and get a good seat!"

Lucy was having a great time. She had spent most of the afternoon necking down the champagne and chatting up the men folk in the hunt and didn't miss a flirty trick with any of them. Their wives of course had other opinions about her but Lucy was oblivious to the silly cows - frumps the lot of them. The good news was that Michael Gainsborough, who was the hunt treasurer, had suggested that she became a member of the supporters club, then she would be on their mailing list and be kept informed of meets and the like. Lucy said it would be a great idea and had promptly kissed him on the cheek - much to the chagrin of his wife. Michael went onto explain that these dates were still pretty hush hush and as a hunt supporter she would be notified if there were any changes to the plans, usually by telephone.

"Apart from today, we don't normally have much trouble with Sabs these days and we keep ourselves to ourselves to be on the safe side." he brayed at her.

Lucy looked at him demurely, thinking pompous old git, but merely gazed admiringly into his drink flushed face, his bulbous nose twitching with importance. He didn't know what he had coming.

Andrew was chatting to Grace, she was animated and excited her pretty face flushed with pleasure; her two hound puppies had done well and she was now in possession of a silver trophy and a beautiful cut glass engraved rose bowl. She couldn't have been more thrilled, her face was creased with smiles and Andrew was saying how very pleased he was for her and he was looking forward to her joining their team. Grace chattered on, she was excited not just about the puppies doing so well, but she had so much to look forward to in her life. Andrew listened indulgently, giving her his full attention, his handsome face not leaving hers whilst she prattled on. He was not particularly interested in the hounds or the etiquette of hunting, but their practice took care of the hunt horses and many of the hunt patrons, so it was an important for him to be here, it was expected of him, as it was of Oli. So far all he had done was make small talk to a lot of his clients, but he was genuinely delighted and pleased for Grace, and he thought she was a great choice for Paulene as an assistant. Colin listening to them amiably. Andrew was completely unaware that he was such a hit with the ladies, with his easy laugh and lop sided smile showing very even white teeth, and for Colin, his wife's contentment was all he wanted and right now she could not be happier.

"No Julia today then Andrew?" asked Colin, "I bet the other ladies are delighted!" Colin smiled benignly, despite his good looks Andrew had never been one to be interested in other women, although he had plenty of offers, Lascivious Libby had always been after him, but had switched her affections to Oli since he'd arrived.

"Ah she has one of her tennis tournaments today, and this isn't really her thing here, not being a rider or follower of the hunt" Andrew smiled at him ironically, "tennis balls interest her far more."

"That's a pity, we hardly ever see her these days. Perhaps you both fancy coming for supper one night, eh Grace?" suggested Colin, turning to her for confirmation and willing her to agree.

"Yes, do Andrew, it'd be so nice to see you both and it's been ages since you came over together." She laughed, her eyes twinkling ,if she didn't know Colin better she would swear he was doing a bit of fence mending between Andrew and Julia, "Although should we be asking my boss to supper?"

"Definitely, we'd love to come, give Julia a ring Grace and organise it." Andrew said quickly, then looked over her shoulder, "Oh, there's Oli, excuse me a moment, I need to speak to him" He kissed Grace on the cheek and dashed off.

"Well he was in a rush" said Colin, "don't forget to ring Julia and organise that supper, that man works too hard. And perhaps we can get to the bottom of this nonsense about Julia and that young man."

"Maybe, but I wouldn't count on Julia wanting to come at all. Not after what Mum and I saw in the garden centre the other day! She has other fish to fry I think and you shouldn't be interfering!"

Andrew hurried away, relieved to have seen Oli to give him the chance to make his escape, not that he didn't like Colin and Grace very much, but he didn't want to talk about Julia, he was always having to make one excuse after another for her absence, frankly it was getting tricky to think of how to make her apologies anymore. He hailed Oli, "Hi mate, gather you had a bad one last night."

"Hey buddy, been looking for you, yep dodgy colic, they operated at the veterinary hospital early this morning, looking less touch and go now though." Oli looked tired with dark rings under his eyes, but was definitely more like his usual ebullient self. Andrew was pleased, for a while since Suse had left he had been quite morose, but he was clearly recovering. "Caitlin's just getting me a cup of tea, shall I get you one?"

"Too late, I'm here" said a soft Irish voice, "Hi Andrew, how are you, been a while since I saw you." She leant over and kissed him on the cheek, her soft dark eyelashes brushing his skin.

"Caitlin, how are you?" Andrew exclaimed, taking the tea and passing the cup to Oli "You look as lovely as ever." This wasn't quite true - Caitlin's eyes were dull and miserable.

"Oh go on with you now." She smiled at him coyly, "Shall I fetch you a drink of tea then?"

"No, honestly, I'm all tea-ed out." He grinned, "How are you, horses okay?"

"Yes, fine thanks."

Oli intervened, slipping his hand around Caitlin's shoulders, "Poor Caitlin, there's been a nasty business up at Nantes."

"Oli, you weren't supposed to say." she hissed, "They don't want it getting out now."

"Sorry, but Andrew won't say anything, he's used to keeping secrets, aren't you mate, besides you can't keep anything quiet in this village for long." Oli whispered back, "he'll find out soon enough, anyway he's family."

"Christ, what's happened?" Andrew looked concerned, "Are you okay? Don't worry I won't breathe a word."

Oli looked at Caitlin, "Luckily, she is, and so is Jennifer, although it was a close run thing. Caitlin here saved the day!"

"Oli, don't be exaggerating now." She looked uncomfortable, her eyes darting about to make sure no-one was listening, and then her face froze in shock, "B'jesus, look who's over there!"

Andrew and Oli stared over to where she was looking, to see juicy Lucy in full flow, chatting to Harry the Whip, with Beebs clutching onto his arm looking seriously pissed off. One strap had fallen down off Lucy's pink dress displaying her shoulder and dangerously near to exposing a nipple and she was laughing and joking with them, her blonde hair twirling as she playfully punched Harry in the chest.

"Christ!" exclaimed Oli, "She's got a bloody nerve to show up here."

"I was rather hoping I'd seen the last of her to be sure" groaned Caitlin, "she's bad news so she is."

"Don't look now" whispered Andrew uncomfortably, "she's seen you."

Lucy stopped in mid conversation, catching sight of the three of them, buoyed up with the champagne, she excused herself from Harry almost ignoring Beebs and swayed over towards them. The vets looked at one another and then back at Caitlin, who was gritting her teeth.

"Caitlin!" slurred Lucy, "Great to see you! I was hoping you'd be here!" She launched herself over to hug Caitlin whose body froze with dislike. Lucy didn't seem to notice, and then turned to Oliver and Andrew. "Well, well, two gorgeous vets, you must share them out Caitlin, you can't have them all to yourself, or can you?" Lucy smirked tottering unsteadily on her heels and hitching her strap back over her shoulder, "Now what are you three talking about?"

"Hello Lucy" Andrew said coldly adding, quite rudely for him, "who invited you?"

Lucy looked at him in surprise, "Now Andrew aren't you pleased to see me?"

"No frankly I'm not, excuse me, come on Caitlin, I think I need that tea." He took the astonished Caitlin firmly by the arm and marched her into the tea tent.

"How rude!" exclaimed Lucy to Oli, who was staring open mouthed, Andrew was never like that, he was politeness personified. "What's got into him?"

"Bad night on call" improvised Oli, "How are you Lucy - since your hasty departure?"

Lucy stroked his bare arm with her fingertips, "Yes it was hasty, but I'm back now, and a little bird told me that you are a single man! We must get together, I could come over and make you supper one night if you like?" Immediately she slipped into full flung innuendo mode as she licked her lips at him, running her snaky pink tongue along her teeth.

Oli tried not to look horrified, God she was ghastly, "I don't think my girlfriend would like it." he countered quickly.

It was Lucy's turn to look surprised, "You didn't waste any time did you big boy! Or did you always have a girlfriend?" she playfully pushed him, "well if you're ever in need of company!" she winked at him, "I'm your girl!"

Jennifer balancing a cup and saucer carefully in her hand glanced at Chloe, who had also been watching the little charade played out with Lucy and Oliver.

"She's such a little cow that one" Sandy exclaimed, "Just look at her."

"Yes, I can't say we aren't glad to be rid of her, although I didn't know her really, but she made Caitlin's life hell." Jennifer said thoughtfully, "we've a new groom starting at the end of the month, thank goodness"

"That's good – what's she like? She can't be much worse than Lucy." Sandy said nastily, "Anything's got to be an improvement."

"Well she's a he and actually he's drop dead gorgeous to look at!" Jennifer laughed, "He's a friend of Susie's."

Chloe grinned, "Yes, I heard he was coming, Susie speaks very highly of him, in all ways."

"Well – good looking and efficient, got to be an ace combination!" laughed Sandy, "might cheer up Caitlin too, she's had a rough few weeks."

"Mmmm, but I think there's a man at the foot of it all, you never know your new Adonis might be just the thing to put a smile on her face" added Katherine, "she's such a nice girl, she deserves someone lovely."

"She and Oliver are very close aren't they? Do you think there's anything going on there? After all - his wife leaving and all that?" Jennifer gave a naughty laugh, "They'd make a splendid couple, and they're always talking together."

"Who knows, but good on her and him, that's all I can say. Makes you wonder though if that was the real reason Suse did a bunk, but Caitlin hardly seems the type to be having affairs with married men does she?" said Sandy, "although Suse was a sour old bag, I suppose who could blame him?"

"You never know what goes on in marriages though do you – after all ..." At that moment the conversation was interrupted by Charles, a bit worse for wear on the champagne, "Come on you lovely ladies, what are you nattering about?" he grinned naughtily slipping his hand around Jennifer's waist, "what's the gossip?"

"Just talking about you dear Charles what else?" quipped Sandy, taking Mark's hand as he joined them, "or maybe not, now you're strictly a one woman man."

"Definitely am!" Charles smiled at Jennifer who flushed with pleasure. "Come on Missus" he added "home time for us I think!"

In the banter, none of them noticed that Chloe had gone quite pale, mulling over what had been said about Caitlin.

CHAPTER 45

By Monday **Pete** was still missing. Charles didn't go into work until late, insisting on having breakfast with Jennifer. He hadn't left her side all weekend and whilst it was lovely for her to know he was so caring, frankly it was beginning to feel like she was in prison.

"Charles darling, please go to work and stop behaving like an old woman!" she complained, "I'm going up to Chloe's as usual and I'll stay there for most of the morning, then I'm going shopping into Penfold's and then I'll be home, where Mrs Fuller will be and Caitlin too, so I'll be fine."

Charles winced, he knew she was right she would be surrounded by people she knew all day, "I know you think I'm over reacting, but it's only because I care."

She got up from her chair and made her way over to him, kissing him on the mouth, "I love it that you do sweetie, but life has to go on doesn't it? I promise to ring you later – okay?"

He kissed her back, "Yep, okay Jen!" He rolled the single syllable with a smile, "Since when were you Jen and not Jennifer by the way?"

"Funny isn't it!" she laughed, "I don't know how that happened, but most of the girls at Chloe's call me Jen, and I quite like it actually, makes me feel ... less frosty somehow! D' you know for years when I was a kid, I insisted on being called Jennifer, somehow had more gravitas than 'our Jen' which is what Mum and Susan used to call me, but with the Mileoak lot – it seems fine."

"Well I think either suits you. Incidentally, have you spoken to your mother lately?"

She was surprised, he'd always been snobby about her family, they'd never been to Nantes, he always preferred that she saw them in

London, and in truth it had quite suited her too, they wouldn't fit in with her lifestyle down here just as she hadn't either. "Well I do try to give her a quick ring every other day or so" guiltily thinking to herself that recently she'd been too busy enjoying herself, although she did send her mum money regularly, which her mother had always been proudly reluctant to take. "I must of course."

"Why don't you ask her down here for a few days?" Charles said stroking her arm, "I think it'd be nice for her – don't you?"

"Charles, do you mean it!" Jennifer exclaimed, "I'd love to, but are you sure?"

"Jennifer, Jen … this is your home, of course you can have your mother here to stay if you like! I know I've not been easy about it before, and I can be a bloody snob and a difficult bastard, but she's your mum and if it makes you happy, it makes me happy too." Charles actually had another motive, it would also be another person to keep an eye out for her whilst this Pete crisis had not been resolved. "Why not get on the blower today and ask her?"

"Darling, you're so lovely, thank you I will!" She looked at the clock, "Come on now, we'd better get cracking – we'll both be late."

Charles threw his napkin on his plate, and got up, "I'll follow you up in my car as far as Chloe's to make sure you're okay."

Jennifer looked at him mildly exasperatedly, "There is no need Charles, what d' you think – Pete is going to leap out in front of me and drag me from the car." Come on ..!'"

"Okay, okay, I'm over-reacting. But I'm going to follow you anyway, enjoy the attention woman!" Charles slapped her bum in the tight fitting breeches, no need for her to hide them now, although she was still not prepared for the staff to see her in them "D' ya know, these are rather sexy on you, have we got time for a quickie?"

Grace had got up early. She hurried out to check the horses, do the chickens and walk the dogs before coming in to make some breakfast. Colin was in the kitchen and had beaten her to it, there was bread toasting on the Aga, and he handed her a steaming cup of tea as she walked through the door.

"Crikey Colin, can I expect this every morning!" she exclaimed taking the tea, "I just hope it all goes okay. Although I'm feeling really guilty about leaving the dogs -I'm terribly nervous but excited too!"

"Now I've got a working wife, I must do my share." Colin affected a gloomy look, drooping his mouth down, "No more lady of leisure for you."

"You're a bloody cheeky sod!" She irritably threw a tea towel at him, "I work hard in my own way."

"Joke darling, joke! Blimey you're touchy this morning!"

"Sorry, yep I am, just a bit uptight, I need to get on with it and hope I'm doing the right thing." She looked sadly at the dogs, "They're so used to having me around all day. She stooped down to fondle their ears."

"Grace, for Christ's sake, it's just a morning! They'll be fine. Come here and give me a cuddle instead, I missed you in bed this morning."

She moved over to him, breathing his fresh lemony scent, "Oh Col, I hope I'm not gonna make a fool of myself."

"Look doll, of course you won't and remember this is a trial for them and for you, if you don't like it or change your mind, that won't be a problem, so try it and see." He hugged her, "Now go and get changed you smell of eau de 'orse!"

She pushed him away feigning offence, "No worse than Oli and Andrew. Seriously what d' you think I should wear today?"

"Short skirt, low cut blouse and stilettos!" he teased, winking exaggeratedly, "stocking tops!"

"Who d' you think I am? Juicy Lucy! Seriously, do you think jeans are too casual?"

Colin laughed, "You're making a big deal of this sweetie, what did Paulene have on when you popped in?"

"Jeans and a polo shirt with the vets' logo."

"Well then, stop panicking and put on some jeans and stop being daft." He pushed her gently towards the kitchen door, "Go on, get on with it, or you'll be late."

Jonty ended the call, looking at his phone and smiling to himself. Little Lucy had come up trumps, things were going his way and he'd make sure she had a nice little sweetener and fuck me she was easy to keep sweet, give her a length and a line and she'd do exactly what he said. Stupid slag.

"Good news?" Laura asked looking at him as she was packing up her laptop getting ready to go to college, she was always a bit worried these days, he was so secretive about what he was up to and he'd hardly noticed her at all lately. He'd become a total stranger and more than that he was frightening, she'd considered just upping and leaving, but she was afraid he'd come after her and find her and the thought of that made her wince; she had been on the receiving end of his back hand more than once now over the last few weeks. Anyway she'd no-where to go, she could hardly go back to her grandparents and her life in London had now been intrinsically woven into Jonty's world - he'd make sure he found her wherever she went.

Jonty glared at her, she pissed him off these days, and once she'd played her part he'd get rid of her. He knew that she was afraid of him; he sadistically enjoyed pushing her fear a little further each time, watching the little beads of perspiration break out on her upper lip. His total control over her was like a drug, even now he knew she was fearful of his response, her eyes not able to meet his as they bored into her. "Come here" he said gesturing for her to join him, relishing her reluctance. He repeated slowly, "I said come here. Don't make me angry Laura"

She hesitated and then came over to the sofa perching on the arm, he leaned over catching her hand and yanked her down next to him, "Jonty please, I have to go in a minute" she pleaded, "don't be so rough."

Jonty's glare turned into a mocking smile, "I have to go, please don't be rough Jonty" he mimicked, "I thought you liked it Laura, you do like it don't you" he whispered his lips very close to her ear, "Say you like it."

Laura whimpered, "I do like it Jonty, I do really."

"I know you do baby, I know" his hand strayed across, pulling open her shirt exposing her bra. He forced his hand inside wrenching out her breasts roughly and he felt her body tense, "relax, relax, I'm not going to hurt you." Laura knew better than to annoy him and lay like stone as he mauled at her trying to take deep breaths without him noticing her rising panic. He squeezed her nipples hard between his thumb and forefinger, smiling down at her, his eyes drilling into hers. She closed her eyes not daring to look at him and pretended to respond, if she didn't resist it would be over quicker and his hand moved downwards pulling up her skirt, prising open her legs and yanking off her knickers. Jamming his fingers roughly inside her, he said nastily, "There baby, that's nice for you isn't it Laura?"

"Yes Jonty" she moaned as he forced his way on top of her, undoing his jeans and stuffing his cock inside her thrusting backwards and forwards, the sweat running down his face with the exertion, she could smell the odour of his armpits as he levered himself up on his elbows.

When he had come, he pushed himself off, "You're a good little fuck, don't say I'm not good to you baby, and by the way I've got a little job for you to do tonight."

Laura had kept her eyes glued together and had to stop herself from yelling out, she opened them quickly before replying meekly "What do you want me to do?"

Things were busy at Mileoak, Patrick was bashing a red hot shoe on the anvil chatting to Chloe while he worked. He hammered away with easy expertise, stopping every now and then considering the shape and beating again until he was satisfied that it was perfect. He walked over to Ksar who was standing patiently, picked up one of his feet and held the hot shoe onto the hoof to check the shape. Pleased with the fit, he tossed the horseshoe to cool into a bucket of cold water where it spat and hissed like a pan of frying sausages. He stood up, rubbing his back and wiping the sweat from his forehead, "Fetch me a glass of water babe, I'm gasping!" he asked Chloe who was leaning up against the stable wall in her shorts and tee shirt, talking about the puppy show yesterday.

"Sure, do you want squash instead, I can do Ribena or Orange?"

"No ta, just the water 'll be fine thanks. Got any lollies?"

"Of course sweet pea, those orange ones you like – although how you can eat so many especially in the morning I don't bloody know!"

"You sounded just like Lily then!" Patrick laughed at her, "Now I know where she gets it from!"

"Gets what from?"

"All that bloody swearing!" his face creased up into smiles as he teased her, "and of course she's gorgeous looking - just like you!"

"Smooth talker, I'll get your bloody lolly." Chloe stopped, "Oh, oh, I see!" she laughed. "Bloody hell!"

Patrick watched her walk across the yard, he was very fond of Chloe, she wasn't only a client she was a friend, and he was worried about her, nothing he could put his finger on, but she looked a bit distracted and was too quiet, not like her normal bubbling self. It was funny but a lot of people seemed on edge. As he worked his mind drifted to the puppy show yesterday. Caitlin had seemed very agitated, he and Sharon had chatted to her for a while and she seemed to be perpetually looking over her shoulder, not like her at all, she was one of the sweetest people he knew, but he felt that she'd hardly been listening to them. Perhaps Ace had been there, lurking with his wife? Who could he be, and whoever he was, they were keeping it damned quiet, there was no hint of any scandal in any of the other yards he went into, despite his bantering curiosity. Of course though she could've been distracted by that little minx Lucy turning up, he couldn't believe the balls of her really! He supposed it was no wonder Caitlin was upset, probably thought she was there for a confrontation, although when he'd spoken to Lucy she had been all sweetness and light, she was pretty pissed though on all the fizz and was right flirty but genuinely seemed to want to make amends. Ah well, what did he know, Sharon had been furious when she had come up to them, he smiled, remembering how cross she had been when Lucy had hugged him - gave her the right evils! It was nice to be given the come on, okay he was probably a sucker for a pretty girl, and Lucy was attractive even if she was a bike, but it had made Sharon stir her stumps, they'd good sex last night and it had been ages since she had put out for him. Women! He was still smiling to himself, hammering and shaping another shoe when a car pulled down the drive. Looking up he was surprised to see Jennifer Parker-Smythe arriving in that flashy motor of hers - here again, what was she up to? Ah, a farrier's life was certainly never dull - there was not much gossip he missed!

He hadn't heard Chloe come back, as she handed him his lolly, "Eat it before it melts. Did I just see a car come down the drive?"

"Now little Chloe, what is it you're not telling me? That was Jennifer PS coming in, and that's the third time I've seen her pull in here – what's going on that I don't know about?"

Chloe looked shifty, "Sorry, I hate keeping things from you, but I was sworn to secrecy – she's learning to ride. Been coming up every day for a while now, let me introduce you."

"Fine friend you are keeping secrets from me" Patrick whined jokingly, "Seriously, I'd like to meet her, heard a lot about her, but she's never around when I go up to Nantes."

"She's really a good laugh, and has had rotten time over the last few days what with ..."Chloe flustered, she could have bitten her tongue out, so much for keeping quiet. It was too late - Patrick never missed a thing – he looked up from the anvil, his face just about to ask the question why, when Jennifer herself walked up to them.

"Hello – glorious morning!" She turned to Patrick, "I don't think we've met, although you shoe my husband's horses I think – I'm Jennifer Parker-Smythe" she held out her hand to Patrick, who carefully wiped his hands on a towel before shaking hers back.

"Nice to meet you, Mrs Parker -Smythe" he said admiringly "I've heard a lot about you."

Jennifer smiled, "All good naturally! Caitlin and Chloe speak very highly of you. Please call me Jennifer."

Patrick laughed, appraising Jennifer up and down, she was bloody lovely he thought, but a bit ice maiden for him – he liked his women with a bit more meat on them.

"I'm learning to ride with Chloe" Jennifer continued, "She's doing a marvellous job on me, although I'd be grateful if you didn't mention it to anyone – it's supposed to be a secret!"

"Chloe's the best there is, if anyone can teach you she can. Don't worry, I won't say anything either if you don't want me to." Patrick although he was a supreme gossip, knew when to keep his mouth shut, it would be more than his life was worth to upset some of his best clients in one fell swoop.

"You'd better not Patrick, otherwise I'd be seriously pissed off – not to anyone - okay! And stop taking the Mick about my teaching!" laughed Chloe, "How are you Jen? Enjoy the puppy show?"

"Yes it was lovely, although it was quite a surprise to see Lucy there, I thought she had upped sticks and done a bunk?"

"Oh take more than that to break through her tough hide, although I felt very sorry for Caitlin, she looked right upset" Patrick gossiped, "although young Oli the vet was more than happy to take care of her seemed to me."

"Well poor Caitlin, she's a lovely girl and from what I understand she handed the debacle with Lucy rather well, but perhaps she was still shaken up after Friday – after all it must have been more awful for her than me I think, she's been in a terrible state." Jennifer shook her head sadly, "I was lucky she came along."

Patrick's ears were almost visibly flapping, "Why what happened?" he asked trying to keep the keenness out of his voice.

Jennifer pulled a face and held out her hands, and gave him a sketchy account of the incident and that Pete had run away.

By the time she had finished Patrick's mouth was hanging open, "Blimey, that must've been who the missus saw running in front of the car on Friday night" he exclaimed excitedly and told them both about their near miss and the strange bloke.

"What time was this?" Jennifer asked breathlessly, "Where did he go, did you see?"

"Nah, it all happened in a flash, we were coming home on the Cuckfield road up alongside the old Abbey, I was dozing in the passenger seat, when suddenly Sharon slams on the anchors claims she's seen a man run in front of her. I didn't take much notice 'cos she's a terrible driver at the best of times and we just drove on, but it must have been him! I didn't even see the fellah, but she was so sure it was a man, no idea where he went."

Chloe gasped, "Patrick you have to tell the police, they're all out looking for him, was he heading out towards Cuckfield then?"

"Well I couldn't say doll, Sharon might have a better idea, but I never actually saw him."

"Right, come on Jen let's go up to the house and ring Charles, he'll know what to do."

Grace had really enjoyed her morning so far, the time had whizzed past and her head was stuffed full of information She had made copious notes as they went along and Paulene was a great trainer, explaining the office procedures clearly and patiently. Andrew and Oli were both out on calls all morning, and the phone had been busy with one thing or another and Paulene was constantly being interrupted, so Grace had used the time to draw breath and make sense of the computer system. Looking at Paulene, Grace wondered how she'd managed without help, no wonder they needed an extra pair of hands.

Paulene put the phone down, scribbling madly on the call log and rang Andrew asking him if he could pop into another client when he was in that area later. Finally she sat down with a thump in the office chair, "Phew, I could do with a cup of coffee!"

"I'll make it Paulene" offered Grace "I had no idea you would be so busy here."

"It's always like this on Monday mornings, all the non-emergency stuff building up over the weekend" sighed Paulene "totally manic. I can't tell you what a relief it is to have you here."

"Well I hope you'll find that I can take some of the pressure off you at least once I get to know the ropes a bit more."

"You'll be fine Grace and it's nice for me to have company as well, it can get a bit lonely on my own sometimes." The phone rang again and Grace signalled she would make the coffee and left Paulene to take the call. She hummed to herself, she had a good feeling about this job, she knew she was going to love it.

When the front door opened and Andrew walked in, it was to find Grace and Paulene deeply pouring over the computer screen, their blonde and brown heads so close as to be touching.

"Hi you two! How's it going Grace, Paulene cracking the whip?"

"Hi boss – we're getting on just fine, been busy here this morning though."

"Hi Andrew" Grace looked up her face a bit flushed, "Paulene's been brilliant! Hope I don't let you all down."

"Don't be daft!" laughed Paulene, "you're picking up the computer side of things really well, and you'll soon be sorting out all the other stuff."

"Well that's good news, well done girls. Paulene any interest in the vet job yet?"

"Bit early boss, it's only Monday. Don't worry as soon as I get anything I'll let you know."

"Are you recruiting for a new vet?" asked Grace, "That's exciting."

"Yes it is – Oli and I can't keep up with all the work, just like Paulene. The Practice is expanding all the time." Andrew smiled at her, "I know I don't have to say this Grace, but I will anyway - anything you hear in the office has to remain absolutely confidential for obvious reasons, but also too we are a very small team here and I like everyone to be included but some of our future plans are a bit hush hush at the moment. We try to have a practice meeting once a week, so you'll be fully updated then."

"Of course Andrew, I totally understand – you can certainly rely on my discretion."

"I know that Grace, I know. We have exciting times ahead and I'm so glad you're going to be part of them." He picked up his diary and went through to the back office.

"That sounds interesting." Grace exclaimed to Paulene, "but before I think about anything else, you'd better just check I've done this right." She indicated to the screen where she had been listing the call outs for the weekend.

Paulene checked the work carefully, "Perfect Grace, you're going to have no problem with this."

The morning raced frantically away to lunch time, the girls had worked practically non-stop. Grace couldn't believe the time as she gathered up her handbag and car keys, Paulene got her lunch out of the fridge and settled down to eat a sandwich. Grace felt guilty going off, "I'm so sorry to be leaving Paulene, but I can't stay any longer – I've left my dogs at home and they're not used to being on their own for long."

Paulene laughed, almost choking "You are funny Grace!" Swallowing her mouthful, she added "Of course you have t' go, you're only part time. Why not bring the dogs in with you tomorrow? They'll be no trouble and if you can't bring them to the vets where can you bring them?"

Grace was astonished, she hadn't even thought of asking. "That'd be fantastic! Are you sure Andrew and Oli won't mind? I don't want to be a damned nuisance."

"Course they won't mind, anyway I run the office – not them. If the dogs don't settle then we'll have to rethink, but worth giving it a try eh?"

"It'd make a huge difference to me, and they're very well behaved. Not like the mad hounds I walked this year." Grace was thrilled, it would make her feel so less guilty. "Okay we'll try it out tomorrow then, thanks Paulene, see you in the morning – don't work too hard.

CHAPTER 46

The same evening Charles was lounging on the sofa next to Jennifer, cradling his brandy, his feet up on the coffee table, the paper discarded on the floor beside him. It had been a worrying day for him - when Chloe telephoned him to tell him what Patrick's wife had seen he'd felt totally sick. For a moment he had remained speechless and then demanded to know more, listening carefully to Chloe's account. He had replaced the receiver and immediately dialled Alex Corbett to be met by the frosty receptionist, and himself shouting and telling her she was a stupid bitch and to put him through straight away. Alex had remained irritatingly calm, and asked him to kindly remain so too, and that he would get onto the police and update them, but that Pete was probably miles away by now. The psychiatric social worker was convinced that he would have probably been lucid enough to get right out of the area, and knowing he'd done wrong, run off – possibly to London. Charles hadn't agreed and his frustrations mounted to Vesuvius proportions – but he was wasting his breath. They seemed to have no conception of how Pete had been behaving or frankly how dangerous was. After the call he had sat staring out of the window wishing he could go home, but there were some tricky negotiations to handle that day with the foreign market and he had been late in enough as it was. Now though he at last felt relaxed as he sprawled beside Jennifer stroking her hair with his spare hand. They were watching an old re-run of Inspector Morse and she was watching engrossed, concentrating on yet another serial killer on a spree of multi-murders. The whole genre was a bit too close to home for him, although she seemed oblivious to connection.

"Did you ring your mother darling?" he asked during the commercial break in the programme, "have you fixed a date for her to come?"

She got up and replenished his glass, "Yes, I did ring her this afternoon, but I didn't mention it."

"Why not?" Charles took his glass, "I thought you'd love the idea?"

Jennifer looked awkward, "Actually darling, I thought you might've changed your mind, after all it was pretty much a spur of the moment thing this morning. You know act in haste, repent in leisure." she laughed, "come on you know what I mean."

Charles sighed, he knew his normal reaction would have been to be cross that she hadn't done as he asked, but all he felt was ashamed – it just emphasised what a selfish prick he was, "No sweetie, I meant it, I was wrong before, please do ask her."

Jennifer smiled, she knew he was worried about her, but still their relationship seemed to be taking a new turn and it was one she loved, "Okay, how about sometime soon then?"

"Great, perhaps over a Friday night to a Monday, then you could have Friday together and I could be here over the weekend and drop her back in town on Monday – how about this weekend coming - what do you think?"

"Sounds great, I'll ring her in the morning. Charles thank you, this means a lot to me."

"Don't say that!" Charles moaned, "I feel bad enough already, I should've said it ages ago."

She went over to the sofa, nestling against him, "You've said it now, that's all that matters." Jennifer too had a tiny agenda in asking her mother to come down, she had already spoken to her sister, who knew more about self-defence weapons than anyone else she knew, and who was procuring some protection for her that very day. Her mother could bring down the innocuous parcel when she came. Perfect, Pete wouldn't know what hit him if he tried anything again, "Oh look" she said "it's started again" as the advertisements on the television finished, "We'd better concentrate."

Laura walked down the high street, it was still quite light and the sodium lamps hadn't come on yet. A police car dodged past, weaving it's way in and out of the evening traffic, it's blue lights flashing and sirens blaring as it wailed past her. She jumped nervously suddenly feeling huge and conspicuous to them, even though she knew that they would never have noticed her - she just felt guilty. The thought of being apprehended with all this stash on her was terrifying; it would be enough to charge her with dealing. Of course she did the odd line herself, but she'd never been involved in this sort of trick. She kept her eyes down marching steadfastly towards the tube, the sooner the job was over the better.

Linda's flat looked empty as she made her way towards it and up the filthy stairwell, the door was firmly closed and she couldn't hear anything as she tapped on the door. Laura waited anxiously, she would be bloody furious if she'd made this journey and no-one was here. She knocked again harder this time and was just turning to walk away when she heard a tiny noise from the other side of the door. There was no letter box to peer through and she tapped on the door again, this time calling out, cocking her head to one side to listen for any response. She heard it again, a feeble little moan coming from inside, she rapped harder, but it was hopeless whoever was inside was not going to open the door. What to do she thought, then had a sudden idea, reaching up on tip toes and fumbling along the top ledge of the architrave, she was in luck – a key She struggled to flip it down, finally it fell with a clunk onto the floor, picking it up and gingerly she pushed it into the lock turning the key until it clicked. She tried to push the door, but it was stuck, she shoved harder opening it as far as she could but meeting a solid obstruction. She edged it open further, squeezing through the narrow gap and gasped to find Linda sprawled on the other side. Laura dropped to the floor turning her over, she was totally comatose spittle drooling out of her mouth. Putting her fingers to her neck Laura tried to feel for a pulse, She fumbled about - God it all looked so easy on the TV; when suddenly Linda's body went rigid and then went into uncontrollable shaking, her head violently twitching backwards and forwards. Fucking hell, she was having some sort of fit, Laura jumped back to avoid the thrashing arms and legs wondering what the hell she should do, she had no idea. She couldn't ring for an ambulance not with all this gear on her, she watched helplessly as Linda's body jerked on the floor - she could just run away, no-one would know she had been here. In that moment she heard the sound of feet thundering up the stairs and Sean blundered his way through the door.

"Shit, Laura, what's going on?" he took one look at Linda and fell to his knees grasping her firmly by the arms trying to stop her flailing about, "Linda, Linda, it's okay babe, it's okay!" He glared at Laura, "What happened?"

"I didn't do anything Sean! I just popped by and found her, she seemed out of it, then started some kind of fit!" Laura tried desperately to explain, "Oh God Sean, will she be all right?"

Linda's body was still thrashing around but the fit was definitely subsiding, although she was still unconscious. Sean relaxed his grip and began to stroke her hair, and then when she was completely still, he moved her carefully onto her side. Laura stood clutching her arms around her, she was astonished at how tender Sean was with Linda and more amazed that he knew what to do. Sean looked up at her, "We'll just stay with her, make sure she's not sick, she'll come round in a minute or two, but she won't remember what's happened."

"What has happened Sean, has she got some kind of epilepsy? I had no idea."

"Don't be stupid, this isn't epilepsy" he stared at her stonily, "this is drugs."

"You're joking! I knew she'd started using but had no idea it was serious."

"Are you fuckin' thick? It's always bloody serious. I smoke a lot of dope, take the odd pills, but this stuff is fucking lethal, I never touch it. Linda started using a while ago - thought she could handle it" He sighed, "like anyone ever can."

Laura put her hand on his shoulder, "Sean I'm so sorry, this is bloody awful."

He shrugged her hand away, "Are you? Why are you here Laura? Were you bringing a little something for Linda? She has gotten so much worse since you started coming round."

Laura recoiled, "'Course not, what d'you take me for? That's a bloody terrible thing to say." She guiltily clutched her shoulder bag closer to her, "I only came by to see you."

Linda was starting to moan and come round, Sean leaned over

her, "Hey babe, I'm here, it's okay, I'm here." He stroked her face, "Come on let's put you on the sofa." He picked her up like she was a bag of sweets, and Laura could see how emaciated Linda had become, her bones sticking out through her tee shirt. At some point she must have wet herself, there was a dark stain on her leggings, and the track marks on her arm were obvious. Her white face was streaked with black make up and her eyes looked vacant. Sean laid her tenderly on the sofa, and put a pillow under her head, and Linda stared at them, not able to speak.

"Look Sean, I'll go eh?" Laura twisted her hands together "I'm no good with this sort of thing."

"Sorry I snapped at you, but I just don't understand where she's getting it from, we've no money for this kinda shit." He looked gloomily at Linda, "Come on babe, you're okay now."

"Do you think we should call and ambulance Sean, she looks dreadful."

"Don't be stupid. She'll come round in a minute, then we've got to do some serious talking."

Laura stood watching, shifting her weight anxiously from side to side with her arms clutched tightly round her, when at last Linda started to moan and her eyelids flicked open and then shut again. "She looks a bit better, you're right she's coming out of it."

Sean leaned over her further, talking to Linda all the time. Laura felt helpless and guilty, this was her fault although she wasn't going to admit to that, instead she said "Look Sean, now she's recovering, I'm gonna go. I'll call you tomorrow – okay?"

Sean hardly acknowledged her, intent on Linda and muttered "okay", as Laura slipped out of the room.

She picked her way carefully down the stinking stairway into the street below where she leaned up against the wall breathing heavily desperately wondering what to do. One thing was for sure, if she went back to Jonty and hadn't handed over the goods she would be in serious trouble, but equally she wasn't going to give them to Linda either. She felt the package in her shoulder bag and made up her mind. She began to walk determinedly towards the tube, surreptitiously taking out the package and tossing it nonchalantly into the nearest bin as she passed.

Miles away at the Old Mill Pete shifted uncomfortably on his makeshift bed. The spores of mildew on the musty old sacks making him cough as they floated up to his nostrils. He was feeling calmer now, the voices in his head had been quiet for a few hours and he was no longer hungry. It had been easy to find food after all and he had enough here to last him for some time. He'd stowed the tins and boxes away under sacks and was careful to clean up after he'd eaten to avoid encouraging the rats. He felt filthy though and it was only at night time that he was able to go down to the mill pond to wash, for fear of being seen.

Earlier today he had heard the sound of a car engine coming up the drive from the lane and peering out through the timber cladding he watched a police squad car pull up and two officers had clambered out. They walked around the mill, trying all the doors and looking through the windows, and then started to make their way over to the outbuildings. His heart was pumping and his mouth had gone dry, and he scampered up the steps to the loft to hide himself under the sacks. He had waited a long time, hearing the men rattle the bar on the small outside door where he had barricaded himself in, listened to the scrunch of their feet as they walked around the buildings. He lay trembling under the sacks expecting at any moment for them to find him, and to his disgust found a trickle of urine seeping down his trousers in his anxiety. All the time he had to stuff his fist in his mouth to stop himself screaming. He had no idea how long he had lain there, it could have been minutes or hours until he was brave enough to put his head out from the sacks and creep down the stairs. He tiptoed across the echoing barn floor and squinted out through the gap, his eyes scanning as far as he could see and to his immense relief the police car had gone. He had leant back against the wall and allowed his body to slide down onto the floor, he was safe.

Now the night had fallen and he could risk going outside to wash. Silvery shafts of moonbeams spun down through the tiny gaps in the roof, and tentatively he crept down the stairs to slide open the barricaded side door. It was a lovely night, warm with a gentle breeze sighing through the rushes, the mill pond reflecting a ghostly light onto the trees. He waited, listening carefully to the night sounds and when he was sure that the coast was clear, shuffled over to the water's edge dipping his cupped hands into its smooth glass surface and the water rippled outwards in perfect concentric rings as he disturbed its stillness. The mild softness of the water soothed his face and he threw off his clothes and slipped his body into the cool water savouring the chill as it engulfed him easing away all the weary dirt of the day. His feet sunk into the squelching mud and he felt it ooze through his toes and turned his face upwards to the moon, and stood motionless like some ethereal spectre as the water became still around him. Some minutes passed as he stood not moving and the bite of the cold water pervaded his body and with a grunting effort he clambered back onto the bank, and stood shivering on the grass, realising with dismay that he had no towel or anything to dry himself. He would have to rectify that he thought, and he could do with some more clothes if he were to stay hidden here. Seizing up his jumper and rubbing himself down over his shivering body he crept back to the sanctuary of the barn.

Dawn was breaking as Andrew drove home, it had been a miserable night with the horse he had been attending dying from a twisted gut. Why oh why, did people leave it so late to call the vet; if the owners had rung when the horse had gone down with the colic that afternoon he could probably have saved it, but as it was they had left it too late calling in the early hours and by that time there was nothing that he could do. He hated cases like this, made him feel useless and angry too, the ignorance of people astounded him sometimes. The sunrise was awesome this morning, as the great ball of the sun crept up over the hills, spreading fingers of warmth over the land, the birds had just started to wake and their song heralded the dawn. His car sped along the lanes, rustling the tall cow parsley awake as he swept past on his way home. As he came to the turning up the lane leading to the Old Mill he was tempted to pull in and have a look round, he slowed right down gazing up the drive and hesitated, but he was dog tired and knew it could wait for another day, and putting his foot down on the accelerator pushed on towards home. Home, he thought, he wondered if Julia was awake waiting for him, but he knew she wouldn't be. It had been a long time since she worried about him and his late night adventures, and to be fair a long time since he had worried about hers. Once upon a time she may even have gone with him, but now they didn't even sleep in the same room when he was on call, as she hated being disturbed. So he would creep in and slide into the spare bed and try and get a couple of hours before he started his day again. Up ahead he saw the five bar gate into his own driveway, and it swung open as he approached and the car glided in beside Julia's little BMW Z3, and carefully locking the Toyota he crept into the house his eyes already heavy with sleep.

The sun continued its slow dawning as it crept up the sky, bathing the sleepy village with a soft mellow haze, the houses on the green had their curtains closed with no signs of life even though the birds had stirred a good thirty minutes earlier. Ravi Gupta however was wide awake and was already busy in the shop, having set out the flowers and vegetables under the awning and was now opening the stacks of newspapers delivered by the paper man. As he arranged them in neat rows on the shelves he pondered on the problem of Fatima. He was really worried about her and he'd left her to sleep on these last few mornings. He'd hoped that it would be easier for him now that the twins were home, but they had announced only yesterday that they intended going on a trip to Europe this summer with their Uni mates. How could he be managing he thought gloomily, it was all he could do to keep it all afloat as it was, Fatima's seemingly tireless energy had evaporated, and although the mind was willing, the ample flesh was not, and it was taking a serious toll on her health. If only he could be persuading her to go to see the specialist as Dr Corbett had advised, but she was determined that she wouldn't be going. He made her so cross, he had hoped that the twins might well have made her see sense, but it was almost worse, she would not be admitting to them that she was unwell. He sighed deeply, his kind face wrinkling with the worry of it all. He glanced down at his hands, they were filthy and blackened with the print from the papers, tutting he went into the kitchen at the back of the shop to wash them. He had just finished running the water when he thought he heard a noise in the shop, wiping his hands on a paper towel, he cocked his head to one side listening, then he bustled out to see who it was, but there was no-one there. How strange, he was sure that he had not been mistaken and then looking on the counter he saw a pound coin, someone must have come in for a paper, but they looked undisturbed and just as he had left them. He quickly checked the till, tossing in the coin, it was fine and untouched and nothing else seemed to have gone. He shrugged his shoulders, and went outside to look up and down the pavement, there was no-one in sight. Slowly he went back inside to get on with his work and promptly forgot all about it.

Colin looked down at his wife as she lay sleeping beside him. She looked lovely in this first light, and he couldn't resist putting out his hand and stroking her hair. She murmured in her sleep and rolled over, slowly opening her eyes to smile at him. He leant down and gently kissed her on the mouth, and she surprised him by kissing him back hard and throwing her arms around his neck and pulling him down towards her. He felt the soft cotton of her nightshirt against his bare chest and inched his leg in between hers, kissing her all the time. He slowly undid the buttons, allowing his hand to stray down over her breast. Grace groaned with pleasure and clenched his hair tighter in her hand, arching her hips into his, rubbing herself up and down on his leg. Colin moved his hand down circling her belly as he went and lifted himself off, opening her nightshirt, as he inched down the bed to suck on the nipples, biting them gently. Laughing, Grace rolled over in a flash, taking him with her, and levered herself astride him, pushing his cock up inside her as she gyrated her hips against him. They came together within minutes and flopped against each other laughing.

"Good morning darling! That was a nice surprise, if this is what that job is going to do for you, then I'm all for it!"

Grace smiled at him, "Nice surprise for me too." She gently eased herself off him and he rolled over onto his side of the bed, "fantastic, for once I don't get the wet patch!" she grinned reaching out for the tissues and handing them to him. "Come on you can make a cup of tea!"

Colin laughed and rolled out of the bed, struggling into some boxers, "Okay – you coming down or shall I bring it up?"

"I'll get up, got lots to do before I go to work. Did I tell you I can take the dogs with me today" she called as he stepped over the pile of clothes on the floor.

"Yes about four times! Crikey Grace why can't you put your clothes away when you get into bed."

"Stop moaning and make the tea." Grace laughed at him, falling out of bed and heading for the shower "and toast."

Colin padded down the stairs and into the kitchen, the sun was well and truly up now and already quite warm, and added to the heat of the Aga the room felt stuffy. He flung open the back door and the dogs sped into the garden, sniffing and rooting about in the borders and he turned round and put the kettle on to boil. He was busy slicing the bread when Grace ambled into the kitchen and plonked herself down on a chair.

"Don't you just love this time of year" she sighed "no horses to muck out, no wellies, no hay nets to fill, no dripping Barbours over the Aga."

"I do indeed darling, here's your tea and the toast won't be a minute."

Grace sat gazing out of the window up over the hills towards her parents' farm, "do you know" she mused "I think this little job is really going to suit me."

Colin came and sat down beside her with his tea, taking her hand over the table, "I'm so glad my darling, I really hope it works out for you, but you know if it doesn't and come the winter you find it all too much, you don't have to do it."

Grace leant over and kissed him, "I know" she sipped her tea and quickly changed the subject, "I'd better get the washing in before I go – I left it out last night, hope it's not damp."

"I'd better give my working wife a hand" Colin smiled and together they got up discarding their cups and went out into the garden. "It's a lovely morning."

"Sure is" replied Grace picking up the peg bag and laundry basket, swiftly unpegging the clothes and tossing them into the basket. "That's funny, I'm sure I hung a towel out here? Have you unpegged it Col?"

"Not guilty, sure you put it out?"

"Yes, I'm sure I did, one of the big fluffy bath ones you know? Perhaps it's blown off into the border, have a look love will you?"

In the end they both looked – but the towel had disappeared.

CHAPTER 47

Jennifer was in her study sipping her Earl Grey, she glanced at the clock it was just after nine and she took a deep breath and picked up the phone.

Her mother answered on the third ring "Jennifer, how lovely to hear from you again, I didn't expect you to call today!" The joy and surprise in her voice when she knew who was calling immediately made Jennifer feel guilty.

"Ah Mum, you make me feel awful when you say things like that"

"Don't be silly dear, I know how busy you are."

Jennifer gulped awkwardly, after all she was never busy really was she? "Listen Mum, I was just wondering if you fancied coming down to stay this weekend, I could pick you up on Friday and Charles says he will drive you back on Monday when he goes to work? " she blurted.

There was a small pause as her mother considered what to say and then replied tentatively, "But Jen are you sure? I mean I 'd love to but what about Charles – what'd he say?"

"Actually Mum, it was his idea. Please say you'll come, I'd love you to!" Jennifer pictured her mother sitting in the spotless flat with its lace curtains and china ornaments and suddenly felt desperate to hug her.

"Well dear of course I want to come. If you're sure?"

"That's settled then. I'll drive up first thing on Friday to pick you up. We'll come straight back here, so we can have the day together. I thought I'd take you out to lunch." Jennifer gushed, aglow with plans.

"Now don't you go spending money love, I can perfectly easy get the tube and a train down to you. I'm sure there's a bus to your village."

"No, definitely not, I'll pick you up - be about ten, if the traffic is good, so be ready to go for about then."

"Well, that'd be lovely Jen, what a surprise! It'll be so good to see you dear. Wait till I tell Mary next door!"

"It'll be good to see you too Mum, we'll have a smashing time."

After they said their goodbyes and Jennifer had replaced the receiver, she sat back in her chair, she wanted to make this really special. They could stop off in Horsham for lunch and she could buy her Mum some bits and pieces, then they could come back and have an hour or two by the pool if the weather was nice. She thought about taking her out for dinner either on the Friday or Saturday but she wasn't sure how comfortable her Mum would feel about that. Perhaps it would be a good idea to get Mrs Fuller to make supper for Friday, and then they could play it by ear for the Saturday and maybe do Sunday lunch out, it would be less formal. Yes, that would be a good idea, she would speak to Mrs Fuller straight away, but before that she quickly texted Charles and told him her plans. She smiled to herself, when he replied immediately saying how pleased he was.

Mrs Fuller was busy in the kitchen on her lap top when Jennifer breezed in her face flushed with smiles.

"Mrs Fuller, guess what - I've got some great news! My mother is coming to stay for a few days. I'm so excited! I want to make her feel really welcome. I know it'll be a bit of extra work for you, I hope you don't mind?"

"Of course I don't mind Jennifer, it'll be lovely to meet her, and it'll be lovely for you too. Good to see you with a bit of colour in your cheeks, especially after all that upset last week." Mrs Fuller beamed at Jennifer "We must plan some menus or will you be eating out?"

"Ah thank you. Well I thought supper here Friday night at any rate. Do you think the pink room would be the best?"

Mrs Fuller didn't hesitate, "By the far the nicest, it's such a lovely room, and the best views too. I'll make sure that Doris has it all ship shape, and has fresh flowers from the garden."

"Fantastic, she'd love that! Thank you." Jennifer flopped onto a kitchen chair, "I so want it all to go well. One thing though Mrs F, I don't want her worried by what happened, you know, don't say anything to her will you?"

"Course not m' dear I understand, that's best all forgotten. Now let me put the kettle on and you tell me what she likes best to eat and I'll get ordering."

Charles put down his mobile, cradling it momentarily in his hand. He was pleased that Jennifer's mother was coming, it would be nice for her, and frankly he meant what he said last night, he shouldn't have been such a cranky sod about if before. Jennifer had made a real effort with his children and he should've made an effort with her family too. Thinking of Jessica and Rupert, he must get a move on and book this safari, that's if that bitch Celia ever deigned to give him the go ahead. He made a move to dial Celia's number, but stopped himself. Before going ahead, he really should make sure that Jennifer really could ride, otherwise it could be a recipe for disaster. They could go this weekend with her mother. Instead of dialling Celia, he scrolled down to find Chloe's number and punched the call button waiting impatiently whilst it connected.

Chloe answered and sounded breathless "Hi Charles, I'm riding, any news?"

"No Chloe, thanks for passing that information on about Patrick, but the police checked that area and found nothing at all. It probably was him, but they think he'll have moved on, most likely gone out of the area, but I won't be happy till he's caught."

"Ah that's a bugger, I was hoping you had good news."

"Well in a way I have. Jennifer's mother is coming to stay for the weekend, she's really looking forward to it. To tell the truth, I don't know her very well and I was wondering if we could come up to you and if you have time to give Jennifer a riding lesson?" Charles went on, "I'm booking a safari holiday for us and the kids; I need to know if you think she'll be up to it riding wise? Thought it might be a good idea to have a look myself."

Chloe laughed, what was it about Charles that always made her a bit wary, "Of course you can come, I'd like to meet Jen's mum, she doesn't talk about her much."

"Well that's probably my fault, I've never encouraged her down to Nantes before. She's a nice woman really …. But well I've been a bit of a snob about it I suppose!" Charles admitted.

I bet you have thought Chloe, but instead remarked, "Well you're making an effort now and that's what counts. A safari sound fab! It shouldn't be a problem for Jen as long as you say that she's a novice, I'm sure that'll be okay. Any way you can judge for yourself on Saturday. Want me to talk to her about it today when I see her?"

"Chloe you're a life saver!" flattered Charles, "by the way any thoughts on a horse for Jennifer?"

"Actually yes, I know of one that would be perfect, but the owner's not quite sure she wants to sell yet, but don't worry I'm on the case. Look Charles gotta go, coming up to the road – I need both hands!"

"Okay, call me then, meanwhile mum's the word" he joked, "ciao."

He ended the call sitting back in his chair and then getting up and striding to the window, watching the cars crawling along in the street beneath him. He tapped the end of his pen on the window thinking hard, then taking a deep resigned breath walked back to his desk and called Celia.

Caitlin stomped up the stairs to the flat, pushing open the door. She stepped in wrinkling up her nose at the smell. She had been quite embarrassed when they showed Felix round the other week and knew that she could delay the inevitable clean up no longer. Jennifer had not asked her to do it, but it was quiet in the yard at the moment and she could spare and hour or two to do a bit of a tidy up. She walked over to the kitchen. God what a messy cow Lucy had been, the sink was full of dirty plates, the debris of the food had dried on and was hard now, the dregs of coffee staining the mugs a dirty brown. She emptied the sink and ran the tap til the water was hot and filled the bowl with steamy bubbles, and put the crockery in to soak. Opening the fridge anticipating the worst and proving not to be disappointed, she picked up a black sack and started chucking out all the old food and sour milk. This was going to take ages she mourned, donning her rubber gloves she reached over and flicked on the radio, wincing as the music rang out, the volume turned up to maximum. She turned it down and started to work methodically to clean the place up singing along to the radio as she sloshed the dirty plates clean in the sink. She felt a vibration before the bleep of a text came on her phone, she wrenched it out of her pocket, peering at the screen.*"Must see you, miss you badly baby. Usual place 3pm? Xxxx "*

Caitlin smiled to herself. She took off the gloves and tapped a reply, *"Miss you too. See you then xxxx"*. She put the phone back into her pocket and glanced at her watch, it was just after midday. If she got a shove on, she could finish this and have plenty of time to shower and change before she met him. Her heart lifted, even the thought of cleaning this shit hole felt better when she could look forward to three o'clock.

John looked at his mobile, turning it over and over in his hand. He knew he couldn't go on much longer deceiving Chloe, and it wasn't fair anyway, he owed her more than that. The thought of losing her and the children and his home made his heart sink. He had never felt so gloomy, but pretty soon it would all come to a head anyway and she would find out, but was it better that he told her? He put down the phone and cradled his head in his hands, rubbing his forehead with his fingertips, what a fucking mess. In a way he was very excited about the future and all the promise and thrill it would bring to his life, but there seemed to be so many hurdles before he got there. His mind was so confused, he just didn't know how to handle things next, but one thing he did know for sure, was the thought of hurting Chloe and the kids was something he wanted to avoid more than anything else, and if he delayed perhaps it would it all sort itself out in the long run. He inhaled deeply, no, he would leave it for a while. Okay it was an ostrich attitude but he just needed to take each day as it came, and today was not the day for revelations.

Chloe on the other hand felt brighter. She was busier than she had ever been. The girls were revving up to go to Rackham Horse Trials and the way the horses were going this should be a good day out for both of them. Rackham was a relatively new event, with an imposing cross country course and some tricky fences, but they were fair and the setting was beautiful. She had offered to take them in the truck, but this time she would take the children, and she might even persuade John to come too. She fantasised about the great day they could have, a good picnic, supplied by Jeremy, and a family day out. She was determined to make an effort and the thought made her feel more secure than she had felt in ages. For the first time in a while, her life seemed to be on an even keel. She kicked Seamus into a canter enjoying the relish of his powerful hocks as they pushed underneath her and they tore up the hill, there was nothing like it! The grass sped away under her feet and she kept her head low and her body forward as she urged him onwards, exhilarated as the wind blew in her face.

Laura was keeping her head down. She was still reeling from the shock of finding Linda last night. Luckily, Jonty had been out when she got back and she had pretended to be asleep when he crawled back in the early hours. He had obviously been out on a job, and she slipped out of bed noiselessly, keen not to wake him. She dressed as quietly and had gone before he'd stirred and then felt and enormous sense of relief when she'd closed the door behind her.

God how had things gotten so bad, she knew that he'd always sailed close to the wind, but over these last weeks she'd inadvertently set him off on some hair brained scheme which had turned him into a spiteful vicious stranger. She couldn't face the confines of the tube and ran her fingers through her hair as she leant against the bus stop. She had made up her mind to go straight over to Linda's this morning to see how she was, and urge her to seek some help. At least it seemed to be something proactive that she could do, she was bloody well not going to be party to Linda's downfall whatever Jonty did to her. Last night had frightened the shit out of her. The bus chugged up to the stop, hissing as the doors spat open to disgorge its passengers and take on its newcomers. Picking up her bag she climbed on board, zapping her Oyster card on the reader and flung herself onto a seat, gazing miserably out of the window. Lurching off, the bus crawled along painfully, stopping and starting endlessly, faceless people climbing on board, all looking drab and fed up. She hardly noticed them wrapped up in her own thoughts until the blue door flashed past and the bus drew up at the next stop. She dragged herself up and jumped off, walking back towards the all too familiar stair way.

She took a deep breath outside the flat door, then knocked and waited. There was no sound from inside, she rapped harder and waited again, still nothing. She glanced at her watch it was not that early, they should be stirring by now. Just as she was dithering about what she should do, the door opened. Sean was rubbing sleep out of his eyes, his feet were bare and he had a pair of grubby sweat pants hanging around his hips.

"Fuck me Laura, what time d' ya call this?"

Laura looked at him guiltily, "Oh Christ Sean, I'm sorry, I was so worried about Linda, I just wanted to make sure she was okay."

Sean peered at her "Well okay, you'd better come in, she's sleeping, or she was." He held the door open and walked back into the flat gesturing for Laura to follow him. The place looked just as filthy, and he plonked himself down on a sofa and started to roll up.

Laura stood awkwardly, "Shall I make a cuppa tea?"

"Yeah, why not, dunno if there's any milk though" Sean did not look up, carefully licking the end of the Rizla.

Laura busied herself in the kitchen, it was even more disgusting than the last time she had seen it. The cups had brown tide marks and were piled high in the sink with dirty plates and cutlery and the worktops hadn't been wiped down in ages, hard little brown blobs all crusty and hard from spilt coffee pitted all over them. Christ she thought, this place is a bloody health hazard. She set to, running hot water into the bowl to wash up, only to find that there was no washing up liquid. She did her best, but Sean had been right, there was only sour milk left out on the counter, so she made black tea and carried it back out into the living room, where Sean lay with his eyes closed and head back on the sofa, the fag protruding from the end of his mouth.

"Here – you're, you're right, no milk, so it's black – okay?"

"Sure "said Sean opening his eyes, he looked at her suspiciously, "why are you really here Laura?"

"I told you Sean, I was worried, been worrying all night. Linda needs help, we need to get her on some sort of programme."

"Pah! Are you joking! Do y' know what you're talking about?" Sean sneered at her, sitting up and taking his tea, "You've no fuckin' idea!"

"Ok Sean, no perhaps I don't but I'm damned well gonna try, not just let her die one night, 'cos she's had a fit. You're right, I don't know about drugs or programmes, but I can't just sit back and let her kill herself, without trying to do something about it." Laura hissed at him, "Just 'cos you're apathetic and resigned, I'm not – Okay!" She came to an abrupt halt, her face flushed, but feeling better having got it all off her chest.

Sean eyed her carefully, and there was a long pause before he spoke, weighing his words carefully. "Laura, since you came into our lives, Linda has gone more and more downhill. But it's true, you've never taken anything that I know of, and I like your passion with this anti-hunting stuff, so sure I'll take you on face value, but I swear, if I find that you've been supplying Linda, I'll kill you – got that? So you show your loyalty – prove it."

"I'm going to Sean" whispered Laura, "I'm going to"

"Good, well when Linda wakes up, we'll try talking some sense into her and try to get her into some sort of rehab, see if we can persuade her to see her GP. It's not going to be easy and she's gonna need a lotta support from us." He took a slurp of his tea, relit the roll up, which had gone out, "you on board for all that?"

Laura looked at him steadily, "I'll do as much as I can Sean, and the first thing I can do is clean this shit hole up. I don't do drugs and neither should you, not any kind, so what you preach you must practise, so no more spliffs – right?"

This time it was Sean's turn to look shifty, "Well, I dunno…"

"I mean it!" Laura spat, "Don't lecture me, if you can't deliver yourself! Right, now I'm gonna go and get some cleaning stuff, buy some groceries and we're gonna get this place sorted for when she wakes up, and when I come back I want all your shit gone." She stood up, brushed off her skirt and marched towards the door.

"Laura" Sean called after her, "It's a deal, I'll get rid of it all. You help me and I'll help you with the other stuff, y' know the Sabs and all that."

Laura turned to look at him and smiled, "thanks Sean, okay, it's a deal."

It was just after three when Caitlin pulled her little Peugeot into High Ridge, the day had turned a bit cloudy and she hoped it would stay dry. What would they do in the winter she mused, they couldn't go on meeting like this then when the rain was lashing down, or worse when there was snow on the ground. Moreover her work load would double once the hunters were in, with or without Felix, so sneaking the odd hour off would be even more difficult. She sighed, squirted herself with some Miss Dior, brushed her mane of hair and put on her lip gloss, glanced around the car park and when she was certain the coast was clear, got out and made her way through the woods.

He was already there, and had set up a blanket and a picnic, jumping up when he saw her. It was always the same, directly she saw him, all her fears and worries just disappeared, it would be all right, she knew it would be. His smiling handsome face affirmed his love for her, and she beamed back at him and threw herself into his arms.

"Oh b' Jesus, I've missed you." she sighed, "It's been a terrible time, so it has. I've never felt so lonely."

He stroked her hair, kissing the top of her head, "Oh baby, I know, I know, you've no idea how much I've wanted to come to you. I was so worried when you told me. I'm so sick of all this subterfuge." He tipped her face up to him and kissed her gently on the lips, cupping her face in his hands, feeling her relax and kiss him back. Her hands slipped around his back, feeling the strength of him, allowing herself to slip into their embrace.

When they finally drew apart Caitlin whispered, "It's so good to feel you again."

"You too sweetie, you too. Now come on sit down, I've got us a picnic. All the things you love! Although only sparkling elderflower – can't have us both going home smelling of Prosecco can we?"

Caitlin frowned, the moment was spoiled, both going home, different homes. Covering up, the subterfuge, the deceit and the lies. She shoved the thoughts away for the moment, knowing that once he'd gone they would storm back to torment her in her lonely world again.

CHAPTER 48

The week was speeding past, Pete was still missing and the hunt for him had all but been abandoned. The police were not willing to commit more manpower, time or money, and both they and the health services believed that he had probably done a bunk and was by now right out of the area. Despite Charles' repeated lobbying the investigation just seemed to fizzle out leaving him frustrated and feeling helpless and very protective towards Jennifer. She on the other hand was excited about her mum coming to stay and had been busy all week with Mrs Fuller organising everything to the last detail, and now at last it was Friday morning.

Jennifer was up early, had gobbled down her toast and ushered Charles off to work. He had smiled indulgently, pleased that she was happy and left her to it. She skipped down the kitchen passage, bubbling with the anticipation of a good weekend ahead to tell Mrs Fuller that she was off, and would be back later this afternoon.

Mrs Fuller glanced up from stirring a pan on the Aga as Jennifer pushed backwards into the kitchen, her arms laden with a tray of dirty breakfast crockery.

"Now Jennifer, you shouldn't have worried about that, Doris will be in shortly and she'd have cleared."

"No trouble! I was just coming to tell you that I'm leaving in about 10 minutes." she fairly jumped up and down in excitement. "I'm so looking forward to this weekend."

Mrs Fuller smiled at her kindly, she was only a kid after all, "I know and we're going to make it right special too. Take a glance at the pink room on your way upstairs. It looks a picture! And I'm making a nice lemon meringue to go with the chicken tonight, so that'll be tasty and not too fancy either."

Jennifer gave Mrs Fuller a hug, "Thank you so much Mrs Fuller, you've been brilliant!" she smiled happily.

Mrs Fuller hid her surprise well at the unfamiliar gesture and hugged her back, "It's been a pleasure, and I really mean that. Now m' dear you get off now and drive carefully."

In fact the first part of the drive had gone relatively quickly as she'd decided to go via the M23/M25 route using the Blackwall Tunnel and then onto the A13. It might have seemed an odd route but on a clear day it was faster, and it had actually not been a bad run, just the normal bottle head at the tunnel. Now though the traffic was awful. Jennifer crawled along in the car, stopping and starting, thank God the car was automatic and these new models cut the engine when in traffic, so at least it was eco-friendly; she sighed as she watched the exhaust fumes belching out from the stacked up vehicles. Irritated, she tapped her fingers on the steering wheel in agitation continuously looking at the clock on the dashboard or the Rolex on her wrist.

She had forgotten how dreary and dingy this part of London was - so grimy compared to the country, especially these main roads threading through what used to be the poorest area of London. Until she had gone to live in the Chelsea flat and then down to Nantes, Jennifer had never lived anywhere other than the East End and now, as she edged her way towards her old home, she realised that despite all the efforts to tart the area up, with bright young professionals buying up all the rows of smutty houses and attempting to rejuvenate them, there was still a huge amount of squalor. There were piles of rubbish heaped on street corners, tawdry signs over dubious shop fronts, with groups of lads in hoodies lurking together in sinister groups. True, the massive ethnic influence of the area gave splashes of the exotic. In fact fast food shops were everywhere, from Chinese, to Caribbean, to Kebab, to Mexican, grocery shops selling every kind of spice, herb and specialist vegetables gaudily displayed amidst the choking carbon monoxide, and inevitably the sinister Halal meat shops. Jennifer wrinkled her nose up, the thought of those animals being bled to death made her feel really queasy. She struggled on along the old familiar roads, the East India Dock Road, Commercial Road, through Limehouse, Stepney and towards Whitechapel, pausing at every junction as the traffic lights seemed to be inevitably red. The smell of a vast variety of foods drifted in the air, people crowded down the pavements; girls in vintage clothes, young Yiddish men proudly wearing their kippahs, Islamic women in hijabs, and youths in low slung baggy jeans with their boxers pants poking out at the top, it certainly was a multi -cultural scene, and one that she now felt completely at odds with. How bizarre, she had always thought it would feel like home, but now it was the most alien place in the world and she longed to back at Nantes and the serenity she had there. A car hooted angrily behind her and she looked up, the traffic light had gone green, she shot forward inching into yet another queue of traffic and began signalling right to turn into Vallance Road - she was nearly there.

Five minutes later, she swung the Mercedes into a numbered parking spot behind an L shaped block of brick red flats, lucky for her - her mum didn't use a car so she could use her allocated space. Purple wheelie bins stood in regimented rows, but despite this all sorts of debris was piled up beside the bins waiting to be collected. Spoden House was where she had been brought up and there at least there was some semblance of green, a small patch of tired grass surrounded the front of flats and was protected by iron hooped park railings. There were no flowers just some stunted shrubs and spindly trees, but it was a lawn of sorts. Once you got away from the hub-bub of the main street, it was relatively quiet here, you'd not think it was so close to Brick Lane. The flats themselves were six stories high, and the upper floors had minscule protruding red brick balconies strewn with washing, bicycles, mops, pushchairs and the like. Jennifer carefully locked the car, you couldn't be too careful around here, and picked her way towards the stair case. Her mother lived on the third floor. She started to climb up, counting the steps, remembering exactly how many there were. She glanced at her watch – it was just past ten, perfect timing.

Jennifer knocked only once and stood self-consciously in her summery red polka dot Joseph dress, with its fitted waist tied with a belt, and her Jimmy Choo flat pumps, a large Hermes bag on her arm. The door flew open and her mother's face was crinkled with smiles and Jennifer rushed forward to give her a hug, "Oh Mum, I'm so pleased to see you, and I'm so glad you're coming down to stay." She was almost sobbing.

Her mother stroked her hair, "There, there now love, I'm looking forward to it too." She pushed Jennifer back, "And just look at you, don't you look wonderful, so tall and slim, although I think you could do with a bit of weight on you! Come on, let's have a cuppa and I've been down to the market and got us a nice Danish."

"Oh Mum, don't worry about me, I thought we'd get straight off. Are you all packed?"

"Yes, I'm all ready to go, but our Susan said she'd pop round to see you before we went, and I knew you'd not want to miss her, she'll be here any minute."

Actually Jennifer hadn't given Susan a thought other than to wonder if she had managed to get the things she asked for, and immediately felt guilty, she looked down at her mum, and realised just how pleased she was to see her and how much she'd missed her. She looked really good and despite the streaks of grey in her hair she'd obviously had it done especially for the weekend and had gone to a lot of trouble with her clothes. She was wearing a pink skirt and top, which had definitely been bought especially for the weekend.

"Of course I want to see her, and Mum you look really nice, are those new? Your hair looks super too– come on I'll put the kettle on."

Her mum looked pleased, smoothing down the skirt, "Yes, I got them down Brick Lane - they look expensive, but they're a real bargain. You know though Jen you don't have to send me that money, I know it's lovely an' all not having to work, but I could manage y' know."

"Mum, I want to, so no arguments – okay?" She put her arm through her mothers and they walked through to the spotless little kitchen.

They were busy chatting when they heard a key in the front door and a cacophony of noise and expletives came from the hallway as bags were thrown down. Susan burst noisily into the kitchen.

"Well little Jen!" Susan laughed ironically "You've become quite a stranger, and just look at you, in your expensive designer gear!"

Jennifer blushed, "I know, sorry Susan, it's been a long time, too long. No excuses but I'm here now – come and give me a hug!" She held out her arms to her sister and smiled.

"Come 'ere our kid!" Susan grinned, "Good to see ya!" She squeezed Jennifer so tightly that she made her gasp, "Hey Mum – where's my cuppa?"

"Oh it does my heart good to see you two!" their mum sighed, "just like old times." She poured Susan's tea, picked up the plate of pastries and they went into the little living room.

A comfortable hour passed, with Jennifer catching up on all the gossip of who was doing what, how Susan's children were, what Wayne - Susan's new man was up to, how Mary next door was doing, and how her arthritis was and all the general chit chat of their London lives. At last she said gently to her mother that it was really time for them to be making a move. She glanced at Susan, a pang of regret that she hadn't asked her sister too, but then she didn't think she could push it that far with Charles, not yet anyway.

Susan gave her sister a warm smile, telling Jennifer it was okay and turning to their mother said, "Yeah, come on Mum, let's get your case then, and I'll help you down the stairs with it. Oh Jen, I've got that little something you asked me about, I'll bring it down and put it in your car. Then I can come back up here and clear up the cups and stuff."

"Thanks Susan, you're a star. Come on Mum then, let's get your things." Jennifer stood up "We're going to have a lovely time, it'll be a super little break for you."

"I know dear, I know, I can't remember the last time I went anywhere"

Susan scoffed, "Give over Mum, you go to the Bingo every week, you don't do so bad!"

Down at the car, Susan whistled when she saw the Mercedes, "Blimey, that's a nice motor! Does the roof come down? How long you had this?"

Jennifer was embarrassed, "Charles bought it for me as a surprise for my birthday. It's lovely isn't it? Yes, the roof does come down. Look I'll show you!" She leant over and pushed a button and the neat little roof folded itself away.

"Well, I never did!" exclaimed her mum, "What fun. Can we

have it down now?"

"If you like – although it might be a bit smelly with all the fumes of the traffic." smiled Jennifer.

"Oh, I don't mind, it'll make me feel like a girl again!"

"Come on then Mum jump in." She flipped up the boot throwing the case in the back and Susan passed her a small brown package, she hugged her, "Brilliant, how much do I owe you? Are there instructions?"

Susan laughed, "Can't think why you need it, but yeah instructions included, and a pony will do it."

Jennifer grimaced, "Only twenty five quid, you sure? Here" she rummaged in her bag and fished out her purse. "Look take this." She handed over two crisp fifty pound notes, "What's left over spend on the kids, I'm grateful sis', I really am."

Susan fingered the notes, "Thanks. I'd like to say no, but they could do with some new trainers."

"Good well, that's settled then. How about instead of Charles bringing Mum back on Monday, I do, and we could go out for lunch?"

"Fuck me – lunch! That's posh! Okay, why not. Yeah, I'd love to!"

"Right, that's settled then! See you on Monday." Jennifer slid into the car and started the engine. They waved gaily to Susan as they drove away down the road in the sleek silver car, and Susan stood there watching them go, pleased for her mum and whistling softly at Jen's good fortune, but why did she want that stuff, they were odd things to ask her to get? Oh well no doubt she'd let on when she was ready, she walked back to the flats to clear up and get back to the daily grind.

Jennifer edged out onto Vallance Road, and once more into the melee of the busy East End and the clamour of the street traders and the rich smell of the take aways. Her mum was in her element, the roof down the breeze ruffling her hair in the swanky car. Once again Jennifer was unlucky and was caught at every red light. They were waiting for what seemed like an age, when they both noticed a lanky skin head with closely cropped hair, and heavily tattooed arms staring at them brazenly from the pavement, his face registering surprise, then a sneer as he eyeballed them with contempt. He was with another smaller man with a sharp pointed face, and he nudged him in the ribs and pointed rudely at them.

"Crikey, who's he staring at?" laughed Jennifer. "Do you know him Mum?"

"Well, yes and no" stammered her mum, "that's Jonty Steele, he's a right bad lot. He's not someone you want to have anything to do with or get on the wrong side of either! Don't look at him."

"Don't worry I won't. These stupid hoods are all the same! All mouth! Forget him." She laughed, put her foot on the accelerator as the lights changed and moved off towards home.

Jennifer wished she had a camera with her when they pulled down the drive to Nantes - her Mum's face was a picture, much the same as hers was she supposed when she first saw it. It did look wonderful bathed in sunshine, with its soft mellow brickwork; the tumbling roses caressed the windows, and the tinkling of the fountain as she swept up to the front door. Charles had engaged a firm of contractors who had done a good job on the lawns and it did look lovely, she pulled up beside the front door, and turned to her mum. "Well here we are – home. What do you think?"

Her mother just sat completely silent looking up at the house, tears in her eyes, taking it all in, finally whispering quietly, "Oh Jen, it's unbelievable."

Jennifer took her mother's hand and kissed it, "It's my home Mum, and I love it and I hope you will too."

At that moment, the front door swung open and Mrs Fuller bustled down the steps - her face creasing with smiles "I just thought I'd come down to welcome you to Nantes Madam, and to say how very pleased we are to have you to stay, and that if there is anything that you need during your visit you only have to ask. Here let me help with your bags."

Jennifer beamed gratefully, "Mum let me introduce you to Mrs Fuller, who is our housekeeper here at Nantes but who is actually much more than that, I simply don't know what I would do without her! Mrs Fuller this is my mother Ivy Bainbridge."

Jennifer's mum embarrassedly shook Mrs Fuller's hand, "Pleased t' meet you Mrs Fuller, call me Ivy, and thank you so much for looking after my little Jen. I'm very excited to be here and to meet you, I'm sure we'll be good friends."

Mrs Fuller shook her hand back warmly replying "It's a pleasure to meet you too Ivy, and you must call me Freda. I hope you enjoy your visit."

Jennifer's mouth almost gaped open, it was a far cry from the welcome that Mrs Fuller had extended to her when she first came to Nantes and she was astonished and pleased at the same time. In her confusion she grabbed the case from the back of the car and ushered everyone into the house saying "Right Mum, let's take this up to your room and then perhaps we could have some tea Mrs F? As it's such a lovely afternoon we could take it on the morning room terrace, what do you think?"

"Good idea, such a nice view over the garden - should be ready in about half an hour then" and with a ghost of a wink she turned away towards the kitchen.

"Perfect, thank you" Jennifer called after her, "Come on then Mum." They climbed up the staircase together, her mother still quietly overawed by it all, until they reached the first light airy landing with its long windows and huge vases of flowers.

"Jen this house is huge! I'll get lost, I know I will!"

"No you won't Mum, it is big, but you'll soon find your way around, and I've put you in the pink room which is just to the right over here, quite close to the main staircase so you can easily find your way down. I hope you like it."

Jennifer walked over and pushed open a wide door into a room flooded with afternoon sunlight. Two tall floor to ceiling Georgian windows were facing them draped with white silk curtains sprigged with tiny pink roses tied back with sashes of vivid pink. Between the windows were matching casement doors, which had been thrown open to lead onto a small balcony with two white wrought iron chairs and a little round table. The room had been painted in ivory white, with an imposing antique French white rattan bed delicately carved on the head and foot board with roses and ivy and dressed with the crispest whitest linen dotted with dainty pink rosebuds and plumped high with fat pillows and cushions picked out in the same hues of pinks and reds. The wardrobe and chests of drawers were French too, distressed in white, with a huge scrolled free standing mirror. On the opposite wall was an ornate writing desk and chair, with a squashy arm chair in the corner and side table strewn with magazines looking out of the long window over the garden. There were bowls of roses and sweet peas on the desk and the chest of drawers and the room smelt heavenly. Despite all the pink touches it was not at all kitsch, but summery and fresh.

"Oh Jen! It's lovely." Ivy gasped, she ran her hand over the bed linen, "this is real quality stuff. It must've cost a fortune!"

"I'm so glad you like it Mum, come and have a look at the views" she guided her mother over to the casement windows and they stepped out onto the balcony together.

"We're looking out over the back lawns here - look there's the pool over there and just below us is where we're going to have our tea in a minute." She pointed to the pool and then down below them to the terrace. "That's our room there look and our balcony" she pointed to the left "so we are not far away."

"It's beautiful, you can see for miles. The pool looks lovely too. Can I see that later?"

"You can see it all Mum – I hope you've brought your cossie?" laughed Jennifer, "and look, those are Charles' horses down there in the water meadow and those are the children's ponies, look can you see?"She pointed them out in the distance.

"Oh yes!" Ivy laughed, "Well you certainly fell with your bum in the butter my girl!"

Jennifer laughed uncomfortably, "I suppose you're right I did," then quickly changing the subject "now let me show you your bathroom and then we'll get our tea."

She guided her mother back into the bedroom and pointed out another door discreetly screened between the wardrobe and the chest of drawers, "and this is the bathroom." She pushed it open. The suite was all white with floors and walls of cream polished marble flecked with pale pink. There was a large corner whirl pool bath and glass walk in shower. The wash basin was set in an outsized marble plinth which doubled as a storage unit, stacked with Molton Brown toiletries and fluffy shell pink towels. Pink slippers sat under the basin, and a soft fleecy pink robe hung on the back of the door.

"I just don't know what to say! It's like being in a hotel – not that I've ever been in one!"

"Not an hotel Mum, a home! Now let's leave the unpacking and I'll give you a quick tour of the house and then we'll have our tea."

It was more than half an hour later when they were sitting under the parasol and Mrs Fuller was loading up the table with the tea things. She had done Jennifer's mother proud, and made some scrumptious savoury tartlets and tiny crustless sandwiches, and the most delicious mini strawberry shortbreads and chocolate éclairs.

"Freda, this looks wonderful, you are spoiling me. Aren't you going to join us?" beamed Ivy.

"No I'd better not, I've got to get things organised for the supper as you're all eating in tonight." Mrs Fuller said kindly, not wanting to hurt Ivy's feelings, who clearly had no idea that it wasn't the *done* thing.

"Go on, sit yourself down" said Ivy, "I can always give you a hand after."

Mrs Fuller glanced at Jennifer, this was going against all protocol. "Well ..." She began

"Come on Mrs Fuller," said Jennifer pulling out a chair, "Mum's right, we can all muck in later."

As the sun shone down on them and they wolfed down the tea,

Jennifer realised that she was starving. She watched her mother chitchat away guilelessly to Mrs Fuller and gradually seeing Mrs Fuller become less and less awkward and chat back to her and the two women laughing, she felt happy. Here was her mum at Nantes on this glorious sunny afternoon, a whole weekend ahead of them and for the first time in months, she felt this really was her home and she was content.

CHAPTER 49

Saturday morning at Chloe's was always bedlam, even though she didn't have to make the usual dash to get the kids to the bus, they still had to be organised and fed – which was like feeding time at the zoo on a good day. John did his best but in his usual gentle way, they played him up and it was always Chloe who waded in with the metaphorical big stick and sorted them out. This particular morning was no different and after refereeing a potential outbreak of World War III, she left them to it and stomped down to the yard with the dogs racing ahead of her. Beebs and Susie had been hard at work already and the horses had been hayed and fed with most of the mucking out done, and they were in the tack room taking a well-earned cuppa.

"Morning boss" greeted Beebs, "What's on the agenda then?"

"Morning girls" Chloe barked, "Jump to it. Bloody busy morning, loads to do. Lessons and liveries."

"Blimey Chloe, hold hard, we've only just sat down. You're in a bait! We've been going as fast as we can y' know!" snapped Beebs, who had a lousy headache, "Give us a break!"

Chloe was instantly sorry, "Christ Beebs - that was unforgiveable, the kids have played me up this morning the little buggers, but no need to take it out on you two. I do know how hard you work, sorry babes."

Beebs grinned, "S' okay, I'm like a bear with a sore head too, 'cos I've got a blinder of a headache. Okay, what's on then?"

"Beebs, if you feel lousy – d' you need to have a lie down? I'm sure we can manage, can't we Susie?" She glanced at Susie for confirmation, "there's nothing worse than working when you feel rotten?"

"I'm fine Chloe, honest I'll live, now come on, what's to be done!" laughed Beebs.

"Okay. Now importantly, Jen is bringing Charles and her mum up this morning and I'm giving her a lesson. I really want this to go well, I'm sure we all do, for Jen's sake, so I thought Ksar would be our best bet – what d' you think?"

"Definitely!" said Susie, "She's doing well on him."

"What's her mum like?" asked Beebs.

"No idea" said Chloe, "Don't know any more than you do, but I'm more concerned about Charles – he's talking about taking her and the kids on a horse back safari."

"Fuck me!" said Susie, "Well it could be a goer I suppose?"

"Well possibly, but we'll let Charles decide after he's seen her ride. Poor Jen, I bet she's in a right state!" said Chloe.

"Shitting herself more like, but one thing she's a bloody trier." added Beebs, "Okay what else then?"

"Loads of lessons for me back to back, and liveries to sort out for you guys back to back too. Saturdays, joy oh joy!"

"Bring it on then!" laughed Susie! "what time do we kick off?"

"Ha ha! Let's hope it doesn't kick off!"

"No! Especially today with Jen's mum, I doubt she knows one end of a horse from another – make her welcome girls won't you? I've a feeling she'll be a bit out of her comfort zone."

"Don't worry Chloe, we will" assured Beebs, "we like Jen, and we'll make a fuss of her mum."

"Thanks. I know I can rely on you. Okay on on then! Here come the first lot!"

Jennifer was inwardly becoming more anxious, she and her mum had had a leisurely breakfast together in the morning room, and now she was giving her a guided tour around the garden. Charles himself could not have been nicer or more welcoming to Ivy last night. She'd thought he would disappear into his study and leave them to it after dinner, but he had spent the whole evening with them, chatting and talking, even playing cards. Mrs Fuller had done a great job with the meal, a plain roast chicken, and her famous lemon meringue pie. All in all it seemed to be going really well as far as her mum was concerned, but this morning the thought of Charles coming to watch her ride was really making her uptight, she felt like a coiled spring.

"What's up love?" Ivy looked at her daughter, "Come on, I know something's wrong."

"Nothing Mum, nothing at all – honestly." Jennifer delved down sniffing a rose to avoid her mother's eyes, "it's so lovely having you here."

Ivy took Jennifer's arm, "Jen, I know you, what's the matter, is it me being here, 'cos if it is, I can easily go back early y 'know. I've had a lovely time, but if it's difficult, it's not a problem."

"Oh Mum!" Jennifer hugged her mother, "of course it isn't that! It's just ... Well, okay, let me tell you then." They sat down together on one of the garden benches and Jennifer blurted out the whole story of the secret riding, and how today was the first time that Charles was going to see her ride, and she was terrified she was going to bugger it up.

Ivy smiled and took her daughter's hand, "Jen, okay, I can see now why you'd be in a state, but you're one of the strongest, single minded people I know – been like it since you were a little girl, so you have. When you set your mind to summat – you do it. Riding won't be any different – you've gotta believe in yourself – this Chloe believes in you doesn't she?"

"Yes Mum, yes she does" whispered Jennifer, "and I know I can but it's just in front of an audience – especially Charles - y 'know?"

"Look Charles loves you, you've only got to see the way he looks at you to know that, he wants you to succeed, so you go and do just that."

"Oh Mum, do you really think so?"

"Yes, I do, and you'll be fine, you'll make him proud of you, I know you will." Ivy squeezed her arm, "and me too!"

Jennifer laughed, "Oh Mum, you're right, of course I can." She glanced at her wristwatch, "Come on upstairs with me, while I go and put my breeches on, and we'll get cracking."

They walked back arm in arm across the lawn to the terrace and Charles watched them from his study. He smiled to himself, as he saw Jennifer talking animatedly to her mother and the old girl nodding and listening to her, and then both of them laughing. He suddenly felt mean, for so long he had denied Jennifer this chance to welcome her mother here, his inbuilt snobbery wanting to shut Ivy out and keep her compartmentalised in London. It wasn't that he had been mean in terms of money, he had been more than happy to give Jennifer an allowance for her mother's maintenance, after all it was only money and he had plenty of that, but to include her in his life was far more than he been prepared to give. Now seeing them together and watching Jennifer unobserved, happy and relaxed with her mother in her home made him see how cruel he'd been. Nearly losing her had brought him up short, okay he couldn't turn the clock back, but hell's teeth, he could try and make up for it now. He'd no idea what would happen today up at Chloe's but however she got on, he was determined that he would make her feel good about herself even if she was just a wobbly beginner. At least she'd been prepared to try for him, and that was more than could have been said for him over the last year or so. No, things were going to change.

Katherine and Sandy had loaded the horses into the trailer and were negotiating the narrow lanes out of the village. They were heading up to the South Downs to do some fittening canter and hill work with the boys in preparation for the next event. Sandy was driving, she looked incongruously tiny in the chunky car, her feet only just touching the floor. Katherine's bobbed hair was tucked behind her ears, as she concentrated on filing down a broken nail. It was nearly quarter past ten, and as they drove past the entrance to Nantes, they saw Charles' Range Rover pull out. Sandy tooted the horn and they both waved.

"Poor Jen, hope it goes okay" Sandy said, "I think it was a good idea us getting out of the way, nothing worse than an audience."

"No, you're right. Although, I feel a bit like the clichéd rat leaving the sinking ship. It might just 've helped with the tension if we'd stayed around to chat to Charles and her mum to take their eyes of her."

"Well maybe, but too late now, and she'll be fine with Chloe and the girls. Anyway our lads need a good work out and it's a perfect morning for a blast. Then this week – I'm gonna concentrate on the flat work."

"Blimey, what's come over you!"

"Gotta get the old boy to respect me a bit more – get some more balance and control. I know Chloe bangs on about it, but she's right and I need to knuckle down and stop pissing about."

"Good on you! Are you talking about Mark too?" Katherine glanced at her slyly, "time to stop pissing about?"

Sandy laughed dryly, "No flies on you Mrs Gordon eh! It is that obvious?"

"No, only to those who know you, but you're serious about this guy aren't you?"

Sandy shrugged her shoulders, "I didn't intend to be, at first it was just fun, an inevitable sexy shag after a great night at Jen's party, then it just grew to be more somehow, and don't ask me how that happened. He says he feels the same, but I suppose I am just such an old cynic, don't trust men you know."

"Not all men are untrustworthy – you've just had a bad experience. Mark's a nice guy - I don't think he's playing you – do you?"

"No, I don't. But how can you tell really and truly? Look at Chloe, and don't say there's nothing wrong between her and John, you'd have to be blind not to see it! Yet three months ago who'd have believed it?

"Don't. It's so bloody hard to credit, poor Chloe."

"Then look at Charles, I know we like Jen, but after all Charles was married before to Celia." Sandy added, "He had an affair, or should I say affairs!"

"I don't think they should have ever have married by all accounts, and he and Jen certainly seemed very solid whenever I've seen them together."

"Well we didn't really know him before did we, but you've only got to take a look around, Oli's marriage, Andrew's wife, who no-one ever sees, Libby Newsome, Angie Ferrers to name but a few!"

"I don't think that's very fair, Mark's never been interested in other women much as far as I know, even when he wasn't involved with you, and God knows there're plenty who offer themselves on a plate."

"Oh, I know, and I'm just an old cynic." moaned Sandy, "Anyway, I think I'm in too deep now."

"I wonder if Jeremy and Mark are having this same conversation?" Katherine laughed, "Do men have these kind of talks at all, or is everything black and white to them?"

"God knows, but sometimes thinking too much doesn't do you any good!"

Charles indicated right and pulled into the track leading to Mileoak and negotiated his way down the drive pulling up beside the horse walker. Jen was fiddling anxiously with her hands, listening idly to her Mum's chatter from the back. Charles leaned over and took Jennifer's hand in his, smiling at her. She smiled back gratefully and took a deep breath. Chloe had walked over to greet them, her tousled tawny hair like a lion's mane whipping around her face in the breeze. Charles got out of the car and walked round to open Ivy's door and help her out, she looked tiny and quite fragile standing beside him, and he surprisingly put his arm around her shoulders and introduced her to Chloe. Jen hovered behind them dancing nervously from toe to toe.

"Welcome, Ivy, how nice to meet you. Jen has told us all about you."

"Well m' dear, an' she has told me all about you too, an' how very kind you've been to her. A real life saver from what I gather" beamed Ivy.

"Well, I'm not sure about that! Actually don't know what we'd do without her. Do you fancy a cup of tea, the kettle's boiling!"

"Well that'd be right lovely dear, and our Jen's going t' have a lesson then?"

"She sure is, you'll be amazed! She's a natural."

"That's good, but she's an amazing girl is my Jen."

"Oh for God's sake" Jennifer spluttered "Let's get that tea!"

They wandered over towards the tack room pausing now and then with Jennifer pointing out various glossy horses to Ivy, and Charles chatted to Chloe as they walked ahead.

"Go easy on her Chloe, I want this to be a success" he muttered quietly, "it doesn't matter to me how much of a beginner she is, she's had a rough old time."

"Charles, credit me with knowing my job" said Chloe crossly, "and actually, you'll be surprised I think"

"Sorry Chloe, course you do, I'm more anxious for it to go well than she is" he groaned.

Chloe realised this was a side of Charles she hardly recognised, and thought he was probably right, this haughty arrogant man had at last found a woman he really loved and one he had almost lost. It had been a hard lesson and he desperately wanted to make it up to her and for her to be happy. "Don't worry Charles" she said kindly "just relax."

Beebs and Susie, who had seen the Range Rover arrive had taken refuge in Alfie's empty stable and were peering out from behind the door and nudged each other as they watched Charles and

Chloe marching towards the tack room.

"Fuck me – they look serious" whispered Beebs, "in fact Chloe looks quite cross!"

"Yep, she does" Susie agreed, "but he's gorgeous looking isn't he? And he's loaded!"

"Mmm, yep he's good looking, but he's an big-headed sod too! But Chloe can handle him, just hope Jen can handle Ksar. What do you think of her mum, not quite what I imagined."

"No, me neither, she looks sweet. Kinda fluffy, still looks can be deceptive sometimes."

"We'd better show our faces, Chloe 'll be mad if we're caught skulking about in here."

They breezed out of the stable and joined the others who had by now reached the tack room, where Chloe was filling up the kettle. Beebs and Susie stood at the door, their bodies casting shadows into the room.

"Ah, girls, meet Mrs Bainbridge, Jennifer's mother," Chloe turned, "Ivy, this is Beebs and Susie, my right hand girls."

Ivy stood up and went to shake their hands, the girls hastily wiping theirs on their breeches before responding, "Ah, I've heard a lot about you two!" she laughed her eyes twinkling "Jen tells me you've had some right laughs together – I'm so glad."

"We have indeed!" grinned Beebs reaching forward to shake Ivy's hand, which was surprisingly firm, "Jen's been great fun to have here."

Susie stepped forward, rather quietly for her, saying "Nice to meet you, Mrs Bainbridge."

"Now you just all call me Ivy please – none of that formal stuff" laughed Ivy "I can't tell you how lovely it is to meet you all."

"Now girls, we're just going to have a cuppa, then Jen's going to give Ivy a quick whizz round the yard, can you have Ksar all tacked up and ready to rock an' roll – say in 10 minutes?" asked Chloe, as she poured the tea, "that should be fine eh Jen?"

"Perfect" smiled Jennifer, glancing at Charles who was lounging on the edge of one of the old armchairs, "okay with you darling?"

"Of course," he drawled, "take as long as you want sweetie - and hopefully it will be the first of many days you come down to stay eh Ivy?"

Ivy laughed with a small inclination of her head towards him, "I'd love to Charles, but you might not say that on Monday morning after you've had me for the whole weekend" It was a funny thing, but as she smiled at Charles her whole face changed and the others could see that exactly where Jennifer had gotten her looks from; Ivy had been and in fact was still very attractive for an older woman, and under the façade of a sweet fragile lady, she was in fact definitely able to hold her own with Charles.

"Oh no Ivy, I mean it, you're welcome to come any time." Charles met her eye for eye, and he thought with surprise, I could really like this woman, she's not over-awed by me at all.

"I should love to then, thank you." Ivy deftly changed the subject and turned to Chloe, "how long have you lived here?"

"Oh donkey's years" Chloe replied, "John and I fell in love with the house, and have been busy pouring money into it ever since."

"Do you have children m' dear?" asked Ivy, "It's such a perfect place for kids to grow up."

"Yes, we've three, no doubt they'll be pelting down here at any moment, although my husband John tries to keep them busy on Saturday mornings – but it doesn't always work!" grinned Chloe, thinking - that's when he hasn't got other things on his mind.

Jennifer finished her tea and stood up, "Do you want me to help tack up Beebs?"

"No, honest Jen, you show your mum around and we'll be ready in a jiff"

"Okay, you finished yet Mum? Charles, are you coming?" Jennifer asked.

Charles scrambled to his feet, "Yep, all ready, come on Ivy, I've never really asked, do you like horses?"

"Never had a chance to find out!" laughed Ivy, "but it's now or never I suppose!"

Katherine and Sandy were galloping flat sticks across the downs, hooves pounding along the ground underneath them, the turf flying out behind. The horses strained as they fought neck and neck to edge into the lead, the wind was whipping their riders' cheeks into a flushed pink. The tears rolled down their faces from the speed, their bodies were almost horizontal along the horses' necks with their stirrups racked up short. Sandy signalled to Katherine to start pulling up and gradually they started to rein the horses in, their strides easing into a more contained canter until finally they were walking. The horses' flanks were heaving, sweaty white foam on their necks, and their nostrils were flared and dilated, the mucous lining red and livid.

Katherine panted, her face shiny with perspiration and her eyes watering, "God Chloe will kill us!"

"I know, but fucking hell that was wonderful!" Sandy gasped, "I'm so definitely a speed freak!"

"We were supposed to just be doing some cantering and hill work." choked Katherine, "but it was just so exhilarating, I couldn't resist it!"

"Me neither!" Sandy dissolved into a splutter of giggles, "I hope their legs are okay, or we'll be in big doodoo!"

"Oh God, I hadn't thought about that!" Katherine gulped, "Shit, d' you think we ought to get off?

"No, but we'd better walk them back, give them a chance to cool off too. It should be okay, it's pretty good going up here, this old chalk grassland has pretty springy turf, not too hard, but we'd better ice tight the legs just in case, and confess I suppose."

"Well you know more about it than me, as long as you think it's okay. They're both bloody fit though eh?" Katherine wrinkled up her nose, "Rackham next week"

"Yeah, I don't think fitness'll be the issue, for me it's the flatwork, but you can never tell – just when you get one phase right, one of the others comes and bites you on the bum!" joked Sandy, "That's eventing for you!"

"All I want to do is get round safe and hopefully clear" said Katherine thoughtfully, "If I get placed it's a bonus."

"Me too, but a place is nice – and you've got eventing fever, like the rest of us! Look how elated you were after Borde Hill."

"Well that's true enough. But it's only my first season, so I've a lot to learn, like not doing what we've just done!" Katherine mused, "I'm dreading telling Chloe!"

"Oh she'll be alright, she knows what it's like, but she'd rather we said than didn't, at least she can do something about it. Prevention better than cure and all that stuff."

They ambled back across the downs, the horses stretching on a long rein, their breathing quickly returning to normal and the sweat on their necks drying their normal glossy coats to a stiff dull matt. From up here on the top of the ridge, they could see for miles, almost right across to the slate grey sea in the distance and the rolling undulating downs seemed to spread out endlessly all around them. Vast fields fanned out covering acres and acres with burgeoning crops, divided by spindly hedges and scrubby trees, their trunks windswept into odd angles by long exposure to the merciless winds driven inland off the sea. Ethereal cumulus clouds had drifted in off the coast and were etched brilliant white against the vivid blue of the sky, and seemed to cling in motionless suspension over the huge patchwork of the downs. The whole scene was breath-taking as the three elements of land, sea and sky melded together.

"It's stunning up here – just look at those views, you can see for miles." exclaimed Sandy, "judging by these crops, we could be in for an early harvest, that'll mean early autumn hunting."

"God Sandy, we're hardly into summer yet." moaned Katherine, "Let's just enjoy this shall we!"

"I know – but I love it when we start early - makes the season so much longer."

"Are you giving Seamus any time off this year then?" Katherine asked, "He'll need a holiday after a busy season."

"Mmmm, I thought maybe, December and January, after all it's the worst time of year isn't it? Who knows what Christmas and the New Year will bring."

"Good idea, I might do the same, but right now, I'm not thinking beyond next week." Katherine sighed, "Christmas! Christ!"

Jennifer had forgotten all about her audience, she didn't give Charles or her mum another thought as she had been concentrating so hard. She'd been on Ksar now for about quarter of an hour. To begin with she had made blunder after blunder, her body stiff and un-responding. Ksar, with his normal patience had just ignored her, doing his own thing which was exactly the opposite of what she wanted. Eventually Chloe on the pretext of tightening the girth had grabbed her leg and hissed under her breath to pull herself together. She'd been really sharp and Jennifer was taken aback, it was so unlike Chloe with her usual endless patience, but actually it was exactly what she'd needed. Furious, Jennifer started again, and Ksar realising she meant business was suddenly putty in her hands, and to her delight was soon performing beautifully. Chloe kept the lesson simple, only asking her to work on things she was really confident doing, and the half hour had soon passed and Jennifer couldn't believe it when Chloe said enough and to let him walk on a long rein, amidst bursts of applause from her mum and Charles.

Flushed - she looked over at them, and to her astonishment Charles gave her the thumbs up sign and her mum was waving her hands in the air. Beebs and Susie who'd been surreptitiously watching from the yard came over to the railings to offer their congratulations. Jennifer slipped off Ksar and threw her hands around his neck hugging the gentle giant whilst he slobbered all over her looking for Polos.

"Well done Jen, that was good, very good." said Chloe, and then added quietly "sorry I had to get tough."

Jennifer stepped back from Ksar, "Oh Chloe, it was exactly what I needed. I was being a right wimp! It went okay didn't it?" she asked "I mean, I didn't make too much of a fool of myself?"

Chloe laughed, "No Jen, no you didn't you rode super, you really are a natural."

"Darling, I'm so proud of you!" Charles had run into the school and was hugging Jennifer, holding her in his arms and stroking her face, "You did wonderfully, I can't believe it!"

"Aw Jen, you did so well m' love, not that I know much, but it looked good from where I was sitting!" Ivy joined them, "Well done, who'd have thought it."

Beebs came over and took hold of Ksar, "Well done, you showed 'em! Good boy Ksar," she gave the horse a rub on the ears "let's give you a nice wash down now."

Jennifer spun round, "Thanks Beebs, but here let me do that please." She walked over and took the reins out of Beeb's hands, "Just gonna finish him off Charles, and then I could do with a large glass of wine."

"I'll give you a hand then Jen" said Beebs, "be quicker."

Charles watched her walk off with Beebs, handling the horse confidently and quietly, and turned to Chloe, "You've done wonders."

Chloe grinned, "She's done wonders, she's worked so hard Charles, every day, can't get enough of it. It was a big thing for her today and I'm thrilled it went so well. What did you think Ivy?"

"Well love you're asking the wrong person, but she's always been terrified of horses, and to see her sitting there so confident and happy was summat else. She may have worked hard, but so have you dear!" enthused Ivy, "To tell the truth, I've been worried sick about her living down here, but it makes my heart glad to see her like this so it does."

Charles looked guilty, "Well you've no need to worry Ivy, not all the time I'm around anyway." he said sombrely.

Ivy gave him a long look, "I'm pleased to hear that Charles, I really am." Then she smiled at him, "She loves you, and as long as you love her, that's what matters.

CHAPTER 50

Saturday night was busy in the Lord Nelson, the dingy old pub sat on the corner of the cross roads and was the archetypical London tavern of a century ago. On the outside, it had dark polished wooden doors with square paned grimy windows and dull brass thumb latches. The walls were a tired red brick, with insets of green ceramic tiling and the same small squared windows set high, which let in little light to the inside. The pavement was littered with dog ends since the smoking ban. One of the previous landlords had attempted to smarten the place up, putting up hanging baskets and benches outside, but they had all been vandalised within a week, so he had given up and moved on; and now it gave no pretence to what it was, a local meeting place for street traders, old men and villains. You didn't go to the Lord Nelson to show a girl a good time that was for sure.

Laura walked nervously down the street, she was even tempted to take Sean's arm - she didn't feel safe. When she was with Jonty, and okay he was a bastard to her a lot of the time, she never felt like this, he commanded R.E.S.P.E.C.T. With Sean, he was a nobody and by default so was she and she didn't like it at all. She kept her eyes down on the pavement avoiding eye contact with anyone. Sean, on the other hand didn't seem to notice anything untoward. He was, as far as he was concerned fulfilling his part of the bargain. They had been all day at a drug rehab walk in centre together with Linda. As with all junkies she was quite pliable to go, still with enough of the drug in her system to make her docile and a bit frightened about what had happened - but they both knew that shortly she would be craving more and would become irrational and angry about any suggestion of help. So they'd acted quickly and she'd agreed to seek help. The upshot was that she'd agreed to be admitted to a psychiatric unit and luckily a bed had been available, so she'd been admitted.

Now true to his word, here they were going to a meeting of hard core Hunt Sabs in the Lord Nelson, a different place from where she had met them before and she was not looking forward to it one bit.

They pushed open the door into the pub, edging their way to the bar and waited to be served.

"Bloody hell, it's a squeeze in here!" moaned Laura, elbowing her way beside Sean, "Are all these people coming for the meeting?"

"Don't be thick, course they're not. Just locals from the stalls and the like. The others are probably upstairs by now, we're late." He managed to catch the bar maid's eye "What you having?"

"Half a pint of lager for me – thanks."

"And I'll have a pint thanks darlin'" he added to the frazzled peroxide blonde who came over to serve them.

They took their drinks and with difficulty threaded their way towards the back of the room and up a set of stairs, carefully carrying their glasses as they went. At the top of the landing there were three doors, two were ajar and one, which was marked Private, was firmly closed, and then the stairs curled upwards. Sean stopped and knocked three times on the closed door, and after a moment or two it was opened by a tall, dark haired man who said nothing but stood back and motioned them to come in. There were about half a dozen people in the room, although it was hard to see it was so gloomy inside. The air was thick with smoke and Laura felt her nose wrinkling with disgust.

A thick set man was obviously in charge and was sitting at the front, a pint of Guinness in front of him and a scowl on his face, Laura recognised him straight away, she had met him before when she had gone to the Sabs meeting that night with Linda, Sean and the others a few weeks ago, but this was a very different scenario.

"Welcome Laura, Sean, good to see you both. I was pleased to hear from you Sean old mate, and from you Laura, we was all interested in what you had to say when we last met" he said quietly to her "but we've to be careful y' know. We've checked you out, just t' be sure and y' seem t' be kosher."

Thanks mate, I said she was cool" grinned Sean, "Got some good ideas too. Aint ya Laura?"

Laura stared hard "I'm passionate about what I believe in" she said sharply, "I think I could help you and the cause."

"You seem passionate enough" said the man, "This 'ere is a small select bunch of hard liners, we're the ones who do the real jobs, the others just make the noise – you'd be one of us."

Laura pulled out a chair and sat down, "I can give you information about a particular hunt, where they go, what they plan, what land they're doing it on and so forth, what days they go out. I can find out all sorts of information for you, which means you can target them in particular throughout a whole year, including their social functions. You can't ask me how I get the information – that's the deal – okay? The actual sabotage is up to you."

"Why? What's in it for you?"

"Because they sicken me, the way they live, the way they treat animals for sport, the way they treat people and that they think they are above the law – that good enough for you!" she spat, "That's what's in it for me."

"Sounds kinda personal to me – why this one?"

She pulled herself together a little, "It feels personal, I hate them and I just happen to be in a position to help you if you want, if you don't – I'll clear off, no more to be said." she picked up her bag and made to leave.

"Whoa, calm down feisty lady! That's good enough for me." laughed the man, "okay let's start talking strategies here, and making some proper introductions."

Laura looked up at him smiling slyly, "Great – you won't regret it."

Down in Fittlebury the Fox was busy too, Patrick had brought Sharon out for a drink and had met up with Grace and Colin in the snug bar. Dick Macey was regaling some thrilling tales of when he was a detective in the police force, and Janice was rolling her eyes exaggeratedly behind his back in a '*I've heard all this before gesture*'. The others didn't seem to mind, Dick was really entertaining when he was in full swing. The bar was pretty crowded, but after all it was Saturday night, and there was quite a lot of passing trade. People returning from the coast through the back lanes stopping for a drink or a bar snack before going home, plus all the old regulars propping up the bar in their tatty tweed coats and their check shirts.

The bar door was propped open, the air was quite mild after a warm day and the evenings were long with light as midsummer night approached. Charles pulled into the car park with the Range Rover, and helped first Jennifer and then Ivy from the back seat. They strolled over into the garden, Jennifer and Ivy loitering to admire the hanging baskets, Charles called for them to hurry up and stepped down into the snug.

"Hi Charles." greeted Colin, "All alone? What're you having?"

"Hi Colin, Grace," he stooped down to kiss her on the cheek, "no Jennifer and her mother are just outside, we've popped down for supper, they'll be here any moment." He turned to Patrick, "Hi Patrick, how are you? Haven't seen you for a long time, is this your wife? I don't think we've met? I'm Charles." He put out his hand to shake Sharon's.

Sharon blushed, and unusually for her was lost for words, finally she stammered, "No we haven't met before although I've heard a lot about you, I'm Sharon, nice to meet you."

"Here let me get this round in, Janice, when you've got a moment." Charles called, clearly unaware of the impact he'd made on her.

It was amazing thought Patrick, the effect that Charles had when he came into a room, as Janice dashed over to take his order patting her hair - the women all ogled him and seemed tongue tied, and the men jumped up to gain his attention. Sharon couldn't stop gawping - her tongue was almost hanging out for Christ's sake! He turned to the door to see Jennifer and her mother coming in from the garden. She looked amazing tonight, her normally pale skin had a really healthy glow and her face seemed to have lost that gaunt strained look. She was wearing a full swing skirt nipped in at the waist and flat pumps which on most women would have made them look dumpy, but with Jennifer's long legs she looked sensational. The woman who accompanied her was a little shorter but just as slim, she was holding onto Jennifer's arm and laughing at some joke between them. Charles immediately brought them over and introduced Ivy to the others.

Jennifer gave Colin and Grace a hug and greeted Patrick like an old friend, and he basked in her attention. Sharon on the other hand, who had not met her before, gave Jennifer a vinegary smile, making her dislike evident from the outset, and despite Jennifer's best attentions to talk to her, Sharon answered her with monosyllabic replies, screwing up her mouth and face into an acidic false smile. Jennifer was dismayed, Sharon's reaction to her was reminiscent of the old times at that first ball, although what she had ever done to her was a mystery, she decided to just ignore it. Colin and Grace were lovely, as was Patrick and they all stood at the bar as Charles organised their drinks.

Ivy watched on the periphery of the group, summing them all up, this was such a different lifestyle for her little girl and on the whole she seemed to be happy. She had worried about her this past year but so far the folk she had met were right decent, bit posh but alright, except this last girl, who stood on the edge with a face like thunder. Ivy had seen her type before - jealous little minx, spiteful too, obviously though Jen had never met her before tonight, but she wouldn't trust her as far as she could throw her.

"It's so nice to meet you Ivy. Are you enjoying your stay?" asked Grace, "Nantes is such a beautiful house isn't it?"

"Oh yes m' dear, it certainly is, I've never seen anything so grand! Charles and Jen have really spoilt me this weekend too, I'm having a lovely time. Although the house is so big, I thought I'd get lost in it at first. I've got my bearings a bit now although I've only been in a tiny part of it."

"How have you found Mrs Fuller, she can be a bit daunting at times! A bit like Mrs Danvers in Daphne Du Maurier's Rebecca."

"Oh I love that film! No, Freda's been a real duck, made me very welcome, we get on well - Jen's lucky to have her."

Sharon stood glowering at them, "Is this your first visit then?" she said snidely, "Surely you've been invited down before now?" She looked nastily at Jennifer, "Why hasn't Jen asked you down - after all she moved in a long time ago, it's been ages since Celia moved out."

Everyone stopped talking and looked appalled at the crass remark, but Ivy didn't hesitate, not giving Jennifer a chance to respond. She looked steadily at Sharon and replied sweetly "Oh, I'm so sorry dear, I've forgotten your name, Tracey was it?" She smiled,

"No, I've another daughter and her two children in London, who've needed a lot of my time, so this is the first time I've been able to come," then she added pleasantly "but you'll be seeing a lot of me now I'm sure."

Having diffused the awkward remark so quickly, the others in their embarrassment all started talking at once to each other, as Sharon folded her arms and looked cross - her moment of confrontation having been headed off at the pass by this seemingly sweet woman. Patrick was absolutely furious and was studiously ignoring her and chatted to Charles and Colin about the forthcoming hunting season, whilst Grace suggested that Jennifer take Ivy to see Charleston either tomorrow or when she was next down.

"Oh Ivy, you'd love it!" Grace enthused, "It's the most charming place, especially on a nice day."

"I've never heard of it." said Jennifer pathetically grateful to Grace for changing the subject, "Where is it then."

"Well, it's not far from Firle on the A27, it was the home of the artists Vanessa Bell and Duncan Grant, they moved there during the First World War and it became the meeting place for the Bloomsbury Group – she was Virginia Woolf's sister. But it's more than that, it's not grand, it's the setting, and inside they painted it themselves in the most original way."

"Gosh, I'd no idea it was even there! I've driven that road loads of times on the way to Lewes, but never noticed any signs." said Jennifer.

"Well you probably wouldn't if you didn't know it was there!" laughed Grace, "it's not just the house though, the gardens are lovely, really quite small, but just ….oh I can't describe them, you'll just have to go and see – but only go if the weather is nice, because it can be damned bleak if it's raining."

"What are you three plotting" interrupted Charles, "because whatever it is, we'd better continue it over dinner, it's getting late."

"Just telling Jen and Ivy about Charleston, you must've been there Charles?" said Grace, "being a Sussex boy."

"Yep sure have, obligatory – it's a crazy place, you'd love it darling – you too Ivy, when we get back home, we can look it up on Google, and if you fancy going we could pop over tomorrow, but right now – I'm starving!" He turned to Colin and Patrick, "You guys joining us for supper, I'm sure Janice can find us a bigger table in the dining room."

"We'd love to." said Colin, "We were going to have a bar snack anyway, so that sounds good."

"Patrick?" asked Charles, "How about you?"

"Well, perhaps not" said Patrick - regret in his voice, looking at Sharon, who still had a face like a slapped arse.

"Oh please do, it's been so nice to meet you and I'm very interested in your job" Ivy smiled mischievously at him, and then turning to Sharon touched her lightly on her arm added "and of course your charming wife, by the way my dear I love your blouse, is it from New Look? Did you get it in the sale? I saw one like it myself and nearly bought it last week but sadly they only had the larger sizes left." Ivy's voice was so benign that no offence could possibly have been taken, but Jennifer recognised the danger signs as clearly as if she had waved a red flag.

Pete skirted his way around the edge of the rhododendrons and around the far perimeter of the lawns, careful to avoid setting off the security lights. He stumbled through the shrubs, tripping every now and then over a hidden root. The lights of the house shone dimly out across the grass casting eerie pools of light, but as much as he squinted he could see no movement from inside. He dare not cross the drive on the gravel for fear of being seen or heard, so he kept behind the bushes where he could watch unseen and safe. He was on the wrong side to see if the cars were in the garages, so he'd no idea if anyone was at home. He'd just have to take his chance. There was one thing that he'd left behind in his haste to leave and it had become an obsession to get it back, and to Pete it was worth the risk of returning. He shook his head, his dirty wild hair whipping his face, tears started to well up in his eyes, he loved this place, it was his home but he knew he could never come back, not all the time she was here anyway. He wiped his eyes angrily, and crept on towards the cottage.

He did not approach directly down the flag stoned path, but slunk around the hedge that encompassed the back of the cottage, squeezing through where the hawthorns were thin. and approached the back door from the far side. Then he crawled on his belly over the springy grass, with the peculiar nostalgic smell of the earth filling his nostrils and he wanted to fade away into it, for it to swallow him up and leave him here at his beloved Nantes. He laid for some while, with his nose pressed into the earth and closed his eyes - trying to shut out all the horrors which haunted him; he started to weep quietly, the wretchedness of his situation once again assailing him. How long he sobbed he had no idea, but then he heard them whispering, and his whole body immediately stiffened, he put his head to one side and opened his eyes, sure that he could see them, beckoning him from the cottage door, calling him. It would be all right, they would tell him what to do. Inching his way towards the door he gradually stood up, looking all around him, he couldn't see them now, but they had told him what to do. He turned the handle on the door, but to his surprise it wouldn't open, he looked down at it unbelieving, he tried it again, more forcefully this time, but it wouldn't yield. This time he fairly yanked, but still it wouldn't budge. He bent down and groped under an old pot by the door, where his mother had always kept a key, although since she had died he'd never locked the cottage. He shoved it in the lock and tried to turn it, but it wouldn't turn either way, he tried to force it, first one way, and then the other, until the key bent and it was stuck fast in the lock. With a rage he hammered on the door, hurling himself against it, but it held fast. He was locked out, he couldn't understand it. He needed that photograph. He had to have it.

He walked around to the kitchen and without hesitation put his fist clean through one of the little square panes in the window, the glass breaking with a little tinkle. He shoved his huge hand through the tiny gap, heedless of slicing his wrist on the broken glass and unlatched it, yanking it open with a huge sigh of relief. Squeezing his bulk through and clambering over the draining board he found himself standing in the kitchen, and strained to listen, he couldn't hear the voices, but he wasn't going to hang around here. He charged through the sitting room, ducking his head out of habit under the low beam and up the stairs, not bothering to be quiet. He dashed into his room, and there it was, the photograph of his mother, he picked it up and clutched it to his chest. In a single moment of lucid thought there was just one more thing, he pulled open the wardrobe door and dragged out his coat and shoes, wrapped them into a bundle and was gone, hurtling back down the stairs and back out of the window.

As he skirted back around the garden, taking the same meticulous route by which he had come, he was suddenly alarmed when all the security lights blazed on, smothering the garden with a harsh white glare. He melted back into the safety of the rhododendrons and froze as the Range Rover sailed down the drive its headlights on full beam sweeping the shadows. The car skimmed around to the back and pulled up in front of the garages, and Pete could hear voices, but this time it was Jennifer and Charles and another voice he didn't know. He strained his ears to listen but he couldn't determine what was being said, only that they were laughing and joking. How dare they he thought, she must be laughing at him, it was her who had locked him out. That bitch, that stuck up cunt he ruminated irrationally. More and more the expletives tumbled into his head, his anger almost making him want to shout out at her. But as the blood pumped around in his head like a beating drum, and the madness subsided, he realised that they had gone inside, the security lights had gone out, just like the light in his heart.

CHAPTER 51

Charles wearily picked up the phone - it was Celia returning his call. He was dreading this conversation.

"Oh hello Celia, thanks for returning my call. How are the children?"

"They're fine - thank you for asking Charles. Now what can I do for you?" Celia asked frostily.

"I wanted to know if you'd thought about this holiday I mentioned last week? I need to have some dates, so that I can fix something up." Charles explained patiently, "I'd like to go about the second week in July, when do the children break up from school?"

"Well of course, if you were any sort of father to them you would know" said Celia bitterly, "but since you have shown an interest – they finish on 9th July. Before you ask, no they can't leave any earlier to go on holiday with you. Perhaps you might consider I might want to take them away then."

"Well I wasn't asking that you take them out of school - since that would suit me perfectly" replied Charles calmly, "and are you planning to take them away then, and if so, where to might I ask?"

"Well no, I wasn't actually, but you just don't consider anyone but yourself Charles, never have and never will. You didn't even think to ask." spat Celia nastily.

"Well as you aren't - it's not an issue is it? Come on don't let's argue, for the children's sake please?"

"You make me sick Charles, you swan in, with your common little wife and expect me to bend over backwards to accommodate you. Well, you can think on!"

Charles felt his temper rising, God she was a first class bitch, but rowing with her would solve nothing, and he bloody well wouldn't rise to it. Instead he replied quietly, "Celia, I think that kind of behaviour is uncalled for frankly. I'm asking if it suits you if I take the children away on holiday that's all. If you're not planning anything and you say you're not, what's the objection?"

"The objection is that I don't like the children spending time with that tart!"

"Well I think you're being ridiculous. They spent a lovely weekend us with us last time, and surely it's in the children's best interests for us all to get along well? I don't object to you having boyfriends, and I understand that you're seeing some chap now and I'm really pleased for you." Charles tried to reason with her, "Please Celia, think of the kids."

"How dare you compare my social life to your sordid affairs!"

"Celia, whether you like it or not, Jennifer is my wife and I love her, and I love my children and they are all part of my life – and I don't think that what I'm asking is being unreasonable, but I do think your reaction is."

"You may think you love her Charles, but I know you, you'll soon be tired of her and be seeking solace elsewhere, if you haven't already, and that's what's not fair on the children." Celia raged.

Charles had had enough, "Alright Celia, have it your own way, I'll take this to court then, is that what you want?"

"You wouldn't dare!"

"Watch me! I've joint custody, control and access, and most of the time I let you call the shots, but not this time, and I won't have you behave like this any longer. Now what are you going to do, behave reasonably – like a civilised woman, or shall we go to court and you can have all your friends know just how irrational you are? Your choice? Hardly good for the children though eh?"

There was a long pause at the end of the line, at first Charles thought she had hung up on him, but he waited - willing her to speak, and finally she replied. "Very well, but I want you to know that I am only agreeing under duress."

"Thank you Celia, I appreciate it, I'll go ahead and book the holiday then and email you all the details. Can you tell the children I'll ring them later?

"Very well. You're a bully Charles, you always have been, I pity poor Jennifer living with you. Goodbye."

Charles was still cradling the receiver in his hand when she put the phone down. She was such a bitch! He knew she'd make it awkward, but not that awkward. How had he lived with her for all those years, well of course the answer was that he had been a serial philanderer and had lived behind the façade of pomp and snobbery. Thank the Lord he had met Jennifer! He'd get one of the girls to nip down to the travel agents and get some brochures, they could look at them this evening.

Rackham horse trials was next weekend and Chloe was revving up Seamus and Alfie in preparation for the event. After Sandy and Katherine's confession that they had galloped them hard at the weekend, she had kept a careful eye on their legs, on the lookout for any filling or swelling, but so far nothing untoward had happened and they were as cold and hard as they should be. Nonetheless, you could never be too vigilant. Sandy was going to have a lesson four times this week and try and get the unruly Seamus more under control, and a day off on Wednesday instead of the usual Monday. Katherine had decided that she would have three, just to hone in on the test skills, and then a jump session as well, so they were both going to be busy. Jen was coming up this afternoon after she had taken her mum home to have a session in the school, as she had not come up yesterday and was starting to get withdrawals. To top it all the haylage had been baled and was being brought into the barn, all in all it was the usual chaotic start to the week.

Chloe herself was feeling a bit brighter, her weekend had been good, John had almost been like his old self, consequently the children had been more settled and so had she. Was it to be short-lived, was the crisis blowing over, or was it the lull before the storm? It was hard to tell, but she was taking any respite she could right now. At least he had agreed that they should all go to the horse trials together and that was something for them all to look forward to. Her mobile rang and she dragged it out of her pocket and peered at the number and smiled, fingers crossed this might just be more good news.

Nantes was bathed in sunshine, its mellow stone walls warm to the touch as the temperature rose with the climbing sun. The horses were dozing in the paddocks and all was very quiet and still. Caitlin was humming to herself in the stable yard, Mrs Fuller was on her laptop doing the weekly order from Ocado, and Doris was upstairs changing the beds, mumbling to herself about her arthritis. The grumble of a pick- up truck pulled down the drive, filled with gardening tools and a large ride on mower on the back. Two men jumped out, one was an older chap and a young guy with him, both in shorts and tee shirts with tanned brown faces from the sun. Fred appeared from behind the garages where he had been pottering about mending the latch on the back gate.

"Morning lads" he called out to them "beautiful morning again."

"Morning Fred" shouted back the older of the two "yep it is, although the forecast next week says it's gonna break. Everyone's haymaking like mad. The roads are choco with tractors and trailers."

"Yes, at least they've got it in dry. Even if it is a bit sparse." laughed Fred, "There's never a perfect year!"

"No" agreed the man, "Now any instructions from the boss?"

"He says, can you do the lawns as normal, but the rose arbour needs some attention; can you have a look at it, the herbaceous borders, and a tidy up round the terrace, the pots are looking a bit straggly. Mrs Fuller says can you pop in for your tea to the kitchen today 'cos she wants to talk to you about the kitchen garden."

"Blimey! We'd better get cracking - Ian, you get started on the mowing the main grass, and I'll start the terrace. Then you can do the cottage garden with the small mower and I'll do the arbour. We'll be ready for a tea and a bit of cake by then I think."

"Okay Tony mate, lucky we set the day aside, it's a bloody big garden!"

"Yeah, well, it's a good contract alright, so let's do a good job."

They dropped the tailgate of the pickup and manoeuvred the mower carefully off down two planks of wood, checked the petrol and Ian chugged off to start on the lawns. Tony donned a canvas apron with big pockets stuffed with secateurs, trowels, fork and gloves, picked up an oversize plastic skip bucket and made his way to the back to house to start. The peace and tranquillity of the morning was humming with the sound of the mower. Fred scratched his chin, he hated Mondays.

Mrs Fuller was just putting the finishing touches to her coffee and walnut cake, she stood back and admired it, mmmm, it smelt delicious! She had the beef casserole in the bottom oven gently cooking and it would be well and tender for tonight's dinner, so she had earned her cup of tea. Just in time too, as she heard Doris chuntering away in the laundry room and the washing machine swishing away. She had just put the kettle onto the hot ring, when she heard a thumping of footsteps down the passage from the back door and Fred burst into the kitchen.

"Fred Windrush, you'd better have a good reason for stomping through the house with those boots!" Freda snapped looking aghast at his feet.

"There's been a break in!" he gasped, his face red with running and excitement, "in the cottage!"

"What d'ya mean! A break in! Calm down Fred, sit y'self down and tell me properly and mind my cake!" Freda pulled out a chair as Doris hurtled into the kitchen.

"What's up!" she demanded, "Fred are you alright?"

"Course he is Doris, now be quiet do, and we'll find out!" Freda barked at her, "Now Fred, what're you talking about?"

Fred sat down and took a breath, "Well those blokes doing the garden were just starting to mow the cottage grass, took the small mower round, when the young'un found the kitchen window had been smashed in and was wide open, blood all over the window sill!"

"No!" squeaked Doris, "who could've done it – there's nothing in there worth taking."

"Only one person of course" said Mrs Fuller "It's got to be Pete hasn't it, who else could it be? Who else would even know about the cottage tucked away at the back there? If anyone wanted to steal anything, they would have gone for the house or the garages, or even the granary or the stables."

"The funny thing was, there was an old key broken in the lock." said Fred, "like someone had tried to go in the door."

"I hope you didn't touch anything you great oaf" snapped Doris "it might have finger prints!"

"A fat lot of good they'll be then." sighed Freda, "ah well, I'd better ring Mr Charles and he'll want me to ring the police no doubt. Where are the gardeners then Fred? Get them in here for a cuppa whilst we wait to see what's wanted, and best keep away until they decide I suppose."

She got up wearily and picked up the telephone on the wall, Doris sat down with a thump on the chair and Fred went to find Tony and Ian. At least Freda had finished the cake, they were going to need it!

It was after half past four when Jennifer was driving back along the lanes towards Nantes, having had a good lesson with Chloe. It felt great to be riding again, she had really missed it and she realised that if Charles was serious about this safari then she was going to have to put in some serious overtime if she wanted to be up to scratch. She pulled down the drive, and round the curve to where it forked to the stables and was surprised to see a police car and the garden contractor's truck in front of the house. She couldn't see anyone about, so drove around to the garages and parked the car. The back door was open, so she made her way along the passage and heard voices coming from the kitchen and went in to find Mrs Fuller, Doris and a lad sitting at the table drinking tea.

"Hi," she greeted, "I'm home, don't get up Mrs F, I'll pour myself a cup of tea. What's going on outside?

"Oh Jennifer you did startle me coming in like that!"

"I'm sorry" Jennifer said her back to Mrs Fuller pouring the tea, "what are the police doing here?"

"Oh dear oh dear!" Mrs Fuller said her voice faltering, "It's the cottage, young Ian here was cutting the grass and found there's been a break in."

"What d' you mean a break in?" Jennifer said startled, "has anything been taken?"

"A window was smashed at the back, some blood on the sill. The Police 've found a key's been bent and stuck in the lock, but of course Mr Charles had the locks changed, so it was useless, so they broke in through the window. Who'd have a key?"

Jennifer went white, the implication was obvious "It was Pete you mean?"

"Well we don't know for certain, but it does look that way" stammered Mrs Fuller, "oh my dear, I didn't want to tell you, but you need to be told."

"Does Charles know?" whispered Jennifer.

"Yes, it was he who called the police, he's on his way home now. He tried to call you but your phone's not picking up."

"No, I've had it on silent, forgot to put it back on." Jennifer picked up her tea, "Mrs Fuller, I'm going up to my bedroom to change, tell Charles when he comes in please. I imagine the police don't want to speak to me."

"Are you all right Jennifer?" Mrs Fuller looked anxious, "Do you want anything else?"

"Thank you, but no, and yes I'm perfectly all right" Jennifer said determinedly and took her tea and went out.

"Well" said Doris, "What do you make of that."

Jennifer sat on the edge of her bed, putting her tea on the bedside table, and couldn't decide if she was upset, frightened or just plain bloody angry. In fact she decided she was a mixture of all three. How dare that man behave like this, they'd been nothing but good to him, Charles' family had given him a home all his life, and okay he resented her because of Celia but she'd really tried to be nice to him, and he'd now created some bizarre vendetta against her. The creepy thing about it was, at some unknown point he'd crept back to the cottage and broken in, although Christ knew why, but the crucial thing was that they'd been totally unaware that he'd been there. He was like some stealth missile, but she was not going to be caught unawares again, she knelt down and groped under the bed and pulled out the paper parcel that she had picked up from Susan last week.

Charles roared down the drive, not bothering to put the car away and slewed it alongside the squad car and ran across the lawn towards the cottage. A uniformed officer was outside and he stopped Charles not allowing him any further and called for another plain clothes officer to come out from the house to see him.

"Mr. Parker-Smythe is it Sir?" the man asked consulting his notebook.

"Yes, this is my cottage, I understand from my housekeeper that it has been broken into, can I ask officer what has been taken?"

"Well I was going to ask you the same thing Sir, from what I can see nothing at all, but if you wouldn't mind stepping inside and having a look around, perhaps you'd tell me?"

"Of course. I gather they got in through the kitchen window?"

"Yes, a small pane has been smashed, and he put his hand through and unlatched the window from inside, made a fair old mess too, cutting his arm when he put it through, there's quite a lot of blood on the sill and the sink. We think he tried to get through the door first though. We found a key bent and stuck in the lock, like he tried to use a key but it wouldn't fit."

Charles sighed, it certainly sounded as though the intruder had been Pete and went on to explain the whole story to the police officer who listened carefully to everything Charles said.

"Well it certainly seems as though it could be him, although of course we mustn't jump to conclusions. Dr Corbett from the village can be contacted I assume about it, can he Sir?"

"Yes, yes definitely. They thought he'd done a bunk, gone

completely out of the area, they could well have been mistaken it seems. Anyway let's go inside and I can see if anything's missing."

The cottage looked pretty much as Charles had left it the last time he was there. Nothing had been disturbed, it still had a very sad unlived in look and only the glass fragments on the draining board were different. He and the police officer moved up the stairs into Pete's bedroom and Charles stiffened, noticing at once that the photograph had gone. The wardrobe doors too were ajar, and he flung them open, the coat and the shoes had gone. The rest of the house had been untouched. It was all very sinister.

"Officer, I must get back to see my wife, she will be home by now and be pretty upset I'm sure, perhaps when you're finished you'll look in and we can discuss what's to be done next?" asked Charles, "If of course there's anything we can do?"

"Yes, of course, you get off now Sir, and I'll look in when we're finished here."

That night in bed Charles hugged Jennifer close, and she snuggled up to him. She loved the feel of his strong arms around her, when they were like this she felt so safe. It had been a horrible afternoon. The police had come in after their examination of the cottage and Alex Corbett had been contacted, along with the psychiatric social worker. The general consensus was that it must have been Pete who had broken into the house, as all that was gone was the missing photograph, the coat and shoes and these items were all obviously important to him. The pills, which were in fact far more valuable, had been left behind. There was also the question of the bent key in the lock. It made perfect sense, especially when you took into account the attack the previous week. But the million dollar question was, where was he now and where had he been all week? The police promised to resume their search, although so far they had been worse than useless fumed Charles, and meanwhile he was worried sick about how to keep Jennifer safe.

Jennifer on the other hand was not afraid now, she was bloody angry, but more than anything she was ready – on the alert for anything he might try. Charles was adamant that she should not be on her own at any time, and tonight he had called the staff together with

Jennifer and been totally firm on this point. Despite Jennifer's initial protests, she had promised - feeling totally pathetic, that she would stay close to them, and let them know her movements over the next few weeks or at least until Pete had been apprehended. Although Charles agreed with her privately that for the time being at least she could still keep the real reason for her visits to Chloe's between themselves only. Charles had pointed out that luckily Felix would be arriving next Monday, which would help, and then after that they would be away for a few weeks on holiday, but meanwhile they must all be on their guard and if anything suspicious at all was noticed, both the police and he should be told immediately. Everyone had meekly nodded their heads, Charles was like a tornado when he was in this mood. Jennifer had her own scheme though, Susan's package contained a powerful mace and dye spray, which she planned to carry with her all the time, the instructions claimed that one squirt in the face would be enough to stop any attacker in their tracks. Tomorrow, she was going to see what else Susan could come up with by way of self-defence stuff – she had heard about Tasers, but thought they were illegal in this country, but what did that matter. She'd definitely call her, no more playing by the fucking rules.

CHAPTER 52

Rackham Horse Trials was tomorrow and Katherine and Sandy had got their times from the BDWP page on the internet. They weren't bad considering that one was in the BE100 and the other in the novice, and it meant they could travel together. Chloe, who was going anyway, had already offered to take them in the truck, provided Jeremy could take John and the children in his car with the picnic. John was all in favour, it meant he didn't have to leave quite so early and he enjoyed Jeremy's company. The times between each phase were pretty tight for both sections so the girls had decided to walk the cross country course today, it would save a good hour or so tomorrow. Chloe had asked Jen if she wanted to come along - even though she was a long way off competing at this level - declaring it would be interesting for her.

"Don't think I don't know why you're asking me Chloe!" admonished Jennifer when they got back from their ride, "I know Charles has asked you to keep an eye out for me, with this Pete business."

"Okay, I admit that's true," laughed Chloe throwing up her hands in surrender "but you'll be inspired by it too. Wait and see!"

"I'm sure I will and" she added, smiling at Chloe, "I'm grateful too."

Katherine and Sandy had already had their lessons earlier and were busy packing the lorry ready for a prompt start in the morning. They were toiling backwards and forwards their arms laden with trunks, consulting their check lists making sure everything had been put in.

"Don't forget to put in a new tub of Green Ice Gel." shouted Beebs, "The one in the lorry is nearly empty!"

"Good job you told me." said Sandy, "have you got anymore?"

"Don't panic!" interrupted Chloe, "There's some in the medicine cabinet, I'll get it."

Jennifer watched them all dashing about like bees around a hive and walked Rufus over to the wash down box, gently hosing him off and feeding him Polos. Susie came over and offered to take him back down to the field. Jennifer watched him go regretfully, she loved that little chap.

"Righto," called Chloe "we'd better get a wiggle on ladies, although Beebs has said she'd pick up the kids from the bus, but I don't want to make it too late back, so I'll get the car."

They piled into the Discovery, Jen and Katherine in the back, narrowly avoiding some sticky old sweets glued to the seats and a complicated Lego model which had disintegrated into smithereens, as Chloe rocketed along the lanes towards Rackham. The countryside was beautiful as they travelled up and over the downs towards the venue, the girls chattering and gossiping together. For a while all thoughts of Pete were driven from Jennifer's mind as she relaxed and laughed with the others, it was a joy not to be looking over her shoulder all the time.

Chloe bumped the car into the field and parked it alongside the other course walkers, and they walked over to the secretary's marquee to have a look at the course plan. Chloe was right - Jennifer was interested, she'd never been to anything like it before. They all poured over the map and studied the course; more or less both classes would run over the same route but the jumps would be of different heights and the novice track would be complicated by combinations and angles.

"Okay, let's get going then" said Chloe, "the start box is over there."

They trooped off in the direction of the distant caravan, pausing to glance at the show jumping arena where the organisers were just putting the finishing touches to the track, erecting the electronic start and finish gates and dressing the fences.

"We'll look at that when we come back shall we?" said Katherine her nerves obviously beginning to jangle, "it looks quite big!"

"Nothing you can't handle" laughed Sandy, "they always look bigger the day before, tomorrow they'll seem much smaller!"

"She's right Katherine, now come on, the cross country calls – on on!" laughed Chloe.

Jennifer was bemused by all this talk, the jumps looked enormous to her, who hadn't even jumped a pole on the ground yet. One day she thought, one day. Taking one last look at the show jumps she hurried after the others.

Jonty was packing up the stall, it had been a shit day. Plenty of people - but crap punters with no money. There was nothing to be made in this game anymore but lucky for him he had fingers in other pies, and if things went his way pretty soon he would be rolling in it! He was planning a little visit to that cock hungry little slag Lucy tonight, but before he went he had a few drops to make. He glanced at his watch, fucking thing had stopped and he only bought it last week, he would have a word with that dodgy bastard Lefty who sold it him – pile of crap it was. It must be getting on though, he shouted out to Moses on the next door stall, who was looking gloomy at the lack of trade. Mind you, who wanted all that African carving trash anyway.

"Hey Moses, wassa time mate?"

Moses turned to him rolling his brown eyes and answered in his usual slow lugubrious way "Gettin' on hal' pas' four man. You packin' up now then?"

"Yeah, no fuckin' punters mate, waste of a day. You?"

"Same 'ere man" he said miserably.

"Oh well, tomorrow's 'nother day, as they say" laughed Jonty, thinking thank fuck he didn't rely on the stall to make ends meet.

He finished the packing and phoned Weasel to bring round the Landrover to collect the gear, and within fifteen minutes they were inching out of Brick Lane and heading towards the lock up.

"What time we gotta be in Horsham?" asked Weasel "I'm sick of that run, it takes fuckin' ages."

"Stop moaning. I gotta do a couple of hits, then we'll go straight down. Our Lucy's gagging for a bit of action and she's got something for us – so it'll be worth it."

Weasel pulled up the Landrover behind a tired block of flats, where, tucked away at the back were rows of garages. He stopped beside one, and looked around him. It was very quiet, no-one much about, just a few young kids in trainers and hoodies kicking a ball against the garage doors. Jonty got out and spoke to them, gave them some money and they scarpered without looking back. He went over to one of the garages, glanced furtively around him, pulled out a bunch of keys, unlocked it and wrenched the door up; and Weasel skilfully reversed in the Landrover, and the door clamped shut behind them. In less than a couple of minutes it was as though they had never been there. Their real business for the day had begun.

For Charles it had been a dreadful week. The only good news on the horizon was that he had booked the holiday and they would be off in ten days. God he couldn't wait. How he'd managed to go to work every day and carry on as normal, let alone make as many successful coups as he had astounded him – he could only imagine that the ruthless way he behaved in business was purely down to the anger boiling away at the surface of his helplessness on the home front. Throwing himself into work was one way of forgetting for a nanosecond about that bloody lunatic on the large. He marvelled at Jennifer, he'd seen a new side of her, and one he admired, she was certainly no simpering pathetic wreck. They were going to have a great holiday – he couldn't believe how she had ridden that day at Chloe's – that had seemed eons away now. Once again showing a side of her he had no idea even existed.

The police had combed the countryside but once again the elusive Pete had not been found, he was like the bloody invisible man! He'd racked his brains to think of a place that he could be hiding but he was a strange old mix, had hardly ever left Nantes as far as he knew, always been afraid of shadows and dark places, and yet now he had disappeared into them without a trace. His greatest wish was that he was dead in a ditch somewhere.

He pondered too about the phone call he had received from Chloe. She had found a possible horse for Jennifer. It was the little mare Polly that Katherine had sold last year. The woman who had bought her had been diagnosed with some illness and it would mean her having to give up riding, and whilst she was not in a rush to sell - Polly would be on the market again. Chloe said the horse would be perfect for Jen and would he like her to pursue it quietly on his behalf? Charles had immediately said an emphatic yes, but then wondered if he should have asked Jennifer first, would a surprise be better or would she want to choose? More and more he was realising that she was her own woman and made her own mind up about things. He'd better ask Chloe what she thought and he would make sure there was a good drink in it for her for all her hard work.

Caitlin couldn't wait for Monday when Felix would arrive. She was knackered and could do with a breather. Although the work was not hard just now, it was just the always having to be on call that was so demanding, just when she wanted to be somewhere else; and now with all this business with Pete taking an extra toll on her time it was wearing to be sure. She'd never forgive herself so she wouldn't if something happened whilst she was having fun when she should have been on her guard.

Felix - she wondered how he would pan out. It was a funny thing that he was coming here for the season, although he seemed like a good craic and it would be fun to have a smiling face around instead of the sulky Lucy! She had tidied up the flat now and would pop down to the Gupta's shop and buy some bread and milk and stuff for him, and pop in some flowers from the garden to make him feel welcome, although thinking about it, flowers might be a bit girly, and he was certainly no girl! When she had spoken to him on the phone, he said he would be arriving at about 8am and was bringing his horse at the same time, and so she had gotten a stable all ready and made some space in the tack room for his saddle and bridle. She had no idea what the horse itself would be like, they could turn out in one of the smaller paddocks to start with, till they saw how it got on with the others, but she couldn't risk Mr Charles' horses getting kicked just before the start of the season that's for sure. That was the only downside, never a good plan to have a groom's horse, or any other come to that! Oh well, she supposed it would be okay, provided she was tough to begin with about priorities.

She picked up some tools and went over to skip out the horses, they were all in, as Patrick was coming late this afternoon to do some trims and check on Queenie. It was a bugger really, as Jennifer was out all day and she had an opportunity to sneak out, but it was the only time he could fit them in, and she didn't want to leave it til next week. Beano nuzzled in her pockets softly as she bent down to pick up the droppings, pulling at her hair with his teeth, she pushed him away gently with her shoulder, crooning at him to wait and she would give him a Polo if he was patient. Suddenly an ugly black shadow was cast over the top of the loose box door, blotting out the sun that had been streaming through, she looked up startled and was momentarily afraid - her heart beating fast.

"If the mountain can't come to Mohammed, then Mohammed must come to the mountain" said Ace, walking into the stable and pulling her to her feet and kissing her thoroughly, "mmmm, you smell nice!"

"Holy Mother" whispered Caitlin, "Whatever are you doing! Supposing you were seen!"

"I'm beginning not to care frankly," he said smoothly, "but as it happens my sweet, I parked a way away, and walked across the fields. Let's nip up to the flat, Felix isn't here till Monday is he, and Patrick's not due for another hour!"

Lucy had finished work and was tarting herself up in the cloakroom. She didn't want to go home before she met Jonty and Weasel even though that wasn't till later tonight. Her mother always wanted to know the ins and outs of a duck's arse, so it was best to avoid her. She'd left a message on the answer phone saying she would be home late and was going for a drink with some friends. Well that part was true anyway, she was meeting Tom for a quickie in the Bear before she met the lads. The news about Pete had spread round the village like a dose of clap, and Tom had promised her that tonight he'd fill her in on all the gory details but he warily said that he couldn't stay long - well little did he know that suited her fine! She'd have some juicy titbits of information for Jonty later which would keep him interested and coming back for more. She wasn't stupid, she knew it wasn't her he was interested in, but for the time being it spiced up her life and anyway it might lead to more – you never knew! She couldn't wait to tell Jonty, but she might embellish the tale a bit!

It was nearly nine o'clock when the lads finally showed up at B52s and Lucy was in a right old strop. She had been waiting for almost three quarters of an hour and was just going to flounce out when they came strolling round the corner.

"Fuck you Jonty" said Lucy as he sauntered over, "I'm going!"

He caught hold of her wrist, "Don't go little Luce, sorry we're late." he wheedled, "come 'n, I'll buy you a nice drinkie and I've bought you a lil' pressie!"

Lucy sniffed, "You piss me right off, and I'm not a slag y'know."

"I know love, I know" he smiled at her, letting go of her wrist, "Weasel get Luce a drink, and one for you, I'll have a coke." he peeled off some notes from a great wedge and tossed them at Weasel. Lucy's eyes nearly popped out of her head - just like he knew they would. "I've been doin' a bit of business, that's why I'm so late."

"Okay, just don't treat me like shite, 'cos I won't stand for it – right."

"Course not love, it couldn't be helped" he stroked her wrist, resisting the urge to slap her hard. Fucking little tart who did she think she was kidding. "What's the goss then hun?"

Lucy's eyes glittered, remembering with glee what Tom had told her, "Well you'll never guess what?" she laughed, "Someone has tried to kill Mrs Perfect- Parker-Smarmy –Smythe!"

"What!" spluttered Jonty, seizing her wrist again, "what the fuck are you talking about you crazy tart, tell me more?"

"Ouch you're bloody hurting me!" yelled Lucy, alarmed

snatching her hand away and rubbing her wrist, "what's up with you!"

Jonty pulled himself together, "Sorry Lucy, I was shocked that's all" he joked, "Who'd have thought it, in a sleepy little village like that eh! Tell me what happened, there's a good girl."

Lucy set off telling the tale, embroidering it with every sentence and watched Jonty's face frown as he listened without speaking.

Weasel clunked the drinks down on the table, Jonty motioned for him to shut up, whilst Lucy carried on with the story, and she paused every now and then to take a sip from her drink. She certainly had his attention now, although she couldn't imagine quite why he was so interested. She finally came to the end, faltering, "Well, that's it really."

"And this Pete has disappeared you say?" he asked, "No idea where he's gone?"

"Nah, blokes a nutter. Mind you, Mrs Frigid's been wrapped up in cotton wool ever since."

Jonty's face darkened. "Has she indeed. Drink up, we need to go, I've things to sort out, sorry Lucy, business babe. We'll drop you off."

Weasel groaned, "We've only just got 'ere Jont'!"

"Shut the fuck up and get that down your gob!" growled Jonty, "plans have changed."

CHAPTER 53

"**Oh** Charles please can we go!" begged Jennifer, "I think it'd be such fun."

"You've really got the bug darling! Are you sure you want to, won't you be bored?" said Charles, "Don't you want to do some shopping or something for the holiday?"

"I can do that anytime, I really want to go to the horse trials, I've never been to one before and it looked great when we walked the course yesterday! John and Jeremy are going, so you won't be the only guy there."

"Oh okay," sighed Charles "but I've got a couple of things I need to do today, what are the girls' times?"

"Well early I think - they're leaving the yard about nine ish?"

Charles laughed, "Alright, you've twisted my arm. I can sort this stuff out later, we'd better get a shove on. The way you're going, it'll be you riding next year."

Jennifer raced round the breakfast table and gave him a whopping great kiss, "I don't think so somehow, but thanks sweetie! I'll go and get changed!"

Twenty minutes later they were in the Range Rover and pulling out of the drive and heading towards Rackham. It was a perfect day, with puffy fat clouds like huge white zeppelins hanging against a clear blue sky, and a ripple of breeze was giving a Mexican wave through the leaves on the trees. Jennifer chattered all the way, and once again Charles was amazed at her sangfroid, she seemed to be completely unfazed by all that had happened, and as the miles sped past he started to relax too. If she could deal with things, then so could he.

They swung into the entrance, and Charles coughed up the tenner to get in and they drove slowly around the lorry park, until Jennifer pointed out Chloe's truck and their Range Rover pulled up next to Jeremy's. Katherine was white faced and tense, already mounted and just about to make her way over to the working in area for the dressage. Chloe was clutching *Old Faithful*, and Sandy was filling up water buckets and getting out the ice tight and bandages ready for the return from the cross country phase. Seamus was stomping crossly in the lorry, annoyed that he was having to wait for his turn. Jeremy and John came over and greeted Charles and Jennifer, they could hear the children whooping and laughing in the lorry, and Mark, who had travelled with them, popped his head out of the living door and waved hello – it was going to be quite a party.

"Morning Jen, Charles" welcomed Chloe, reaching over and giving them a hug, "it's pretty hectic, so just bear with us."

"You carry on Chloe, we'll just tag along and tell us if you want us to do anything." laughed Charles, "We'll be fine."

"We'll be finished by lunch, and I've packed a great picnic" said Jeremy, "after Borde Hill I've got quite into this eventing lark!"

Chloe shouted to Katherine that they should be making their way over and Sandy said she would join them in a while when she'd got herself organised. Mark offered to stay and help her and the others all trooped off in the direction of the dressage arenas.

Jennifer was holding Charles' hand and was spell bound at the marvellous looking horses riders "Wow" she said "This is so posh!"

"You make me laugh Jen" said Charles slipping into the vernacular, "I had no idea you were so keen, I'm seeing a whole new side of you."

She grinned naughtily at him "Oh I'm sure you've seen most of me darling but perhaps this might add a few new dimensions!"

Charles squeezed her around the waist, "Promises" he murmured in her ear.

"Come on you two, that's enough, you're an old married couple now!" laughed Jeremy. "I'd better get this video out, Katherine 'll kill me if I miss the damned test!" he groaned fiddling about with the camera.

"Do you need a hand with that?" asked Toby, "Shall I show you how to use it?"

"Well, thank you Toby" grinned Jeremy, "You youngsters are always better at this high tech than us oldies." He handed the camera over to Toby, who expertly started to pan in and out on the riders.

John, who had Rory on his shoulders, and Lily by the hand struggled along behind them, "Be careful with that Toby" he warned, "Best let Jeremy do the actual videoing of Katherine then if it goes wrong, you can't be blamed."

By the time they finally got to the warming up area Chloe was taking off Alfie's bandages and giving last minute instructions to Katherine, who was nodding sagely and concentrating on everything that Chloe was saying. The others gave them a wide berth not wanting to interfere with the training, and stood by the white fence tape demarcating the dressage arenas. Finally, Chloe came over to stand with them dumping *Old Faithful* on the grass as Katherine trotted off to her arena.

"Christ it's so much worse than when I used to compete myself!" she complained, taking Lily's hand, "Are you having a nice time darling?"

"Well it would be nicer if you weren't always bloody working Mummy!" said Lily exasperatedly.

John stared at Chloe and she immediately felt those nauseous pangs of guilt as she looked down at Lily, and at Rory sitting on John's shoulders, playing with his hair. Toby, who was now bored having had to relinquish the camera, was tugging at John's hand. These moments with her family were so precious and here she was buggering about with horses! "I know my sweet, but it's only for an hour or so, then you can have my undivided attention – I promise!"

"What's undivided mean? Does it mean multiplied?" Lily said sweetly.

"Yes darling – that's exactly what it means."

Jonty was in the flat with Weasel, Tubby and a couple of the lads. The atmosphere in the room was charged with his foul temper as he crashed and banged his fist on the table.

"After all our fuckin' hard work, that stupid mad bloke has ballsed it up for us, and now they'll all be on their fuckin' guard and so will she!"

"Well mate, p'rhaps we should just give this 'un a miss? It's a big old scheme and okay the pickings rich, but it's bleedin' dangerous!" suggested Tubby wheezing on his fag, "they'll be other scams."

"Shut the fuck up Tubby!" snarled Jonty turning on him, "I'm not letting it drop – got it! We'll find another way!"

"Jont, the tart's gonna be surrounded by people looking out for her, there's a nutter on the loose, and every bit of filth in the county are searching for him, and every tossing country yokel too. How ya gonna lift her, tell me eh? Gonna be impossible – let alone get away with it." sighed Weasel, "You heard what that bint Lucy said."

"There's gotta be a way you arsehole, I know it, just let me think." Jonty put his head in his hands, "Pass me another Stella."

Tubby started to roll a joint with practised ease, and handed it round to the others for a toke, Jonty waved it away. He sat silently while the others muttered quietly to each other, turning his lighter over and over in his hands deep in thought.

Finally Weasel had had enough, "Jont, give it up mate, forget it, let's just move on. We've got a load of gear to deal tonight, just let's get on with it cutting it eh?"

Jonty stood up, violently shoving the table aside, "Just get the fuck out - all of you, you're a bunch of losers. I can make this work you see if I fuckin' don't! I'll cut the stuff myself, you can come back later and make the drops, now piss off and leave me alone!"

"Have it your own fuckin' way" Weasel spat pushing back his chair and gesturing for the others to follow, "but I'm telling you Jont, you're losing it mate!"

They slammed out of the flat and Jonty sat there for a long time, his face blank gazing unseeing out of the window. His mind was working overtime, churning over and over as to how he could turn this to his advantage. Finally he got up, prised open a floorboard and dragged out a white plastic wrapped package and put it on the table. Walking over to the bathroom, he opened the cabinet, took out a mirror, razor blade, some talcum powder and latex gloves, went back over to the table and started the painstaking task of cutting the coke into deals ready for the night's work.

At Rackham, things were going well, Katherine had jumped a clear round in the show jumping, which Toby had filmed perfectly, and the reliable Alfie had taken her round the cross country safely to finish with a double clear on her dressage score of 29.5. The results were taking ages, so although it looked as though she was going to be in the ribbons there was an agonising wait for the last scores to be put up.

Meanwhile Sandy had done her dressage with the feisty Seamus who after a week's drilling in the school had decided to play ball and performed a fair test with no mistakes, even if he was a little tense at times. Sandy was delighted and was now revving up in the practice ring for the show jumping where Seamus was doing his customary bucking and farting. Chloe was standing in the middle altering the jumps, whilst the others sat around the edge of the ring waiting for Sandy's turn. Toby was panning in and out with the camera, ready for action, whilst Mark could hardly contain his excitement - he was more on edge than Sandy! Jennifer had not enjoyed herself so much in ages, she was really enthralled with the whole competing thing, and Charles, Jeremy and John were all having a laugh together.

"Christ, - look at the size of her thighs in those breeches" sniggered Charles at some unfortunately proportioned woman, "she'd crush you to death!"

"That's if her bosom doesn't suffocate you first!" laughed John "Look at the size of her!"

"Pity the poor nag that's got to carry her round the cross country course!"

"Daddy, that's not a very nice thing to say is it?" said Lily, "you'd tell me off, if I said things like that."

"Uummm, no kitten you're quite right, we didn't mean it, did we Charles, Jeremy?"

"Of course not sweetie" smiled Charles, "She can't help being fat."

"I didn't mean about her" scoffed Lily, "She is fat and obviously eats too much, I meant the poor horse."

"Oh, I see." said Charles suitably admonished, "Of course, I see exactly what you mean."

"Quiet on the set, cameras rolling." called Toby, "It's Sandy next."

In came the big grey Seamus, with his huge bouncing canter, eyeballs rolling and nostrils flared as he saw the jumps. Sandy's face was grim with determination as she waited for the bell to start. Mark had gone quite white, gripping the edges of his trousers with anticipation. Chloe slid down beside them, with her fingers crossed as Rory crawled onto her lap, his thumb in his mouth.

They were off, over the first, a fairly straightforward rustic, and then into an inviting spread, followed by a sharp left hand turn into an upright of planks. Sandy managing to control the exuberant Seamus and make him wait to give the right number of strides, rather than plunge over the fence with his usual gusto. Then it was the combination, she steadied him up, but he snatched at the reins and dived out of control at the line of poles and fillers, bounding over them with glee – mercifully clearing them all. Sandy red in the face, managed to steady him before urging him into the next big oxer, which was huge, and took him by surprise enough to make him steady up for the upright which followed it. Each jump was a case of haul and go, and finally they were at the last, Sandy not taking her eye of the game for an instant, made a Herculean effort and cleared the last – to a massive cheer from her supporters – she had gone clear – it was a bloody miracle, as Lily would say!

They all raced over to Sandy as she came out of the ring, but Mark was the first to reach her.

"Darling I'm just so proud of you! You were wonderful!" He beamed, "Just bloody wonderful!"

Sandy slid off Seamus, after giving him a huge pat, "he was awesome wasn't he?" she laughed, high on adrenalin, "but you know sweetie, it's just so good to have you here too!"

"Come on you lovebirds!" interrupted Chloe "It's a quick turn round, let's get the cross country gear sorted, and see if we can get down to the start - they might let us go early."

Charles and Jennifer had wandered back to the lorry, whilst John took the children off for an ice-cream and Katherine and Jeremy had gone to the scoreboards to see if her results had been put up. Chloe busily started exchanging tendon boots for brushing boots, whilst Jennifer held the excited Seamus. Once the studs had been checked, Chloe brought over another bridle with a stronger bit for the cross country phase and at the same time Sandy came out of the lorry.

"All set?" asked Chloe, "Medical armband on?"

"Yep. Can you just tighten up my back protector?"

"There you go" said Chloe, adjusting the straps, "Comfy?"

"Well as you can be in these bloody things!" winced Sandy, "like a suit of armour. Help me on with my air-jacket can you?"

"Don't knock it, they're life savers. Right we're all done here. Katherine has refilled all the water buckets for when you get back, so all sorted."

Alfie whinnied softly as Seamus moved off in the direction of the start, but then carried on contentedly munching his hay, tired after his day's exertions. Seamus on the other hand couldn't wait to attack the course, he danced and pranced, bouncing Sandy around on his back as fresh as a daisy, the others scurrying behind to catch up.

Rackham was not the best viewing course, but the others had walked to a small hillock, more or less in the middle, where you could see quite a few of the fences, and Toby had decided he could film best. Charles and Jennifer joined them, whilst Mark and Chloe elected to stay at the start/finish line. The starters were an efficient bunch and they were running well on time. The course was riding well, with the usual pitfalls in the combinations but no serious hold ups. Having been instructed by Chloe not to jump anything until it was almost her turn to go, to avoid over-exciting him too much, Sandy was circling Seamus round in the collecting ring. To Mark the waiting was the worst, he was counting down the number of competitors before it was Sandy's turn and he wondered how on earth she was managing to stay so cool and composed. Chloe touched his arm and smiled reassuringly, but said nothing.

Jennifer gazed out over the lovely parkland, the sun sparkling on the water fence, and the thud of the horse's hooves as they pounded round in the distance on the course. She was amazed at the skill and bravery of these horses and riders and the speed at which they took the fences was breath-taking and inspirational. The children were chattering, and the others busy making small talk, when over the loud speaker the commentator announced that Sandy was just about to start on the course – they spun round, their heads craning to see the first fence and the grey blur that was Sandy setting off on the over-excited Seamus.

They watched transfixed as Sandy tore off over the first three fences and then disappeared into the woods, and then an announcement from the commentator.

"Sorry everyone, they've stopped the course, there's a faller, we've no more information yet!"

The little party on the hill froze. Toby stopped filming and Jennifer clutched Charles.

"Oh my God, it must be Sandy" gasped Katherine, "She must have fallen in the woods, it was bloody twisty in there!"

They saw the First Aiders tearing off from the start bumping over the fields in their four wheel drive, and Chloe running off in hot pursuit with Mark in tow, but miraculously the ambulance veered off to the right, and Chloe suddenly stopped running, looking after them. It was obviously not going to the woods but off in the direction of a small copse about three quarters of the way round. Whoever had fallen, thank God it had not been Sandy, but some other poor unfortunate. Everyone waited for what seemed ages before finally there was another announcement.

"The faller was No 474 Emily Payne, riding Storm Fire, but both

rider and horse are fine, just winded. We'll be starting again as soon as the course is cleared."

Katherine gave an audible sigh of relief, "Thank the Lord, but not good for Sandy, awful to be held up, especially on Seamus, he won't like that!"

They looked over to the start and saw Chloe and Mark hug each other in relief, but it was still an interminable five minutes before the ambulance returned and a rider-less horse was being led back across the course by a dejected groom and the announcement was finally given to restart.

Only seconds later a grey flash flew over the silver birch pile into the daylight from the woods, heading up to the combination of parallels and charged onwards over the sunken road surging down over a man-made drop and away into the distance. The hold-up seemed if anything, to have made Seamus keener! He was simply streaking, not breaking rhythm, just galloping and jumping each fence as it came, eating up the ground underneath them, they made it look easy. The viewing party on the hillside cheered as Sandy disappeared into the ominous copse, and willed her to come out unscathed the other side. What seemed an eternity passed as they waited and suddenly appearing out of the gloom of the trees, they saw Sandy and Seamus leap out over a vast log and into the open parkland again. Seamus hardly taking a pause as he splashed through the water and then surging on, leaping several tricky combinations to gallop up and away, passing quite close to the hill as they wound their way over the course. The final few jumps left were mainly straightforward which required big bold riding, but should present no difficulty for them, although there was still a nasty corner fence to negotiate. Seamus had seen the collecting ring in sight and was still full of running, high on adrenalin and tugging hard at the reins; Sandy looked exhausted, a tiny little dot on the enormous grey horse. The party on the hill could see Chloe standing cross legged and Mark jumping up and down with excitement at the finish as Sandy now came into their vision as she neared the last fences. Seamus lunged at the corner fence and hit it hard with a sickening crunch, and for a moment faltered desperately trying to balance and right himself, seemingly hanging in mid-air for a nanosecond with Sandy desperately clutching onto his breast plate, as they floundered above the corner in slow motion. It was all over in a flash, with a massive effort Seamus had managed somehow to sort himself out and cleared the odd angled jump, although stumbling on

601

landing. Sandy had miraculously managed to stay on board. Katherine and Jennifer were clutching each - other hardly daring to look; the men with a collective groan and then a rousing cheer, as they watched the indomitable horse and rider storming home to take the last jump and gallop through the finish – they had gone clear!

Two hours later, Jeremy had spread a large tartan rug on the grass, set out picnic chairs and an umbrella, had champagne chilled in a cool box and loaded up a table full of grub! Charles was loafing in one of the chairs, Jennifer sitting in front of him, her back cradled between his legs while he stroked her hair; Sandy and Mark lounged on the blanket, and Katherine, Chloe and John sat in the other chairs. The children who had their own blanket and a supply of jam sandwiches were busy squabbling over a bottle of coke. The horses were dozing in the back of the truck, intermittently having a chew of hay; they had been walked off, washed down, legs iced and checked for any injuries and were quiet now after their busy day.

"Great spread Jeremy!" said Mark, "I'd no idea we'd have a picnic afterwards!" he laughed, picking up another chicken drumstick.

"Strict instructions from the boss!" mocked Jeremy, "more than my life's worth!"

"If I'd known I could've brought a contribution" mumbled Jennifer, her mouth full of prawns, "I feel awful you've provided all this, you didn't even know we were coming."

"Don't give it another thought dear heart, more than enough to feed everyone, although I'm sure the kids prefer the jam sarnies that Chloe brought."

"Believe it or not those disgusting squidgy things and the coke are a treat for them." grinned John "helps keep them quiet! Mind you J you've done a brilliant job on the food – you've put us all to shame, these Samosas are delicious!"

"Ah, Mr Gupta's specials! What did we all do before they took over the village shop."

"True and they also do a good line in Mr Kipling's Fondant Fancies – a must for kids – especially the pink ones!"

"Perhaps it's all those E numbers that make them so hyper!" laughed Chloe, "maybe Seamus sneaks out in the night and snaffles them!"

"God he was strong today" sighed Sandy happily, "he was awesome!"

"I'm glad you thought it was awesome, I had my heart in my mouth" moaned Mark, "much more terrifying to watch!"

Katherine suddenly leapt up "it's no good, I can't sit around here idling, I'm going to the scoreboards – coming Sandy?"

"Whoa Katherine, don't want you want a top up?" asked Jeremy brandishing the champagne.

"No thanks. They must have the results up for my section by now, and I can't stand the suspense any longer. I'll be back in a jiff, you don't have to come."

"I'll come with you Katherine" offered Jennifer, she levered herself up, and brushed the crumbs off her jeans, "I'd be interested to see how they work out the scores."

"Great! Thanks Jen." The two women walked off together across the field towards the huddle of tents in the distance.

There was a small silence, which was broken by Chloe. "How is Jennifer bearing up Charles after all the traumas?"

"She's damned remarkable" drawled Charles, "It's me who isn't doing so well. I see that crank around every corner. It's hard to credit he's not been found yet. I can't thank you enough though Chloe for keeping an eye out for her this week."

"Well to tell the truth Charles it's been easy, Jen's good company and she certainly has a passion for the horses now. I think she's going to love this holiday and it'll bring her on a treat"

"I wanted to ask you, do you think we ought to tell her about that horse you mentioned – Polly was it called, or should it be a surprise?"

"Oh God Charles, I don't know. It's your call – but she's a big girl and a surprise is one thing, but I think when you buy a horse you need to sit it on and see if you like it, she might hate Polly!"

"Mmm, you're right of course," he murmured, not fazed by Chloe's abruptness and more talking to himself, "I'll talk to her later then."

"John - how's business?" asked Jeremy topping up his glass, "busy?"

"Actually it's pretty tough at the moment, I seem to be working harder and longer and getting less."

"Same for us all." brayed Jeremy, although in his case this wasn't strictly true.

Charles looked guilty, thinking of his ruthlessly successful week, but something in John's face made Charles take a long look at him, and he made a mental note to probe into John's company next week and see how it was faring in the market these days, he had an instinct for trouble.

CHAPTER 54

All the previous week Pete had kept his head down in the barn, only coming out at dusk to wash in the mill pond, drying himself on the stolen towel, and stealthily creeping around dustbins in the village searching for food. Although he still had quite a stash left over from the cache taken from the Puppy Show, it was not going to last forever and some of the cake now had specks of green mould growing on the edges. The night visits has yielded some interesting finds, and he was becoming more adept at living rough.

It didn't matter to him not to be out in the sunlight, he felt safe in the gloom of the barn. He had become a creature of the night now, the darkness suited him just fine as its inky blackness folded around him like a comforting cloak. He enjoyed the stillness, he was at peace especially now that he had the photograph back. The voices still nagged him, but he was content to know that she would be dealt with and that for the time being this was to be his home.

He was sprawled on his straw bed, eyes open staring into the dimness of the barn, the odd trickle of sunlight shafting through the slats, casting laser beams across the murky air. The photograph was in his hand and although he couldn't see it, it was good to know it was there. His hand was hurting from where he had slashed his way through the window, although he'd been careful to wash it in the running water under the mill race that night and wrap it in the towel, but now his whole arm was smarting, it felt hot and painful. Of course it was so difficult to keep himself clean, he should have taken the carbolic soap, that would have sorted it. Gingerly he touched his arm, he couldn't see it, but instinctively he knew it must be infected, tonight he'd have to try and get something to clean it up otherwise it would be serious. He closed his eyes and willed the voices to come to him and tell him what he must do.

Lucy was miffed, after Jonty's hasty departure leaving her high and dry she'd made up her mind to have nothing more to do with him. She was pretty certain he was more than just a bad lot anyway. In a way of course that was his fascination, but for once she almost agreed with her mother, she should be out having a good time with people of her own age and surely she could do that locally, she still had a few friends around here. Trouble was they were so bloody boring, so dull, never wanted to take a risk or do anything exciting. Take Tom - good looking, decent, hardworking, good career ahead of him - at least when he finished his degree, wealthy parents, but would wet himself at the thought of doing a line, or drinking and driving! Still he was someone to go out with and it was better than no-one. Jonty had pissed her off big time, he could go screw himself. She picked up her phone and tapped out a saucy text to tempt Tom, and was pleased to receive a reply almost straight away, *'pick you up 8pm – usual place.'* She smiled with satisfaction, that was easy she would make a real fuss of him tonight, she'd bought some kinky new underwear, actually for Jonty and Weasel, but after the fiasco of last night it'd been wasted, it was clean enough to wear again, she'd give Tom a treat instead. He'd have a nice surprise!

Whilst she was contemplating the delight of what she would do to Tom, her phone beeped a message, Jonty's name flashed up on the screen. She opened it triumphantly, *'sorry about last nite, c u 2nite ?'* She threw the phone back in her bag, let him wait, he was too late, she'd made other plans.

Jonty waited for her reply. Five minutes past and still she hadn't responded. Fuck her, his instinct was not to bother but right now he needed her. Okay, he thought let her play her little game, he could play that too, and when the little white package he'd given her last night had been used, she would come begging back. He'd leave it a couple of days.

Laura looked at him, "Everything okay?"

"Sure baby, it's fine, let's do something tonight, I feel like having fun" he reached over and pulled her towards him, "I'm not working, what d'ya fancy doing?"

"Christ, I dunno Jonty, we could go clubbing if you like? Or a movie and a meal?" Laura moved closer to him, "What d' you fancy?"

"Right now baby I fancy doing you" He began undoing her jeans and peeling them off her hips and dropping them to the floor, nuzzling into her belly with his face, "Mmm you smell nice."

Laura kissed the top of his head, feeling the bristle scratch her chin, "Fancy a bath?"

"Yeah, go run one – I'll be with you in a minute."

She stepped out of her jeans, and he slapped her arse as she trooped off towards the bathroom. Picking up his phone which he'd left on silent, he checked for texts – nothing, and tossed it onto the table and followed Laura into the bathroom.

She was standing in her knickers leaning over the bath, swirling the foaming suds round with her hands. He pushed her off balance so that she was splayed over the tub and he pushed aside her panties, enjoying her gasp of surprise. His other hand stroked her back, and expertly undid her bra' so that her breasts tumbled out, her nipples dangling down almost touching the white enamel of the bath. Abruptly he stood up and undid the belt on his trousers, and stepping out of them, turned her to face him, his cock huge and erect bouncing out in front of him. Dropping to her knees she took it into her mouth, sucking, licking and gently biting, then working it backwards and forwards, whilst massaging his balls with her hands. She felt them tighten under her hold, as he became more and more excited, and suddenly she stopped, getting up off her knees, took his hand and invited him to step into the foaming bathtub. The water surged up over their bodies as they squeezed in, with Laura levering herself astride him, pumping up and down with increasing intensity, creating a huge swell of water to gush over the edges of the bath

"Turn round baby" he murmured, "on all fours"

With a lot of sloshing of water, she manoeuvred herself round, so that her bottom was pointing towards him, Jonty took the soap and lathering it well between his hands, dipped his fingers between the cheeks of her bottom, and his soapy fingers explored her thoroughly, probing and sinking into her, moving them expertly round and round, every now and then tapping gently on her clitoris, till she was almost shouting with the exquisite pleasure. Then his hand moved around to her arse, first inserting his soapy little finger into her anus, feeling the tightness of her, and his other hand moved around to the front and rubbed her throbbing clitoris as she panted and gasped.

"Don't come yet my little darlin', not yet" and just as quickly he withdrew the contact and she collapsed into the water frustrated.

"Oh my God, you tease! I was so nearly there!"

He stepped out of the bath, holding out his hand to help her out, and wrapped a towel around her, leading her into the bedroom. The bed was unmade and he gave her a little push and she tumbled over backwards onto it, the towel falling open as she landed.

"You know Laura, you've a lovely pair of tits. He reached down and cupped them in his hands, his cock dangling onto her stomach, "I thought we'd play a few games tonight – how about it?" He squeezed her breasts, breathing hard.

Laura didn't reply, she was a bit afraid but excited at the same time. She arched her back up towards him and gave him a small smile. He didn't smile back, but got up and walked over to his rucksack and pulled out a tangle of leather straps, and from where she was spread-eagled she couldn't really see what he was up to.

"Sit up baby" He pulled away her hair and fastened a dog collar around her neck, attached to which were two chains with cuffs at the end, he took her wrists and strapped them securely in, so that her hands were pinioned back at shoulder height. "There now, I think you've been a naughty girl Laura and perhaps you need a thorough fucking and a little bit of pain to go with it – lie back and try to behave."

Laura pinioned in the shackles had no option but to obey and felt a frisson of excitement course through her and, Jonty leant over her smiling slightly, then staring at her body. The way he gazed at her was very sensual and Laura could feel herself becoming more aroused, her helplessness was a big turn on. He traced one finger slowly and erotically over one breast and then the other, trickling his hand tantalisingly downwards, and then asked her to open her legs as wide as she could. Laura could feel her heart beating fast wondering what he was going to do next, when he said softly "Close your eyes" and she felt her clitoris being lubricated and massaged and she relaxed and sighed with pleasure. Then there was a sharp pain, excruciating in its immediacy and then a sudden glowing of warmth, she snapped her eyes open, wriggling and pulling at the leather dog collar confining her hands.

"What the fuck Jonty!" She gasped, as she saw him with a needle and syringe in his hand, "bloody hell!"

"Keep your eyes closed, or I'll have to blindfold you!" snapped Jonty, pushing her back roughly and replacing his hands between her legs, her clitoris felt as though it was on fire! She did as she was told, and once again she felt the coolness of the lubricant and this time she was ready, but when it came once again the intensity of the pain took her breath away and she almost screamed out loud, and then the warmth spread through her – it was a weird feeling. She could not say how many times this happened, by this time she was wrapped up in the warp of pain and pleasure. Eventually Jonty could contain himself no longer and rammed his way inside her, she was wet and slippery and so ready for him. She lost all control of her mind and senses and when she came, her orgasm seemed to go on and on.

Lucy on the other hand had a very different evening as she met Tom, dressed in a short denim skirt and skimpy blue sequinned top. It was a lovely night, still light and the air was warm after the heat of the day. Tom looked good, he was really quite brown, having been working outside all day. Lucy clambered into the old Landrover, he had the canvas hood down and as they pulled off the breeze whipped up her hair and it flew around her face sticking to her lip gloss.

"I thought we'd head off towards Brighton, it's always rocking on Saturday nights" Tom said nonchalantly, anxious to avoid Fittlebury and any confrontation, "Honey Club is always favourite."

"Blimey Tom, it was the last thing I was expecting, I'd have dressed up a bit more" whined Lucy, "but yep, love to, you're full of surprises!" She was glad she'd worn the sexy underwear now, this could turn out to be a good evening after all, and she'd only texted him to spite Jonty!

They drove down the A23, Tom urged the old Landrover along as fast as it could manage, which to be fair was pretty dire, but Lucy didn't care, it was kind of a trendy vehicle to be seen in anyway. They threaded their way slowly through the town centre, managing to catch all the lights, arriving at the roundabout with the Palace Pier straight ahead of them. The sun was setting a burning orange glow and the sparkle of the lights from the Pier danced on the gentle waves of the sea. The place was humming with people of all shapes and sizes, it was full of colour, and music boomed out all along the seafront, as Tom turned right at the roundabout, and drove along looking for somewhere to park. They were lucky and Tom squeezed the old beast into the space with some difficulty, going red with the effort of struggling with no powered steering.

"I've gotta put the tilt up Lucy, you'll have to give me a hand" said Tom, tugging at the old canvas and dragging it over the cab and lashing it down, "you take that side."

"For fuck's sake Tom, I might break a nail!" moaned Lucy, "Do we have to?"

"You'll be glad it's up on the way back" he laughed, "it'll be cold I can tell you! Now drag it back over the frame – like this." He showed her, and grumbling all the time she finally managed to get it in place. Tom came round and fastened the hood down, then put his hand in hers and they sauntered off down the promenade heading for the roar and thump of the music below.

It must have been one o'clock in the morning, when they reappeared, Lucy supporting herself on Tom's arm, singing at the top of her voice and was pretty much worse for wear. Tom was sober but he'd had a good evening, although his feet were killing him from all that dancing. He managed to bundle Lucy into the Landrover, her head lolled over the seat, bloody hell so much for hot sex he thought, he wasn't into comatose fucking! He strapped the seat belt round her and she smiled up at him.

"Just give me a half hour snooze Tomo" she said, "Then let's pull over somewhere shall we, I'm feelin' kinda randy."

"Lucy Hun, you're out of it, what d' you take me for?"

"A sexy hunk, and yes I fancy taking you babe!" she mumbled, "Give me a shake when we get near Fittlebury."

Tom sighed, and pulled the Landrover out into the quiet streets, making his way down the A23 towards home. It was a lonely old drive back, with Lucy gently murmuring in her sleep, oh well he thought, it'd been quite a good evening on the whole, although he had thought he'd get his end away. He pulled off left and headed across country along the back lanes towards Horsham, although the roads were was twisty it was a shorter in the long run.

Lucy started to stir beside him "You gonna pull up somewhere?" she murmured huskily, arching her back sexily, "that little zzzz was just what I needed."

Tom briefly glanced over at her, "You sure Luce, you looked pretty out of it to me."

"Don't be such a wet Tom, take more than a few drinks – course I'm alright. Unless you don't want to of course?" she said teasingly.

Tom didn't need to be asked twice and started to rack his brains where he could park, there were loads of field gates, but had the disadvantage of the odd passing car, even at this time in the morning and he didn't want to get caught with his trousers down. Then it came to him, High Ridge Woods – perfect, and it was pretty much en route.

Fifteen minutes later he had stopped and was snogging with Lucy on the front bench seat, cupping her breasts with his hand and getting mighty excited. She was bloody sexy.

"Have you got a blanket?" she whispered "It's a lovely night."

Tom his breath coming in panting rasps at the thought of having Lucy outside in the woods didn't hesitate and reached over into the back and dragged out a rug.

She glanced knowingly at him, "Condoms?"

He patted his wallet pocket, smiling at her "Let's go!"

They scrambled out of the car, giggling together as they found the path into the woods. The night was very still, with a gibbous moon shedding an eerie light, every sound being magnified tenfold, as Tom spread the blanket down on a mossy spot between some trees. Taking her hand he pulled her down and started to nuzzle her neck, edging off the straps of her tee-shirt to reveal the lacy balconette bra underneath.

"Mmmm, that's very nice" he murmured, "Let's take this tee-shirt off shall I, so I can have a proper look."

Lucy obliged him by pulling the top over her head, her breasts full and springy in the tantalising underwear, "Glad you like it." She wriggled out of her skirt, to reveal the matching thong "I bought the set" she giggled.

Tom's eyes were out on stalks and the sight of her was enough for him, he leapt on top of her and pretty soon she was tearing off his clothes and he was totally naked as they rolled about on the blanket grunting and moaning.

Pete had been on one of his night sorties and had heard the Landrover arrive; slipping into the shadows of the woods he watched them unobserved. He saw a girl and a boy leave the car and make their way down the track. He knew immediately it was Lucy, he would know her anywhere, and warily he followed them. Although it was quiet, they were making quite a lot of noise themselves, and he stood observing, his huge body dissolving into the security of darkness. He could hear her voice carried on the night air, urging the boy on, she took off her tee-shirt and skirt and then the boy leapt on top of her and they were laughing and rolling around with Lucy tugging off his clothes.

Pete felt the hot uncontrollable rage sweep over him like a red mist clouding his judgement and the voices popped into his head '*kill him, kill him*', he threw his hands up to his ears to shut them out and the intense pain in his throbbing arm shot through him like a sword, bringing him abruptly to his senses. No, he must do tonight what he had set out to do, he grabbed his wrist squeezing the injury till he could stand the agony no more, and as the pus oozed from the wound the voices vanished as did his anger. Lucy by this time was lying supine and Tom's white bum was pumping away between her legs, his brown tan line clearly visible as he thrust back and forward. Pete turned away disgusted and made his way back towards their car - he had another idea.

CHAPTER 55

The next week was a busy one for Jennifer, she wasn't sure what to pack for the holiday, despite researching it on Google, the one thing she did know was not to wear anything that looked like camouflage or army stuff! Natural beiges, browns and greens apparently, and a large hat were the norm. She'd been down and had her vaccinations from Alex Corbett as had Charles, and the children had complained bitterly to him, when he telephoned them about theirs. They were all equipped with the anti-malaria medication, although the mosquitoes were supposed to be at their least worst at this time of year. In fact this was, according to the company who had organised the trip, the best time of year to go, but there again they would say that, it was costing a fortune! Typical Charles though had booked the best of everything and because they had children with them, he'd had to have private vehicles for the game drives, and make special arrangements for the horses. Money talked, there was no doubt about it, and Charles certainly couldn't be called mean.

Last week he'd really surprised her by saying that he thought she might consider getting herself her own horse, which obviously she would keep at home, if she was serious about going out hunting with him. The autumn season would soon be starting, which would be an ideal time for her to begin as there was little or no jumping involved. On the whole they were easy days of cantering about and then checking and then having another canter – perfect for her, but sadly he didn't think Rufus would be up to it. Chloe had found a horse that might fit the bill and wondered if she might be interested. Jennifer had been astonished and also a bit concerned, it was all going really well up to now, with Chloe and the girls' continuous support, and riding under their guidance, but having one here at Nantes might be different altogether. She would miss them all dreadfully - the laughs they had, and the friends she'd made and she was reluctant to lose that, it had become special to her. She said as much to Charles, who agreed and totally understood how she felt and urged her to think about it and maybe talk to Chloe - there was no pressure.

The other thing of interest that happened was the arrival of Felix on the Monday morning. Jennifer had forgotten momentarily that he was coming and was bringing her tray into the kitchen catching Mrs Fuller gossiping with Doris.

"Morning, just brought in the tray Mrs F." She called and was surprised to see Mrs Fuller was quite pink about the cheeks, and Doris was patting her perm coquettishly. "You two okay?"

"Felix has just popped in to say hello, you've just missed him. He's a charmer that boy." smiled Mrs Fuller.

A charmer he certainly was too, as when Jennifer had popped in to the stables later to welcome him, she'd been surprised to see Caitlin quite like her old self, laughing and joking with a spring in her step. Felix had immediately stopped what he had been doing and came over to shake her by the hand, fixing her with his extraordinary eyes; then introducing her to his horse - Admiral, despite Caitlin insisting that Jennifer was not that keen on horses. They had seemed to be getting on like a house on fire thought Jennifer, and she had been pleased, truly hoping this would prove to be a real success story.

As for the Pete business, nothing had been heard of him since the break in and the police were pretty sure it had been him. Once again the trail had gone cold. She carried the mace spray with her at all times, but she thought less and less about him. She was still careful, not going out after dark on her own, but generally she felt much safer and in truth she was so pre-occupied with other things she was rarely on her own anyway and she was excited about her holiday.

Charles was also looking forward to his holiday, although his arm was aching from the bloody jabs. He'd been busy this week and rung Chloe to say that Jennifer was going to think about the horse situation and whilst she liked the idea – she was worried about losing Chloe's support and that of the girls in the yard. Chloe said she could understand that, and Charles agreed with her, and suggested that she pursue the horse when it became available and they could sort the problem out if Jennifer tried it and liked it.

He'd also looked into John's company. On paper it was okay and there seemed nothing amiss, but there'd been something in his face that day at Rackham that had alerted Charles, and he was rarely wrong about business. He couldn't think what it could be and had made a few phone calls to some of his chums in that line but to all intents and purposes, all was well; the company was thriving and John was highly thought of and worked hard just as he claimed he did. He stored the information away and made a mental note to check again when he came back from holiday.

He was also pleased with the way Felix was panning out, although it had only been a week, the lad seemed willing to please and Caitlin had texted to say that all was going well and that he was a hard worker and very obliging. Charles had sent a message back asking that Felix come over to the house later, as Charles wanted to meet him and that he would see him in his study. When Felix had walked in, Charles was a bit taken aback, the boy was too good looking by half, which didn't please him at all, but his handshake was firm, and after talking to him for a while, Charles had started to thaw out. After he had left he decided he actually quite liked the lad. Oh well, time would tell.

Felix himself had enjoyed his first week, he liked the flat, it made a real change from having to share with others and Caitlin had done a good job of clearing it up and it was sweet of her get the bread and stuff in for him. He liked being able to be near the yard and the horses, it meant he could fall out of bed in the morning and go to work, and late stables would be a doddle when they were in at night. Caitlin seemed to be really nice too, wasn't pulling rank and happy to show him the ropes, saying how the boss liked things done and what he was a stickler about, and what annoyed him. She filled him in on the goings on in the household, about the mysterious Pete, who sounded like a right head case to him, and Mrs Fuller and Doris. He had asked Caitlin about Jennifer too - who said she was really nice and very supportive to her when Lucy had left, but that she didn't know anything about horses and didn't ride either, so she rarely saw her.

All in all it was going well. Admiral had settled in as though he had been here for years, and at the moment he had plenty of time to fit in exercising him around his work, although Caitlin had made it clear that one thing the boss would not tolerate was if he found out that his own horses were neglected in favour of Felix's – fair enough he could deal with that, although the work load was not great, so he was sure he could cope.

The second night he'd been there Caitlin had taken him down to the local pub and introduced him to a few people and they'd all seemed like a good bunch, mainly hunting folk, and Susie had joined them and it'd been great to see her again. They chatted away, catching up on the gossip about old mates, Susie asking him how he was settling in and saying he must come over and have supper with them one night and meet Beebs the Head Girl where she worked. She talked about Chloe's yard and how busy they were, especially now the eventers were in full swing, and he told her about Admiral and the high hopes he had for him.

Susie had been surprised that he'd brought a horse saying "Blimey, will there be enough room, if Jen gets one?"

Felix had thought it an odd remark to make, and replied "Do you mean Mrs Parker–Smythe? But surely she doesn't ride, does she?"

Susie had blustered out an excuse, saying how stupid of course she didn't, but Felix couldn't help but wonder why she'd said it and also she had called her Jen – like she knew her. Bloody odd - but Susie had hailed some friends and started introducing him and the time to ask her more questions had gone.

Andrew and Oli were sitting in the back office pouring over the applications for the veterinary assistant post. There were quite a few, it seemed it had been a good time to advertise.

"God this is going to be hard - eh mate?" moaned Oli, "It's going to take ages."

"Let's split the pile in two, you take one, I'll take the other. Then we each make a pile of rejections and the second looks and then swap, that might work!" laughed Andrew rubbing his forehead with the thought of it all.

"Okay, here's your half then and bloody good luck!"

They worked steadily for the next hour, shuffling papers into piles, whilst Paulene and Grace manned the phones and made much needed coffee and finally they'd come up with a bit of shortlist.

"Right" said Andrew "out of all that lot, it seems we have six that we both think are worth an interview."

"Christ, is that all." moaned Oli, "What happens if none of them are any good?"

"Then we'll advertise again – this person has got to be right for the practice - this is a big step for us all. Have a look in your diary and let's fix a day next week shall we?"

Grace breezed in, "I'm off home now, anything you need before I go?"

"Nope you get off Gracie, see you tomorrow."

"Bye then." They heard her whistle to her dogs and the clunk of the door close behind her as she left.

"Grace has turned out well hasn't she?" said Oli, "Hard to imagine the place before she was here."

"Yeah but that was a given really wasn't it, she's one of us, it was lucky she was looking when we were, hope we're as lucky with the assistant. I'll get Paulene organising the interviews."

"Any more news on the mill?" asked Oli, "you haven't said much lately."

"No news – all in the hands of solicitors and you know how slow they are. I was going to try and get the price down a bit with all the red tape about English Heritage, but Mark thinks Lady V will probably take umbrage and just not sell at all, so I don't want to risk it, so for the time being I'm just letting things take their course. We're getting it for a good price in the first place. Mark actually said it could work to our advantage as we could be eligible for grants and stuff, so he's looking into that for us which was decent of him considering he works for her."

"He's a decent bloke. I gather he's seeing a lot of Sandy Maclean - they got close that night of the Parker-Smythe's party y' know."

"I was there dumbass, - course I know." Andrew grinned, "Good for them, they make a great couple!"

"Mmmm, I'm a bit jaded about the couple thing" lamented Oli thinking that was the night Suse had left him.

"Me too buddy, me too" said Andrew sadly.

Jonty was getting anxious, that fucking Lucy - he hadn't heard a word from the slag. It had been nearly a week now. Initially it occurred to him to just drive down and catch her after work and rough her up a bit, he was fuming. He had been in a bad mood for most of the week, until bingo he realised that actually he could turn things around very nicely to his own advantage if he played his cards right and that meant keeping Lucy on side, so he would have to make an effort and butter her up nicely.

He had despatched Laura out to see Sean and the odious Linda who was struggling in rehab, and make sure that she maintained her contact with the hard core Sabs. She had moaned about it, but had gone, reporting back to him on their plans, it was the usual crap about disruption, blaring horns, scratching cars, letting down tyres, targeting specific vulnerable members of the hunt - that sort of rubbish. They wanted to start the campaign early and continue a systematic war throughout the season and it seemed that this autumn hunting malarkey would start almost immediately after the harvest, which could be about eight weeks away. It seemed ages but it would give him plenty of time to organise everything to the very last detail. He couldn't afford any mistakes. He needed more information and Lucy was the source. He picked up the phone and sent her a text '*U still cross with me*".

Lucy got the text at a vulnerable moment, she was fed up, sweaty and bored, she texted back straight away '*r u sorry*'.

Jonty looked at the text, thinking - no but you will be if you don't fucking buck up bitch, but instead he replied '*pick you up tonight after work*'

Lucy thought for a moment, she wasn't doing anything, but he hadn't said sorry had he? Oh well - she tapped back, 'gr8 6.30 B52' and pressed send . Too late to change her mind now.

Jonty was pleased, he would make sure he wasn't late and rang Weasel to get his arse up to the flat, they would go down early just to be certain.

When Lucy sauntered around the corner at a quarter to seven she was pleased to see that Jonty and Weasel were waiting, although she caught the look on Jonty's face before he saw her and it was black with bad temper. Good she thought, now he knows what it feels like to be kept waiting. When she came over though his expression changed completely, he was all smiles and contrition, despatching Weasel to get the drinks in and kissing Lucy on the mouth, giving her tit a quick squeeze.

"Missed you doll" he smiled "How've you been?"

"I've had a great week – you?" Lucy felt she had the upper hand - he was all sweetness and light.

"Haven't you missed me?"

"A bit, but I've been busy y' know, out with my other mates."

"Ah okay, who's that then, that hunting lot?"

"As it happens yeah, we've had some laughs. Doing the Brighton scene" she exaggerated, "The Honey Club – you heard of it?"

Jonty smiled, it was one of his biggest customers on the drug scene, "Yeah I know it. What gossip you got then? What happened about your nutter"

Lucy looked at him strangely "You mean Pete? Dunno why you're so interested but he's just disappeared - they never found him. Who cares anyway, but those lucky fuckers are going away so I heard, on a safari. Even taking the kids with 'em, bloody mad if you ask me, she can't even ride!"

"Whatdya mean" said Jonty trying to take the edge out of his voice, "they all ride don't they!"

"Nah, she don't, she's his second wife, the kids live with their mum, so fuck knows how she'll get on! Makes me laugh!"

Jonty couldn't believe his ears, the extra security with the wife and then he finds she can't fuckin' ride! He'd have to have a major rethink. "The kids ride though don't they?" He nearly added that he knew they did as he'd seen them, but managed to stop himself in time.

"Why you so interested?" Lucy questioned, as Weasel slapped their drinks on the table, "you're like the Spanish fuckin' Inquisition! Yeah the kids ride when they come over to stay with their dad, snotty little bastards!"

"Just curious to know that's all babe." Jonty took a swig of his diet Coke, "I hate these hunting bastards, stuck up toffee nosed cunts, the ruling classes. Look what they did to you."

"Yeah that's true" sighed Lucy, "Don't worry as soon as they've anything planned I'll give you the wink!"

"That's my girl" he reached over and squeezed her hand lightly, "I know I can rely on you Luce! We're gonna have a great night!"

After they left the Travel Lodge that evening having treated Lucy to a thorough screwing and several lines of the best for good measure, Jonty was deep in thought. Everything was bloody going wrong. He had just assumed that the fucking woman could ride, all these bleedin' nobs could – except her it seemed! But okay he knew the kids did, so he would just focus on them instead. Charlie boy would pay just the same, maybe more. Maybe his cloud could have a silver lining after all. Just doing the kids would be easier to handle too, although if they lived with their mum the logistics of when they came to stay with their dad might be difficult. It was a pity though, as he was looking forward to spending some quality time with the ice maiden missus and thawing her out, but that couldn't be helped.

As he drove along with Weasel dozing in the seat beside him, he started to work it all out in his mind, yes it would pan out just the same, in fact it would be easier. The imperative thing was that he needed to have a mole who could tell him when the kids were staying and the dates and places that the hunt planned to meet. Lucy was that mole and if handled her the right way, she could give him all he needed. He smiled to himself. It was bloody risky, but there again that was what he loved - the danger, and the spoils of course.

CHAPTER 56

The month of July had come in just like a summer should be, warm and beautiful but by the end of the second week, the rain had set in and hadn't stopped. The skies were a solid dull grey and full of persistent drizzle, it wasn't cold but it was miserable. The grass grew at an alarming rate, the hedgerows were unruly and out of control and the verges a mass of long grasses and the wild flowers stooped down heavy with fat raindrops. The hanging baskets at the Fox swung forlornly their bonny blooms drooping, the flagged path was wet and shiny underfoot, and the parasols from the benches were stacked in the shed to keep dry. Rain dripped ceaselessly off the awning outside the village shop and discouraged trade and Mrs Gupta kept the door firmly closed. No-one stopped and chatted on the village green, and if they did it was only momentarily to shelter under the pump. Even the vicar scurried from vicarage to church under a large black umbrella and did not stop to talk. Mums picking up the children who were still at the state primary school hurried them quickly into their cars and drove back home sloshing through the puddles, disappointed that sports day had once again been cancelled.

Nantes was quiet. Mrs Fuller had gone away, taking advantage of the family's holiday to stay with her sister in Eastbourne and left Doris and Fred to housesit. They were in their element, lording it in the house enjoying all the luxuries, despite the strict instructions from Freda not to let their feet get too far under the table. Caitlin was taking the time back owed to her after all the extra work she'd put in, and had decided to have some afternoons off, now that she had Felix to take the strain. She'd stayed put in the Granary hoping for some illicit hours with Ace, but the weather had put paid to any meetings in High Ridge and she gloomily thought that this was probably a sign of things to come. She couldn't even use the pool the weather was so dreadful. They'd only managed the odd few snatched meetings which had been far from satisfactory, and made her feel really smutty. On the upside Felix was brilliant, strong and capable and above all reliable. He didn't moan and was enthusiastic about the coming season, which she herself had been dreading, not because of the horses but she just couldn't see where her own life was heading. She could see him from the Granary window during his lunch break in the sand school training his horse, deftly turning circles, concentrating hard, and patiently teaching the horse the tricks of dressage, oblivious to the rain. He was a joy to watch, a natural and once again she wondered what on earth he was doing here at Nantes.

Mileoak was busy as always, despite the dismal weather. Horses were a twenty four seven job and Susie and Beebs were constantly changing their clothes, and the horses' too - they all had their lightweight rugs on which was a chore and made the work harder. The rug room was damp and smelly, full of dripping exercise sheets hanging out to dry leaving pools of water on the floor.

Katherine, whose children had broken up for the long summer break, had been coming up sporadically, fitting in Alfie as much as she could and juggling doing stuff with the children in between. The only thing about Susannah and Marcus being away at boarding school was that they were pretty independent, which she liked in one way and hated in another, but at least they didn't whine when she went off to do her horse. They were all off soon on their own family holiday to their house in Portugal, where Jeremy could play golf all day, and she could laze around the pool; so she was doing as much horse therapy as she could before they left.

Sandy had a big case on, and they hadn't seen much of her since her triumph at Rackham where she had ended up second and would have won the section if her dressage had just been a tad better, but Sandy had been delighted, as were the rest of the team, it was an awesome achievement! She still had the Cheshire cat grin on her face when they did see her, so whilst she didn't have the time to hang around and gossip, they read the signs that all was going well with Mark. Beebs had seen his car parked outside her cottage early one morning when she was coming home from a weekend away at her mum's, obviously Mark had stayed the night – leastways, he wasn't delivering the milk, as the curtains were still drawn.

Chloe was still looking a bit drawn, although she and John had been getting along okay, but okay was all you could say about it really. The mistrust that Chloe felt could not be totally hidden and she was constantly watching him for the tell-tale signs of an affair. He was still cagey about his phone, but was desperately trying not to be, although he fell upon it when it rang, and then looked guilty when he picked it up. He was also trying too hard with the family, bringing her flowers, which he'd never done before, and playing with the kids and dogs, and asking her about the yard and how she was doing work wise. That was strange too, he'd never bothered much before about it, he'd always been the breadwinner, and she provided the jam to go on top, it was as though he was wondering if she could survive if he left her, or that was how it seemed to her anyway. Chloe knew that she was probably being unfair to him in a lot of ways, he may just be trying to be interested, but it was a funny thing, once trust had been challenged in a relationship it was bloody hard to get it back. Luckily though the children seemed to be blissfully unaware, as apart from that one outburst from Toby a few weeks back, they seemed happy and well adjusted, but maybe that was because the rows had subsided and the atmosphere was to them back on an even keel. Although to Chloe it was a fragile temporary truce until the inevitable shit hit the fan.

Down at the surgery the interviews had gone ahead for the new veterinary assistant and Oli and Andrew had squabbled over whom they should appoint. Paulene had been in on the interviews whilst Grace fielded all the calls in the reception area. The candidates had been an interesting bunch, ranging at each end of the spectrum from an older newly divorced guy wanting to make a new start in a different area away from his ex-wife, to a glamorous fake tanned, fake eye-lashed, sexy blonde with endless legs encased in leggings and fake Dubarry boots who frankly it was hard to believe had even qualified! The others came in varying degrees somewhere in between.

By the end of the sixth candidate they were all exhausted and frazzled by the experience and sick of asking the same questions. The definite rejects were easy to weed out, but in the end the final shortlist was between the older guy, whom Andrew liked because he had experience and whom he felt would be able to work more on his own and need less babysitting; Oli's objection was that he might be stuck in ways and didn't trust why he wanted to leave his old area. A just qualified but highly recommended attractive young woman, who came across as dynamic and energetic, with lots of ideas for improving their systems, and who was full of theories and certainly talked the talk; Andrew's objection was that she was too pushy and

624

Paulene totally agreed with him and thought she would be a pain in the neck and was too up herself. And finally another girl, excellent qualifications, a Kiwi, who had been an intern at an Equine Hospital in Oz for two years, and now wanted to come over to England to gain experience here. They all liked her, but wondered if she would want more then they could offer her at the moment. After all the Old Mill might be a year or so at least before anything much happened, and if she had worked at an up and running equine hospital – that's probably what she wanted right now. They decided to call back the Kiwi and the older guy for second interviews, Oli was outvoted on Miss Pushy! Paulene said she'd organise it and meanwhile chase up their references.

London had also been having its fair share of rain, and the roads were slick and wet, the rubbish soggy and sodden on the pavements. People scurried along with brollies up, avoiding eye contact with each other hurrying on to their homes or work. The markets were suffering from dire trade and the stalls were sparse either not bothering to turn up at all or packing up early because there were no punters.

Laura was spending more and more time with the Sabs, and had now become a familiar face at the Lord Nelson. The big guy whom she had first met and she now knew as Ryan, no longer looked at her with suspicion and she listened to them planning all sorts of campaigns. It was not just about fox hunting but they were serious about all animal rights, down to fishing, farming, animals used for experiments – just about everything. But whatever they did their sabotage was seriously planned and seriously carried out, not just a bunch of amateurs mucking about. Although at the outset she'd said that she would provide the information and they'd to do the rest, it was impossible for her not to become involved in what they were doing.

Their strategies about foxhunting astonished her. She had just thought it was vandalism really - but it was real scientific disruption, the idea being to distract the hounds from the huntsman and prevent them from catching the fox. Ryan explained that the huntsman controlled the hounds with the hunting horn and his voice, different sounds meant different things – that amazed her really, it all certainly sounded the same to her! It also signalled to the riders what was going on too. In the group the others practised on the hunting horn, listening to recordings endlessly, until they were as expert as the huntsman, the level of their dedication and patience was surprising. The same went for the voice calls, which were so weird – more like old English and hardly recognisable as real words at all! She helped prepare the hand held sprays which would reduce the scent for the hounds to follow, which was easy – water and oil of citronella - it actually smelt quite nice. They had hunt whips with long thongs and an apparently vital piece of equipment was a small loudhailer attached to a dvd player which magnified a recording of hounds in full cry after a fox, which they told her would distract the hounds and they would follow the sound rather than take notice of the huntsman. The preparations were elaborate. Her information was going to be important to them, if they knew exactly where the hunt was going to be, they could plan their route and rather than just follow them aimlessly, they could lie in wait for them - it would be invaluable. The intensity on their excited faces alarmed Laura - as she realised that these people were total fanatics.

After one gruelling session she dropped over to see Linda, who was still in the rehab unit, having finally ended up being sectioned after a particularly psychotic episode. She had calmed down a lot on heavy medication, and was a pitiful sight, and it had now been a few weeks since her admission and she felt an obligation to her.She felt responsible although she could never let Sean know that obviously, he thought she was Miss Wonderful the way she had stood by Linda - if only he knew she thought guiltily. Sean had been as good as his word and she was now validated as a Sab herself, so as much as she hated going, she was going to stick to her part of the bargain. Anyway Jonty was pleased with her and was actually being quite nice to her – for how long she didn't know, but she wasn't going to rock any boats.

Jonty himself, although he'd been furious to find out that snotty cow couldn't ride had decided to turn things to his advantage, he would just lift the kids instead, anyway he reasoned if the tart was the second wife she was probably worth less anyway. As for the nutter, who according to slag Lucy, still had not been found, he could turn that to his advantage and blame their disappearance on him! The Sabs would do the disrupting and while they were all running around like headless chickens he would do his bit. The important part was to have the plan formalised, and in his head he knew exactly how and where, and then Lucy would give him the wink as to the when. They could then spring into action at a moment's notice! He rolled himself a joint adding an extra crumble for good measure of the fine skunk he'd just picked up and was currently mixing the rest with some rubbish to sell on, and inhaled deeply. As the drug took its effect and the feeling of heady calm overcame him he sat back in his chair and sighed deeply it would be as easy as pissing he thought!

Lucy was enjoying herself, she was still working at the Bistro and that was grotty it was true, but the filthy weather had kept the shoppers at home and the outside tables were empty, so it was just the office workers and the odd passing trade stopping in, so they were not that busy. Gino was worrying, Maria was getting bigger and her feet were swelling up and she needed to sit down more, it would not be long before she had to give up coming in, and he was fussing around her all the time. Then it would just be down to her and the confrontational 'Cesca and she was a fat bitch! Lucy however couldn't have given a flying fuck about them – she was seeing more and more of Jonty, he was paying her a lot of attention and she loved it. He and Weasel were coming down about twice a week, and he was always bringing her a little present, he was so thoughtful. At first she had been a bit wary, the odd pill in a nightclub, or joint she was fine with, but she had always fought shy of doing coke – mainly 'cos it was so bloody expensive, but blimey he was generous, and it just made you feel so good, and it had made her very randy. It was funny though she never saw him doing it - although he claimed he did - when he went to the bog – or so he said. She was still seeing Tom in between, and they'd gone down to the Fox a couple of times, so she'd kept up with all the local gossip, which she'd happily passed onto Jonty when she saw him and it made her feel important as he listened to her, so intently hanging on her every word about the village, especially when she talked about the hunt. He told her a little bit more about the Sabs he worked with and how it would be good for him to have any dates that she could supply of when they were meeting and that sort of thing. He said if she could get the information he needed he would definitely make it worth her while in all sorts of ways. Lucy didn't need asking twice, and promised that she would find out - after all what was it to her, it would be a good laugh to have a bit of disruption up their stuffy arses! So running between Tom and Jonty was fine with her, gave her the best of both worlds – it even made the Bistro bearable!

Pete was in a filthy state, living rough was taking its toll, and despite his nightly ablutions he now had a bushy beard, and his hair was even longer. The cuts on his arm had healed now, although he had run a fever for a few days and the arm had started to become infected. The lucky raid on the Landrover and finding the first aid box had helped just in time. Some sterile dressings and antiseptics, coupled with the Paracetamol and he'd managed somehow to pull through, although he'd had to scrub his infected hand blisteringly and had run a temperature for a few days. One thing though, he had now become adept at stealing, he took every opportunity he could, although he still only went out at night, but it was amazing how careless people were. They left their cars open, their sheds, their back doors and their garages. He made use of everything he found in dustbins, even down to discarded bits of soap and partially squeezed toothpaste tubes. Of course it wasn't that he didn't have money to buy things he needed, but he couldn't risk being seen. At night he could blend into the shadows, creeping about until he was sure the coast was clear, and after all he was very good at that - he had been doing it all his life. On one particularly successful night he found himself at the Pillsworthy's place where he had found an old barn unlocked, which obviously was some kind of storage shed for stuff that had not been looked at for years. It was like an Aladdin's Cave! He had been careful though not to take too much at one time - only filching small items, but that evening he came away with an old fashioned pump up primus stove, a small can of paraffin and some matches! Every now and then he had stolen back, being more careful each time he went, just in case they were laying a trap for him, his paranoia working overtime. He had now quite a little stash of useful bits and pieces, an old sleeping bag, some candles, and a pair of old scissors. He was mindful not to disturb the other rubbish that lay around the stuff he had taken, so that if anyone glanced in, it would not look as though anything had gone.

The long days did not trouble Pete entrenched on his straw bed muttering to himself. Once or twice he had heard a car draw up alongside the mill and he'd scampered down the loft stairs and peered through the slats of the barn, craning to see who had come with his heart pounding, but they had never come near him. Most of the newcomers had seemed more interested in the mill itself and one lot were a couple with loads of papers and maps in their hands, measuring this and that, and scrambling around inside it. They didn't seem to be much interested in the surrounding buildings other than giving them a cursory look. Another time he saw that vet's car, the one that had called at Nantes all the time, and he just got out of his car and wandered about, sitting by the edge of the mill pond gazing at the buildings – peculiar he had thought it was. None of them had disturbed him, but the voices nagged him and told him he should make an escape plan should anyone come into the barn. Talking quietly to himself, he combed the ground floor, exploring with his roughened hands the wooden cladded walls. There were the huge doors at the front and the small one he used in the side, but he could find no other; but after days of painstaking searching, finally, in the workshop right at the back, he found a neatly concealed door which led directly out to the fields and out over the park land towards Fittlebury Hall.

There was another thing too, he knew that he couldn't live out of dustbins much longer – food wise he needed more, and the only thing for it was a trip to the shop. The village was out of the question, and there was nowhere in Priors Cross, but he might risk further afield towards Cuckfield. He was sure there was a late night garage with one of those express shops which would have the stuff he needed. He talked the problem through mouthing the words in the darkness, waiting for the reply, his head jerking slightly as he thought. Yes, he could do that, and he immediately felt a wave of calmness flood over him. Once again the voices had told him what he must do.

CHAPTER 57

By the first week of August Felix mused that he had been here just over a month and the time had flown past; he felt as though he'd been at Nantes for ages, slipping into the routine easily. He'd made some alterations to the flat, painting out the garish colours that had been Lucy's choice and now everything was a chalk white, with iconic black and white posters on the walls, which was much more his thing. He liked living on his own, and loved having Admiral in the yard just at the bottom of the stairs. Caitlin was good to work with too, a grafter, and as long as he did his share she was easy going about him riding his own horse in his lunch time break. She often sloped off herself at odd times, although where she went he had no idea, she didn't say and he didn't ask her, it was her business.

Anyway, things were about to start hotting up now that August had arrived and he wasn't thinking of the weather, although a bit of sunshine would be a welcome change. They'd already brought the hunters up to start getting them fit and ready for the season and spent the last two weeks walking to strengthen their legs, with plenty of hill work which would have been dull if Caitlin hadn't been such good company. At last they could begin trotting and then the faster work would start about two weeks after that, which would be much more interesting. Caitlin said that the boss hunted most weekends and some weekdays, so his horses needed to be fit, but the ponies didn't as the kids would only go out occasionally – the odd weekend and school holidays, but they had to be ready just in case. Felix privately thought it was a bit of a waste of time keeping them and it would be better to use hirelings for the kids for the odd day, but who was he to argue, it paid his wages after all.

Jennifer and Charles had been away now for three weeks and were due back any day, and he was not sure how his life would change when they returned. He'd had hardly had any opportunity to get to know them before they left, but perhaps that was just as well, as least it had given him time to settle into his routine. Mrs Fuller had come back a week ago and was a sweet old thing - a real duck, she made a right fuss of him, baking him cakes and stuff. Caitlin thought it was highly amusing when she saw her trooping over to the yard, cooing over him like an old mother hen and teased him mercilessly about it. Yeah, life at Nantes was working out just fine, long may it continue!

John sat in his car in High Ridge Woods, his head slumped forward, his hands gripping the steering wheel. He had never felt so wretched. He had no idea how long he could keep this up, all this lying to Chloe, pretending nothing was wrong, you could cut the atmosphere between them like a knife, although he was trying so hard to act normally - too hard, but she wasn't stupid. It wasn't her fault that things had turned out the way they had, nothing she had done or said, but he'd changed, his whole life had, and that was going to affect her life too and the children's and their home. Every time he looked at them he felt guilty about what he going to do, what he was risking, but he knew that he just couldn't help himself any longer; he was going mad, he couldn't see the future as it was now and however much the truth would hurt her, in the long run this had to be better than living this awful lie. He sat back with a jolt, throwing his head back against the seat and exhaled deeply, he could put the inevitable off no longer, he would set himself a date, wait till the end of the summer holidays at least for the children's sake, the beginning of September then - he would tell her then.

Andrew was content as they'd at last made an appointment for the new veterinary assistant and had all unanimously agreed on Alice Cavaghan the girl from Oz, who was joining them next week. Actually in the end it had not been a difficult choice, as when the older guy's references had come in, whilst not actually saying so in black and white, they'd all agreed his reasons for leaving his old practice seemed a bit ambiguous. So Alice had been appointed and she was just what they were looking for, young, bright, and enthusiastic and had enough experience not to need babysitting in an ambulatory practice, and would be fantastic to have on board if they ever got going with the diagnostic centre at the Old Mill. The new vehicle had arrived and was now equipped and ready to go, although it had seriously hurt spending all that money, but it was a drop in the ocean compared to how much more expenditure lay on the horizon.

Grace had come up with a good idea, she thought they should have a drinks party to welcome Alice and introduce her to their clients, reasoning that as a client herself it was nice to know who was new on the team. Vets were like doctors in that respect, you needed to have confidence in your practitioner and not have Alice just pitch up at their yard with no introductions. In fact Grace had come up with good ideas altogether, suggesting a monthly newsletter to clients that could go out on email, make a Facebook page, making sure their webpage was kept up to date and have a blog of their activities, and perhaps bi monthly lectures on interesting subjects in informal evenings in the village hall. If they were to expand she said, then they also needed to market themselves and invite new clients. Andrew and the others had been delighted, they'd been so busy with the logistics they hadn't even considered this aspect. So Alice's welcome party had been organised for the Wednesday evening of her first week and they had decided to hold it in the reception area of the surgery. Grace had printed off invitations for Andrew and Oli to hand out to clients on their rounds and had emailed, posted and hand delivered the others. It was difficult to know how many people would come but she and Paulene were going to cater for the about fifty and hoped it would work out!

At the brief staff meeting that Friday morning, they were all settled down with coffee huddled in the back office, with half an ear open for the front door should anyone come in, although Grace's dogs would soon bark if anyone arrived.

"Right!" began Andrew "This has to be quick as we're manic, but we need to get together before Alice starts on Monday. Now Oli, she's staying with you, have you had time to sort the spare room out and tidy up the house?"

"Oi! I resent that mate!" laughed Oli, "You saying I live like a pig!"

"Yes! You know you do!"

"I can pop over if you like Oli and give you a hand" offered Grace, "I could go this afternoon, or Sunday if you like, change the sheets that kind of thing?"

"Oh Gracie, you are a love, would you? It's not my bag really. We've been so busy I haven't had much time to keep the place tidy!"

"Yep course I will, just don't expect me to do it every week, after that, you're on your own!" teased Grace, "leave the key under the rain butt."

"Sorted then" said Andrew "Now the reception do, how we doing with that?"

"Invitations are out, I'm getting the booze and nibbles when I go to Sainsbury's this weekend" said Paulene, "Grace and I are going to push all the chairs and stuff to the back of the reception area and there should just about be enough room. It's difficult to say how many people'll come, but it should be okay. If the weather's fine we could spill outside I suppose."

"Good. Grace, have you ordered the new business cards and stationery for Alice?" Andrew asked, "And Paulene have you set up the computer systems for her and updated our webpage?"

"Done boss!" they said simultaneously and both laughed.

"Good girls, what would we do without you. Now just a bit of feedback about progress on the Old Mill. English Heritage have paid a visit and it definitely is a listed building, so that restricts what we can do with it - but the good news is that there are grants available. The planning department are not adverse to what we are proposing and neither are they but it would have to be done in keeping. The Highways are in consultation about access though as apparently they feel it may increase the amount of large traffic going down that lane so they are looking into that and we may have to widen the entrance, but that is all underway. Our solicitors are doing land searches, as although there's a small paddock included with the sale I'm hoping to buy an extra few acres attached to the mill, so that we can have turn out for any horses and put in a school at a later date for diagnostic purposes. Sadly all this takes time, so meanwhile it's still all under your hats, but equally it's still all systems go and all looking really exciting I think!"

His long update was greeted with murmurs of approval and assurances that no-one would say anything. He pushed back his chair, picked up his coffee draining it in one gulp, "Right I'm off to do a lameness work-out, I'll see you all later." and with that he was gone.

"Christ he's like a bloody whirlwind!" laughed Paulene as she watched Andrew fly out of the door - a bloody good looking one too she thought.

Oli pushed back his chair, "Thanks for helping me out Gracie, I owe you one."

Grace gave him a hug, "No problem, you haven't had an easy time lately, you never know, this new vet and you …" she tailed off, looking at him and winking.

"No, sweet, never mix business with pleasure - besides I have other fish to fry!" he winked back and disappeared after Andrew.

Chloe had been to see the woman who owned Polly and talked about selling her. It was a tragic story, Emily was a really nice woman, who loved the horse, but had been diagnosed with a degenerative heart condition which meant no strenuous exercise and she had been advised against riding. She said that it would break her heart to sell Polly and she would rather leave her in the field than sell her to the wrong home. Chloe felt sorry for her, it must be awful, she couldn't imagine how she would feel if that happened to her. Gently she explained that she may just possibly have the right home for Polly if she was prepared to sell her, and although she named no names, Emily said she would consider it, and that she trusted Chloe, and why not bring the lady over to try Polly when she was ready but there was no hurry on her part. Chloe had left feeling sad, but it might be a good outcome for them all though, Emily could keep in touch with the horse, Polly could have an excellent home and have a useful life. Jennifer could have a safe and reliable known horse to ride that would be perfect for her, and that Jessica could progress on to when she was older. It all certainly seemed to fit nicely, but Chloe was a realist where horses were concerned, just when you thought it was going well, something came along and buggered it up, just like life in general she thought grimly.

Jennifer was back this weekend although Chloe doubted that she would see her till Monday. Their weekend would be taken up by delivering the children back to Celia - good luck with that thought Chloe! It had been a long holiday and she wondered how they'd all got on, and whether or not Jen had managed the riding. It hadn't all been on horseback, Charles had apparently organised all sorts of private driving safaris too, and then light aircraft trips and all sorts – must've cost a bloody small fortune! She really hoped it had gone well, Jennifer needed this sort of bonding trip with Charles and the kids, it was a pity that she couldn't do the same with her and John. She shoved that idea to the back of her mind – it was no use wishing, when she had broached the subject of a family holiday with him this summer he had managed to avoid the issue, saying he couldn't take the time off work at the moment. Anyway, she forced her thoughts firmly back to Polly, she would see how Jen felt, and take her over to see the little mare when she came back – only if she wanted to go along that route. If she was serious about going out hunting, it would not be long before autumn hunting began and it was a perfect place for her to start and Polly would be the just the right horse to take her.

Celia was waiting anxiously for Charles to arrive with the children, it had been a long while to be separated from them and she had missed them terribly. They had telephoned her often and said they were having a marvellous time, prattling on about the animals they'd seen and the things they were doing, and how much fun they were having. Frankly it pissed her off, but she couldn't say so. She paced up and down, growing damned impatient. The plane had landed at Heathrow at six forty five that morning, she had tracked it on the internet and it hadn't been delayed and it was now after eight thirty – where the hell were they? She reasoned that it would have taken about an hour to get their baggage and then get the car and then another hour to drive down she supposed, so they should be here any moment, but she hated the waiting. She poured herself another coffee, and forced herself to sip it slowly and continued her pacing. She had even insisted that Anthony go home last night as she didn't want Charles to know that he had stayed here whilst the children had been away. At this rate he could have just left early and there would have been no need for all this subterfuge.

It was not until twenty minutes later and she was pouring herself another coffee that she heard the sound of a car coming down the drive, she dashed to the window, yes, it was Charles' Range Rover, and she rushed outside to greet the children. They spilled out of the back seats running across to meet her – laughing and talking at once and throwing themselves at her.

"Mummy! We've had the most brilliant time!" shouted Rupert hugging her hard, "And you'll never guess what – Jennifer can ride!"

"Rupert, don't crush me dear please." said Celia, pushing him away from her lightly, "My goodness, that must have been an interesting sight!" she said sarcastically.

"She was really good!" smiled Jessica naively missing the nasty tone completely, "we had no idea! So she rode with us every time, it was great fun! She helped us choose some presents for you too!"

Charles had got out of the car and was getting out the children's bags and Jennifer hesitantly walked over towards Celia and Jessica rushed up to take her by the hand.

"Hello Celia, sorry we're late, the bags took a long time to come through. Hope you weren't worried. " She said apologetically, "The children have had a lovely time, they've really missed you."

Celia eyed her coldly, "I don't expect someone like you to have the good manners to be on time dear. I'm pleased my children seem to have had a good time with their father, now if you'll excuse me, I don't have anything to say to you and I want to see to Jessica and Rupert, I'm sure they must be tired." She turned on her heel and left an open mouthed Jennifer astonished at her rudeness.

Charles who had overheard stepped forward intent on retaliation but Jennifer held him lightly on the arm, so he merely stooped down, kissing and hugging both kids, "We've had a great time haven't we? Now don't forget we're going to see each other very soon! Love you both very much."

"Oh Daddy we love you too" whispered Jessica, her eyes full of tears, "And Jennifer, as well."

Jennifer knelt down to join them and she felt Jessica's little arms around her neck and whispered back, "I love you too sweetie and we'll see you again very soon – I promise." As she stood up - to her surprise Rupert came over and hugged her hard around her waist, and she responded immediately, hugging him back and kissing the top of his head.

"Thank you" he muttered, "I've had a wonderful time, you're such fun to be with."

"So are you Rupert, and we're going to have lots more great times together I promise you."

"Right" fumed Celia, "That's enough of that nonsense, Jessica, Rupert indoors now please, I'm sure you've seen plenty of daddy." she barked. "Good morning Charles" and with that she walked back into the house and slammed the door.

Charles started to laugh at the ridiculous situation, "Well no change there then. Come on darling, let's go home." He opened the car door for Jennifer and spun the Range Rover round in the drive and headed back towards Fittlebury, watched by a stony faced Celia from the drawing room and a tearful Jessica from her bedroom.

CHAPTER 58

Wednesday morning had come and Jennifer was nervous, she was going with Chloe that morning to try out Polly. It was a big step for her to be contemplating a horse of her own. It was one thing to ride safe old Rufus, and Ksar in the confines of the school, and even the trail horses who were used to amateurs such as herself, but if things went wrong she could always give them back. Charles was all for it, he'd been impressed with the way she had ridden on holiday but he had explained quite gently to her that Rufus would not be up to taking her much further, if that was genuinely what she wanted to do, and it was not fair on the old horse to expect him to either. She'd talked it through with Chloe, who had finally said that she should at least go and try Polly before she worried herself into the ground about it all.

Jennifer's heart was thumping like a dog's tail as she and Chloe drove up to Emily's house. It was a pretty place, just on the outskirts of Cosham, with a small yard at the back with two timbered loose boxes and a hay barn attached, a small sand school, and paddock. Out of one of the stables a fine grey head looked out of them as they arrived.

As Chloe and Jennifer walked out to the yard with Emily, Polly called to them, and immediately nuzzled into Emily who rubbed her ears as she put on her head collar and led her onto the yard. She was a really pretty horse, her dark grey dapples were fading now and in places she was almost white, and she had the longest eyelashes Jennifer had ever seen.

"I shall be so sorry to see her go, she's been such a friend to me, but you can hear from my breathing, I'm not really fit enough to ride now, and really she's too young to just chuck in the field and retire" said Emily sadly patting Polly, "but I told Chloe, there's no rush at all, I just want her to have a lovely home – that's the most important thing to me."

They tacked her up, and Emily rode around the sand school for about five minutes but it was clear that she couldn't manage much more, so Chloe offered to get on. Jennifer was amazed - she didn't often see Chloe ride in the school and she certainly put Polly through her paces, and transformed the look of the horse in what seemed minutes to her.

"Ah she's such a sweet little horse!" smiled Chloe, as she got off. "Could do with a bit of flat work though eh Emily?"

"I know, I've let it all go a bit really, what with the illness, only been hacking her out, but you made her look lovely Chloe. Makes me realise that she'd be wasted if I kept her."

"Come on Jen, your turn now" said Chloe gently to Jennifer, who was stroking Polly's head and giving her a Polo. "Up you get."

Later Jennifer was to recall, it was a funny thing but the moment she sat on Polly all her nerves disappeared, coaxed by Chloe, she was walking trotting and cantering without a problem at all. Her face must have been grinning from ear to ear, because when she finally got off, Chloe's only remark had been, "Well, I take it that you like her then?"

On the way home, she just couldn't stop talking, she was just so excited!

"I absolutely loved her Chloe, she's so pretty, just the right size, and I felt so safe – straight away, you know really safe, and well, when you rode her, you made her look fantastic, and perhaps I could do that in time too; and I felt she really liked me, and Emily said she was really good to hack out, and easy to do in all ways, I'm sure I could manage her, and …"

"Whoa, whoa!" yelled Chloe amicably, "calm down! There's a lot more to buying a horse than a first try! Like the price, having her vetted, don't you want to hack her out, have me jump her - anything like that?"

Jennifer looked deflated, "Oh, I hadn't thought about any of those things. I'll be guided by you," she added more soberly "and Charles of course."

"Look, actually I know she's good to hack out, and as for the jumping, she'll be fine for you to learn on, although she's never going to do huge tracks, but you don't want her for that do you? Why don't we suggest to Emily that she comes to me at for a week on trial, during that time we can have her vetted, negotiate the price, sort out insurance and stuff and if you get on okay we can go from there. I think she'd agree to that, she's known me for years and she'd trust me with her, and honestly I think Emily's pretty unwell so it might be a relief for her."

Jennifer beamed "Oh my God, I might have a horse!"

"You might well indeed!" smiled Chloe.

Felix and Caitlin were out hacking on Dandy and Beano, they'd been for a good ride over by the Abbey ruins and were now coming towards the village on their way home to Nantes. The horses were ambling along on a long rein, their riders enjoying the sun which had finally made an appearance this morning.

"Fancy stopping at the shop for a lolly?" Felix asked Caitlin, "I'll jump off and get them."

"Go on then, why not! You're getting me into bad habits."

They reined the horses in and Felix leapt off and handed his horse to Caitlin whilst he ran in.

Caitlin waited outside, the horses stamping impatiently for him to come back when a car slowed down to pass her, she turned to nod her head in thanks and was surprised to see it was Jennifer's silver Mercedes with the roof down and Chloe Coombe was sitting beside her, they pulled over and Chloe got out.

"Everything alright Caitlin?"

"To be sure Chloe, Felix's just popped in for a lolly!" she laughed, "sorry to have made you stop."

"Just wanted to make sure you're okay." Chloe turned and got back into the car, Jennifer waved at her and they drove slowly away.

Felix bounced out of the shop, took his horse and jumped on. Caitlin admired the way he did that, he was certainly fit!

"Who was that who stopped?" he asked his mouth full of lolly, licking juice of his lips.

"Chloe, with Jennifer, thought I had a problem. I wonder where they've been now?"

"Dunno, what does Jennifer do with herself all day?"

"Good question to be sure. Anyway I was saying how about going to the vet thing tonight – it's an open invitation to meet the new assistant, would be a good chance for you to meet people in the area. You know how you love to charm everyone!"

"You're getting to know me only too well Caitlin. Networking! Great let's go then!"

Oli was relieved, to tell the truth he hadn't been looking forward to sharing his house with Alice until they found her accommodation. Since Suse had gone, he'd let the place go a bit and the thought of having to pick up his boxers from the floor and keep up to date with the washing up didn't appeal to him one bit. Gracie had been an angel and had come in on Sunday and spruced the place up, but the look on her face spoke volumes. When Alice arrived on the Monday, it looked great. Grace had even put flowers in her room and the kitchen and bathroom were spotless, even if she told him that from now on, it was up to him to find a cleaner!

Alice was cool though, easy going and liked the odd beer - especially since she wasn't doing on calls yet. She was tall, slim and strong and bloody intelligent. So far he thought they would get on just fine, she was never in your face and didn't hog the bathroom. She was good looking too, but not in the sweetly lovely way that Caitlin was he thought fondly, or the perfect beauty that Jennifer Parker Smythe had, or even sexy like Chloe, but in a striking Scandinavian way somehow. Not his type at all, but easy on the eye nonetheless. What's more she was on his level intellectually, could hold her own in any conversation but wasn't overbearing either – yes on the whole she was okay.

The first couple of mornings she had gone out with him, getting to know the country, and meet people, and in the afternoons gone out with Andrew to meet his clients. Tomorrow would be her first day on her own. Grace and Paulene got on well with her too, Alice was great with them, taking their advice about stuff and careful to never make them feel inferior to her in anyway. Everyone agreed they had made a good choice, and tonight was the welcome party.

Grace and Paulene had shoved all the chairs and desks back in the reception area and put two tables out, one with drinks, and one with nibbles. On a whiteboard they had pinned a big photo of Alice smiling and listed below her achievements and specialities, and around the room placed business cards with her contact details. They hoisted up a welcome sign, with some balloons, which privately Paulene thought looked a bit corny, but Grace said added to the familiarity, so she had gone along with it, and some light background music and they were ready.

"Let's hope people come now!" Paulene said, a bit worried "be bloody embarrassing if no-one turns up!"

"They'll come!" said Grace confidently, "Out of curiosity if nothing else, you know what this village is like!"

By seven thirty the car park was almost full, and Caitlin squeezed her Peugeot into a narrow gap between a Landcruiser and an Audi. She glanced at herself in the mirror and put on some lipstick.

"Someone here you wanna impress?" teased Felix

She slapped him on the arm, "Only you sweetheart, only you! Can't walk in with the best looking guy in Fittlebury and no lippy to be sure!"

"Okay now I know you're joking."

"You'll never know darlin' – will you?" she teased amicably.

They walked over to the door, it was pretty crowded, Oli was greeting people and he leant forward to hug her as she came in and she introduced him to Felix but they hardly had any time to exchange a word as other people were behind them waiting to come in.

Andrew was deep in a serious conversation with Rachael Pillsworthy and what must be the new vet. They had been joined by Lavender Clarke, the amateur whip for the hunt, and Jay who had come instead of George.

Colin was talking to young Oli and Tom and then Patrick had joined them, stuffing his face with sausage rolls and sidling up to them, her blouse half undone was Libby Newsome. Caitlin nudged Felix and they went over to join them.

"Hi," said Caitlin in her husky soft voice, "I don't think you've met Felix have you Libby?"

Libby turned and her mouth fell open, "No, I don't think I have, you've been hogging him all to yourself have you Caitlin?"

Caitlin laughed, thinking good luck with this one Felix, but instead replied "Not a bit now Libby, Felix is working with me up at Nantes, so you'll be seeing him a lot this season to be sure."

"Lucky you Caitlin," Libby purred, and then turning to Felix, "I certainly hope to be seeing a great deal more of you Felix" winking sexily at him emphasising the great.

Felix looked aghast but replied smoothly enough, "I shall certainly look forward to it Libby."

Patrick who had finished his mouthful laughed, "You be careful with Libby now young Felix! Tom, what you been up to – seen any more of Juicy Lucy?"

Tom immediately flushed red, "Yeah, she's all right, I know she was a cow to you Caitlin, but I think she's genuinely sorry y' know?"

Caitlin felt a huge surge of pity for him, poor Tom, he was a nice boy if gullible, "Don't worry your head about it Tom, Lucy did me a favour!" she looked at Felix, "Tis all water under the bridge. I've no axe to grind with her now!"

"You know Caitlin you're a really lovely person." said Tom, "really and truly lovely – I mean it!"

Two hands appeared on Caitlin's shoulders, "I'll definitely second that!" said Oli, kissing the top of Caitlin's dark curls "She is lovely!"

"Oh God, I'm gonna be sick" spat Libby, "Come here Oli, you haven't said hello to me properly." Luckily for him, Oli was rescued from the fate of Libby by the arrival of Chloe and the girls from Mileoak who joined them making a lot of noise.

"God it's crowded in here." said Chloe squeezing in beside Colin, "the world and their wife are here."

"Yes, I'm glad it's a good turn out for them" Colin grinned, "Grace has been going around like a spider on speed all week organising it."

"Well, she's done a good job" laughed Chloe, "Glad she's enjoying herself here Colin, she's in her element." They glanced over to watch Grace animatedly handing out glasses of wine and chatting to clients. "She's settled in well, hasn't she?"

"Yes, it's done her the world of good" said Colin enthusiastically, "Loves it!"

Andrew was making the rounds with Alice, introducing her to the various gaggles of groups and finally made it to them. Chloe liked her straight away, the direct eye contact, her firm handshake, the confident but pleasant way she had about her, but the dynamics between Alice and Libby were very interesting. Libby was quite high handed almost dismissive with her, hanging onto Oli's arm immediately questioning her previous experience, but Alice remained charming and friendly but was seemingly not put down in any way, it was really quite amusing! Chloe warmed to Alice all the more. The other person who was very interested in Alice was Felix, who couldn't take his eyes off her.

Caitlin was dying to ask Chloe what she and Jennifer had been doing that morning but didn't get the opportunity to get her on her own. She chatted to Colin and Patrick and watched Oli trying to extricate himself from Libby, and saw Felix watching Alice, and then Chloe talking quietly to Andrew on their own for a moment, and before she knew it, everyone was starting to talk about going home. As they started to drift away the opportunity to ask Chloe had gone. Ah well it was none of her business anyway.

By Friday lunchtime Polly had arrived at Mileoak. Chloe had picked her up in the truck and she was now installed in a stable where Jennifer was grooming her like she was a dusty china ornament. Beebs and Susie made all the right noises, about how beautiful and perfect she was, although of course they knew her from before when Katherine had owned her. Chloe had said that today would be a quiet day for Polly, perhaps a just quick lunge in the school would be best and tomorrow Jennifer could ride her. However frustrated Jennifer felt and how keen she was to ride her that day, she knew that Chloe was right, so she contented herself with fussing over Polly and getting to know her in the stable. Beebs showed her how to lunge her, without getting dizzy, and Polly stood and waited patiently when Jennifer got herself in a tangle with the lunge rein and eventually got the hang of it.

That night at Nantes Jennifer was so excited when Charles came home, she dashed out to meet him, hugging and kissing him, and thanking him for letting her try Polly, and she couldn't wait for him to see her. Charles was pleased, good old Chloe! So far so good, she had really come up trumps finding a horse, but he knew only too well, that horses were great levellers and one minute you were on top of the world and the next you were down in the dumps. He looked at Jennifer's beaming face, he didn't want to burst her bubble though, saying he couldn't wait to meet Polly either and they could go first thing in the morning but how about a drink and an early night. Jennifer smiled at him, touching his lips with her fingertips and then letting them run down towards his belly, linking through the belt of his suit trousers, and pulled him towards her, what a wonderful idea she said.

Down at the Fox, Dick Macey was pulling pints with one hand and shouting food orders to his wife over his shoulder. It was going to be a busy night, the sun had brought out the customers and they were rushed off their feet.

The usual crowd were in the snug, Patrick was propping up the

645

bar with a pint of lager, chatting to Colin and Grace, when Oli and Alice walked in.

"Hi you two! Over here" called Colin, "What you having?"

Oli and Alice made their way over to them, "Busy in here tonight mate! Mine's a lager, what about you Alice?"

"Fine for me too – thanks Colin."

"Dick, when you're ready mate." called Colin to the flustered landlord, "Two pints of lager."

"In a minute Col, I'll give you a shout."

"Well Alice how's your first week been then?" asked Patrick, "What's the gossip?"

"Now take no notice of our Patrick Alice, he's a right old woman, never tell him anything you don't want the world and his wife to know!" laughed Grace.

"Whatdya mean!" demanded Patrick, "I only ever tell one person at a time, and actually I'll have you know, I can keep a secret!"

Alice laughed, "Well Patrick, I've had a right dandy first week thanks, everyone's been great and I'm starting to find my way about, and I don't start my on call till Monday, so right now – it's brilliant!"

"She's settled in really great, haven't you Alice, no problems at all." Grace confirmed, "And I can even read her handwriting, which is more than can be said for yours Oli!"

"You've been talking to Paulene Gracie!" Oli laughed. "Look there's a table over there – shall we grab it?"

As they moved over to the empty table, the door opened and in walked Caitlin and Felix, they made their way over to them "Can we join you?" asked Caitlin.

Oli immediately stood up giving Caitlin a hug, "of course, let me get you both a drink, give me a hand Caitlin eh?" They sauntered over to the bar together and left Felix to sit down next to Alice.

"Guess we're both the new guys in town" he said to her, turning

646

up the charm to max strength, "we should have a lot in common."

Alice looked appraisingly at Felix taking in his startling blue eyes, and replied "I guess we must have."

"Mmmm, we must find out then" he replied oblivious to the astonished stares of the others.

CHAPTER 59

The Fittlebury and Cosham Hunt had four masters, Rachael Pillsworthy, who usually acted as the Field Master, and her husband Giles; Ian Grant and Duncan Worthington-Barnes. George was Huntsman, and Jay the assistant, they had Harry who whipped in and Lavender Clarke was the amateur whip. Michael Gainsborough was the Hunt Treasurer, Felicity Coleridge was the Secretary, and Lavinia Appleton Lacey was Chairman of the Hunt Committee itself. Amanda Lewington Granger was Chairman of the Hunt Supporters. When the main season was on most of the masters came out each time, but during early autumn hunting they often took it in turns, only Rachael and Ian hunted every time and were the senior masters.

However that Saturday morning they had all met down at the hunt kennels, and were busy planning the beginning of the season which could start by early September or with any luck by late August, which was only a couple of weeks away. The earlier rain through July had made everything grow madly - now the warm weather had set in again, and the baking August sun demonstrated just how hot it really could be at this time of year. The plump grain was ripening fast and it would be an early and abundant harvest if the weather held. Deciding they had better call an emergency meeting they began by inspecting the hounds with George and Jay, who reported that they were in fine fettle and they were now exercising them with the horses rather than hikes and the new intake had settled well. The horses were fit and ready too, and they were up to the full compliment.

The masters needed to keep an eye on the farm harvest schedule and decide which country they would hunt first. Traditionally the land over towards Haywards Heath was the last to be brought in as the land was the wettest, and the other side of Cuckfield came first, the rolling downs with its exposed land somewhere in the middle. The amount of followers were usually small for autumn hunting unless the days fell at the weekends and coincided with kids off school, and this year it seemed like that might well happen. Everyone loved autumn hunting, it was a time to introduce new hounds, for new followers to gain experience and for children to have some fun without having to jump the big fences. The meets were much more informal, the mounted field wearing what was called ratcatcher, which meant jackets of varying tweeds rather than the heavy black coats etiquette dictated when hunting proper started. There were no lawn meets as such at this time of year, where to plait the horses was obligatory, although at some meets, their hosts still provided refreshments before they moved off. Still the Fittlebury and Cosham, like most hunts was steeped in tradition and they were fierce about protecting them, and the respect for the hunt staff and masters was paramount, as it was for the farmers over whose land they hunted. Followers still greeted the masters with deference when they were out, and when they left to go home always chorused *"Goodnight Master"* to them - as tradition required. The huntsman himself was rarely addressed, and he and the whips usually kept themselves and the hounds well away from the mounted field. The Field master for the day was in charge of the mounted riders, and woe betide any rider who was out of control and overtook them or disobeyed their instructions. Often the huntsman would take the hounds off in an entirely different direction to the field itself – only to join up with them later, it was all very well planned.

Hunt Meet cards were produced and sent out to farmers, subscribers, members and supporters informing them of venues and up and coming events, but owing to the massive disruption caused by hunt saboteurs, not just at the meets but at social functions too, the information was precious. At one time, when the Sabs had been at their most aggressive they had stopped producing them entirely, but ever since the ban - when the threat of disruption should have been minimal they had been re-introduced, but the dates of autumn hunting were never published. Interested parties were informed by email or telephone as to what was going on - that way the hunt could vet to whom their information was sent, and their database was very well screened security wise. It worked well, and no information was in the public domain and they had little or no problem with disruption - although there had been the incident at the Puppy Show, it had never been proven that this was the work of Sabs. So they were not that concerned when after a busy morning they had drawn up a schedule of meets starting at the end of August, going up to the end of September, which they would review week by week. It was to prove one of the most disastrous decisions they had ever made.

Charles sat by the arena watching Chloe put Jennifer and Polly through their paces. The little mare was certainly smart, a good size too for Jennifer, not too big at 16hh, but not too small either. She was a quality sort, with a fine head, and good limbs, and the Connemara cross Thoroughbred was a good mix, enough stamina coupled with sensibility was a perfect combination. She moved well too, although she needed work on the flat, and Jennifer wasn't skilled enough by a long way to get the best out her yet, but that was good because it gave her something to work towards.

They finished the session and Jennifer was all smiles and Chloe was pleased too and they came over to him to see what he thought.

"I really like her ladies, very much, but Chloe - can she jump? How about I stick up a fence and you pop her over it for me?" he said.

"What me!" squeaked Jennifer

"Not you silly! I meant Chloe!" Charles laughed, "That's if you don't mind Chloe?"

"Course I don't Charles, it'd be nice for Jen to see her jump too, hang on I'll fetch my crash hat." She disappeared into the tack room.

"Darling what do you really think, isn't she just lovely!" sighed Jennifer, patting the grey neck "I feel really good on her!"

"You look good too, and it's important you feel safe darling. Yes, I do like her very much." Charles grinned, "You need to hack her out next though."

Chloe reappeared with her hat on and Charles strode out into the school and dragged out some wings and poles and put up a cross pole to start. Obligingly Polly cantered over the jump in both directions, and then Charles altered the jump to an upright and once again over they went.

"She makes quite a nice shape Chloe, and is quite economic in the jump" called Charles. "That'll be good for Jen, we don't want her being thrown off by something that jumps too big."

"I like the way she keeps the rhythm into the fence too" shouted back Chloe, "doesn't pull either. Put up a spread - let's see how she copes with that."

Jennifer had no idea what they were talking about but watched as Charles altered the jump and Chloe cantered around and once again Polly just popped over it – to her exactly the same way as she had done the others.

"That'll do I think" said Charles, as Chloe pulled the horse up, "She seems really genuine."

"Yes she is, quite a find really, they don't come along like this every day do they?" she laughed to Charles.

Jennifer rushed over and gave Polly a Polo, tugging at her ears, as Chloe dismounted.

"That horse 'll be spoilt rotten" said Charles, "not too many titbits darling! Now Chloe, I think we need to talk tactics here, if you've got time for a coffee can we do it now, as I won't be about in the week."

"Good idea Charles, I'll get one of the girls to see to Polly"

Directly they sat down, Charles switched into business mode, and Chloe could immediately see why he was so successful at what he did. Half an hour later it had all been decided. Polly was to stay with Chloe for the full trial week, during which time Jennifer could hack her out and have lessons. Chloe would arrange for Polly to be vetted and provided she passed and Jennifer still wanted her, he would definitely buy her – Charles wouldn't haggle on the price, he said she was worth every penny. In the meantime Charles asked that Chloe, her staff and liveries not mention anything about Polly outside Mileoak, as he hadn't spoken to Caitlin yet about another horse at Nantes, and he would want to be the one to tell her. He also said that it may well be that after the first week, if Jennifer felt the need, perhaps Chloe might have them for a further week, until she felt confident to have Polly at home. Once though Polly did come to Nantes, he would very much like Chloe to come several times a week to teach Jennifer if that would be possible. It seemed a really sensible plan, and Chloe agreed to it all, and Jennifer sat there hugging herself, hardly believing it was all happening!

During the next week the hunt secretary and the hunt supporters' club secretary sent out a round robin email to its members telling them that autumn hunting would commence at the end of the month and to watch out for emails over the next few weeks as to the venues for the meets. Jennifer was very enthusiastic when Chloe told her, especially now she was pretty certain she was going to keep Polly, and one of the first meets was almost certainly going to take place from Fittlebury itself, and they usually met at the Fox. Chloe thought that this would be a relatively quiet day and a good one for Jennifer to try for her first outing.

Oli, who had been sworn to secrecy, had been out the previous day to vet Polly and she had passed with flying colours and the more Jennifer rode her the more she liked her. Chloe had spoken to Charles on the phone and he'd agreed to go ahead with the sale and said he would transfer the money to Emily's account the following day. There was the minor issue of some tack for the horse, as up till now they had been using Emily's – Charles asked Chloe to sort it out, either buying it separately from her if Chloe thought it was good enough, or organising new things from Penfolds in Cuckfield and making do until it arrived.

"Just let me know how much you need Chloe, and the account details and I'll transfer it straight away." He had said tersely and ended the call abruptly.

Chloe looked at the phone when she realised he had disconnected - really she thought he could be extraordinarily rude at times! But hey, the horse was perfect, Jen was happy, Emily was happy, it was a good outcome and she could sort it.

Caitlin was making the most of the lovely weather and nestled up in the arms of her man. She hadn't been able to see much of him lately, having to make do with texts and snatched phone calls, and the odd stolen kiss in a steamed up car. With this glorious weather it was just so much nicer to lay back under the springy turf, feeling the softness of the grass under her toes as they wriggled in ecstasy under his touch.

Right now, he was urgently kissing the side of her neck, down over her shoulder and along the edge of her arm, as he slid the edge of her tee-shirt down. Her hands ran through his hair, her head arched back, as she opened her body up to him. God she had missed him, and she knew from his hungry response to her that he had missed her too. But it wasn't just the sex, she wanted to do normal things, like cook a meal together, and more than anything to be able to spend all night together, like a proper couple. She pulled him down onto her, her lips finding his and kissed him hard and he responded as desperately as she had.

"Oh Holy Mother Darlin', how much longer, I am dying with the waiting!" she moaned, "It's driving me insane."

"Caitlin, Caitlin my sweet, within the month, September, I promise you darling."

"You promise me now, really?"

"Yes, I do – I can't wait any more either, I feel exactly the same." He kissed her again "I love you, I truly do."

Slowly he began to peel off her clothes and his mouth moved from hers slowly down over her body, she murmured with anticipation and opened her legs.

Suddenly the stillness of the woods was split by the shrill electronic beep of a ringtone, "Christ!" he jumped "What the hell's that?"

"Oh b' Jesus, tis my phone – sorry, I'll turn it off." She leaned over and pulled it out of her jean's pocket, "Oh bugger, I'd better answer it, it's Charles."

"Caitlin, is that you?" Charles barked

"Yes boss, what can I do for you?" Caitlin asked nervously.

"Come to the house when I get back tonight please. My study –

6.30pm." The phone clicked and he disconnected.

"Bloody hell." said Caitlin sitting up looking worried, "What's got into him?" She relayed what Charles had said.

"He's probably just having a bad day at work darling, don't panic, come on, we have so little time together" he pulled her back down again, but it was no good Caitlin was in a right state, supposing Charles had somehow found out.

Lucy was crowing with the information! She rang Jonty and left him a voice mail, not something she normally did, but she couldn't be bothered to type it all in a text. He'd be pleased with her though she knew that! About half an hour later she got a text back *'cant talk babes, gud girl, get down to c u Fri 4 info x'* She idly wondered why he couldn't talk, obviously something to do with his work, although she wasn't quite sure what he did. She was always hoping that he might offer to take her up to London, but he never did. She was beginning to get a bit twitchy when she didn't see him. Tom was alright as a stop gap, but Jonty was something else. She loved the buzz that the coke gave her too, the feeling of absolute invincibility that she could do anything, it was fucking amazing! Trouble was the day after , it left her bad tempered and with a headache, so Jonty always left her with a little stash so she could take away that bad *'next day'* feeling, but it always left you wanting more. She knew she'd never get addicted, she was too sensible but just the odd bit each day wouldn't hurt her she reasoned. Now Jonty was coming down on Friday, so he would bring some more, and hopefully the dates and venues for the hunt meets might be out by then; but on the other hand, if they weren't then he would have to come again another day, and that would be to her advantage – just feed him a little bit of info at a time.

Charles was in a foul temper which was not improved by a tortuous journey home on the train. He got into the Range Rover and drove home, forcing himself to go slowly as he was in the mood to take risks and drive like a maniac. That was the trouble when he was away from work for any length of time, they were fucking idiots and he had had to sort out all sorts of crap this last week and as a consequence had ruthlessly fired a couple of city boys who thought they were shit hot but in fact had bombed hopelessly. He'd cleared up the mess but it had been a close run thing and the one thing he hated was fools at work.

He swept down the drive and parked the Range Rover in the garage and went in through the back door, shouting hello to Mrs Fuller as he came in. He made his way into the drawing room but Jennifer was not there to greet him. He frowned, that was odd, she was always waiting for him, where was she, he waited impatiently and then a sickening thought occurred to him – Pete! He hadn't even considered him since he came back from holiday! He turned round and ran up the stairs two at a time, bursting into their bedroom, tossing his jacket and briefcase onto the bed, but the room was empty - she was not there either. He sat down heavily, trying to think and feeling helpless, where was she? Suddenly he leapt up and dashed down the stairs - only to find Jennifer on her way up.

"Darling, I was just coming to find you, what on earth's the matter, you look dreadful" she said worried, "I was just in my study when you came in."

"Oh my God, I thought something had happened to you, when you weren't in the drawing room."

"Sweetie, course I'm all right, why wouldn't I be?"

He wrapped his arms around her, kissing her hard on the lips, "I'm just being paranoid, take no notice of me. I've had a seriously bad day! As long as you're okay, I'm okay. You're all that matters!"

They both turned as they heard footsteps crossing the hall and the sound of a knock on Charles' study, "Oh God, I'd forgotten, that's Caitlin, I'm going to tell her about Polly, pour me a drink will you sweetie." He called down the stairs, "Go in Caitlin, I won't keep you a moment."

"Oh God!" said Jennifer, "she's going to be in for a shock, I hope she's okay about it."

"Well she'll be fine I'm sure darling, after all it's what we pay her for, and it's not exactly hard work is it – especially now she has Felix to help, they're hardly overworked are they?"

"Well good luck with it."

"Thanks!" He laughed " but it'll be a piece of cake after what I've already had to do today."

CHAPTER 60

Whatever Charles had believed, the news that he'd bought Jennifer a horse, and that she'd learned to ride had come as a surprise to Caitlin. The mystery of what she did with her time though now became clear, and also why she'd become so matey with Chloe. Thinking about it, so much now made sense, and the idea hadn't even crossed her mind at all. Even so she was still amazed that she hadn't heard about it on the grapevine from Susie and Beebs who'd obviously known, or somehow on the jungle drums that beat constantly through the village. It had been kept very hush-hush for sure, or maybe she'd just been keeping herself to herself now because of her own secrets these days?

The manual work of coping with an extra horse wasn't really going to be a problem, especially not now that she had Felix, although the knock on implications of whose horse it was could be. Not only would Jennifer be a total novice, and as such would need complete supervision she supposed – just like the children in a way, but coupled with that, she was also in effect - her boss, or her boss' wife - not an easy combination. Up till now her work at Nantes had meant that she pretty much did things her own way - would Jennifer's presence in the yard change this situation? It would be impossible to tell. Charles had been quite short with her that evening and said that Jennifer would come over to the stables herself at some point to talk to her and Felix about the new horse, but that he was just letting her know what was happening. For the time being the horse was being kept at Mileoak, but would be arriving at Nantes sometime within the next week, so could she get a stable sorted out.

When she had left, her mind racing with unanswered questions, she wandered back to the Granary, suddenly asking herself if Ace had known about this, and if he had, why hadn't he said anything to her, after all the horse was being kept at Mileoak and he must have seen Jennifer there too. He must have known! She was disappointed in him that he hadn't mentioned it.

She thought about going over to see Felix to tell him the news but then decided against the idea, she didn't want to appear pushy or that arriving on his doorstep uninvited could be misconstrued in any way. Instead she went home, poured herself a large glass of wine and slumped down on the sofa trying to watch the TV, but her mind was churning, not just about Jennifer, but if Ace hadn't told her about this, which was a relatively small thing to him, what else wasn't he telling her?

Mrs Fuller jumped out of her skin when Jennifer burst into the kitchen the next morning, nearly dropping a loaf she was putting in the Aga.

"Good morning Mrs F! Another beautiful day."

"Good morning to you too. You're on top of the world!" smiled Freda, glad that Jennifer was so happy, she'd hardly seen her this week.

"Oh I am, I am, have you got five minutes for me to tell you all about it!" Jennifer said as she plonked herself down in a chair.

"Of course" said Freda –"I'll make a cup of tea shall I?" she turned to the Aga and put the kettle over, "Earl Grey?"

"Please" said Jennifer, "Oh I see you've got your Elephant apron on."

Mrs Fuller stood back smoothing down her apron, "I have indeed, it's very nice, and right kind of you to think of me too." Jennifer smiled, she'd brought back the quirky native apron and a book with local recipes as a little present when they came from the safari, actually she'd bought everyone something, but she hadn't told Freda that.

"Oh it was just a little thing, to say I thought of you" Jennifer smiled, "but guess what? Charles has bought me a horse!"

"No!" Freda sat down, this was news indeed, although of course she did know that Jennifer had been taking lessons, indeed had seen her dashing out every morning in her breeches, but had been told by Charles that she was to say nothing to anyone about it to anyone, including the other staff, and when Mr Charles gave an order it was more than your life was worth to disobey him.

"Yes, she's called Polly and at the moment she's up at Chloe's but is coming home next week, and I'm going to be going hunting at the beginning of the season on her! Isn't it amazing!"

"Well you're right there. I'm very pleased for you m' dear, but you be careful, that huntin' is a dangerous old game y' know!"

"I'll only be doing the easy days to begin with Mrs F, don't you worry - Charles and Chloe won't let me do anything else, but I'm terribly excited. Charles told Caitlin last night so I'll try and go over and see her later, but I'm going up to ride Polly this morning, but meanwhile you don't have to keep mum about me riding anymore."

"That's a relief – don't know how she hasn't found out before to be honest! Still she'll be pleased for you too I'm sure. Now that kettle's humming, let's have our tea and you can tell me all about Polly." She shifted off her chair adding, "have you told your mum yet?"

"Yes, I was straight on the phone to her, she was dead chuffed for me, I'm hoping to ask her down again – maybe next week or the week after, that okay with you?" adding awkwardly, "Charles and I are were hoping to have the children too, although Celia is being a bit tricky about it, as we took them on such a long holiday, but hopefully the weekend before they go back to school."

Freda didn't comment about Celia, just replied, "Well that'll be lovely, just let me know when m' dear, I'll get everything ready for them, now let's have that tea."

Jennifer was not the only one to be excited, Jonty was feeling the adrenalin rush he loved when he was going to pull off a job, except this was the mother of all jobs! He couldn't believe it, after all this fuckin' time, in a couple of weeks and it would be on. Just the final planning stages and he'd called a meeting today when they would draw it all together.

They were a hardnosed bunch. Weasel of course was his right hand man, Tubby, Hawkeye, Nathan, Freddie and Nora his bitch, were all seated round the room waiting for him to begin. He had worked with them all plenty of times, and he trusted each and every one of them. There were no cans of lager open this time, Jonty expected and had their full attention – everyone's wits very much about them.

"Right – here's the job." He began. "We're gonna lift two kids and hold them for ransom."

"Fuck me!" exploded Tubby. "This is big stuff Jont!"

"Yep, it is and the pickings too, a rock or more." Jonty looked around him at the serious faces, "Say now, you in or out?" He paused, waiting for them to respond, "Say now, 'cos once we start talking, you're in and no going back – right?"

They all started mumbling and arguing, and Jonty waited biding his time, but he knew them well, and when finally they agreed they were in, he smiled he knew that the lure of the big money was too much to turn away.

"Okay – here's how we'll do it." He spread the map of Fittlebury on the table, indicating where he had marked out the key areas. "This is the Fox, the local pub, this is an old Abbey, which is ruined, this 'ere is an old derelict water mill, and this is what we're gonna do."

They all craned over the map – looking at the locations.

"These people go hunting, y' know fox hunting and they start in a couple of weeks Charlie boy, their Dad takes kiddies out, and they start from here," he pointed to the pub, "they'll go along this road here," he traced the route with his finger, "and they go in here" once again he pointed to the bridleway leading up to the Abbey ruins. "As they go past the ruins, we'll be waiting, I've organised a diversion, we snatch the kiddies whilst daddy is otherwise engaged, going back down the way we came, to the Landrover which we've left here." he pointed to the bottom of the hill.

"Look Jont, I don't want to shoot you down in flames mate, but there's holes in this plan, fuckin' great holes!" moaned Hawkeye,

"For a start, it's gotta be some kind of bleedin' diversion for us not to be seen."

"It will be mate. Laura has befriended some fanatical Hunt Sabs, and I'm talking nutters here. Got all the gear, they wear camouflage, wear balaclavas, use horns, sprays the fuckin' works, she's gonna feed them the info, they'll create the diversion just where and when we need it, gonna be a right old rumpus and we can do the lifting. Here's the thing tho' neither these sab cunts nor Laura know what's really gonna happen though right, she's a stupid tart and they're nuts, but that works in our favour, they can't give us away."

"Okay, so the diversion is good, but if we leave your motor at the bottom of the lane, every fuckin' toff will be sure to see it when they ride past and every other fucker too! Hardly inconspicuous is it? How you gonna get the kids back down the hill without being seen, into a beaten up old Landrover that everyone has by now noticed anyway and make a hasty exit back up to the smoke - leave it out! You're off your bleedin' rocker mate!" said Freddie.

"Calm down and listen" soothed Jonty, "We'll dress the same as the Sabs, they won't be able to tell us apart, they all drive these old Landrovers, they'll be loads parked down there but here's the best bit." He laughed his eyes gleaming, "You haven't heard the half yet."

An hour later, they cracked open the cans, rolled some joints and relaxed, "it's fuckin' brilliant Jont, a masterpiece!" laughed Hawkeye.

"Yer it fuckin' is, but it's all down to timing and keeping our heads, everyone has to be ready to stick to the plan, don't get side-tracked or lose focus – right." said Jonty sharply to them all, "We'll meet again tomorrow, but not at my gaff from now on for obvious reasons. Nath, we'll come to you – three o'clock. Nora – start shopping gal."

They nodded their assent, finished their beers and left one by one, until only Weasel was left.

Jonty took a slug of his lager and inhaled heavily on the joint passing it to Weasel, he let the smoke filter through his nose before saying "the beauty mate is if it all goes tits up, you and me get away scot free!"

Weasel snorted, choking, "I like it Jont, I like it!" he laughed.

That same afternoon Jennifer decided she must stop off and see Caitlin and Felix before she went into the house, so she parked her car by the garages and strolled over to the stables, looking forward to telling them all about Polly.

The sunlight bathed the yard and the tack room door was wide open with the radio blaring out pop music, so she guessed that they must be cleaning tack. Walking over towards the open door she stopped for a moment when she heard them talking - realising it was about her.

"Well we'll just have to make the best of it, it's probably just a phase and she'll get fed up and it'll be a five minute wonder and the horse 'll be sold before you know it" she heard Felix say.

Jennifer paused, waiting to hear Caitlin's response, "It's just I've always been my own boss y' know, and it'll be like someone looking over my shoulder all the time. And she's a real novice too, so she knows nothing really, couldn't have been riding more than a few months to be sure, so it means it'll be a babysitting job."

Jennifer heard Felix laugh, "You mean three children instead of two, come on, it won't be that bad!"

Caitlin replied gloomily, "I wouldn't be taking bets on it now! The boss would have my guts for garters if anything happened to her, you don't know what he was like after the incident with that bloody Pete! Christ knows he' be furious – what a bloody nightmare it's going to be for sure."

Jennifer was absolutely livid! How dare they talk about her like that! She'd done nothing but try and be kind to Caitlin, babysitting indeed, is that how they saw her! Well think on.

She stalked into the tack room, switched off the radio and turned to both of them, fixing them with a steely glare and said coldly, "I've just overheard every word you both said, and I'm really sad to know Caitlin that's how you see me as nothing more than someone who looks over your shoulder all the time, and who knows nothing and whom you imagine you'll need to babysit. I've never been like that with you and if you're honest you'll admit that's true. I've always tried to be friends, let you use the pool, take time off whenever you wanted, never checked up on you - and I certainly don't need you to babysit me and was eternally gratefully when you rescued me from the pool that day." She turned to Felix, "As for you, thinking that riding will be a phase that I get fed up with, you're hardly in a position to comment, as you simply don't know me, nor likely to have the opportunity either after that remark."

"Oh Jennifer" whispered Caitlin, "I'm so sorry, I don't know what to say…"

"I rather think you've said everything don't you?" Jennifer stared at her "I was so excited about coming to tell you about my horse and bringing her home, and there are you two being spiteful, you should be ashamed of yourselves. Chloe, Susie and Beebs have been fantastic and they don't seem to think I'm a nuisance, and I've loved being there and thought you'd welcome me too, how wrong could I be. It's a sad day that I can't bring my horse home, because of two small minded people. I'd rather keep her at Mileoak any day. Anyway I won't keep you, I'm sure you two have lots to talk about."

Jennifer, her heart thumping, and feeling tears pricking the back of her eyes, held her head high and turned abruptly around and marched back to the house, leaving Caitlin and Felix open mouthed.

"Holy Mary!" sobbed Caitlin, "What have I said, I didn't really mean it, it wasn't like me at all. Jennifer has always been lovely to me so she has, and now she'll be going and telling the boss and we'll both be out of job, so we will! What on earth can we do?"

"Christ Caitlin, I don't know. Perhaps she'll calm down and not say anything!" groaned Felix, "You said she's a really nice woman!"

"Well so she is now, but that was before y' know, she's fricking furious, and I don't blame her! I'd feel the same wouldn't you? She's right in what she says, always been very fair – never interferes or asks what I'm up to, doesn't care – I don't know what made me say it! After all this is her home and Jesus knows she entitled to have a horse here if she wants, and I have to go and say that. I feel awful, I never normally say things like that, what's come over me?" She started to sob again, and this time Felix could not console her.

Jennifer tore into the house through the back door, only to bump into Mrs Fuller who was coming out of the laundry room. She took one look at Jennifer and was aghast.

"Whatever is it my duck" she asked, "it's not that Pete is it?" She put her arm around Jennifer who had started to cry and she led her into the kitchen. Jennifer sat heavily down on a chair and Mrs Fuller pulled up one beside her, "Now m' dear, what's happened?"

"Oh, God, I'm sorry, you must think me very stupid" Jennifer sobbed, "I'm fine, it's not Pete, don't worry."

Mrs Fuller sighed, thank the Lord for that she thought, but what on earth had distressed Jennifer so much, she tried again, "Then what Jennifer, something's upset you?"

"It's my own fault, they say eavesdroppers never hear any good of themselves, and I dropped over to the stables and overheard Caitlin and Felix talking about me. They weren't being very nice, that's all. It upset me, and I stupidly told them so," she faltered "I shouldn't have said anything."

"Yes, you should" said Mrs Fuller angrily, "they'd no business talking like that in the first place, and good for you pulling them up. No better than they ought to be – they have it too cushy by half!"

"You don't think I did the wrong thing then?" asked Jennifer looking up at her, "I thought I should've kept quiet."

"Certainly not" Freda said emphatically, "This is your home, they're paid to do a job, they want to get on and do it and stop gossiping! Doesn't hurt to be told now and again, you're a right old softie really!" She took Jennifer's hand and squeezed it, "No, you did the right thing, but what're you going to do about it now, that's the issue?"

"Well, it was all about me bringing Polly here, they implied that I would be a pain to have around, so I said I wouldn't be bringing her now, and implied that Felix had better watch his step more or less!" Jennifer laughed ruefully, "I see what you mean, they think I'll go and tell Charles don't they!"

Mrs Fuller laughed too, "Oh yes, that's what they'll be thinking especially if you said you'd keep Polly at Mileoak, and serve them right too! Won't do them any harm, might make them respect you a bit more! What will you do?"

"Well of course I'm not going to tell him, he'd go bonkers and fire the lot of them, I wouldn't want that. You know what he can be like."

"If I was you I'd let things lie for a bit and see what happens next." smiled Freda, "let them make the first move eh! Things have a funny way of turning out!

CHAPTER 61

Friday night came and Felix and Caitlin watched from the Granary window as Charles parked his car and walked into the house. Neither of them spoke a word to each other, they were sick of talking, they'd churned over and over what had happened all afternoon, trying to decide what they should do, or moreover what they thought Jennifer would do.

At first they thought she might have come back to the stables, either to talk to them again, or demand an apology, but they hadn't seen her.

They then surmised that she'd have been straight on the phone to Charles, but now this seemed unlikely as he appeared in a good mood when he walked into the house, quite unhurried with his jacket slung over his shoulder. They waited in the Granary expecting at any moment for him to come whizzing out, or for Caitlin's phone to ring asking her to come to the house, but nothing happened at all.

An hour later the back door opened again and Jennifer and Charles came out together, he in a dinner jacket and she was in a cocktail dress, they were obviously going out for the evening. Caitlin and Felix heaved a sigh of relief - nothing was going to happen that night then.

Felix had a brainwave, "I know, I could ring Susie, she'd know if Jennifer had rung Chloe this afternoon wouldn't she and how long the horse is staying at Mileoak?"

"Well she might I suppose, but would she tell you? They're obviously pretty good at keeping secrets up there aren't they?" she said with a touch of irony, "How about you come clean with her and tell her what happened, she's more likely to tell you then isn't she?"

"Good idea" he said tapping out the number.

Caitlin stood half listening to his call and half in a world of her own. How did her life suddenly go from grey to downright black in an afternoon? It'd been unlike her to be so bitchy, she wasn't normally like this, but the strain of this business with Ace was getting to her, changing the person she was. What was it Tom had said just the other night, she was a truly lovely person, she could hardly call herself that now could she – she was truly a bitch, no better than Lucy.

Felix got off the phone, his face was red. "Well I just got a right ear bashing from Susie!" he moaned, "I did what you suggested, and she told me we were the most stupid pair of wankers she knew."

"Oh b' Jesus" groaned Caitlin "go on."

"According to Susie, Jen – she called her Jen if you please - is great fun, never afraid to get her hands dirty, very generous, works hard at her riding and is doing really well; lovely to them, a great livery, gives them super tips, never complains etc etc, the list is endless. She says she hopes we get kicked out 'cos she'd love the job."

"Did she say anything about her moving the horse?"

"According to Susie, next week sometime , so I guess Jennifer hasn't done anything at all."

"Okay, well we might be in luck then, come on, I think we need Mrs Fuller's advice on this." Caitlin marched over to the door, "get your skates on, while they're out."

Freda was in her little sitting room just off the kitchen when she heard the back door, she knew immediately it was Caitlin, she'd been expecting her. She shuffled down the corridor and opened the door wide for them to come in and they followed her back down to the kitchen.

"You'd better sit down Caitlin, Felix" she said, her voice quite frosty, "what can I do for you?"

Caitlin took one look at Mrs Fuller's cross face and burst into tears, "Oh Mrs F, I've been very stupid." Out poured the whole sorry story, with Felix looking embarrassed, the self-confident lad looked like a little boy lost.

"Well I don't need to tell you both that you should be ashamed of yourselves do I?" Mrs Fuller admonished, "but what are you going to do about it now?"

"I don't know what to do" sighed Caitlin, "I feel dreadful, I didn't mean any of it y' know, she's always been so kind to me. If she tells the boss – we'll both be out on our ear."

"She won't tell Mr Charles, she's a decent woman, and a kind one, not that you deserve it - either of you. You both need to eat a large slice of humble pie and apologise properly and truly mean it, and when she brings her horse here make her genuinely welcome. Of course she's going to need help, and you should give it willingly, not because she pays you but because you want to. When she goes out on that damned huntin' malarkey make sure you take care of her, as you should do and stop being so damned spiteful the pair of you."

"Do you think she'll accept our apology Mrs F?" asked Felix "she was pretty upset."

"Well wouldn't you have been upset? Yes, she'll accept it because she's one of the good ones, and I'll speak to her too. Just you make sure you treat her properly in the future, otherwise you'll have me to deal with, and God help you if Mr Charles ever finds out! Now out you both go, I'm missing Eastenders."

The weekend brought more hot bright weather, and on Saturday morning Jennifer had gone up to ride Polly and Charles had gone with her, he was enjoying every moment of her success on the little mare. He was grateful to Chloe whose skill as a trainer was brilliant - she was so patient and he could almost see Jennifer grow in confidence with the lessons. Afterwards Chloe had invited them up to the house for a lemonade, but Charles declined saying he had some urgent business stuff he had to do this morning, but suggested that she and John bring the children up later to Nantes to have a swim and a game of tennis. If they fancied it - he could do a barbeque as the weather was so good – and it was agreed they'd come after four o'clock when Chloe had finished teaching.

Jennifer and Charles sped off in the Range Rover and he turned off in the direction of Cuckfield, swooping along the dusty lane alongside the old Abbey.

"Where are we going?"

"Just want to pop into Penfolds and get you a tweed jacket for hunting and some breeches and boots and stuff, then some food for the Barbie. I'll nip into the butchers and get some steak and burgers and sausages for the kids too."

"You are lovely Charles" Jennifer said, "It was nice of you to ask Chloe up."

"She's been good about Polly and the kids 'll enjoy the pool on a day like today, and we so rarely use the court, it'll be fun for us."

They were back home within a couple of hours and Jennifer said she's pop the meat down to the kitchen and let Mrs Fuller know. Charles said he needed to do some work in his study and disappeared.

Jennifer pushed open the door to find Mrs Fuller beaming from ear to ear.

"Sit yourself down m' dear, where's Mr Charles?"

"In his study, he won't be out for a while – why?"

"Developments!" said Freda winking at her.

Jennifer had to smile when Mrs Fuller told her about Caitlin and Felix - she told the tale with real relish. "Oh they're right sorry those two are!"

"Oh well, shall I go over and put them out of their misery then?"

"No, I'd leave it till Monday if I were you - make them sweat a bit, no harm done."

"You're the boss!" laughed Jennifer, "thanks Mrs F, I knew I could rely on you. Now Charles is going to do a barbeque this evening about six ish, Chloe and John Coombe are coming over with their children, he's bought this meat. Could you be an angel and do some salad and pasta, and perhaps a pud?"

"No trouble at all, I'll do a nice rice salad, new potatoes, and green salad. I've some of my home made coleslaw too. How about I do a trifle? Kids always like that with a nice treacle tart and cream."

"Mmmmm – makes my mouth water thinking about it." grinned Jennifer.

Lucy was bad tempered today, she had a terrible headache and a runny nose, in fact her nose felt bloody sore. She was really low, perhaps she had a cold coming - she seemed to be permanently sniffing. She'd had a blinding night with Jonty and Weasel, and good sex with Weasel to finish, although it was a funny thing, she was as randy as hell, but the orgasm had been hard to achieve. Jonty was a great bloke, he was always so interested in her and what she was up to, she really fancied him but he never touched her, just took photos of her and Weasel. He was generous too always doling out the coke and listening to her prattling on when she was high and felt invincible. Last night he had got her on the subject of the Parker-Smythes again and all the old hate festered out in the form of what she wanted to do to them, moaning about the spoilt kids and Caitlin, and the stuck up wife. How they had all just come back from their fucking holiday and there was her sweating it out in the Bistro. Jonty asked how often the children were there, Lucy had shrieked with unnecessary laughter and it had been all he could do to calm her down.

The last thing she felt like doing today was running around taking fucking sandwich orders from a load of poxy Saturday shoppers who couldn't make their minds up. Maria hadn't come in, and that bitch Cesca was running the show indoors and giving her hell, she was gonna tell her to shove her tuna mayo up her arse if she wasn't careful. If she had felt more like her normal feisty self, she probably would have, but all she wanted to do was go home to bed and go to sleep. Even that though wasn't going to be possible – she'd promised Tom she'd go out with him tonight. She felt she had to go, she might learn a bit more about what was going on first hand and Jonty 'd been so pleased with the information she'd given him last night, asking her the exact route the hunt took when they met at the Fox and all kinds of random stuff. She'd had no idea he was such a keen sab, but she liked to encourage him, anyway what was it to her if the fuckin' hunt got disrupted. He was sweet really, left her a line or two to keep her going til he came down next week, she could do one before she met Tom, that would help her get through the evening.

Chloe, John and the kids pitched up at Nantes at four thirty, the children spilling out of the car, to be greeted by Jennifer, who swooped up Rory and gave him a hug. Charles followed her outside and shook John and then Toby by the hand, and kissed Chloe on the cheek and sombrely kissed Lily on the hand Her little face flushed with pleasure.

They followed Jennifer through the house onto the back lawn and over to the pool, and pretty soon, the children were all splashing about, although Rory still used his arm bands. Chloe and Jennifer laughed and shrieked in the water with them, throwing balls and plastic toys about whilst Charles and John watched from the loungers on the edge. It was a glorious afternoon, the sun toasting everything nicely and the garden was looking beautiful. It made Charles realise what a crap job Pete had done all these years, the contractors were much more efficient and he said as much to John.

"Yes it really does look beautiful, I'd love to do something like that you know, be more creative." John mused, gazing out over the garden.

"Would you?" asked Charles surprised, "But you're doing very well at your job aren't you, highly thought of?"

It was John's turn to look surprised, "Well I wouldn't say that, but perhaps I'm having a midlife crisis Charles," he looked sadly at Chloe and the children "I'm not sure I want this anymore."

"What Chloe and the children you mean?" asked Charles intrigued and desperate to find out more.

"Daddy! Daddy come in and play with us!" yelled Toby, "The water's lovely!"

John got up immediately, "Coming!" he called, "Excuse me Charles."

The afternoon sped past with the kids and grown-ups in and out of the pool, then racing around the lawn playing rounders. Charles whisked up a feast on the barbeque and Mrs Fuller produced some great salads and puddings for the children. The tennis court was sadly forgotten and by seven o'clock the children were tired and getting ratty and Chloe was collecting their things into the car.

"We've had a great afternoon, thanks for asking us" she enthused, "What do you say children?"

"Thank you very much for having us" they chorused dutifully.

"Chloe, I have a little something for you" said Charles quietly, slipping an envelope into her pocket, "open it when you get home."

"Charles, there's really no need honestly." Began Chloe, "I …"

"There's every need Chloe, please take it graciously," he turned to the children, "and do come again everyone."

Eventually when the children had been strapped in their seats, John sped off down the drive in the grubby old Discovery and Charles stood at the front door arm in arm with Jennifer. Her face was full of smiles, but Charles was frowning - he was really concerned, he had a nasty feeling something was going to happen to them.

The following week rolled in and Jennifer took Mrs Fuller's advice and waited till the Monday before she went over to see Caitlin and Felix. She walked into the yard to find them both looking very embarrassed. Caitlin was wringing her hands and started to stammer out an apology - not able to meet Jennifer's eyes. Felix hovered behind her, not knowing quite what to say. She looked at them both and smiled and told them to forget what had happened, because she certainly had and she was looking forward to bringing her horse home later this week. Poor Caitlin, Jennifer certainly didn't want her to have to crawl and she almost visibly saw them sigh with relief. Deep down Jennifer knew that Caitlin was not a nasty person, probably not Felix either, and Caitlin had her own personal problems, although she was not sharing what they were. Jennifer knew only too well from personal experience how misery could alter the way you behaved.

672

The matter was put behind them and forgotten as far as she was concerned.

For Caitlin, though she'd never forget how Jennifer had been decent about it all, and was determined that she would prove to Jennifer that she'd do her utmost to help her in any way she could. Felix, who didn't know Jennifer, nonetheless felt his respect for her go up several notches, and he thought that Susie was right, she really was a lovely person, his remarks had been crass and stupid and he was genuinely sorry.

Polly was coming to Nantes on the Wednesday, and Felix was driving their horsebox down to pick her up. Her stable was all ready and Charles and Jennifer were going to have a hack out together on the Saturday – a real first! Jennifer was going to miss Mileoak and the girls, and on the Tuesday she rode early and drove down to Brighton to the Lanes and bought Chloe something special as a thank you for everything she had done for her - little knowing of the generous envelope that Charles had already given. On the way back she dropped into Penfolds and bought Beebs and Susie a really expensive smart coat each, ones which they had both wistfully admired in a catalogue - so she knew they would love them.

When they had loaded up Polly to go to her new home, they had all cried together, in a group hug, whilst Felix looked on embarrassed by this evident display of genuine affection, and once again felt ashamed of the things he and Caitlin had said. Jennifer had left the presents surreptitiously in the tack room, so that they could find them when she had gone. She could never thank them enough for what they'd done for her, and she would never forget either and the tears rolled down her cheeks as she waved goodbye - even though Chloe was coming on the Friday to give her a lesson!

Laura, on Jonty's instructions had fed the information to Ryan about the forthcoming autumn hunting and he assured her that they were all set and ready to go. She said that surprise would be the best form of attack and to let the first few meets go by and lull the hunters into a false sense of security, and then hit them hard when they least expected it. The Sabs were all for that, and she said that she could tell them exactly what route they were taking on a particular day - so instead of converging at the meet itself, when the hunt could change direction and outwit the Sabs easily, it was best to plan the disruption where they would least expect it. Ryan listened intently, it was a good idea. Laura said, they had to be ready to go within a few days' notice, and they needed plenty of bods to disguise what the real Sabs were doing. He said none of that would be a problem - they would be ready when she gave the word.

Jonty meanwhile had met the rest of his cronies several times, being careful never to be seen in the same place twice and they were now clear what roles they all were to play. They'd gone over the scenario a thousand times, covering every angle, every possible problem and every possible outcome. All the necessary tools for the trade had been procured one way and another, and stored separately, each being responsible for their own equipment, so that nothing could tie them in one to another, if anything should go wrong. Jonty was in his element, he loved it – the planning, he often thought he should have gone into the armed forces, special operations would have been his thing. The others were more stoic, it was fuckin' risky, but you had to hand it to Jont, he could organise a job, covered every bloody aspect, but this all hinged on whether or not these fucking kids went riding on that particular day. The other thing about Jont was that he never did a line, never smoked a joint, never did alcohol for at least a week before a job, and he didn't let them either, once it was over, you could do what the fuck you liked, but not before. They were all jittery though, waiting for the nod, and no dope either, fuckin' nightmare.

By Friday Jennifer felt as though Polly had been at Nantes for years, she went out every morning and tried to beat Caitlin to mucking her out, but the horse was always immaculate by the time she got to the yard. Although Jennifer drew the line at grooming and tacking her up, explaining that she really wanted to do it herself. On the Thursday Caitlin had watched her riding in the school and had been pleasantly surprised and on the Friday Chloe pitched up to give

Jennifer a lesson. So far so good.

Chloe had brought exciting news telling them that the hunt was meeting at the Fox in Fittlebury on the following Saturday, which was when they were having the children to stay. In theory, if all the horses were sound, and Jennifer was still progressing with Polly, they could all go out together. At first Jennifer had been concerned that she would not be able to cope, but Chloe had assured her that there would be no jumping and anything else she'd manage just fine. Anyway if Jessica was going out too, she'd have to be on the leading rein, in which case Caitlin would be going out too, so they could all go sedately at the back, especially as it was Jennifer's first outing. Rupert could stay with Felix, which meant that once things got going, Charles could hunt up front if he wanted. It should work perfectly. It would probably be a bigger field than usual for autumn hunting, as Katherine and Sandy were bound to go, and Colin and Grace too, and all the usual stalwart members especially as it was a Saturday meet. Jennifer couldn't believe it, her debut had finally arrived. She was delighted and terrified at the same time.

CHAPTER 62

Saturday morning had arrived and Charles and Jennifer were up early clip clopping along the road through the village toward the Fox. It was a lovely morning and heaven to be out with Charles, and the sun was already quite warm. Polly was walking along quite happily beside Beano and Jennifer didn't think she could be more content.

He was going to take her along the route that they would hunt next week, so that she would know where she was going, even though she'd be with Caitlin, who wouldn't leave her side, and knew the country well. However he said it was best to have an idea, and there were some good steady canters which would be fun.

"Autumn hunting is really different to hunting pukka" he said, "This is a time when the Huntsman is teaching the new hounds their job, people bring out their new horses, and a time for new riders too." He went on, "So it's much less full on, more sedate and quite a bit of standing around. There's quite a bit to learn about the science of working hounds, but don't worry too much about that, I just want you to enjoy the ride, and the experience. Once you come out more – you'll start to see what I mean."

"Will they kill any foxes?" she asked nervously, "I'm not so sure about that."

"No!" he laughed, "Since the Act was passed, we're not allowed to, but it doesn't stop the hunt functioning or losing its tradition of hunting. They lay false trails and the hounds follow those. One of the problems with this time of year is that with the warm weather the scent is poor, so we have to start really early, or sometimes even hunt in the late afternoon when it's a bit colder."

"Crikey, what time do we start then?"

"Well, we won't find out for certain until a day or two beforehand, but usually between six and seven in the morning, might be later but depends on the weather."

"Let's pray for a bit of a cold snap then!" she laughed.

They trotted on, Polly gamely keeping up beside Charles and they turned in towards the Abbey, and once through the gate, they kicked on into a good canter up the hill and stopped at the top to admire the view. Charles pointed out the various little bits of woodland which he called coverts where the Huntsman would send in the hounds to flush out the scent, saying that experienced members of the hunt would position themselves around these areas to make sure that the hounds ran in the right direction, it was called 'holding up the coverts'.

They carried on with the ride, and Polly behaved superbly – didn't pull once even when on one occasion Beano was quite mad to get his head and zoom away. The thoroughbred in her certainly gave her enough speed too, but she never got silly and Jennifer felt quite safe on her. They'd made their way back in a big loop and were approaching the Fox from the opposite direction walking sedately back home, Charles remarked that he thought Polly was a great find, and couldn't be more perfect for Jennifer and that they were all going to have a fab day on Saturday and Jennifer couldn't help but agree.

Saturday night saw the usual crowd down at the Fox except that had Lucy pitched up with Tom. Even though once again she had become a familiar sight in the village, she was not liked and apart from the men ogling her tits, that was about all she had to offer. She sat on the periphery of the crowd and unbeknown to them took in all they were saying, which included the autumn hunting so far and the meets planned for this week - especially next Saturday when they would be leaving from the pub, although no-one knew what time it would be yet.

Grace said she had an interesting piece of news but that up until now she had been sworn to secrecy, and that was that Jennifer Parker-Smythe had been taking secret riding lessons at Chloe Coombe's place and had actually bought herself a horse! Oli had vetted it last week and apparently she was going to take it out on Saturday! Lucy's ears pricked up - fucking hell she thought, but she managed to make no comment as Grace went on, saying that it was rather sweet as Charles' children were going out too. The evening wore on, they gossiped about the new vet Alice, who turned out to be a bit of super star. According to Grace she had made the most fantastic job of stitching up a horse that had been caught in barbed wire, and that she'd made a hit with the clients she had met so far.

After a while Lucy started yawning, she was so bloody tired these days and her nose constantly dripping, but no cold had come out, she had nudged Tom and they had left, stopping in High Ridge Woods for a quickie on the way home. Before she went to bed, she texted Jonty, "*Fox @ Fittlebury, Saturday, no time yet but early am. Parker Smythe cunt has horse & going with kids!*" She'd waited for a reply "*G8 work – txt l8r*". She smiled and blew her nose, which was really sore and fell into bed.

Jonty was irrationally ecstatic, he contacted the others and they met the following day in a dive of a pub in Whitechapel. He was almost dancing when he told them they would have an additional valuable prize for the plucking - and the fucking he added, laughing maliciously. The date had been confirmed, it would be early in the morning but the mole couldn't confirm the exact time yet – but they were on!

Hawkeye was concerned, he hated last minute changes, they all did - how would they know they had the right ones, it was a bit vague wasn't it?

Jonty's face clouded over with dark anger, "Well I know the cunt don't I, and I'll be there, so don't go fuckin' soft on me now." he raged.

The others had looked away, they were in too deep now to turn back. Nora and Freddie broke the tension and lamely said they'd get finished this week, they were more or less set up anyway, just the last part to do. The others looked at each other, shifting uneasily in their chairs and confirmed they were ready too. Jonty looked down on them all, this was his baby and it was gonna work.

Laura contacted Ryan, and met him and the others at the Lord Nelson on the Wednesday. She took a map, and carefully showed them exactly where they needed to be, and the relevant woodlands, the Abbey itself and its location to the woods and the path. Ryan nodded his approval, clapping her on the back, his eyes gleaming. He picked up the phone, organising a bus load of Sabs for the Saturday, students from the local college. He congratulated Laura and asked her if she wanted to come with them. She squirmed saying she couldn't risk blowing her cover, and he smiled understanding at once, but saying they would do her proud and would take photos and a video.

Laura had left, she felt a real shit, these people were fanatics, but they truly believed in their cause, and she was using them for some fucking hair brained scheme of Jonty's, and Christ knew what he was up to – she had no fucking idea at all. She made her way to the rehab centre, the only consolation was that Linda seemed to be marginally improved, but as it was her who had put her there in the first place it didn't make her feel a whole lot better. She didn't like herself one bit, for two pins she would just piss off out of London and not come back.

As the week progressed down at Nantes, Mrs Fuller got the house ready for the children's visit and ordered in their favourite food. Jennifer enjoyed having Polly at home more and more, and Chloe started to teach her to jump. She went hacking with Caitlin and Felix. She rang her mum often and promised that next week she would pick her up and bring her down to stay for a few days. On the Friday afternoon Charles picked up the children from Celia, and Jennifer was heartily glad that she didn't have to go with him, and wasn't looking forward to taking them back on the Sunday. Still that was another day she supposed. She'd heard via Chloe that they were to meet the following morning at seven. Blimey that meant leaving the yard at six thirty!

Friday night was a happy, excited evening with the children reliving the fun nights they had spent under canvas on the safari, and Jennifer had made a tent for them in the drawing room and they decided to have supper on the floor laughing their heads off at the shocked face of Mrs Fuller when she brought in the trays! They all went to bed early in anticipation of the day ahead. It was a lovely happy evening and one that haunted Charles for the many nights that were to come.

The harsh beep beep of the alarm woke Charles and Jennifer with the kind of jolt that shouldn't be allowed, but Jennifer had only slept fitfully anyway and without disturbing Charles, she slipped out of bed and into the shower. The very thought of the day ahead made her heart thump with the anticipation of it all. She stood under the heat of the powerful spray jets allowing the water to cascade over her, the steam of the water vaporising on the glass screen, she rinsed her hair one more time and stepped out, the cold air gushing onto her. Towelling dry her hair, she went over to shake Charles, who moaned and turned over, and then she padded out across the landing to rouse the children, who were already wide awake and half dressed in their jodhpurs. Jennifer had said for Mrs Fuller not to get up, but to leave breakfast out in the kitchen - so giving Charles another shake, she and the giggling children crept downstairs together. They were half way through their second bowl of cereal when Charles materialised, bleary eyed, and poured himself a cup of coffee but smiling nonetheless. Jennifer went into the pantry and doled out Kitkats, Mars and Twix bars – one of the tips Chloe had given her was to fill up your pockets with chocolate as you were bound to get hungry and need a sugar fix! Giggling excitedly, she grabbed Jessica by the hand and they all tiptoed out to the stables, collecting their boots by the door as they left.

Caitlin and Felix had been busy and everything was well under control. The horses were gleaming and already tacked up and waiting. Charles was riding Beano, Felix his own horse, Rupert was obviously taking Scooter, and Caitlin was leading Jessica from Dandy and Jennifer on Polly. Everyone looked very smart in their ratcatcher gear. Charles handed Felix a hip flask and went into the tack room to get his hunt whip and one for each of the children and Jennifer. Felix courteously helped Jessica climb onto Queenie and handed the lead rein to Caitlin, adjusted Scooter's girth for Rupert, held Polly whilst Jennifer mounted, and then swung on to his own horse and they were ready to move off.

They rode in pairs along the road, Jennifer and Charles together, then Rupert and Felix, with Caitlin and Jessica behind. All along the lane horse boxes were parked in random gateways, with riders struggling to get on excited horses as they danced about, and Charles called good morning as they passed. It was quite chilly, and Jennifer was glad that she had put on two pairs of socks, again at Chloe's suggestion. Their own horses were keen, sniffing the air with anticipation and Beano was finding difficulty in walking and kept jogging. Polly clearly couldn't understand what the fuss was all about and kept up her usual steady pace. As they neared the pub, more horses joined them and there were piles of droppings on the road steaming on the early morning air. Jennifer spotted Grace and Colin Allington on their horses and to her delight Katherine with Alfie and Sandy on the farting Seamus! She waved hello to them and they shouted back to her.

Everyone piled into the pub car park, and Charles steered them into a quieter corner where Jennifer could watch comfortably without worrying about being in the way. It was a wonderful sight and she was enthralled by it all. There must have been horses and riders of every shape, size and dimension! Children on ponies, fat women on fatter cobs, sleek ladies with red lipstick on smart thoroughbreds, gentleman on old fashioned hunters and young lads on eventers, in fact a whole spectrum of equine enthusiasts. There were quite a lot of people on foot too, some of the oldies Jennifer knew from the pub, Dick and Fred, with their feisty Jack Russells. Oli and even Patrick had turned out, and rather surprisingly she saw Tom with Lucy, what was she doing here? Lucy glared at her and turned away.

She could hear the hounds baying excitedly from somewhere but she couldn't see them, she asked where they were, and Charles explained that they were not out yet, and were still in the hunt lorry at the back of the car park. He laughed and told her too, that hounds never barked, they only "gave tongue" or "spoke" and were counted in couples.

They'd made good time and it was only ten to seven, when she heard a loud cry -"*hounds please!*" There was a murmur from everyone and huge cacophony of noise as about twenty of them hurtled round the corner, and old George and Jay came with them, mounted on two very smart bay horses, and Lavender brought up the rear on her chestnut. They skilfully manoeuvred them over to the side of the green where the hounds waited running around in small circles, sniffing the air, cocking their legs, and the odd errant one trying to make a break for the road, but Lavender and Jay kept them under control with sharp cries of "Come - Larkin", "Back - Anchor" holding out their long white leather thonged hunting whips to guide them back into line. It was all very colourful and as they watched some of the horses were getting more and more excited but dear Polly just stood quietly for Jennifer, as though she had been doing it all her life, but the same could not be said for Beano, who couldn't wait to get going.

A woman was coming around on foot speaking to each of the riders, and then they gave her some money which she pocketed in a leather pouch and ticked off their names in a notebook, when it came to Charles she just shouted good morning and moved on to the next group.

"She's collecting the 'cap' for the day" explained Charles, "that's the money the riders pay to come out, I pay annually - an agreed sum with Michael Gainsborough which covers all of us every time we go out, as I can't be bothered with it on the morning – it more often than not works in their favour though!" he laughed ruefully.

Jennifer smiled there was an awful lot for her to learn. Suddenly everyone jumped to attention. Rachel Pillsworthy was standing up in her stirrups asking for quiet.

"Well Good morning to you all on this lovely day, and welcome to those of you who've not been out with us before. We have a good field today of about thirty – excellent for one of our first autumn meets! For those of you who don't know me, I'm Rachael Pillsworthy one of the Masters and your Field Master for the day. The other Master out today is Ian Grant." She indicated a man standing next to her on a black horse. "We're going up towards Priors Cross this morning and draw across the Abbey plain, there'll be quite a lot of cantering up there but no jumping today." There was a little moan from some of the riders. "However" she continued, "All being well, we're moving onto towards the Cockroost Nine, so there are a couple of small hedges, and tiger traps for those who want to jump them. Jumpers should follow me, non-jumpers follow Ian here. Remember we have young hounds out today, so make sure you give way to the Huntsman and Whips at all times, and at no time leave the headland unless instructed. Have a good day and be safe!" She nodded across to Old George, "Hounds please!"

Jennifer whipped her head round to hear George blow a quick note on his horn and move off with a clatter of hooves onto the lane out towards Cuckfield, the hounds trotted after him followed by Lavender and Jay at the back.

Rachael and Ian and waited for a moment and followed them, with the main body of horses moving off in pairs after them along the road. Beano was almost beside himself with excitement, leaping about and struggling to go with them. Charles looked grim, and Jennifer urged him to go ahead and said she would stay at the back with Caitlin and Jessica. Caitlin said for Felix to go with Rupert and Charles, they'd be fine, as she was on the steadier Dandy.

Charles looked back as her rode away and called "Have a wonderful day darling – stay safe!

CHAPTER 63

Jonty had been waiting in the Abbey ruins since six that morning. They had a stash of equipment hidden behind some of the fallen stones. He was bloody freezing and wrapped his green anorak tightly around him, taking a swig of water from a bottle he had in his pocket. The others were cold too and even though the sun was up now it was still chilly. They were all dressed the same – green camouflage combats, black hoodies, balaclavas and green anoraks, and they all wore latex gloves. His phone beeped a message, it was from Lucy, *"just moved off from the pub"*

"Right" He forwarded the text to Laura in London, and she immediately sent it onto Ryan who was waiting in the woods below. From the gaps in the Abbey stones, they watched dark figures swarming all over the valley dashing in and out of the woodland, and moving out onto the plain. "Here we go lads" he said breathing heavily as he pulled down his hood.

The Hunt by now had more or less reached the bridleway; there were the usual foot followers' Landrovers and four wheel drives parked alongside the road, and Patrick who had cadged a lift with Tom and the others, got out. That's funny he thought, there was that old dog of a Landrover again, the one he'd seen before - it must belong to one of the hunt supporters but he was buggered if he knew who. The hounds and the huntsman had congregated to the far left of the gateway inside the field, whilst the rest of the mounted followers filed through and waited behind them. The horses' nostrils were smoking out steamy breath in the chilly air. The terrier men and the rest of the foot followers stomped around the bottom of the field towards the woodland about a mile away where they would have a good view of the hounds working and where they could see them go off over the plain towards Cockroost Nine. The Masters spoke with the huntsman for a moment and they stood waiting. Caitlin told Jennifer that they were checking, which was a hunting term for waiting, whilst everyone was in position until they started and that it was often like this during autumn hunting, there was a lot of hanging around.

Jonty was watching, what was happening or rather not happening, from his vantage point at the top of the hill.

"What the fuckers waitin' for?" he growled, straining to see what was going on. It looked like people on foot were skirting around the edge of the field at the bottom, close alongside the hedge, heading towards the woods. "What are those geezers doing over there?"

"Fucked if I know Jont," muttered Weasel his raspy breath stinking so close to Jonty's face.

Jonty pushed him away irritated. He felt so tense he could explode with the agitation, clenching his fists so hard that he nearly burst the latex gloves.

"We'll just wait and see then." He slowly exhaled his breath willing himself to stay calm.

Down below, the Huntsman glanced at Rachael who nodded and he gave two short bursts from his horn and kicked his horse forward into a strong and fast canter up the hill towards the Abbey, followed by the hounds which streamed out to the side of him and the whips, followed closely behind. Rachael waited, holding the field back for a good couple of minutes and then urged her horse into a gallop and the mounted followers careered after her, heads down going as fast as they could. They tore up the path heading for the ruins, the turf flying out in all directions, the horses straining and pulling, and then once they reached the top, the leading riders were lost from view as they hurtled down the other side. Caitlin leading Jessica cantered slowly up the hill with Jennifer behind. There was no way they could keep up with the rest of them at that speed, Queenie just didn't have it in her, and besides it wasn't safe. Caitlin assured them they would catch up with them when they checked at the covert over the hill on the plain down below.

Jonty couldn't believe it, these people were fuckin' nuts, it was like the charge of the bleedin' light brigade. He watched horrified as a sea of riders stampeded towards the Abbey and galloped past his hiding place at break neck speed! How the fuck were they going to weed out the two he wanted from this lot, and they weren't even going to stop! He groaned with frustration, he hadn't read the situation at all, he'd had no idea it would be like this! All his carefully laid plans were just galloping past and there was fuck all he could do about it! He turned to the others who looked as horrified as he did, it was fuckin' carnage!

Suddenly from the woods way down below them, there came a lot of noise and horn blowing, he narrowed his eyes trying to focus on what was happening in the distance. By now most of the riders had gone past him and the Sabs were doing their job, running around spraying stuff all over the place, blowing horns, calling to the dogs which were dashing over to them to be given treats, and the hunt was in complete disarray. The guy in charge of the dogs was rushing around with the other two blokes on horses, lashing them with whips and shouting and screaming at them, whilst the Sabs surged out of the woods, yelling back and laughing. The mounted followers were standing back clearly not knowing what to do.

By the time Caitlin, Jessica and Jennifer cantered to the top of the hill, they had heard the noise going on the other side and pulled up to see what was going on but Caitlin knew straight away.

"It's Sabs" she said to Jennifer, "Antis. Holy Mother, there're masses of them! We'd better wait here I think till it's over, it can get quite nasty sometimes, and we'll be safer! Bastards! We're hunting quite legally. Why don't they just leave us alone!"

Charles who was hunting right at the front with Felix and Rupert pulled up quickly behind Rachael.

"What the hell's going on!" he yelled to her "Where did this lot come from!"

"It's bloody Sabs Charles, they just appeared from the covert, they've sprayed the whole frigging place with citronella and started up with the horn! The hounds are running amok, they don't know if it's goodnight or Good Friday!"

Charles looked in horror at the disruption. There were what seemed to be hundreds of them all dressed the bloody same. Some were blowing horns and some were calling out to the hounds which were bounding up to them and being given titbits. George was dashing about with his whip, shouting and blowing, and Jay and Lavender were doing their best, but this was well organised and planned there wasn't much that they could do.

The field were held up about a hundred yards away with Rachael and Ian, and he suddenly had a horrible thought, Jennifer where was she? He searched amongst the waiting horses for her and Jessica but couldn't find them, and then looking up the hill along the path beside the Abbey, to his relief he saw that Caitlin had seen what was going on and sensibly stopped at the top. At least they were safe right up there and well away from the action. He turned his horse back and cantered back to join the fray. By this time the foot followers had joined in, and there was a lot of barracking and barging going on. The Sabs had their cameras and videos out and he could see Patrick take a swipe at one, knocking it to the ground and victoriously stomping on it with relish! There was a howl of rage from the Sabs and a one of them took a swing at Patrick only to be tripped over by Dick. Charles sighed, this was going to turn nasty – he just knew it.

Caitlin, Jennifer and Jessica were horrified at what they saw and stood watching for what must have been a good few minutes, and Jonty couldn't believe his luck. Perhaps it was going his way after all – that was the bitch and one of the kids right there under his nose! He signalled to Weasel, but he'd seen them too, as had the others, and they all yanked their hoods down further, slipping quietly out of the ruins behind the horses.

Before the riders knew what was happening, two large figures had grabbed the horses' bridles and held them fast, whilst Jonty and

Weasel grabbed Jennifer and Jessica by the legs and dragged them to the ground, stuffing rags over their mouths and noses sitting on top of them until their struggling ceased. Caitlin shouting in anger, lashed out with her whip, but another figure had emerged and caught hold of the thong, as he dragged it out of her hand, she lost her balance and tumbled off backwards onto the ground. She fell hard, hitting her head with a dull thud on the stone wall of the Abbey and lay completely still. The man rolled her over with the toe of his boot and then kicked her viciously in the ribs.

"Quick" hissed Jonty, dragging Jennifer by the legs, her head banging up and down on the ground as he pulled her into the ruins. Weasel following closely behind with Jessica and the others brought the horses, lashing them to a small tree which taken root by the stones.

"What about the other tart Jont?" muttered Weasel, "We can't leave her out there."

"Sneak out and drag her in Hawk" commanded Jonty, taking rope out of the backpacks. "Tie these two up fuckin' quick!"

Nathan and Tubby worked fast, lashing Jennifer's ankles and wrists together, and did the same to the unconscious Jessica. Searching their pockets, he whipped out Jennifer's mobile phone and tossed it to Jonty. Securing duct tape tightly over their mouths and eyes they took out two blankets and rolled their bodies up in them. By this time Hawkeye had dragged Caitlin back, chucking her inert body down in a heap. "She's a gonna mate, blood coming out of her ears, mouth – you name it - hit her head on the rock when she fell."

Jonty didn't have time to think about her, "Dump her then - get going Tubby and Nathan, don't stop till you get there, and then you know what to do – right."

"We're going, we're going!" Tubby threw Jessica's little body over his shoulder and slid off carefully, wearing the smooth soled shoes Jonty had insisted upon to limit any possible tracks they might make. He disappeared down the footpath right at the back of the Abbey, followed closely by a grumbling Nathan who was carrying Jennifer - the ruins totally obscuring them from the view of anyone on the plain below.

Jonty peered out across towards the woodland again, the whole operation so far could only have taken a few minutes, and it was starting to get nasty down there. Looked like a punch up going on! He ran back, to see Hawkeye injecting the horses savagely in their necks, their eyes rolling with fear, as one by one their legs buckled and they sank to the ground, where he gave them a satisfying kick. Weasel was now picking up two identical blankets each of which had been stuffed with a long bolster pillow, Jonty picked one up and threw it over his shoulders, and Weasel followed him. Hawkeye glanced around making sure they had left nothing incriminating behind and ran down the path after Nathan and Tubby spraying the citronella wildly behind him as he went. Jonty grinned at Weasel and then they ran as fast as they could, their bundles flapping about on their backs, down the bridleway, towards the lane and the Landrover.

Down with the Hunt things were going from bad to worse, and Rachael had called for backup from the police, despatching Mike Lister, one of the terrier men to go back to the entrance to the lane to direct them. There was little that they could do but wait and not get involved. The hounds by now had settled down and were enjoying an impromptu and early breakfast much to the crowing delight of the Sabs. George had given up trying to get control and was just occasionally and rather feebly blowing his horn to try and encourage them back, whilst Jay and Lavender looked on helpless. The Sabs were having a field day, laughing and taking the piss out of the riders at every opportunity. Of course the land was private property, they were only legally allowed to be on the bridleway, but the laws of trespass were pretty sketchy at the best of times. Patrick had been hauled away by his mates, and so had Dick, although you could see they wanted to punch the Sabs' lights out, but they didn't touch them. There was a lot of insulting name calling going on, swearing and threats, but luckily no fisticuffs.

Lucy was huddling behind one of the trees on the edge of the wood, she had no idea it would be quite so aggressive, and nor did she know which one Jonty was, they all looked the same. What did give her a lot of pleasure though was the look on that smug bastard Charles Parker-Smythe's face - he was fucking livid! She couldn't see Caitlin or Jennifer, they were probably cowering at the back of the field. Serve them right she thought, it had certainly spoilt their day out, and all because of her! She had got her own back all right!

Mike Lister hurried back along the headland, angry and frustrated by these bastard Sabs, how fucking dare they, they were hunting quite within the law. It was those bloody lefty bastards that were trespassing and breaking the bloody rules – not them. He was seething. Poor old Patrick, no doubt they'd try and get him in court now too. Still they'd been plenty of witnesses to say he hadn't actually touched the bloke with the camera, it had fallen out of his hand. As he stomped along, half running, half walking, he wondered who on earth could have tipped them off? It had to be somebody from inside – these meets were never published and were by invitation from the Masters only - even the time was only confirmed a couple of days before. The clever bastards hadn't even been at the Fox, they'd know where they were going to draw right from the outset and were waiting for them to arrive, otherwise the Masters could have just taken a different route. It had to be an inside job. He was nearly at the gate now, and was alongside the hedge on the field side of the road, when he saw two of the fuckin' Sabs bundling a couple of rolls of what looked like old carpet into the back of a Landrover. What were they up to now? He hollered angrily out to them, but the blokes took one look at him and just jumped in the vehicle and drove off at full steam – fucking cowards he thought! There was a wail of sirens coming from the other direction – and he ran over to the field gate yanking it open, as the Police Landrover spun in the entrance. Mike jumped in the back and they sped across the field towards the woods, and about fucking time too he thought.

Charles saw the police arriving with their blue lights flashing, and offered Felix a swig from his hip flask. Rachael and Ian went over to speak to them, and three burly officers in black combats got out. One of the Sabs walked over and they all started talking heatedly, the man stabbing his finger angrily at Patrick and Dick and the broken camera; Rachael waving her arms around indicating the hounds. Everyone just watched and waited to see what the police were going to do. It all seemed to take ages. They went over and took Patrick's name and address, and that of Dick too, then the bloke whose camera had been damaged. The big guy who was obviously the leader was insisting that Patrick be arrested. The Police were shaking their heads and all the time the sun was getting up and the day was getting warmer.

After what seemed an eternity, Rachael came back standing up in her stirrups to make an announcement, "I'm so sorry about this everyone, but in view of the fracas and disruption to our legal activities this morning caused by the saboteurs, and what with the heat rising now, the scent is too poor to continue, so Ian and I have decided that for today we will have to abandon. If you would like to follow me, we'll make our way back to the Fox. Sorry once again." She turned her horse around and rode sedately right across the plain with the mounted field behind, in a show of defiance that they did not need to use the bridleway and had every right to be there.

Charles glanced up to the Abbey, Jennifer, Jessica and Caitlin were no-where to be seen, "I think they must have gone back already" sighed Charles, "poor Jennifer, she was so looking forward to her first day out. What a bugger!" He took out his phone and rang Jennifer, but it went straight to voice mail. He tried Caitlin but once again it did the same. "They must be trotting and can't hear it." he said, "We'll catch them up at home."

The police had asked the Sabs to leave, and once they saw that the hunt had been abandoned, they decided to go home and trailed after them across the field, yelling victory calls as they went. Nobody went back up the hill past the Abbey, and the police waited until the last person had left and the Sabs had got into their vehicles and driven away before they too closed the gate firmly behind them and went back to the station to file their report.

Charles was in a hurry now to get home and they trotted most of the way, but true to tradition the three of them forced themselves to walk the last mile back. Caitlin would give him a right telling off if he brought the horses home sweated up. He was thoroughly fed up, what a waste of a day! He felt more sorry for Jennifer and the kids though, they'd been so looking forward to it. They rode into the yard, expecting Caitlin to be there waiting for him as she normally was, but it was eerily empty. The tack room door was locked and there was no sign of her or the horses. He jumped off, and looked around, shouting for her, but there was no answer.

"That's bloody odd." he said to Felix, "I thought they'd have been back ages ago. I'll try ringing again." He pulled out his phone, but got the same responses as before – voicemails. "Felix take care of the horses can you, and Rupert can you give him a hand, I'll pop into the house and see if Mrs F has heard anything from them."

Five minutes later he was back, "I'm really worried, she's not heard a thing, where the bloody hell can they be?"

"They can't be far away sir" said Felix, "they were waiting at the top of the hill when all the trouble was going on so they definitely weren't involved in anything, and perhaps they just went off for a hack instead?"

"Maybe, but somehow I don't think so, not with Jessica, she'd be tired by now and Queenie's not that fit is she?"

Charles felt sick, his thoughts immediately turning to Pete, "Right, Rupert old chap, you go indoors with Mrs Fuller and stay by the phone in case there's any news. Ring me if you hear anything. Felix you get your car and drive around the lanes looking up all the bridleways they might have taken, there might have been an accident or something, and I'll go back towards the Abbey which is where we last saw them. Make sure you take your phone."

CHAPTER 64

Charles' thoughts were racing by the time he got to the bridleway gate, he had an awful feeling about this, something wasn't right, why wasn't Jennifer answering her phone, or Caitlin either? He glanced at his watch, it must be at least a couple of hours since he last saw Jennifer up here, where could she have possibly gone? The sun was quite strong now and he was sweating under the thick jacket and hunt shirt and stock. He was buggered if he would walk up to the Abbey – so he threw back the gate, leapt back into the Range Rover and hurtled up the hill. He pulled up outside the ruins and looked down on the plain at the exact same spot where they had stood earlier, you could see for miles up here and there was not a damned sign of them.

He looked down at the ground studying the hundreds of imprints of the horses' hooves where the field had galloped over the ridge earlier, searching around to see if he could find any that had gone off in a different direction, and then he froze in shock as he saw some blood on the grass and splattered on part of the stone wall of the Abbey. Frantic, he looked all around him, shouting out their names, nothing, it was totally still and quiet, and then he ran into the ruins.

He saw the three horses first, they were lying almost flat out, except for their heads, which were yanked upwards at funny angles where their bridles had been tied to a tree but their bodies had somehow collapsed underneath them. He ran over, they were breathing but totally out for the count, he couldn't get any responses from them. He loosened the reins which suspended their heads and they thumped dully to the ground, still they did not stir but apart from that they looked unhurt, and he couldn't see any blood or any damage to them. He stood up mystified, and looked around, calling out, and his voice resounded around the old walls. He wandered around behind the fallen stones and suddenly stopped, hardly able to take in what he was seeing. He clutched at the stones for support, and felt the colour drain out of his face. There was a body lying slumped, half fallen to one side on the grass, blood trickling out of the nose. His hands flew to his mouth, fucking hell - it was Caitlin. Trembling he ran over to her, bending down he touched her cheek, she was quite cold and he knew straight away that she was dead. Her face was pale, her lips almost white and he could see from the side of her face that she'd had a whacking blow to the side of her head just below her hat and right on her temple.

He got out his phone and dialled 999, demanding both the police and an ambulance, willing them to hurry as he gave them directions. Bloody hell, what was going on, Caitlin! Where the fuck were Jennifer and Jessica, he was yelling on the phone as he ran around the ruins, until he had covered the whole area searching for them, urging the emergency services to hurry. He rang the Vets, who said they would send someone up straight away and to try to stay calm. Calm, fucking calm! He screamed, he shouted, but there was nothing, not a sound - it was useless calling, they had completely disappeared. He went back over to Caitlin and stroked the side of her face wanting to cry, what a tragic end to this lovely girl, and moreover what had happened to her? Where were Jennifer and Jessica, and what had happened to the horses?

What could he do, he could only wait for help, and he slumped down beside Caitlin and took hold of her cold hands between his, as though warming them up might help, and he sat there trance like for what seemed ages, until he heard the throaty roar of a four by four charging up the hill. The engine cut and two doors slammed and he heard a voice calling him.

"In here, I'm in here." he shouted replacing Caitlin's hand reverently and getting up abruptly, running outside. It was Andrew and the new vet Alice, thank Christ - they must have been in the surgery when he called.

"There's been some kind of accident - the horses," he pointed "over there, I don't know what happened - they look like they're dying." Charles started to shake, "And Caitlin's dead, must've fallen off and hit her head, and I can't find Jennifer or Jessica"

"What did you say?" shouted Andrew, "Not Caitlin, Christ no! Not Caitlin, where is she?"

"Andrew!" snapped Alice, "Pull yourself together! The

emergency services are on their way, if she's dead, there's nothing we can do for her, but we might be able to save these horses and that's our job here!"

"Fuck the horses!" stormed Andrew "You look at them, where's Caitlin Charles?" He gave Charles a shove and he led Andrew around the back of the fallen stones to where the body was and Andrew fell to his knees. "Oh my God! Caitlin my little love, what's happened to you?" He put his fingers to her neck and leant forward and listened to her chest for a long time, then put his fingers to her wrist, and then her neck again. "She's not fucking dead you moron, she's unconscious, but she's breathing - just and she's got a faint pulse." He examined her head, being gentle with the wound and not taking off her hat, then cautiously supporting her head, he carefully rolled her into the recovery position and put his jacket over her. "Keep talking to her Charles and tell me if she is sick or changes in any way." He leapt up and dashed back to the horses to help Alice.

"They've been doped for sure" said Alice, "Difficult to say what with, my guess looking at them is Ketamine, but we can't be certain until we've done bloods. Whatever they've had, there was evidence it was done in a vein," She showed Andrew "Whoever did this wanted them right out of it for a couple of hours and I don't suppose they cared much about the outcome."

"Okay" said Andrew, "It's more than likely to be a cocktail, Ketamine, Valium and maybe Dormosedan, that'd be favourite if they know what they're doing. Get some blood testing kits out of the car so we can be sure. They should come round spontaneously and when they do it'll be rapid, so be ready and I think just observation till then – heart rate, pulse usual. I'll get Oli up here to give you a hand and he can bring some giving sets just in case we need fluids." He picked up his phone speaking quietly and quickly, and then dashed back over to Caitlin.

The sound of sirens once again screamed across the valley, Andrew sent Charles out in a daze to direct the Ambulance, which was already steaming up the hill. Two green clad paramedics jumped out, clutching bags and raced past him towards Caitlin.

Andrew was still bending down beside her, he looked up when they arrived, "She's been unconscious for about two hours we believe, and was found about 30 minutes ago. She has shallow breathing, but I've not located a chest injury, her pulse is weak, but evident. She has an obvious but non penetrative injury to the right temple, and is bleeding from the ear and nose on the right side. I moved her to the recovery position and tried to keep her warm. She was very cold when we found her, lips and face white, and I think she was in shock."

"Thank you sir," said the paramedic politely and what is the young lady's name?"

"It's Caitlin" Andrew whispered, "Caitlin Montague."

"Okay now Caitlin, can you hear me? My name's Tony I'm a paramedic and I'm here to help you now, you're going to be fine."

The other paramedic took Andrew by the arm, "It's okay sir, you've done a fantastic job, probably saved her life, but we can take over from here, let us do our job now. We'll let you know what we're doing as soon as we've assessed the situation."

Suddenly there was an ear splitting scream from Charles who could stand it no longer, "Where are Jennifer and Jessica, you've all forgotten them, where are they!" he howled.

Down at Mileoak Katherine and Sandy had long since hacked back and washed off their horses, and were now sitting down to clean their tack and enjoy a cup of coffee.

"What a waste of a day" moaned Sandy, thinking she could've had an extra hour in bed with Mark

"Tell me about it. Bloody Sabs!" agreed Katherine, "You've got to hand it to them though, it was well planned."

"Too well planned if you ask me. There's a mole somewhere, has to be. They took us completely by surprise."

"You could be right, how horrible to think that someone is pretending to be a supporter but is really in cohorts with those bastards."

"Got any ideas who it might be?" asked Sandy "must be someone pretty in the know."

"No, no idea at all, you?"

"No but I'm going to find out." Sandy grimaced, "If it's the last thing I do."

Susie breezed into the tack room, "You all right ladies? Can I leave you to it? Chloe's just asked me to go up to the house and babysit the children. She and John are going out for a bit, they need some peace and quiet to talk apparently, so I'm going up there now. Beebs is in the cottage if you need anything, she's covering from lunchtime."

"No you go ahead Susie, we're fine" said Katherine. When she'd gone, she looked at Sandy, "Christ that sounds ominous, I think John is about to reveal all, it's confession time – poor Chloe, I hope she's okay."

"That bastard, I'll tell you one thing, if he's having an affair, I'll take him to the cleaners for her, and he won't leave with the clothes he stands up in!" spat Sandy.

Oli's heart was pounding - he dashed into the surgery, picked up the stuff he needed and more besides, locked everything up carefully after him and threw the whole lot into his car. He spun out of the car park and floored it up the road towards the Abbey. The gate was already wide open and he could see an ambulance and two police cars with their blue lights flashing at the top of the hill. He slewed the car through the entrance and gave it full throttle up to the top.

As he walked towards the ruins, he was stopped by a uniformed police officer who said he could go no further. Totally frustrated he demanded to be let through and that he was the vet coming to attend to the sick horses and that he was needed urgently. The policeman remained adamant, but after consultation with a colleague, was escorted into the ruins. It was like a scene from a horror movie. The horses were all completely comatose and Alice was craning over them, he hurried over to her.

"Christ, what's been going on here?"

"Thank God you've come Oli," sighed Alice, "It's nasty, I need all the help I can get here!"

"I can see that, where's Andrew?" he asked, "I spoke to him, but he didn't say much, just told me to get here as fast as I could and I brought the stuff over he said he wanted."

"Good, I'm bloody glad you're here, this lot should be coming round soon with any luck. Charles has called Felix and he's on his way up to help. Andrew's with Caitlin, but it's not looking good for her. Charles thought she was dead but luckily Andrew found a faint pulse – but it's a bad head injury, temporal area, I'm thinking subdural or epidural haematoma, but that's only my guess and it's not been confirmed. They're getting the air ambulance, but even if she survives - which is doubtful, who knows what the damage will be."

Oli blanched "Fucking hell, that's unbelievable! She's such a sweet, lovely girl. Do they know what happened?"

"Nope, no idea yet, just dealing with the casualties first, then the questions I think, but Charles' wife and daughter are missing, no-one's any idea where they are, there's no trace of them, and that's a big concern obviously." Alice grimaced, "Come on mate, let's do our bit here eh, try and sort out these poor buggers."

They bent over the horses, Dandy was now struggling awkwardly to his feet, and then toppling over again onto his knees, but the others still hadn't stirred. Oli and Alice leapt out of the way lest he fell on them, and then tried to help him up. Overhead they heard the whirring rotor blades of the helicopter circling round and round looking for a place to land. The great monster hovering lower and lower as it teetered in the sky.

Oli looked up as Andrew beckoned him over, "Oli, I'm going to the hospital with Caitlin. Alice can drive my vehicle back. If they don't respond spontaneously, get in touch with Equine Hospital, in fact do it anyway, so they can be on standby just in case you need them. I'll ring you later."

"Andrew, you look terrible, are you sure you need to go, why not just let the medics do their stuff and stay here?" asked Oli, "You could always ring and find out how she is later on?"

"You don't understand Oli, I do need to go, she's the only thing I care about and she may well die, and she's not going to be on her own!" Andrew snapped, "That's the end of it – okay!"

Chloe and John drove up to the downs in stony silence and he pulled over right at the top in a car park designed for walkers with spectacular views to the sea beyond. The sun was warm through the car windows, even though there was a stiff breeze blowing in from the coast.

"Chloe" John began, "I don't know how to start"

"Just get it over and done with John, I'm tired of all the bloody games - sick of it." Chloe said, trying to keep her voice calm "I've given you all the time you asked for, it's time to be a big boy now and come clean."

"God, Chloe, you're not making this easy for me are you."

"No! Why the fuck should I?" Chloe exploded "I've been patient and stupid for long enough. Pussy footed around you for bloody months whilst you worked out what you wanted to do! Have you given a bloody thought to me and the kids – no!"

"That's not fair - it's for you and the kids that I've been hesitating, to try to do the right thing."

"Well actually I think you're pretty bloody selfish – and whilst you've been doing some thinking so have I! So perhaps I should go first – I don't want to be with you anymore – you're not the man you used to be, you're miserable, self-absorbed, and dull. I think you're a liar and a cheat, and I want you to pack your stuff and go and the sooner the better. The kids and I are better off without you!" Chloe was getting into her stride now "Fuck off with your other bloody woman and don't come back!"

"Chloe, you don't mean that and what are you talking about – what other woman? You've got it all wrong!" John shouted at her exasperated, "There's never been anyone else but you."

"So you say!" said Chloe huffily, "What about your bloody phone. All those secret texts and stuff, you're always late back from work, I never know where you are or what you're doing – you're so bloody secretive."

"Stop, stop!" John implored her, "Look let me explain, I see now, I should have said this ages ago, should have confided in you, but I didn't want to say anything before, because I didn't think I could go through with what I am going to do, and it will affect you, the kids and possibly our life and even our home."

"What are you talking about John?"

"Listen, just let me tell you then! It's my job."

"Really" Chloe said disbelieving him, "like I was born yesterday!"

"For Christ's sake! Okay, my job is fine, safe, doing well, too well, but I hate it. Hate going there every day, have done for years, but I do it for you and the kids, to keep Mileoak. But now, they want me to work overseas, Dubai, it would mean a contract over there for five years, uprooting and taking you and the kids with me, or I go alone."

Chloe gasped, "Why on earth didn't you say this before?"

"Because I didn't want to worry you, I didn't want you to have to be involved in this decision. You would feel you had to go and you love Mileoak and what you do, it's your life, the children's lives. How could I ask you to give that up?" He smiled at her, "and I don't want to go without you all – it's as simple as that."

"What are you going to do then?"

"Well, perhaps it's time for me to make a life change Chloe? That's what the phone calls and texts are about, I've been thinking about starting my own business and working from home. I've got some great ideas, and to be truthful I can't wait to start. It'd be tough and we'd have to make some financial adjustments, but if we pull together we could do it, I know we could." John took her hand and kissed her fingers, "that's if you still want me to stay?"

"Oh John, of course I do, I was just panicking – I thought you had someone else!" Chloe laughed, "I think it's a marvellous idea and of course we can do it, in fact I know it! I want to hear all about it!"

She turned in her seat and kissed him softly on the lips and he returned the kiss, the first real embrace they'd shared in months. They parted and both looked at each other and they started to laugh! "We're a couple of bloody fools, but I wish you'd just told me!" she said contentedly, snuggling into his arms and sighing with relief. Unbeknown to them, high above their heads the rhythmic thudding blades of the air ambulance was whirling in the blustery thermals, struggling on its way to the major trauma unit at the Royal Sussex Hospital.

CHAPTER 65

Jennifer was dimly aware that she couldn't move, she couldn't see or speak either. Her head felt detached from her body and the pain that was shooting through her was so intense she could cry. She was being smothered, struggling to breathe, a cloth was wrapped around the whole of her - like a shroud, and this overwhelming panic was rushing over her. She was going to suffocate, and in her terror she started to thrash and wriggle, rolling and struggling, trying desperately to breathe and free herself.

Suddenly she felt herself being roughly tumbled over and over, being unwrapped like a parcel and the rush of cold air flood onto her face calmed her a little, although she couldn't open her eyes and mouth - they seemed to be taped shut. Her arms had been tied behind her back and she couldn't move them, but felt a rough hand yanking her left elbow out from under her and scissors snip away her new jacket from the wrist, then a sharp pain, and the prick of a hypodermic needle as once again she drifted into blissful oblivion.

Now that Caitlin had been airlifted to hospital the Abbey had become a potential crime scene. The uniformed police had completely sealed off the area with blue and white tape and two officers were interviewing a frustrated Charles, who was becoming increasingly angry that they weren't taking the situation seriously. He told them what had happened that morning, about the abandoned hunting, and the Sabs, and the last time he had seen his family, and they asked if he knew of anyone who might have a grudge against him. He reluctantly told them about Pete and his previous attempt to harm Jennifer, saying he thought it was unlikely to be him, as where would he have got the stuff to dope the horses, and moreover Pete would not have harmed Jessica and Caitlin. He was positive that the Sabs were responsible, it must have happened when the fracas was going on down by the woodland.

The police officers made careful notes, but reminded him of the dangers of speculation and that actually there was no evidence that either Jessica or Jennifer had been harmed and from the looks of the groom and her injuries, she could had fallen off her horse and hit her head, even doped the horses herself. They looked gloomily at the abundance of footprints around the fallen stones, they would need to get a team of specially trained forensic officers to check the area properly, although as a crime scene it was pretty fucked up, but it would have to be done, and get a specialist search team and dogs organised which would all take time.

Whilst they were waiting, they asked Charles to give them the names and contact details of anyone who was hunting that morning who may have seen or heard anything that might help. Charles perked up, yes, there had been lots of people - somebody must have seen something! He went to his car with one of the uniformed officers and painstakingly they started ringing round.

When Charles spoke to Rachael she was obviously shocked and desperate to ask more, but quickly pulled herself together understanding the urgency of his questions and suggested he ring Mike Lister, as he was the only one who had gone back to the gate to wait for the squad car and perhaps might help. She gave him Mike's number and address and he hastily rang off. The copper next to him took over and made the call, explaining carefully her reasons for calling, "Right Sir, someone'll come over and take a statement now, as I expect you'll appreciate the urgency. Thank you." She looked at Charles, "He saw two hooded figures, Sabs, chucking what looked like rolls of carpet into the back of a Landrover and driving off, I'll tell the Guv."

The uniformed chaps looked almost relieved when they heard the constable's report and put in a call to CID, they could definitely hand this little lot over to them.

The police had urged Charles to go home, insisting that nothing could be gained by him staying and it may well be that Jennifer had tried to ring home. They would come round later to see him and they were sure there were people that he had to contact. He also said that he would contact the Family Liaison Officer Co-Ordinator and ask if an officer could be sent along to help him, who was skilled in helping families cope in these situations. Normally Charles would have told them to fuck off, but he realised they were right and he was grateful for the support. He couldn't imagine what he was going to tell Rupert, let alone ring Celia and Jennifer's mother, then there was his own family and worst of all Caitlin's family – it was going to be tough to know what to say.

In London, Jonty and Weasel were on a high, they'd done it!

"Fuck me Jont mate, that was a close run thing, but we pulled it off!"

Jonty sucked the froth off his top lip from his can of lager, "Yeah, we did, a few hairy moments when those bleedin' horses charged past, but we had luck on our side eh!"

Weasel laughed, "I know, I nearly shit my pants!"

"Now, we gotta move quick, and give the filth something to think about. What the fuck's keeping them?" He toyed anxiously with his phone. "They'd better not fuck up!"

"Cool it Jont, they know what they're doing. It's only been a couple of hours."

Jonty tapped the edge of his nose, "it's all about the timing" he growled.

DS Neil Berry who was on call, was not thrilled at being interrupted yet again that weekend and apologised to his long suffering wife and headed back to work. Neil was an astute officer and met his colleague DC Dianne Scott at the scene, the only thing that could be said was that at least it wasn't raining. The uniformed boys had gone so far, and the SOCOs had arrived a few minutes before them, but the crime scene was carnage and to say compromised was a fucking understatement! He'd never seen so many hoof and footprints and to top it all two of the horses were now on their feet and being walked slowly all over the shop and the other was still sparko on the ground! There was a stink in the air too, which he couldn't immediately identify either. The search boys would take longer to arrive, but the dog unit was here, although not having much luck by the looks of things with the dogs running around aimlessly to the frustration of their handlers. He had rung for the helicopter to be scrambled with its heat seeking imagery equipment to scour the area, but being a warm Saturday afternoon, he did not hold out much hope. There would be loads of walkers out and anyway whatever had gone on here happened a good few hours ago now and it was unlikely to be of any value unless the missing pair were lying unconscious in a field somewhere. The only immediate and possibly valuable piece of information was this Mike Lister who'd seen some suspicious activity going on. He went off with his DC to get a statement and then he'd come back here later to see how they were getting on, hopefully this was all just a storm in the old teacup and the woman and the kid would turn up at home any minute.

Word spread round the village like a rampant virus that afternoon, especially once the police had started asking questions and Mike Lister's story became common knowledge. Speculation as to what had happened was rife, but the general consensus was that the Sabs were responsible. In the Fox, feelings were running high and everyone was lamenting about what a lovely girl Caitlin had been, it was as though she was already dead. Lucy who was sitting with Tom and Oli felt really uncomfortable. She had sadistically enjoyed the debacle at the hunt this morning and seeing all those snotty beggars having been taken down a peg or two, but abduction and the attack on Caitlin that was a different thing altogether. If they ever found out it had been down to her – God, it didn't bear fucking even thinking about. She sat quietly in the corner feeling paranoid.

Probably the last person to know was Chloe. She and John got home around two, not wanting to leave the kids for too long and obliviously sauntered into the kitchen like love's young dream to find Susie agog with the news. Chloe was absolutely stunned and sat down heavily on a chair, her head in her hands hardly able to believe it. She immediately picked up the phone to ring Charles, but the line was engaged.

"I've got to go over there, he'll be in a dreadful state – he can always tell me to go, but at least I know I've offered."

"I'll come with you Chloe" John offered, "Susie, can you hold the fort here?"

"Of course – take as long as you need, I just hope that when you get there they've been found. Oh God though, if anything happens about Caitlin - you promise to ring me."

"Definitely, and thanks Susie, I really appreciate it. When I know more I promise I'll ring you - okay?"

Chloe and John drove straight over to Nantes, they parked round by the garages and rang the back door bell. Mrs Fuller opened the door to them, her eyes red with crying, "Oh Chloe my duck, thank goodness you've come, Mr Charles is in a right state – we're in the kitchen. They're not back yet."

When Chloe saw Charles she couldn't believe it, he must have aged ten years; she went over to him and put her hand on his shoulder, "We came as soon as we heard Charles, I hope you don't think we're intruding."

Charles squeezed her hand, "No, I'm really glad you came, thanks so much, both of you. I just can't believe it. Oh Chloe where can they be? And Caitlin, poor Caitlin, I thought she was dead, but Andrew saved her I think. He's gone off in the air ambulance with her, but she was unconscious and probably has brain damage."

"Oh Charles, how awful – I don't know what to say" stammered Chloe - what could she say?

Charles started to talk, he muttered on and on, almost as though he were talking to himself. Chloe and John just sat there listening to him. The kitchen door opened and a large woman came in with

Rupert who was looking ashen, his little face pinched and drawn.

"Hello Rupert" said Chloe, "We've come over to keep you company for a while."

"Thank you" he whispered, "Has Daddy told you about Jennifer and Jessica?"

"Yes darling he has, but the police will be doing all they can to find them."

"Mummy is so angry with Daddy" he said, his voice quavering, "she said it's all Jennifer's fault - it isn't you know! She's coming over now to take me back, but I don't want to go, I want to be here." He started to cry.

Chloe went over to him, bending down and looking at him seriously, "No, of course it isn't anyone's fault Rupert, Mummy's just upset that's all, and worried of course. We all say things when we get upset."

"Yes we do" said the lady kindly, "I'm Sandra by the way" she offered her hand to Chloe, "I'm a Family Liaison Officer"

"Hello, we're Chloe and John - friends and neighbours" said John, "is there anything that you need us to do?"

"Well, I think perhaps we need to get this young man sorted out with his mother, and I'm going to try and arrange for someone to pick up Jennifer's mum to be brought down from London – I think it'd be best for her to be here under the circumstances until we have any news."

Charles interrupted, "I know that Jennifer 'd want Ivy to be looked after here and not be kept in the dark, but I just don't want to leave Nantes at the moment, just in case they come back – you know."

"I can fetch her" offered John, "that's no problem."

"Oh God John – would you?" begged Charles, "I'd be so grateful."

"No problem at all mate, I can go now if you like?"

"Thank you so much - look take my car," he tossed John the keys, "the address is programmed on the Sat Nav. That's such a relief." He slumped back in his chair.

"I'll ring and let her know" offered Sandra.

"You go now then John, I'll finish up your horses Charles, as I don't expect they were done when you got back, and I'll get in touch with Felix and find out what's happened to the others" said Chloe, "that'll be something that I can do to help."

John and Chloe made their way back outside, looking up at the Granary where only a few hours ago Caitlin had been happily getting ready for hunting.

"What a fucking mess" said Chloe, "drive safely darling for Christ's sake"

So far the SOCOs had come up with nothing much, although they were still working at the scene, but it had been hugely contaminated by the number of people that had trampled all over the place. Although of course, in the scheme of things that couldn't have been helped, but it was still exasperating. The search dogs had been hampered too, these fucking antis knew a thing or too when it came to polluting a scent and the trouble was the place was open to the public and all sorts of people could have been there over the last few days. The police helicopter had been circling around for a while now but had found nothing.

The only thing that had been of value was the statement that had been taken from Mike Lister who had confirmed seeing two hooded people, dressed in camouflage gear, acting strangely. He described them as heaving two bundles - looking like rolled up carpet, which could have been the missing woman and child, into the back of an old Landrover and hot footing it down the road heading towards Cuckfield. This happened whilst their mates carried on with the disruption by the woodland and before the arrival of the squad car. It wasn't sounding good, and as Neil headed back to Haywards Heath HQ he thought he ought to give his chief a ring to bring him up to speed.

The arrival of Celia at Nantes was heard by Chloe long before she saw her storming into the house. She had hurtled down the drive like a maniac, spraying gravel all over the place as she swerved to a halt in front of the house. Chloe watched her from the shrubbery as she was walking back from the stables having sorted the horses out, thinking poor Charles, that was all he needed. She could hear Celia's hysterical screaming from where she was and pondered whether or not she should go back to the stables and leave them to it, or go in and try to calm Celia down. She thought back to Rupert's anxious little face and decided for his sake, if no-one else's, she should try and get Celia to pull herself together a bit.

She tiptoed in through the back door and up to the kitchen where Mrs Fuller had taken refuge.

"Lord above, she's in a right temper, shouting and screaming in there Chloe, I don't think that'll help." Freda whimpered, "That poor little lamb Rupert, it's not good for him either."

"Where are they?" asked Chloe, "Is Sandra there?"

"Yes, but Celia's trying to chuck her out, and she went mad to find us all in the kitchen!"

"God she's such a snob!" chided Chloe, "Okay, I'll go in and see if I can smooth anything over."

Celia was holding court in the drawing room, stalking up and down, waving her arms in the air, "This is your fault Charles, that common little slut you married, you might have known she couldn't be trusted to look after Jessica! Now this has happened, you aren't fit to be a father!" she yelled.

"Hello Celia." Chloe said tentatively looking at the others who were looking aghast at Celia's ranting and raving.

"What are you doing here?" Celia demanded, glaring at Chloe, "Come to gloat!"

"Celia, don't be so ridiculous." said Charles wearily, "Chloe's been helping me, everyone has, it's you who's making a scene and behaving badly."

"I want her out of my house, and this woman too" shouted Celia pointing at Sandra, "people like us don't wash our dirty linen in public to the likes of them."

"That's enough, I've had enough!" Charles stood up, towering above her, "This isn't your house Celia, it's mine and Jennifer's. Chloe is welcome here, as is Sandra, it's you who isn't. You're bullish behaviour is frankly disturbing and uncalled for, and bordering on the deranged. Perhaps you need to be thinking about our children for once instead of yourself and what people might think, because to be honest I don't care. All I want is for my wife to come home through that door with my daughter, and for you to stop shouting and to comfort our son who is thoroughly traumatised by all this!"

"How dare you speak to me like that Charles!" Celia said flabbergasted, "I am thinking of Rupert."

"Well if that's true, stop screaming like a fish wife and calm down then" Charles said coldly, "behave yourself and stop acting like a brat and consider his feelings rather than your own for once."

Sandra had been watching the dynamics between the couple with interest, she was of course here to support the family but above all she was a police officer and any intelligence she garnered was passed to the investigating officer. It was a sad fact that often harsh secrets came out and Charles' ex-wife certainly had an axe to grind with his current one.

This heated display was interrupted by the beep beep of a message on Charles' mobile, he wrenched it out of his pocket and saw it was from Jennifer! He gasped in relief and quickly opened it, but his smiling face froze to abject horror when he saw what it was.

"Oh my God!" he whispered, "oh my God!"

Sandra went over and took the phone from him. He had been sent a photograph. It was a full length picture of a woman and a little girl, they were tied to chairs, heads hanging limply to one side at an odd angle - obviously drugged. Their mouths and eyes taped closed with silver duct tape, both were dirty and dishevelled and wearing tweed jackets and beige breeches, and around the woman's neck was a printed sign *"How much are we worth?"*

CHAPTER 66

Andrew was sitting in the Critical Care Unit at the Royal Sussex Hospital, gazing at the still figure of Caitlin who looked so tiny and frail in the bed. He was holding her hand and talking to her, he didn't know if she could hear him but that didn't matter, he carried on anyway.

It had been a nightmare journey in the helicopter, being bucketed about against the wind as they hovered into Brighton. He'd really had to insist that they let him come – and in the end they'd reluctantly agreed, when he said he was her partner and she had no other relatives over here, and as she was unconscious it was important that someone be there for her.

The care had been first rate though and you had it hand it to these guys, their team work was exemplary, but there was no oddsing it, Caitlin was in a serious way, and it was very much touch and go. Her GCS score was only three, which meant that she was deeply unconscious. The wound to her head had been cleaned and although it was nasty it did not seem to be penetrating, but the worry was a large bruise which had formed behind her ear. A Consultant Neurosurgeon had taken him to one side explaining that the next step was to do an urgent CT scan, to see if there was any fracture and bleeding going on in the brain, but that he had to warn Andrew that the bruise was indicative that there may well be and to be prepared that immediate surgery might well be indicated.

Although the surgeon had said that this was urgent, they seemed to have been waiting for ages, but in reality he knew it was only a short while really. He kept thinking of all those sunny days they had been together in High Ridge Woods and wondered why he had been such a fool not to have told Julia to sling her hook ages before. Caitlin meant the world to him and without her – well - he didn't want to imagine his life if anything happened to her. He'd give anything to hear her voice. God he just hoped that he could have one more chance to show her how much he loved her.

The photograph had changed everything. When Neil received the call from the FLO he'd gotten on to his boss straight away, who had contacted the on call SIO for the Major Crimes Team, and things had snowballed from there.

An incident room had been set up pro temps at Haywards Heath and the SIO had brought with him his own outside enquiry team which he'd selected himself, consisting of a DI, a DS and four DCs, and he included Neil and Dianne and their own divisional DI, Raymond Burns. The SIO, was a man named Jim Farrell and he'd called a briefing after acquainting himself with what had happened and was now addressing them all. He was a burly bloke, known to his subordinates as Diamond Jim, not only because of his rise up the promotional ladder from a lowly rank, or because of his large belly but for the large gold ring with the flashy diamond he wore on his little pinky.

He was abrupt and to the point.

"Right, this is the first briefing of Operation Icarus, the time is two thirty pm on Saturday 4th September 2012. "You've all read your briefing notes I assume?" he looked around at the assembled grim faces. "Now the phone that sent the photograph to Mr Parker-Smythe was his wife's, and we need to get a fast triangulation as where that phone was when it sent the message, and if we can - where that phone is now. Peter, get on to that straight away."

He paused consulting his notes, "Linda, get hold of all the animal rights organisations and known hunt saboteurs groups and see if you can find out which one of them organised the disruption today. Ken, I want you to get some statements from the folk who were out hunting this morning and see if anyone else noticed anything untoward, like strange vehicles, that sort of thing – it doesn't matter how trivial it seems. Ray perhaps you and Neil can give Ken some support with that, as it might be a long task and local knowledge will be good here – go to the village shop, the pub that sort of thing."

He stopped for a moment watching them all taking notes, and

took a sip of his coffee. "Dianne can you get an update on the injured girl's condition, and on those horses too. Find out if the vets know exactly what they were doped with. Terry and I," he indicated to his DI, "will be going to see Mr Parker-Smythe and the family. I've been in touch with National Specialist Law Enforcement Centre, who'll be sending down some officers tomorrow who are trained in the management of kidnap and extortion and I don't want to issue any press statements till I've spoken to them. One more thing, there'll be no time off until further notice." He stood up "See you all tomorrow morning six thirty sharp." He nodded in dismissal.

John struggled up to London in the Saturday traffic, his mind bursting with the traumas of the afternoon. His revelations to Chloe had been completely overshadowed by the simply awful news about Jennifer and Jessica's disappearance. He tried to imagine how he would feel if it'd been Chloe and Lily. The thought was inconceivable, it just went to show that you could have all the money in the world but it didn't always help life run smoothly. He thought about the life ahead for him and for Chloe, it would be tough he had no doubt about that, but Chloe was a grafter and he knew they'd survive somehow.

He indicated right, listening carefully to the Sat Nav. God he was dreading this journey back with Ivy, he didn't even really know her, only met her the once briefly when Jen had come up with her a few weeks ago. What could he say to her on the long journey home?

Unbeknown to John, not ten miles away as the crow flew, Jonty had just forwarded, on Jennifer's phone the photo of her and the kid to Charlie boy's mobile, which Nora had sent on a pay as you go mobile. He imagined the shock on the bloke's face when he opened the message, it must've been priceless! It was a great idea, the pay as you go was untraceable and Nora wouldn't use that phone again, but he knew that the old bill would be able to trace that Jennifer's phone was somewhere in London, and the next photo he sent from it would be from the same area but not quite the same street! The trace could pinpoint almost to the exact road where the phone was but he wasn't going to fall into that trap – he could lead them a right old dance! But as long as it was in London, they would not be looking for her in Fittlebury. He switched it off now in satisfaction and made his way back towards the East End.

DCI Jim Farrell knocked on the front door at Nantes, with his DI Terry Bates beside him, and they didn't have to wait for long before the huge door was opened almost immediately by a tall, imperious man, and behind him a couple of women. They flashed their warrant cards and introduced themselves and the man's face fell when he told them there were no further developments.

They trooped into the drawing room and sat down, Jim taking in every opulent detail of the furnishings and honing in to the crackling tension, caused not least by the situation but by the scowling, confrontational woman who immediately demanded what rank he was, and what steps he had taken so far. Jim had dealt with women like her many times before, patiently giving her his rank and explaining that he headed up the MCT which had been called in, but then went on to address the room as a whole, saying that they would talk to them all individually and perhaps he and Charles could go somewhere more private. The woman immediately started kicking up a rumpus, which he quelled sharply, saying that she would have her opportunity to make her complaints later, and to let him get on with his job and that his colleague would speak to her. Poor old Terry he thought grimly, still that was the privilege of rank.

As the gloaming set in, and the night air became colder, Pete stirred in the barn, it was almost time for him to go out on his nocturnal foray. As the weeks had gone by, he didn't mutter out loud so much, but had conversations in his head now, in fact he behaved more and more like a night creature, his senses tuned acutely to the merest noise and his eyes now hated the bright light of the sun. For the huge man he was, he moved surprisingly quietly, light on his feet and his reactions were keen and sharpened to sudden movements.

Like a foraging rat, he rummaged in the increasing darkness in one of the Tupperware boxes which now contained bits and pieces of food he had bought in the garage, and anything edible he'd retrieved from bins. He chewed mechanically, trying to avoid getting any debris in his beard which was now quite long, but wasn't as itchy as it had been, but he hated it nonetheless, it made him feel unclean and it was matted, like his hair. He took a sip of water from a plastic bottle, and tipping his head back finished it in one gulp. Tonight, he must replenish his supplies.

Ivy Bainbridge sat upright in the passenger seat beside John as they drove back towards Sussex. John marvelled at her, his first impression when he had met her before was of a sweet thing, downtrodden and a bit pathetic, but not so now. She was angry, very angry, and feisty with it. Any thought that Jennifer had just simply walked off with Jessica and was lost she had clearly dismissed, claiming that they simply didn't know her Jen, if that was what they thought! No, she was adamant something had happened, and she was damned if she would sit back and do nothing! John admired her spirit and placated her, but privately thought there was little she could do herself, no matter what had happened. His job was to get her back to Nantes and to Charles, and hopefully there would be more news when they arrived. He had to admit too, that he'd been pretty surprised when he saw the part of London that Jennifer had come from, it was rough to say the least, and he wasn't a snob either. Jennifer's sister Susan had been a revelation, you wouldn't have thought they could possibly have been related, but that both her sister and her mother cared very deeply about Jennifer was not in question. They were both anxious to know exactly what had happened – but he was woefully unable to give them much information, but Ivy had promised Susan that she would ring her directly she got down to Nantes to let her know more news. Susan's last remark to her mother, as they put her case in the car was that she would get Wayne to put the word out and see what was going down, and not to worry, if anything was, he would hear about it. John felt as though he was on the set of some sort of TV drama, and was glad when they were underway.

They crossed the Queen Elizabeth II Bridge over the Thames and John slid down the window and chucked in money to the automatic booth at the Dartford Toll, the gates were raised and he accelerated out, converging into the traffic going southwards. He felt more comfortable driving now, it was a pretty straight motorway run back, and he sat back in his seat, feeling less tense. It was all well and good taking Charles' car, but it was a bit stressful driving it in London. He cruised down the road, careful not to exceed the speed limit, and glanced at Ivy, her face was set and rigid as she stared ahead of her.

"Do you want the radio on?" he asked, trying to make conversation.

"No I don't" she snapped back, then almost immediately added "look I'm sorry lad that was rude of me, but I'm worried sick."

"Of course you are, we all are. I'm sure it'll be okay though Ivy, there must be a rational explanation."

"Look lad, coming from where I do, you always think the worst, because there're some right villains in this world. Charles is a rich bloke, lifting his wife and kid would be easy picking to some, and easy to do, so I don't do rational often, because there's not been much rational in my world."

"Well, let's hope that it's not that Ivy for everyone's sakes."

After that John shut up, he didn't want to think about what Ivy had said, she couldn't possibly be right, could she?

Lucy was worried shitless. That afternoon in the pub had been the worst she'd ever spent. She couldn't wait to leave and had made Tom take her home saying she felt sick. She had gone straight upstairs to her room, and sat on her bed. Supposing, just supposing Jonty had been involved? She'd told him all about the meet, where they'd be going, and she'd seen his Landrover parked in the lane, so she knew he'd been there. It'd been gone when they had abandoned the hunt, but she hadn't thought anything about it at the time, but she was thinking about it now. The other Sabs had not left till after the hunt supporters, so why had his vehicle gone before? Should she contact him and ask him what he was up to, or should she just leave it? She took out her phone, turning it over in her hands, and then laid it down. What could she say, and if he was implicated did she want to know? What would she do then - she should go to the police, but that would mean telling about her involvement, and there was no fucking way she was going to do that. She could ask him she supposed and see what he said, and then she could tip the police off anonymously? No, it was just best not to know and not to say anything, she'd said enough. She'd wait to see if he contacted her and then she would she think about it again.

The surgeon was making his way back towards Andrew and he could see from his face that it wasn't good news. Caitlin had gone in for the CT scan and had not come back. Andrew was waiting in the relatives' room, and was sitting with the umpteenth cup of coffee which once again he'd let grow cold. Andrew stood up as he approached, the man bade him sit down and pulled over a chair for himself.

"Andrew" he began, "I'm afraid, there's no easy way to say this, but the scan has shown that Caitlin has an intracranial bleed, an epidural haematoma. This type of bleed is quick and is usually from the arteries, causing the brain to move and lose blood supply or be crushed against the skull. The larger the haematoma the more damage they cause. They can be life threatening and can reach their peak size within about six to eight hours of the trauma. Often the patient can appear to be fine after the accident and then lapse into coma, but the fact that Caitlin has been unconscious since she was found is a worry. So you can see that I need to operate immediately if we are to save her, so we are preparing her for surgery now."

Andrew put his head in his hands, "My God" he muttered "I know this is hard for you to say, but what are her chances?"

"Well, as I said, she has been unconscious for a while now which is not a good sign and her GCS score is only 3, but the sooner I can reduce the pressure and remove the haematoma the better the prognosis. At the moment she probably has a 50/50 chance of pulling through the operation but as to making any sort of normal recovery I can't say; but I may be able to tell you more a day or two after the surgery, but I'll do my best – okay?" he stood up, shook Andrew's hand and made a hasty departure.

Andrew stayed where he was, hardly able to believe what he had just been told, how he was going to get through the next few hours he had no idea.

Jim Farrell came back into the drawing room from where he and Charles had been closeted in his study. Charles look drained and sat down wearily. Chloe looked up expectantly, she'd been sitting with Rupert her - arm around his shoulders. Celia was no-where to be seen. Sandra stood up as they came in, and Jim waved at her to sit down again and he pulled out a chair for himself.

"Now" he said speaking directly to Chloe, "It's Mrs Coombe I gather, could I just have a brief word with you please, as Mr Parker-Smythe tells me you are a friend and a neighbour."

"Yes, that's true" replied Chloe, "but I wasn't out hunting today, so I don't see how I can help?"

"Everyone who lives locally will be interviewed Mrs Coombe, so whilst you're here, we might as well ask you some questions now, if you don't mind?"

"No, of course not, ask away, I'll do anything that I can to help."

Jim took out his notebook, and once he had confirmed Chloe's name and address asked "We have had a statement from a Mr Lister saying that he saw two people, he thinks men, dressed as saboteurs, bundling what he described as rolls of carpet, into the back of an old Landrover parked in the lane by the Abbey during the hunting yesterday. I know you weren't out then, but have you seen any such vehicle loitering around, out of place in Fittlebury or the area recently. It may not have been over the last few days even, but think back over the last few weeks."

Chloe grimaced, "Well Landrovers are pretty common in these rural areas to be honest, can you give me any idea what type of vehicle, you say it was old, what do you mean – soft top, long wheel base?"

Jim consulted his notes, "A long wheel base with long, home-made, elongated blacked out back windows apparently, just described as an old type."

Chloe exclaimed excitedly, "Well, I did see one of those – they are quite unusual, actually I saw it twice, but it was weeks ago! I noticed it because, the first time I saw it I was waiting for the school bus to arrive and the bloke who was driving it was going along the lane like a bloody nutter! Oh sorry, forgive the French!"

Jim was immediately interested and sat on the edge of his chair, "Can you tell me anymore Mrs Coombe? Did you see the driver?"

Chloe thought back, she could remember the incident clearly, it had been just before the spring half term and the weather had been very hot. She shut her eyes momentarily and tried to picture what she had seen. "Yes, I remember very well as it happens. It was a man driving, young with a shaved head, which I thought was odd at the time, as not many young people round here have them. I remember thinking he was driving way too fast, and that I didn't know him – which in itself was odd, because in this village everyone knows everyone else. He had a girl with him."

"You said you'd seen the Landrover again, when was that Mrs Coombe?"

"Yes I did see it again. Now hold on, I must get this right. I was with Susie and Beebs, they're my grooms and we were going into Horsham to buy dresses, as Charles and Jennifer were having a party – that must have been … well I suppose about two weeks later, the party was in June wasn't it Charles?"

Charles nodded eagerly, "yes it was, I can get you the exact date from my diary!"

"Well hold on a moment sir" said Jim, "what happened Mrs Coombe?"

"As I said we were going into Horsham in my Discovery, it was about two o'clock I think, and all round the one way system I was being tailgated, this bloody Landrover was right up my bum , even at the lights, it practically jumped them to keep up with me. We parked in Piries Place, which is about the only car park in Horsham that takes high vehicles, but it was definitely the same Landrover that I'd seen before, because I remember thinking that at the time!"

"Well that's very helpful Mrs Coombe, thank you."

"Wait, I haven't finished, later in the charity shop, I saw the driver again, it was definitely the same man, and he was with a girl."

"Are you sure Mrs Coombe? Could you identify the man?" asked Jim "or the girl?"

"I could try" said Chloe nervously.

Jim sat back in his chair and closed his notebook, looking at his watch, it was getting on for six, "Could you come to Haywards Heath Police Station tomorrow morning at ...say eight thirty? We've set up an Incident Room there for the time being, and one of my officers will go through this again with you and we'll try and to get together a description of the man and woman."

"Yes, of course I will, if you think that it might be of some use."

"Every little scrap of information is of use Mrs Coombe" said Jim his tone deadly serious.

CHAPTER 67

The night air was cold and Pete wrapped his overcoat around him and tied it with bailer twine, slipping quietly out through the barn door. There was no moon tonight but the sky was cloudless and the stars were bright, but it didn't matter to him, the darkness was his friend. Silently he slipped alongside the fields keeping to the grass headland. He had planned to go up behind the mill and away towards Priors Cross tonight and see what he could find in that direction. The Mill stood majestically etched against the back drop of the woods, alongside it the cottage with the ramshackle lean to outhouses and he edged his way around the back of them heading toward the shelter of the trees.

The soft hoot of a barn owl made him pause for a moment and he heard the swish of its wings as it passed quite close by making its way across the field searching for mice. He smiled to himself – just another night friend out hunting. He tightened the twine around his coat and crept on circling wide of the buildings and keeping to the shadows. He stopped abruptly again, he could hear voices, but they were not the normal voices, not his friends - the ones that he heard in his head. He listened hard again, sinking to his knees and cocking his head to one side like an animal. There they were again - more definite this time, he was quite certain now. Pete's heart started to pound and he could feel a pulse beating in his head, a small trickle of urine ran down his leg. He crawled like a dog towards the sound, sniffing the air, his senses totally alert and ready to run. Someone was talking and they were in the cottage. He crept up to the back kitchen window and crouched underneath it, listening. A very faint glow was creeping out from the grimy panes and warily he pulled himself up until he could peep through. Someone had put a piece of cardboard roughly across the window from inside, but there was a tiny crack where it did not quite fit - he squinted, adjusting his eyes to peer into the room.

A wiry woman dressed in black was pacing back and forth, she had tattoos on her arms, and piercings on her lips and eyebrow, with jet black hair and was smoking. She was talking to an unseen person on the other side of the room. Every now and then though, he could catch a glimpse of someone else too, who seemed to be fast asleep on a chair. He tried desperately to see the person, but the woman kept walking backwards and forwards obscuring his view. This woman was angry, she was having a hard job to stop herself from shouting that much was evident, and then in her rage, she turned to the person on the chair and stubbed her cigarette out on their leg. The person on the chair jerked a little but did not move or scream, and it was then that Pete saw that they were tied up and had something over their mouth. The woman walked back again, so that once more he couldn't see. It was very frustrating, as he craned his neck watching the woman ranting and raving, and then just as suddenly she left the room and he had a full view of the captive on the chair, and he realised with a feeling of enormous satisfaction that it was the person he hated most of all in the world – Jennifer - the bitch that had ruined his life! The voices had told him that she would be dealt with, and that he must trust them, and here she was! He knew he must not interfere. He slid back down the wall smiling to himself, thanking the voices for delivering Jennifer to her fate, and knew that before long he would be able to go home to Nantes - but for now he would continue on his nightly errand into Priors Cross.

It had been hours since the surgeon had left Andrew feeling helpless in the relatives' room. He felt shrunken, defeated and useless. What would his life be without Caitlin, how could he have procrastinated all this time? Images of Caitlin tumbled around in his head - of happy times together, and anger too for all the precious time he'd wasted whilst he hesitated about making a decision. It wasn't as though he was in the least bit uncertain about their future, but he wanted to make sure that the plans for the Old Mill were underway before he told Julia. Well he would make a decision now. He went outside and spoke to one of the staff at the nurses' station, saying he needed some air and would be back in an hour. They looked sympathetically at the exhausted handsome man, his eyes dull with worry and agreed this would be a good idea and said that Caitlin would be gone for a good while yet.

He wandered outside and sat on a low wall watching the world go by, the plethora of people hurrying past, leading their busy lives, having no idea that his was hanging on a precipice edge. He picked up his phone and took a deep breath and rang Julia, it was time to come clean. Frustratingly but unsurprisingly it had gone to voice mail. He felt totally deflated - there was no way he could leave what he wanted to say on a message. He picked up the phone again and rang Oli, who picked up straight away and reassuringly reported the horses had all come round spontaneously as Andrew had predicted they would, but that Jennifer and Jessica were still missing, and it now seemed that they may well have been abducted and told him about what Mike Lister had seen earlier. Andrew tried to tell him about Caitlin but found himself breaking down. Oli didn't know what to say. Andrew ended the call abruptly, saying he would get back to him. He tried Julia again, but still she didn't pick up.

He returned to the relatives' room, nodding to the staff as he came back, and sat a crumpled heap in the vinyl armchair trying to keep himself together, but it was no good, he'd never felt so alone. The hands of the electric clock silently moved around the hours as he waited, and he heard the tap of footsteps coming down the corridor. The door opened and he looked up, his eyes desperate and afraid but to his amazement it was Oli standing in the doorway.

"Thought, I'd better come down and give you a bit of moral support mate, sounded like you needed it. Alice is holding the fort." He came over and put his hand on Andrew's shoulder, "You okay?"

Andrew stood up and put his arms around Oli, "Thanks buddy, I'm a bit fragile y' know" he said bleakly, "Caitlin, I …."

"How long you been together then?" asked Oli, "I never guessed, not once."

"Oh God, I'm so sorry, I've been so fucking stupid. I just wanted to wait for the right time, y' know with Julia and all, but in the scheme of things, what did it bloody matter. Nothing matters now. We've been together for months, started one night when I went out on a late night colic at Nantes. We spent all night out in the stables with one of the horses, we were just talking, but the chemistry was just sparking – right from that night; went out for the odd drink, texting, flirting, you know and it just went on from there."

"She's a lovely girl Andrew, you make a lovely couple" said Oli genuinely, "much better for you than Julia."

"Julia – Oh God. Don't remind me, she doesn't know of course, although I've tried to ring her tonight, but she never picks up. She'll be shocked, good old dependable Andrew, but I don't care anymore, it's always been her that's been the one to play around, and Christ knows there's been enough of that, but whatever happens to Caitlin, I'm not living this bloody lie any longer."

"What have the surgeons said about Caitlin?" asked Oli, "How long has she been in theatre now?"

Andrew glanced at his watch, "Over five hours now, Christ, I'll go bloody mad!"

"What did they say though Andrew?"

Andrew sighed, and told Oli exactly what the consultant had said, and put his head in his hands again. Oli didn't know what to say – it was in the lap of the gods, and all they could do was wait and pray.

The dawn had just broken as the members of the MCT were assembling in the incident room clutching paper cups of coffee and yawning. They settled down, taking out their notebooks, and DCI Farrell looked around him waiting for their attention.

"This is the second briefing of Operation Icarus, the time is six thirty am on Sunday 5th September 2012. Right. Most important, Peter do we have any information as to where that phone was when the photo message was sent yesterday?"

Peter Southern looked up, "Yes, the tech boys have made a triangulation point of the phone and have pinpointed it to Walthamstow, more precisely Greville Road, in E17. The phone has now been turned off, so no further info there."

"Okay, so the message was sent from that area, but of course that doesn't prove that's where the woman and child are being held. However, the fact that this Mike Lister saw them being bundled into the back of the Landrover which was being driven off in the Cuckfield direction does indicate that they are no longer in the local area. Cuckfield is close to the A23/M23 which does have good access to London. One thing that does interest me, Landrovers use a lot of petrol or diesel, whoever did this would've made sure that this vehicle was full of gas, probably filling up just before they arrived at the job to be on the safe side. Assuming that they came from the same direction they left – that is the Cuckfield direction - Peter, can you check all the petrol stations along that route – say the A23 up to the Pease Pottage services on the CCTV and see if anything comes up. We know it would have been early that morning, so set the parameters from say – five am to six thirty am."

"Got it guv." Said Peter, scribbling in his notebook.

"Linda, what news on the animal rights lot?"

A small blonde woman took the floor, she was pretty and animated, pushing her designer specs down from the top of her head onto her pert nose, "Well I contacted as many as I could and nobody knows much about what happened yesterday, not any of the local bunch anyway. I've got in touch with some colleagues in the Met and they are getting back to me, as they've some groups that operate up there, more into radical action and hard line. I've got a few more leads to chase up today."

"Well keep on it, although I expect that today we'll get another message and then we'll know more about who we're dealing with" sighed Jim resignedly. "Okay Ken, what news on the local statements?"

"Well we've done pretty well there guv. The pub in the village - the Fox was full of people willing to offer up opinions. General consensus was that this was a well-planned disruption, normal anti-hunting Sabs apparently go to the meet, kick up a bit of a rumpus, follow the riders down the road, shouting and screaming that sort of caper, make themselves pretty obvious and unpleasant right from the outset. This time though, no-one saw sight or sound of them till they ran out from the woods and the hunting had actually started, and then it was planned like a military operation. Folk seem to think there was a mole, too much insider information, knew exactly where the hunt was going to be going apparently. Two interesting things though, we took a couple of preliminary statements which seem promising. One from the local farrier who swears he's seen this Landrover before - several times and also noticed it in the lane yesterday, he's coming in this morning to give a full statement. The other from the landlord of the pub, a retired copper – who said he'd had an odd young couple in, back in the summer, driving a similar vehicle. He's coming in too. "

Ray added, "There's also an interesting addition, the woman who runs the village shop – a Mrs Gupta told me that some time ago, before the summer holidays, she had a visit from some suspicious looking characters who were looking for Nantes Cottage – they said they had a friend that lived there. She said they were odd looking, not from round here, and she was suspicious and watched them leave and they were driving a Landrover with blacked out windows. This lady is not well though guv, so we need to take a bit of care with her."

"Now that is interesting," said Jim and he went on to tell them what Chloe had said, "She'll be coming in at eight thirty, so can one of you take a statement from each of them. See if you can get a proper description, it might be this lot could work together on that and we could get a pretty good photo fit. Dianne, what've you got for us?"

Dianne Scott flushed, it was the first time that she'd worked with a team like this, although her part so far had been minimal. "The report on the injured girl is not good. It has been confirmed that she had an epidural haematoma and had a long operation last night. She is in intensive care, and the next few days will critical. The horses have all recovered and it has been confirmed that they were doped with a cocktail of drugs – Ketamine and Valium."

"If this girl dies, it may be that murder, rather than attempted murder is added to the kidnapping charges" Jim said ominously, "these are dangerous bastards. This was well planned, and by the looks of things well in advance too. Ketamine is an easy drug to get on the street, could be our boys are into drugs, if we can get a photo fit set up from the descriptions from the witnesses, we could try and match anything up to know drug villains as well as Sabs. So these are priorities. Dianne, you're a local lass, I want you to go over to the village shop and try and persuade this Mrs Gupta to come over this morning to work with the others to get a description sorted, and of the woman too, but be gentle with the old girl."

"Right boss" said Dianne, pleased to have been given a special job.

"Once we've got these photo fits, I want a couple of you over to the village – see if anyone else saw these two hanging around in the last few days or so. Sandra, how are the family bearing up, anything you need to report to us from that angle?" demanded Jim.

Sandra gave an account of the home situation. "The ex-wife is a real piece of work, a right snob, hates the new wife with a passion. The boy is a sweetie and definitely didn't want to go back home with his mother at all and I can't say I blame him – you saw her Gov! I spoke at length to the housekeeper who says that Jennifer, is a really nice woman and they all like her, and Mrs Coombe confirmed this. They also said the husband doted on his wife and they were very good together and there were no apparent problems between them."

Jim thanked her, but said to keep her eyes open, and not to forget that statistically crimes were committed by people known to the victims and said she should get back over to Nantes and spend the day at the house, adding to the others, "Okay, later today the negotiators will be here, and we have a waiting game, but that doesn't mean we sit on our laurels. Terry, get in touch with the Press Office and get them to prepare a statement. Next briefing four pm this afternoon. Any developments ring me immediately and be prepared to be back here at a moment's notice."

The atmosphere at Nantes was dreadful, as grey as the day outside. Charles had not gone to bed, he sat in the drawing room not able to move from his chair, Ivy had sat with him, and although they'd hardly spoken both had been grateful the other had been there. Celia had finally gone home with poor little Rupert who hadn't wanted to go, but had been gently persuaded that it was probably the best place for him to be at the moment. Before she had left though, Celia had been rude beyond belief to Ivy. Charles had been staggered, as had everyone else, but Ivy simply ignored her completely, leaving Celia mouthing her insults to herself.

Later though just before she left, as Celia had been coming out of the cloakroom, Ivy was waiting for her, sticking her foot out so that Celia fell with a splat, landing heavily on the floor. Ivy loomed over her sticking the heel of her shoe in her face - no longer the pathetic woman she portrayed.

"Don't ever speak to me like that again" she hissed, "or you'll be sorry."

Leaving Celia gasping on the floor, Ivy had gone back to the drawing room as though nothing had happened, and shortly afterwards Celia had gone home without mentioning anything.

Mrs Fuller brought in some tea, she looked awful, her face was blotchy with crying, and her hands shook as she set down the tray. Ivy urged her to sit down and join them, Mrs Fuller looked anxiously at Charles, who gestured towards an armchair. It was no time to stand on ceremony. They sat gloomily drinking their tea, when Ivy asked if she might use the phone later. Charles said of course and that there was no need to ask. Ivy said she wanted to keep Susan up to date - she'd been worried sick.

There was a knock on the front door - Charles leapt up and dashed into the hall, upsetting the tea tray. He wrenched it open to find Sandra, looking bedraggled from the drizzle outside, and she just shook her head and smiled sadly at him as she came in and he knew immediately she had no fresh news.

She came and joined them in the drawing room, and Mrs Fuller took her mac and went to get more tea and Sandra gave them a brief update on what was going on. They lapsed into silence, there seemed little to be said or done if it came to that. Ivy excused herself and went to ring Susan, using the phone in Jennifer's study.

Susan answered straight away, "Mum, gawd, I thought you'd never ring, what's happening?"

Ivy told her that apart from the photo, which had been traced now as coming from Walthamstow, they'd no more news. It was a waiting game for the next contact to be made.

"Blimey fuckin' Walthamstow!" moaned Susan, "You say though, that a couple of Jen's friends might've seen this geezer hanging about do ya?"

"They're in the nick this morning doing a photafit."

"Get hold of it Mum, soon as ya can. Wayne and I'll get onto it, ya never know, we might get summat. Look gotta sort the kids out, they're killing each other, ring me soon as ya know. Try not to worry, if he's a smoke bloke, some one round 'ere will know 'im!"

"Alright love. You mind how you go then." She replaced the phone thoughtfully, she just hoped Susan was right and it wasn't all just big talk.

Chloe arrived at Haywards Heath Police Station early and was surprised to see Patrick pulling into the car park just after her.

"Yo Chloe" he called as he got out of his van, "What you doing here?"

"Oh Patrick isn't it awful about Jennifer! I've come to make a statement about yesterday" Chloe answered grimly. "What about you?"

"Me too. The police were asking questions in the pub yesterday and it turned out that me and Dick both saw summat. It's bloody terrible, and you can't tell me this wasn't well planned" he speculated, "I saw that Landrover in the lane yesterday, and I've seen it hanging around a few times before then too."

"Oh God, so did I, several times in fact, it's hard to believe isn't it?" she took his arm, the unique scent of hoof and horses that he had on his damp work clothes adding a sense of comfort to the horrible situation.

"Come on chick, let's get it over with."

The interviews took ages and were done separately but Chloe, Patrick and Mike Lister had all described seeing an identical vehicle. Patrick and Chloe spent some while with a patient police officer trying to make a picture of the man and girl they had seen, until at last they were satisfied that it was a reasonable likeness. They were surprised to see later when they'd finished Mrs Gupta coming from another interview room with a police woman. Fatima looked tired, her big body sagging and her swollen feet spilled out over her shoes.

"Mrs Gupta!" exclaimed Chloe, "I didn't expect to see you, are you alright, you look exhausted."

"Hello my dear, yes I'm fine, but this is a terrible thing I'm thinking. I knew those two were trouble when they came in that day."

"Did you see them too?" Chloe said surprised.

"Now" one of the woman police officers interrupted, "you've all given us descriptions and we'd like to compare the two identikits, with the one that Mr Macey, the landlord of the Fox has given and see if we can perfect them a bit, if that's okay with you?"

When they sat down together and looked at the sinister pictures they were all astonished, staring back from the screen there were very similar images, except in one the man did not have a goatee but the unmistakable thing was the man's light blue eyes.

Jonty was giving Laura some cause for concern. He'd been on a high since Saturday night, and she knew for sure he had been up to no good. The Hunt Sabs had been out that day to Fittlebury but what part Jonty had played she had no idea. Ryan had texted her on Saturday afternoon, to say that it had gone really well, the hunt had been abandoned and to thank her for her information, and was looking forward to the next time out. She felt very uneasy about everything, the pleasure of thinking about spoiling that bastard's day out hunting had been overshadowed by the worry that Jonty had taken over and had kept her very much in the dark about what he'd been planning – only to tell her that she'd had her revenge - just as she wanted. What form that revenge had taken terrified her, and she was convinced his manic behaviour meant that whatever had taken place had definitely succeeded as far as he was concerned, but she dared not speak to Jonty for fear of his reaction. She was certain that there had to be more to it than the innocuous misdirection of hounds.

When the morning news came on the TV the next day, her heart sank when Fittlebury made the lead story. She watched with dread as the anchor woman told of how hunt saboteurs had planned an attack on the local hunt, and that during this siege one person had been critically injured, several horses attacked and two people were now missing. TV crews showed the Fox, and shots of the Abbey with the blue and white police tape. A brief statement was given by the Senior Investigating Officer outside the Police Station, who confirmed that this had been a particularly vicious attack, and that a woman and child were missing, presumed abducted by the saboteurs. One rider had been badly injured and whose condition was still critical. The police, he said, were following up several leads, and an eye witness statement had proved invaluable. They were not able to give any further information at this time and that they did not believe that the woman and child were any longer in the area.

Laura was stunned, she was in no doubt as to who the missing people were, and who had been responsible. Kidnapping for Christ's sake, she wanted no part of that and what the hell would Ryan think when he heard about it! He was a fanatic and an idealist, but he was no sodding kidnapper and once they found him, he'd tell them all about her involvement. She couldn't decide what to do, but her instinct told her to pack her bag and make a run for it.

CHAPTER 68

Jennifer was dimly aware of pain in her arms and legs which seemed to be forced into an unnatural position, and she had a swimming feeling in her head. Her mind was muzzy and she felt as though she were floating. She couldn't open her eyes, nor her mouth, but she could hear voices muttering around her. An innate instinct told her to remain as calm as she possibly could, and try not to let the overwhelming panic that she felt welling up inside her to override her sensibility - that the stiller she was the more likely she would be to find out what was happening to her. She tried to force her mind back to the events and knew that she had been riding, and someone had pulled her off her horse, after that she couldn't remember anything, or could she? Yes, there had been saboteurs, they had been watching them down in the valley, her, Caitlin and Jessica - that was what they'd been doing at the time. Now she was here and she could only presume that she had been targeted and abducted.

She listened to the fragments of conversation murmuring around her, catching odd words, *'photo, Jonty, kid, food, time'* and wondered what they all meant. Suddenly and without warning she felt a sharp slapping around her cheeks, someone trying to rouse her, and the tape fastening her eyes was pulled off with a stinging yank. She blinked rapidly, her vision was blurred, and she desperately wanted to rub her watering eyes.

"Wake up, wake up, come on you silly tart, wake up!" barked a voice at her, and as her eyes gradually focused she saw a hooded figure staring at her, "That's better, now you can see me can you!"

Her eyes darted around the room, it seemed to be an old kitchen, and there were three of them, all with hoods on that she could see, but no sign of Caitlin or Jessica and with anguish she wondered what had happened to them. The one who had slapped her took out a knife and she quelled when she saw it, but he merely bent down and slashed the ropes free from her legs and arms that fastened her to the chair.

Holding the knife to her throat, he ordered her to stand, and with wobbly legs she did as she was told. The others came over and manhandled her through into another room and dragged her up a set of stairs, but not before she had a glimpse of another tiny figure in the room, tied just as she had been and clearly unconscious – with horror she realised it must be Jessica.

Her legs just didn't seem to want to work, and as much as she tried she couldn't stand up. Whether it was from fear or weakness she had no idea as they hauled her along a little corridor - her feet dragging behind her and into a small room with a tiny window threading the pale gloomy light of early morning onto the floor. She was thrown down onto an old iron bedstead, and someone was strapping her right hand to the bedhead with a cable tie.

Jennifer had never been more terrified in all her life, the man above her, and she was sure it was a man, still had the knife and he looked so menacing with just his eyes visible in the hood. One of the others came over and to her horror started removing her clothes, using scissors to cut them off. She tried to wriggle but she was just so weak, and eventually gave up until she was lying on the bed totally naked, and laughing they threw her clothes into the corner. She had never felt so embarrassed, vulnerable or ashamed, she squirmed on the bed and the tears rolled down her cheeks.

"Nice pair of tits" said one of them, giving one of her nipples a tweak. "We could have a right game with her!"

"No! Jonty said we wasn't to touch her, other than this remember! Get the fucking phone and take the picture!" snarled another and this time it was a woman's voice.

Jennifer shut her eyes in humiliation, as they posed her for the photograph.

Jonty was itching to know what was happening in Fittlebury. What were the police doing and had they taken the bait? Whatever - if they found the others at the mill, he was confident he couldn't be implicated could he - even if they found him in London, there was nothing incriminating here other than the tart's phone, which he could easily dump if things got too hot! No it was a great plan! Then he suddenly he had a horrible thought – what about Lucy? She had worked at Nantes, had a grudge against the Parker-Smythes, it wouldn't be too long before they questioned her. The old bill weren't stupid and neither were these hunting nobs, they'd know someone gave the Sabs the info, and it wouldn't take Einstein to work it out. Plus, he thought angrily, he'd been seen with her loads of times in Horsham and in the fucking Landrover too, she even had his mobile number! Unlike Laura who knew how to keep her mouth shut, that stupid slag wouldn't. The more he thought about it, the more he realised that Lucy could be a real threat to him, and after all she had served her useful purpose now. He glanced at his watch, time he was making his way over to Walthamstow, and then he would deal with Lucy.

Ryan had seen the news too and was livid, what the fuck – they'd had nothing to do with any of that shit! Sure they had been there, sure they had disrupted the hunt and bloody successful it had been too, but this, no way! He rang round his cronies and they decided to meet in the Lord Nelson.

The others were as horrified as he had been, it must have been that bint Laura, she'd set them up. Ryan was fuming, pacing back and forth in anger, normally he saw through people but she had well and truly hoodwinked them. He wondered if that bloody Sean had anything to do with it either, after all it was he who'd introduced her. The police were gonna come calling at some point, although their little cell of Sabs were pretty covert, their surveillance guys were bloody everywhere and they weren't stupid. If this turned out to be kidnapping and a murder charge too, there was no fucking way they were taking the rap for that. The others agreed, the only course of action was to be the ones to contact the police and own up to it being their group that was out that day, but say they'd had nothing to do with anything else. As much as he had a dislike for the filth, he disliked traitors and villains even more. The others listened in, as he made the call to his contact in the Met.

Thirty minutes later they were being interviewed by a DS and a DC, who listened carefully to every word he said, with the other guys adding bits and pieces to the story. Finally the DS showed them a photocopy of a photo fit picture which had been faxed over, asking if this was the girl known as Laura. Ryan almost spat at it in disgust, and confirmed that it was definitely her. The police officers could hardly contain their excitement, asking where she lived. Ryan explained that he had no idea, but gave them her mobile number and Sean's, and they then left in a hurry, saying they'd be in touch.

Later that morning Jim Farrell had driven in the rain, which had now become more persistent, over to Nantes with the photo fits to see if Charles recognised either of the two people that had been seen in the Landrover. He'd rung beforehand to say he was coming and when he arrived Charles almost snatched the pictures out of his hand and studied them, but his face registered nothing. He thought there may be something familiar about the girl, he stared at it for a long time, but he couldn't place where from. Ivy, who was sitting on the sofa, asked if she could have a look, and Jim handed them to her, she scanned the first quickly, and put it aside and then looked at the other - her face lighting up with surprise.

"I know who this!" she exclaimed, "He's from round where I live!"

Jim was astonished, "Are you sure Mrs Bainbridge?"

"Definitely! His name is Jonty Steele, he's a right bad lot, into all sorts. Runs a stall in Brick Lane Market, but everyone knows it's just a front for drugs."

"Do you know the girl?" asked Jim.

"No, never seen her before, but it's definitely Jonty Steele, I'd know him anywhere on account of the eyes."

Jim picked up his phone and dialled through to the incident room, "We may have a break. See if you can pull up anything on a Jonty Steele, from Brick Lane area in London, we've got a positive ID on the photo fit. Call me back straight away."

"Oh God" said Charles, "do you think he's got them?"

"Well, it's certainly a possibility, and it won't take us long now we've got a name to check out. You've been really helpful Mrs Bainbridge" said Jim to Ivy, "Did Jennifer know this man?"

"No, well, we did see him once, when she was bringing me down here the other week. We had the roof down on her car, and he was staring at her when we were stopped at some lights, but she just laughed about him. You don't think that sparked him off do you? He's got quite a reputation for being a nasty piece of work if you cross him."

"I don't think so, this has been planned for months, according to Mrs Coombe and the other witnesses the Landrover has been seen periodically around here for weeks now. I think he'd already planned it, that's of course if he's involved at all."

"Oh nothing would surprise me where he's concerned" cried Ivy, "my poor Jen and that little girl, I dread to think what he's doing to them!"

Charles groaned, "Don't Ivy, don't, I can't bear it, I feel so bloody helpless! What good is all this fucking money, if anything happens to them!"

Mrs Fuller said "Excuse me Mr Charles, may I have a look, I've just thought about those two intruders, that night of the party, that was a man and a girl, do you think it might've been them?"

"What was that Mrs Fuller?" asked Jim, "What intruders?"

"God, you may well be right Mrs F, I hadn't thought of that till now! It was the night of our party, the one Chloe Coombe mentioned. Late that night we had some gate-crashers. Well that was what we thought they were at the time, nothing in the house was taken, and Mrs Fuller disturbed them in the garden and they ran off. The next day we found that Jennifer's dress, which had been left by the pool after we'd been swimming had been ripped to shreds. We just forgot about it."

"Does it look like the two people in the pictures Mrs Fuller?" asked Jim

"Well, it was very dark and I only glimpsed them so I can't be certain" said Mrs Fuller grimly, "but it seems an odd co-incidence

737

doesn't it?"

Jim stood up to go, "It does indeed. Look, I'm leaving you with Sandra, as I need to get moving with this new piece of information, so …"

They were all paralysed with shock as Charles' phone beeped an incoming message. He jumped visibly and with quaking hands whispered, "It's from Jennifer's phone. Oh my God!"

Jim didn't hesitate, he rang the incident room, "The victim's phone has been switched on there's been another message, get onto it now, once you get the location, get somebody over there!" he yelled. Walking over to Charles he took the phone and looked at the photograph, the picture was of a naked woman tied to the bed, her mouth taped shut, her eyes terrified, it was enough to put the fear of God into anyone. There was no accompanying demand, just the photo. These were sick, nasty bastards. He looked beyond the woman, she was tied by the right hand to an iron bedstead, just a blank wall as a back drop, no window, nothing to give away where she was being held, in fact she could have been anywhere. His phone rang, it was Terry.

"Walthamstow Jim, the Met are on their way, the phone's still on at the moment."

"Good work. Anything on this Jonty Steele character?"

"Better than that, Peter's come up lucky with something on the petrol stations. A Landrover, long wheel base, blacked out windows, driver answering the description of our man filled up at Pease Pottage Services at 5.12 on the Saturday morning and we've got a licence plate – vehicle registered to a Jonty Steele and we've got the address."

"Right, get round there, and start checking ANPR, see if you can pinpoint that vehicle's movements now we've got the plate. I'm on my way back." He stood up abruptly, "I have to go" he said to them, "the net is drawing in Mr Parker-Smythe, Mrs Bainbridge, I know how difficult this is for you, but we've got some positive leads now, and I'll be keeping you posted. Meanwhile Sandra here'll answer any of your questions."

Charles, Ivy and Mrs Fuller watched him go, and Sandra saw

him out to the front door, whispering to him in the hall way for a moment or two. She came back, her face tense, she suggested that they should phone Celia to let her know that another message had been received.

Charles was in a bad way, distraught enough as it was and he just couldn't face dealing with Celia, but Ivy interrupted him, asking if he wouldn't mind her giving Susan a quick ring first. She'd only be a moment. Charles was grateful – it'd give him time to compose himself and he and Sandra were talking in low voices when she made her call.

Susan listened carefully, "Okay Mum, I'm onto it. Call you back soon as."

Jonty turned off Jennifer's phone, pulled the woolly cap down further over his head and drove off to the next street in the Vauxhall Corsa he'd borrowed from Hawkeye. He parked and watched in the rear view mirror with amusement as two cars tore down the street, obviously unmarked police cars, then laughed as they slowed, scouring up and down the road. Stupid fuckers he thought.

He would like to have gloated for longer but it was too risky, so he drove carefully back towards Bethnal Green, singing his head off to the radio. There was not much traffic on the road, being a Sunday and he'd just gone past the tube, when up ahead he saw there was some kind of activity going on. People were out on the street, hovering around in a crowd, staring down his road, traffic was going right slow, rubber necking as they drove past. He had no choice and eased off the gas too, although he'd like to have floored it out of there! As he got nearer to the end of his street, the crowd were all peering and pointing and he couldn't resist having a look. There were blue bleedin' lights everywhere! He quickly shoved on some shades and pulled his hat down further, and forced himself to look ahead, Christ, they looked like they were right outside his flat! His heart was beating, what the fuck! How had they gotten onto him so quick! Well they could have nothing on him anyway, the Landrover was tucked away in the lock up which he rented off a mate, there was no gear stashed in the flat, but he wasn't gonna hang around and take any chances. He took the next left turn to hook up with Whitechapel Road and Mile End Road, heading out towards Bow, and then made for the Blackwall Tunnel, it was time he paid the luscious Lucy a visit before she grassed him up, but before he did, he just had to prepare a little gift for her.

Jim was back in the incident room. By this time the special negotiators had arrived and been fully briefed; he had also called in SOCU, the Serious Organised Crime Unit, who were specialists in surveillance work and could work in conjunction with the Met. Terry reported that Steele's gaff had been empty when they arrived, and they could find no evidence of either Jennifer or Jessica having been in the flat – although a forensic team were in place going over it now. When questioned and showed the photo fit pictures, the neighbours confirmed that both Steele and the girl lived there and that the girl was known as Laura, but she'd been seen leaving about an hour before they'd got there, lugging a suitcase. Jonty himself had left sometime earlier that morning and that he did have a stall in the Brick Lane Market. Terry said they were checking that out now. A description of them both had been circulated to all departure points in London, to apprehend them if they were seen.

Jim nodded, they were doing all they could, as fast as they could, but his mind kept wandering back to the photo of the naked woman on the bed. What would they be doing to her now he wondered, and worse still what had they done to the little girl? Another grim thought flashed through his mind - if as he suspected, they had done a bunk, would they ever find her and the kid? Let's face it, you could have all the specially trained negotiators you liked, but they were worthless if the bastards made no demands and this wasn't about money at all.

Andrew had not left Caitlin's side since the accident. She had not regained consciousness for over thirty hours now, and to him it seemed as though he had sat beside her for a lifetime. The consultant had seen him after the operation and explained that he had removed the blood clot, and the next few days would be critical in terms of her recovery, although her life was no longer in danger, unless there were complications following surgery, which at the moment were unlikely. Andrew had asked what he actually meant, and the surgeon had explained that the worst way was that Caitlin may never regain consciousness, and be in what was called a permanent vegetative state, that is able to breathe on her own, but not able to come out of her deep coma. The best was that she would make a full but slow recovery, or it could be a mixture of something in between. Perhaps her short term memory might be affected, her sight, her speech, her ability to co-ordinate her movements, some or all of those things, and they would have a better idea in a few days' time. Andrew hadn't quite known what to say, and the consultant had patted him on the shoulder and said they would talk again tomorrow and to try and get some rest himself.

He went outside to sit on the wall, to try to clear his head. One thing was for sure, whatever the outcome, he wasn't going to desert Caitlin now, no matter what - he'd be there for her. The fact that she had pulled through was enough for him, he wasn't giving up on her. He dragged out his mobile, the sooner he got this over and done with the better, and dialled Julia's number and this time she answered.

CHAPTER 69

Patrick was restless after the morning at the police station, his mind kept drifting back to the occasions when he'd seen that bloody Landrover, racking his brains about it all. He dropped into the Fox at lunchtime for a pint, not something he normally did, he wasn't a lunch time drinker, booze, made him too sleepy but the thought of staying indoors with Sharon clinched it for him.

It was a miserable day, the rain had come back with a vengeance and the path was wet and slippery and nobody was outside, except for a few desperate smokers snatching a drag before being driven back indoors. Patrick stepped down into the snug, Colin and Grace were there, Tom and young Oli, Dick the terrier man and a couple of the other hunting folk. Naturally the talk was of yesterday, with Dick adding his bit in between pulling the pints. The others were all eager to ask Patrick his version of events at the police station that morning.

"Well, Chloe was there too, seems she saw that Landrover as well as Dick and me and got a look at the driver and the girl too, so did Mrs Gupta from the shop. They were able to give a good description which is more than I could do as I only saw them fleetingly" he said regretfully "but from what I can gather, they've definitely been abducted."

"No, that's terrible!" said Colin, "Bloody Sabs!"

"I think there's a lot more to this than meets the eye Col" said Patrick, "I saw that Landrover weeks ago, and so did the others, this has been planned for months."

"Well the disruption was well planned yesterday, that's for sure" said Oli, "Didn't even come to the meet and follow the field, which is what they'd normally do, they love all that heckling - they knew exactly which covert we would draw first, so someone in the know told them."

"But who?" asked Colin, "and why would they do it?

"It has to be someone pretty close to us all to know something like that?" said Grace angrily, "Someone with an axe to grind, someone that has something against Caitlin, Jennifer and Charles, and to do something like to the children – it's hard to credit." Suddenly she stopped speaking and looked hard at Tom, "You don't think it could be Lucy do you?"

Tom flushed his usual red, "No, I don't, you're always against her Grace, I'm sure she wouldn't."

"Well she did fall out big time with Caitlin and has never made any secret that she thinks the hunting brigade are up their own arses!" snarled Grace. "It could be her, she's ingratiated herself back with us hasn't she since she stomped out. Been here when we've talked about it"

"She was there yesterday though Grace" said Colin, "following on foot, she'd hardly do that would she if she were involved?"

"She was probably tipping them off as to where the field was. Did she make any phone calls Tom?" demanded Grace

"Well - she did, just the one actually, said she was texting her mum, but I did think that was odd, because it was seven in the morning and she can't stand her mother! It was just as the field moved off." Tom said sheepishly.

"That's it then" said Grace triumphantly, "she's the mole, I'm damned sure of it. I think we should tell the police!"

"Hold on Grace, you can't be sure" Colin said reasonably, "this is all supposition!"

Patrick who had been thoughtfully drinking his beer chimed in, "No, I think Grace is right, we should tell the police. Okay she may have nothing to do with anything, and if that's the case no damage done - but if she does and we don't say anything, how would we all feel if Jennifer and Jessica were harmed. Remember Caitlin's already in a critical way, they didn't care about what they did to her. "

They all looked at Patrick stunned, he was usually the one full of jokes and humour, but his face was deadly serious, and when he put it that way, he was right, they should tell the police.

Colin broke the silence "You're right mate – of course we should."

Patrick fished in his pocket and brought out a card, "the copper gave me the direct line for the incident room this morning, just in case I remembered anything else, let's give her a bell eh?"

Jennifer lay spread-eagled on the bed, she was frozen with the cold, and desperately thirsty. After they had posed her for the photograph, they had secured her other arm with a cable tie too, and she had been left alone. She wept with tears of frustration, and helplessness and fear. She had no idea what they were planning next, and all she could think of was little Jessica in the downstairs room trussed up like a chicken. She tried to think logically. Kidnappers wanted ransom, so presumably the photograph they had taken would be sent to Charles to demand money, which she knew he would pay. She had read somewhere that to deprive someone of their clothes gave the other person power, that was certainly true she grimaced. She had also read that it was important to try and develop a relationship with your abductor, that way it made it more difficult for them to harm you if the time came. Well, it was bloody hard when your mouth had been taped shut. She must keep focussed, pretty soon they would have to give her a drink, if they didn't want her to die of dehydration, she would try then. In the meantime she would force herself to forget her nakedness, imagine that she had really nice clothes on, she was bloody determined not going to let this make her even more vulnerable than she already felt. She craned her head to see her clothes piled up in a bundle on the floor, it was laughable when she thought of the mace spray tucked in her jacket pocket, a fat lot of good that had been.

She had no idea how long she had been there, they had taken her wristwatch, and the light that was coming from the dirty windows was very grey. She heard the heavy sound of footsteps coming up the stairs, and along the passage at the top. As the door opened she willed herself to stay calm. The hooded figure came over to the bed and just looked down at her, the malevolence in the eyes was terrifying, she found her swallowing hard, but defiantly returned the stare. In an almost leisurely way, the eyes roamed down taking in every part of her body, and a latex gloved hand pushed between her legs, roughly fingering her and she dived and squirmed away. He pushed down on her belly and shoved the fingers in harder, watching her eyes roll in terror.

"Pack it in wanker!" shouted a voice from the doorway, "keep it in your trousers!"

The man pulled his fingers out, and laughed, "just having a little fiddle that's all!"

"Well don't" snapped the voice, it was the woman, "help me instead." She bent down beside Jennifer, "Now listen up. I've brought you some water and something to eat. I'm gonna take the tape off your mouth, but if you make one sound you'll regret it eh?" she nodded towards the man, "I'll let him do what he likes with you – got it?"

Jennifer nodded her head dumbly, all her determination had disappeared, and the woman ripped off the duct tape and Jennifer felt as though her lips had been taken off with it. "Thank you" she said, but the moment the words were out, there was a resounding slap as the woman gave Jennifer the back of her hand.

"I said not one fuckin' sound and that was just a taster!"

Jennifer her face smarting from the blow, nodded dumbly as the woman offered her water from a bottle which she gulped down greedily, choking as she went.

"Not so fast you greedy cunt" the woman growled, "you can have more in a minute!"

Jennifer gasped, making herself drink more slowly, feeling the bruise coming up on her cheek. The woman produced a packet of custard creams, broke one in half and pushed it into her mouth, and told her to eat it. The stodginess clogged in her teeth and stuck in her throat, but she said nothing and did as she was told, the fear was back, all the strength and resolve of getting the kidnappers on her side was hopeless and forgotten.

The phone rang making everyone jump at Nantes, Charles rushed to answer it and they all hovered around expectantly, but it was Susan wanting to speak to Ivy. He handed over the phone and she went out into the hall to take the call.

"Mum, I've got something for you" Susan said excitedly, "The old bill have been over to Jonty Steele's place and turned it over, he's not there and the girl he's living with has done a runner. Wayne put the word out and saw that smelly Frank in the pub who had something for him. Apparently Jonty's got a lock up he uses, it's just off the Colombia Road, rents it off someone he knows!"

"Go on!" said Ivy, "Do you think that's where they might be?"

"Dunno, but worth a shot, get a pen and I'll give ya the address."

Ivy ran into Jennifer's study and found a pen and paper and wrote it down as Susan spelled it out for her mother, "okay, I've got it!"

"Another thing Mum. Jonty's right hand man is a bloke called Weasel, looks like a fuckin one too, you'd know him."

"Yeah, I've seen him love, but do ya know where he lives?"

"Wayne's bin busy – got it right here, proper name's Willie Thorpe. Now word 'as it, that they've been sortin' a job. Wayne said Frank thought that evil bastard Hawkeye was involved, and that spiky tart Nora Buxton. But you can guarantee where she is that dopey thug Freddie will be too."

"Well done our Susan" said Ivy excitedly, "I'll pass that on straight away!" She turned and ran back into the drawing room.

Jim issued instructions quickly, as soon as he got the phone call from Sandra. SOCU were despatched ahead of two teams of officers going to the lock up and one of the negotiators were already on their way. Another team were going to lift Willie Thorpe aka Weasel. The net was closing he just knew it. A DC came in, waving a piece of paper.

"Guv, I've just had a call from that farrier, apparently they've been talking in the pub and they think they may have a lead on the mole. A girl that worked for the Parker-Smythe's, and walked out a few weeks ago, she's been hanging around with the hunt supporters lately and sent a suspicious text or phone call during the meet yesterday. Want me to follow it up?"

"Definitely, who is she?" asked Jim, "no-body mentioned her before?"

"No, her name's Lucy Phillips, lives in Horsham and works in a Bistro on the Carfax apparently."

"Ring Sandra, and get her address from Mr Parker-Smythe, and pay her a visit, might be nothing, but might be something."

Jim sat thinking, could the woman and the child be in the lock up? Where the hell was this Jonty character and had the girl Laura done a bunk and if so why? Did Lucy Phillips have anything to do with it, she certainly had a motive. If they could lift this Weasel character then they may well be able to get him to talk, if they could get his mobile phone too, that would be very useful. God it was the waiting part he hated, but they were getting closer.

Jonty decided not to text her, but to catch her as she left work. He parked the Corsa, keeping on the hat but taking off the glasses, and stood under cover of the Swan Centre by Boots watching her from a distance as she scurried back and forth inside the Bistro, the rain was preventing the shoppers from sitting outside. It was Sunday and the stores shut early, so he assumed the Bistro would too, so he wouldn't have long to wait. He loitered about, getting himself a coffee from Costa and strolling back, just as the stores were closing. The Bistro had put up the closed sign and she'd be out in a few minutes, and he got the car and waited by the bus stop.

"Hey Lucy!" He called, reaching over and opening the passenger door "jump in, I'll give you a lift!"

"Jonty!" she said, looking anxious, "Fuck you gave me a shock!"

"Come on babes, get in – you're getting soaked! Let's go for a drink!" he laughed, "like my new motor?"

Lucy hesitated, reluctant to get in the car, "Yeah, what happened to the Landrover?" she said warily.

"Got rid of it last week, Weasel had it off me, got too juicy to run – bought this little run about. Bought you a little something too." He tapped the side of his nose.

"Jonty what happened at the hunt last week, did you go then?" Lucy asked suspiciously.

"Nah, Weasel went, I had ta work, pity in one way, but as it happens, gather it all got a bit nasty, so glad I wasn't there!" he laughed. "Got time to go the Travel Lodge? I know a way to dry you off!"

"Okay, that'd be good." she smiled at him, she felt relieved, he hadn't been involved after all, and she had always fancied him and he'd obviously made a special effort to come down to see her. She got into the car shaking her dripping hair.

They drove towards the Travel Lodge, the windscreen wipers hardly clearing the screen as the rain started to come down harder and the car splashed through the puddles that had begun to accumulate on the road.

"Bet you're glad you're not waiting at that bus stop." Jonty laughed, "What a day!"

They pulled into the car park, Jonty reversing the Corsa into a space in the corner. He squeezed Lucy's knee, "I've just gotta make a call doll, my phone's almost dead – lend me yours. Here take some cash and get us a room will ya – use your name, and," he pulled a package out of his pocket, "have a line and be ready and waiting for me when I come up, I'll only be a minute!"

Lucy felt excited, oh she'd be ready and waiting alright, she couldn't wait to get started, the thought of it made her wet already! She greedily took the money and the little plastic bag with the white powder.

"It's good stuff!" He laughed, "Enjoy a line or two while you're waiting, get you revved up for me!"

Lucy gave him her most seductive look, and said huskily, "Oh I will babe, I will!" she handed him her mobile and jumped out of the car, running across the car park in the rain.

Jonty watched her go into the reception, she turned and waved to him as she went in, and he lifted his hand in acknowledgement, pretending to be on the phone. He waited for a full five minutes, before he started the car and drove off.

Jonty stopped the Corsa in High Ridge Woods, the rain was lashing down now and there were no walkers out today. He glanced at his new watch, it should be all over by now he thought grimly, pity, but it had to be done – the stupid cow had even given up her phone! He considered his position, he couldn't go back to London for the time being, he'd no idea what happened to Laura and frankly he couldn't care. She didn't know anything anyway. He'd lie low for a while, and have a well earned snooze, and then he'd pay a little visit to the mill and give them a surprise! He licked his lips in anticipation of the fun he could have with his hostages! Re-parking the car, so that it was totally obscured from the road or any causal mad dog walker in this weather, he pushed down the door locks and fell asleep.

The constant drumming of the rain on the roof of the barn had kept Pete awake today, and he felt restless and anxious, wringing his hands together, and nodding his head back and forth constantly. He didn't like the rain, nasty wet stuff. He felt hungry, and groped around for the remains of some muck he had found in a restaurant bin last night. Cold chips and some fragments of meat, glued together now with congealed sauce, but it would have to do. He opened the

Tupperware container, and began his methodical chewing, eating always comforted him, although he longed for fresh bread like the stuff he used to buy in the shop. He sat in the half-light , thinking about the woman the voices had told him would be punished. He knew he could trust them, but could he trust what he had seen? His old paranoia irrationally came flooding back into his head. Should he just go back and check that it was definitely her - had *he* really seen her? He had often imagined seeing things before, could this be another one of those times, it had only been a glimpse after all. The more he thought about it, the more worried he became that he'd made a mistake. His head was nodding faster and faster back and forth the more agitated he became, until his whole body was rocking. He didn't go out during the daytime, he knew he mustn't, but he also knew that he couldn't wait till dark, he had to be sure.

As desperate as he was, he had to be careful, so he used the door out of the workshop and went through the back of the fields towards Fittlebury Hall. Although it was still daylight, it was dreary outside, with no break in the dark grey clouds or the slashing rain which cast a claustrophobic murky gloom over the whole landscape. He skirted around the other side of the hedge from the mill and dived into the woods behind it, and clambered over the stile about one hundred yards further away. The rain was teeming down and he could hear the swollen mill pond pounding through the sluice of the mill race. He stood hiding in the trees, a dark shrouded figure blending perfectly into the undergrowth on the dismal day, intently watching the kitchen window of the cottage for signs of life. It was very quiet and still, no-one was in the kitchen and he slithered on his belly, towards the outhouses at the side, using the overgrown garden as cover. Fat drops of rain had found their way down inside the neck of his coat, and his hair was hanging in wet strings around his face, but he hardly noticed, all he could think of was affirming what he had seen before. Sliding alongside the underneath of the kitchen window, he chanced his luck and looked over the sill, cupping his hands over his eyes to see inside.

Yes, there was the figure again, tied to the chair, but she looked so much smaller this time and there was no tape over her eyes or mouth. He pulled himself up a little further, pushing harder against the window, craning to see the forlorn face. The sudden shadow at the window made the captive woman look up and as she recognised him, her expression changed to one of hope and she suddenly screamed out for all she was worth!

"Pete, Pete, help me! Help me!" she begged "Help me!"

He staggered back, it was not that bitch at all, but his darling little Jessica that looked at him! He rushed to the window again, and he was right, it was Jessica, but this time she was not alone - the hooded thugs had heard the commotion and run in from the front of the cottage and now stared at him pointing their fingers, yelling and shouting. They were unbolting the back door and wrenching it open and the largest of them all now was lunging at Pete with a knife. With a lightening reaction Pete kicked it out of his hands and hit him as hard as he could, the man flew back in astonishment and Pete landed another blow. By this time, four others had come out and were circling around him, like snarling predators surrounding a wounded animal intent on their prey. He was out-numbered, no matter how strong he was, he was no match for them and had no option but to make a run for it. He shouldered the smallest one out of the way, knocking them to the ground and kicking out with venom, punching another as he flew past, running as fast as he could, and leaping around to the front of the cottage he hurtled down the drive towards the lane.

Mrs Gupta was really tired, had had to be resting after lunch, the interview at the police station had been quite upsetting for her. Ravi had manned the shop, but she had said she was quite alright now and could easily manage a quiet Sunday afternoon, especially a wet one like this, there wouldn't be much trade today and it was nearly closing time anyway.

She was sitting on her stool behind the counter, eating a Fry's Turkish Delight and reading her favourite magazine - Prima. Ravi popped his head around the door from the back asking her if she was wanting a cup of tea. He was so good to her Ravi, what would she be doing without him she thought. What a terrible business it had been yesterday, that poor Mrs Parker-Smythe and that dear little girl - what was this world coming to? She had known that those two were no good the day they walked into her shop, perhaps she should have been saying something straight away, but who was to know?

Thinking like this made her feel quite unwell, she was feeling very breathless all of a sudden, and her heart was beating very fast. She groped in her pocket for her pills, when the door crashed open

751

and smashed back violently against the newspapers. Mrs Gupta leapt up in alarm from her stool, to see a huge man, one of those tramps, with a filthy beard and hair, looming in the doorway, his breath coming in dry rasps, his eyes mad and wild. He rushed up to her, and grabbed her by the shoulders, his stinking breath in her face, and she screamed out in terror and the pain in her chest tightened like a vice around her.

"Mrs Gupta" gasped Pete breathless from running, "It's Jessica, Jessica the little girl from Nantes Place, she's a prisoner up at the Old Mill! Do you understand what I'm saying! Get someone straight away to help! I'm going back there now!"

Just then Ravi came through the back door with her tea, Mrs Gupta had collapsed behind the counter, the pain in her chest agonising and she could hardly breathe. Ravi dropped the cup in horror as he saw a massive man run out of the door and Fatima gasping on the floor. He rushed over to her, willing her to be okay. She was very breathless and couldn't speak, and little beads of perspiration had broken out on her forehead. Ravi rummaged about and found her pills, putting one under tongue and waited holding her hand and talking to her.

Fatima was desperately trying to talk, but Ravi was just telling her to hush and not try to exert herself in any way. She was becoming more and more agitated though, and Ravi was just on the point of thinking he should ring for an ambulance, when Patrick breezed in through the open door.

"Blimey Mr Gupta, what you got the door open for, it's bucketing down out there – just gonna buy Sharon some chocs as I've been missing since lunchtime playing cards in the pub!" Then he stopped - looking in horror at Mrs Gupta's bloated body sprawled on the floor, "Oh Christ, what's happened?"

"Patrick, thank goodness you're arriving" said Ravi, "Mrs Gupta's had a terrible fright! That mad gardener has just been in here ranting and raving! She's collapsed as you can see!"

"What Pete? He's not been seen for weeks! I'd forgotten all about him. Poor Mrs G, is she okay? Should I ring for an ambulance?"

They squeezed around the counter and tried to get the enormous bulk of Fatima into a sitting position and Ravi pushed another pill under her tongue, she was waving her arms around and trying to speak. As the minutes ticked past the angina attack was at last subsiding and finally she managed to gasp out in fits and starts what it was that Pete had said to her.

Patrick leapt to his feet, "Fucking hell! You stay with Mrs G, I'd call an ambulance if I were you to be sure. I'm gonna call the police and head straight up to the mill, but that must have been almost half an hour ago now!"

CHAPTER 70

When Jonty woke up, he realised he'd been asleep for quite a while. He stretched and felt refreshed, grabbed his jacket from the back seat and stepped out into the rain. Fucking weather, he locked the car and made his way into the woods, at least it was dryer in there, although the bloody trees were dripping all over him. He picked his way through the undergrowth, stumbling every now and then, and cursing as he righted himself. It was a longer walk than he thought, but he couldn't risk going any closer by car, he imagined with delight their uncomfortable surprise when he arrived and how much fun he would have with the ice maiden.

As he neared the mill he waited in the woods and watched for a while. All was quiet, just as it should've been he thought with satisfaction, other than he was bloody wet through. He walked over towards the back door of the cottage and to his uneasy surprise saw that it was half open - that wasn't right. Diving for the cover of the out houses, all his senses on full alert and with his heart beating a tattoo on his ribcage he stood very still. There was not a bloody sound – other than the fucking noise of that water. He edged out again and made his way back to the kitchen door and went in. The kid was tied up to a chair - her mouth taped up, and she was obviously doped up to the eyeballs and out for the count. He prodded her spitefully and she didn't respond. He walked cautiously through to the next room, there were sleeping bags on the floor, some empty cans of lager, remnants of joints in the fireplace, rubbish piled in a corner, but otherwise empty. It was like the fucking Marie Celeste. He crept up the stairs, pushing one door open after another - in the last one along, he found Jennifer, still quite naked and fastened to the bed, her mouth taped shut and completely out of it, the red pin prick of a needle mark in her arm and a livid cigarette burn on her leg. He pinched her nipple hard between his fingers, she didn't move at all, she was totally sparko. There was no sign of the others at all, where the fuck were they all?

He turned around and stormed down the stairs - he was bloody furious, they had fucking abandoned ship and done a bunk. What a load of wankers! He strode back into the little sitting room and kicked around the sleeping bags and went over to the camping gas stove they had brought with them, touching the kettle, it was still warm. So they hadn't been gone that long - he was surprised he hadn't seen them in the woods, because he was fucking sure they wouldn't have scarpered down the lane. Perhaps they were coming back then? That might possibly be it. He'd wait for a bit, make himself a cup of tea, might warm him up, he was bloody frozen after getting so fucking wet. He lit the stove and waited for the kettle to boil.

Patrick jumped into his van driving like a maniac through the village taking the road to Priors Cross, if Mrs Gupta was right, and Pete was involved Christ knew what he was capable of doing. He phoned the direct number he'd been given that morning and was connected directly to the MCT, he explained what had happened and impatiently gave the location of the mill, and said that he was on his way there now. He didn't wait for a response, threw the phone on the passenger seat and put his boot hard on the accelerator. By his reckoning Pete had a good half hour on him, and although he was on foot, he would still probably make it to the mill before he could. This bloody rain didn't help, the van didn't corner too well on the slick wet roads, and Christ knew he didn't want to have an accident on the way there. He slowed down a bit, picked up his phone and rang Nantes, Charles answered immediately and breathlessly he told him to get over to the mill straight away. Charles didn't need asking twice, and ended the call abruptly.

Patrick drove on grimly through the downpour, it would take Charles at least fifteen minutes to get there and the police probably longer, and suddenly he had another idea – Colin and Grace! They lived close by and he had them on speed dial. He pushed hard on the digit and the phone started to ring - please, please answer Col mate he prayed.

"Patrick you old reprobate!" Colin laughed "Has Sharon chucked you out?"

"Get up to the Old Mill as fast you can!" Patrick yelled "Pete has got Jennifer and Jessica up there, he's gone mad, nearly killed Mrs Gupta in the village shop just now! God knows what he's going to do! I've rung Charles and the police are on their way, but I need help right now!"

"What .... you winding me up Patrick?"

"Don't be fucking stupid Col, course I'm not, get up there now! I mean it" shouted Patrick, "before something awful happens!"

Jonty heard the sound of the back door being pushed open – he looked up thinking the others were back, but there were no voices – that was funny. He went over to the kitchen door to see a massive man, towering over the kid, he had a bushy beard with long dirty hair and wild eyes – he recognised him straight away, it was that mad gardener. Pete took one look at Jonty and gave a howl like a wild animal and lunged for him. Jonty dived back into the sitting room with the bear of the man thundering after him, he shot to one side to avoid him, but the man grabbed his jacket and caught hold of him swinging him round like a puppet. Jonty was caught off balance and sprawled on the floor, into the lager cans and overturning the gas stove, the boiling water from the kettle splashing over his legs. The man hurled himself on top of him, but Jonty had dived to one side and managed to wriggle away. The man took hold of his leg and they brawled on the floor, arms and legs flying in all directions, until Jonty fought his way out of his grasp and struggling to his feet made a dash for the door. The giant was not to be deterred and ran after him gaining on him with every stride on his long legs. They ran around to the front of the cottage and Jonty found himself once again floored by this enormous hulk of a man, they rolled over and over on the soaking ground, the brambles tearing at their clothes, and all the while the little blue flames of the gas stove were licking away at the old wooden floor of the cottage.

Patrick tore down the drive in his van, the windscreen wipers going at full pelt to find Pete and another man wrestling on the ground, he leapt out and stood helpless wondering what on earth to do. Pete was pounding his fists into the smaller guy screaming at the top of his voice that he would never let anyone harm Jessica! Patrick glanced around, he was already soaked, the rain driving hard into his clothes and face, as he heard another car racing up the drive, it was Colin's Land cruiser with him driving and Grace in the passenger seat. Thank the Lord he thought, reinforcements had arrived.

The two men were still brawling, he guessed they would have to try and part them, but he didn't fancy it much to be truthful. Pete was a big bloke and mad with it, anyway, Jennifer and Jessica were the important ones. Suddenly with a huge inhuman growl Pete, yanked the smaller man to his feet, and Patrick recognised him as the shaven haired driver of the Landrover. With Pete's massive hands around the man's throat they swayed from side to side, staggering alongside the reedy bank of the mill pond and then both over-balancing tumbled into its murky depths swollen and engorged with all the rain, and they immediately sank under the water. The three onlookers on the bank froze in horror, Grace clutching Colin's arm as they waited for them to surface. Moments later a shaven head bobbed to the top, and then appeared to be yanked down again, and then Pete's head appeared, his long hair plastered across his face. His eyes were maniacal, intent on destroying this man, they grappled together and Pete seized him by the throat, choking the life out of him, the other man pushed his thumbs in Pete's eyes and once again they both disappeared under the surface, only to come up again, but all the time the driving force of the water was pulling them closer and closer towards the mill race. The tug of the water was strong, and their sodden clothes hampered them both as they fought with less and less power. The smaller man was the first to be sucked through the funnel of the race chute, he was immediately stuck fast, head first and face down, with his arms pinioned to his sides. The water tumbling angrily over the top of him, he flayed and struggled, arching his back upwards in increasingly futile attempts to keep his head above the torrent, his shaven head thrashing uselessly up and down. There was nothing he could do, wedged in the race, no matter how hard he struggled and fought, his efforts becoming more and more feeble, until finally his body was still, rippling only with the mad eddy of the water. Of Pete there was nothing to be seen, he did not resurface again, the mill water was swirling, muddy and disturbed and they had no idea what had happened to him.

Grace held her hands to her mouth in shock at the horrific scene. Colin folded his arms around her. Patrick turned his head away not wanting to look at the floating body being tossed about by the water, and then gave out a huge yell of alarm.

"The bloody mill is on fire!"

They ran to the front of the cottage and could see through the window into the living room, the fire had started in the corner and was now teasing its way up the walls and licking along the tops of some sleeping bags. They tried to open the front door - but it was firmly locked and there was no way they could force it, no matter how hard they heaved their shoulders against the wood.

"Quick! Let's go round to the back" yelled Patrick

They ran around past the out houses, the brambles tearing at their trousers, and the rain pelting down on their faces. The back door was half open and the smoke was already seeping out in long tendrils into the garden.

"Grace!" shouted Colin, "Call the fire brigade! We'll try and find Jennifer and Jessica!"

Patrick and Colin ran inside, immediately gagging and choking, their arms flying up to protect their faces and found Jessica in the kitchen tied to the chair.

"I'll go upstairs mate – you get her out" wheezed Patrick, choking on the smoke that was already filling the room.

Colin was gagging and nodded to Patrick, managing to gesticulate to Grace to give him a hand to lift the unconscious girl. Patrick dodged around the flames in quick darting movements into the sitting room and fought his way up the staircase, he felt as though his lungs were on fire, his eyes were stinging from the acrid fumes. He pulled off his damp sweat shirt and wrapped it round his head and fumbled his way through the rooms upstairs. It was getting hard to see - Christ he had to find her, if Jessica was there, so Jennifer must be too.

He stumbled along the landing and opened the last room, luckily the door was closed, and so not much of the smoke was in here yet, he looked aghast as he saw Jennifer's body, totally naked and out of it, sprawled on the bed. He had no time to be shocked – fucking hell she was cable tied! He whipped out his penknife and cut the ties, threw her over his strong shoulders and started for the stairs. Directly he opened the door the smoke billowed in thickly, the yellow flicker of flames licking the top of the landing - bloody hell there was no-way he could get down there – the fire was out of control, the wooden walls of the cottage were like a tinder box! Desperately he made his way back into the bedroom and shut the door. He laid her back on the bed and forced opened the window, shouting out to Charles who had now arrived with Sandra and Colin and were standing below in the garden.

"We can't get out, the fire's got the stairs, we've only got minutes at most – I'm gonna smash this window out, and you'll have to catch her, she's doped, totally out of it– okay?"

He raised his leg and started kicking at the window, the glass splintering all over the place. He could see the smoke coming under the door now, where was the fucking fire brigade? He started kicking frenziedly, over and over, glass shattering everywhere, the wooden struts snapping under the weight of his boots – but there was no way you could lower someone through such a small gap! He became more desperate, as he could hear the roar of the fire getting closer. Ramming more and more force against the window until suddenly the rotten old frame gave away completely – the whole thing just tumbling out to the watchers below.

"Ready!" he shouted to Colin. With all his strength he lowered Jennifer feet first out of the window, leaning out as far as he could manage without falling himself, hanging onto her arms and then dropped her the last few feet to where Charles and Colin caught her, stumbling backwards with the impact but otherwise unhurt. "Now me mate, fucking hurry, or I'm burnt toast!" He clambered out onto the ledge, swinging himself round and lowered himself down till he was clutching on with his fingertips, and then let go, landing hard on his ankle and yelling out before collapsing, coughing his lungs out on the wet ground.

Grace had brought some picnic rugs from the back of her car, luckily the plastic backed ones, and so that when she covered Jennifer, the rain slicked off in little rivers along the creases. Charles cradled Jennifer in his arms, and carried her carefully to his car, setting her down gently on the back seat. Colin carried Jessica, and propped her in the passenger seat. Grace and Patrick followed behind, with her supporting him, hobbling painfully on his leg, they needed to get as far away from the fire as possible, the heat was becoming so intense and the noise of it was incredible.

They looked up to hear the wailing sirens of the emergency services coming at speed down the lane, there was no need for them to worry about them finding the secluded entrance to the mill, the roaring greedy fire was like a beacon guiding them in.

CHAPTER 71

The next morning the rain had finally died down, to leave a murky grey day, the air thick with the tainted acrid stink of the smouldering blackened remains of the cottage and the mill. One fire crew was still there, alert for any signs of the fire flaring up again, but it was a precaution now, and they leant against their truck, their faces dark with soot, yawning after a long night.

The police had been busy too, a wide area had been taped off and an officer was on duty at the entrance to the drive checking people in and out. He had just authorised entry to the Specialist Search Unit, which had sent a team of divers to search the pond and they trundled up in their van to meet the other SOCOs already at the scene. Jonty's body had been recovered the night before, at great risk not only because of the rushing water, but the fire which was rapidly spreading to the attached mill. The fire team had pumped water from the pond in great shooting arcs to try to arrest the spread of the flames, whilst the precarious job of retrieving the body took place. As for Pete, no sight had been seen of him since he had last disappeared under the water, and it was decided to wait until the morning to look for him.

Jennifer and Jessica had been taken by ambulance to the Princess Royal Hospital in Haywards Heath, where their condition was deemed to be stable. They had both been heavily sedated, and should recover spontaneously albeit slowly. Charles had stayed with them both, and rung Ivy and Celia, asking that Sandra bring Ivy to the hospital as soon as she could. During that evening they had started to come round, but were not really with it, and could remember only snatches of what had happened, drifting back into sleep. Sandra reported their condition back to DCI Jim Farrell, who said that any questions could be left until tomorrow and left her to it, although another officer was posted to ward off any unwanted visitors, including the press.

Patrick went by ambulance to Haywards Heath too, it was fairly obvious that his ankle was broken and had swollen to huge proportions and was at an unnatural angle. The initial adrenalin charge of getting away from the fire, when he hadn't felt the pain, had gone, and the agony of the injury took hold. The break was a complicated one, and he'd been taken into the operating theatre, where his ankle was pinned and he was now recovering in a ward.

SOCOs were crawling over the scene like ants at a picnic, and eventually moved their attention to the barn across from the mill, discovering Pete's living quarters, and began the meticulous task of gathering evidence. It was obvious he must have been here for months, living like an animal. They found a wrinkled photograph and carefully stashed it in a plastic bag and labelled it, moving on to the stack of tins and Tupperware boxes, turning their noses up in disgust at the stinking remnants of food.

The specialist search team was getting organised, preparing for the grisly task of finding Pete's body and were already in their inflatable grey dinghy. There were two divers on the boat, all kitted up, but without their masks, their eyes glued to the sonar screen. A helmsman guiding the craft skilfully alongside the mill race and the rotting wheel, as one of the divers shouted out and the dinghy slowed and the diver dropped a marker buoy. Obviously something odd had come up on the screen. The divers masked up and dropped into the water, carrying a body bag, attached themselves to the boat by a bright cord and a supervisor on board watched them as they sank below the surface. The pond was not that deep, but it was murky and it was not long before they lugged up the massive bulky remains that had once been Pete.

Nantes itself was quiet, Mrs Fuller was in the kitchen with Doris and Fred, Charles was at the hospital, and she herself felt exhausted after the traumas of the last few days. She made the tea, and sat down at the table with them, whilst they waited impatiently for her to tell them what had gone on the night before.

"Well" she sighed, "I don't know where to begin."

Doris was impatient, "Try Freda!"

"Now Doris, it's been a dreadful time up here, you don't know the half I can tell you." she said crossly, pouring the tea "from what I can gather, those Sabs, or whatever they call themselves, had Jennifer and Jessica hidden at the Old Mill, although they'd laid a false trail for the police in London. What they didn't know what was that Pete was living rough up there, he saw what was going on and ran down to the shop just as they were closing and told Fatima Gupta."

"Yikes!" said Doris relishing every word, "what happened next then?"

"This is a terrible story Doris, not some bit of tittle tattle" snapped Freda, shocked at the enjoyment in the woman's voice, "We're talking about little Jessica here and our Jennifer."

"Sorry Freda," Doris said meekly, "of course we are, go on then."

Freda carried on telling the story, sipping her tea in between, whilst Doris and Fred listened with no further interruptions, their faces agog as it went on.

"So they're unharmed then?" asked Fred, "Lord be praised."

"Well, if you call being drugged and kidnapped unharmed, I suppose they are" argued Freda, "God knows how they'll both be coping. Our Caitlin may never recover properly and Patrick with a broken ankle! But I'll tell you one thing, it made me realise what a lovely woman Jennifer was, when that bloody Celia turned up here, shouting and raving and screaming!"

"No!" said Doris, "What happened?"

"We was all in here, Mr Charles in a right state of course, she marches in here shouting saying what was he doing in the kitchen–sitting with the staff! I ask you, bloody cheek, at a time like that!"

"She was always a snob Freda, I know you always thought the sun shone out of her backside, but she could be a right cow!"

"Then she starts shouting at the policewoman sent over to help, giving her her marching orders, and when the big chief comes over, she says she's making complaints and all sorts, and there's poor little Rupert shivering and shaking in the chair – she never gave a thought to that little boy." Freda complained, "Made me really appreciate Jennifer I can tell you."

"Lawks I can imagine how she was with Ivy then." Doris said, "Poor duck."

"Well" said Freda thoughtfully, "she was right rude to start with to Ivy, and then it was as though she had suddenly pulled herself together and by the time she left she was almost civil, but I'll tell you one thing and that's not two, I'm mighty glad I don't work for her anymore."

"Poor old Pete" said Fred thoughtfully, "he had a rotten life really."

"Yes, he did, but let's not forget a few weeks ago he tried to drown Jennifer, and he ended up being drowned himself. I know he was ill, but you can't get away from it can you?" said Freda

"He came good in the end though, he came good in the end."

Andrew was where he'd been for the last forty eight hours sitting beside Caitlin, holding her hand, gazing into space, isolated in the bubble of Intensive Care, completely oblivious to what had been happening in Fittlebury. The mechanical pump and beep of the machinery rhythmically going on around him almost unheard now, as his thoughts strayed to his conversation with Julia.

When he'd finally managed to get in touch with her, apologising for not letting her know where he'd been, Julia laughed sarcastically, saying she'd not even noticed he hadn't been at home and had just assumed he was working. Andrew started to explain about the accident and that he was with Caitlin now, and about their affair. So when he had blurted it all out, there had been a silence on the end of the phone.

Julia had then said cuttingly "So you want to spend the rest of your life with a paraplegic then? Well Andrew that's your affair – and speaking of affairs, you're not the only one, I'm leaving you anyway, for Lance, my tennis coach, he's taken a job in Australia for the winter, and I'm going with him."

Andrew had been stunned, not by her admission, which was no surprise to him, but by her callous behaviour, he'd just replied quietly, "Well good for you Julia, I hope you'll be very happy together. I'm sure we can divorce amicably."

"I doubt it" Julia had said coldly, "I'll make sure I get every penny out of you" and with that ended the call.

As Andrew sat watching Caitlin, he thought about what Julia had said, he was glad she was going away, it made things a lot easier, because one thing for sure was, he was with Caitlin for the duration.

In the incident room, they were beginning the arduous task of tying up the loose ends of the investigation, although finding the abducted woman and child had taken the pressure off, there were still people to arrest. Now they had to piece together what had actually happened, and as each piece of the jigsaw was unearthed, they were at last beginning to see the big picture.

In the lock up they had found the Landrover complete with the rolled up blankets, and discarded hoods and green anoraks. The SOCOs had gone over the place and found a stash of drugs worth a great deal of money, and plenty of fingerprints. They'd also found a quantity of stolen goods from a variety of previous jobs which had been unsolved in the city over the last few months – it was quite a haul.

Weasel, when he'd been picked up, had eventually talked and talked, especially when he discovered that his pal Jonty had done a runner and left him in the shite to carry the can. They'd not told him yet that Jonty was dead. Although Weasel wouldn't give the names of anyone else involved but the incriminating texts on his phone were enough, and finally, faced with this indisputable evidence he cracked and admitted everything. The others had been picked up later that same night. After they'd left the cottage, they'd split up and tried to get back to London. Two of them were arrested for attempting to steal a car, and the others when they had ran slap bang into a squad car in Haywards Heath, where they trying to get to the station.

"Guv?" asked young DC Dianne Scott, "that Lucy Phillips, the one that might've been the mole?"

"Yep, I know who you mean" Jim answered irritably, "how're you getting on with that?"

"Well, when I called round to her home address yesterday afternoon, she was still working apparently. I asked the parents to let me know when she got home. They've been on the phone this morning, she didn't come home last night. They've rung the Bistro and she's not turned up for work either. She's not answering her mobile either."

"Ring the parents yourself, find out what time she left yesterday, and if anyone picked her up, or if she spoke to anyone while she was at work, but it sounds as though she's done a runner to me. Get round to her home and ask the parents for an up to date photo. Let me know asap." Jim grunted, turning to the reports on his desk and making notes in his policy book. He was going to have to interview Jennifer next and he wasn't looking forward to it much, but he couldn't leave it to a junior officer and Christ knew what state she'd be in after the ordeal she'd been through. It was going to be a long day.

The team assembled later for the briefing at 6pm, they all looked worn out, they had been at it non-stop since Saturday.

"This is the fourth briefing of Operation Icarus, the time is six thirty pm on Monday 6th September 2012."

"As you all know, thanks to the gardener Pete and the quick thinking of the farrier Patrick Hodges, Mrs Parker-Smythe and her step daughter were recovered last night, but the with loss of life of the gardener and the suspect Ionty Steele. Have we got statements from the woman who runs the shop and her husband, and the other two people who were involved?" he consulted his notebook, "Mr and Mrs Allington?"

Linda answered immediately, "Yes Boss. Mrs Gupta confirms that this chap Pete Bowyer, who was the gardener at Nantes Place but left several weeks previously because of psychotic behaviour, ran into the shop saying he had seen the little girl at the mill and that she was a prisoner, and he needed help. Mrs Gupta was terribly frightened bringing on an angina attack. The farrier, Patrick Hodges, arrived and when Mrs Gupta managed to recover told him and her husband what had happened. According to her, then Mr Hodges ran out of the shop heading towards the mill. It was on the way there that he rang the incident room, and also Mr and Mrs Allington, whom he knows well and who live close by to help him. He also rang Mr Parker-Smythe. This is all corroborated by the other statements given."

"That seems clear enough" said Jim, "and the rest we know. The body recovered from the mill pond today has been identified by Mr Parker- Smythe as that of Peter Bowyer, there will be a post mortem tomorrow but it would seem likely that he drowned. SSU divers reported that the bailer twine wrapped around his coat had hooked up on a metal stave of the mill wheel - right under the water line and he obviously couldn't free himself. The body of the other man is presumed to be that of Jonty Steele." Jim continued "Any sightings of the accomplice – Laura?"

Peter answered "No Sir, not yet, but I don't think she'll get far, we have her phone number and directly she turns it on we can trace it, we've also circulated her picture now, and the press office has managed to get us a spot on Crimewatch."

"Good" said Jim, "I've been unable to interview the victims, as apparently the medics say they're not up to it yet, but tomorrow they will be, and possibly even be sent home. So we'll have to be patient on that one. Linda, did you get anything from Mr Hodges – the farrier?"

"No, he was drugged up to the eyeballs on painkillers, it was a bad break, he was lucky to get out of the house alive by all accounts."

"Brave bloke" said Jim, "see if you can get anything tomorrow. What about these Hunt Sabs – what's the score with them?"

"Right Guv, the Met interviewed them first but we haven't followed it up yet. Seems they were pretty much duped by this girl Laura. She fed them the information about the hunt's activities, fuelled their fire so to speak, but they say they had no knowledge about the kidnapping or the real intent of the exercise." Linda grinned "When I spoke to the Met guys, they were inclined to believe them, after all it was the Sabs who notified us it was their branch that was involved, by all accounts this bunch were pretty angry that their altruistic ideals were infringed for criminal purposes if you please!

Still we'll get onto it and take statements obviously and then of course it'll be up to us to make a case and pass it on to the CPS – but I'll be getting on to that."

Jim gave a rare smile, "Well keep me posted – we'll have to see what we can make of it, I think on the whole though intent probably would be difficult to prove."

At that moment the door burst open and DC Dianne Scott charged in panting, "Sorry to be late Guv and sorry to barge in like this, but there's a development I think!"

"Sit yourself down lass and tell us calmly" placated Jim, "what development?"

Dianne sat down on a chair, and looked around at the others anxiously, "This morning, I've been following up on the whereabouts of Lucy Phillips, she went missing after work last night about four pm" she explained. "At lunch time today, the Travel Lodge in Horsham rang reporting the death of one of their guests. Apparently one of the chambermaids went in to make up the room and found the body of a girl. She had checked in the previous day at about four fifteen in the afternoon, paying cash for the room, and they assumed she had just checked out - seemingly she was a regular short stay customer – if you know what I mean" she flushed as she carried on, "A constable went out, and the medics at the scene thought the death was owing to a lethal dose of cocaine and strychnine. She had a considerable amount of what appeared to be cocaine in her possession. The contents of her handbag were examined to identify her and bingo, it was our missing girl – Lucy Phillips. The parents have been notified and have given a positive ID. A post mortem is being held tomorrow to confirm the cause."

"Well done Dianne. Pour yourself a coffee, you probably need one. Well I think we can assume that Steele was in some way involved in the death of Lucy Phillips. See if there's any CCTV in the car park at the Travel Lodge or reception, if she was a regular visitor, chances are we might get an idea of who she was with. How did she get there too? We know it wasn't in the Landrover, that was in the lock up, so either she walked – unlikely in yesterday's weather, or she was picked up by car? Get on to the local traffic and patrols, keep an eye out for abandoned cars - one things for sure, Steele isn't coming back for it. If she was going home by bus, check the CCTV in the town centre and see if we can trace her last movements before she got to the travel lodge, he may have been waiting for her after she finished work. If the cocaine is in a plastic bag, check it for prints, it might implicate Steele." He smiled, twiddling his ring on his finger, "Dianne, check that handbag for a phone will you, if it's not there, then where is it? Find out the number, – if it's still on, can we get a trace on it? If we can get anything off Steele's phone once the lab boys have had a go at it too, that will be useful. Okay, get moving plenty to do! Next briefing nine am tomorrow."

Jennifer lay back on the pillows in the private room, Charles was sitting beside her holding her hand, he had spent the whole day, flitting between her and Jessica. She smiled at him wanly, her head still felt fuzzy, and she'd never been so tired. The events of the last two days felt as though they'd happened to someone else, the few tortuous things she could remember made her cringe inwardly, and hold Charles' hand more tightly. He'd been marvellous with her, not forcing her to talk, but told her that Jessica was doing really well, that everyone sent their love and spoke of silly inanities, and she just smiled at him, hardly taking it all in. Jennifer knew that Celia was with here too with Jessica and she made no comment, she felt too tired to think about it. Her mum had been in too, and she felt like a little girl again the way she fussed over her.

The consultant had been in to see her several times and was very kind, sitting on the edge of the bed talking to her. He said that physically she would be fine, but she had been through a dreadful emotional shock, and perhaps she should consider having some psychological counselling over the next few months, which may well help. Jennifer was adamant that she would be fine, and if she felt she needed help she would ask, but when he asked her if she thought she felt well enough to go home tomorrow, perhaps in the afternoon, and she didn't know how to answer. In the hospital, in this little room she felt so safe - outside how would she feel? When Charles was out of the room, she confided how she felt to her Mum, and Ivy brushed the hair away from her eyes and looked at her seriously,

"Look Jen, I can understand exactly how you feel, it'd be odd if you didn't, you've had a terrible ordeal. You know though, it'll pass, what happened to you is over, done and forgotten and my best advice to you, is to try and forget it too, get on with your life and enjoy it, make the most of every moment."

"Oh Mum," whispered Jennifer, "I don't know if I can, just when I was getting it all together. Now this."

"But this isn't your fault, this is something you'd no control over, and was something that happens so rarely. You'll recover, come on, this isn't the tenacious girl I know!"

"Will you come back with me Mum? Stay for a while?"

"Course I will love, try keeping me away!"

CHAPTER 72

The village was in shock with the tsunami of news, the sleepy hamlet of Fittlebury had been woken by a maelstrom of appalling events which just seemed to go on and on. Not only the devious kidnapping of Jennifer Parker-Smythe and her step daughter, but the deaths of Pete and Lucy, and the still comatose state of Caitlin, and Patrick's broken ankle. All of their lives and those close to them had been altered or lost within such a short space of time.

This Tuesday morning, the sun shone periodically through a pale turquoise sky, and the leaves on the horse chestnut trees were starting to curl at the edges, heralding the autumn. The rain had left the grass squashy and lush, and the horses left deep imprints on the tracks down to the fields when the girls turned them out. The summer was waning and the thought of autumn and the hard slog of winter ahead, coupled with the awful events of the last few days had taken its toll on moral in the yard at Mileoak. But the horses still had to be fed, watered and worked, no matter what had happened.

Chloe felt responsible, thinking if she hadn't found Polly, Jennifer would never have gone out hunting that day at all, but it was no good thinking like that, life was full of what ifs. Lucy had been a cow, but did she deserve the end that she'd had - to get hooked up with that low life who subsequently murdered her? No, no-one deserved that, and Pete too, he was mentally ill, how culpable were they all? None of them had cared enough not to notice before, and at the end if it hadn't been for him, how long would it have been before Jennifer and Jessica were found?

All this thinking Chloe decided was not a good thing, look at how she had misjudged John. She had convinced herself so much that he was having an affair, and all the time it had been nothing of the sort. Since Saturday they had talked a bit about how their lives would change when he gave up his job, and his plans to start up on his own. There was a lot more talking to be done, but now they were pulling

771

together again and despite all the terrible things going on around her, it was a huge relief.

Down at the surgery, Oli and Alice were coping well in Andrew's absence, although they both admitted they would be glad when he was back. There was something very solid about his knowledge and experience, and his calm way of dealing with things. Paulene missed him too, they had worked together for years and the fact that Andrew and Caitlin had been having a secret affair for months really shook her, she'd simply had no idea at all. Oli had always thought that Paulene had a bit of a soft spot herself for Andrew even though she was married – a girl could dream after all. For Oli, he thought they made a perfect couple, certainly more of a match for Andrew than Julia could ever have been - how cruel life was.

Grace had not come in the day before, as she'd had to make statements to the police, so when she arrived that morning, she was plagued with questions about the fire and the drama of Sunday evening. Colin, Patrick and she had agreed on the night of the fire, that outside of the police, they would tell no-one else about the condition in which they'd found Jennifer – Lord knew, she had suffered enough. When the others told Grace about Andrew and Caitlin's affair she was surprised, but not about Julia pushing off with her tennis coach. She went on to tell them that she knew that Julia had been with someone else and how she had seen them together weeks before. God it was a mess they all agreed and now the future looked bleak - Caitlin still had not regained consciousness and the plans for the mill were over.

Patrick was in less pain, the drugs in the hospital were powerful and effective, and the surgeon had said that although the break was nasty, he should make a full recovery Even Sharon had been nice to him, and he'd found himself the hero of the piece. Charles had come to see him offering his thanks for saving Jennifer and Jessica, and saying he was not to worry about anything, he would make sure that he had the best aftercare and physio to help him make a speedy recovery. Patrick would like to have been in a position to tell him not to worry about that, but he knew being laid up like this would seriously affect his livelihood. Although he had insurance it would in no way recompense him for the loss of his earnings in real terms. But Patrick being Patrick would dine out on the drama for months to come – all except for some of the details which he'd never let on about.

He'd had quite a few visitors already, young Oli and Tom, Grace and Colin, and Chloe and John. They'd filled him in on what had happened since, and he was sorry to hear about Lucy, no matter what she was, she didn't deserve to die like that. The surprise of course was Ace – Andrew Christopher Edward Napier, the love of Caitlin's life, was the married man, who'd have thought it? He remembered all those months ago when that late spring day when he and Chloe had gossiped in her yard and speculated about who it could be, he never in a million years thought it could be Andrew! According to Grace though his wife had been running around with her tennis coach for ages, you never knew what went on in other people's lives! He prayed that Caitlin would recover at least some form of a normal life, she was such a decent person, what was better to die like Lucy, or live the life of a cabbage?

The thought too of spending weeks at home with Sharon filled him with gloom, he was bloody determined to work hard at the physio and get back to work as fast as he could, it would drive him mad to be at her mercy all day and night!

At Nantes Felix beavered away in the yard, he'd never realised how hard Caitlin had worked until she was no longer there, and it would be months before she came back, if she ever did he thought ruefully. Despite his personal ambitions he liked it at Nantes, he was pretty much his own boss and he liked the way things ran here. He was coping okay, and Chloe had sent Susie over to give him a hand when she could spare her and that had been a bonus. He knew he could manage, but at some point he would have to speak to the boss and ask him for some extra help, even if it was only part time.

Mrs Fuller had aged a lot over the last few days, the worry showed in her face, even though now Jennifer and Jessica were safe, she was concerned at how long she could go on working like she did. The little holiday she'd had with her sister whilst the family were away on that safari seemed a long time ago now. Mr Charles had told her that Jennifer would be coming out of hospital today, and that Ivy would be coming to stay for a while to be with her. It was a good idea, but it would mean a lot of extra work, and neither she nor Doris were getting any younger. She was thrilled though that Jennifer was coming home, although she had no idea how she would be feeling or how much affected by what had happened, it would be difficult to know what to say.

She took a cake out of the oven putting it on a rack to cool, and stirred the meat bubbling away on the top of the Aga. She pulled the pan to one side ready to put in the casserole, and thought she'd better get on with changing the beds ready for when they came home. She gathered up the linen and went to find Doris who was vacuuming the sitting room.

As they worked they could hear the thrum of the contractors' mowers outside, breezing over the lawns for probably the last time that autumn, and the constant snip snip as they cut back the roses and climbing shrubs ready for the onslaught of the colder weather.

The two women gossiped together, tossing the sheets across the bed, smoothing them down and folding in the edges

"Little Jessica's going home with her mother I suppose" said Doris, plumping up a pillow.

"Yes, according to Mr Charles, she's not too bad, they kept her drugged most of the time and she can't remember much about it apparently, but I pity her going home with Celia."

"Blimey, you have changed your tune a bit Freda" remarked Doris, "she has always been a right a right snob, but that night she was obviously upset and didn't know what she was saying."

"I've been thinking Doris," said Freda, "when I look back to those years when she lived here playing lady of the manor, all that stiff upper lip stuff, I realise now that there were plenty of cracks, but I never saw them then. She was never a truly nice person."

"It's taken you all this time to realise that!" Doris laughed, "They say there's no fool like and old fool!"

"Who you calling old?" grinned Freda hurling a pillow at Doris, and realised it was true, there was plenty of life left in her yet!

Mark had been given permission to survey the scene at the mill, which was still part of the on-going police investigation, although they had largely finished now. The fireman had established the cause of the fire, and all the evidence they needed had been collected. One or two officers were still lurking about and he gloomily surveyed the wreckage that was left. The fire had cause havoc, the cottage and the attached out buildings were all gone, just charred stumps were left, and heaps of rubble and blackened junk. A lot of the mill had been damaged too, although some of it was still standing on the pond side, and the wheel, which did for Pete, was still intact, but a cursory glance told him that the best route would be to pull the whole lot down. To try to restore it would be hopeless and expensive. The barns on the other side of the drive were completely untouched, which was something he supposed.

The place was insured of course, but not for the kind of money that would be required to rebuild here, and it was a blow to the estate that was for sure. He made initial notes to report back his findings to Lady V, and they would have to get surveyors out here when the time was right, and they could go over the place thoroughly but right now it was not looking good. You also had to factor into the resale, how many people would want to live here, a place tainted with such a horrible history - purchasers were funny about that sort of thing. He thought back to Andrew and how excited he'd been about his plans for the place and it all seemed eons ago, and what future did he have now? By all accounts he'd not left Caitlin's side since the accident, and Julia was bad mouthing him all over the county. For the people that really knew Andrew and Caitlin, and Julia come to that, they would take no notice, but some mud sticks and people loved to gossip. He sighed, when he'd discussed things with Sandy in bed last night, she'd been furious, claiming that Andrew need not worry and if that silly Julia thought she was getting a penny more than she deserved she was wrong. When the time came she would represent Andrew and that bloody woman wouldn't know what had hit her! He'd hugged his little Rottweiler, his little pocket rocket, and knew that she would do exactly that.

His thoughts strayed to Sandy, he was in very much in love with her, he knew it, there was no pretending otherwise and he knew she loved him. Where did their relationship go from here? They had both been married before and divorced, and at the start neither wanted any commitment, but as their love had grown stronger, and they had become more comfortable with each other, he was beginning to feel differently. He wanted more, wanted to know that every day she would be there, not that she wasn't now, but to seal it - almost like a contract. Like a marriage – yes why not he thought excitedly, would she feel the same way? If he asked her would he frighten her off?

Andrew felt the bristle of his unshaven face, and the tiredness overwhelm him as he sat in the overheated confines of Intensive Care. The nurses were constantly bustling from one patient to another checking monitors and machines, dragging curtains around beds to minister treatment and medication. Patients came and went, some new, some recovered and some died. It became a never ending diurnal lifestyle, which he watched at first with some interest and then dispassionately as the hours had rolled past into days.

Oli had been great and brought him clean clothes and some books too, so that he could read to Caitlin. The doctors had said that it was important to keep talking to her, and that was something positive that he could do. Oli had told him that Julia had gone from the house when he went to fetch his things, her clothes were not in the wardrobe or in the drawers, so he doubted whether she would be back. Andrew had said that he was glad, it made it easier for him. He'd also brought him up to speed about Patrick and the dramatic rescue and about the demise of Pete and Lucy. Andrew had listened aghast, but to him the greatest casualty of all was Caitlin.

Caitlin's mother had phoned regularly and was due to arrive that afternoon, and he was dreading meeting her, how would she feel when she saw him. She was a good Catholic woman and would almost certainly disapprove of their relationship, and he remembered how Caitlin had struggled to juggle her faith with her love for him.

Charles too had been in regular contact, saying that he would come down when he could, but in the meantime he was not to worry about anything. If Caitlin needed anything extra in terms of care he would pay for it, and if Andrew needed a locum pro-temp, he would pay for that too. At first this had irked Andrew, if they needed anything, then *he* would bloody pay for it, who did Charles think he was! Later thinking about it, he realised that Charles was not showing off, or swanking about with his money, he had offered because he felt a genuine guilt, that in some way it was his fault that Caitlin was in this state.

He opened the book and started to read again, it was the first Harry Potter Book and he was now almost a third of the way through.

Silly choice really - trust Oli, but at least it was easy reading. He propped the book on the bed, and held it open with his hand, leaving his other hand free to hold Caitlin's. He'd just got to an exciting part of the story and Andrew was getting into his stride, when he felt Caitlin's hand slightly tighten against his. He stopped reading, and looked at her, she seemed just the same, he must have imagined it, so he carried on reading where he'd left off. Once again, he felt her hand tighten against his, and this time he was sure he wasn't mistaken. He leant over her, talking directly to her now and whispering

"Caitlin, darling, can you hear me, it's Andrew, if you can hear me, squeeze my hand." Once again he felt her hand tighten in his, "Oh my God Caitlin, you can hear me, hold on darling, you're in hospital, you're fine, we're fine, I'm going to get the doctor."

Charles had purposely driven back home to Nantes so that they wouldn't pass through Priors Cross, the last thing he wanted Jennifer to see was the remnants of the police activity and the place where she'd been held captive. She was in a fragile state, having been interviewed by the DCI this morning, even though he had been very gentle with her. She could really remember very little, she couldn't say what happened to Caitlin, when she and Jessica had been pulled from their horses, Caitlin had still been on hers. Other than when the photograph had been taken upstairs in the cottage and she had been given something to drink and afterwards when they had injected her in the arm, she had no memory of anything else. Her abductors had all worn hoods, the only thing she could say for certain was that one of them was a woman, and they referred to a man called Jonty. Jim had left it at that, there would time for more questions later, but there was no doubt who had orchestrated this and he had paid the ultimate price for his wickedness.

There had been a tearful farewell between Jennifer and Jessica, the little girl, who was remarkably robust considering, grabbed her waist and clung onto her begging to come back with her. Celia had stood back with a stony face, but one look at Ivy quelled any remarks that were on the tip of her tongue, and eventually Jessica went home, reassured with promises that Jennifer would ring her that evening to say goodnight and to give her love to Rupert. Ivy had brought in some clothes for Jennifer and after she had dressed, they took one look around the room and left. To Jennifer it was a big step, her mother smiled at her and nodded, and they made their way out to the car.

As Nantes came closer, Jennifer started to relax a little, they swept through the village, and it all looked just the same. The shop had the door open, probably for one of the last occasions till next spring, the mums were starting to arrive to pick up their children from school, the Fox had a few stragglers sitting in the garden enjoying a burst of autumn sunshine, and across the green the vicar was gossiping with a couple of women with dogs by the pump. Everything looked so normal.

The car slowed down to turn into the drive and Charles put his hand out and took hers, kissing her fingertips - saying how much he loved her and how lucky he was. She smiled at him and leant over and kissed him back, whispering how much she loved him too and that she was the lucky one. The horse chestnuts bowed gracefully above them, the leaves were starting to turn, their greens transforming into patches of golds and reds, and soon they would be ablaze with glorious colours. They swept on down the drive, over the bridge and towards the house, and she recalled the first time she had seen Nantes all that time ago, and again when she had brought her mother here too, but today was different. Charles pulled up outside the front door, and Mrs Fuller ran out to greet them, her face flushed with pleasure.

"Well darling" smiled Charles, reaching down and unclipping their seat belts, "Welcome home."

Jennifer looked up at the grand old house, the mellow walls smothered in the last of the roses, and then around the gardens towards the paddocks and saw Polly's elegant head looking over towards her, "Yes," she grinned back at him, "I'm back home with you, where I belong."

EPILOGUE

Nine months later.

The weather was glorious, the sun beat down from a perfect blue sky and there was the merest hint of a breeze, the scent of Nantes' famous roses and honeysuckle drifted up from the gardens below through the open balcony. The horses were grazing peacefully in the paddocks beyond and the church bells were ringing in the village.

"Come on sweetie, or we'll be last ones in the church" called Charles to Jennifer, as he adjusted his cravat. "Bloody things!" he muttered to himself as he struggled with the pin.

"Don't panic Mr Mainwaring" laughed Jennifer, coming out of the bathroom and over to help him, "I'm ready, here let me do that."

Charles looked at her reflection in the mirror and whirled round, "Wow, you look sensational!"

"Do you like it?" she said, giving him a twirl. She did look fabulous and she felt it too. Sophie had done her proud once again, in a very pale pink silk dress, delicately printed with large cabbage patch roses and leaves. The frock had a fitted bodice with a full skirt, falling just below the knee, and she was wearing a small and subtle matching fascinator, with nude coloured shoes and clutch bag and a waist length silk jacket "I don't want to be in a competition with the bride."

"It's perfect, you're perfect!" said Charles delightedly "Now give me a hand with that pin, or we'll never get there in time."

The small village church at Fittlebury was packed to capacity to see Sandy Maclean and Mark Templeton tie the knot on the glorious June day, and Charles and Jennifer slipped in at the back, next to Katherine and Jeremy who had saved them a place.

Caitlin was across the aisle from them with Andrew, and she smiled and waved hello, and Jennifer and Charles waved back. It had been a long and slow recovery for Caitlin, but she was pretty much there now, although she had not returned to Nantes and now lived with Andrew, where he fussed over her like a mother hen. The organist started to play Mendelssohn's Wedding March and the congregation stood up for the bride, Caitlin leant on his arm, and he proudly kissed the top of her head.

Chloe and John were in the pew in front, trying to keep the children quiet, but when the evocative music started, Jennifer saw John reaching out to find Chloe's hand and squeeze it between his. They'd had a tough few months with John starting up on his own but they had got through it. Charles had been great, he'd always liked John, and from what he had learned about him in the city, he knew he had talent and had given him a lot of help and advice and even invested some money in the new company. With Charles' support, which created a lot of kudos and sending him clients, and twisting a few arms on the way, plus the severance money from his old job, they'd paid off their mortgage, and were starting to make money.

In front of Andrew and Caitlin, stood Colin and Grace – waiting for Sandy to sweep down the aisle. Grace had come over all emotional, and was dabbing a hanky to her eyes and Caitlin reached out and gave her arm a squeeze and smiled. Graced grinned back with a little lift of her eyebrows, and gave her burgeoning tummy a stroke, Colin looked down at her, and his face shone with pride, their baby was due in three months.

Sandy looked amazing, no-one could have outshone her today, with her petite elfin features and her white blond hair, studded with pearls and rosebuds, but it was the vintage dress that was so sensational. In off white, inspired by Monique L'huillier - an Alencon lace overlay with a silk under slip, in a figure slicking mermaid style with a sweetheart neckline. It was drawn across the shoulders behind and fastened with a small rose and a daring open scooped back fastened very low over her bottom with tiny buttons, to fall away into a swirl behind her. She was truly the radiant bride.

The party that followed the wedding was fabulous, everyone drank and ate far too much, laughed through the speeches, and cat - called during the cutting of the cake. They danced to the blues band, and waved goodbye to the newlyweds with much hilarity as they sped off on their honeymoon. The party rocked on until the early hours and there were going to be some mighty hangovers in the morning. Jennifer leant against Charles and he held her close as they danced.

"I'm so happy darling, it's been a wonderful day" she sighed, a little tipsy from all the champagne, "I have you, wonderful friends and a wonderful life, I am without doubt the luckiest person alive."

Charles leant forward and kissed her, a long deep kiss, and she felt her toes curling in her shoes, "Mmmm, it's me who's the lucky one, when I met you." he murmured, "you turned my life upside down and right now you're turning me on too!"

"Charles!" she said huskily, running her leg up between his and rubbing herself against him through the silky flimsy dress, and then she kissed him again, running her hands through his hair.

Charles could feel himself getting hard, his hands straying around the curves of her bottom, "Jennifer" he whispered "You're a naughty girl – you're not wearing any knickers!"

"No, haven't had any on all day – and what are you going to do about it then" she teased, her hands moving downwards.

"Come on you wayward hussy" he said, "Let's go home and I'll show you!"

The End

The sequel to **Rough Ride**, and there is a rip roaring sequel, is hotting up and brewing well! More romps and riding in steamy West Sussex! Happy reading!

Rough Ride is also available in e-book format on Amazon.co.uk. and shortly as an Audio book abridged by P J King and read by Chris Stafford.

For updates on the sequel and the Audio book – please refer to the website www.pjkingauthor.co.uk

ABOUT THE AUTHOR

P J King was brought up in the country on a small farm, her father being a horse dealer, and she could ride before she could walk! Despite her rural upbringing and love of horses, she decided to pursue a career on the front line in an acute psychiatric hospital with a multi-disciplinary medical team. After some years, the innate draw and passion for horses lured her back and she is now a dressage trainer, judge and sports psychologist, living on her own stud farm in the South East of England. She is married with three children, and has a host of dogs and horses, together with the inevitable uniform of Hunter wellies and Barbours! Drawing on her own life experiences in the medical and equine industry, she decided to write about what she knew best, and to recreate some of the wonderful (or otherwise!) characters that she has met and weave them into a novel. *Rough Ride* is that story.

Find out more about P J King

www.pjkingauthor.co.uk

https://twitter.com/pjking_author
https://www.facebook.com/roughride.pjking

Printed in Great Britain
by Amazon.co.uk, Ltd.,
Marston Gate.